D1808359

Tables of Content

Chapter 1:   The Mysterious Lady in Yellow Robe

The secular sect Eternal Ice Palace was one of the three most influential outer fraternity clans in the martial fraternity.

It was located on top of the misty mountains of the Heavenly Mountains in the far north of the northern fraternity. At the top of the Heavenly Mountains was a great lake and it was where the Eternal Ice Palace was said to be located.

The Eternal Ice Palace was forbidden to men and naturally, the Eternal Ice Palace consisted of only women.

The sectarian leader of the Eternal Ice Palace was the Celestial Fairy. It was not her beauty that lured Yi Ping to the Heavenly Mountains for the Celestial Fairy was said to be a ninety year old hag.

The Celestial Fairy was greatly feared in the vicinity and in the martial fraternity. She was also highly accomplished in her martial skills; a single martial stroke from her would usually spell the end for her opponents!

It was rumored in the fraternity she had just passed away after leading the Eternal Ice Palace for the past twenty years.

When the news of her death broke out in the martial fraternity, it immediately caught the attention of the martial pugilists. The imagination of her wondrous secret martial arts caught on like wildfire among the pugilists.

Therefore pugilists from all over the fraternity had been making their way north to the forbidden Heavenly Mountains, hoping to lay their hands on the fabulous martial treasures of the Eternal Ice Palace.

Yi Ping had come for the very same reason.

There was another reason that drawn him into these desolate mountains; to witness a possible conflict between the martial exponents which to him, was even more exciting than the secret martial arts of the Celestial Fairy!

He was young and a roving swordsman. He was not from any major clans, orthodox or not. He was just a busybody and was like many pugilists took every opportunity to meddle into the affairs of the martial fraternity.

Even if he was killed, he had to witness one of the most important events of the martial fraternity. Or at the very least, befriend some heroes of the martial fraternity. It would be even better if he could gain some recognition in the fraternity!

Therefore with this in mind, Yi Ping had set off to the bitter cold and harsh lands of the north!

On the third day, while walking and whistling, he heard the sound of trees crushing onto the ground. At first, he thought nothing of it until the thunderous sound of the trees gets louder and louder.

Then an injured middle age man was running and tripping onto the ground. When he saw Yi Ping, he immediately cried out, "Young hero, help me!"

Yi Ping responded by drawing out his sword. He thought, "Is the man being chased by bandits?"

Yi Ping shouted at him as he ran towards him, "Get behind me!"

A foolish hero usually died young. Yi Ping was not even thinking of how many bandits were chasing him. Fortunately, there was only one and it was a yellow dressed lady with a yellow veil.

She had appeared in the horizon and she did not even have a weapon in her hands. So then why did this man flee from her? From his expressions, he seemed to be terrified of her.

Even though that yellow dressed lady was veiled and Yi Ping could not see her face clearly, he could tell she must be a beautiful maiden. Her complexion was extremely fair and appeared flawless, her eyebrows were thin and delicate and her eyes were sparking and mesmerizing.

The yellow dressed lady walked elegantly in a straight line. Even though she appeared to be walking slowly but the paces covered by her was astonishing; Yi Ping had never seen anyone who could walk as swiftly as her yet she appeared like she was taking a stroll!

But when a tree blocked her, she gently kicked the tree and the tree flew off in another direction as she continued to walk towards them!

Yi Ping was astonished and he looked on with disbelief!

An inner strength practitioner might take sixty years of practice to do what she did with considerable efforts but she did that effortlessly.

Yi Ping looked into her eyes. She had beautiful and sharp eyes. When he looked into her eyes, she too paused in her tracks and looked back.

Yi Ping heart was pounding fast.

Yi Ping mustered his voice and said, "Lady, why are you chasing him?"

The yellow dressed veil lady replied, "Do you know who he is?" Her voice was unmistakably youthful.

Yi Ping was shaken by her reply, "I do know who he is. But a man in dire straits requires help, if I do not help, can I still be considered a man?"

The yellow dressed veil lady hummed coldly, "He is the Bandit King Yao Duo, a vicious killer of the innocents! And you still want to protect him?"

The Bandit King Yao Duo was the most brutal man in the martial fraternity in recent years. His martial accomplishments were high too. Even the renowned Eagle King Yin Tianzheng was not his match! He gained his renown through sheer notoriety! His victims were many and his evil deeds were too numerous to be accounted for!

Even the seven major orthodox clans dare not offend him lightly after a few attempts to get rid of him. And moreover, his evil cohorts were many too.

Yi Ping was shocked and he turned to the stranger to ask, "Are you really Yao Duo?"

The middle-age stranger laughed aloud, "Indeed I am! A true hero will never change their name…"

"Good and you can now be a dead hero!" All of a sudden, the yellow dressed veil lady kicked Yao Duo in his face and crushed his skull. That happened so fast that Yi Ping was unable to stop her at all.

Then the yellow dressed veiled lady turned around and said, "If you want a long life, don't meddle into the affairs of others especially for those that you did not know."

There was a weird expression in her eyes but at that moment, Yi Ping did not notice it. She said, "If you are thinking of going to the Heavenly Mountain, you are only courting your own death. Even if your martial skills are as good as the Bandit King Yao Duo, a cruel fate awaits you in the mountains. Turn back if you cherish your life!" With that, she started to walk away.

Yi Ping rubbed his nose and watched her disappeared into the background. It was as if she had never appeared.

He began to dig a hole into the ground as he said, "Even if you are a notorious man, how could I bear to let your body be food for the wild beasts and birds when you have tried to ask for my help? Since you have died, everything should be buried under the earth."

Unfortunately, Yi Ping had already decided to proceed to the Heavenly Mountains despite the advice that he had been given. He was still young and he got nothing but courage in his heart.

It was not too long when he reached the foot of the Heavenly Mountains that he started to see dead corpses and abandoned emblems littered along the mountains route. There seemed to be a battle not too long ago and he hurried his pace.

All of a sudden, he heard menacing voices in the corner of the mountains. Out of curiosity, he sped towards it.

"It seems that this lovely damsel here is in distress and there is no one here to save her."

"Who would expect that we can find such a beautiful woman here?"

"We did not make it to the Heavenly Mountains in time but we got ourselves a prize here. Hahaha."

An extraordinary maiden of great beauty, dressed in silky white dress had her back against the cliff. She looked badly shaken. She was teething with rage and fear. Even then, her grace was extremely enthralling.

Yi Ping was stunned at her beauty for she was like a fairy that had descended onto the mortal realm.

In front of her were three men, wielding swords and halberds. From the looks of it, they had already decided to devour this young maiden in their minds.

Yi Ping stepped in angrily and shouted, "What are three despicable men doing here?" He brandished his long sword and pointed at them.

The three men were taken by surprise. They quickly turned around and saw a young man. They looked at one another before roaring out loud.

One of the men with a long bushy beard stared at him and said fiercely, "So what are you going to do with us? Kill us? Do you know we are the Three Evils of the West?"

There was a glitter of hope in the eyes of the extremely beautiful maiden when Yi Ping had first appeared but that hope was soon crushed at the mention of the Three Evils of the West.

Yi Ping was taken aback. The Three Evils of the West was renowned in the martial fraternity for their wickedness and brutality! Not only that, they had killed countless highly skilled pugilists as they rampaged the martial fraternity for twenty-years! That was why they were greatly feared.

Another man with the moustache laughed, "Or are you thinking of joining in the fun after we are done?"

This aroused Yi Ping anger. Even though he had to die, he could not abandon the righteousness in his heart. Yi Ping eyed them fiercely and smirked, "If you scram now, I will be forgiving."

The third man with a short beard and wielding a halberd in his hands suddenly attacked him, "Outrageous! I will kill you today and cut your body into many pieces!"

Yi Ping was surprised at the speed and ferocious of his halberd attack. He barely managed to parry the attack and was knocked back. But before he could steady his footing, he received a kick in his chest and was knocked down to the ground.

The short beard man laughed, "I thought he is some daring hero. But he turns out to be an amateur. A sword in your hand is like a piece of worthless metal!"

Yi Ping coughed out blood and wiped his mouth, "This is not over yet!" All of a sudden, he lifted his sword and pieced the throat of the short beard man who was still laughing!

When the short beard man collapsed onto the ground, he was still staring in disbelief! What a swift sword!

Yi Ping had succeeded for two reasons; His opponent had underestimated him and let down his guard.

The other two men were experienced pugilists and after seeing one of their own had fallen, they did not dare to be careless anymore and had immediately attacked Yi Ping with their swords! All their attacking strokes were lethal!

They immediately attacked Yi Ping in all directions! There was a saying; two hands were hard to beat down four hands. It was not long before Yi Ping had been pierced in his chest and hacked on his back!

He soon collapsed on the ground, barely taking ten strokes from them.

Now the man with the moustache, who was the more cunning and vicious of the two, stabbed Yi Ping in his heart again.

The man with the long bushy beard asked him angrily, "What did you do that for? He is already dead!"

The man with the moustache laughed wickedly, "I want to make sure that none disturb us later."

The man with the long bushy beard paused and laughed wickedly, "True, true…" But before he could finish laughing, he was grasping a dagger in his throat for breath! When he fell on the ground, his eyes were still staring at the man with the moustache!

The man with the moustache turned and looked wickedly at the extremely beautiful young maiden, "Such an extraordinary beauty. You belong only to me and there is no one else to share in my enjoyment."

The young maiden pursed her lips and there were now tears in her eyes. All of a sudden, her alluring eyes were staring in bewilderment.

When the man with the moustache saw her expressions, he quickly turned around and got a fright of his life!

The young man that he had just killed was standing in front of him! Before he could react, he felt the cold metallic length of a sword piercing through his stomach! When he had died, he was still in disbelief!

The young and extraordinary beautiful maiden nearly fainted from fright as she asked, "Are you a ghost or a man?"

Chapter 2: The Celestial Fairy

When Yi Ping regained his consciousness, he found himself in what seemed to be a dimly lit cave. His first thoughts were that he had already died and he was in hell. But when he saw that his wounds had already been dressed and that he was aching painfully, he knew that somehow he was still alive.

That was because a dead man would never feel pain.

Then he noticed there was a small bonfire in the cave which kept the cave warm.

He tried to sit up and that took all his efforts. As he looked in front of him, all of a sudden, he saw the young and extremely beautiful maiden that he had seen earlier. She appeared to be mediating but before he could say anything, the maiden moved her small alluring lips and spoke, "You should rest more. Your wounds are extremely severe and you may lose your life because of that."

Yi Ping stared at her dreamily. He could not imagine it was real!

The alluring maiden soon flushed deeply as she interrupted gently, "Why are you staring at me? Don't you know that is a rude gesture to stare? And who are you?"

Yi Ping was snapped of his trance and he quickly bowed with his hands, "Maiden, I thank you for saving my life from The Three Evils! I, Yi Ping am in your debts! May I know my benefactor name?"

The alluring young maiden said coolly, "They are not the Three Evils of the West. They are imposters and their martial skills are mediocre. Or else even with your Icy Heavenly Tears Energy protecting you, you will still die."

Yi Ping was bewildered and asked, "What Icy Heavenly Tears Energy?"

The alluring young maiden was silence for some time before she said, "You can call me Maiden Xian. Let me ask you. Who is your protégé master? Why did you come to the Heavenly Mountains?"

Yi Ping replied, "I have no protégé master. All my skills are self-taught…"

Maiden Xian opened her eyes and interrupted angrily, "Nonsense! I have examined your pulses earlier and your pulses emitted the Icy Heavenly Tears Energy Pulses. That is what is protecting your heart from harm. Or else even if you have ten lives, you still will not survive!"

Yi Ping was astonished and puzzled, "Maiden…this is the first time that I have heard of that name…"

Maiden Xian looked intently at him for a few moments before she said, "Do you know Shui Yichi?"

Yi Ping said, "Maiden, I do not want to lie to you. She is my late mother!"

Maiden Xian was momentarily stunned as she was heard saying in a low voice, "She is no longer in this world?" She seemed to be shaken by the news before she asked, "How long was that?"

Yi Ping was curious as he said, "She passed away when I was little…" His eyes were teething with tears as he recalled his sad childhood. "Maiden Xian, you know my late mother?"

Then he paused and almost punched himself. How could she possible know his late mother? She looked younger than twenty. Even he himself, was older than her!

Just as he was recovering from his foolhardy words, she gave him another shocker.

"Indeed! She was my protégé sister. She left the Eternal Ice Palace twenty-years because of one man. She must have imparted all her martial energy to you…that explains why I can find our sect intricate energy in your body meridians…"

Just as he wanted to ask her who she really was, a wicked laughter filled the cave; a large bulky man with red beard had just barged into sight.

The red beard man laughed, "If it isn't for this bonfire here, I would never find this place! What have we here? A couple?"

Maiden Xian said, "He is Huo Fu the Flaming Fist, the sect leader of the Fire Tablet Sect. He must be here to look for an opportunity to loot the Eternal Ice Palace."

The red beard man laughed, "I didn't know I am so famous that even junior pugilists can identify me. Don't we all have the same motives? I am getting cold and this fire is just nice!" But all of a sudden, he took a second look at the dress of Maiden Xian and said, "You are from the Eternal Ice Palace?"

Maiden Xian looked at him hatefully and replied coldly, "That's right!"

Huo Fu laughed, "Good, good! You have two options. Either you show me the way to the Eternal Ice Palace or be subjected to my merciless torture. I can assure you that I won't let you die so easily." He took a deep breath before laughing out again, "After all, I can see that you are a rare beauty and I won't let you die so easily."

Yi Ping was shocked as he stood up, "The Fire Tablet Sect may not be an orthodox clan but they do have some repute in the martial fraternity. How can you say such a thing?"

Huo Fu had a wicked smile on his face, "Who do not covet after the martial secrets of the Eternal Ice Palace? Now that the Celestial Fairy had passed away, countless legions of pugilists have already been making their way here. Among them, are several supposedly heroes from the orthodox clans. Naturally, they did not dare to use their real names. Some did not even dare to travel boldly and travel under a disguise for they are men of high repute in the fraternity! When it is time for them to strike, they will make all sorts of excuses like passing by and claiming that they are righting the wrongdoings of evil men!"

Yi Ping hummed coldly.

Huo Fu looked at him, sensing his hostilities. "I thought you are on my side. The Eternal Ice Palace is a forbidden ground for men. Surely, you can't be from the Eternal Ice Palace too?"

Then Huo Fu clapped his right fist on his left palm as he said, "The intrigue of the martial fraternity is not to be underestimate!"

He pointed his finger at Yi Ping and said, "You must be trying to seduce this young maiden here and almost on the verge of succeeding. You are trying to be the first to sneak into the Eternal Ice Palace, am I right?"

Yi Ping was speechless. He replied coldly, "Senior, you think too much!"

Maiden Xian looked away. Her cheeks were momentarily flushed from his audacity.

Huo Fu laughed, "The young uses their wits while the old uses their strength!"

Yi Ping was indignant and he raised both his palms to attack Huo Fu, "Senior, be prepared for my attack!"

Huo Fu suddenly smiled as he raised both his palms and there was a thunderous clap when both palms impacted together. Yi Ping was thrown off and sent flying backward, knocking against the wall of the cave and crushing into it!

Maiden Xian got up as she cried out, "Hold!"

But it was too late! It happened too fast! She could see that this Huo Fu was an experienced exponent. He had purposely provoked Yi Ping into attacking him so that he could see what stance his opponent would use. As Yi Ping was with her, and was still wary of the martial of the Eternal Ice Palace therefore he had used a ruse.

Huo Fu laughed, "Such simpleton! I was expecting some forms of secret projectiles. Despite knowing that I am the sect leader of the Fire Tablet Sect, he still dares to receive my Fiery Palms. When he attacks me, I already know the depth of his martial strength!"

He looked intently at Maiden Xian, "You seem to be smarter than him but unfortunately, your reaction is too slow. That speaks volumes of our martial strength differences. If your martial skill is to be on par with me, you will be able to intercept him."

This Huo Fu, even though he was big and bulky, seemed to be clumsy and slow wit but he was actually a cunning and experienced exponent! If he was not, how will he be able to survive in the treacherous martial fraternity? He would have died a hundred times over!

Maiden Xian had no choice but to nod slowly. Even though she looked composed, she was extremely upset now.

Huo Fu laughed aloud, "Now maiden, will you choose to tell me the location of the Eternal Ice Palace on your own accord or will you choose to die a slow death?"

Maiden Xian full name was Shui Yixian. Shui Yixian was none other than the Celestial Fairy and the sectarian leader of the Eternal Ice Palace.

But why was she here? She was supposed to have passed away already? Was she not a ninety- year old woman?

The Icy Heavenly Tears Divine Skill was a secret martial skill of the Eternal Ice Palace. When the practitioner reached the ninth and the last stage, they would cease to age. Unfortunately, every thirty-six years after reaching the last stage, the practitioner martial power would be lost for thirty-six days. In order to regain the lost martial power, the practitioner would have to relearn the intricate formula of the Icy Heavenly Tears again.

She had attained the ninth stage of the Icy Heavenly Tears when she was eighteen years old. That was why she had ceased aging and looked like eighteen! She was considered a martial prodigy. For hundreds of years, none of the past practitioners had ever reached the ninth stage of the Icy Heavenly Tears before they were fifty and half of them did not even reach the seventh stage of the divine skill. Even her martial protégé mistress attained the ninth stage of the Icy Heavenly Tears when she was only fifty-five.

There were only two exceptions. One was her and the other was her oldest protégé sister.

Her protégé mistress had two other direct protégés. She was in fact the youngest. The oldest protégé sister was Shui Yichi and her second protégé sister was Shui Yisi. Shui Yichi was also a martial prodigy. She had attained the ninth stage of the Icy Heaven Tears when she was thirty. At that time, she was only fourteen year old and had looked up to her.

Even though they all shared the same surname of Shui, they were not related for they were orphans who did not even know who their parents were. It was customary for the direct protégé disciples of the Eternal Ice Palace to use the clan surname of Shui.

But when she had attained the ninth stage of the Icy Heavenly Tears through sheer hard work and self-cultivation, her second protégé sister was envious and she began to plot against her protégé mistress and her eldest protégé sister. Fortunately, her plot was discovered by her protégé mistress. Her second protégé sister had her martial skills disabled and was driven out of the Eternal Ice Palace!

So this powerful enemy of hers knew that she would lose all her martial power during this period. Who else but her second protégé sister knew the timing of her martial weakness? Who else but her would spread rumors of her death and stirred up the passions of the pugilists in the fraternity of the glorious martial secrets of the Eternal Ice Palace?

Fearing for her life and in need of a secular place to regain her lost martial power, she picked a cave away from the Eternal Ice Palace to meditate as the location of the Eternal Ice Palace was known to her nemesis. In turn, she left the Eternal Ice Palace to her two protégé disciples, Beautiful Sword Fairy Shui Meijian and Jade Sword Fairy Shui Yujian to be in charge.

Unfortunately, her two young protégé disciples were not as highly gifted in martial skills. She was hoping that nothing would go wrong till she returned. But she knew that even if she returned, she would still have to battle countless number of pugilists who would not give up at this point.

The throngs of pugilists that seek to traverse the Heavenly Mountains did not know the exact location of the Eternal Ice Palace therefore they were randomly combing the mountains for clues and a route up to the mysterious Heavenly Mountains. Unfortunately, one group of pugilists found her and she was forced to flee. And that was when she had first encountered Yi Ping.

She had only ten days more before she could fully regain her martial power but that day would not come. While Huo Fu was talking to her, she had already forcefully started to channel all her internal energies into her fingers. In this way, she would temporary regain half of her martial power but afterwards, she would surely die from the forceful exertion!

And she was already preparing to die!

When Huo Fu had just stopped speaking, she had attacked him with both her fingers! Her speed and the windforce that accompanied her fingers thoroughly caught Huo Fu by surprise as he quickly raised his Fiery Palms in retaliation!

There was a huge thunderclap sound as Maiden Xian's fingers impacted upon Huo Fu's palms.

Huo Fu could not believe his eyes as his large bulky body was sent flying backward and out of the cave! He simply could not believe that this young maiden here could be capable of such tremendous force!

Maiden Xian coughed out blood but her focus was still on her enemy. She staggered out of the cave to look for Huo Fu. But he had already escaped very far. She could see his large and bulky figure in the distance as he ran in a stagger manner; for he had been badly injured.

It was said that the swiftness movement skill of the Fire Tablet Sect, the Fiery Chaser was one of the epitome movement skills of the martial fraternity. Its claim was definitely not a boast. If Huo Fu was not injured, she might not even caught sight of him given the head start that he had.

As she had no strength left to pursue him therefore she returned to the cave.

She was now staggering. She had forcefully gathered her internal energy and expended her vital force. Voided of internal energy, it was only a matter of time before she died!

Her eyes were one of sorrows. She cared not that she died. But if she died, the lives of more than a hundred protégés of the Eternal Ice Palace would perish as well! Why was fate so cruel to her?

She staggered to the collapsed wall which Yi Ping had fallen.

When she had reached him, he was convulsing with blood in his mouth. She straightened him and put her palm onto the back of his head. She started to use the last of her vital energies in an attempt to clear his injured channels of any blood clogs.

Even though Yi Ping was severely injured and in a daze, he could see that this young maiden had sustained internal injuries and from the looks of it, her condition was gravely critical. She was very pale now. If she attempted to treat his internal injuries now, she would surely lose her life!

And that was something that Yi Ping did not want to see!

Looking at her, he had forgotten about Huo Fu. He could only remember after he got hit, he had lost consciousness for a while. When he regained his conscious, she was beside him.

Yi Ping said weakly, "Maiden, don't expend your vital energies for me. It is futile. You and I are both dying. I don't wish to see you die before me! Even if you expend all your vital energies for me, my injuries are really far too severe."

Maiden Xian said gently as she looked curiously at him, "If it weren't for me, you will not get yourself injured and be in such a sorry state. Even if you cannot be saved, let fate decide alright? As for me, I am already dying. Nothing in this world can save me now. As for you, young hero, you still have a chance to live. So, don't let it gone to waste…"

Yi Ping was shaking all over and his eyes were in tears, "I don't want you to die! Why should a kind maiden like you die while I live? I don't want to live if you died!"

Shui Yixian's tears flowed down her cheeks as she smiled weakly, "Silly boy! You sound as though we are a…" Her cheeks began to redden for a quick moment as she added, "couple."

She added quickly, "If you only know how old I am, you will not want me. Moreover, the only reason why I am saving you is because you are the son of my eldest protégé sister…."

Yi Ping turned and looked at her gently, "You are you. I like you when I first look at you."

That came from the bottom of his heart and was his honest thoughts.

When a person was dying and in a daze, they tended to speak only the truths. At this moment, Yi Ping had already casted away the painful severity of his injuries and was speaking from the bottom of his heart.

Shui Yixian looked at his eyes with a thousand affections. She burst into tears again as she cried, "Yi Ping…" All of a sudden, she began to cast away her iron shell, forgetting that she was the sect leader of the renowned Eternal Ice Palace. She was now a young maiden again, undoing her years of emotionless cultivation that had made her cold and emotionless! To her protégés, she was always the stern protégé mistress.

How could she forget how touched and grateful she had been when Yi Ping saved her from the three wicked men? Just when she thought that she had escaped from an evil fate, another one had suddenly befall her?

Yi Ping grabbed her hands and said gently, "Since we are both dying, why don't we be man and wife here?"

Yixian nodded without hesitation as she wiped the tears in her eyes with her sleeve, "My husband…"

Yi Ping said gently, "My wife…"

Yi Ping held her hand as he bowed onto the ground, "Heavens above, I, Yi Ping, is willing to take Maiden Xian as my wife, be it through joys or woes, she will always be in my heart!"

Shui Yixian bowed onto the ground too and said, "Heavens above, I, Shui Yixian, is willing to be Yi Ping's wife, be it through joys or woes, through all crisis, I am forever his wife!"

They bowed again onto the ground three more times after they said together, "Heavens and Earth be our witness!" Then they collapsed into embrace together.

Even though they did not exchange a word more, they knew that they were now the most blissful couple and that content to die in one another embrace.

All of a sudden, Yi Ping pointed to the same carvings and drawings of the wall, "What are those?"

Shui Yixian opened her eyes and she began to look at the wall that Yi Ping had indicated. There were many words and drawings on the wall just as Yi Ping had said.

Shui Yixian's eyes shone as she gasped, "These are the intricate formulas of our sect Icy Heaven Tears and the Divine Emerald Skill. Someone must have carved it into the walls of this cave and then sealed it afterwards. And we have accidentally barged into this sealed section."

That sealed wall section was revealed earlier when Huo Fu had sent Yi Ping crashing into it.

Yixian used all her efforts to stagger to the wall as she examined it, "This ninth stage of the Icy Heavens Tears is slightly different from what I have practiced…This one, this one…" Her eyes were beaming with tears.

Yi Ping was curious as he asked weakly, "Something is amiss?"

Shui Yixian nodded, "This one version is more polish than the one that I have been practicing and it seems that someone from our sect have rewritten the intricate formula here." She immediately pointed to the carving and words on the wall for Yi Ping.

Yi Ping could not understand the meanings of the carvings of the wall therefore he replied wryly, "We are dying now. Even if there is a divine skill in front of us, we don't have the lives to practice it."

Shui Yixian said gently, "Others maybe can't but I can!"

While speaking, she had already memorized and organized all the minute details of the intricate formula in her mind. Normally it would take years of dedicated efforts to even grasp the intricate formula and put it into use but she had effortlessly did it.

She had immediately identified the true essence of the intricate formula and found a solution to her loss of martial power state. She immediately proceeded to sit down in a mediation pose and soon there was three wisp of smoke arising from her head.

She opened her eyes once more and wiped away her beads of perspiration before saying, "Yi Ping, I have recovered half of my internal strength. Let me lend you a hand first!"

Before Yi Ping could protest, she had flown to his back and was channeling her vital energies into his body!

Chapter 3: The Icy Heavenly Tears

Yi Ping said to Shui Yixian, "Xian'Er, now that we have almost recovered from our injuries, we should leave the mountains and head south. There are many top exponents like Huo Fu that have gathered here. You are from the Eternal Ice Palace and the way home is no longer safe for you. If the pugilists know that you are from the Eternal Ice Palace, they will not let you off."

Shui Yixian exclaimed, "Do you really don't know who I am?"

Yi Ping said, "You are from the Eternal Ice Palace and is a protégé of the Emerald Mistress."

Shui Yixian sighed. It seemed that he really did not know that she was the Divine Mistress of the Eternal Ice Palace. But it was not surprising. Very few people in the martial fraternity knew her real name.

She asked, "Surely you have heard of the Celestial Fairy?"

Yi Ping smiled, "She is the Emerald Mistress of the Eternal Ice Palace. That is her fraternity name."

Shui Yixian said, "The Celestial Fairy is me. I am the Celestial Fairy!"

Yi Ping was shocked, "That can't be. Xian'Er, you must be playing a joke on me, right?"

Shui Yixian was solemn and she looked intently at him.

Yi Ping embraced her and said, "It doesn't matter who you are. You are you. That is what matters."

Shui Yixian was touched as she gasped, "Yi Ping…"

Yi Ping said, "Even if we were to die in the Heavenly Mountains, I will still follow you!"

Shui Yixian said lovingly, "The Eternal Ice Palace is renowned for these three skills, the Jade Icy Finger, the Divine Emerald Skill and the Frosty Icicle Swordplay. These skills are not suitable for you. Even though your internal strength is our sect Icy Heaven Tears, it is not suitable for men. I can however teach you how to utilize your martial skills…"

Over the next few days, Shui Yixian helped Yi Ping to refine his martial skills. Yi Ping was a quick learner.

He had not met a renowned master and most of his martial skills were picked from the streets and from fighting with thugs.

Shui Yixian explained the meanings behind the stances and taught him to look at various martial strokes in different perspective. Even though it was only for a few days, it was like a sudden enlightenment to him!

Shui Yixian was surprised at how fast Yi Ping could absorb her teachings. He was studious and could practice hard while she meditated upon the Divine Emerald Skill.

Three days later, she could completely circulate her vital energies in her meridian channels and had completely regained her martial power.

At the end of three days, Yi Ping saw a rainbow halo on her head. He was astonished and asked, "Xian'Er, are you alright?"

Shui Yixian smiled and opened her eyes, "Ping'Er, don't you worry. Not only have I completely regained my martial internal strength, I have also figured out the tenth stage of the Icy Heavenly Tears intricate formula. I have never dreamed that such a stage could exist. This crucial stage could be the key to unlock the mysteries of the Divine Emerald Skill. The master that left behind these cravings must be closely related to our sect."

She got up and demolished the carvings on the wall with her palm force. In a few moments, the carvings on the wall were all but unrecognizable!

Yi Ping asked, "Xian'Er, why did you do that for?"

Shui Yixian said, "This martial knowledge is too dangerous to be left behind especially with so many pugilists in this vicinity. If it falls into the wrong hands, then it will be a disaster for the martial fraternity."

Yi Ping nodded in agreement.

Chapter 4: The Battle at Mt. Heavenly

At the lofty peaks of the Heavenly Mountains, more than fifty pugilists from different sects and clans had gathered. There were sect emblems and heraldries of all kinds. After many difficulties, they had gathered together and there seemed to be an uneasy alliance if it exists at all.

Their goals were identical and it was the Eternal Ice Palace.

Unfortunately, to reach this point, there been many bloody encounters and only the fittest of the remnants survived. And these pugilists knew it and were wary of one another.

A yellow dressed maiden in a veil was standing loftily alone. From her visible eyes and enthralling confident posture, everyone was guessing that her beauty must be extraordinary. No one knew who she really was and quite a few pugilists had tried to hook up to her and they got more than what they had asked for.

One of them was Young Master Qiu Wufeng the Windless Swordsman. Who had never heard of the Windless Swordsman? He was in his early thirties yet he was now ranked as one of the four most prominent young men of the martial fraternity.

Of course this had to do with the fact that his father was the Master of the Qiu Martial Clan. The Qiu Aristocracy Clan had been recognized as one of the four most powerful martial clans in the fraternity.

Naturally, the other three renowned young men of the martial fraternity were also from renowned aristocracy or major orthodox clans of the martial!

They were Gongsun Jing the Benevolent from the Gongsun Aristocracy Clan, Zuo Tianyi the Heartless Sword from the Infinity Sword Clan and Nangong Le the Joyous from the Nangong Aristocracy Clan.

As for Young Master Qiu, his Silence Swordplay was one of the most feared swordplay in the martial fraternity, able to come in any direction without a slight movement; his swordplay was silent and windless!

Not only that, in his company today were three equally formidable exponents; Ye Lu the Lightning God, Qiao Feng the Shadow Kicker and Lu Baiyun the Heartless Scholar!

Ye Lu the Lightning God and Qiao Feng the Shadow Kicker were old men who had found fame a long time ago. That they chose to be in the company of Young Master Qiu Wufeng was proof of his clan prestige and renowned!

Lu Baiyun the Heartless Scholar was in his early forties. Even though he was younger than the Lightning God and the Shadow Kicker, he was a prominent swordsman even at the age of eighteen when he defeated the clan protégé master of the Ironclad Clan, one of the seven major orthodox clans!

Young Master Qiu Wufeng approached the yellow dressed maiden and greeted her, "I am Qiu Wufeng the Windless Swordsman. Maiden, may I have the honor of knowing your name?"

What followed was a slap across his face! It happened so fast that he could not react!

The yellow dressed maiden said softly, "If you do not want further humiliation, I suggest you move away from me."

Young Master Qiu Wufeng was stunned. He was a handsome and dashing man. Few women could ever resist him, let alone embarrassed him like that! And he showed his displeasure with his eyes! He swore that he would make her pay!

But the Heartless Scholar stepped in and said, "Maiden, you have offended our young master. Do you think you can get away with this so easily?"

The yellow dressed maiden hummed coldly and she seemed that she did not care.

There was strong malevolent aura coming from the Lightning God and the Shadow Kicker as well. No matter who offended any one of them, it was not an easy matter to get away scotch free. Much less the three of them at the same time!

The Heartless Scholar laughed, "Either you apologize to our young master and accompany him for a few days or you be terribly sorry."

The yellow dressed maiden looked at the Heartless Scholar in his eyes and said, "What if I don't?"

The Heartless Scholar said sternly, "Then forgives me for what I will do next!"

All of a sudden, he was interrupted by a laughter that came from the Clan Chief of the Six Rivers, Long Wudi. "You are a renowned figure in the martial fraternity. If this matter gets out that you uses your martial skills to harass a young lass, won't you be a laughing stock? I am not worry about you but for the repute of the Qiu Clan!"

Even though Long Wudi might not be able to defeat the Heartless Scholar, what he said was like an arrow piercing through the heart.

Young Master Qiu thundered sternly, "Let's us go!"

A young man from among the pugilists laughed coldly, "To think that the reputable Qiu Martial Clan is also interested in the treasures of the Eternal Ice Palace. What laudable action. He is also a womanizer…"

But before he could finish, the Heartless Scholar had sprint next to him and given him two tight slaps!

His swiftness skill was so astonishing that more than half of the pugilists could not help but gasped in awe of it!

The Heartless Scholars said, "Know this, our young master had originally wanted to visit the Emerald Mistress to receive her instructions and to pay her a visit! This is a small lesson for insulting our young master!"

All of a sudden, an old man attacked the Heartless Scholar with his fists.

The Heartless Scholar was startled by the windforce of the fists as he quickly stepped backwards.

The Heartless Scholar could not recognize him and he asked, "Senior, who you are?"

The old man laughed, "I have long retired from the pugilistic fraternity. However, I am not afraid to say that I intend to demolish the Eternal Ice Palace on my own!"

Quite a few pugilists from the crowd laughed at his boast.

The Lightning-God sighed, "Maybe we shouldn't be here. Only Tian Kui is able to execute the Beholder Hands and pushed back the Heartless Scholar with a single strike."

The faces of the pugilists turned ashen at the mention of Tian Kui.

Tian Kui was the number one heretic exponent ten years ago. The bloodshed that he had caused were too numerous to be counted. During his time, there were three more powerful major orthodox clans, the Divine Sword, the Hexagon Spear and the Hyperion Clan. These clans had since been completely annihilated by him.

It was said that ten years ago, he took his rampage to the Eternal Ice Palace. But no one knew the result of that secret duel with the Emerald Mistress.

Everyone assumed that he had lost and had been killed! But it seemed otherwise now.

Tian Kui laughed, "I must be getting old. Even a junior can avoid my strike so easily!"

The Heartless Scholar pay respectfully with his hands and said, "That is because Senior, you have stayed your hand or else I will not even have the chance to back off."

Tian Kui roared with laughter, "Good! At least you respect your elder. I am actually spoiling for a fight." It was true. When he saw the Heartless Scholar displaying his martial skills, he had the interest to spar with him.

The Heartless Scholar turned ashen, "Senior, you…."

Tian Kui pointed at the Lightning God and the Shadow Kicker, "You and you, all of you can fight me at the same time. I want to see if my martial skills have any improvements…"

But before he could finish, he had suddenly frozen.

Everyone looked in the direction that he was looking at and caught sight of two strangers walking towards them.

One was a young man. He was handsome and had a refine and noble air. The other was a young maiden with long black flowing hair. She was so beautiful that she was like a heavenly fairy that had decided to grace the mortal realm. When she saw the pugilists, she began to smile slightly. Immediately, all the pugilists' heart skipped a beat and thought, "Did she just smile at me?"

When the yellow dressed maiden saw Yi Ping, her heart too skipped a beat as she thought, "Why is he here? And why is he with her?" That day after they had met, she had secretly stayed away from his view and saw him burying the villainous bandit king. She had observed him for a while before she left. With his martial abilities, she had doubted he could even cross the lofty peaks of the Heavenly Mountains. She had never been moved by a man before and was constantly worried if he could survive the trek. But now when she saw him, she was comforted but she was also none the pleased. That was because…

Tian Kui was shaking all over. Why was he trembling? Was it because he was trembling with joy and moved by the sight of this heavenly maiden?

Quite a few pugilists immediately thought that even though Tian Kui was old enough to be her grandfather, he was still a lecher after all.

Tian Kui looked at Shui Yixian and asked, "Is that really you?"

Shui Yixian alluring eyes looked at Tian Kui and said softly, "Yes I am!"

Everyone was taken aback. Was Tian Kui acquainted with her?

Tian Kui trembled uncontrollably, "All these years, you have not changed. I have grown even older. Since then, I have trained my martial skills non-stop. I practiced twelve hours daily and now my level of martial expertise has reached a level that even you could not have imagined!"

Tian Kui paused for a while before saying, "I have come for you. Today no matter what, I have to take you as my wife and if you lost to me, you must come with me!"

Ten years ago, Tian Kui challenged the Celestial Fairy and he was soundly defeated by her. His spirits was crushed and since then, he had trained every single day, hoping to meet her again and to defeat her!

He had never seen any maiden as elegant and noble as her. It was love at first sight. When he was defeated by her, he was thoroughly shamed. Unable to cope with the defeat, he thought of ending his own life. But when he thought that he might still have a chance, he resolved to train his martial abilities to perfection so that he could once again challenge her and win her heart.

But when he had heard that she had passed away, he was so upset that he had to go to the Heavenly Mountains and had a look.

He had trembled uncontrollably because she was still alive! And he could still fulfill his desires that he had dreamed of every single night!

All of a sudden, Tian Kui roared aloud and he was filled with martial power. His shout was so terrifying that the pugilists were all forced to take a couple of steps back!

As soon as he had quieted down, he had suddenly attacked the heavenly maiden!

Everyone was stunned and confusion immediately broke out from among the pugilists! They had thought that Tian Kui and the heavenly maiden were acquaintances! They immediately feared for the heavenly maiden.

Every punch, every fist by Tian Kui had so much martial force that he could easily smash the rocks into powder!

But the heavenly maiden instead of dodging his attacks, received his attacks with her hands. She countered his fists with her palms and his palm with her fingers!

In that single moment, Tian Kui had struck at least twenty times and each blow of his could have incapacitated his target! But the heavenly maiden had countered all his blows and retaliated. She had struck Tian Kui on his head with her finger and she had struck her palm on his chest!

It happened so fast that most of the pugilists could only see Tian Kui flunking backwards and he had coughed out blood! There was a red mark on his forehead and his chest seemed to have been burnt by the heavenly maiden!

The result was a shocker as no one had expected Tian Kui to be beaten back in split second!

Tian Kui wiped the blood from his mouth as he got up, "This is not over yet. I have not yet used my best martial skills..." However his voice was shaken. He had never expected himself to be beaten back in such an effortless manner! It was exactly what had happened ten years ago...

Young Master Qiu Wufeng too, had been captivated by this heavenly maiden and was eager to be acquainted with her. Therefore he stepped in and asked Tian Kui, "Old Senior, surely there must be a misunderstanding here. Why are you attacking this maiden?"

Tian Kui laughed, "You still do not know who she is? All of you are here today to attack the Eternal Ice Palace and yet you do not know who she is? What a joke!"

Then he turned and said to Shui Yixian, "Only I am the exception!"

Qiu Wufeng asked, "Can Old Senior please enlighten us? I really do not know." He too, was curious about her.

Tian Kui laughed, "She is the Celestial Fairy! She is none other than the Emerald Mistress of the Eternal Ice Palace!"

Everyone was taken aback. How was it possible? She was supposed to be dead and she was supposed to be an old woman?

Shui Yixian smiled coldly at the pugilists, "That is right. Under the gaze of the Celestial Fairy…" She paused and all of a sudden, there was a cold, malevolent killing aura that radiated in her presence as she said slowly, "There…are…no…survivors!"

All of a sudden, she swung her sleeves and multiple secret projectiles flew in all directions! Those who were unable to dodge were either killed or maimed on the ground!

Young Master Qiu Wufeng had barely dodged her secret projectiles when the Lightning God and the Shadow Kicker sprint in front of him.

The Lightning God shouted to everyone, "If we don't fight her now, sooner or later, we'll be killed!" With that he raised his fists at the Celestial Fairy.

All of a sudden, the pugilists remembered the legend of the Eternal Ice Palace. The Celestial Fairy spared no one that dared to intrude upon her forbidden grounds. If they want to live, they had to fight! But some of the pugilists who had survived her secret projectiles were secretly waiting for the others to attack her while they seized the opportunity to run!

However, when Yi Ping saw that Shui Yixian was about to be attacked by the Lightning God and the Shadow Kicker, he stepped in to interrupt them!

The Shadow Kicker said to Yi Ping, "Outrageous! If I don't incapacitate you within ten moves, I am not the Shadow Kicker!"

The Lighting God said to Qiao Feng the Shadow Kicker, "You alone, is more than enough for this lad! I will go and help the Heartless Scholar!"

Shui Yixian hastily cried out to Yi Ping, "Ping'Er, be careful."

Even before she had barely finished speaking, she was attacked in all directions by the Heartless Scholar, Tian Kui, Long Wudi and the rest of the pugilists.

Only Young Master Qiu and the yellow dressed maiden did not make any move yet.

Qiao Feng the Shadow Kicker was renowned for his powerful shadow kicks. He gave Yi Ping a series of kicks with one continuous attack. Yi Ping had never seen so many kicks moving so fast in his life before. He tried to parry with his sword but he could not avoid the many kicks that struck him on his forearms and legs.

Qiao Feng was kicking relentlessly. He knew that no one could survive his powerful kicks if they kept defending. They would only get themselves seriously injured and had their strength quickly drained away!

Yi Ping barely avoided having his face smashed by Qiao Feng's kick. Yi Ping was already fighting frantically while Qiao Feng appeared to be relaxed and he had only kicked five times!

Qiao Feng said, "This is the sixth move!"

Yi Ping was faltering and he could felt his strength draining away. Yet at the same time he was wholly fascinated by the martial abilities of Qiao Feng.

All of a sudden, Yi Ping started to display the Shadow Kicks as he kicked back at Qiao Feng!

Qiao Feng was momentarily stunned, "Where did you learn that?"

Yi Ping hummed coldly, "I just learnt it!"

Qiao Feng shouted angrily, "That is impossible!" He was now kicking faster and faster, even displaying several secret kick techniques that hid a kick within a kick. In an outburst of few strokes, he had unleashed dozens of shadow kicks!

But Yi Ping heart was pounding as he got more and more fascinated with the Shadow Kicks Skill. He had never known a renowned master and had the personal experience of witnessing an epitome upper martial skill like the renowned Shadow Kick! Unconsciously, he had begun to practice the Shadow Kick as though someone had just been instructing him!

Yi Ping began to kick more and more furiously, improvising the Shadow Kicks as he got along.

Qiao Feng was now breaking into cold sweat even in the cold weather. He had expended a huge amount of martial power and was surprised that an inexperienced pugilist like Yi Ping could hold on for so long and was even matching his kick with a kick, with some moves that were even better than his own!

Before long, Qiao Feng legs were hurting! He could not believe that this young man could even match his decades of dedicated martial foundation! Moreover, how was it possible for this lad to know the Shadow Kick Skill? Even an experienced pugilist could not kick as well as him; much less repeat the kicking feat of his shadow kicks!

Qiao Feng said suddenly, "The Mirror Reflection Skill? You are using the Mirror Reflection Skill?!"

The Mirror Reflection Skill was a skill that could replicate the martial skills of others according to the rumors of the fraternity.

But Yi Ping was not listening.

Yi Ping eyes were glowing as he looked intently at Qiao Feng's kicks! A normal young man would have fallen long ago even if he could parry a kick from Qiao Feng! But Yi Ping was so fascinated with the Shadow Kick Skill that every conscious of his was in it.

So engross was he that he was not aware that he was in pain; nor was he aware that with his present fortitude and martial limitations, he could not possible accomplish these kicks without practicing. Because he was not thinking, he had done the impossible and transcends his limits.

And of course, this had to do with the fact that Yi Ping had a natural ability to memorize any moves. Indeed, most of his martial moves that he had picked up were from looking at the fights of others.

This had also to do with the superb martial instructions that he had received from Shui Yixian while in the cave and he was also somewhat protected by the Icy Heavenly Tears coupled with his natural flair for enduring pain.

Shui Yixian had said, "A fist for a fist, a kick for a kick. That is basic martial basis. Fighting is about dismantling stroke for stroke until you can find a solution to completely overcome your opponent. When an opponent attacks, they will expose themselves to opening. Most pugilists in the martial fraternity are more eager to prove their martial superiority by attacking. Adopting defense is also the best offense to defeat these opponents."

She added, "I am going to teach you the intricate formula of the Listening Rhythm. This will allows you to follow the breathing and movements of your opponents much easier."

Shui Yixian was delighted that Yi Ping was able to learn the Listening Rhythm without any trouble. Normally, this skill requires years to master and perfect…

Yi Ping did not know how to overcome Qiao Feng. Instead of utilizing the Listening Rhythm Skill to follow the moves of the opponent and awaited an opportunity to attack, Yi Ping used his natural flair for memorizing to kick back at Qiao Feng.

If Qiao Feng was not so powerful, Yi Ping would never be forced to the desperate act of pushing his own limitations to keep himself alive.

When Qiao Feng saw him repeating his Shadow Kicks, he changed his kicking stances to breech his kicks. But h was also unwittingly showing Yi Ping how to counter his very own Shadow Kicks with each new move!

Yi Ping was also unconsciously learning the Shadow Kicks and using his gut feeling to look for an opening. Then when he saw an opening, he kicked Qiao Feng on his face directly with a tremendous impact!

Both Qiao Feng and Yi Ping fell onto the ground at almost the same time. Qiao Feng was the one being struck? What about Yi Ping? It was because even though he had not taken a direct hit from Qiao Feng, he had taken serious injuries in his non-vital areas. Moreover, the pace of following Qiao Feng drained him both mentally and physically. And he fell onto the ground, drained of all his strength.

With Qiao Feng martial prowess, if he could stay calm and restraint from anger, it was impossible for Yi Ping to gain an upper hand over him. But when he saw Yi Ping replicating his kicks with familiar moves to his Shadow Kicks, he was indignant. So when he got a hit, his rage emotions attacked his heart and he fainted!

Even though Shui Yixian was fighting several opponents at the same time, she had kept a watchful eye for Yi Ping. Because of that, her martial movements were restricted and only the weaker pugilists had fallen.

When Yi Ping won the duel with Qiao Feng, she was relieved and was also glad. It was because with Yi Ping present martial progression, it was not possible to defeat a top martial exponent like Qiao Feng. But he had done the impossible!

But her distraction had made her opponents bolder!

The Lightning God said, "We can win her!"

Even though Shui Yixian was fighting more than ten top exponents from the martial fraternity at the same time, including Tian Kui, her martial movements were still graceful as she met strokes for strokes and moves with moves. No one could imagine she could manage against so many martial exponents in so many different directions at the same time!

But any experienced pugilists could see that she was now on the defensive and in no time, she would be exhausted and beaten! That was why the Lightning God encouraged the others to make more efforts in their jointed attacks against her!

Tian Kui just got another blow in his chest. He took a deep breather and raised his martial power again before joining in the battle fray again!

The pugilists were using a wolf pack tactics to bring her down as they attacked and retreated at the same time.

Because Shui Yixian was being attacked in all directions, her martial power was not sufficient enough to deal a much more serious impact on stronger exponents. Moreover, she had no chance to take a breather!

The Lightning God raised his martial power to its zenith and unleashed the Lightning Hand Skill with his palm but he was knocked when Yixian struck his palm with her finger.

The Lightning God shouted, "I have finally witnessed the Jade Icy Finger. Excellent! The martial skills of the Eternal Ice Palace are indeed powerful!"

Long Wudi stepped back from the battle fray and said, "This is not a real duel at all. There so many of us against a lone woman. That is not honorable to me. I bid my farewells!

Today, I have witnessed the martial skills of the Eternal Ice Palace and still live. That is something that I shall be proud of!" With that, he left.

No one could spare any strength to say a formal goodbye to him or to force him to stay. That was because this duel was required all their attention. A moment of distraction would mean instant death!

The Heartless Scholar displayed his Whirling Sword Techniques while cursing silently. He could not believe that an unarmed person could avoid his whirling sword techniques so easily.

Shui Yixian was astonished at the sudden speed and intricate strokes of the Whirling Sword Techniques. This forced her to raise the Divine Emerald Skill with her left finger as she deflected the on-slaughter of the attacks of the Heartless Scholar as she evaded at the same time.

All of a sudden, the Celestial Fairy reached out to the tip of his sword blade with her fingers and broke his sword into halve! The Heartless Scholar hastily took a few steps behind. He could not believe anyone could break his precious sword with their fingers!

It seemed that the martial power of the Celestial Fairy had suddenly increased!

Everyone was expecting the Celestial Fairy defense to break down soon as Tian Kui was still attacking her relentlessly.

But the weird thing had happened. Instead of waning, the Celestial Fairy's martial strength appeared to have suddenly increased. Why was that?

It was because Shui Yixian could not focus on the fight while worrying for Yi Ping. So when Yi Ping had defeated his opponent, she was now able to put all her attention on the duel at hand!

All the pugilists were astonished and another three pugilists fell in the battle. Only seven pugilists were still standing. Among then, only Tian Kui, the Heartless Scholar and the Lightning-God had suffered fewer injuries while the remaining four were seriously injured!

More than twenty corpses were now lying on the ground!

Young Master Qiu was watching the fight intently. He saw how a group of thirty pugilists had surrounded and attacked her in all directions. Very slowly, the number of pugilists dwindled down to less than ten. The pugilists in the fight did not take note of their dwindling advantage as their attention was completely in the fight. It was because any small distraction could be fatal!

No matters how intrigue and powerful her opponents' attacks were, the Celestial Fairy would patiently dismantle and neutralize it without any expressions.

So when the Celestial Fairy attacks increased, Young Master Qiu immediately noted the number of dead and feared for the Lightning God and the Heartless Scholar. It was because if the Celestial Fairy were to win, they might not live. If Tian Kui were to win, this merciless villain might not let them live too!

When he heard of the rumors that the Celestial Fairy had passed away, he had assumed correctly that quite a few pugilists might seize the opportunity to give the Eternal Ice Palace some troubles. At the end of the day, it would be better if the secret martial arts of the Eternal Ice Palace were to fall into his hands than to some villainous hands. Therefore he asked his father to lend him three top martial exponents that were guests at the Qiu Martial Clan.

The Lightning God, the Shadow Kicker and the Heartless Scholar were considered as the very top fighters of the martial fraternity. Moreover there were three of them. But he had not expected to find Tian Kui here. Nor did he anticipate that that the passing of the Celestial Fairy to be just a rumor; unless of course this maiden had been lying.

But her martial executions and finesse were all seasoned moves. Only someone who had years of martial practice and progression could do it.

All of a sudden, Young Master Qiu shouted, "Uncle Lu, Uncle Ye. Let us go now!"

Why did he order a sudden retreat?

It was because he had suddenly seen a dozen maidens approaching from afar! Those maidens looked beautiful in the distance but they were like roses with thorns. They could only be from the Eternal Ice Palace. With the number of top pugilists dwindling to just a few, any hope of assaulting the Eternal Ice Palace was no longer possible. Moreover, the Celestial Fairy might not be the only top exponent from the Eternal Ice Palace.

Young Master Qiu was young but he was also a lot wiser than most. He did not want to die from either the hands of the Eternal Ice Palace or from Tian Kui. So what else could he do?

He turned to the yellow dressed maiden and said, "Maiden, I suggest that you escape with me too! Things are not looking good and you'll be safe in our company till we reach somewhere safe."

The yellow dressed maiden looked at him with her beautiful eyes and whispered softly, "How do you know that I am not from the Eternal Ice Palace myself and that I will not kill you myself?"

All of a sudden, Young Master Qiu turned ashen and he immediately fled! However the yellow dressed maiden made no move.

The Heartless Scholar and the Lightning God heard the commands issued by Young Master Qiu. They were sweating and breathing heavily. This fight had been a tough one for them. So when they heard that Young Master Qiu had ordered them to retreat, they had already made up their minds to seize an opportunity to leave the battle.

The Lightning God was the first disentangle from the battle and his first thought was his friend, the Shadow Kicker. Had he fallen?

The Lightning God was dismayed to see the Shadow Kicker onto the ground. He inspected him for signs of vital life and was glad that he was still breathing. He said, "Old friend, you are still alive! Hold on!" He picked the Shadow Kicker and carried him onto his shoulder.

The Heartless Scholar was next but not after he had taken a crushing blow on his chest! He thrown up blood and barely avoided a second blow. Tian Kui had indirectly saved his life when he attacked the Celestial Fairy with a vicious claw! The Celestial Fairy simply flung him onto the side with the windforce generated by her sleeves!

With just two opponents left, the Celestial Fairy was able to regain her vital breath now and with that, her martial internal strength! Her strokes became more and more intricate and powerful, growing in complexity and harder to avoid!

He barely fled from the Celestial Fairy and when he took a second look at the battle scene, only Tian Kui and the Celestial Fairy was still fighting. His body was now trembling with fear. This was the first time he had known fear! Only when he had left the battle, did he realize how frightening the martial levels of the Celestial Fairy had been!

At the same time, Yi Ping had barely regained his conscious and was struggling to get on his feet as he was still being gripped with aching pain. His body had taken a lot of punishment from being hit and he had extended over his physical limits.

Tian Kui laughed and said to Shui Yixian, "Very good. Now there are just two of us left!" All of a sudden, his body seemed to grow even more muscular and bigger as he struck the left and right accupoint channel on his chest.

Shui Yixian raised her thin eyebrows slightly, "The Unholy Possession Skill?"

Tian Kui laughed, "That is right! I didn't think that you can recognize it!"

The Unholy Possession Skill was used by the heretic sects three hundred years ago. It was an evil skill that could sap away the martial power of the opponents while boasting one's martial power.

Tian Kui was reserving the use of this epitome skill to the very last. That was because while this skill could boast his martial power by many folds, it was also a skill that could drain away all his internal power. He had waited until the Celestial Fairy had expended considerable internal strength as she fought the pugilists. Now it was the time to use it.

Shui Yixian had no choice but to raise her martial power to fight against Tian Kui. She raised the martial power of the Divine Emerald Skill to the ninth level, her highest. Even with the invisible force generated by the Divine Emerald Skill, she could still feel her strength being sapped away as Tian Kui landed blows after blows on her. Each time when she met his palms with her fingers, her fingers would tremble slightly.

Tian Kui was surrounded by a martial force that rendered normal strikes useless. This battle could not be decided by martial techniques and strokes but by sheer martial power!

Yi Ping saw that Shui Yixian and Tian Kui were fighting one another so furiously that they were like shadowy images moving all over the place. He wanted to go over to help her but there were constant burning windforce that were generated by their attacks that wept everything onto the ground! There was simply no way to approach the two of them!

Tian Kui attacked even more furiously than ever before as he gained more and more strength. All of a sudden, he turned his palm strikes into claws as he torn away Shui Yixian's sleeves. He laughed, "Even though the martial arts of the Eternal Ice Palace are epitome, it is not without their weakness! I will like to see you fighting without clothes!"

Shui Yixian was indignant but she kept her cool. Instead of trying to land a strike onto her, Tian Kui was aiming at her long dress and sleeves, attempting to outrage her modesty which was a lot easier!

Soon Tian Kui had ripped her sleeves, revealing her white porcelain skin. Tian Kui could feel her attacks falter as she was concerned about her modesty. He could see that her ears had turned red even though she was still without any expression.

Tian Kui grabbed her dress and torn part of it away.

Shui Yixian cried out, "You are a beast! Outrageous!" All of a sudden, Shui Yixian took a few steps back and had coughed out blood. She was really upset and that caused her blood to reverse.

To the practitioners of the Icy Heavenly Tears, emotions were a taboo. That was why the Eternal Ice Palace had no men and its protégés spend their time refining their emotions through mediation.

Tian Kui knew that he had succeeded and he quickly sprint towards her to disable her. He muttered, "I have finally won…"

All of a sudden, the yellow dressed maiden who had been watching had appeared from behind him and gave him a fatal blow on his head!

Tian Kui simply could not believe that anyone could approach him without him knowing! Moreover, the burning inertia windforce generated by the epitome skills of the Divine Emerald Skill and the Unholy Possession Skill were still present and had not died down yet. It was not possible for anyone to interfere in the duel, unless that person possesses uncanny martial power!

It was precisely that Tian Kui did not believe anyone else could possess their level of martial power and it was precisely why he was not on guard. That was when the yellow dressed maiden had approached him from the back and had succeeded in dealing him a fatal blow!

Even more astonishing, Tian Kui was protected by a huge amount of tremendous martial force. Even if he was hit by the Celestial Fairy, he could still continue fighting.

So when he had died, his eyes were still open and staring in disbelief!

Yi Ping was astonished too even though he had witnessed her martial power before.

Shui Yixian had seen the yellow dressed maiden approaching Tian Kui and was surprised that she could move though the burning windforce with ease and what was more, she could not believe her eyes too that the yellow dressed maiden had actually killed Tian Kui with just one blow!

Shui Yixian said gratefully, "Maiden, thank you. If not for you, my modesty will be outrage…" Indeed she was extremely grateful to her. She had almost thought that it was all over. "May I know your name, maiden?"

The yellow dressed maiden replied coldly, "You don't have to be grateful to me. This beast fight dirty and I don't want you to die in such a pathetic manner…"

All of a sudden, the yellow dressed maiden had dealt Shui Yixian a blow on her heart! That sent her flying backwards!

Shui Yixian was completed caught off-guard. She had never expected someone who had just assisted her to attack her! When she had raised her fingers to raise the Divine Emerald Skill, it was too late. The force that struck her heart was the same as the one that she had used on Tian Kui!

Even though the battle between Tian Kui and the Celestial Fairy had stopped some time ago, the burning winds from the battle did not cease yet. Yi Ping had to crawl toward Shui Yixian as he cried out, "Xian'Er! Are you alright?!"

Yi Ping caught hold of Shui Yixian's hands as he asked again, "Xian'Er, are you alright?"

Shui Yixian could not reply but she smiled weakly. She knew that this blow had been fatal and that she could feel her very life seeping away.

Yi Ping pointed at the yellow dressed maiden, "We are not your enemies. Why did you suddenly attack Xian'Er for?!"

The yellow dressed maiden said, "You know her well? Do you know that she is the Celestial Fairy?"

Yi Ping laughed aloud, "How will I not know? She is Xian'Er, my wife!"

The yellow dressed maiden was startled, "Your wife? Do you know that she is actually a ninety-year woman? That is because she has reached the highest epitome of the internal arts that she cannot age."

Yi Ping said hatefully to her, "How would I know? Why should I care? I love her and her alone. I don't care about any other things! How vicious are you!"

The yellow dressed maiden was startled as she answered coldly, "I am vicious? Do you know this woman in front of you is capable of killing anyone without batting an eyelid? If I am vicious then she is even more vicious!"

Yi Ping cried out, "No matter if she is the most vicious woman under the heavens, in my heart she is an angel. She is the kindest hearted maiden that I have never known. She is my dear wife and we swore to go through woes and joy together!"

Shui Yixian was crying now as she gasped, "Ping'Er…"

Even the yellow dressed maiden seemed to be moved as her eyes turned watery. But she said coldly, "Before you die, I will tell you the truth so that you will die peacefully. I am the grand-daughter of Shui Yisi!"

Yixian was startled even though as she had expected her enemy to be Shui Yisi, "Where is Shui Yisi?"

The yellow dressed maiden replied coldly, "She had died five decades ago. You have no idea that when she had died, she was still bitter and filled with hatred towards you. That curse did not end with her. My mother was also afflicted by her bitterness that her whole life was to pursue means to end your life. That bitterness did not end with her death. She had passed on that bitterness to me. All my life, I have only known a purpose. That is to kill you."

Shui Yixian could sense her cold bitterness in her tone. Indeed, she could imagine her sufferings. If she had not suffered a great deal of ordeal, she would never have reached her level of martial accomplishments to injure her. She could imagine that her mother went through an even greater ordeal to realize her daughter martial accomplishments.

Therefore she could only say weakly, "Yi Ping, when I am gone, don't avenge for me. You are not her match." She looked at the yellow dressed maiden and said weakly, "I hope that you can spare him…"

The yellow dressed maiden said coldly, "My target is only you."

Shui Yixian said, "Good…may my death bury all these feuds between us."

Suddenly, a dozen maidens in light blue dressed descended around them and they were crying, "Protégé Mistress! What exactly has happens?"

The yellow dressed maiden hummed coldly and began to walk away.

Shui Yixian said weakly and said to a young maiden who was holding her, "Yu'Er. I am dying now. When I am dead, bury me in the ice casket at the inner sanctuary that I have prepared…"

Yu'Er, who was also the Jade Sword Fairy Shui Yujian, cried out, "Protégé Mistress, you will never die! Who did that to you? I will slice him into a million pieces!"

She turned and looked at Yi Ping as she said coldly, "This is the filthy man that did it?" She was about to stab him with her sword when Shui Yixian interrupted panicky, "He is…my husband."

Shui Yujian was shocked and so were the others.

Shui Yixian said, "He is to be the next protégé master of the Eternal Ice Palace, Mei'Er and you, are to serve him faithfully in my stead…"

She smiled weakly and closed her eyes, "Ping'Er, you have to live on…"

Yi Ping cried out, "Xian'Er! Xian'Er…Don't leave me!"

But Shui Yixian did not and could not reply anymore.

Yi Ping trembled and fainted; the shock of witnessing his wife died right in front of him was too much to bear for him…

Chapter 5: Jade and Beautiful Sword Fairies

When Yi Ping regained his consciousness, he found himself in a large feathery bed. The bed was fragrant and comfortable. He could not believe such a comfortable bed could actually exist. He was feeling so relax in the bed that he did not want to wake up.

"Protégé Master, you have awakened?" A sweet voice was heard.

Yi Ping had a sudden shock. He had suddenly remembered the events that had taken place at Mt. Heavenly. He called out panicky, "Xian'Er, where are you?"

He looked around him and saw two young beautiful maidens standing in front of the bed who were smiling at him. He blinked his eyes. He had recognized Shui Yujian voice but there were two 'Yujian' now!

Yi Ping said, "Yujian?"

The exquisite young beautiful maiden that had just spoken laughed softly, "No, that is my sister. I am Shui Meijan. We are twins! You can also call me the Beautiful Sword Fairy."

Shui Meijian was delighted that Yi Ping had awakened. When she looked at him, her heart was fluttering. She was a little disappointed that he had called out her sister first. But soon she had forgotten about her disappointment as she introduced herself.

Shui Yujian sighed in her heart. She was more reserved than her twin sister. She pursed her lips and wished that she could respond quicker than her sister.

Yi Ping nodded and asked, "Where is Yixian? Is she…"

Shui Yujian burst into tears, "Protégé Mistress had passed away. We have laid her body into the inner sanctuary." This time, she was quicker than her sister.

Yi Ping was silent for a long time while Shui Meijian and Shui Yujian looked at him quietly; they did not dare to disturb his thoughts.

Yi Ping was suddenly aware that he was clothed in a new and clean garment. He muttered, "My clothing…?"

Shui Yujian said, "Protégé Master, Sister Mei and I have showered for you and help you get dressed. As for your old clothing, it is too dirty and too difficult to mend. So we have thrown it away. Protégé Master, don't be upset with us…"

Yi Ping turned flustered, "It is not that…I am a man, the two of you are still young maidens…I…"

Shui Meijian giggled softly, "Protégé Master must be shy! You are our master now and we are all your properties. It is our duty to serve you and to take care of your daily needs."

Yi Ping tried to change the topic by asking them, "You are Beautiful Sword Fairy Shui Meijian and Jade Sword Fairy Shui Yujian?"

Yujian and Meijian said at the same time, "That is right, Protégé Master!"

Yi Ping said, "Take me to the inner sanctuary. I want to take a look at Yixian."

Shui Yujian appeared to be panicky, "Protégé Master, the ice casket has already been sealed! We can only bring you to the inner sanctuary chamber."

Yi Ping sighed, "Is that so? It's alright. Just bring me there."

Shui Meijian and Shui Yujian bowed respectfully, "Yes, Protégé Master!"

Yi Ping said awkwardly, "Disperse with this 'Protégé Master' formalities. Err…I don't feel comfortable with it."

Shui Meijian and Shui Yujian took a look at each other before saying, "Yes, Master!"

Yi Ping sighed and said, "That Master word too."

As they walked along the passageways, Yi Ping noticed that it was colder than usual and asked out of curiosity, "The Eternal Ice Palace seems to be a cold place. How can the two of you bear this unbearable cold?"

Shui Meijian laughed softly, "Mas…We are used to the cold. The Eternal Ice Palace is situated beneath the Heavenly Lake. That is why none of the pugilists can find this place."

Yi Ping was astonished, "We are under a lake?" He looked around him and admired the marbles of the passageway. "This must have taken a lot of effort and time to construct…"

He imagined the hardship of the laborers and wondered if anyone of them would be allowed to leave the Eternal Ice Palace alive. It was because even though the Eternal Ice Palace was not an unorthodox clan, it was a mysterious place which is off-limits to outsiders and shrouded in secrecy.

Shui Meijian smiled, "I do not know. It has been here when we are here. And the Eternal Ice Palace is centuries old. But we do have sisters that are skilled in masonry here. I will ask them later."

Yi Ping replied, "Oh. That won't be a necessary. I am just being curious..."

But as they walked along the passage, Yi Ping saw many more maidens that were dressed in refinery, he could not resist commenting. "These maidens are all so young and beautiful; to think that they have to spend all their eternity here. It is really such a pity."

Shui Yujian had misunderstood and said shyly, "We are all your women. If Master desires any one of us, please feel free to summon us to your presence…"

Yi Ping was startled and he quickly said, "This is not what I mean. And can you imagine the boredom of staying here all your life? All of you deserve to find a partner, have a family and knows what is happening to the fraternity at large."

All of a sudden, both Shui Yujian and Shui Meijian burst into tears.

Yi Ping was at a loss as he asked, "I…I am so sorry. What has happened?"

Shui Meijian sobbed, "Master, you may not know that the Eternal Ice Palace does releases our older protégés when they are twenty-five so that they can get married. But their fates often ended up in misery. The outside fraternity is crude and fraught with dangers. If they were discovered to be from the Eternal Ice Palace, they would be tortured by the pugilists for our clan martial secrets. "

Shui Yujian added, "As Sister Mei and I are the direct protégés of our late Protégé Mistress the Celestial Fairy, we the only exceptions and we cannot leave the Eternal Ice Palace. However, the rest of our sisters have to leave the Eternal Ice Palace when they are twenty-five. This is an unbroken rule. Unless Protégé Master is willing to accept them as direct protégés, they are not allowed to stay."

Yi Ping asked, "Why not allow those who want to stay to stay and let those who want to leave to leave?"

Shui Yujian replied, "It had been like this in the distant past. But some protégé sisters either regret their decisions to stay or leave, so it was finally made into a clan golden rule that all non-direct protégé disciples have to leave when they reach twenty-five. Since then, there have been no exceptions."

Yi Ping asked, "The clan rule can't be changed?"

Shui Yujian said, "It cannot be changed. It is considered a great disrespect and dishonor to past venerable leaders to do so."

Yi Ping nodded for he understood that clan honor means everything to the people of the martial fraternity. But he added defiantly, "The Eternal Ice Palace is off-limits to men. I am sure that it is a clan golden rule as well. That I am here, does it mean the clan rule has been broken?"

Shui Meijian laughed and interrupted cheekily, "That is not entirely true. We do have men guests from time to time. Moreover, the first founder of the Eternal Ice Palace is a man!"

Yi Ping was taken aback, "The Eternal Ice Palace is founded by a man?!"

Shui Yujian giggled. "That is right! In fact, several of our past Eternal Ice Palace leaderships were helmed by men. But because our past few protégé mistresses had been women and it not convenient for men to be in the Eternal Ice Palace, so it is generally off-limits to men."

Shui Meijian added, "Moreover, the skills of the Eternal Ice Palace are not wholly suitable for men. So generally, the leadership of the Eternal Ice Palace is often passed to a woman."

Yi Ping asked, "I don't understand. Since the founder of the Eternal Ice Palace is a man, how is it possible for him to invent the Icy Heavenly Tears and the Divine Emerald Skill among many which are more suitable for women?"

Shui Yujian laughed softly, "That is because the martial origins of the Eternal Ice Palace come from his wife! The founder was said to be a scholar who did not know any martial skills."

Yi Ping rubbed his nose for warmth and looked at Shui Yujian and Shui Meijian directly for the first time. Only a blind man would fail to see how beautiful and appealing they were.

Indeed, other than Shui Yixian, he had never seen anyone else as beautiful and captivating as them. To think that just a few days ago, he had been so fearful of the reputation of the Eternal Ice Palace.

Shui Meijian raised her alluring voice, "Master! Are you alright?"

Yi Ping woke from his trance and quickly replied, "I am alright. You really shouldn't keep calling me Master…"

Shui Meijian giggled, "Master…alas I forget so fast. I'm so sorry!"

Yi Ping awkwardly replied, "Never mind…"

Shui Yujian laughed softly, "Master, you are looking at us so intently just now. Is there something wrong?"

Yi Ping said quickly, "No, nothing is wrong. I am just day-dreaming. You also, alas I am not your Master…"

Shui Meijian teased, "Master, you been sleeping for two days and you still feel sleepy?"

Yi Ping had completely given up on correcting them as he sighed in his heart. It seemed that they were too mindful of their manners and found it hard to adjust their etiquettes.

Shui Yujian gave Shui Meijian a quick tug and she quickly kept quiet. When Shui Yujian had tugged her, she realized that she was acting inappropriately and forgot that Yi Ping was their protégé master.

Yi Ping soon realized that Shui Yujian was more refined and careful in her speech while Shui Meijian was quick in speech and would say anything she thought of.

While walking to their destination, Shui Meijian began to hymn softly as she began to sing in a low voice.

Yi Ping was startled. Her voice and music was very beautiful. Yi Ping asked, "Mei'Er, you know how to sing too?"

Shui Meijian was startled and asked panicky, "Something wrong, Master?" She hoped that she had not offended him. She was almost in tears as she asked fearfully, "Did I disturb you…"

Even Shui Yujian was startled.

Yi Ping quickly said, "Oh no. Your lyrics and the melodies that you have just hymn, is just too beautiful. I enjoy music too." And he began to whistle beautifully too.

Shui Meijian was delighted as she happily clapped, "My sister and I love to sing too!"

Shui Yujian was also absolutely delighted that Yi Ping also appreciated music as she hymned a quick melody.

Yi Ping praised her, "This tune is so unique. I have never heard of it. It is simply too heavenly. If I can hear this every day, I will be content."

Shui Yujian flustered as she lowered her face, "We can play the zither, pipa and the erhu too."

Yi Ping gasped, "That is not easy. The two of you must be really talented in your musical accomplishments."

Shui Meijian laughed captivating, "Our Protégé Mistress does not really encourage us, and thinks it is a waste of time…"

Shui Yujian tugged her hard and said, "Let us continue now. We are reaching soon."

Yi Ping nodded.

It was not long before they had reached the inner sanctuary chamber.

Shui Yujian said, "Master, we have reached."

The chamber was large and freezing cold. In the middle of the chamber was a white marble casket.

Yi Ping immediately ran to the casket and fell onto it. He muttered, "Yixian, Yixian, why have you left me…"

Yi Ping was clearly inconsolable for a long time. Shui Yujian tried to console him but he had not heard her.

Yi Ping was too sorrowful. He wailed to heavens for separating Shui Yixian and him as he replayed his memories of her.

It was not long before tears appeared in the sisters' eyes as well as they watched him expressed his sorrows for their late protégé mistress.

Shui Yujian could feel her heart aching. Her impressions of men were generally not impressive until she had met Yi Ping. Even though she had only known him briefly, he already had a place in her heart.

Shui Meijian was clenching her hands together onto her bosoms as she held back her tears. She had secretly fallen in love with him. At first when she was notified by her sister that they got a new protégé master, she was in shock. When she had saw Yi Ping, she was even more startled with his noble air and looks. It was love at first sight for her…

Yi Ping suddenly stood up and said tearfully, "I got to leave this place now."

It was because he had a sudden realization what he was going to do next. If he could not avenge for his wife's death, then his wife would never be put to rest.

Shui Meijian hastily asked, "Master, where are you going? You can't just leave the Eternal Ice Palace."

Yi Ping said, "I am going to avenge my wife's killer and I am going to find her no matter where she is!"

Shui Yujian asked, "Master, you know the killer?"

Yi Ping hummed coldly, "Even though I did not see her face but I will never forget her martial display! I will find her and offer her blood to my dear wife!"

Shui Meijian said, "Master, then let us accompany you!"

Yi Ping shook his head, "I have no idea how long it is going to take. Moreover, the Eternal Ice Palace needs someone to take care of and to protect it from external threat. As the most senior protégés, that responsibility will be yours."

Shui Yujian cried, "Don't we have the same responsibility to avenge our late protégé mistress too?"

Yi Ping had already made up his mind. And moreover, Shui Yujian and Shui Meijian had never been to the outside fraternity. They had no idea how dangerous and treacherous the people of the martial fraternity could be. Besides with two beautiful maidens accompanying him, it could be more of a hindrance.

But he had no idea how much he had hurt them. It was because they had thought that he did not like them and did not want them to be in his company.

Chapter 6: Gongsun Jing

Yi Ping did not know how long he had been wandering since he had left the Eternal Ice Palace. Was it days, weeks or months? He could not really remember.

That was because all he could remember on the eve of leaving the Eternal Ice Palace, was that he got very drunk; Very dead drunk. When he was awake, he was in bed naked; and so were Shui Yujian and Shui Meijian besides him.

That was why he left the Eternal Ice Palace in haste and he was in a daze for a long time. What did he actually do? He could not believe what he had done and what had happened.

"Yixian, Yujian, Meijian…forgives me…"

He cursed himself for hurting Shui Yujian and Shui Meijian and losing their trust in him. He could not imagine that he had actually destroyed the lives of two innocent maidens in his drunken state. After that he was in low spirits for a really long time and was often in a daze as he thought of Yixian, Yujian and Meijian.

Yixian had entrusted her two protégés to him and yet he did something so unthinkable to them. He could never forgive himself for what he had done.

He thought of taking his life on numerous occasions but when he remembered that he had not found his wife's killer yet, he reluctantly pulled himself together again.

He was Yi Ping of old again. It was as though he was still a wanderer and had never been to the Eternal Ice Palace. Everything was just a beautiful dream. No one would ever believe him even if he tells anyone.

But he could not forget the fact that Shui Yixian was his wife and that she had died in his embrace. He could not forget the blood feud that he had with the yellow dressed maiden. He had no idea where she was. He did not even know her name! It was as though she had never existed.

He was confused. Was everything just a dream?

He was drinking wine as usual in a tavern. He did not have a habit of drinking before he went to the Eternal Ice Palace. But because drinking was the only way for him to forget his unhappiness and the tragic death of his wife, he retorted to it. That was another reason why he could not remember how long he had been wandering or the passage of time as he was drunk most of the time.

He thought he had a purpose but he had since lost that purpose. Even if he could find his enemy, could he be able to defeat her?

All of a sudden, someone greeted him, "Young hero, why are you drinking alone? Do you mind if we sit beside you?"

Yi Ping looked up and saw a handsome young man. He was the one that had greeted him and he looked like a refine scholar. There were two others with him; one was a one-arm old man but he was anything but old for he exudes strength and vitality. The other was a middle age monk with a thick white eyebrow.

The refine scholar added, "I apologize for not properly introducing myself. I am Gongsun Jing."

Those with the clan surname of Gongsun were few and only one martial family carried that clan name. This refine scholar was none other than Gongsun Jing the Benevolent from the

Gongsun Aristocracy Clan. He was said to be a highly regarded and won the respect of the pugilistic heroes for his kindness and thoughtfulness.

Even Yi Ping had heard of his renown and had once wished to be acquainted with him! But that was in the past and all he wanted now was to be left alone.

Gongsun Jing had seen a handsome young man drinking alone. Judging by the sword that he had besides him, he garnered that this young man must have come from a renowned martial clan. He was eager to recruit the likes of him as his friends and followers. The younger they were, the easier to be acquainted with!

It was not a one sided friendship. Likewise, the pugilistic heroes from the martial clans would also like to befriend Gongsun Jing for he had the renowned and would be a powerful backer in the future.

Unfortunately for Gongsun Jing, Yi Ping was not from any martial clan. The sword that he had with him was just a sword that he had grabbed from the Eternal Ice Palace on a whim as he had lost his own sword. And today, he was only interested in drinking and had just started.

The sword that Yi Ping had randomly grabbed was one of the four most precious swords of the Eternal Ice Palace, christened the White Emerald Phoenix.

Gongsun Jing was eying Yi Ping's sword and said, "Do you mind that I take a look at your sword?" He had said so casually as the white emerald sword that Yi Ping had on him caught his attention. He was a swordsman and interested in all kinds of swords.

To his surprise, Yi Ping simply said. "You can take a look." He placed the sword onto the table.

In the martial fraternity, the pugilists regard their weapons dearly and would never allow strangers to inspect their weapons. A weapon weight and its characteristic would often give their opponents' clues on how best to counter it.

And moreover, a swordsman would never part with his sword unless he was dead.

Therefore Gongsun Jing had not really expected this young man to surrender his sword so readily. He had expected the young man to either reject him nicely or rudely and he would have a good idea if he was a friend or foe.

Gongsun Jing took the White Emerald Sword and inspected it. There was a 'White Phoenix' and an 'Emerald' inscription on it. The emeralds that adorned the white long were real and the blade of the sword was exceptional sharp!

Even the one armed old man who did not appeared to be interested in the sword at first, was exclaiming when Gongsun Jing had just unsheathed the sword, "What a good sword! It is surely one of the few top tier swords in the fraternity!"

When the White Emerald Sword was unsheathed, the brilliant chilling malevolent aura of the sword was brilliant and everyone could feel its chill piercing through their bones!

Gongsun Jing was bewildered. The owner of this sword had to be from a renowned martial clan in order to protect this sword and would be zealous of it.

But this young man did not seem to care very much for his sword.

And he did not seem to be very interested in acquainting with him even after he had reported his name aloud in an attempt to awe him. Yet he was generous enough to show him his sword.

Even in the Honor Manor, there were no swords of this quality and Gongsun Jing was secretly covetous of the White Emerald Sword.

He reluctantly returned the White Emerald Sword to Yi Ping, who took back the sword without saying anything.

Gongsun Jing smiled and said, "I am interested to be acquainted with heroes from all over the martial fraternity. Do you mind telling me your name and your martial clan of origin, young hero?"

But Yi Ping was too despondent and disheartened to say anything. And moreover he was just a nameless nobody while Gongsun Jing was a renowned figure in the martial fraternity.

Gongsun Jing was embarrassed by his silence and added, "I can buy you all the drinks that you want, young hero."

Pugilists in the fraternity were mostly lovers of wines and would hardly reject such a generous free offer.

But still, Yi Ping continued to ignore him.

This enraged the one-arm old man who shouted, "What insolence! You have no idea what is good for you, young man!" He threw a punch at Yi Ping.

Yi Ping saw the incoming punch and barely blocked the attack. This seeming innocuous move was like an unstoppable force and had actually pushed him backward and he was forced to get off his seat! The one-armed old man was a more powerful opponent than he had looked and his martial level was not beneath Tian Kui!

Gongsun Jing exclaimed aloud and praised Yi Ping, "Good! To think that he can actually block Uncle Gu attack!"

This rejuvenated Yi Ping fighting spirit and he began to attack the one-armed old man with his fists and palms.

The one-armed old man blocked his attacks easily and without any effort. The one-armed old man laughed and shouted, "Do you know who I am? You dare to raise your fist against me? Let me tell you. I am Gu Tianle the Warrior-God!"

Yi Ping was startled. Who had never heard of Gu Tianle before? He was the only one that deserved the title of Warrior-God. His martial abilities were renowned throughout the martial fraternity for the past twenty-years! Twenty-years, he had single-handedly stormed into the most powerful heretic sect in the martial fraternity, the Holy Hex Sect and defeated the most powerful heretic martial exponent leader Ji Yunzhong. That earned him the title of Warrior-God!

From then on, the various heretic sects and unorthodox clans began to lie low. This was the result of his resounding act!

Gu Tianle shouted, "If you still do not display your true martial origin, don't blame me for not warning you!"

Yi Ping knew that Gu Tianle was only playing with him and he could sense that his incoming blows were getting more and more furious and more intricate.

He decided to display the Shadow Kick Skill that he had picked up from Qiao Feng the Shadow Kicker. But to his surprise, Gu Tianle simply blocked his shadow kicks with his forearm and all of a sudden, he became enraged, "Who is Qiao Feng to you?"

This time, he was no longer teasing with Yi Ping and struck him on his chest. This sent Yi Ping violently backward with a crushing sound. Yi Ping was stunned that despite the Shadow Kicks and the frontal defense that he had positioned, Gu Tianle could punch through him so easily!

Yi Ping rubbed away the blood off his mouth and spat, "I have nothing to do with Qiao Feng!"

Gu Tianle hummed coldly, "If you are not related to Qiao Feng, where did you learn the Shadow Kick Skill from?"

Yi Ping said coldly, "I do not need to explain to you!"

The reason why Gu Tianle had been so upset with Qiao Feng was because he had lost his arm in an ambush by Qiao Feng the Shadow Kicker and his sworn brother, Ye Lu the Lightning God.

Gu Tianle raised the martial power in his palm and shouted, "Let see if you can withstand this!"

Yi Ping stood up defiantly and raised all his martial power in both his palms to accept the incoming attack.

Gongsun Jing shouted, "Young hero, it is dangerous for you. You risk death by…"

But Yi Ping paid him no heed. There was a crashing force and a thunderous clapping sound as Yi Ping was flung all the way till he crashed onto the wall!

Gu Tianle had only use miniscule strength but he was surprised that Yi Ping had so much martial power for a young man like him. He thought, "Isn't he the old freak's disciple?" It was because at the moment of impact, he had felt the cold negative radiance force of his internal strength.

Gu Tianle did not know that Yi Ping internal strength was the Icy Heavenly Tears or else he would surely be in a greater surprise.

Most internal strength forces displayed by the martial fraternity were positive types. Only a few such as the Eternal Ice Palace, the Holylight Sect and the Southern Sword Sect used the negative types. It was because negative type progressions were generally slower and dangerous to practice alone. That was why these sects were usually seclusion sects and rarely interfere in the affairs of the martial fraternity.

But before Gu Tianle could ask him further, Yi Ping had jumped off from the second floor of the tavern!

They were astonished that Yi Ping still had the strength to escape.

Gongsun Jing sighed, "We have injured him and if he dies, I will not feel good. All I want is just to befriend him…"

The Monk who real name was Jue Yuan said, "He is severely injured and cannot go too far away. Let me get him to the residence to recuperate so that we can show him we do not mean him any harm."

With that, Jue Yuan jumped down from the second storey of the tavern as well!

A crowd had already gathered when the commotion started. They began to praise Gongsun Jing, "Young Master Gongsun is a compassionate hero that is kind even to his enemies!"

Someone cursed Yi Ping, "It isn't Young Master Gongsun fault. I witness the act. That young man was just an insolence and arrogant thing. He is probably an enemy of the Gongsun Residence in the first place!"

Chapter 7: The Divine Horizon Hands

Yi Ping had run outside the town. He struggled with his injuries till he got out of town. He knew that he was being pursued but his pursuer did not seem to be in a hurry.

He sat down to recuperate and waited for his pursuer to appear.

Sure enough, a monk appeared in the horizon.

Yi Ping hummed coldly, "You have come."

Jue Yuan laughed, "Yes, I have come. It seems that you been expecting me."

Yi Ping said, "We are now in an isolated place. This place is the perfect place for you to kill me."

Jue Yuan laughed, "Indeed! I, Jue Yuan the merciless, will send you to the heavens today!"

Yi Ping said coldly, "What a name! And I thought that a monk is someone merciful!"

Jue Yuan said proudly, "Not me. To be merciful to the enemy is to be merciless to ourselves, am I right to say so?"

Yi Ping replied, "Indeed."

He added, "I will never think that the Gongsun Jing the Benevolent will be someone who is malicious to a stranger."

Jue Yuan said, "You have made two mistakes. Firstly, you have rejected the friendship of our Young Master Gongsun and secondly you are the protégé of Qiao Feng the Shadow Kicker. Any of these deserves the death penalty, don't you think so?"

Yi Ping got up and drawn his long sword, "So this is martial fraternity justice! Those who are not on your side are your enemy! What a joke! Even a nameless nobody like me deserve to have the great monk Jue Yuan to dirty his hands!"

Jue Yuan laughed as he rubbed his prayer beads that were in his hands, "You are not a nameless fellow. The fact that you can withstand a blow from Gu Tianle and still survives proves that. Even if you are not a threat now, you will be one in the future when my Young Master Gongsun wants to unite the martial fraternity."

All of a sudden, Jue Yuan broke his prayer beads and each of the beads sped towards Yi Ping with tremendous speed and force!

Yi Ping was surprised and he quickly raised his sword in defense.

But the weirdest thing happened. All twenty of the prayer beads fell onto the ground right in front of Yi Ping as though it had all struck an invisible barrier!

Both Yi Ping and Jue Yuan were surprised!

Jue Yuan was dumbfounded. He was famous for his killing prayer bead projectiles. At this distance, no one could ever dodge all twenty of his prayer bead projectiles.

To suppose that this injured young man with his current martial level could do so was highly improbable. Moreover, this young man had not even begun attempting. His prayer beads seemed to strike an invisible wall!

"A monk bullying a wounded man and attempting to kill him, this is humph interesting…"

Yi Ping and Jue Yuan looked up and saw a young maiden with black flowing hair sitting on top of a tree branch. It was not her exquisite beauty that caused them to hold their breath even though her beauty was impossible to describe and her looks was peerless! The fact that someone could move within their sight and yet they were not aware was simply too extraordinary!

Yi Ping heart was pounding fast. At first he had thought she was Shui Yixian but when he looked carefully, he realized his mistake. Both of them shared the same unparalleled beauty and were extremely beholden to gaze upon!

Yi Ping heart sunk immediately in disappointment.

The extraordinary beautiful maiden jumped onto the ground. Her descend was unhurried and she landed on the tips of the grass gently.

She said, "I didn't want to interfere in your affairs but the conversation is too much for me to bear."

Jue Yuan could not believe his eyes. This 'Tipping on Grass' like the 'Walking on Grass' was the highest epitome of any levitation skills. That she was just hovering on the tip of the grass spoke volumes of her breathing technique and martial progression. He simply could not believe that this young maiden would be capable of such a feat!

Jue Yuan asked, "Who are you?"

The extraordinary beautiful maiden said coldly, "It seems that you are not only a merciless monk but also a lecherous monk. Not only a lecherous monk but a shameless monk to ask a maiden her name in broad daylight!"

She did not mince her words at all. This instantly angered Jue Yuan.

Jue Yuan angrily said, "No matter. I know who you are soon!" He unleashed his Triple Merciless Palms at the young maiden!

Jue Yuan was famed for his deadly Triple Merciless Palms and had killed countless number of pugilists.

Yi Ping warned the maiden, "Be careful, maiden…"

She had interfered because of him and he did not want anything to happen to her.

The Triple Merciless Palms were indeed extraordinary and deadly. No wonder it was ranked so highly in the martial fraternity! The extraordinary beautiful maiden was taken by surprise as she barely avoided the first three strokes of the Triple Merciless Palms.

Jue Yuan was surprised as well. He had never seen anyone evading the likes of her before. When he attacked with the Forceful Bale Stroke from the Triple Merciless Skill as he charged, it could be followed by any strokes. This forces his opponent with no other choices but to fight him in close quarter.

This caused him to waste his ingenious stroke and to end the combat quickly.

Jue Yuan however, did not hesitate at all and rained down blows after blows on her.

The extraordinary beautiful maiden displayed a variety of martial strokes to counter his blows. Therefore, Jue Yuan was not able to guess her martial origins. It seemed that she was intentionally hiding it.

He wryly mocked, "It seems that you are intentionally hiding your martial origin. Even if you are a charming lady, you will soon learn that I, Jue Yuan am like no others before you. That is why I am known as the merciless monk!"

And he increased his strength and the martial power of his palms. "I will take you down in under thirty moves! I like to see if you are still able to hide your martial origin!"

The extraordinary beautiful maiden was aware that Jue Yuan meant what he had said. All of a sudden, there was a sudden shriek and her smooth silken right hand was imbued with an extraordinary force that projected a mighty tremendous force onto Jue Yuan!

Jue Yuan was struck by that mighty projected force and was flung backward!

Even Yi Ping was exclaiming aloud, "What an extraordinary martial skill!"

It was because projected force would get weaker away as the distance increases. But this extraordinary palm technique extended the projected force of the palm by a short distance. Even though the projected distance of this palm technique was extremely short, it was this aspect that was truthfully frightening! Normal pugilists could not block against it and this palm technique could also weaken the strength of the opponent before a clash.

As Yi Ping was standing behind the extraordinary beautiful maiden, he could see that she had withdrawn her right hand to her back and her fingers were trembling!

Jue Yuan could not believe what he had just seen. He shouted madly as he escaped, "The Divine Horizon Hands, the Divine Horizon Hands! That is impossible!"

It seemed that Jue Yuan was not seriously injured by the projected force. Rather, he was more afraid of this palm skill.

The extraordinary beauty did not give chase as she heaved a sigh of relief, "Whew. Lucky! I don't know how to handle him if he is to persist further."

Yi Ping was looking intently at her.

The extraordinary beautiful maiden said, "Hmph! Instead of thanking me, you stared at me. You should at least tell me your name, yes no?"

Yi Ping shook his head and muttered, "You are not her..."

This puzzled the extraordinary beautiful maiden, "I am not her?"

The extraordinary beautiful maiden was none the pleased and it was all written in her expressions and Yi Ping could keenly feel it. She looked intently at Yi Ping. Wordlessly, it seemed that she was warning him not to compare her with other maidens.

Yi Ping said, "I am looking for someone. Sorry I am just muttering. I am Yi Ping. I am grateful to you, maiden. How do I address you maiden?"

The extraordinary beautiful maiden smiled, "You are in luck today. It is because I have decided to tell you my name. My name is Ji Lingfeng."

Yi Ping said, "Maiden Ji, I will repay you in the future."

Ji Lingfeng asked, "It seems that you have some issues with that monk. Why is he after you?"

Yi Ping shook his head, "I am not really sure. I was drinking in town when Gongsun Jing, Gu Tianle and Jue Yuan approach me suddenly..."

He began to relate the day happenings to her.

Ji Lingfeng smiled, "It is well known that Gu Tianle had a blood feud with the Shadow Kicker and the Lightning God for the loss of his left arm. Why did they accuse you? Is there really no relationship between Qiao Feng and you?"

Yi Ping said, "We duel at the peak of the Heavenly Mountains some time ago. I just unconsciously pick up his kicking style. I really do not know any Shadow Kick Skill..."

Maiden Ji said doubtfully, "That is amazing, isn't it?"

All of a sudden, Yi Ping stepped forward and displayed the strokes that she had displayed in the duel with Jue Yuan and even the Triple Merciless Palms!

Ji Lingfeng gasped and was amazed, "You can really remember every detail of the fight vividly! I thought that only happens when top exponents reached the level of 'Martial Unifying'. At that level, they would be able to display any martial strokes that they had seen or observed with the martial unifying principle. But that won't happen to someone as young as you. Mere copying is useless I must warn you first and there will be too many openings for your opponent to exploit."

Ji Lingfeng did not know that Yi Ping had indeed reached the 'Martial Unifying Level'. Any martial skills that he had picked up after he had observed for a time were not mere copying and in actual combat, he was also able to improvise and gasp the martial principles fairly quickly as though he had actually practiced the martial art for years.

But for now, Yi Ping was really merely replicating what he saw without polishing it as he had no flexible opponents to practice upon. He did not know that the Triple Merciless Palms that he had observed would be able to aid him tremendous in the future as he had observed sufficient strokes from it to grasp some of its principles.

However, he could not grasp Ji Lingfeng martial skills as she was using a mixture of strokes from different clans and sects.

She laughed, "I better remember to get away from you when I am using my secret techniques. You must know that pugilists in the martial fraternity are hostile to people that steals their martial skills. Therefore even if you can remember all their strokes and moves, you must not display it. This is for your own good! That is why top exponents always duel in a secret place, away from prying eyes. Those who are extremely proficiency in martial arts are able to remember their secret skills or use it to their own advantage. "

She added, "The advantage lies in seeing and learning; not recklessly displaying any half-pick skills. You got to have your own set of martial skills so that you will appear to be unfathomable and able to continuously improve your own skills. Only then can you be a true master."

She said, "That is why the seven major orthodox clans have existed for hundreds of years. They are not afraid of the pugilists attempting to steal their skills. But rather, their martial skills lie in continuous refining and improving to reach the epitome. The changes, the flexibility and the complexity of their martial skills caused their clan skills to withstand the test of time. "

"Even though their skills can be identified quickly and their strokes may be a common knowledge, countering it is a totally different matter. Because they know others know their strokes' weakness, they are able to react with even more unfathomable changes to your counter."

When Ji Lingfeng saw his despondent look, she changed her tune and encouraged him, "Martial foundation can be built. One day, you may be able to defeat Jue Yuan. Even I am not his match. Sometimes we got to use our wits."

Yi Ping was astonished that a young maiden that was younger than him would know so much. He was suddenly enlightened and bowed respectfully to her, "Maiden, your advice is golden and I am forever grateful!"

When Ji Lingfeng saw his grateful eyes, she was delighted.

Ji Lingfeng smiled, "You…you did not bow to me when I save your life. When I am merely imparting to you about the common taboo of the martial fraternity, you give me a bow. You are indeed strange!"

Yi Ping said, "I have longed to look for a good martial master but I am unfortunately not to find any. Just now, when I see the palm technique that Maiden had displayed, I am truly impressed. May I know the name of that palm technique?"

Ji Lingfeng said, "Oh that. I believe it is called the Asper Horizon Hand. That what the old man said. I learnt it a few days ago when I am passing through a valley. He took the wine that I have on me and insist on repaying me by teaching me a technique from the Divine Horizon Hands. As the old man had meant me no harm and I got nothing to do anyway, I learnt just one technique from him."

She added, "This skill is hard to master. It requires a good foundation in internal strength. Just now after I have used it, my blood almost reverse its flow. If Jue Yuan persists in fighting with me, I do not know what will happen next."

She smiled and blinked her eyes at Yi Ping, "It seems that you are interested to learn the Horizon Hands?"

Yi Ping said earnestly, "Maiden, it is actually as you said. Can you tell me where this Old Senior is? I will like to pay him a visit."

Ji Lingfeng sighed, "My brother warns me not to meddle in the affairs of the martial fraternity or I get myself into endless trouble. I should really have listened to him…"

Yi Ping asked, "Maiden, will you help me?"

Ji Lingfeng sighed again, "Since I have nothing to do for the next few days, I will help you. But first you have to go town first!"

Yi Ping was startled, "Go to the town? What for? Aren't we going to the valley?"

Ji Lingfeng smiled, "That old man is a weirdo but he likes to drink. If you can go to the town and get some jars of good wine, he may consider you accepting you as his disciple!"

Yi Ping said excitedly, "Why didn't I think of that? Maiden, you are most helpful. Let us go now!"

Ji Lingfeng said, "I will wait for you here."

Yi Ping was startled, "You are not coming with me?"

Ji Lingfeng smiled, "If I go into that town, very soon, everyone will be after you and me. Therefore it is better for me to be staying put."

Yi Ping asked, "You have enemies in the town?"

Ji Lingfeng sighed, "Do you think that a beautiful lady like me will go unnoticed in the town? Very soon, Gongsun Jing's men will know our every single movement. You have better leave your sword with me too. Their eyes and ears will be after someone with a white precious sword."

Yi Ping was startled.

What she had said made sense. What astonished Yi Ping was that she was able to calmly analyze the situation and advise him.

He handed his sword to her, "Maiden, wait for me. I will be back in a short while!"

Ji Lingfeng asked, "This sword has an inscription onto it, the 'White Phoenix' and an 'Emerald' inscription. Is this long sword from the Eternal Ice Palace?"

Yi Ping said, "That is right. I have picked this sword from the Eternal Ice Palace."

Ji Lingfeng laughed softly, "This is a precious sword that is only used by the leadership of the Eternal Ice Palace. It is amazing how you can obtain this sword unscathed. Does it mean that it is unsafe to travel with you? I don't want to antagonize those bitches from the Eternal Ice Palace. "

Yi Ping said, "Maiden, don't you worry. I am assured you that no one will be after this sword for a long time!"

Ji Lingfeng asked, "Hmph, you can assure of it?"

Yi Ping had already started running as he shouted in the distance, "I will explain to you when I am back!"

Ji Lingfeng laughed captivating, "Hey! Don't exert yourself and run so fast. You…have not recovered from your injuries yet!"

Chapter 8: The Treachery of the Martial Fraternity

When Yi Ping got back with two jars of the best wine that he could purchase, tossed around his shoulder, it was nearly nightfall.

Yi Ping could not find Maiden Ji anywhere in the vicinity. His heart sunk. Had she lied to him? Not only was she not here, he had also lost his precious sword to her.

It was said that the pugilists of the martial fraternity were full of wiles and trickery. The first rule was always, never to trust anyone. Some pugilists meant no malice but would not hesitate to make a mockery out of others. And it seemed that Maiden Ji had helped him in order to trick him into giving her his precious sword on his own free will.

After shouting for some time for her, his heart sunk. He was crestfallen and cursed, "Her name, her name is probably not her real name! How foolish I am. This is an important lesson!"

He composed himself and after a while, he said to himself, "I have only lost a sword but has acquainted with an extraordinary lady. She has saved my life and I have yet to repay her. If she likes that sword, I would have given it to her even if she has not asked for it. She has asked me to go to the town to buy some wines. Isn't that a good idea too? I can't drink in peace in the town but now I can drink peacefully in this serene place!"

He started to uncork a jar of wine and began to appreciate the wine. The feeling was soothing and he was comforted.

But once again, he was interrupted.

"I have asked you to buy some wines for the old freak yet you have taken to drinking all by yourself? I have thought that you have the sincerity to find that old freak to be your martial master? Hmph, you are really…" A familiar voice could be heard scolding him gently.

Yi Ping had a skip in his heart. He looked up and saw Maiden Ji walking towards him. He rubbed his nose and was secretly overjoyed to see her again. He said, "I thought that you are gone and so I decide to drink alone."

Ji Lingfeng smiled, "You thought that I am gone? Do you not miss me? If I am gone, why didn't you search for me then?"

Yi Ping was speechless and said, "I didn't think so far. If you want to leave, who am I to stop you?"

Ji Lingfeng smiled, "It seems that you are really a heartless fellow. Here, take this back!" She threw the White Emerald Phoenix precious sword at him.

Yi Ping caught the sword in mid-air and placed it on his side. He said, "I really thought that you are gone…"

Ji Lingfeng sighed, "It is your entire fault!"

Yi Ping asked, "My fault?"

Ji Lingfeng unhappily said, "I am waiting for you and playing by the waters. All of a sudden, two identical young beauties attacked me just because I had that sword of yours. They kept accusing me of stealing their sword. From their martial origins, it is obvious that they are from the Eternal Ice Palace."

She added sarcastically, "So that is your assurances earlier that no one would be after this sword?"

Yi Ping was startled and he asked hurriedly, "They are twins? Are they alright? What did you do with them?"

Ji Lingfeng was clearly displeased and she replied coldly, "Shouldn't you have asked if I am alright first before you ask of them? Or are you acquainted with them?"

Yi Ping said, "You are standing right in front of me now. It is obvious that you are unharmed. Hurry and tell me what happens to them?"

Ji Lingfeng hummed coldly, "I didn't do anything to them. We duel for a while but their Divine Emerald Skill and swordplay are too unfathomable. They are even harder to deal with than that Jue Yuan. I didn't want to waste my time fighting and messing with the protégés of the Eternal Ice Palace so I fled from them. I took a detour back here again and yet you are not worried about my safety?"

Yi Ping sighed solemnly, "They are my friends. You are my friend too. I don't wish for anyone of you to be harmed."

Ji Lingfeng said coldly, "The Eternal Ice Palace is a forbidden ground for men and they had strict rules on that. It is unlikely that they are your friends. It must be your wistful thoughts. They seem to care more about this sword. Did you steal it from them? Like all men, you are dishonest! I have thought that you are different but now, I know otherwise!"

Yi Ping panicked and said, "Maiden, I don't want to lie to you. I am the new Master of the Eternal Ice Palace. As for the twin sisters, they are Yujian and Meijian."

Ji Lingfeng was equally startled and she asked, "How can it be? Isn't the Eternal Ice Palace a forbidden ground for men? With your mediocre skills, you aren't even fit to be their opponent!"

Yi Ping sighed and said, "It is a long story…"

Ji Lingfeng was saddened in her heart. It was because she did not want to be associated with a liar and the young man that she had saved was just a common thief. If Yi Ping had said that he had stolen the sword, she would not mind. But a liar was a person that could not be trusted.

Ji Lingfeng said coolly and there was mocking in her eyes, "I have the time. Go on, convince me."

Even though she was beginning to distrust him but she had decided to give him a final chance to explain.

He began to relate to her what had happened to him during his sojourn to the Heavenly Mountains. How he had met Shui Yixian and how he had accidentally become the new leader of the Eternal Ice Palace.

After Ji Lingfeng had heard his accounts, her expression of disbelief did not go away.

Even though she had prided herself on her superb intellect, yet she could not tell if Yi Ping was telling the truth. When he was talking about Shui Yixian, his eyes were emotional and he seemed to be in a place far away. A liar would not possible display such sentiments unless he was really an experienced actor. She was deeply moved.

She sighed in her heart, "He must have taken a great deal of beating. That is why he is now delusional. What a pity…"

His accounts had too much inconsistency in it for her to believe. It was because his martial level was too weak to inherit the helm of the Eternal Ice Palace. That was as good as destroying the repute of the Eternal Ice Palace, something that a rational leader of the Eternal Ice Palace would never do.

Moreover, even though she knew nothing much about the Eternal Ice Palace, it was well known in the martial fraternity that there was currently no men in there and the Emerald Mistress Celestial Fairy sworn herself to celibacy a long time ago! And she was said to be a ninety year woman now if she was still alive.

Yi Ping virtually told her everything except the part where he had to leave the Eternal Ice Palace in a hurry.

Ji Lingfeng looked away and said, "No matter if you are telling the truth or not. Let's us pay that old freak a visit. He is an erratic fellow. I dread to visit him so soon but because you are asking for it and I have no heart to say no to you, consider it my bad luck."

She had never expected that the first man that she took a liking to was a broken down wanderer and was a delusion fellow that had lost his mind. She had not really expected her first possible romance to be so screwed up.

Yi Ping was overjoyed and he said, "Good, let us hurry now!" He immediately started to walk rapidly.

Ji Lingfeng looked at his back view and sighed in her heart.

She immediately said, "Hmph. That is the wrong way, you know…"

Yi Ping immediately froze in his tracks and he looked awkwardly, "If that is the case, may maiden lead the way."

Ji Lingfeng said, "So I am your tour guide now?"

Yi Ping was stunned by her question. He fumbled and said, "I don't know the way…"

Ji Lingfeng sighed, "Actually I don't really remember the way very well too."

Yi Ping was startled, "You don't remember?"

Ji Lingfeng averted her eyes and said, "It somewhere in that direction. I don't have a map and I was eager to travel to the main road. I didn't really pause to observe my surroundings for any landmarks as I was traveling too rapidly."

Yi Ping asked, "You really don't remember? Surely you can't have forgotten the paths that you have taken. We can just back track. It is really a simple matter. We can look for your old tracks once we are there."

Yi Ping had been a wanderer for a long time. He was a superb pathfinder and had rarely lost his way even when he had no maps.

Ji Lingfeng pondered for a while, "I don't think we can find an easy path."

Yi Ping asked, "Explain?"

Ji Lingfeng sighed as she pointed to the stretches of mountainous hills in front of them, "I…crossed at least seven hills and had jumped down at least twenty times on those steep cliffs. Jumping down is easy but can we fly up? Can you fly up?"

Yi Ping blinked his eyes in astonishment. He finally said, "What can we do then?"

Ji Lingfeng asked him, "You asking me what to do? It is you that want to go to that accursed place. I don't even want to go there."

Chapter 9: Ji Lingfeng

Ji Lingfeng adjusted her long white sleeves and put on a veiled straw hat behind her back.

Yi Ping asked, "Why did you do that for? It is not as if you cannot be recognized by anyone. I surely will be able to recognize you even if you turn into ashes."

Yi Ping had said that because he had a blood feud with the maiden in yellow and anyone with a veil irked him.

Ji Lingfeng did not seem to mind. In fact, her thin eyebrows had a mischievous expression. She soon chuckled softly, "You will soon know. Is it true that even if I am turned into ashes, you will still be able to recognize me? I didn't know you are paying so much attention to me. If you are a pile of ashes, I surely wouldn't be able to recognize you."

Yi Ping did not want to argue with her. He said hurriedly, "Let us set off now. It is getting dark soon. You don't have to keep adjusting your attire and grooming yourself by the river."

This time round, Ji Lingfeng was none too pleased. She murmured, "It just a few minutes. Why are you being so impatient?"

Yi Ping heard her and he said, "I have been waiting for you for the past two hours. First, you start mending your dress and now you tidying your attire. Isn't that enough already?"

Ji Lingfeng said, "During the ruffle with the bitches from the Eternal Ice Palace, they have torn parts of my clothing. Of course I have to mend my clothing to look presentable. Don't you think so too? After all, I am a girl and I should protect my modesty."

Yi Ping said, "They are not what you think. And please don't use vulgarities on them. A pretty maiden like you wouldn't mouth profanities."

Ji Lingfeng laughed softly, "Unfortunately, that is my mouth and not yours. If you do not want to listen to me, you can simply go far away from me."

Yi Ping had never met a maiden the like of her before. He was speechless and he began to sit down onto the grass patch. He did not know how long he got to wait for her.

Actually he had felt bad arguing with her. That was because she had saved his life and instead of being grateful, he was now arguing with her. It was just that he could not help feeling that she was trying to make a fool of him.

All of a sudden, he had a thought, "What if she has made up that old master? Who would impart anyone their secret martial skills just like that?"

Just as he was about to question her again, she said. "I am ready. Let's us go now."

Yi Ping was about to question her when he noticed that she was already very far. What an astonishing swiftness movement that she possessed!

Therefore, he had no choice but to run after her.

Yi Ping soon realized why she had been so mindful about her attire. In this wilderness, there was plenty of biting insects. Now he knew why her eyes were secretly beaming with laughter. In no time, he was bitten by numerous insects. He quickly took out some extra clothing from his bundle and turned it into a makeshift cloth to wrap around his face.

Ji Lingfeng was a unique lady. It seemed that her expressions portrayed her emotions. Even if she did not speak, her body mannerism and facial emotions tells it all. She had very thin eyebrows, her eyebrows and forehead had numerous expressions all the time.

When Ji Lingfeng turned back and saw Yi Ping hastily covering his face and looking for a robe with long sleeves, she was seen clasping her hands onto her mouth as she bent to and fro. She was obviously enjoying what had happening to Yi Ping.

Yi Ping was covered in perspiration from the running as he complained aloud, "You…did not warn me!"

But he had no strength left to complaint further for she had turned around and danced away again. He had no choice but to follow her white figure in the distance.

From time to time, she would pause briefly for him to catch up but as soon as he was near, she would continue to move again.

Yi Ping was astonished at her swiftness movement and her breathing techniques. He thought, "How long did she train in order to reach this level of expertise?"

He was immediately ashamed of his own martial achievements.

He did not know how long he had been running. There were a few times that he had lost her and he was panicky. But each time, she would appear in front of him.

It was night now. Yi Ping was thankful that there was a full moon tonight and thousands of stars illuminate the darkness. But even with the full moon, he could barely see any foot path. On several occasions, he tripped and fell down.

When he had lost his footing again and slipped down a treacherous slope, Ji Lingfeng had suddenly appeared on top of him and gripped him on his shoulder.

Her grip was surprising strong and Yi Ping was pulled up from the slope.

Yi Ping was instantly grateful to her as he said, "Thank you!"

Ji Lingfeng rebuked him gently, "Don't misunderstood. I am only worried for the wine jars."

His eyes that were filled with gratitude soon turned gloomy as he said breathlessly, "Maybe you can help to carry the wine jars…"

But before he could finish speaking, she said coolly. "Inhale deeply and follow me."

Immediately, Yi Ping could feel a powerful force pulling him forward alongside with her as she caught hold of his hand. This time round, his runs became a lot easier even though it was still as hell as ever.

Ji Lingfeng was waiting for him to collapse onto the ground or to beg her to stop. But he did not. Worried about his injuries and guilty about misleading him, she supported his runs with her martial power and pulled him along with her.

Even then, it was not going to be easy for Yi Ping as he had to run at her pace even though the pressure on his breathing had eased considerably.

Yi Ping's heart skipped a beat when she touched and held him with her left hand. He began to flush deeply as his ears turned terribly red as he felt her silken smooth hand. Even her scent was so intoxicating so up close to him.

This was the first time that Yi Ping really looked at her closely even though it was at her back view.

She had looked relax and it was as though she was taking a stroll while he was half dead from climbing up and down the hills! But looking at her, made him forgot about his exhaustion…

Ji Lingfeng almost messed up with her breathing regulation as she was distracted by thoughts of him; she could feel the warmth of his right palm in her hand. It was an assuring palm, strong and comforting. This was the first time she had held a man hand other than her brother. It was a wonderful feeling yet she could not describe it…

After running for some time, Ji Lingfeng was secretly amazed at his endurance even though his breathing techniques and swiftness skill were mediocre. She really could not believe that he had endured till now even though he looked as though he would collapse at any time!

Astonished by his inhuman endurance, she thought, "Is he human?"

Yi Ping was in a daze and he already seeing stars as he thought, "Is she even human? How is it possible for her to run up and down the hills for this long…?"

Ji Lingfeng was already feeling the stress of expending her internal strength to support him and she was worn-out.

Yi Ping did not even realize the passage of time when Ji Lingfeng coolly said aloud to him, "It seem that I have found the valley. Lucky us!"

As soon as she had released her grip off his hand, Yi Ping fell onto the ground in sheer exhaustion.

Yi Ping nearly died of exhaustion. Now he really knew what she had meant by she was traveling rapidly! He silently sighed, "I never want to travel with her ever again."

Ji Lingfeng suddenly gave a long sigh, "We have climbed ten hills and got lost. This valley was actually just besides the third hill that we had passed. We really are lost."

When Yi Ping heard that, he did not know whether he should laugh or cry. He felt like banging his head onto the ground in misery.

Ji Lingfeng said, "This path leading down should lead us to the valley. Let us go now. This time round, I am not going to walk you there."

She began to move on but when her sharp ears did not pick up any sign of movements from behind, she turned back instantly.

Yi Ping was still lying on the ground.

She asked softly, "Hmph, are you there?"

There was no response.

She asked again, "Are you alright?"

Still, there was no response.

She was panicky, "I have killed him…?"

Drain of all his strength and having reached the limits of his endurance, Yi Ping was knocked out cold.

All of a sudden, he began to recall a time when he was a five year old child again. His mother was frail. At that age, he was already helping her to gather woods among many other menial tasks…

Shui Yichi looked dreamily as she stared out of the window, wishing every day that she could see her husband again. She was frail and her health worsened every day. She feared that she might not live for long.

If there was anything that she could not let go in this world, it was her only child, Yi Ping.

Even though she was once Emerald Mistress of the Eternal Ice Palace before she passed the leadership to her younger protégé sister Shui Yixian, she did not miss her previous glorious position. She had no attachments for her protégé sisters or anyone in the Eternal Ice Palace.

Even though she was once close to Shui Yixian and they had spent five decades together, their affections toward one another cooled over the years.

Maybe it was the Emotionless Rhythm that they had been practicing that made them indifferent to one another even though they were in the same sect together. Or maybe it was because they were both the best in many generations and not wanting to disappoint their protégé mistress, they strove to perfect their skills.

It was also precisely why she did not have any protégé disciples.

Shui Yixian was striving for the ninth level of the Divine Emerald Skill and was in her final stage of breaking through the eighth level of the Divine Emerald Skill. As for her, she stopped her Divine Emerald Skill at the eighth level and focused on the Jade Icy Fingers. With her intimate understandings of the Jade Icy Fingers, her Icy Heavenly Tears was even more intricate than Shui Yixian, even though they had both attained the ninth level of the Icy Heavenly Tears.

In time to come, she had even evolved her Jade Icy Finger into the Jade Icicles Finger. So intricate was her later understanding that she was able to prolong the backlash of the Icy Heavenly Tears and was even able to choose an opportune time herself. Even the time that she needed to recover her martial level was more than halved!

Even though Shui Yixian was a martial prodigy and had achieved the ninth level of the Heavenly Tears when she was eighteen while she only achieved the same level when she was thirty, her Icy Tear Heavenly Tears energy had always been purer.

She took on the challenge of mastering the jade Icy Fingers to perfection. It was an extremely arduous and monument task but eventually she had overcome all difficulties and she had even created the Jade Icicle Fingers. When she had achieved the Jade Icicle Fingers, her Icy Tear Heavenly Tear energy became so pure that she could even neutralize the defensive force of Shui Yixian Divine Emerald Skill!

But it was also the creation of the Jade Icicle Fingers that caused her much harm. Through the Jade Icicle Fingers, eventually she found a possible way to resolve the weakness of the Icy Heavenly Tears and started to look for another way for a breakthrough in the current state of her icy Heavenly Tears. Therefore she started to experiment with another skill that she created with the pure negative energy of the Icy Heavenly Tears and the Jade Icicle Fingers, the Eternal Heavenly Tears.

By this time, she had already handed over the leadership of the Eternal Ice Palace to Shui Yixian because she had found the love of her life, Yi Tianxing, a man that dared to challenge the Eternal Ice Palace.

When she thought of Yi Tianxing again, her eyes were tearful again and her heart began to ache terribly with great sorrow.

After leaving the Eternal Ice Palace, Yi Tianxing had imparted to her the Divine Revelation, an intricate formula and mediation skill similar to the Emotionless Rhythm. She was inspired by it and began to write with her fingers in a cave near the Eternal Ice Palace on her untested theories on the ultimate Icy Heavenly Tears and even on the hidden stages of the Divine Emerald Skill that she meant to practice once she had fully mastered the Jade Icicle Fingers and the Eternal Heavenly Tears.

Because she was afraid that outsiders might found her inscriptions, she sealed the cave as a precaution even though only a direct protégé of the Eternal Ice Palace might be able to understand it. Moreover, she deemed the theories too dangerous to impart. She herself would not practice the theories as she had found a safer way in the Eternal Heavenly Tears.

And with her protégé sister, Shui Yixian present martial level, there was also no need for her test her unproven theories and wasted years of her time.

She did not know that more than twenty years later, her protégé sister Shui Yixian was still not been able to progress much further because she had been too hasty in her Icy Heavenly Tears in her earlier years. In fact, she was forced to spend the next twenty years researching the Icy Heavenly Tears over and over again in order to combat the forthcoming Divine Calamity that had killed their protégé mistress.

And Shui Yixian in a lucky happenstance had found the inscriptions that she had left behind.

When she was eight months heavy with child, her husband Yi Tianxing was betrayed by his sworn brother. That vile sworn brother of his had even tried to outrage her and harm her. As she was in a heavy stage of pregnancy and because she had not fully mastered her Jade Icicle Fingers yet, she had overtly exerted herself and irrevocably damaged her health, losing much of her internal strength that she had painfully gained over the years.

Her thoughts were suddenly interrupted by little Yi Ping who had accidentally scalded himself. She gasped weakly upon seeing it but Yi Ping did not say anything or cry.

She looked at Yi Ping, her beloved child who was boiling hot water for her with the fire woods that he had gathered in the woods. Her heart ached for him when she saw his numerous bruises and knew that that he was bullied by the neighboring children again. But he would never cry in front of her.

It was as though her child could sense her sadness and grief even at a very young age.

All of a sudden, five men broke into the house. When they had entered the house, they were stunned at her enchanting beauty. It was because they had never expected to find such a beauty in this desolate countryside.

The strongest of the five, who appeared to be the leader, broke the silence, "Brothers we are in luck. We have heard that there is a beautiful widow here but I have never expected to find a peerless beauty here."

The other four began to laugh wickedly. Their laughter was full of malice and ill-intent.

Little Yi Ping began to shout and charged at the leader.

Shui Yichi gasped aloud, "Child, don't!" But it was too late…

But the leader just laughed and he kicked Yi Ping real hard. This kick was so powerful that it sent Yi Ping flying backward and he was flung against the wall with a loud bang!

Shui Yichi eyes turned red and teary. She leaned her hands onto the side of the wall as she walked as soon as she could towards her child. She was so weak and her movements were limited.

But before she could walk to her child, the five men had surrounded her and began to seize her in all directions.

All of a sudden, the five men could feel a bitter cold that pierced through their spines. It was so cold that it felt that their skins had been burnt. They could feel their bones cracking and when they fell down dead onto the ground; their eyes were wide-opened in disbelief.

In that swift instant, Shui Yichi had struck them with her Jade Icicle Fingers. Even though she had lost much of her internal strength, her Jade Icicle Fingers was still an extremely potent skill against ordinary men.

Shui Yichi comforted her child, "Child, are you alright?" She sobbed and held little Yi Ping into her embrace.

Little Yi Ping muttered, "Mum, I am alright. Are you alright?"

Shui Yichi wept even louder, "Child, your mum is alright. Don't you worry about me…"

Little Yi Ping was bleeding from his nose and mouth but he said, "Mum, you know how to fight? Can you teach me how to fight?"

Shui Yichi held him tightly, "I will. Child, you must be strong…you mustn't die…"

Little Yi Ping said, "Mum, I won't die. I don't want mum to die too…" He had turned completely white but still he refused to cry.

Shui Yichi wept, "Look, my child."

She sketched her hands in front of him. Immediately, the air around them turned bitter cold.

It was so chilly that the tiny flies around the house began to drop dead onto the ground.

Shui Yichi wept as she laid her hands on her child's small body, "My child, you will feel terrible pain, even awful terrible pain but you mustn't be afraid. You will not die. But it is going to be very painful."

Indeed, little Yi Ping must be feeling terrible painful because he was now shedding tears and his body was trembling nonstop. But he did not cry aloud or plead to his mother to stop. He simply did not want to make his mother sad and fearful.

Negative energy, especially negative cold internal energy like the one that Shui Yichi possessed was ill-suit to treat internal injuries. Moreover, hers were the extreme cold negative energy. If the receiver was seriously injured, their body would not able to take it. It would be so agonizing that it would only worsen their injuries.

But Shui Yichi had no other choice as she began to transfer all her internal strength into her child in an attempt to save his life.

When she had finished imparting her entire Icy Heavenly Tears energy into him, little Yi Ping eyes were still opened even though his face had turned entirely white.

Little Yi Ping shivered and bit his purple lips, "Mum, I am alright. Teach me how to fight. I want to protect you…"

Shui Yichi smiled weakly as she got up. She immediately displayed seventy gestures, eighty stances and ninety strokes. All these movements were the most ingenious fighting movement that Shui Yichi had ever known; it was collected from the vast martial scrolls of the Eternal Ice Palace and the numerous opponents that she ever fought with in her entire life.

After Shui Yichi had finished displaying those profound fighting moves, she collapsed onto the ground, never to awake.

And these fighting movements were to be ingrained deeply into little Yi Ping's mind. In time to come, he would slowly intuitively remember it again…

Chapter 10: Aspire Invocations Intricate Recite

When Yi Ping opened his eyes with a sudden jerk, he had just broken into a cold sweat! He seemed to have fallen into a deep slumber and had a nightmare. This nightmare was always the same, haunting him constantly. He could not forget how his mother Shui Yichi had died yet he must live in constant denial.

He dreaded to lie but he had lied to Shui Yixian. Even though he was honest about his mother maiden name to Shui Yixian, he had lied to her that she had passed away shortly after giving birth to him. It was because he still had to search for the people that had harmed his parents.

Even though he was a five year old boy back then, he could remember his father name was Yi Tianxing and his mother maiden name was Shui Yichi. His father had a sworn brother and it was this sworn brother that had betrayed his father and harmed his mother.

He did not know that his mother was from the Eternal Ice Palace therefore when Shui Yixian questioned him about it, he told her a half-truth. That was before he knew that his mother was actually her older protégé sister.

No wonder he found himself drawn irresistible to Shui Yixian, she indeed had many similarities to his mother…

Before he could confess to her on the truth, Shui Yixian had passed away…

Yi Ping thought, "Am I destined to lead a lonesome life?"

An alluring voice was heard calling out to him, "You have awakened? I have thought that you have died. Your pulses are so weak. I…I am so sorry…"

He had not heard her apologies for he was still in a daze. When he saw it was Ji Lingfeng, he stared at her and turned as white as sheet. He was instantly panicky and got the fright of his life as he tried to flee from her!

Seeing her again was worse than the terrible nightmare that he just had!

Ji Lingfeng called her to him, bemused by his actions. "Why are so afraid of me? Do you really think I will eat you up? What am I? A demoness? Have you forgotten that it is you that want to pay that old freak a visit in the first place?"

After Yi Ping had heard her, he began to turn back. He asked hesitating, "Are we really reaching?" He was really afraid of her.

Ji Lingfeng laughed softly, "Of course, it is just down this path. Quickly, follow me!"

Yi Ping sighed and walked staggeringly behind her, "If I know that this trip will be so difficult and nearly cost me my life, I would never agree to come. Even before I can find the martial master, I would probably die in her hands first…"

This time, Ji Lingfeng was just taking a gentle stroll. When she saw that he was struggling to even walk, she immediately took him by his arm to support him.

All of a sudden, Yi Ping felt she was not that bad after all.

They were now walking very close. Both Yi Ping and Ji Lingfeng averted their eyes and were awkward.

There was a few times that Ji Lingfeng or Yi Ping wanted to say something but they could not find the courage to say a word. It was as though they were afraid of disturbing the tranquil air between them.

Soon after, Yi Ping saw a small broken down hut. He was astonished that someone had actually built a dwelling here in this desolate forested valley.

Ji Lingfeng smiled, "We are here! Go on and go in." The way she had said it, was like it was none of her concern and that she was only a speculator waiting to see what would going to happen next.

But before Yi Ping could walk into the hut, a voice was heard saying, "Young lass, you are back so fast? You didn't forget me? I catch the sniff of the fragrant of the Bamboo Leaves Wine. Excellent! But you seem to have brought someone here. I don't like strangers. You can ask him to leave!"

Ji Lingfeng laughed gently, "I am not the one that bring you the Bamboo Leaves Wine. This young man did. If you don't want to see him, he can simply leave."

An old man with a cane opened the door of the hut. He had a cane with him and he seemed to have difficulty in walking.

The old man growled and said, "Lass, why did you bring him here for?"

Ji Lingfeng replied, "He would like to learn superior martial arts from you."

The old man looked at Yi Ping from head to toe as he said, "He looks like he is almost dead and he still wants to learn martial arts from me? Anyway, I won't accept any disciples. He can leave immediately. I don't have the habit of coaching strangers anything."

Ji Lingfeng said, "Oh? Did you not teach me the Asper Horizon Hands just a few days ago? Am I not a stranger?"

The old man said, "I also have another habit. When I take something from a stranger, I will never owe them anything. You are just lucky that I have a craving for good wines that day."

Ji Lingfeng said coolly, "Do you know that in order to find you, he has run throughout the night, searching hills by hills for you? Does this not prove his sincerity and willingness to shoulder hardship?"

Yi Ping was touched that she had actually stepped in to persuade the old man for him. He knew that he was asking for the impossible and that this would likely be a futile trip. He was just trying his luck.

In the fraternity, the martial masters would never reveal their martial secrets easily. Even if they would want to find a successor, it was likely to be someone that they had raised since young. That was so in order to reduce the odds of their skills from falling into the wrong hands.

Yi Ping was expecting a reclusive martial hermit and the sight of this old man disappointed him. But nevertheless, he truly believed that this old man was the one that could help him in improving his martial advancement.

So he respectfully said, "Old Senior. I, Yi Ping, pay my respects to you. I have the wish to meet a worthy master…"

The old man muttered, "Yi…" All of a sudden, his expressions changed. "What is your name again?"

Yi Ping replied weakly "Yi Ping."

The old man stumbled backward. He looked at Yi Ping carefully and when he saw the White Phoenix Emerald precious sword, he trembled. How this young man got hold of the White Phoenix Emerald precious sword that was once used by Shui Yichi? He remembered very vividly that this sword had been passed to Shui Yixian…

He asked, "Who your mother?"

Yi Ping was puzzled that this old man had suddenly asked of his mother. He asked, "Why did you ask me that?"

The old man gripped his shoulders and asked again, "Your mother, where is she?"

Yi Ping could feel the strong grip of the old man that was upon him. He could not breathe and his face had turned purple. But he refused to say anything. It was because this old man might well be the very enemy that he had been searching for!

Ji Lingfeng was panicky as she attacked the old man with her palms. She said aloud, "Old freak, what you think you are doing?"

In three successive attacks, she had forced the old man to release his grips off Yi Ping as he took a few steps backward.

In her panicky state, she had just used the 'Moonlight Cut' stroke of the Sacred Heart Skill. The Sacred Heart Skill were her real skills. Unless she had no other choice, she did not want to use it. She tried to hit the old freak on his shoulder and face at the same time, followed by another attack but he had evaded it all!

Yi Ping fell onto his knees weakly.

Ji Lingfeng was besides Yi Ping in an instant as she voiced her concern for him, "Are you alright? If he did not want to teach you anything, I will teach you!"

Yi Ping was too weak even to reply her. His vision had gone blurry. He felt really unlucky today. Three times in a single day, he had almost died. The first time was by Gu Tianle, the second time it was by Maiden Ji and the third time was by this crippled old man.

The old man said sternly to Ji Lingfeng, "Surrender him to me or else I will be ugly. I don't want to lay my hands on you."

Ji Lingfeng replied coolly, "Funny! You did not want him as your protégé disciple, so why are you asking for him now?

The old man said, "Now I have changed my mind and decided to make him my martial protégé!"

Ji Lingfeng stepped in front of the fallen Yi Ping regally as she displayed a defensive posture as she answered icily, "What if I am not willing to allow this to happen?"

The old man raised his cane and said, "Then I will surely teach you a lesson that you will never be able to forget."

Ji Lingfeng said coldly, "A martial master like you will raise your hands on an unarmed junior and a weaker sex? It is indeed very laudable. Why don't you tell me your name so that I can tell everyone in the fraternity what you have done?"

The old man said, "In a real fight, there are no senior or junior, nor men or women and only fighters. Only survival matters. Moreover I have been a hermit for so long. What do I care for the honor of the martial fraternity?"

Ji Lingfeng hummed coldly as she prepared her forthcoming strikes. This old man was a crippled and had difficulty walking. Even though he was an experienced opponent, she might not lose to him with her superior swiftness skill and with some luck.

The old man added, "And you are definitely not unarmed. From your top to bottom, there are at least three hundred secret projectiles that you can use. Others may be fooled by your deceptive outlook but not me."

Ji Lingfeng was stunned that he could see through her. This would make her surprise attacks difficult. Was he simply guessing? Therefore she replied calmly, "You think too much. I have no secret projectiles."

The old man said coolly, "Is that so? What about the dozens of needles in your straw hat? What about the crystal wrist beads in your wrists? What about the poisonous polish in your smallest finger nail on your left? What about the three hairpins on your head and the dozens of secret projectiles underneath your outer garment?"

Ji Lingfeng could not hide her startled expression as she took a step backward. This old man had extremely sharp eyes.

The old man said, "If I still fail to see that you are from the Holy Hex Sect after using the Sacred Heart Skill, then I am surely blind. The Holy Hex Sect is famed for its poisonous secret projectiles and techniques, especially the 'Consecrated Meteor Shower' technique and the Meteor Rain needles."

Yi Ping was startled that Ji Lingfeng had so many weapons on her. He disapproved of using secret projectiles, seeing it as an underhand means in a fair fight.

No wonder she was intentional hiding her martial origins. It was because the Holy Hex Sect was an unorthodox heretic sect and in recent years was at odds with the general orthodox fraternity!

In his dizzying state, he muttered, "How vicious!"

Ji Lingfeng lifted her right foot backward and kicked Yi Ping. She exclaimed in displeasure, "Shut up. My secret projectiles may well save very your life."

Even though the kick was not hard, in Yi Ping current condition, it was more than enough to knock him out cold. Yi Ping was heard muttering before he was knocked out, "Why… did… you… kick… me… for…"

Ji Lingfeng said coolly, "Serves you right! Whose side do you think you are on?!"

The old man said angrily, "Why did you hit him for?"

Ji Lingfeng said, "Because he is rude!"

The old man said angrily, "You don't have the right!"

Ji Lingfeng said coldly, "Hmph, does it matter? If I don't have the right, you have the right?"

The old man said angrily, "I have the right. I am his father!"

Ji Lingfeng said coldly, "If you are his father, I am his mother then!" Then she lifted her right foot again and kicked Yi Ping, not once but twice. "See!"

All of a sudden, the old man attacked her with his cane furiously, forcing her to somersault backward as she did not want to use her bare hands against his cane.

Just as she was about to attack him with her Meteor Rain Needles, the old man was already besides Yi Ping, shaking him and examining his pulse, "The Icy Heavenly Tears energy pulses! Yichi must have imparted to him the Icy Heavenly Tears! He is really my son!"

The old man was wailing, "Son, who cause you to be in this dire straits? Who is that heartless fellow?!"

Ji Lingfeng gasped in shock, "You are really his father?"

The old man said, "I am! Tell me, who is the heartless fellow that had injured him and caused him to be in such a bad shape?"

Ji Lingfeng said sheepishly, "Err…it is Jue Yuan. We are no match for his Triple Merciless Palms and were pursued by him throughout the night."

The old man sighed, "More than twenty years ago, I have actually spared his life. I should have ended his life long ago. His Triple Merciless Palms is indeed extraordinary and could be ranked among the top skills in the fraternity."

But he was secretly thinking, "You really think I am an old fool. At first, you say you searching hills by hills for me and now, you saying you are being pursued."

Ji Lingfeng tried to distract him, "Is Yi Ping going to be alright?"

The old man said solemnly, "Come with me! If he dies, I am going to hold you accountable too." The old man carried Yi Ping on his back and had walked into the hut.

Ji Lingfeng protested, "What has it got to do with me?"

The old man turned and said sternly, "Because you just claim to be his mother and has given him three kicks!"

Ji Lingfeng sighed deeply as she said, "Those kicks are not even real kicks at all…" But because she was concerned for Yi Ping, she followed the old man into the hut.

When Yi Ping opened his eyes again, he saw the old man smiling at him. "Son, are you alright?"

Yi Ping was startled and quickly looked at his surroundings. He was in a small room with this old man. He also saw Ji Lingfeng.

Ji Lingfeng was sitting on a chair, looking serenely as she looked back at him. She was even smiling at him.

"Are you alright?" she said with genuine concern.

But when he saw her smiles, he was terrified. It was because he remembered the torturous runs with her and the kick that he had received from her…

Yi Ping had plenty of courage. He was not afraid of death and pain. In fact, fear was always the last thing in his mind and he had almost got himself killed many times in the past.

But when he saw her, he was truly terrified of her. It was because Maiden Ji was at times warm and at times cold towards him. He did not know when she would suddenly be cold again.

Even though her kick was not hard, it was so suddenly that he was startled and he could still remember it vividly. Stunned by her sudden kick, he was knocked out cold.

Yi Ping thought, "They are supposed to be fighting with one another. Why are they now together in the same room? Are they putting on an act or has Maiden Ji sold me out to this old man? She is after all, from an unorthodox clan and is capable of anything. Alas heavens, I am so pitiful…"

The old man was shaking him and shouting excitedly, "Son, I am your father Yi Tianxing! Your mother is Shui Yichi! Son, I have thought you had died many years ago. Heavens have eyes!"

When Ji Lingfeng heard his name, her smiles had sudden vanished. It was because her father, Ji Yunzhong the previous protégé master of the Holy Hex Sect had died because of Yi Tianxing. In that moment, her facial expressions underwent a tremendous change…

Even though Yi Tianxing was a late comer to the martial fraternity and disappeared just as quickly, he had gained fame as one of the top swordsmen in the fraternity with his Horizon Swordplay as well as his numerous chivalrous acts.

Yi Ping was stunned as he stammered, "You know my mother…You…are really my father?"

Yi Tianxing nodded sadly, "Son, where is your mother? Is she still well?"

Yi Ping shook his head sadly, "Mum passed on when I was five…"

Even though Yi Tianxing had expected the worst, he was still emotional. He said, "Son, it must be hard on you all these years."

Yi Ping asked, "Father, where have you been all these years? If you are with us, maybe mum would still be alive today."

Yi Tianxing sighed deeply, "It is a very long story. Let me start from the beginning first."

He said, "Twenty-five years ago, with just an iron sword with me, I went up the Heavenly Mountains to challenge the Eternal Ice Palace. It was there that I first met your mother, Shui Yichi. At that time, she was the Emerald Mistress of the Eternal Ice Palace. We fought over a three days period."

He paused for a while as he recalled the past, "On the first day, we fought with our martial power and were evenly matched. On the second day, it was a contest on who had the superior swordplay. Again, we were evenly matched. On the third day, we decided to contest which of us had the superior willpower, the one that moves first on the icy peak of the Heavenly Mountains would be the loser!"

Ji Lingfeng interrupted, "Then you must be the one who had lost! She could probably meditate for days without moving, even in the snow."

Yi Tianxing laughed, "You are wrong! The contest was in fact over in less than a day!"

Ji Lingfeng gasped, "That is impossible. The mediation technique of the Eternal Ice Palace is well known and I don't think Shui Yichi would be afraid of the cold."

Yi Tianxing laughed, "That was true but after the contest went on for six hours, Yichi, she opened her eyes as she thought I was dead. So I won."

Ji Lingfeng was astonished.

He added, "It turned out that she was not concentrating on her mediation but was worried that I got frostbite. Truthfully, I was freezing and my limbs had already turned purple. I was already injured by her Icicle Fingers on the first day and did not realize the severity of my injuries. However I was stubborn and refused to say a word. She saved my life and brought me back to the Eternal Ice Palace to recuperate."

Yi Tianxing laughed merrily, "I may have won the contest but I lost my heart to her. We would have retired peacefully and freed from the affairs of the martial fraternity."

Yi Tianxing said, "Son, do you know why your name is Ping?"

Yi Ping was startled, "You know my name even before I was born?"

Yi Tianxing nodded slowly as his eyes were brimming with tears, "We have already decided to name you Ping no matter if you are a girl or boy. It was because we want you to lead an ordinary life unlike us…"

Ping means Peaceful.

His eyes seemed to be in a far off place.

He finally spoke again after a few moments of silence, "At that time, Yichi knew her days were probably numbered and she wanted to lead an ordinary life with me and our unborn child. So we decide to name you as Ping, which mean ordinary and peaceful."

Yi Ping was startled, "My mum was ill?"

Yi Tianxing shook his head, "Not at all. Her health was fine. It just that those high level practitioners of the Eternal Ice Palace knew the end of their days through the Divine Calamity, just like practitioners of our Divine Horizon Hands knew ours too. That was the reason why she forced herself to train so hard in order to avert the Divine Calamity."

Ji Lingfeng curiosity was aroused. It was the first time she had heard of such a thing as the 'Divine Calamity'. What was that?

Yi Ping too asked, "What is the Divine Calamity about?"

Yi Tianxing seemed to be reluctant to discuss it as he changed the topic, "I used to have a very good sworn brother. He was the first person that I have met when I left the mountains…"

Yi Ping was silent. He only knows that much for his mother used to murmur to him that his father had been betrayed by his best sworn brother. "What is his name?"

Yi Tianxing looked at Yi Ping's eyes and asked, "You knew?"

Yi Ping nodded bitterly, "Mum only tells me this much but she had never told me his name!"

Yi Tianxing sighed deeply, "That is because this sworn brother of mine, Gongsun Bai, has great influential in the fraternity. He has many powerful friends and many exponents under his wing. Your mother did not want you to waste your life."

Both Ji Lingfeng and Yi Ping were stunned to hear that his sworn brother was Gongsun Bai. Gongsun Bai was from one of the major martial clans in the martial fraternity, the Gongsun Clan and it was also one of the four major aristocracy martial clans in the martial fraternity.

Yi Ping said, "Gongsun Bai is the father of Gongsun Jing. I have met Gongsun Jing and he is as crafty as his father! Father, I swear that I will avenge you!"

Yi Tianxing shook his head, "I am afraid that Gongsun Bai may now be too formidable. It is best that you avoid the Gongsun family."

Yi Tianxing sighed, "I never expected Gongsun Bai to turn upon me. Of all my friends, he is the only one that I could trust the most for he was a benevolent man and held in high regard in the martial fraternity. Also he was from a respectable and rich clan but alas he…"

He added, "One day, Gongsun Bai tricked me by telling me that the Three Evils of the West were back in the fraternity and that only I could stop them. Wanting to prevent a catastrophe from happening to the martial fraternity, I left Yichi who was heavy with child and rushed with Gongsun Bai to stop the Three Evils of the West. I promised her I will be back in no time…"

"I trusted him because he was my sworn brother but he laid a trap for me and ambushed me. I fell down into this valley, breaking my back and legs. For a long time, I could not move. Maybe I was lucky. The mud that was in this valley seemed to have a healing properties and my broken back slowly recovered. Till now, I have not fully recovered and my movements are severely limited."

He sighed, "As soon as I could move again, I went back to the village to look for your mother but I could not find anyone. No one stays there anymore. Disappointed and aimless, I came back to this valley as my back was aching badly. Only the mud here can ease my pain."

Yi Ping said, "The village was destroyed by a flood many years ago and since then everyone had evacuated. Moreover, Gongsun Bai had gone after my mum; she had since fled the village even before that great flood."

Everyone was silence. That was because no one could imagine what exactly happened and what ordeal Shui Yichi was forced to go through during that dark period. Gongsun Bai was a wolf in disguise and there was no better way to harm someone other than pretending to be a friend.

Ji Lingfeng asked, "What was his reason for betraying you?"

Yi Tianxing went silence for some time before he slowly said, "He told me he was envy of me. He wishes to take Yichi as his wife and to take possession of her martial secrets. Therefore he tried to kill me so that he could get close to my wife."

All of a sudden, Ji Lingfeng said coldly, "Great Hero Yi, do you know who I am?"

Yi Tianxing laughed aloud, "How would I not know? You are from the Holy Hex Sect and must be related to Ji Yunzhong."

Yi Tianxing said, "I knew when you first come into this valley with. Even though you did not make a sound but I recognized the Fairy Breezes weightlessness skill of the Holy Hex Sect. You may not see me but I had already seen you from afar!"

Ji Lingfeng was startled, "You knew back then?"

She said coldly, "You know who I am from the first day and you even taught me the Asper Horizon Hand?"

Yi Tianxing laughed, "Who you are is another matter. I only want to drink the wine that you had on you then."

He added, "Moreover, even though I have taught you the Asper Horizon Hand, I didn't really expect you to be able to use it so soon. When you are able to use the Asper Horizon Hand, you will have to visit me again with more wines."

Ji Lingfeng said coldly, "Why? Do you think I really want to learn more of your martial skills?"

Yi Tianxing laughed, "Oh no. That is because if you have used the Asper Horizon Hand a few more times, your vital energies will be erratic. And the only one that could help you is me! The Asper Horizon Hand is not suitable to be used by anyone. Without my Aspire Invocations Intricate Recite to control the vital force of your Asper Horizon Hand, it will only harm the body. If you don't believe, you can feel free to press against the accupoint that was five fingers below your heart."

Ji Lingfeng did as she was told and could feel a pressing pain! She said coldly, "I thought you are a pugilistic hero and yet you use this despicable means to harm me!"

Yi Ping said, "Maiden, I think this may be a misunderstanding. Please calm down. My father is not an evil man."

Yi Tianxing said, "I only want you to pay me a few more visits and get me some good wines to ease my boredom. I can lift your alleviations and impart to you the basic intricate formula of the Aspire Invocations. After all, I won't really harm you."

Yi Ping knew nothing about the risks of internal martial intricate formulas. He exclaimed happily for her, "Maiden, congratulations! My father is going to teach you the Aspire Invocations. He is not going to harm you."

Ji Lingfeng smiled bitterly. It was not a joyous thing that she got to learn the Asper Invocations Intricate Recite. It was because imparting to her the Asper Invocations Intricate Recite could actually harm her more.

All internal martial intricate formulas had an unbroken rule, the practitioners must master it and able to utilize it in the shortest time as possible to the best of their understandings. That was why the same intricate formula could end up differently and affected the purity of the resultant vital internal energy for different practitioners.

Even though internal martial intricate formulas were able to realize the martial advancements of the practitioners, it was not to be recklessly learnt.

If the practitioner advanced too fast without first fully grasping the essence of the intricate formula of the previous level, they would suffer in consequent levels and also affected the purity of the internal energy. If the practitioner got struck for too long in the lower levels of the intricate formula, it would affect their future martial progression and the strength of their internal energy.

Therefore, many practitioners of the martial clans would spend years building up their martial foundation and their martial understandings, even taking years to ponder and research a particular internal martial intricate formula!

But of course, once they lay their hands on a precious internal martial intricate formula, they might not be able to resist the temptations. The martial masters of the major martial clans in the martial fraternity knew the risk of the internal martial intricate formula. That was why they only imparting it to suitable protégés or even only the next leadership candidate.

This led to envy and many pugilists would ignore the risks for practicing the internal martial intricate formula as everyone wanted to be more powerful than their rivals, believing that they were the ones who had the intellect and the talent for the skill.

And as the time passed by, due to the numerous conflicts in the fraternity, many internal martial intricate formulas were lost; it became a covetous thing for the pugilists to lay their hands upon. Even the previous warning of old was lost on most pugilists in their pursuit for more powerful skills.

If Ji Lingfeng got struck with the Asper Invocations or if it was in conflict with her existing internal martial formula the Holy Amalgamate Intricate Recite, the backlash would be terrible.

She had to find a way to merge the Holy Amalgamate and the Aspire Invocations first. It would possible take many weeks and even years for her to safely even start practicing on the Aspire Invocations.

Once she had begun on the Asper Invocations Intricate Recite, she could not turn back anymore. And this old freak could only teach her the basic intricate formula of the Aspire Invocations as a solution to her internal injury. Without looking and knowing what contained in the later stages of the Asper Invocations, it would be a dangerous practice.

Therefore, she would never have believed that this old freak was not trying to harm her.

Perhaps Yi Tianxing had seen what was bothering her. He laughed, "Don't you worry so much."

If she was not worried, that was impossible. She nearly fainted by those dreadful thoughts and afraid that she might lose or cause her martial power to deteriorate!

All of a sudden, Ji Lingfeng said coldly, "Since you already know that I am related to Ji Yunzhong then do you know that you are the one that caused him his death? How vicious are you. Now you are trying to harm me!"

Yi Tianxing was startled, "Your father is no longer in this world? Young lass, surely there must be some misunderstandings? I didn't kill your father."

Ji Lingfeng began to tremble as she said, "He was killed by Gu Tianle twenty years ago and because of this victory, the pugilists in the fraternity gave him the title of Warrior-God. That was what everyone had thought. The real cause of his death was his injuries that you have caused him twenty-five years ago from which he had never recovered."

Yi Tianxing asked, "So you wish to avenge your father?"

Yi Ping was shocked at the revelation that her father was indirectly killed by his father.

He remembered that his mother had indirectly died when she was trying his life. The real perpetrator was Gongsun Bai who had caused her to sustain severe injuries previously. That was why he had secretly sworn to find the real perpetrator behind the disappearance of his father and the indirect death of his mother...

Chapter 11: The Martial Secrets of the Mysterious Yellow Dressed Maiden

Ji Lingfeng had ranted at Yi Tianxing in a moment of ire.

Yi Tianxing had asked, "So you wish to avenge your father?"

Ji Lingfeng shook her head, "My brother and my mother told me, even though that you have caused him to be injured but my father had never blamed you. The duel had been honorable and you had even saved his life by teaching him the Divine Revelation Skill so that he would never need to be plagued by the curse of the Holy Amalgamate Skill that caused his internal organ injuries."

She added, "My father had never expected you to teach him your clan most secret skill to him. Your righteousness touched my father. But even though he had retired from the martial fraternity, the Holy Hex Sect had never had a moment of peace. Pugilists like Gu Tianle were always organizing attacks on our sect to gain renown for themselves."

Yi Tianxing gulped down the wine that Yi Ping had brought as he sighed, "So did I. Your father Ji Yunzhong was the number one top exponent of the heretic sects. I challenged your father in order to gain fame too."

He added, "Even though I have defeated your father, I realized that he was suffering from internal injuries that impaired his ability to fight optimally. Even though his skills were powerful enough to defeat most first rate exponents but when two equally top exponents fought with one another, it would determine the vanquished and the victor!"

He said, "Not wanting to take advantage of your father, I imparted to him the Divine Revelation Skill and no one else knew of the secret duel that we had."

Ji Lingfeng had a tear in her eyes, "That is why my father had been grateful to you. You have helped him to prolong his life."

Yi Tianxing said, "It is undeniable that I have caused your father internal injuries to worsen."

Ji Lingfeng said, "However, my father was glad to have you as his worthy opponent. He often said that if he had met you a few years ago, things might be differently. Even when he was defeated by Gu Tianle, he still said that the one that defeated him was you and not Gu Tianle."

Yi Tianxing sighed, "His martial skills must have deteriorated a lot during those five years."

Ji Lingfeng said, "Since then, the Holy Hex Sect disappeared from the martial fraternity. Only in recent years was it revived by my brother."

Yi Tianxing said, "I remembered your brother…"

Ji Lingfeng's brother was a full twenty years older than her. When her father died, she was only a three year old baby.

Yi Ping did not know that Ji Lingfeng had such a tragic past as he begun to empathize with her. He asked, "How old are you back then?"

Ji Lingfeng sighed softly, "I was only three…"

Yi Ping looked at her with great empathy, "It must be hard on you all these years. That means you are now twenty-three of age now."

All of a sudden, Ji Lingfeng kinked her eyebrows as she looked back coldly at him.

When Yi Ping saw her cold stares and her sudden change of expressions, he began to be fearful and thought, "Why is that every time I say something, she will be so cold to me? It not as if I say something awful? Or is it because she doesn't want me to take pity on her?"

When Ji Lingfeng heard him saying to her, "It must be hard on you all these years" she was deeply touched. But when she heard him describing her age, she was displeased. Like many young maidens in the fraternity, they were sensitive about their age once they were past eighteen. If she was near to him, she would definitely kick and slap him.

Yi Tianxing sighed deeply, "Why bother returning to the martial fraternity? Your family should lead a life of seclusion and retreated from the intrigues of the fraternity. There are simply too many bloodshed."

Ji Lingfeng said, "Even if we want to, the pugilists would not spare us. Over the years, we had been betrayed and pursued numerous times. The blood of our elders and our clan protégé, we must definitely avenge upon. Old Senior, you don't have to worry for us. Thanks to your Divine Revelation, my brother, Ji Wuzheng has now perfected the Holy Amalgamate Skill."

Yi Tianxing was startled, "He has?"

Ji Lingfeng said, "Completely. Without your Divine Revelation Skill, my brother would have suffered internal injuries as he progressed. In fact, my brother had defeated the Sword Saint, the top exponent of the orthodox clans last year!"

Yi Tianxing was even more startled, "Old Man Zuo of the Infinity Sword Clan?"

Ji Lingfeng said, "That is right!"

Even in his time, Old Man Zuo was renowned for his Infinity Swordplay and was already conferred the title of Sword Saint by the martial fraternity for his superior swordplay. His twenty-two infinity sword strokes were renowned throughout for its offensive stances and extraordinary strokes.

The Infinity Swordplay was unusual in the sense that the weakest sword stroke started from the twenty-two stance, the Infinity-Twenty-Two. When the stance numbering dropped, the infinity swordplay got more intricate and powerful.

Most senior protégés of the Infinity Swordplay rarely got past the eleventh stance of the Infinity Swordplay. Even then, those that had reached the eleventh attainment stance of the Infinity Swordplay were top swordsmen that very few exponents in the fraternity would be able to match.

It was said that Old Man Zuo was the first person in the Infinity Sword Clan that could attain the Infinity-First of the Infinity Swordplay. He was closed to unravel the full mysteries of the Infinitude Recite and it was rumored that he had already achieved the Infinity-Zero, a swordplay that was so supernatural that it was out of the world.

Yi Tianxing muttered, "Even with my Horizon Swordplay and your sect Hexagon Swordplay combined, it cannot even come close to the Infinity-Two. I know because my grand protégé master was a bosom friend of Old Man Zuo's protégé master and they had sparred on numerous times. So how did your brother manage to defeat Old Man Zuo?"

Ji Lingfeng said mysteriously, "Of course it cannot be compared. Or else my brother would be dead many times over."

Yi Ping could not resist interrupting, "Why do you beat around the bush. How did your brother defeat the Sword Saint?"

Ji Lingfeng said, "Old Man Zuo knew that my brother would never be his match and he is a junior. Therefore they contested with their inner martial arts. After a titanic fight, my brother's Holy Amalgamate Skill emerged victorious over the Sword Saint's Infinitude Skill. Again, your Divine Revelation Skill played a huge part in the victory."

Yi Tianxing blinked his eyes and said, "I am sure your brother will not stop till he dominates the martial fraternity?"

Ji Lingfeng smiled coldly, "Old Senior, you do not have to worry about this. You only have to know that my clan is forever grateful to you that we are able to revive our sect. I can ask my brother to wipe out the Gongsun clan for you. I have heard that Gu Tianle is now a guest of the Gongsun clan. Our enemies are the same."

Yi Ping said, "This blood feud is only between Gongsun Bai and us. We don't need outside help to kill Gongsun Bai."

Ji Lingfeng said coldly, "Hmph you...I am just trying to help you. Do you know that killing Gongsun Bai is not easy? His martial level is way out of your league! Or else, my brother will have already led his men to lay waste to the Gongsun Manor."

Yi Ping said, "I don't need you to worry for me, I can..."

Ji Lingfeng said, "Did you forget that I have helped save your life? If...if something happens to you, how do you repay me this debt? Is this the righteousness that you have in mind?"

She added, "Don't forget this that without me, you would never have united with your father. So you owe me two debts!"

Yi Ping was speechless and said, "Maiden..."

Yi Tianxing laughed, "Son, this maiden obviously cares for you and wants to help you. Yet, you keep rejecting her overtures."

Ji Lingfeng flustered and said, "No, I am not obviously cares for...him! He is just a rascal that does not know what is good for him!"

Yi Ping thought sadly, "In her eyes, I am only a rascal?"

Yi Tianxing said, "That is why he is admirable, isn't it?" Even though he was an old man now but the passionate eyes that Ji Lingfeng had for Yi Ping could not escape from his eyes.

He added, "The two of you are like a little couple. Why don't you get married right now and I will be your witness?"

All of a sudden, Yi Ping kneeled onto the ground, "Father, your son is already married!"

Yi Tianxing was startled and he asked, "Who may she be?"

Ji Lingfeng trembled lightly in shock, "He is really married?"

Yi Ping said, "She is Shui Yixian."

Yi Tianxing was taken aback and asked, "Shui Yixian? He knew Shui Yixian as the third protégé sister of his wife, Shui Yichi. But there were many people with similar names in the fraternity.

Yi Ping said, "You know her too. She is the Celestial Fairy."

Yi Tianxing received a jolt in his head.

Yi Tianxing roared with laughter, "Like father, like son. You married her with your mediocre skills? This is unbelievable."

Yi Ping began to relate his accounts with Shui Yixian.

Ji Lingfeng began to tremble as she thought, "He really is not lying to me. I am the one that does not believe him...That means he is not delusion and is of sound mind?"

When Yi Ping had finished related the accounts, he added, "My wife had just passed away. I should observe a three year of mourning for her. I shouldn't get married at this time."

Ji Lingfeng turned away as she coldly said, "Even if you want to marry me, I may not agree too. I don't want ever to be your guardian for life."

Yi Tianxing looked on with an interesting expression on his face. Sometimes, a lady meant entirely the opposite of what she had said. It would be a pity to give this fine lady up, even if she was not from the orthodox clans.

Yi Tianxing roared with laughter, "So Maiden Ji, do you still want to learn the Aspire Invocations?"

At the mention of the Aspire Invocations, Ji Lingfeng expressions turned sour.

She said coldly, "Why are you still trying to harm me?"

Yi Ping defended his father, "Maiden Ji, why do keep saying that? My father has only good intentions towards you."

Ji Lingfeng looked coldly at Yi Ping and almost threw a secret projectile in his direction, "Why don't you keep quiet for a while?" She wanted to say shut up to him but decided to soften her tone at the last moment.

Yi Ping did really keep quiet, afraid to even look at her.

Yi Tianxing began to recite the Aspire Invocations Intricate Recite and said, "This is the basic Aspire Invocations Intricate Recite."

Ji Lingfeng was startled after hearing it, "This is the intricate formula of the basic Aspire Invocations? Why does it sound like it is a dissolution skill? It doesn't seem to be related to the Asper Horizon Hand?"

Yi Tianxing laughed, "You are so smart. It is a dissolution skill but it is used only to neutralize the erratic vital energies for the practitioners of the Asper Horizon Hands. Our clan uses it to test the martial advancements of our protégés before imparting the real staging of the Aspire Invocations. If you really want to improve the prowess of the Asper Horizon Hand, you have to learn the Aspire Invocation Intricate Recite and the Divine Horizon Hands."

He paused for a while before continuing, "So, are you willing to be my protégé disciple and learn my Aspire Invocations?"

Yi Ping said to his father, "Since Maiden Ji thinks father is trying to harm her and unwilling to learn it, let don't force her. If she doesn't want to, I want to! Moreover the Aspire Invocations Intricate Recite is our clan martial secret and shouldn't be taught to outsiders."

Ji Lingfeng was excited. It was because the Holy Amalgamate Skill was a type of dissolution skill too. If Yi Tianxing could explain to her the dissolution intricate formula of the Aspire Invocations, it would further her understandings of the Holy Amalgamate Skill and helped her in her martial progression tremendously!

Moreover, Yi Tianxing had explained that to her the basic Aspire Invocations was a standalone skill that could help her control her erratic vital energy and would not require her to practice it as another inner martial intricate formula.

Therefore she flew to Yi Tianxing and said alluringly, "I want to learn. Alas, protégé master! Your protégé disciple Ji Lingfeng pays my respect to you!"

Yi Tianxing laughed, "That is my good protégé disciple!"

Yi Ping was left bewildered, "Didn't you say you won't learn the Aspire Invocations?"

Ji Lingfeng turned back and smiled alluringly, "Hmph, when did I ever say so? It seems that your hearings are bad."

Indeed, she had never said so. She was just giving the impression that she did not want to learn it.

Yi Ping was speechless.

Ji Lingfeng had a mysterious look in her eyes as she said to him, "From now on, you have to address me as your older protégé sister and listens to me."

Both Yi Tianxing and Yi Ping were stunned.

Yi Ping asked, "When… did you become my older protégé sister? You are younger than me…"

Ji Lingfeng said proudly, "Just now. Hmph, didn't you just hear from your father that he has just accepted me as his protégé? You haven't even joined yet. Since I am the first to join, then I am your older protégé sister."

That was the rule of the martial fraternity; the one that joined first under the same protégé master was to be the most senior.

Yi Tianxing recovered from his surprise and said, "True, true…"

Ji Lingfeng batted an eye at Yi Ping and said, "Quick, address me as your older protégé sister."

Yi Ping was amused, he began to rub his nose as he pondered, "Actually it is a good feeling to have an older protégé sister." All of a sudden, he felt that he was no longer alone.

So he said, "Greetings older protégé sister!"

Ji Lingfeng smiled alluring, "Greetings my younger protégé brother!"

Ji Lingfeng was secretly joyful for she now had someone to talk to. It was because as the Holy Maiden of the Holy Hex Sect, she had no friends and no one to talk to except for her brother.

When she had heard of an upcoming major congregation that was going to be held by the Gongsun Clan for a punitive action against her brother, she was panicky and decided to take actions into her own hands to visit the congregation against her brother wishes.

It was because her brother had not yet recovered from his internal injuries from his duel with the Sword Saint even though it had been nearly a year now.

It was no coincident that she had met Yi Ping. She was aware that Gongsun Jing was in that particular town and was waiting for an opportunity to teach him a lesson but as he was always in the company of top exponents like Jue Yuan and Gu Tianle, the opportunity that she been waiting for never came.

When Jue Yuan had attacked Yi Ping, she decided to interfere even though it would mean exposing her true identity and bring her plans to disrupt the congregation futile.

Yi Tianxing said to them, "Our clan is renowned for the Horizon Swordplay, the Divine Horizon Hands, the Aspire Invocations Intricate Recite and the Divine Revelation Skill."

Yi Tianxing said, "The Divine Revelation Skill is a breathing technique that controls the breathing and vital energy in the body. What makes it special from other breathing techniques is its ability to re-energize the breath and allowing practitioners to hold on to the vital breath as long as possible."

"When used together with the Aspire Invocations, it is able to unleash the full potential of the Divine Horizon Hands and our secret techniques, the Asper, the Asper Continuum and the Asper Divinity Horizon Hand."

"When top exponents fight, the first breathe is always the most important as well as the most powerful. That is the essence of vital energy and the key to release our martial force in the forms of internal energy. As a fight continues and consumes more and more martial strength, breathing becomes harder and harder."

He paused for a while before adding, "In a real fight, your foes will not give you rest and will seek to overpower you through exhaustion and fatigue. There are no respite and chance to rest. The Divine Revelation retains unused vital energy and reconverts it back as vital breath."

He said, "As proficiency in the Divine Revelation Skill grows, the practitioner will be able to retain the vital breath in the body channels to be used later. This is unlike the breathing technique of the Emotionless Rhyme of the Eternal Ice Palace that tries to retain the vital breath as long as possible."

Yi Ping suddenly recalled that when Shui Yixian fought with her opponents, she rarely spoke and was entirely composed. All of a sudden, he recalled the killing stance of the yellow dressed maiden.

Yi Ping asked, "The yellow dressed lady that killed my wife has the ability to muster her martial power in a short confine of time and her killing power is lethal. What type of martial arts is she using? If she had lifted her vital breath, Yixian would have notice and would not be surprised by her." And Yi Ping described her moves.

Yi Tianxing was surprised, "A sudden burst of martial power? It is true that most offensive martial skills required the practitioner to muster and gather their vital energies for the offensive. That is why it is impossible to surprise top exponents like Yixian."

He clapped his hands, "I got it now. She must have known the Emotionless Rhyme too! You said that her grandmother was Shui Yisi, the second protégé sister of Yixian. If she does not know the Emotionless Rhyme, then it really is a weird thing. Therefore she must have slowly re-energized her vital breath and muster her martial power in secret, unnoticeable by anyone."

The Emotionless Rhyme was a breathing technique that could allow the practitioner control over their heart-beat and kept the opponents from knowing if their vital energy was truly spent and also muster martial power in secret.

Ji Lingfeng suddenly said, "That is the Penetrating Hand. Unlike most other martial arts, this unique skill is able to display the most power at point blank, without any hint. So if she knows the Emotionless Rhyme of the Eternal Ice Palace, then these two techniques when used together is a deadly combination."

Now it was Yi Ping turn to be surprised. He quickly asked, "Do you know that yellow dress maiden?"

Ji Lingfeng shook her head and said, "Two years ago, my brother fought with a young maiden on a chance occurrence. The duel was a draw but my brother told me that in a few years' time, that lady martial progression may surpass him and he warned me to be wary of this type of martial art and described it to me."

Ji Lingfeng said coolly, "Accordingly to him, her Penetrating Hands were extremely swift to execute, she could actually displayed six to ten strokes of it in the blink of an eye. Every strike executed by her was lethal and filled with martial power. My brother took a few hits due to carelessness and the internal injuries suffered by him were not light!"

Yi Tianxing said, "Even though this type of martial art may be mustered at a short notice, it is likely to restrict her movements too. If she cannot land her hits, surely your brother can overcome her?"

He pointed out, "It is highly incredible that your brother would not be able to overcome her. There aren't many exponents in the fraternity that can match his Holy Amalgamate Skill in terms of technique and martial power. Why is the fight a draw?"

Ji Lingfeng nodded, "My brother had noticed as well but it was only after he had been surprised by her Penetrating Hands and were almost killed by her. He had actually wounded her with the full martial power of his Holy Amalgamate Skill."

Yi Tianxing was astonished, "She survived that?"

Ji Lingfeng said, "That is because besides the Penetrating Hands, she has another powerful defensive skill."

Yi Tianxing's eyes started to glow as he wished that he had not lost his martial power. He almost wished that he could try out her Penetrating Hands versus his Divine Horizon Hands.

He asked, "Is it because she learnt a protective energy aura skill or iron shroud type of skill that can deflect physical attacks?"

Ji Lingfeng smiled, "Protégé Master, you are right. It is not an energy impervious skill that protects her but something else that is subtle. My brother is able to identify the skill as the 'Golden Impervious Skill'. That is why even though my brother had dealt her fatally, it was still not fatal enough."

Yi Ping sighed. He had never expected his enemy to be an even more frightening opponent that he had thought. But his will was absolute and his wife had to be avenged.

Ji Lingfeng added, "If my brother was not surprised by her and was not injured, that lady would never be able to survive a duel with my brother. "

Yi Ping interrupted her, "That was two years ago. If your brother was surprised by her two years later, he might not survive too. Yixian and Tian Kui were killed by her with a single hit. Her martial progression within these two years must be astonishing."

Ji Lingfeng said coolly, "I think you are overrating her martial abilities. She relied on the element of surprise to bring forth her strikes to the greatest effect. Since my brother knew of her techniques, it is difficult for her to succeed again."

Yi Tianxing said, "Nothing is sure in a duel. But it is a lucky thing we are able to learn so much. When top exponents fight, they always conceal their best techniques unless they have no other choices. It seems that your brother is able to force her to display more than necessary."

But he was already sighing in his heart, "The Golden Impervious Skill. A young maiden has actually mastered this long lost epitome skill?" He really found it hard to believe.

Yi Tianxing said, "We have side tracked and let us continue on the introduction. The Divine Horizon Hands is our clan most powerful skill. It contains three hidden secret techniques, the Asper, the Asper Continuum and the Asper Divinity."

He said, "Normally, to even begin the first secret technique of the Divine Horizon Hands the Asper Horizon, the practitioner will need forty years of martial power."

Both Yi Ping and Ji Lingfeng gasped, "Forty years?!"

Ji Lingfeng immediately recalled that after she had used the Asper Horizon Hands, her fingers were trembling and she felt as though all her strength had been drained from her executing arm!

Yi Tianxing said, "That is right. I practiced for forty-years before I am allowed to descend from the mountains by my master."

Ji Lingfeng said, "Didn't I manage to use the Asper Horizon Hand already?"

Yi Tianxing said, "I was surprised that you can use it so soon. It may be because you have been practicing the Divine Revelation Skill for a long time to enhance your Holy Amalgamate Skill therefore you already have a certain foundation in internal strength. That is why you are able to pick up the Asper Horizon Hand fairly quickly"

Ji Lingfeng blinked her eyes at Yi Ping and smiled.

Without exchanging a word, Yi Ping was annoyed by her. She was gleeful that her martial strength was higher than him.

Yi Tianxing quickly added, "However, without the Aspire Invocations Intricate Recite to refine the Asper Horizon and knowledge of the Divine Horizon Hands, it is almost impossible to fully realize the full power of the Asper Horizon. Not to mention the Asper Continuum and the Asper Divinity."

Yi Tianxing continued, "The Asper Continuum Horizon Hand requires sixty years and the Asper Divinity Horizon Hand requires eighty years of solid internal strength to use."

Yi Ping sighed and muttered, "Isn't that too hard?"

He would be an old man by then.

Ji Lingfeng said, "At most I will take a few more years, compare to you know who."

Yi Ping unhappily said, "Only time will tell. Your clan has so many enemies. You are probably too busy avenging your clan to practice as much as I do."

Yi Tianxing held him in his wrist and examined his pulse, sighing. "Son, because you have the Icy Heavenly Tears energy in you, it may be difficult for you to even begin on the Aspire Invocations. Therefore you won't be able to wield the Divine Horizon Hands to its full potential. If you try to begin on the Aspire Invocations, the risk of deviation phenomena is great. You will end up paralyze or dead."

Yi Ping nodded and replied, "Father, it doesn't matter to me. I am so glad to see you again. Even if my skills are mediocre, I will avenge on Gongsun Bai even if it takes me years of hard work."

When Ji Lingfeng glanced at him, she could see the determined look in his eyes and the mesmerizing righteousness air around him. She felt herself drawn irresistible to him and believed in him…

All of a sudden, Yi Tianxing gasped, "Even though you have the Icy Heavenly Tears in your pulse but your heart pulse seem to be devoid of it at the same time. How is it possible?"

Ji Lingfeng grabbed Yi Ping wrist too and examined his pulses, "That is weird. Sometimes I can feel a cold piercing negative pulse but sometimes I cannot feel it."

Yi Tianxing muttered, "Don't tell me it is Yichi… she had purposely left Ping'Er internal strength in a clean slate? How is it possible? Don't tell me she had finally grasped the mysteries of the Eternal Heavenly Tears in her last final moments? That is just the remnants of her Eternal Force in Ping'Er pulse and not the Icy Heavenly Tears that I think it is?"

He needed more time to ponder over it. But for now, it might be possible for Yi Ping to practice on the Aspire Invocations under his watchful guidance.

All of a sudden, he turned solemn and said, "I must warn the two of you first. In the future, should you have the opportunity to grasp the mysteries of the Asper Divinity; you must not practice or use it. If you pass it to future generations, remember to forewarn them as well."

Yi Ping asked, "Father, what do you mean? If the skill cannot be used, what is the use of it being there?"

Yi Tianxing sighed deeply before he said painfully, "That is the warning left behind by our grand protégé master. If you manage to learn this forbidden skill, in three years' time, you will surely die!"

Both Yi Ping and Ji Lingfeng gasped at the same time, "How come?"

Yi Tianxing said solemnly, "The Divine Calamity." But he refused to say a word more.

Yi Ping and Ji Lingfeng exchanged looks before Yi Ping mustered his courage and asked, "Father, what exactly is the Divine Calamity? You mentioned that mum was fearful of it and even our clan must be wary of it."

All of a sudden, he seemed to be muttering to himself and he was making no sense.

The only legitimate words that they could decipher were, "Bloodsuckers and Celestial Palace."

Ji Lingfeng and Yi Ping looked at one another. They seemed to be thinking of the same thing. There was only one place in the entire fraternity that was called the Celestial Palace…

The Celestial Palace was located in the western fraternity. Like the Eternal Ice Palace and the Virtuous Palace, it was one of the three most forbidden places in the entire martial fraternity.

Even though many of the powerful unorthodox clans were situated in the western fraternity, few dare to intrude on the forbidden grounds of the Celestial Palace. Those that did never returned.

The Celestial Palace was said to be situated in the Nirvana Mountains and was so mysterious that no one had ever seen a single protégé from that place, yet it continued to exist for centuries. No one really knew if the Celestial Clan really did exist.

In the western fraternity, mere mention of the Celestial Palace among the older pugilists would bring great fear and a great silence.

Ji Lingfeng was even more startled than Yi Ping.

It was because the Holy Hex Sect had a brief but stern warning not to mention its name and to visit that place. The Holy Amalgamate Skill was said to be a secret skill that was derived from the Sacred Celestial Skill of the Celestial Holy Clan. That warning and the origin of the Holy Amalgamate Skill was passed down only verbally to the members of the Ji Clan.

Chapter 12: Nangong Le

The streets of the town were noisy and filled with many activities. The town was more crowded than usual. It was because the Gongsun Martial Aristocracy Clan, who controlled the town and its vicinity areas, had invited heroes from all over the fraternity to participate in a rare fraternity assembly.

The death of Old Man Zuo the Sword Saint had sent a shockwave throughout the fraternity and emboldened the heretic sects; there were at least a hundred clashes between the orthodox clans and the heretic sects in the past year alone.

The main purpose of the congregation was to seek a solution to the current martial affairs and to select a new orthodox leader from among the major orthodox clans.

Nangong Le looked bored and was looking for entertainment in the streets of the town. He had come to this town at the invitation of Gongsun Bai. Accompanying him were two renowned tranquil middle-age swordsmen Priest Liu Qingcheng the older protégé and Priest Ling Kongquan the younger protégé of the Tranquil City who acted as his escorts as well as his friends.

Priest Liu Qingcheng was also the protégé master of the Tranquil City.

The Tranquil City was one of the oldest martial clan in the fraternity, famed for its Tranquil Swordplay and the Tranquil Fists. Even though the Tranquil City was famed for its swordplay, the most powerful skill in the clan was actually their Dual Inertness Intricacy, a divinity state of 'Exchanging spirit intricate from a thousand miles, sensing from a million miles', and 'Absorbing the essence of Heavens and Earth'.

Also, Priest Liu Qingcheng and Priest Ling Kongquan were also top inner martial experts and their martial skills were not beneath any of the major orthodox clans' skills.

Nangong Le did not want to go to the Gongsun Manor so early and deliberately stayed in the town to find interesting entertainments. That was typical of his usual style and action.

Priest Liu Qingcheng and Priest Ling Kongquan may look like they were lofty priests that would never partake in such meaningless pursuit, it was actually the opposite.

Also their Dual Inertness Intricacy was all about sensing the emotional elations of others to elevate their state of divinity further. There no better ways than to follow Nangong Le to advance their cultivation!

That was exactly why they were Nangong Le's friends.

Priest Ling Kongquan asked, "Is it good to keep our orthodox friends waiting? I know that many had left early this morning for the Gongsun Manor. Surely the congregation will be crowded and it is even more interesting there."

Priest Liu Qingcheng laughed aloud, "The orthodox clans have always belittled and looked down on the Tranquil City. Even though they did not say that, their hearts tells otherwise. It will only affect our cultivation if we associate ourselves with such negative emotions."

Priest Ling Kongquan smirked, "Alas, I still derive so much pleasure from their hypocrisy."

Nangong Le laughed aloud, "The pugilists of the orthodox will only look up to the influential and not the weak. In their eyes, only the seven major orthodox clans and the Gongsun

Martial Clan deserve their true respect. Small clans and inactive clans like us are just small fries in their eyes."

Priest Liu Qingcheng said, "You are really too humble, Young Master Nangong. You are now one of the four young masters of the martial fraternity and you even got a gold invitation for this congregation. That unruly Gongsun Bai only sent us a silver invitation."

Nangong Le shook his head, "My martial skills are beneath you. I really do not deserve to have the gold invitation. The only reason that I am one of the young masters of the martial fraternity is only because they are short of one person for that honorific to make it sound more pleasant and only because of the wealth of the Nangong Clan."

Indeed, the Nangong Clan was the wealthiest clan in the entire fraternity and well-known for their immerse holdings and banks.

All of a sudden, Nangong Le, Priest Liu Qingcheng and Priest Ling Kongquan halted their steps. It was because they had suddenly heard the most enchanting music that they had ever heard in their entire lives!

Even though the streets were busy and full of a great multitude of different noises that overshadowed the enthralling music, their sharp ears were able to pick it up.

The melody of the music was slow, enchanting and extremely moving to the listeners but it also carried a sad melancholy to it.

They were stunned that such an intricate melody actually existed, despite having listened to hundreds of music from all over the fraternity.

Nangong Le muttered in awe, "What beautiful heavenly music. It is too out of the world."

Priest Liu Qingcheng was so enthralled by the music that he dared not say a word but closed his eyes as he was afraid to miss it.

He had a tear in his eyes; the music was so heart wrenching that he was trembling uncontrollably! All of a sudden, he gained a new inspiration for the Dual Inertness Intricacy...

Priest Ling Kongquan was stammering and trembling, "It comes...from around the...alley!"

Priest Ling Kongquan grabbed Priest Liu Qingcheng and said, "Eldest Protégé Brother, let's us take a look!"

Priest Liu Qingcheng was startled from his stupor as he quickly replied "Yes, let's take a look!"

They soon turned into an alley saw a high wall that blocked them.

Luckily, this high wall was not too high for them to display their wall scaling skills and they soon scaled over it.

They were soon stunned at the sight of the other side after they had scaled over the high wall.

This was so unlike the dirty and confine alley that they were in earlier.

This courtyard was large and very beautiful. It was clean, decorated with all kinds of trees and fragrance flowers.

There was a small artificial large pond with a bridge over it and the enchanting music comes from beyond the courtyard.

Nangong Le muttered, "Did we arrive at the Gongsun Manor by mistake?"

Priest Ling Kongquan smiled weakly, "That is in the other direction?"

Priest Liu Qingcheng said, "That appear to be so."

Nangong Le too smiled weakly, "Who else but Gongsun Bai can afford such magnificent place in this desolate town. Even if this place is not the Gongsun Manor, the owner must be related to him."

The enchanting emotional melancholy music seemed to have come from beyond the courtyard. Therefore, they continued to walk through the courtyard while admiring the beauty and grandeur of the place.

When Nangong Le, Priest Liu Qingcheng and Priest Ling Kongquan came to another courtyard, they could see two exquisite beautiful maidens playing the zither and the pipa with white curtains in the background.

The melancholy and enchanting music had come from them. What astonished them was that these two young maidens had looked exactly alike!

Nangong Le thought, "They are twins?"

Nangong Le was immediately attracted by them and started to appraise them silently. They were in black velvet silk dresses and he was fascinated by their dedicated eyes.

He noticed that they had a long sword besides them. Normally, only pugilists and nobility would carry a long sword with them although there were many exceptions; they could be using it for sword dances and sword plays as it was a popular pastime with many.

He had never seen anyone as beautiful as them in black as it was an ominous color and was not a color of choice for most maidens.

He could only gasped, "So beautiful." And he was instantly hypnotized by them.

All of a sudden, when he saw the translucent jade bangles on their left wrists, he was stunned.

It was because these translucent jades could only be found in the Heavenly Mountains, was extremely rare and priceless. Even if someone had those translucent jades, they would never dare to wear or carry it for fear of damaging it.

When he saw their musical instruments that were made of red purple sandal wood, which was so highly prized and rare that it was worth its weight in gold, he was dumbfounded.

At first, he thought he could use his wealthy background to entice them but now he knew that if he had tried that, it was a terrible mistake for they had no material lack! He began to smile bitterly for he realized he had spent most of his gold in the last few days and was terribly poor at the moment to offer them a decent gift.

The few jewelries and gold that he had were too embarrassing to be taken out as a first time social gift. And he might be looked down upon and lost their first good impressions of him. This was the first time that Nangong Le had felt that he was poor.

Ling Kongquan was solemn as he said, "Be careful. For them to appear in such a place, they may be vixens. We should leave immediately now that we got the chance…"

Nangong Le said, "Even if they are thousand year old vixens, I must still know their names!"

Priest Liu Qingcheng was taken aback, "Brother Nangong, you…"

But before he could stop him, Nangong Le had immediately mustered his courage to introduce himself, "I am Nangong Le. These two are Priest Liu Qingcheng and Priest Ling Kongquan. May we have the honor of knowing the names of both mistresses?"

The two sisters stopped playing and looked into their direction; their dedicated eyes were looking at them intently.

When Nangong Le saw their eyes looking intently at him, his heart began to beat very fast as he thought, "Both of them are so beautiful and so beholding. So which one should I woo? Which one should I woo first? Or shall I woo the two of them at the same time?"

The young maiden on the left asked in a soft voice, "Do you know that you are trespassing?"

Priest Liu Qingcheng hurriedly replied, "Maiden, please forgive us for trespassing. We really meant no harm at all. When we are outside, we suddenly heard an enchanting melody. Out of curiosity, we have come to take a look."

The young maiden on the left said softly, "Now that you have already taken a look, what do you want to do now?"

Priest Ling Kongquan was the first to reply, "Nothing but are…are you both humans?"

The young maiden on the right laughed softly, "Do we look like we are not humans to you?"

Priest Ling Kongquan managed a weak smile, "No…"

Nangong Le smiled, "You are both like heavenly fairies and not humans."

The young maiden on the right seemed to be flattered as she replied, "Is that so?"

Nangong Le said, "That is so!"

Then she looked intently at him, "We can also be vixens and we like to feast upon your blood."

Nangong Le laughed, "Maiden you must be joking. Even if you want to eat me, I will not struggle at all."

The young maiden on the right said, "Really? You will not struggle?"

Nangong Le laughed, "I won't struggle, not even once!"

The young maiden on the right smiled, "What if we are not joking?"

These two young maidens in black velvet were looking at them intently.

Nangong Le, Priest Liu Qingcheng and Priest Ling Kongquan broke into cold sweat. They could not really tell if they were joking.

It was indeed strange that two extraordinary beautiful young maidens would appear in a small isolated town that only pugilists would bother to visit and they were staying in a place with such splendor that seemingly out of place. Moreover they were exactly the same and had so much finery on them yet there were no servants anywhere. And their enthralling music was too supernatural to be found in the mortal realm. Was everything just an illusion?

The young maiden on the left added, "Unfortunately, it is real and we need blood to maintain our youthful appearances, especially men with such vitality such as you."

Priest Ling Kongquan turned ashen as he stammered, "Who…who are you…?" He wanted to run but his legs had grown soft.

Even Nangong Le had turned completely white as he thought, "I have toyed with numerous women in my life and now my life is going to end in their hands. I swear if I can survive this, I will surely turn over a new leaf. Alas Heavens, please help me…"

Priest Liu Qingcheng roared aloud with laughter, "For a moment, I am almost fooled. They are not vixens."

Nangong Le and Priest Ling Kongquan looked at Priest Liu Qingcheng with startled expressions. They were not vixens and they were joking?

Priest Ling Kongquan asked, "Eldest Protégé Brother, you can tell?"

The young maiden on the left smiled, "Of course we are not vixens. Do we look like foxes to you?"

Nangong Le heaved a sigh of relief when he heard that they were not vixens as he slowly recovered his composure.

Priest Ling Kongquan smiled weakly, "I have never seen any vixens in my life but I know that they can take human shape."

The young maiden on the right sighted softly, "Unfortunately we are really not vixens."

Priest Ling Kongquan said nervously, "Vixens are also liars and would never admit they are not vixens."

Nangong Le was alarmed. What Priest Ling Kongquan had said made sense. Only a priest would be able to identify a supernatural being such as a vixen.

The young maiden on the left smiled, "We are actually waiting for a real vixen and were in fact baiting her but you have come instead. If you want to see a real vixen, you can stay here and wait. Maybe you get to see a real vixen real soon."

Priest Liu Qingcheng smiled, "Vixen or not, I don't care. I am Priest Liu Qingcheng, the master of the Tranquil City. I am thinking if both maidens are willing to be my protégés, I would like to impart to you our clan most extraordinary skill, the Dual Inertness Intricacy."

The two young maidens, even Priest Ling Kongquan and Nangong Le were startled!

Priest Liu Qingcheng was straightforward and had declared his intentions.

It was startling because even direct protégés of the Tranquil City may not get the chance to learn the Dual Inertness Intricacy. And he was offering them the Dual Inertness Intricacy if they were willing to be his protégés. Was it not astonishing?

Nangong Le had been acquainted with them for five years. Even though he was always pressing Priest Liu Qingcheng to reveal some of the secrets of the Dual Inertness Intricacy to him in exchange for fabulous wealth and other martial treasures but he would never indulge even an intricate word to him. But today, he was offering it for free to these two maidens?!

Nangong Le smiled bitterly, "Brother Liu, are you sure that you are not spellbound by them? You know that I am willing to be your protégé…"

Even though he had asked to be his protégé on many occasions, Priest Liu Qingcheng would always kindly reject him.

All of a sudden, Nangong Le was alarmed as he thought, "Don't tell me Brother Liu had been bewitched by them already?"

Even Ling Kongquan was taken completely by surprise by his protégé brother as he said, "You are for real? That is our clan secret skill and we know nothing about their backgrounds…"

When the young maiden on the left recovered from her surprise, she smiled faintly. "You don't even know who we are or our names and yet you talk about wanting us to be your protégés?"

The young maiden on the right added, "He is really a weird guy."

Priest Liu Qingcheng did not seem to mind as he asked, "Then may I know your names?"

Perhaps because he was courteous, the maiden on the left said coolly, "I'm the Lady Yu."

The maiden on the right said, "I'm the Lady Mei."

The Lady Yu was in fact Shui Yujian the Jade Sword Fairy and the Lady Mei was Shui Meijian the Beautiful Sword Fairy.

They still refuse to divulge to him their full names but Priest Liu Qingcheng did not mind.

Priest Liu Qingcheng asked again, "Will you be my protégés?"

Shui Yujian answered amusingly, "Unfortunately we already have a protégé clan. It is impossible for us to be in your protégé clan. You can leave now."

Priest Liu Qingcheng said, "You can quit your protégé clan. I can assure you that there are no other martial clans that are better than the Tranquil City. The intricate heart formula of the Dual Inertness Intricacy is unique in the fraternity and is considered one of the most sought skills. You won't regret learning it and joining the Tranquil City!"

Shui Meijian looked at her sister before she said, "If we can betray our protégé clan, then we can betray yours too. You will not want us as your protégés if we are such a person, right?"

Priest Liu Qingcheng said, "With this level of musical accomplishments, it is unlikely that you can be easily tempted by greed or else you wouldn't possible achieve it. Maidens, please reconsider…"

Priest Ling Kongquan interrupted, "Eldest Protégé Brother! Since they do not appreciate your gestures, it is pointless to say anymore to them. Let us go now. We have trespassed long enough."

Priest Liu Qingcheng ignored him and continued to say, "Maidens, please reconsider. It is a rare opportunity…"

Shui Meijian was bewildered, "You…you are begging us to take up your offer? Shouldn't it be we are begging you to take us in?"

Priest Liu Qingcheng said, "It doesn't matter who take who in as long as you are agreeable to be my protégés, I will teach you the Dual Inertness Intricacy."

It was getting comical and even Priest Ling Kongquan felt embarrassed while Nangong Le was feeling awkward.

Nangong Le and priest Ling Kongquan had even forgotten the tense situation that they were in just a few moments ago!

It really seemed that Priest Liu Qingcheng wanted them to be his protégé disciples and he was absolutely serious.

Priest Liu Qingcheng said. "What about this? You can remain in your protégé clan and you still join my protégé clan, I will still teach you the Dual Inertness Intricacy!"

Priest Ling Kongquan was shocked, "Eldest Protégé Brother, you can't do that. There isn't such a thing in the fraternity! Are you nuts?"

Priest Liu Qingcheng said solemnly, "I am sane of course. You have no idea on their latent potential. They may be the only ones that can advance the Dual Inertness Intricacy. Our clan has been on a decline for a long time and they may be the ones that can revive the position of our martial clan in the fraternity."

Priest Ling Kongquan said, "Even if they can advance the Dual Inertness Intricacy but can they fight? They are just good in the musical instruments and when the clan is in crisis, it is pointless to just have internal strength. They don't look like the types that can take hardship therefore their martial abilities will be limited."

Shui Yujian kinked her eyebrows and said, "That is enough. Just leave or you will be sorry." In fact, she had already drawn her long sword.

Nangong Le, Priest Ling Kongquan and Priest Liu Qingcheng gasped at the drawn out long sword; its blade was so shiny and its sound was tingling that they knew instantly that it was a very good sword. What was more, they could feel the cold piercing sword energy of that precious sword at this distance!

All of a sudden, Priest Liu Qingcheng said. "The person behind the white curtain, can you say something? What do you think?"

Both Priest Ling Kongquan and Nangong Le were startled. There was a person behind the white curtains?

Priest Ling Kongquan was stunned. His mastery of the Dual Inertness Intricacy was on the same level as his eldest protégé brother, yet he could not sense any breathing or heartbeat behind the curtains. Was his eldest protégé brother suffering from delusions? There was obviously no one behind the curtains.

But Priest Liu Qingcheng continued to say to the curtains, "What do you say?"

Nangong Le was unhappy with Priest Liu Qingcheng for causing him to be driven out of the place even before he could have the opportunity to exchange a meaningful dialogue with these two extraordinary exquisite maidens. He was about to rebuke Priest Liu Qingcheng when he heard a gentle feminine voice from behind the white curtain.

"How did you know that I am behind the curtains?" A soft gentle feminine voice was heard from behind the curtains.

Only when Nangong Le and Priest Ling Kongquan had heard her voice, they were jolted! There was really someone behind the white curtains!

Priest Liu Qingcheng said honestly, "Actually I do not know and is making a lucky guess. I can neither sense any breathing nor heartbeats behind the curtain. At this distance, no one can remain undetected by me, except for you."

"Oh?"

Priest Liu Qingcheng explained, "But when I saw Maiden Mei took a quick glance at the curtain and hesitating, I immediately sense that she seems to be awaiting instructions from someone. So I made a lucky guess."

Nangong Le smiled, "So there is another person behind the curtain. Let me take a look at you!" He too, was intrigued by the person behind the curtains, especially since he knew it was a lady.

Immediately, he began to sprint past Shui Yujian and Shui Meijian towards the white curtains.

What an astonishing swiftness movement speed! Even Shui Yujian and Shui Meijian gasped softly in astonishing surprise as they tried to intercept him but they were unable to stop him!

As soon he touched the white curtains, he could sense a force slowing him down. He was caught by surprise by the invisible force and before he could muster his martial power to push through the force, his chest was struck by a small porcelain cup and he was flung back!

Priest Ling Kongquan immediately caught of Nangong Le and said, "Brother Nangong, are you alright?"

Nangong Le was caught totally by surprise and his chest was now bursting with pain. He clasped his chest and was terrified. In all his years in the martial fraternity, he had never felt such an unfathomable presence before! When he was struck on his chest by the porcelain cup, he thought he was going to die!

Priest Ling Kongquan said, "It seems that you have broken one or two ribs…"

Nangong Le turned ashen as blood foamed from his mouth.

When Priest Liu Qingcheng saw how easily Nangong Le was defeated by an awkward shaped cup that was ill-suited to be a secret projectile, he immediately knew that the lady behind the curtains was a super exponent.

Even though he may not lose but he was not here to fight.

So he said, "You must be their protégé mistress or elder? What do you say?"

"The Dual Inertness Intricacy is indeed a formidable skill. If Yu'Er and Mei'Er are able to learn the intricate heart formula of the Dual Inertness Intricacy, it will be useful for their future martial progression. I have no objections to it if you are willing to impart to them."

Priest Liu Qingcheng was delighted as he clapped his hands, "Good! Brother Kongquan, can you take Brother Nangong Le to recuperate first? I won't be long and will look for you shortly."

He had asked Ling Kongquan to take Nangong Le away because he did not want Nangong Le to eavesdrop on the Dual Inertness Intricacy.

Priest Ling Kongquan sighed as he muttered, "I hope you did not make the wrong decision…" He began to support Nangong Le up to his feet and departed together with him.

Priest Liu Qingcheng said, "Before I impart the intricate heart formula of the Dual Inertness Intricacy, may I know who you are and which protégé clan are you all from?"

"Indeed you should know. I'm the Celestial Fairy of the Eternal Ice Palace."

Accordingly to the protocol of the fraternity, because Shui Yixian was his senior generation, there was no need for her to reveal her name to him. Few people in the fraternity actually knew her by her true name.

Priest Liu Qingcheng was taken aback as he took a step back, "I…have heard that the Celestial Fairy had passed on. You are really the Celestial Fairy?"

Shui Yujian interrupted softly, "You don't believe my protégé mistress? If you don't want to impart to us the Dual Inertness Intricacy, we do not mind at all."

She really did not mind at all.

Priest Liu Qingcheng laughed aloud, "Don't be mistaken. I am just surprised that I have the honor to talk to the Celestial Fairy today. It is said that the martial skills of the Eternal Ice Palace are profound. Today I have seen it, I am truly convinced. The Eternal Ice Palace may not be an orthodox clan but it is also not an unorthodox clan. I can now feel assure that I did not impart the Dual Inertness Intricacy to the wrong hands!"

The Celestial Fairy nodded and said gently, "But you mustn't tell anyone who we are and where we are from, including the two men that are with you earlier."

Priest Liu Qingcheng said solemnly, "I give you my word."

The Celestial Fairy said gently, "It is not proper that I should stay while you are imparting your clan most secret skill…"

Priest Liu Qingcheng interrupted, "Old Senior, you can stay. I am certain that with your martial cultivation, you won't hanker over anything. If you stay, I may even get some useful advice."

The Celestial Fairy replied, "That is because you are thinking that I am already too old and already hovering at death's door. If I stay and listen to the intricate formula, do I have to be your protégé disciple too?"

Priest Liu Qingcheng smiled awkwardly as Shui Yujian and Shui Meijian chuckled softly. He quickly replied, "Of course not!"

The Celestial Fairy said, "Since you are generous to impart the Dual Inertness Intricacy, I will impart the Tranquil Spirits to you then."

Priest Liu Qingcheng was stunned. This Tranquil Spirits was one of the secret intricate formulas of the Tranquil City and was actually a crucial key to understand the Dual Inertness Intricacy and many of the skills of the Tranquil City but had been lost for several centuries!

He stammered excitedly, "How did you get hold of the Tranquil Spirits?"

She simply said, "It has been with the Eternal Ice Palace for centuries. How it ends up in the Eternal Ice Palace, I really do not know."

When she stepped forth from the curtains, Priest Liu Qingcheng got the shock of his life and nearly got a heart attack.

It was because the Celestial Fairy was anything but old!

When she had appeared in front of him, in her light blue long sleeve silk dress, he thought he had seen a goddess. Even though Shui Yujian and Shui Meijian were already extraordinary beautiful, they were at least human. The Celestial Fairy was so breathtaking, so awe-inspiring yet her presence was so forbidding that she was anything but human!

Even with his Dual Inertness Intricacy, he could not even sense any mortal emotions from her. Was she delighted that he was going to impart the Dual Inertness Intricacy to her and her protégés? He got no hint at all and she was like an impassable wall. It was like she was standing on top of the world, looking at everything loftily.

At this distance, he was surprised that he could sense no breathing and heartbeats from her even though she was just standing in front of him. He had once heard that a person could actually solidify themselves and blend with the surroundings once their internal strength developed past a certain point of cultivation. This was the first time that he had actually witnessed this feat and moreover she was in full visible view!

He thought, "No wonder Nangong Le cannot avoid her secret projectile, she was in front of him all along. It is just that he did not see her…"

Top exponents like Nangong Le, were trained to detect and avoid missile projectiles in their early martial trainings; it was almost impossible to succeed with an open attack using missile projectiles against them.

He was suddenly embarrassed that he was going to impart an intricate formula that may be of no use to someone like her.

Perhaps she could see his discomfort, she smiled gently and said, "Yu'Er and Mei'Er, bow to your new protégé master. From now on, you must also listen to Priest Liu, got it?"

Shui Yujian and Shui Meijian immediately greeted courteously, "Respects to protégé master!"

Shui Yujian said, "I am Shui Yujian and this is my sister, Shui Meijian."

Priest Liu Qingcheng exclaimed aloud, "Good, good! I have only a simple request. I hope that once you are able to discern the mysteries of the Dual Inertness Intricacy, you can let me know. Alas, I have been struck for so long that I am growing more and more disheartened every day. This intricate formula is really too profound for me."

Shui Meijian said curiously, "Is that why you want us to be your protégé disciples?"

Priest Liu Qingcheng said, "That is right! When I heard your music, I know that you are the ones that can break through the intermediate stage of the 'Linking Spirits' progression of the Dual Inertness Intricacy."

The Celestial Fairy smiled gently, "Let me begin first. The heart of the intricate formula of the Tranquil Spirits is 'Absolute Defense through Tranquil'. To reach this stage, tranquil your divine state with absolute emptiness, when formless, from nothing, there something. It is partitioned into three portions, the beginner stage of 'The Defense Harmony, the intermediate stage of 'The Infinity Folds' and the advanced stage of 'The Infinity becoming One and One becoming the Void'…"

Priest Qingcheng was trembling as he said, "This is really the Tranquil Spirits. I only know the stages. The exact intricate heart formula has been lost…"

The Celestial Fairy had not only recited the entire intricate formula to him but also explained to him many new principles that could help him understand the Tranquil Spirits quickly.

After he memorized the Tranquil Spirits, he began to recite the Dual Inertness Intricacy.

Shui Yixian was astonished that there was such an extraordinary dual intricate formula that existed in the world as she muttered, "The spirit exchanges but not the shape, the affection exchanges but not the look, the vital energy exchanges but not the body, the divinity exchanges but not the physical…the essence of heavens and earth as my vitality, the divine state of heavens and earth as my divine state, the changes of heavens and earth as my changes…"

She muttered, "The Dual Inertness Intricacy is really an unfathomable skill… this is indeed a superior intricate heart formula…"

Shui Yujian said, "If even protégé mistress cannot fathom it, we have no hope…"

Shui Yixian smiled, "Everyone has their fates. I cannot but you may be able to. It may take days, months and years but as long as you put your heart into it, you may unravel the secrets one day."

Priest Liu Qingcheng laughed, "Yes, take it slowly. I am already struck for so many years, I don't mind waiting a few more years…"

Shui Meijian sighed in misery, "Now I know that I got two irresponsible protégé masters that expect their protégés to know everything yet refuse to spend the trouble to teach us."

Shui Yixian rebuked her gently, "Mei'Er, I haven't punished you yet for giving me away. Your Emotionless Rhyme has not reached the stage that I have required of you. You know what your punishments will be right?"

Shui Meijian turned ashen with fright, "Protégé Mistress, I…"

When Priest Liu Qingcheng left the place after imparting the Dual Inertness Intricacy, he was shaking his head and thought, "I have thought that with my current level of Dual Inertness Intricacy, I cannot be tempted by lust in any forms. Alas, my cultivation is ruined…"

When Priest Liu Qingcheng had left, Shui Yujian said to her protégé mistress. "It does seem that the protégés of the Virtuous Palace are not in this vicinity and may not be attending the congregation that is hosted by Gongsun Bai. We have been lying in wait for several days now and the only persons that turned up are those three."

Shui Yujian was close to tears, "Master will be alright. We had met a maiden in white a few weeks ago. Even though she had our white emerald precious sword, it did not mean anything…"

Shui Yixian averted her eyes quietly…

She had recognized the Penetrating Hands of the mysterious yellow dressed maiden as a secret skill of the Virtuous Palace. While the Virtuous Palace was renowned for their swordplay, only a few had exactly known that they were equally deadly in close quarters. This combination was extremely deadly and fatal to most of their enemies who were not in the known.

Shui Yixian had thought she was going to die when she was surprised by a direct struck on her heart. That blow was calculated to kill her. She was only saved and fell into an animate dead state because the maiden in yellow had made two mistakes; her first mistake was that she did not know that her Icy Heaven Tears had already progress to the tenth staging at that time. Her second mistake was that she had been too confident.

When she had recovered from her state of animate dead, she did not know what to make of her affections for Yi Ping. Therefore she continued to pretend to be dead and instructed Yujian and Meijian to take of him instead.

Perhaps it was heaven's will that they should be together. But when this love was placed in front of her, she did not cherish it.

Indeed, she had chosen to hide from him as she thought it was just at a spur of a foolish moment. It was because she did not know what love was and was even afraid of it. She simply had too many considerations and hesitations.

But when Yi Ping had insisted on leaving the Eternal Ice Palace to seek vengeance for her, she panicked.

She could tell that although Yujian and Meijian had only known Yi Ping briefly, they had already developed took a liking to him.

In order to keep Yi Ping in the Eternal Ice Palace, they had decided to use an unorthodox method and drugged his drink, making it appear as though he had got himself drunk and did something foolhardy. But they had never expected that Yi Ping reaction would be the opposite of what they were expecting and he had actually fled from the Eternal Ice Palace.

That was when Shui Yixian had decided to leave the Eternal Ice Palace to look for Yi Ping so that he would not get himself killed by the yellow dressed maiden. If she failed to find Yi Ping, she had to find her and killed her first.

Unfortunately she had no news of him till now except for a young maiden in white that had their clan emerald white phoenix precious sword that was last seen in the vicinity.

She hoped that Yi Ping had not been killed by that maiden in white yet…

Because she had suspected that the Virtuous Palace might be secretly monitoring the congregation that was hosted by Gongsun Bai, they setup a trap to bait the Virtuous Palace. If there was any clan in this town that could find the Eternal Ice Palace, it had to be the Virtuous Palace! Moreover, they were already very obvious!

But it seemed that the Virtuous Palace was not here.

Shui Yujian suddenly asked her sister, "Why are you so quiet?"

But still Shui Meijian did not reply to her and she was looking stoned.

Shui Yujian was panicky, "Sis, are you alright?"

Even Shui Yixian was looking at her in surprise. It was because Mei'Er would never keep quiet if she had an opportunity to say something.

Shui Meijian looked somewhat sad as she suddenly said, "I am doing my wordless exchange with my mouth. But it is a pity that none of you could hear me at all."

Chapter 13: Gongsun Manor

Nangong Le was looking pale as he walked in the streets. Even though Priest Ling Kongquan wanted to support him but Nangong Le refused.

Priest Ling Kongquan was surprised that Nangong Le could continue to walk so dignifiedly despite breaking his ribs.

He asked, "Are you really alright?"

Nangong Le smiled bitterly, "What do you think?"

Priest Ling Kongquan managed an awkward smile, "You really can smile. I have heard that you been practicing the Exuberant Divine Skill for more than ten years now. That is indeed a most extraordinary inner martial skill."

Actually Nangong Le was feeling real awful and miserable now. But he had to maintain his refine mannerism and his dignity for the congregation. He did not want his enemies and opponents to know that he was injured.

All of a sudden, Nangong Le began to increase his walking pace much to the surprise of Priest Ling Kongquan. It was as though his injuries had suddenly vanished!

Nangong Le was heading towards a handsome young man and an alluring beautiful lady in white. In fact, it seemed that the entire street was also looking in their direction!

A handsome young man with a charismatic aura with a white long sword walked down the street. If anyone were to look into his face, it seemed to be glowing and untainted with malice. He was pleasing to look at and caused everyone to remember that there was still righteousness and goodness in the world.

As for the alluring maiden that was beside him, was like a fairy maiden that had descended upon the mortal realm. She was extremely beautiful and graceful. Even though she was very pale and white, she was filled with vitality. Her smiles were wondrous and piercing, everyone instantly thought she was amicable and intimate, an illusion that caused everyone to think that she alone was smiling and friendly to them alone.

They were indeed Yi Ping and Ji Lingfeng.

When Yi Tianxing had left the valley to visit the grave of his late wife Shui Yichi, he warned them not to look for Gongsun Bai and instead spent the time to practice hard on their martial skills until he was back.

Yi Ping and Ji Lingfeng knew that he would be away for at least six months.

So when Ji Lingfeng had said to him, "In a few days, there will be a huge gathering hosted by none other than Gongsun Bai himself. With so many people, there is no better time than this to sneak into the Gongsun Manor amidst the confusion. What more, we can take the opportunity to embarrass him in front of the heroes of the martial fraternity."

He had asked her, "How did you know and what is your purpose of going there?"

She said, "I was already aware of it three months ago. Moreover, this gathering is not a secret and almost everyone in the fraternity knows about it. I want to attend the gathering and if possible, to disrupt it. However I am acting alone as my brother disapproves of it. The orthodox pugilists would probably fight for leadership and it is an excellent opportunity for me to witness their martial skills so that I can forewarn my brother."

With that in mind, they had set off hurriedly for the Gongsun Manor.

He turned to ask her in a low voice, "You say that today is the day the Gongsun Clan will host a grand congregation that invites the majority of the orthodox fraternity. And it is the best time to infiltrate into the residency of the Gongsun Clan and to kill Gongsun Bai. Why is that as soon as we entered the town, we seem to be monitored? Have they already known of our plans or because they know who you are?"

Ji Lingfeng smiled and said endearingly, "I have never walked in the martial fraternity before. It is not possible for anyone to have ever seen or heard of me. Look at you, getting nervous even before we are there. To be honest, we don't have any invitations. Even though the number of pugilists and renowned people that have been invited are numerous, the Gongsun Clan will be vigilant against strangers and will not allow any heretic and unorthodox exponents into the gathering."

Yi Ping growled softly, "You are the one that says that there will be confusion with so many people and there is no better opportunity to sneak in than this."

Ji Lingfeng was smiling at him endearingly, "I have thought that we may be able to sneak into the Gongsun Manor but look at all the attention we are getting. Now I don't think it is possible now."

Yi Ping asked, "Then how?"

Ji Lingfeng said, "We just have to try our luck and look for an opportunity."

All of a sudden, Yi Ping halted his steps. It was because he suddenly saw a refine man approaching him. Behind him was a middle age priest in his fifties.

The refine man bowed respectfully with his hands and asked, "I apologize for interrupting. Are you going to the Gongsun Manor as well?"

Even though he was bowing respectfully, his eyes had never left Ji Lingfeng.

Yi Ping was forthright and he answered without hesitation, "That's right."

Perhaps the refine man sensed that he was not being recognized or being look upon favorably by Yi Ping and Ji Lingfeng, so he quickly said, "Alas, what a coincident! I too, am going there. I apologize again for intruding all of a sudden. I, Nangong Le, enjoy making friends from all over the fraternity. May I have the honor of knowing your name and this maiden?"

Who had never heard of Nangong Le the Joyous from the Nangong Aristocracy Clan? He was one of the four most influential and renowned young masters of the martial fraternity and was destined for greater things in the future. Among the four young masters of the martial fraternity, he was said to be the richest and his wealth rivaled that of the imperial treasury.

Nangong Le pointed to Priest Ling Kongquan and said, "This is Priest Ling Kongquan. He is a prominent elder of the Tranquil City."

Priest Ling Kongquan was startled at how spirited Nangong Le was. Just a moment ago, he was looking so pale and weak. He sighed to himself, "Is that how he got his nickname of Nangong Le the Joyous?"

Yi Ping simply said, "I am Yi Ping." He did not introduce Ji Lingfeng or appeared to be interested in the conversation.

Nangong Le was slightly startled. Usually when he announced his name, everyone would be trying to flatter him and be acquainted with him. But this young man did not appear to be interested.

Nangong Le awkwardly said, "Young hero must be someone who comes from a renowned clan or an established orthodox clan to be invited to the Gongsun Manor. May I have the honor to know your illustrious background?"

Ji Lingfeng smiled and said, "My younger protégé brother Yi Ping is the son of the Yi Tianxing. We don't have any invitations from the Gongsun Clan. But because Gongsun Bai was the sworn brother of our protégé master, we thought of paying him a visit. That is all."

Nangong Le was startled that Yi Ping was the son of the Great hero Yi Tianxing who had seemingly disappeared from the martial fraternity twenty-five years ago. His exploits were many and till today, was often mentioned by many. He was even more startled that this maiden took the initiative of talking to him.

So he thought, "Is she also interested in me? That is excellent! So she is the older protégé sister of this Yi Ping. This must be their first time that they are traveling in the fraternity. They seem to lack caution."

So he said amicably, "I have heard of the exploits of the Great Hero Yi Tianxing. In all my life, I have only admired him!"

When he noticed that Yi Ping's eyes had shone, he quickly added, "Today I can be acquainted with his descendant, I am greatly honored! If I am born twenty years earlier, I might have the opportunity to be acquainted with this legendary hero…alas!"

Yi Ping said respectfully, "My father will be pleased to know that!"

Even Priest Ling Kongquan had heard of the renown of Yi Tianxing and he quickly said, "Young hero, you are the son of Great Hero Yi? I am Priest Ling Kongquan. I enjoying making friends and if young hero did not feel I am unworthy, we can be friends too."

Yi Ping quickly said, "The Tranquil City is a renowned clan in the fraternity. It is my honor to be acquainted with you instead."

Ling Kongquan smiled and said, "That is my honor as well. Is your father well? The martial fraternity has not heard of him for a long time."

Yi Ping sighed, "It is a long story. Maybe I can share with you later."

Ling Kongquan said, "I am not a nosy parker. If it is not convenient for Young Hero Yi to share, I understand."

Ling Kongquan could sense his sorrows but he kept it to himself.

As for the maiden that was with him, he had never seen anyone as beautiful as her. Even though the twin sisters were extremely beautiful, they were icy cold. It was their coldness that reduced their attractiveness to him. But this maiden was personal and was smiling happily while they were talking. It was as though she was a close friend who was paying a great deal of attention to them.

Nangong Le said, "You must definitely come with me so that I can have the honor of befriending you. Since Brother Yi did not have any invitation and I have, I can easily invite you as my entourage and bring you into the Gongsun Manor!"

Yi Ping was surprised at his magnanimity, "Brother Nangong you are too kind to me. I apologize for my rudeness earlier!"

When Yi Ping knew that Nangong Le was his father's admirer, his attitude towards him changed and he began to regard him as a friend!

Ji Lingfeng sighed in her heart, "He is so gullible! This Nangong Le has his eyes on me. He may have fooled Yi Ping but he cannot fool me."

Indeed, Nangong Le quickly said, "I forget to ask for your older protégé sister's name?" Yi Ping replied, "Her name is Lingfeng."

Ji Lingfeng glanced fiercely at him but in a blink of an eye later she was smiling again.

She had almost fainted from incredulity! How could he have given her name to anyone just like that? Normally, when the pugilists roamed the fraternity, they would use a fraternity name to hide their clan of origin or identities.

It was not that Yi Ping was not aware of this pugilist practice especially with a dubious background like Maiden Ji. But when she had intentional introduced him as her younger protégé brother and even revealed his father name, he was none too pleased about it even though he knew that she was trying to get an invitation from Nangong Le to enter the Gongsun Manor.

He did not want to make use of anyone to enter the Gongsun Manor. Even if he had to barge into the Gongsun Manor to confront Gongsun Bai, he would do it.

Nangong Le remarked to Ji Lingfeng, "What an enchanting name! I have also never seen anyone as beautiful as you. May I know if maiden is married?"

Ji Lingfeng said, "Even though I want to but unfortunately I am not."

Nangong Le pretended to be disappointed and said, "Why is that so? With your wondrous beauty, I can imagine you surely have hordes of suitors and admirers?"

Ji Lingfeng sighed and she was instantly sad, "I hate to mention this but none of my suitors ever lived long enough to even engage to me. They all died of mishaps after they had sent the engagement gifts. It is like a deadly curse to me."

Her sad countenance caused everyone to feel sad too. It was as though her emotions could affect everyone and the first thought was to comfort her.

Nangong Le was secretly pleased that she was still unmarried and he said, "Even if there is a curse, it is my privilege to die for you."

Ji Lingfeng smiled alluringly, "We have just met and yet you are willing to die for me?"

Nangong Le laughed, "What I say is the truth!"

All of a sudden, Yi Ping could feel a boiling jealousy in his heart. He gritted his teeth and thought, "Maiden Ji has the right to choose her suitor. I cannot stop her. Moreover, my first priority is to avenge my parents and Yixian! Moreover, Nangong Le is rich and is compatible with her… "

Yi Ping thoughts were disrupted when Nangong Lei said, "Brother Yi. Then, let us settle it. We shall go to the Gongsun Manor together! I am sure to be given a good seating position in the hall!"

Yi Ping bowed with his hands and said, "Let's us go then!"

Priest Ling Kongquan whispered, "Brother Nangong, are you sure that in your current state, you can still go to the Gongsun Manor?"

Nangong Le laughed it off, "Do I look like I am injured to you?"

Yi Ping asked, "Brother Nangong, you are injured?"

Ji Lingfeng looked concerned at the same time as she asked, "You are injured?"

Nangong Le said, "Earlier I had a fight with someone. It is just a small ruffle and I sustain a slight injury."

Ji Lingfeng smiled, "For that someone to pick a fight with the renowned Young Master Nangong of the Four Martial Young Masters fame, his injuries may be even worse."

Nangong Le laughed merrily, "Of course, of course! It is a one side victory for me!"

Priest Ling Kongquan could not believe his ears as he sighed deeply, "He does anything to impress…"

When he looked at Nangong Le again, he was back to chatting merrily with Maiden Lingfeng and Yi Ping.

The Gongsun Manor was not an ordinary residence. It was located in the middle of the town and it had high walls around it. It was more like a fortress and there was a large moat at the entrance.

The Gongsun Clan ruled this town. This town had been built by the Gongsun Clan over the centuries. Most of the people in the town were actually associated with the Gongsun Clan.

There were guards everywhere, from the steps of the Gongsun Manor and to the top of the castle walls.

Because Yi Ping and Ji Lingfeng were the guests of Nangong Le, they made it through the gates of the Gongsun Manor without any hassle.

As they went through the gates and into the manor, one of the guards said to the other, "That Nangong Le is really something. I have never seen such a beautiful maiden in my life and probably never will. He is famous as a womanizer and it is said that everywhere that he goes, he will be always be companied by beautiful ladies. Now I truly believe!"

The other guard said, "Look at us. When we saw that maiden, we have actually forgotten to record Young Master Nangong Le's guests' names."

The steward also sighed, "I too, have forgotten about it. I can recognize Priest Ling Kongquan. As for that young man and young maiden, I do not know."

The first guard that spoke earlier said, "Surely, the guests of Nangong Le will not be troublemakers and none would be from the unorthodox clans. Let's close an eye and get over it. There are still many more guests that are waiting."

The steward nodded and signaled for the next group of guests to be brought in.

Chapter 14: Zuo Tianyi

The grand hall of the Gongsun Manor was huge and majestic. It was divided into three colored walls, gold, silver and bronze colors. And the pugilists were partitioned within these walls according to their clan repute in the martial fraternity.

Gongsun Bai was the most powerful and most influential man in the entire martial fraternity for the past ten years. The Gongsun Martial Clan under his leadership had attracted many top martial exponents into the clan. Even top exponents like Gu Tianle the Warrior-God and Jue Yuan the Merciless was now in his protégé clan, the Honor Manor.

As the Grand Master of the Honor Manor, Gongsun Bai was also well-known for his martial abilities, the Ironclad Claw Skill and the Invincible Divine Force Skill.

In the martial fraternity, there was no one else other than Old Man Zuo the Sword Saint and Gu Tianle the Warrior-God that could rival his martial level. Old Man Zuo the Sword Saint had passed away last year and Gu Tianle the Warrior-God had joined the Honor Manor.

Now Gongsun Bai was not only the most powerful man in the entire martial fraternity, he was also the martial fraternity number one top exponent.

To be invited to the Honor Manor, even for those at the bronze seating, was a great prestige and honor. There were countless pugilists that were denied this opportunity and because of this, hundreds of small fights broke out in the martial fraternity to seize the invitations.

Needless to say, all the pugilists here presented today were fearsome exponents and experienced pugilists.

Nangong Le had a gold invitation. Naturally he was supposed to be a seated in the golden section, the closest to the host.

When he had entered the grand hall, he was instantly recognized by many. Unlike the other three young masters of the martial fraternity, Nangong Le spent most of his time in the martial fraternity and was acquainted with many.

Nangong Le fraternity name was 'The Joyous' for he was always smiling and in light spirits. And today he had reasons to smile.

When he first entered the grand hall, there was a sudden silence. Everyone seemed to turn their attentions to him. Even though his role in this congregation was minor, he seemed to be stealing the limelight and that he was causing great envy among many of the guests.

When Yi Ping and Ji Lingfeng entered the grand hall with him, the pugilists had never seen such a matching couple in terms of looks and magnetism. They had instantly captivated the attention of everyone, causing them to be awestruck.

Young Master Qiu Wufeng and the Heartless Scholar were among the guests presented. Even though they had met Yi Ping before but they failed to recognize him. It was because the Yi Ping they had briefly known then was a rugged traveler and this Yi Ping was clean and had a noble air around him. Moreover the Yi Ping then was just a nameless nobody. No one would pay him scant attention.

But today, he was in the company of Nangong Le and the opponents of Nangong Le would naturally be interested in anyone that was with him.

Ever since Young Master Qiu Wufeng retreated from the Heavenly Mountains, he had been thinking of the Celestial Fairy. He began to lose interest in his food and in other ladies. It was because he had never seen anyone as mesmerizing as the Celestial Fairy, until now.

Gongsun Jing recognized Yi Ping immediately. He wanted to recruit him to be his follower but a fight broke out between them. He thought, "No wonder he rejects my overturns. It is because he is already Nangong Le's follower. What a pity!"

Jue Yuan had recognized both Yi Ping and Ji Lingfeng. He had tried to kill Yi Ping back then and had thought that Yi Ping was a protégé disciple of Young Master Qiu Wufeng. The Qiu clan had always opposed the Gongsun Clan. His first thought was, "Have the Qiu Clan and the Nangong Clan forged a secret alliance already?"

Gu Tianle the One-Arm Warrior-God had recognized Yi Ping and was relieved that this young man was well. He did not know that instead of helping Yi Ping that day, Jue Yuan had actually tried to kill him. Even though he had a grudge with Qiao Feng the Shadow Kicker, his intent was not to hurt him. He had thought that Qiao Feng was nearby and had wanted to settle a score with him.

Yi Ping however recognized them all. He thought, "Good! Even though I am being outnumbered today, I am not afraid of death. Let settle our scores once and for all today!"

He scanned his eyes for Gongsun Bai but it seemed that the host had not arrived yet.

He took a quick look and saw that only six out of the seven leading major orthodox clans were presented in the golden wall section. Judging from their colorful banners, the six major orthodox clans that were presented were the Infinity Sword Clan, the Zen Sect, the Monument Monastery, the Divine Sword Martial Clan, the Universal Truth Clan and the Traverse Clan.

The Ironclad Clan was inconspicuously absent from this meeting.

It was well known that the Ironclad Clan and the Heartless Scholar who was a follower of Young Master Qiu had a feud with one another and the Ironclad Clan would often be absented from any meetings that involved the Qiu Aristocracy Martial Clan.

There were at least thirty other clans that were seated in the silver and the bronze sections of the hall.

Yi Ping thought, "This Gongsun Bai is indeed influential. He is able to invite so many martial clans to this congregation. But where is he? Why is that I can only see Gongsun Jing? Maybe it is not the time for him to show up yet? His status must be really prominent to keep the martial congregation waiting for him."

Gongsun Jing laughed gently and walked over to Nangong Le respectfully, saying. "Welcome, welcome Young Master Nangong! We have been waiting for you to start the meeting."

Nangong Le laughed, "I am so honored. I don't think I am so important to keep everyone waiting."

Gongsun Jing smiled, "Not at all, Brother Nangong. We are honored that you have decided to grace the congregation with your presence."

Nangong Le smiled bitterly, "Not at all. Unless I am really weary of living, I would never think of not attending the congregation."

Gongsun Jing asked quietly, "What do you mean by that? ..."

But before he could finish, he was interrupted by Priest Bai Chongzhen, who was the protégé master of the Traverse Clan, "Brother Ling, how are you?"

Priest Ling Kongquan smiled awkwardly, "Not as well as the Traverse Clan for sure. Look at the Tranquil City, we only got a silver invitation." He purposely looked at Gongsun Jing for a second.

Gongsun Jing smiled, "Next time, we are sure to issue the Tranquil City a gold invitation."

Jue Yuan the Merciless smirked, "It still depends if the Tranquil City is fit to deserve a gold invitation from the Honor Manor."

Priest Bai Chongzhen stared at Jue Yuan and questioned, "What do you mean?"

Jue Yuan said, "If the Tranquil City thinks that it deserves a golden seat, then its protégés must be able to prove that they are deserving of the honor."

Jue Yuan looked at Yi Ping, Ji Lingfeng and Priest Ling Kongquan before saying, "Just because they are acquainted with Young Master Nangong Le, they think they deserve a seat in the golden section? Is it fair to the other pugilists?"

He deliberately said it aloud and aroused the attention of many of the pugilists.

Gongsun Jing smiled awkwardly, "Master Jue Yuan…"

But Jue Yuan ignored the awkwardness of Gongsun Jing and continued to say aloud, "Do you think you deserve the honor?"

There were muttering among the pugilists and quite a few were shouting, "Prove to it that you are deserving of the honor!"

Gongsun Jing continued to smile awkwardly. It was because Jue Yuan was his protégé master and as his disciple, he had to pay due respect to him even though he had a higher status than him in the Honor Manor.

Gu Tianle knew immediately that Jue Yuan had wanted to embarrass Nangong Le and his acquaintances.

But of course, he did not know the Jue Yuan was still sore that Yi Ping and this beautiful mysterious maiden had escaped from his fists. No matter, he would teach them a harsh lesson that they would never forget today!

Priest Bai Chongzhen smiled wryly, "Have you forgotten that the Tranquil City and the Traverse Clan hail from the Emei Clan?"

Jue Yuan said unhappily, "There are so many Emei Clans in the Western Fraternity. Just because the Tranquil City is also an Emei Clan, they deserve the golden seating? Fat hope! I afraid the Priest Ling Kongquan still has to prove it!"

Priest Ling Kongquan was really upset, "You stupid monk! Are you really picking a fight with the Tranquil City or just me?"

Yi Ping was amused. It was obvious that Jue Yuan was intentional provoking them. Just when he was about to step forward, Ji Lingfeng inconspicuously pulled his sleeve and he stayed his cool.

Zuo Tianyi, the young protégé master of the Infinity Sword Clan and also one of the four young masters of the martial fraternity fame, was staring at Ji Lingfeng with bewildered eyes. He had taken over the mantle of the leadership of the Infinity Sword Clan when his grandfather the Sword Saint had passed away last year after a deadly duel with Ji Wuzheng, the Holy Sect Leader of the Holy Hex Sect.

In fact, besides Zuo Tianyi, many other pugilists were also staring at her mesmerizing beauty. Only a blind man would fail to notice her. Only the protégés of the Monument Monastery did not stared at her.

It was because the clan protégés of the Monument Monastery were all monks. When they saw Ji Lingfeng, they lowered their heads and looked the other way. The younger monks who were accompanying their elders were blushing all of a sudden and began to chant softly.

The Monument Monastery was famous for its seventy-two epic martial skills, with each warrior-monk practicing at least one epic martial skill in their lifetime.

But the real reason why Zuo Tianyi was looking at Ji Lingfeng was because he had recognized her!

His father died in a duel when he was still very young and he was brought up by his grandfather. And now, his grandfather, Old Man Zuo the Sword Saint had died because of her brother!

The reason that Zuo Tianyi had recognized her was because they were both presented at the duel between the Sword Saint and Ji Wuzheng, the Holy Sect Leader of the Holy Hex Sect!

Zuo Tianyi's fingers began to twitch and tremble slightly...

One year ago at the summit of the Lofty Green Mountains, Ji Wuzheng had the tenacity to challenge the Sword Saint. At that time, he was with his grandfather and Maiden Ji was with her brother.

The Sword Saint asked, "You have come to challenge me?"

Ji Wuzheng said coolly, "I dare not!"

The Sword Saint asked again, "Then why did you send me an invitation to come here for?"

Ji Wuzheng smiled, "It is not me that is looking for a challenge but you are."

The Sword Saint said, "Oh?"

Ji Wuzheng said, "You are a peerless swordsman and there are none in the fraternity that is your match. Don't you feel lonely at the very top?"

The Sword Saint said, "Indeed. No one else understands my feeling. There were once two super exponents during my time that could be my match. One was Yi Tianxing and the other one was your late father."

Ji Wuzheng asked, "You seem to have forgotten about the renowned Gongsun Bai and Gu Tianle the Warrior-God. In the martial fraternity, they are ranked among the very top."

Old Man Zuo the Sword Saint stroked his long white beard and said, "Indeed they are but not twenty years ago."

Ji Wuzheng said, "And yet you did not mention them?"

The Sword Saint answered, "Twenty-years ago, they are nowhere near my martial level and I didn't notice them."

Ji Wuzheng said, "Don't forget that Gu Tianle had killed my father."

The Sword Saint said, "Even though I was not there, I know that your father had a secret duel with Yi Tianxing that worsened his existing internal injuries. To say that Gu Tianle had really defeat your father, is an overstatement."

Ji Wuzheng said, "You know that my father had internal injuries?"

The Sword Saint nodded slowly, "I was there when Yi Tianxing and your father fought against one another. It was just that they did not notice me."

Ji Wuzheng and Ji Lingfeng were both stunned as they both asked together, "You are there?"

Old Man Zuo the Sword Saint looked at the drifting clouds and said, "I too, want to challenge your father with my Infinity-Two. After watching that duel, I knew how unfathomable their martial levels had been. Inspired by that duel, twenty years later, I have finally achieved the Infinity-One."

Ji Wuzheng said, "In the present fraternity, Gongsun Bai and Gu Tianle are formidable fighters and their martial levels are unfathomable. They have few worthy opponents too. Are they worthy to be your opponents?"

The Sword Saint said, "They are now."

Ji Wuzheng asked, "What about me?"

The Sword saint said, "I presume that you have sent me an invitation is because you have mastered the Holy Amalgamate Skill?"

Ji Wuzheng said, "Indeed I have."

The Sword Saint laughed, "Excellent! I have waited for over twenty-years to find a match."

Ji Wuzheng said coolly, "Unfortunately, I am still not your match in swordsmanship. I have long heard that you have fully mastered the Infinite Swordplay. I am still young and have no wish to experience your invincible Infinite-First."

The Sword Saint said, "What do you propose?"

Ji Wuzheng said, "I have heard that you are seeking a breakthrough for the Infinite-First. But without meeting a worthy opponent, no matter how long you meditate upon it, it is extremely difficult for you to unravel the Infinite-Zero."

The Sword Saint stroked his long white beard and said, "Indeed! And this is my greatest regret."

Ji Wuzheng said, "You are so close yet so far from it."

The Sword Saint nodded sadly, "Indeed!"

Ji Wuzheng said, "The secret to unraveling the Infinite-Zero lies with the Infinitude Recite Skill. The Holy Amalgamate Skill and the Infinitude Recite are two of the top epitome skills in the fraternity. If there is a skill that can help you to gain a new understanding of the Infinitude Recite, it has to be another unfathomable skill like the Holy Amalgamate Skill."

The Sword Saint said, "Indeed. You are not afraid to die?"

Ji Wuzheng said, "If I am afraid to die, I won't be here."

The Sword Saint roared with laughter, "Marvelous! Let us go then."

Ji Wuzheng laughed, "Good! Let us go now!"

Zuo Tianyi and Ji Lingfeng were the only ones that were left behind. It was because it was a secret duel between Old Man Zuo the Sword Saint and Ji Wuzheng.

They had left at dawn and returned at dust.

Needless to say, Zuo Tianyi and Ji Lingfeng had spent a full day together.

When Ji Wuzheng and Old Man Zuo had returned, they were both seriously injured and were supporting one another as they walked towards Zuo Tianyi and Ji Lingfeng. But their eyes were beaming and they were laughing aloud.

Zuo Tianyi could still remember that day very well; his grandfather had gripped him very hard as he was exclaiming excitedly, "I have finally deciphered the last intricate word of the Infinitude Recite! I no longer have the mental strength to unravel the Infinity-Zero but you can!"

Not long after, his grandfather the Sword Saint crumbled to his injuries and passed away. The Sword Saint had never blame Ji Wuzheng and the Holy Hex Sect even in his final hours. In fact, he was grateful and hoped that Ji Wuzheng would survive his injuries and be a worthy opponent for his grandson, Zuo Tianyi.

It was because even though Zuo Tianyi knew the final intricate formula now but it would still be many years of hard work and meditation before he could even grasped the true essence of the Infinite-First and Infinite-Zero. The final intricate formula was just a clue and would still change depending on the martial progress of the practitioner. But it was a huge step forward.

Zuo Tianyi was a prodigy since he was young. At the age of twenty, he had grasped the Infinity-Five and by the time he was twenty-eight, he had attained the Infinity-Two. His grandfather, the Sword Saint had only grasped the Infinity-Two when he was forty and the Infinity-One when he was sixty.

In this fraternity, no one other than his grandfather knew the progress of his Infinity Swordplay. It was rumored that he had mastered the Infinity-Nine but none had dared to try.

When Ji Lingfeng saw Zuo Tianyi looking at her intently, she immediately averted her eyes and Yi Ping noticed it immediately.

Yi Ping thought, "They know one another? Isn't that the insignia of the Infinity Sword Clan? This man, he should be the Zuo Tianyi, one of the four young masters of the martial fraternity and is also the clan leader of the Infinity Sword Clan. Does Maiden Ji know him as a friend? Or does he recognize her as his enemy?"

He really wished that it was the latter.

All of a sudden, Jue Yuan was shouting angrily, "He can stay but they must not stay!" He was pointing at Yi Ping and Ji Lingfeng.

This did not make Nangong Le, Priest Ling Kongquan and Priest Bai Chongzhen glad at all.

It was like Jue Yuan was giving Priest Ling Kongquan the honor of sitting in the golden seat because of Priest Bai Chongzhen.

Nangong Le said solemnly, "They are my guests and I have personally invited them. Moreover, do you know this young man Yi Ping is the…"

Jue Yuan interrupted, "I know this young man. He is nothing but a trouble-maker. If he wants to sit in the golden seat, he must prove his martial abilities first!"

Jue Yuan began to display his merciless strokes which he had innovated against Yi Ping.

Yi Ping could feel a flurry of windforce raining down against him. He immediately raised his hands to counter-attack. Judging down by the downward poise of his attacker and after exchanging a few blows, he knew that Jue Yuan was using a type of martial arts that could neutralize his opponent strength.

As he had already been forewarned by his father of this deadly martial art that could neutralize the strength of the opponent and its devastating effect, Yi Ping did not dare to move lightly but focus on exchanging blows with Jue Yuan with his forward fists.

Jue Yuan was confident that in less than twenty strokes, this young man would be subdued by his merciless subduing stances. But to his surprise, Yi Ping was able to block, disengage and to counter attack against him no matter how fast his strokes were!

Jue Yuan was mystified. How was it possible for this young man to fight like an experienced exponent and the speed that Yi Ping had disengaged from his blows were startling!

All of a sudden, Yi Ping rolled his hands together and struck hard into the face of Jue Yuan! Jue Yuan was forced immediately to take five steps backward!

Jue Yuan was not injured seriously but he was enraged. He immediately mustered his martial power and thought, "If he dares to accept my blow, then I can overpower him with my martial power. If he dodges it, then I have an opening to subdue him. Either way, it will be advantageous to me!"

Yi Ping knew that Jue Yuan incoming blows had been charged with his martial power and if he did not dodge it, the consequences might be fatal. But he raised his martial power to accept the incoming blow…

All of a sudden, there was a huge clashing thunderclap and Jue Yuan took six steps back before he could steady himself while Yi Ping took three steps back.

As they steadied themselves, both were coughing out blood. The clash of martial power drained the practitioners of strength and could cause the vital energies in the body to be erratic, leading to death.

Jue Yuan could not believe that this young man had the internal strength foundation to withstand his attacks.

Rather than taking time to restore his vitality channels to prevent further internal injuries, the enraged Jue Yuan mustered all his martial power and charged towards Yi Ping once more!

When Yi Ping saw that Jue Yuan was charging towards him with all his martial power, he quickly displayed the Asper Horizon Hand and there was a shrieking explosive power in his palm as he met Jue Yuan's two hands with his right hand!

Again, Yi Ping took three steps back as he coughed out more blood while Jue Yuan was sent flying back across the hall, much to the astonishment of the crowd!

Jue Yuan was one of the top exponents of the martial fraternity and was greatly feared by many! But today, a young man from nowhere had defeated him; it was truly unbelievable!

Gongsun Jing was stunned that Jue Yuan, a top exponent and his martial master was defeated by Yi Ping. He trembled and quickly said to the men behind him, "Quickly check on Master Jue Yuan condition."

Gu Tianle was enraged and shouted, "You dare to go against the Honor Manor with your insolence?!" He immediately attacked Yi Ping.

But before he could land a hit on Yi Ping, he was intercepted by a shadow that dashed from the entrance of the hall. He immediately parried the attacker blows and retreated five steps backward!

Who had dared to fight with Gu Tianle the One-Armed Warrior-God?

It was Priest Liu Qingcheng, the Protégé Master of the Tranquil City!

Many of the pugilists had recognized him.

Yi Ping was grateful for the sudden help as he had not recovered his strength yet.

Ji Lingfeng had wanted to intercept Gu Tianle but Priest Liu Qingcheng was even swifter.

Gu Tianle smirked, "You dare to fight with me?"

Priest Liu Qingcheng said, "I dare not!"

Gu Tianle took it as a challenge, "But you have. And those that dare to challenge me will end up dead or crippled. Surely, you know my rule."

Nangong Le quickly said, "Calm down. This is just a misunderstanding. This is only a matter of seating positions. I...we can sit in the silver seats. There is no need for us to harm our harmony."

Gu Tianle said, "You are given a golden invitation and chooses not to sit in the golden seat. By not respecting the seating arrangements of the Honor Manor, you are not respecting our Master. Are you thinking of going against the Master of the Honor Manor?"

All of a sudden, Nangong Le felt a chill in his spine and he broke into a sweat. He began to take two steps backward as he could not stand straight. He had suppressed his injuries with his internal strength and the chilling speech of Gu Tianle broke his concentration and he had felt extricating pain from his injuries. He stammered, "Easy, I don't mean that."

Gu Tianle stared at Yi Ping, Nangong Le, Priest Ling Kongquan, Liu Qingcheng and Priest Bai Chongzhen before he said, "So the Nangong Martial Clan, the Tranquil City and the Traverse Clan intend to go against the Honor Manor?"

All of a sudden, Yi Ping took a giant step forward even though Ji Lingfeng had caught hold of his sleeves, "So what if I am?"

All of a sudden, uproars erupted from the hall as the pugilists were talking among themselves. It was because no one had dared to challenge Gu Tianle the One-Armed Warrior-God so openly before. And this young man had dared to!

Nangong Le turned ashen immediately. He had thought he could savage the situation and he was now in a real dilemma!

Ji Lingfeng nearly fainted from his imbecile actions. He was lucky enough to overcome Jue Yuan but Gu Tianle was on a different league altogether.

Yi Ping had thought that if he could win Gu Tianle, then he was one step closer to avenge his father. Therefore he did not think much. That was his intention today and he saw no point in disguising his purposes.

Gu Tianle stared at him and said slowly, "Then you have to pay for your audacious words today. You will regret for every single word that you have muttered and wish that you have never said it."

Nangong Le was feeling awkward and at a loss. If he back off now, the Nangong Martial Clan would lose their honor but if he helps Yi Ping, the Nangong Martial Clan may risk extermination by the Honor Manor. And moreover, this was their territory and they were surrounded by numerous top exponents.

Gu Tianle said to Yi Ping, "You can make the first move first."

Yi Ping said coolly, "Then I won't be courteous anymore."

Ji Lingfeng gasped and her eyes were beaming, "Let us go now..."

Chapter 15: The Grand Master of the Honor Manor

Just when Yi Ping had taken a step forward, Liu Qingcheng said gravely to him. "The first challenger should be me. My fight with Gu Tianle has not ended yet. You should wait a little while longer, young man."

Liu Qingcheng stepped forward and raised his fists.

Many of the pugilists in the hall shook their heads.

Priest Bai Chongzhen said, "Brother Qingcheng, you are not his match. It not worth it to lose your life over a small matter…"

Priest Ling Kongquan said, "It is really not worth it, let us go now…"

Gu Tianle said, "You should use your long sword."

But Priest Liu Qingcheng had already attacked Gu Tianle with his Tranquil Fists as he said, "No need!"

Gu Tianle dodged the intricate strokes of the Tranquil Fists and raised his palm forward and struck Priest Liu Qingcheng hard!

Priest Liu Qingcheng parried in time but he lost his footings and he was forced to take seven steps backward!

The martial difference between the two of them was too great.

Gu Tianle had displayed his famous 'Ultrapowerful Force Hand' and it was all it was required to push back Priest Qingcheng!

Yi Ping saw that stance before when he first met Gu Tianle. It was like an irresistible attack and he remembered he had to parry it three times to steady himself, only this time Gu Tianle was not showing any mercy at all.

Gu Tianle immediately seized the attack opportunity and he flew to Priest Liu Qingcheng again with another strike!

All of a sudden, Priest Liu Qingcheng had counterattacked with his Tranquil Fists again.

Gu Tianle was surprised that his martial force seemed to be neutralized by Priest Liu Qingcheng Tranquil Fists!

Everyone had thought that Priest Liu Qingcheng was a goner but all of a sudden, Priest Liu Qingcheng and Gu Tianle was suddenly on par and had exchanged more than thirty strokes nonstop!

Priest Ling Kongquan was stunned as he thought, "When did older protégé brother becomes this good? This is still the Tranquil Fists but it seems to be alive now. It appears as if he has become the Tranquil Fist and the Tranquil Fists is him."

Even Priest Bai Chongzhen gasped, "This is the true strength of the Tranquil Fist? It is too amazing!"

Actually Priest Liu Qingcheng had no confident. But when he had successfully parried Gu Tianle's 'Ultrapowerful Force Hand', his doubts disappeared and his confidence grew.

With the Tranquil Spirits intricate formula that he had earlier learnt from the Celestial Fairy, his Tranquil Fists seemed to improve and grow more and more intricate as he fought even though he did not have the martial power of Gu Tianle!

Gu Tianle was astonished. He really could not understand why each time he was so close to sound the death knell for Priest Liu Qingcheng, his very attacks would seem to be neutralized at the last moment!

Yi Ping was staring at the fight with excitement. This was a rare fight between two top opponents! Their attack moves, their defending moves, their swiftness skills and evading skills were all too intricate and extraordinary!

Not only Yi Ping, all the other pugilists were awed into silence as more than three hundred moves had passed between Gu Tianle and Liu Qingcheng. Whoever could endure to the very last would win!

All of a sudden, Gu Tianle struck Priest Liu Qingcheng with an explosive force on his chest and he was sent flying away!

Priest Bai Chongzhen and Priest Ling Kongquan immediately executed their swiftness movement skills and caught hold of Priest Liu Qingcheng!

Priest Liu Qingcheng muttered before he fainted, "I hope I didn't disgrace the Tranquil City…"

Priest Ling Kongquan said gravely as he trembled, "Older Protégé Brother, you did very well…"

In the end, the martial power between Gu Tianle and Priest Liu Qingcheng was still too great a difference.

Yi Ping prayed that Priest Liu Qingcheng condition was not critical as he stepped forward, "Now it is my turn!"

Ji Lingfeng sighed silently, "Yi Ping you…As much as I want to extract vengeance on Gu Tianle, he is really above our league. Moreover, there are other top exponents in this hall too. You are really too impatient…"

All of a sudden, there was a malevolent aura that seemed to come from Zuo Tianyi.

Everyone seemed to have sense his malevolent aura and turned to look in his direction.

Zuo Tianyi had unsheathed his long sword and he was walking slowly towards Yi Ping as he said slowly, "Old Senior Gu needs a small rest first. Why don't we spar for a while first?"

Yi Ping looked at Zuo Tianyi and said, "I don't mind."

Gu Tianle said solemnly, "I don't need a rest."

But Zuo Tianyi had already walked in front of Yi Ping and there seemed to be a forbidden killing malevolent around him.

Gu Tianle thought, "This is a good opportunity to see how good this new protégé master of the Infinity Sword Clan is."

So he said, "If I fight with this young man, I afraid I will be mocked by everyone in the fraternity and accused of bullying him. But since Young Master Zuo wants to teach him a lesson, I will relent."

All of a sudden, there was loud earth-shaking laughter coming from the end of the hall! The internal strength of the person was astonishing powerful! The weaker pugilists immediately felt dizzy and their vital energies were disrupted!

Who else possessed such almighty internal strength?

It was Gongsun Bai!

When Gongsun Jing saw him, he immediately said respectfully. "Father!"

The grand hall was filled with a resounding shout by the protégés of the Honor Manor, "With great respect to the Grand Master of the Honor Manor, with great honor to the Grand Master of the Honor Manor!"

Yi Ping looked hatefully in his direction.

Gongsun Bai was an imposing bearded man in his fifties and he was dressed in finery. He was heavily muscled and of strong build.

He began to look at everyone in the grand hall; everyone could feel the piercing gaze of his sweeping stares!

The legs of many of the pugilists became jelly and many looked to the ground in discomfort.

Gongsun Bai said imposingly, "Who has dared to injure a member of the Honor Manor. Don't you know this is my domain? Do you know my rule?"

All eyes turned and looked at Yi Ping, who remained standing relentlessly without flinching.

Zuo Tianyi said, "I am about to teach this insolent fellow a lesson on behalf of the Honor Manor."

Gongsun Bai stared fiercely at Zuo Tianyi and said, "Who do you think you are that you think you can act on behalf of the Honor Manor?"

The pugilists immediately feared for Zuo Tianyi. It was because no one made any decisions for Master Gongsun Bai. He was always the master and the rest were his subordinates!

Zuo Tianyi smiled bitterly and said, "I am who I am. The enemy of the Honor Manor is my enemy as well. The friend of the Honor Manor is my friend."

Gongsun Bai stared at Zuo Tianyi for a while before he said, "Very well. You are indeed a righteous knight errant like your grandfather. This congregation is partly held in honor of the Old Sword Saint. You may teach this young man a lesson on behalf of the Honor Manor."

He then proceeded to sit on the golden throne.

Even though the majority of the pugilists were uncomfortable with Gongsun Bai arrogance but there were nothing they could do. It was because Gongsun Bai was the most powerful man and the Honor Manor the most powerful martial clan in the martial fraternity for the past ten years!

While the Old Man Zuo the Sword Saint was still alive, the seven major orthodox clans could still stand on equal footing with the Honor Manor. But now, they were no different from a second tier martial clan, which had almost all submitted to the Honor Manor!

Zuo Tianyi said, "Then I thanks Master Gongsun for this honor."

He turned and looked at Yi Ping before saying coldly, "I am Zuo Tianyi. What is your name? I do not kill nameless fellow."

Yi Ping looked at everyone and said aloud, "I am Yi Ping."

Zuo Tianyi looked past Yi Ping and looked at Ji Lingfeng.

When Ji Lingfeng saw Zuo Tianyi looking at her, she averted her eyes again.

Zuo Tianyi said to Yi Ping, "I will like to see how outstanding you are."

Yi Ping drew out his long sword without hesitation. He thought, "Even if I were to die today, I must never disgrace my father."

Ji Lingfeng looked at Yi Ping and seemed to want to say something but she hesitated.

Zuo Tianyi displayed his sword stance, the Infinity Pose Stance and pointed his sword towards Yi Ping from the top of his head while his left fingers were posed and readied with the sword finger stance.

Yi Ping readied his sword to the top of his head too and lifted his palm in front of him, with the Divine Horizon Hand Stance.

Both stances were similar but had a subtle difference.

The weird thing was that both continued to stand in this tiring pose for some time.

Zuo Tianyi was waiting for an opening to strike against Yi Ping but his opponent stance surprised him. It was similar to his. This type of stance was the perfect defensive sword stance, able to defend from the top to the feet at the quickest time.

Moreover, Yi Ping's stance had no opening for him for an instant win.

Therefore he waited for Yi Ping to be tired and soften his stance or to attack him. But that did not happen. Zuo Tianyi thought, "This young man is a practicing swordsman too? It looks like this battle is not going to end fast."

Yi Ping broke the silence and said, "Are you going to attack or not? I am still waiting! I have never heard of a challenger who is a tortoise!"

Zuo Tianyi had recognized Ji Lingfeng and he could tell that she had her eyes only on Yi Ping.

If Yi Ping were to fight against Gu Tianle, he would surely lose his life. Therefore he had decided to interfere so that he could find a way to get him out of this awful situation.

He had thought, "This young man did not know his limits. He dares to offend the Honor Manor? Even the Infinity Sword Clan dare not offend the Honor Manor...interesting."

But Yi Ping's sword stances intrigued him more and aroused his interests...

Zuo Tianyi was amused, "I have never known a person that can't wait to die." And he instantly displayed a dancing barrage of sword strokes.

Yi Ping attacked with the Horizon Swordplay and met stroke for stroke!

When Gongsun Bai saw that Yi Ping had displayed the Horizon Swordplay, his stares turned murderous and this was noticed by Ji Lingfeng.

Ji Lingfeng sighed softly and she could feel a terrible ache in her heart, "Yi Ping, Yi Ping, perhaps we shouldn't be here at all. I am so sorry. I shouldn't have brought you here..."

It was not wrong to say that Zuo Tianyi was one of the top swordsmen in the martial fraternity and his swordplay was extremely fast and lethal! No one expected Yi Ping to hold his ground against Zuo Tianyi but he did!

Everyone began to hold their breath as their sword techniques became faster and more extraordinary!

However the older and experienced pugilists were able to see that Zuo Tianyi was attacking more and that Yi Ping was defending more. Therefore it was not wrong to say that victory would eventually belong to Zuo Tianyi!

Yi Ping was amazed at Zuo Tianyi swordplay and he almost lost his focus.

The duel amazed the pugilists. Zuo Tianyi swordplay was steady and calculating. It was as though there was no weakness in his swordplay while Yi Ping swordplay was so fast like lightning that the sword tip of his sword vanished from sight!

The Infinity Swordplay was a swordplay that split from one stroke to a great multitude of sword strokes, with each splinter hiding additional strokes and secret techniques. That was how it got its name. Those that did not know the origin of the Infinity Swordplay would not be on guard against it and would often lose, the price of losing was often heavy; death or maimed.

Few pugilists in the fraternity had recognized the Horizon Swordplay. The meaning of the Horizon was to strike beyond the horizon and out of the blue from somewhere. Only a few pugilists presented like Gongsun Bai, Yue Yuan and Gu Tianle had recognized it!

Gu Tianle expressions turned deadly solemn. It was because twenty years ago, Gongsun Bai, Jue Yuan and he had ambushed Yi Tianxing together. They had thought that he was dead and had no more descendants. And this young man had the same surname Yi as him.

Zuo Tianyi was secretly surprised that he had used more than sixty strokes and yet to defeat Yi Ping. This was a huge loss of face in front of the crowd and a loss of prestige among the swordsmen that were presented.

Few opponents had rarely forced him to use beyond the Infinity-Seven and this Yi Ping had forced him to use too many of his secret techniques in front of the crowd.

As soon as he got the opportunity and the opening that he needed, he immediately displayed the Infinity-Three sword stroke!

Just when Yi Ping swung his sword to parry it, there was a burst of cold energy from the tip of Zuo Tianyi sword.

Yi Ping was caught by surprise by the sudden cumulative brilliant flare of Zuo Tianyi's sword stroke and reacted slower. He was instantly sent flying backward by the tremendous martial force of the Infinity-Three!

Just when Zuo Tianyi had thought that he had won, he was stunned to see Yi Ping was on his feet again!

He immediately raised the martial power of his Infinitude Recite to its zenith and developed it into multitudes of sword energies that charged his long sword!

The pugilists could feel the chilling cold energy that was radiated from Zuo Tianyi and they were all forced to take several steps backward!

Shangguan Qingyun, the Old Protégé Master of the Divine Sword Martial Clan was stunned. He had dedicated all his life to the sword and could yet he could not breech through the physical forms of his swordplay.

He had thought that Old Man Zuo the Sword Saint was an exception and there would be no others in the future. But this Zuo Tianyi who was barely thirty had already achieved the sword energy form!

Zuo Tianyi had used the Infinity-Two! The Infinity-Three was a sword stroke that merged the physical form and enveloped the sword with deadly sword energies while the Infinity-Two was an even higher stage that enveloped the practitioner with sword energies aura.

Zuo Tianyi had wanted to conceal his true strength but when he had met a worthy opponent, he had actually forgotten about it.

When Yi Ping had stood up again, he was stunned. It was because it seemed that he was not affected by his sword energy!

He had even forgotten that it was just a mock duel and had raised all his martial power to its zenith!

When Yi Ping had been struck by Zuo Tianyi sword energy, it felt as though his vital energies had been dispersed and he thought he was going to die. But all of a sudden, he felt a smoothing and renewed energy flowing through his entire body! Unwittingly, Zuo Tianyi attacks had helped him to clear his Conception Vessel and the Governing Vessel temporary, two of the most important eight wondrous meridians!

Zuo Tianyi immediately thought, "He is protected by a body impervious force?"

The truth was that Yi Ping was protected by the Icy Heavenly Tears Intricate Energy that was inside him, which was similar to the cold piercing sword energy.

That was why when Zuo Tianyi had raised his Infinitude Recite to its zenith, Yi Ping was still unaffected!

Even Ji Lingfeng was stunned as she thought, "He is unaffected by Zuo Tianyi's sword energy?"

Yi Ping could see the visible energy that radiated from Zuo Tianyi and from his sword. He did not notice that everyone else had been affected by the unnerving cold piercing of that energy.

In fact, he did not even realize he was the only one that could see the invisible sword energy other than Zuo Tianyi!

Yi Ping raised his spirits with the Divine Revelation and imbued his long sword with the martial power of the Asper Invocations Intricate Recite to its zenith. He knew that Zuo Tianyi martial power was at its zenith too and he dared not be careless. He could not afford to die before he could avenge for his parents!

Even before Ji Lingfeng had recovered from her astonishments, Yi Ping had attacked Zuo Tianyi with the Horizon Swordplay, as mirror images of his sword flew against him!

Zuo Tianyi raised his Infinity Swordplay and in that split second, he had executed thirty-six strokes followed by eight-one strokes of the Infinity Swordplay!

The two swordsmen clashed against one another so fast that there were clashes of brilliant light that the pugilists could hardly see their body movements and even their sword strokes. In fact, no one had believed it was possible to achieve such supernatural speed and attacks!

The pugilists could only held their breath in awe as they watched their spattering blood that flew in all directions amidst the dozens of brilliant lights and ear-shrieking clashing sound that rung nonstop!

Ji Lingfeng could not hold back her tears anymore as she saw their blood flying in all directions even though it was impossible for her to see whose blood was it.

Even renowned swordsmen like Young Master Qiu Wufeng, the Heartless Scholar, Shangguan Qingyun and Old Priest Yan Nanfei the protégé master of the Zen Sect was astonished. It seemed to them that the swordplay level of Zuo Tianyi was at a much higher progression than they had thought!

Nangong Le was even more startled. He had never thought that the new friend that he had just befriended possessed such unfathomable swordplay and his martial level was not beneath that of a young master of the martial fraternity!

He began to sigh as he stole a glance at the tearful Maiden Lingfeng, "If this Yi Ping does not die, I really do not have any hope."

And so he silently rooted for Zuo Tianyi but he was saying to Ji Lingfeng, "Maiden, Brother Yi Ping will surely be alright and be blessed by the Heavens above. Don't worry…"

All of a sudden, a sword flew with such sudden speed into the midst of Yi Ping and Zuo Tianyi that it broke their fight!

Both Zuo Tianyi and Yi Ping began to stagger several steps backward as they stared at a beautiful long sword that not only broke their fight by piercing through them; this beautiful long sword had even rebounded against the wall and was thrust into the ground that had just divided them!

They were both bloodied and covered with numerous sword wounds but they were staring in utter disbelief at this beautiful long sword that was thrust into the ground!

They had sensed and saw this sword flying towards them. Both had exercised their martial power to deflect this sword away but instead of deflecting this sword, both were pushed away by the martial force that was imbued in this flying sword!

They simply could not believe their very eyes that a weapon without a master could withstand the zenith of their martial power at the same time!

Most pugilists could not tell from their bewildered expressions. But they were stunned that a long sword from nowhere could interrupt the duel and rebounded with such almighty force against the wall; it was able to thrust itself precisely into the same ground that it had interrupted the duel!

Ji Lingfeng did not care for all these. She simply flew to Yi Ping embrace and took out her handkerchief. She began to clean his wounds as she asked, "Hmph Yi Ping, are you alright? Why are you so foolish? You should know your limits and where we are…"

Yi Ping nodded silently and he could feel exhaustion seeping in…

Ji Lingfeng said, "Don't try to talk. Adjust your breathing first…"

It was as though they were alone in the grand hall and many of the pugilists were filled with envy especially Nangong Le and Qiu Wufeng.

Zuo Tianyi had suffered fewer wounds than Yi Ping but he too, was drained of his martial strength once he had stopped. He was immediately supported by his clan protégés to his seat!

Zuo Tianyi was staring in shocked silence at his trembling sword. He could not believe that he could fail to deflect this flying sword given his martial strength and almost lost his grip too…

Gongsun Bai was enraged as he thundered aloud, "Who is that? Since you are already here, why don't you come in?"

Almost all the pugilists immediately guessed that it would be a super exponent that used a sword but none could guess who it was given that almost all the renowned top exponents were here.

A wrinkled old man in his seventies with an empty scabbard and a demure maiden with a long sword were standing in front of the entrance. The old man was dressed in a simple gray robe while the demure maiden was also dressed in a simple outfit but it still could not hide her attractiveness.

It was obvious it was the old man that had threw the beautiful adorn long sword.

When Zuo Tianyi saw the demure maiden, his eyes almost popped out…

Gongsun Bai said solemnly, "Do you know the rules of the Honor Manor? Are you courting your own death? Did you throw that long sword?"

The wrinkled old man smiled, "I didn't throw that sword but so what if I did?"

Gongsun Bai asked, "You didn't throw that long sword?"

The wrinkled old man looked at everyone in the hall and his eyes lingered at Ji Lingfeng for some time before he laughed aloud, "Did anyone of you see me throwing a long sword? How do you throw a long sword?"

Gu Tianle the One-Armed Warrior-God said, "It is obvious that you are here to find trouble. Who are you and where did you come from?"

Then he shouted to the guards, "Why didn't anyone of you stop him? Summon all the guards later; I will flog them twenty lashes!"

Gongsun Bai said, "There is no need to check. They are all dead. There is a heavy stench of blood around this old man. Who are you and where did you come from? If you don't give me a reasonable answer, don't expect to leave this place alive."

All of a sudden, the wrinkled old man raised his hand and slapped the demure maiden hard on her left cheek and she fell onto the ground!

Her left cheek immediately turned red and there was blood snoozing from the tip of her delicate mouth.

Venerable Master Deng Zhong, the Head Abbot of the Monument Monastery immediately said, "Why did you hit her for? You have to be reasonable!"

He was not the only one who had reacted in that instant.

Nangong Le, Qiu Wufeng, Gongsun Jing and many others were all startled and were feeling indignant for the demure maiden.

All of a sudden, it seemed that the entire congregation was united again!

The wrinkled old man said, "I am unreasonable? Just a moment ago, you are all demanding for her blood. She is the one that throw that sword. I have merely passed her my sword but she has failed to announce herself and interrupted the duel. This is just a small punishment for her."

This demure maiden was the one that threw the long sword? No one in the grand hall believed such a blatant lie!

The demure maiden had quietly picked herself up and stood beside the wrinkled old man once again.

Yi Ping was angry and he scolded the wrinkled old man, "No matter, you shouldn't have lifted your hands on her! Who do you think you are?"

The crowds were all experienced pugilists with vast experiences in the fraternity. Most of them would not act rashly for fear of offending the wrong person. And Yi Ping was scolding this wrinkled old man! Even Gongsun Bai had yet to berate this old man yet!

The demure maiden looked up and looked at him intently.

The wrinkled old man said to Yi Ping, "Young man, are you sick of living already?"

But before Yi Ping could say a word more, he was dragged away by Ji Lingfeng who had struck him on his back!

Ji Lingfeng nearly fainted from Yi Ping boldness. She pulled him back to the side and said nervously, "Yi Ping, this is between Gongsun Bai and this old man. Don't get drag into this."

Yi Ping was already seriously injured, sustaining both serious external and internal injuries. When Ji Lingfeng had struck him hard onto his back, his entire vision became a blur!

He could only mutter, "Whose side are you on again…"

Gongsun Bai said, "Don't let me repeat myself again. Who are you?"

The wrinkled old man looked at the demure maiden and smiled for a while.

When they followed the glance of the wrinkled old man, they were stunned to see the bruises on the demure maiden face had totally vanished! It was as though she had never been slapped!

The wrinkled old man said, "I am Xiao Shuai, the Master of the Virtuous Palace."

When the pugilists heard the name of the Virtuous Palace, there was a sudden great silence in the grand hall.

Gongsun Bai solemn face had flinched for an instant.

The Virtuous Palace was one of the three most forbidden places in the entire fraternity and was located in the Far East Fraternity. It had rarely interfered in the affairs of the martial fraternity. Few pugilists bothered with the Virtuous Palace too for those that tried to enter its forbidden premise never made it back alive.

The Virtuous Palace was renowned for a type of swordplay known as the Flying Sword Swordplay. Was that the Flying Sword Swordplay that was displayed earlier?

No one had really seen the martial skills of the Virtuous Palace or knows how high the martial level of its practitioners was.

Gongsun Bai said, "The Honor Manor and the Virtuous Palace has no dealing with one another whatever so. The Virtuous Palace has rarely meddles in the martial affairs. So what do you want?"

Chapter 16: The Virtuous Palace

Xiao Shuai began to scan his eyes around the grand hall before he sighed softly, "It seems that she is not here and she has purposely lured us here."

Even though his voice was not loud but the crowd could hear it clearly.

The demure maiden nodded silently.

Xiao Shuai said, "If I tell you that I am looking for someone here, will you believe me?"

Gongsun Bai said coldly, "What do you think?"

Xiao Shuai smiled coldly, "It seems that you are master of this place. Very well, let assume that you are the only one that is fit to talk to me then. Who are you?"

The numerous pugilists that were eagerly watching the outcome were stunned that he did not know who Gongsun Bai was?

Gongsun Bai roared with tremendous laughter, "You don't know who I am?"

Xiao Shuai said coldly, "You have asked who I am. I have told you. Surely you will return me the courtesy and tell me your name?"

Gongsun Bai was furious that this old man had actually blatantly declare that he did not know him yet he dare to barge into his domain? In the entire fraternity, even a commoner knows who he was.

Virtuous Palace or not, there was no one in the entire fraternity that he feared now. Moreover, the Virtuous Palace was a legend and no one had ever seen any protégés from the Virtuous Palace in the fraternity before.

Gu Tianle and Gongsun Jing immediately shouted, "How atrocious! You don't even know who Master Gongsun Bai is?!"

Gu Tianle added, "You must be tired of living already! Let me teach you a lesson! Master Gongsun is the Grand Master of the Honor Manor and you are now in his place. If you do not bow before him, don't blame me for not warning you!"

Xiao Shuai hummed coldly before saying, "I have no ill-intention and I am already being extremely tolerant."

Gongsun Bai said coldly, "You have no ill-intention and yet you have killed my men?"

Xiao Shuai laughed aloud, "Don't be misunderstood. I have merely taught them a lesson. They are still alive."

Gongsun Bai asked, "They are alive?"

Xiao Shuai said, "Really, you can take a look if you want."

Gongsun Bai said, "If they are alive, then where are they now?"

Xiao Shuai said, "If you lose an arm then the pain will be agonizing, am I right? If you are in pain, will you have the strength to do anything else?"

Gongsun Bai said coldly, "And you are saying you are coming to help the Honor Manor?"

Xiao Shuai said, "They are rude to me and refuses to allow me to enter the Gongsun Manor even after I have said I am from the Virtuous Palace. Therefore I have to teach them a small lesson."

Gongsun Bai said coldly, "Unfortunately, you have already offended the Honor Manor. Do you think I will let you off just like this?"

Xiao Shuai looked at the pugilists slowly, "It seems that there are so many top exponents here. It seems foolhardy for me to fight against everyone, am I right?"

All the pugilists began to smile bitterly. In fact many of the pugilists were secretly hoping that this 'Xiao Shuai' would help them to teach Gongsun Bai a lesson. It was because under his dominating influence, many of the martial clans had suffered exceedingly.

Gongsun Bai said coldly, "Is there anyone in the congregation that believes your nonsense?"

Zuo Tianyi had been looking intently at the demure maiden who was standing beside the wrinkled old man for a long time…

She had not changed at all.

She was Ding Yunzi, his distant cousin.

They were both around the same age.

He remembered that when Ding Yunzi was just a young girl, she would often visit him with her mother. In time to come, the visits got less and less frequent and turned into a bi-yearly visit. When he was eighteen, her visits had totally stopped all of a sudden…

And ten years had almost passed since they had last seen each other…

Each time when she had come, she seemed to hide a terrible sorrow and would often cry alone in the night. He knew because he had secretly eavesdropped outside her room.

Even though everyone had called him a prodigy swordsman but it was not entirely the truth.

It was because many of his improvements were attributed to her.

She would secretly impart to him several sword techniques and corrected his sword strokes so that he would be able to improve. He had no idea how she had acquainted her sword skills and she had never discussed it.

In his heart, she was his little protégé mistress and the very reason why he was always training day in and night out so that one day, he would proudly be able to demonstrate his skills to her and earned her praise.

He sworn that one day, he would be her protector and dreamed of the day that she would be his wife…

But that day had never come because she had suddenly disappeared from the face of the earth.

He would often ask his grandfather on her whereabouts and her origins but the Old Sword Saint would shake his head and said, "She is in a faraway place."

When he asked his grandfather when he was twenty-two that he would find her and bring her back as his wife, his grandfather flew into a rage and scolded him, "With your puny skills, do you think you are able to reach that immoral place alive? You have better forget her, the sooner the better!"

He replied coldly, "I have nothing to fear…"

Before he could finish, the Old Sword Saint had slapped him hard and rebuked him sharply, "That is an immoral place and she is an immoral woman. Do not ever mention her in front of me, ever again!"

He had tried to enquiry others on her whereabouts but no one was willing to tell him. Finally an elder had secretly told him, "That place is a fearsome place and one of the martial holy grounds of the martial fraternity. No one really knows where it is. If you want to go there, you have to be as good as the Sword Saint. Otherwise you will really die there."

He had never forgotten her; she was the only reason for his existence and the reason why he pushed himself so hard. He was lonely, very lonely…

It was only when he was practicing his sword, could he feel her presence and of the times that they were together.

He could only mutter now, "Is that really you? I have grown old yet you look exactly the same as ten years ago…"

When Ji Lingfeng saw Zuo Tianyi looking intently at the demure maiden, she began to recall the time when she was alone with him a year ago…

She had asked him, "Why are you closing your eyes? Are you shy or are you blind? Or you are despising me because I am from the unorthodox sect?"

Zuo Tianyi opened his eyes and smiled, "None of the above."

Ji Lingfeng asked coldly, "Hmph, then why are you not looking at me?"

Zuo Tianyi sighed and he seemed to look at a faraway place, "If only you are her…"

Ji Lingfeng asked coolly, "So you already have a sweetheart. Who is she?"

Zuo Tianyi began to tremble as he said, "She is someone that I will never see again in my entire life…"

Ji Lingfeng looked at the demure maiden and thought, "She is the one that Zuo Tianyi is longing for?"

Her thoughts were interrupted when Gongsun Bai roared mightily and everyone could feel his martial power. He began to take a step forward and immediately, the stone flooring beneath him began to crack!

Gongsun Bai had just attained a new level in his Invincible Divine Force and he was lamenting of an opponent to test his new martial power.

And this old man here may be a suitable target for him!

In front of the pugilists today, he was going to demonstrate his martial power and to awestruck them so that none of them would go against him in the future.

Xiao Shuai said, "What a mighty martial power! Is this the Invincible Divine Force?"

Gongsun Bai replied coldly, "That's right!"

Xiao Shuai said, "This skill needs at least sixty years of martial power to even begin to start practicing and it is an extremely difficult to learn but powerful skill. Even if you train day and night, most people will not be able to go past the basics even when they are sixty. And you have reached the advance stage already. Very Impressive!"

Gongsun Bai said, "Indeed. This skill has many difficulties…"

Xiao Shuai replied, "And it is incomplete too."

Gongsun snarled, "How do you know?"

Xiao Shuai hummed coldly, "It is not only incomplete and dangerous to practice too. I know because the Invincible Divine Force that you have is a copy from the Virtuous Palace!"

The pugilists began to rumble among themselves.

Xiao Shuai simply added, "The Virtuous Palace deliberately left it in the central plains thirty years ago. I didn't expect that you are actually its new owner. How on earth did you manage to decipher it when so many of us had failed? This is so interesting."

Gongsun Bai refused to answer him because there were many other pugilists in the grand hall. And moreover this old man knew that a fight was forthcoming and the two of them were actually maneuvering for the best advantage.

The one that helped him to decipher and added to the intricate formula of the Invincible Divine Force was Shui Yichi, the wife of Yi Tianxing. He hated Yi Tianxing for having such a good wife when he should be the one that she ought to marry.

He glanced at Yi Ping briefly with his murderous intent.

Gongsun Bai said, "You are not weak either, judging by your martial power when you throw the sword."

Indeed, the two of them had peak their martial power. A decisive win would depend on their true skills and techniques.

Gongsun Bai said, "But today, you will surely die here. I will not allow another person to undermine my authority and will not tolerate anyone to be a threat to me."

Xiao Shuai looked solemnly at him, "Is that so?"

Gongsun Bai said, "When top exponents duel with one another, besides martial power and techniques, the human factor and the timing are also an important factor."

Xiao Shuai shifted slightly, "That is right!"

Gongsun Bai said, "We are almost equal in martial power and strength. I have the full support of the congregation and that is the human factor. I can attack you with no fear of hesitation but you can't. This is my domain and I have the timing. Timing, Terrain and human factor, which one have you got?"

Xiao Shuai lowered his gaze before saying, "Indeed, I have none of it."

Gongsun Bai said coldly, "If you bow to me, I may consider sparing your life."

Xiao Shuai hummed coldly, "You are asking an old man that is twenty-years your senior to bow to you?"

Gongsun Bai laughed, "Everyone bows to me in the fraternity and you are no exception!"

Yi Ping had regained some of his conscious and strength. He was clenching his fists in rage at Gongsun Bai's arrogance.

Xiao Shuai said coldly, "So if I don't, you will surely kill me. So will the pugilists all attack me at the same time or you will?"

Gongsun Bai laughed, "You don't have to go around in circles. I am looking for a good fight. It is too easy to crash you by asking others to do so. But I want to let the whole fraternity to know this; anyone that dares to offend me will rue the day they are born! I will let them die in the most painful manner."

Venerable Master Deng Zhong, the Head Abbot of the Monument Monastery immediately muttered, "Merciful Buddha!"

Many of the orthodox clans were silent. No one dared to mutter anything against Gongsun Bai out of fear.

Xiao Shuai said, "When I fight with others, my disciple will fight side by side with me…"

The demure maiden shook her head in panic and took several steps backward!

Gu Tianle interrupted and raised his voice angrily, "You cunning old man! Two versus one? You really know how to take advantage. Then you don't mind that I take a part too?"

Xiao Shuai smiled bitterly, "I really don't mind. It is my style to fight in pair."

Gongsun Bai looked at the attractive demure maiden and smiled, "If she is not afraid of getting killed, then she can join in. I will hate to kill someone like her. More hands don't mean more advantage."

The less confident his opponent had, the higher his odds of winning!

Gongsun Bai said, "What is your weapon?"

Xiao Shuai said coldly, "My sword of course. What about yours?"

Gongsun Bai smiled, "With my bare hands. I have stopped using a weapon ten years ago. As long as the weapon is my heart, I can kill."

Xiao Shuai exclaimed aloud, "That is the extraordinary martial stage of without a weapon in your hand and having a weapon in the heart. You have attained that stage?"

Gongsun Bai replied proudly, "That is right."

The pugilists presented were awestruck. It was because even though many pugilists understood that principle but few people could really reach that level of attainment. Only a few super exponents like Gongsun Bai, Gu Tianle, Jue Yuan and the Celestial Fairy could possibly reach that stage.

Even the Sword Saint who was highly acclaimed for his martial prowess did not reach that level of attainment...

Xiao Shuai sighed, "It seems that I have met a formidable opponent today. Yunzi, fetch me my sword."

Now the pugilists knew that her name was Yunzi.

She walked unhurriedly to the beautifully adorned long sword that was thrust into the ground, pulled it out before walking back to her protégé master and handing the long sword back to him.

Some of the pugilists were secretly jeering at Xiao Shuai. They were cursing, "He had denied that he was the one that threw the long sword and now he was asking for his sword. What a joke!"

The demure maiden began to distance herself from Xiao Shuai by walking all the way to the entrance!

Xiao Shuai looked annoyed and sighed, "Nowadays, even my own disciple cannot be trusted. In times of crisis, each is on their own."

Gongsun Bai said coldly, "Are you done yet?"

Xiao Shuai brandished his long sword, "I'm ready!"

Gongsun Bai immediately raised his martial power and charged at Xiao Shuai!

That Gongsun Bai could raise his martial power in such a short time astonished the pugilists presented!

Xiao Shuai immediately swung his sword in a circular movement and thrown it towards the charging Gongsun Bai!

The flying sword sped like lightning and flew towards Gongsun Bai! This was the exact flying sword technique that everyone had seen earlier!

The flying sword was filled with extraordinary powerful martial power as it sped towards Gongsun Bai!

Even though this flying sword was startling fast, it was simple too straightforward and it was all too easy for Gongsun Bai to dodge it!

As soon as Gongsun Bai evaded the attack and charged towards Xiao Shuai again, the flying sword struck the wall behind Gongsun Bai and rebounded again with a startling force towards him again!

Gongsun Bai hummed coldly; this was just a small nuisance to him.

He simply raised his right hand and used his famous Ironclad Claw Skill with the full martial power of his Invincible Divine Force.

As soon the flying sword flew back towards him and impacted onto his right hand, it was deflected and dropped onto the ground!

Gongsun Bai was now in front of Xiao Shuai and was exchanging blows with him!

They were exchanging blows so fast that the pugilists could only see their body being stationary but their hands and legs were just shades of shadow!

Gongsun Bai was heard saying, "It is no use. Nothing can penetrate my Invincible Divine Force!"

To prove his point, he no longer defended against Xiao Shuai attacks once he had gauged the strength of his martial power!

Xiao Shuai attacks had landed on him harmlessly!

Gongsun Bai laughed coldly and said, "Now you will die…"

But before he could finish, Xiao Shuai had smashed through his Invincible Divine Force, not once but several times on several parts of his body, including his head and face!

Both Yi Ping and Ji Lingfeng gasped to themselves, "That is the Penetrating Hands?!"

Gongsun Bai was momentary stunned and startled…

He had not sense any martial power increase coming from Xiao Shuai and yet when he was struck, it seemed that Xiao Shuai attacking strength had increased several folds!

Just when he was about to step backward…

At this moment of time, the demure maiden had silently drew her sword and had whirled it in a circular movement around her more than a dozen times in less than a split second and had sent her long sword flying towards Gongsun Bai!

Qiu Wufeng was famous for his silent swordplay and was given the fraternity name of Windless Swordsman. He was proud of his fraternity name. No one else would attack as silently as him.

But this demure and attractive maiden, she had actually drawn out her long sword so silently and so quickly that it was unbelievable!

If he had not witnessed it personal himself, he would never have believed it!

He was not the only one that was staring in disbelief, the rest of the pugilists that had noticed it were staring in complete disbelief!

Qiu Wufeng and Nangong Le had noticed it because they were looking at her lecherously! They were thinking if this Xiao Shuai had died, then this poor maiden would suffer a terrible fate and it would be a great pity should that happened. So they were looking at her and watching her expressions. But all of a sudden, she had brandish out her long sword…

And her flying sword too, was filled with martial power as it sped towards Gongsun Bai!

In that split second, she had brandished her long sword, whirled it more than a dozen times and sent it flying towards Gongsun Bai in the same second!

Her flying sword flew with startling speed between Gongsun Bai and Xiao Shuai!

Gongsun Bai still had his arms extending in front when he was suddenly struck multiple times by Xiao Shuai!

So when her flying sword flew across between them, it sliced off the arms of Gongsun Bai!

Gongsun Bai yelled aloud in pain as blood from his arm came rushing forth in all directions as Xiao Shuai leapt backward!

While he was still yelling in pain, the flying sword rebounded against the hall pillar and back towards him again, cutting off his head!

When her sword had cut off Gongsun Bai's head, it continued on its path and back into the hands of the demure maiden who whirled the long sword again, cleaning its blade from the blood stains before she sheathed it back into her scabbard!

All these happened so fast that no one was able to react to what was happening!

This quiet, seemingly innocent and attractive maiden was actually a top exponent! It just did not match her age and image!

The numerous pugilists of the various sects and clans were stunned into silence! Gongsun Bai, the most powerful man in the entire fraternity was now a dead man! He had died very quickly but in great agony...

Gongsun Jing had immediately fainted on the spot when he witnessed his father's death and several protégés of the Honor Manor began to crowd around him panicky to check on his condition.

Xiao Shuai had picked up his long sword as he said, "It is still safer to have a weapon in the hands. Alas, he is all talk and no substance. Martial skills, timing, terrain and human factor, I have none but yet I have won?"

He muttered to himself, "If you have the patience to practice for another twenty years, then maybe you would be truly invincible."

No one could really understand how this mysterious old man and maiden could bypass Gongsun Bai's Invincible Divine Force!

No one else but Yi Ping! He had personally witnessed the martial power of the Penetrating Hand! When the Penetrating Hand had breached the Invincible Divine Force, Gongsun Bai's martial power had dropped considerably that even the demure maiden's flying sword could slice through his arms...

Yi Ping wondered if Gongsun Bai still had his Invincible Divine Force at its full martial power, would he still be able to deflect her first flying sword strike? He could still remember how hard his sword arm had trembled after he had used his full martial power to deflect the flying sword earlier...

Then it suddenly occurred to Yi Ping that this old man was trying to conceal his Penetrating Hands from the eyes of the onlookers and created an illusion that a sneak attack had been made by the demure maiden! It seemed that they had planned it right from the very start...

Zuo Tianyi too was stunned.

Her sword strength was even more powerful than him even after so many years had passed?

Yi Ping could not resist laughing coldly, "Good! Gongsun Bai is dead!"

Xiao Shuai said coldly, "Let's us go. There is nothing that interests us here."

Gu Tianle had stepped forward in rage, "Do you think the Honor Manor will let you off so lightly after what you have done? How despicable are you! There are two of you against one. Where is the martial justice?"

Xiao Shuai laughed coldly, "Are you deaf? Right from the start, Gongsun Bai had said he had agreed to fight the two of us together."

He paused for a while before adding, "He deserved to die because he was too suspicious. I have already warned him that the sword was hurled by my disciple but alas, he did not believe me. If he had believed me, he wouldn't be killed."

He began to turn back and walked slowly towards the entrance.

Gu Tianle began to shout, "Everyone, get him together! Avenge for Master Gongsun!"

But no one dared to move and was looking at one another for leadership.

Some of the pugilists were even thinking; if they were to all charge at the duo and if they suddenly throw their flying swords at them, would they be able to evade from it with so many people pushing around them?

There were many pugilists that were even thinking; so that was how they had thrown the sword and it could fly just like that? They were all thinking of trying it as soon as they got the chance. However, they did not know that the secret technique to turn it into a flying sword was more complex that it appeared. Without knowing the secret techniques to do so, it was just a futile and clumsy try.

Gu Tianle looked at everyone. They had never disobeyed the Honor Manor before. The minute Gongsun Bai had died, everyone seemed to have rebel!

Gu Tianle shouted again, "Avenge for Master Gongsun!"

Venerable Master Deng Zhong responded, "Merciful Buddha."

That was the only response so far!

All of a sudden, Yi Ping had freed himself from the embracing support of Ji Lingfeng and stepped forward as he trembled uncontrollably!

Yi Ping raised his voice, "Maiden, hold your steps!"

Was this maiden the one that had killed his wife?

Zuo Tianyi was surprised that Yi Ping still had the strength to move as he thought, "Is he human? There are so many deep slashes on him and his wounds are still bleeding…"

Yi Ping shouted again, "Do you know me or been to the Heavenly Mountains before?"

The demure maiden turned back and took a glance at him before she replied simply, "No. I have never been there before."

Yi Ping was startled and he thought, "No, that is impossible. It has to be her. But her voice is different…"

She seemingly looked at everyone. But she was actually looking intently at Zuo Tianyi and Yi Ping before she disappeared from sight.

Just when Yi Ping was about to go after her, Gu Tianle had immediately confronted Yi Ping and said, "They can leave but not you. You have insulted our Master and who knows, you may be in cahoots with them. If I let you go off just like that, how am I going to account to all the heroes that are here?"

Ji Lingfeng was besides Yi Ping in an instant as she said coldly, "You are the so call Warrior-God of the martial fraternity? Just a few minutes ago, you are like a lamb when they are still here. The minute that they had vanished from sight, you are like a lion. You are really a coward!"

Yi Ping was worried for Ji Lingfeng as he knew that sometimes she could not mince her words, so he added icily, "He is only capable of bullying the weak. Where was he when Gongsun Bai got killed? If he is really not a coward, he would have confronted that Xiao Shuai just a minute ago!"

The pugilists began to turn and murmured to one another. All of a sudden, the grand hall became very incessantly noisy!

Gu Tianle was enraged; he raised his martial power and attacked Yi Ping with the 'Ultrapowerful Hand Force'! A seemingly unstoppable force began to hurl itself onto Yi Ping as he shouted, "Don't be too haughty, young man! There is always a sky above a sky!"

Yi Ping raised his right palm to meet the incoming blow!

Even as Yi Ping had mustered all his remaining strength to accept the incoming blow, Ji Lingfeng was even more agile and had flown past him to intercept the blow on his behalf!

She had raised all her martial power in her right palm and she had clashed headlong with Gu Tianle!

When the pugilists saw that, many in the crowd began to shake their heads and many had already imagined that the young maiden would die instantly on the spot!

There was a huge thunderous clap in that instant and true to the predictions of the pugilists, Ji Lingfeng spit out blood as she flew backwards and fell onto the ground!

In that instant, Ji Lingfeng had used the Holy Amalgamate Skill and had gathered all her martial power into that one blow! But Gu Tianle's Ultrapowerful Force Hand was simply too powerful and she was seriously injured in just one clash!

Gu Tianle's palm began to tremble as he shouted angrily, "You are from the Holy Hex Sect?"

The pugilists were startled. This young maiden was from the Holy Hex Sect?

The Holy Hex Sect was now the leader of the various Unorthodox Clans and also the enemy of the Orthodox Fraternity!

In that clash of blows, Gu Tianle could feel the martial power drain in his palm! The Holy Amalgamate Skill was one of those few martial skills that could cause a draining effect. Luckily, his opponent martial power was much weaker than him and the drain effect had only a minor effect on him.

Ji Lingfeng smiled weakly on the ground, "Yi Ping, don't worry about me. I will be alright. Run please…"

Nangong Le wanted to rush to help Ji Lingfeng but his chest was hurting. He was also afraid of Gu Tianle and the rest of the pugilists…

When Yi Ping saw how badly Ji Lingfeng was injured as she fought to defend him, his entire body was filled with burning rage!

He immediately attacked Gu Tianle, using all his remaining strength with the Asper Horizon Hand!

Gu Tianle was not slow to react and had mustered his Ultrapowerful Force Hand again!

With that, their palms clashed against one another and there was a huge thunderclap!

Gu Tianle was pushed back five steps and as he stumbled back, he quickly lifted a breath of vital energy and steadied himself!

Yi Ping was pushed seven steps back and he was coughing a lot of blood!

The orthodox pugilists were stunned. A seriously injured young person like Yi Ping could actually withstand a blow from Gu Tianle and still stood, it was indeed a miracle!

Even Qiu Wufeng and Zuo Tianyi thought, "This young man, he can still stand? Is he made of steel?"

Ji Lingfeng was in tears as she said to herself, "No good! He has already been injured in the earlier clash with Jue Yuan and Zuo Tianyi. His breathing has not recovered yet and now he has exerted himself further."

Gu Tianle said, "Young man, it is wiser for you to surrender!"

Yi Ping replied angrily, "I will not give up…" His eyes had now turned red and his entire body was now trembling.

The crowd was stunned that he could still stand on the ground. It was obvious to the pugilists that Yi Ping was now in a daze judging from his blood shot eyes and from the amount of blood that he had coughed out!

Gu Tianle said, "Very well, I shall grant your very wish and sent you to the maker with a blow!" Once again, he charged at Yi Ping with his hand forward.

This time, Gu Tianle had decided to use all his martial power.

Yi Ping laughed coldly, "You think that I dare not?" He mustered all his strength and displayed the Asper Horizon Hand!

Ji Lingfeng cried out, "Yi Ping! Don't force yourself!" It was because when the practitioner vital energy was not in harmony, especially after sustaining internal injuries, further use of the Asper Horizon Hand or any skill that required martial power would only add on to the injuries!

Moreover this was already the third time that Yi Ping had used the Asper Horizon Hand without any respites!

Again, there was a thunderous explosive impact when both palms met! The windforce created by the impact was so strong many of the pugilists could barely stand still!

Gu Tianle took three steps back and coughed out blood!

Yi Ping took three steps back too! But he had turned extremely pale in appearance and was not moving!

Gu Tianle and the rest of the pugilists were stunned as they thought, "Is he not human? Why didn't he fall yet?"

The very old pugilists knew that when a person was closed to death, their last vital breath was actually the most powerful and this Yi Ping had used up all his martial power!

Ji Lingfeng knew instantly that something had happened to Yi Ping!

Before anyone could react, she dived forward towards Gu Tianle and attacked him!

Gu Tianle immediately raised his hand again and thought, "This young maiden still have the strength to stand?"

When he saw the wavering images of her incoming hand, he was startled and mustered all his martial power! This was because the young maiden had just displayed the Asper Horizon Hand too and he could not afford to be careless as he thought, "She knows the Asper Horizon Hand too?"

Even before the pugilists could steady themselves, there was yet another thunderous clap that sent everyone moving backward again!

Gu Tianle was seen moving five steps backward and coughing out blood!

Like the Asper Horizon Hand, even though the Ultrapowerful Force Hand was an epitome powerful attack skill, it was too powerful and the practitioners of such a deadly attacking skill would risk overextending themselves. Gu Tianle had used it consecutively four times in a row and the backlash for overextending was severe internal injuries!

Ji Lingfeng stumbled onto the ground again and her face turned extremely pale!

But before Gu Tianle and the rest of the pugilists even knew what was happening, she had suddenly picked herself up again!

She grabbed Yi Ping and both quickly disappeared over the high walls of the Gongsun Residence in an instant!

As if Yi Ping extraordinary endurance was not astounding enough, many of the pugilists were further amazed at her extraordinary swiftness movement skill! They had never seen anyone vanished from sight this fast!

Chapter 17: The Secret Celestial Group

Xiao Shuai said to Ding Yunzi, "She is not here."

Ding Yunzi asked, "Could she be in that another location?"

Xiao Shuai said, "No matter what, we must leave this town as soon as possible."

Ding Yunzi asked, "Master, you are injured?"

Xiao Shuai shook his head, "But I have expended a great deal of my martial power. If there is another opponent like Gongsun Bai here, I cannot fight at my peak."

Ding Yunzi said coolly, "There shouldn't be anyone that can contest with Master. If she is not here, surely she could be in that another location? That is the most suspicious location after all. We should investigate it."

Xiao Shuai said, "I have a very uneasy feeling about that villa. I don't have that feeling for a very long time. Call it instinct if you want but sometimes we need to know our limits and be extra vigilant. That Gongsun Bai had thought that he was invincible and became careless. If he had been more wary, the final outcome would be hard to predict."

Ding Yunzi said, "Master, you are too caution. At your martial level, no one is your match anymore. Even without me, you can still defeat Gongsun Bai on your own."

Xiao Shuai said, "You are too young. Even an invincible fighter will have a moment of weakness and if the enemies have the heart to kill you, they will have already studied your weakness. That is why we mustn't reveal too much of our true skills to gain the best advantage in every situation."

Ding Yunzi said, "But there are only two young maidens in that villa. Surely, we have nothing to fear from them."

Xiao Shuai said, "Precisely that is why. There are too many unanswered questions about that villa. It is like they are enticing us to enter the villa."

Ding Yunzi sighed, "If I can be within three hundred paces of that villa, I may be able to know if Xiao Youxue is there…"

Xiao Shuai said solemnly, "Five hundred paces is the safe distance. Anything closer than that, we risk exposing our whereabouts."

All of a sudden, Xiao Shuai looked at the forested surroundings and sighed. "Just as I feared, they are here."

Ding Yunzi scanned the surroundings and immediately she said aloud, "There!"

She immediately unsheathed her long sword, whirled it several times and threw it as a flying sword in front of her!

Her flying sword flew into the dark recess of the forest and there was a mighty jarring sound as her flying sword struck against something metallic.

Ding Yunzi had extended her fingers out and to her surprise; her flying sword did not rebound back. It had simply vanished.

Xiao Shuai looked intently at the direction that she had thrown her flying sword and said, "They are still there and they are no ordinary opponents…"

Ding Yunzi immediately raised her scabbard in front of her in a defensive posture as she raised her fingers into the sword fingers stance. Even without a sword in her hands, she could still kill with her fingers and scabbard alone!

Two lookalike young maidens appeared from view out from the forest and walked very slowly towards them.

They were in black velvet silk dresses. Their black dresses were almost translucent and their faces were very white in contrast to their dressing. In their hands, they had brandished their long swords.

Xiao Shuai immediately brandished his long sword, whirled it in a circular motion and threw it towards them!

He said aloud, "I will like to see how you can deflect my flying sword!"

His flying sword flew and burst with startling speed against them!

The two young maidens immediately raised their long swords in front of them and when the flying sword struck their swords with a mighty impact; it was mysterious seized by another circular force as it spins in a reverse direction before dropping to the ground!

The two young maidens had taken three steps back as they deflected the mighty force of the flying sword with their Divine Emerald Skill using their long swords!

Xiao Shuai muttered, "These two young maidens have the martial power to withstand my flying sword directly?"

But even before they could steady their footing, Xiao Shuai and Ding Yunzi had immediately saw an opening as they filled their scabbard with their martial power and sent it flying towards the two young maidens at the same time!

The two young maidens gasped at the same time, "Oh no…"

It was because their opponents had seized the opportunity to launch another attack at the same time even before they could steady themselves. They had never fought against opponents that would react with such astonishing speed!

But to the surprise of Xiao Shuai and Ding Yunzi, just when their scabbards were about to strike their targets, another young maiden had appeared in front of the beautiful twins and deflected their scabbards to the other direction with her sleeve!

This newcomer was very beautiful and had the grace of a goddess. It was as though she was not from this mortal realm. Even Xiao Shuai who prided himself on his willpower was somehow moved by her sight…

It was not her unearthly beauty that caused Xiao Shuai and Ding Yunzi to be taken aback but they were startled at how easy she had deflected their scabbards!

It was because their flying scabbard technique was also one of their martial clan most powerful secret techniques and was even more powerful than their flying sword technique!

Even though their flying scabbards were a straightforward attack, it was charged with their entire martial power and deflecting it was even harder than their flying swords. Much of their martial power was lost when the flying sword was spinning. But for their flying scabbards, the martial power retention rate was much higher and it was three times as fast!

Moreover they had thrown their flying scabbards at the same time. Deflecting one of their flying scabbards was difficult enough and moreover there were two…

And this young maiden from nowhere had simply deflected their flying scabbards with just her sleeves!

When Xiao Shuai had recovered from his initial surprise and looked at her face, he was even more startled even as Ding Yunzi analyzed coolly, "They are using a secret technique that is similar to the Invincible Divine Force. No one can deflect our secret techniques with just their martial power alone and if I am not wrong, they are using the Divine Emerald Skill, the nemesis skill of all missile projectiles. And in this fraternity, only the Eternal Ice Palace knows this secret skill."

Ding Yunzi had raised her right hand and moved her little finger slightly. As soon as Xiao Shuai nodded, she would attack again with another secret technique of the Virtuous Palace!

The newcomer was indeed Shui Yixian the Celestial Fairy. The two young maidens at her back were Shui Yujian the Jade Sword Fairy and Shui Meijian the Beautiful Sword Fairy.

The Celestial Fairy nodded slightly and said, "Your analysis is correct. We are indeed from the Eternal Ice Palace. Only the Virtuous Palace is capable of using the Flying Sword Technique. It seems that this battle between the Eternal Ice Palace and the Virtuous Palace is inevitable."

Ding Yunzi said coolly, "If you think that we are weaponless and defenseless, you are making a great mistake…"

Shui Meijian interrupted coldly, "Oh yes? The Penetrating Hands, the Penetrating Slash Technique, the Divine Virtuous Force, the Golden Impervious Skill…right, I am so afraid."

Shui Yujian smiled. She knew that her sister was purposely provoking her opponent. She immediately took a deep breath as she amplified her senses with the Dual Inertness Intricacy, a skill that she had newly acquired.

Ding Yunzi turned pale as she asked, "How did you know?"

Shui Yujian had immediately sensed that the heartbeat of this maiden had increased and she was nervous now. She blinked at Shui Meijian, hinting her of the information.

Xiao Shuai sighed deeply, "It is because I am the one that leak it…"

Ding Yunzi was shocked as she asked, "Master? You told the Eternal Ice Palace our secret techniques?"

The Celestial Fairy begun to look at Xiao Shuai closely, "You are Brother Shuai?"

Xiao Shuai laughed and he began to tremble, "Indeed I am. Sister Xian'Er, you have not really changed at all…I almost couldn't recognize you all these years. Or rather, you have become more and more beautiful. How long have it been now? Fifty years? I have never known that you are from the Eternal Ice Palace or else I would surely look for you there…"

The Celestial Fairy averted her eyes, "I didn't know you are from the Virtuous Palace as well…"

Shui Yujian, Shui Meijian and Ding Yunzi were stunned that their protégé mistress and master had actually knew each other!

Ding Yunzi was even more startled, "This young maiden is actually the same age as my protégé master?! But she looks so young…" She began to look at Shui Meijian and Shui Yujian who looked equally young as well…

Xiao Shuai laughed bitterly, "Fate plays a cruel joke on all of us. Where is Han Shaodong? Are you together with him now?"

The Celestial Fairy shifted uncomfortably as she said, "The last time that I had seen him was also the last time that I had seen you."

Xiao Shuai laughed, "That is good news to me. You have left so suddenly that day…"

Ding Yunzi had never seen her protégé master laughed so merrily before.

Fifty years ago, a group of pugilists were all that were left from the aftermath of a bloody battle over a lost martial treasure trove. The survivors of that bloody aftermath were all above average pugilists. The reasons that they had survived were because they were not as greedy as the others or because they were smarter.

It was because the underground palace ruins that they had found had too many deadly traps and many had died.

Han Shaodong looked at the nine remaining pugilists; Xiao Shuai and Shui Yixian were among the group as well. He said in disbelief, "We risk our lives for just one small flask and some copper coins?"

Xiao Shuai said, "If you don't want that flask, you can give it to me. Maybe the pills in the flask are worth more than anyone of you think it is."

Han Shaodong laughed and he tossed the flask to him, "I will not have the courage to eat some unknown pills. They can be poison you know."

Xiao Shuai laughed, "Or miraculous pills you know."

Shui Yixian smiled softly, "So what are we going to do now? Continue the fight that some of us have left unfinished earlier?"

Xiao Shuai turned and looked at everyone, "It is a coincidental that we have all survived until this point and yet at the same time, we are all reluctant to reveal our true identities. We may not be friends as we may come from over all the fraternity and even the names that we use may be faked. But let us introduce ourselves anyway. You can call me Brother Shuai, Shuai being handsome!"

Shui Yixian laughed softly as she covered her mouth with her hands, "Hello Handsome!"

Xiao Shuai laughed, "Beauty, now it is your turn to introduce yourself. I am sure everyone would like to know your name. I had seen you kicking the asses of so many pugilists during the past week. Everyone seems eager to know your name."

Shui Yixian looked at everyone and she started to stammer, "I…err…Yixian…no…you can call me Xian'Er."

Everyone thought it was funny. It seemed like she was not an experienced liar and everyone secretly made a quick mental note to remember her real name.

Han Shaodong said, "I am just a nameless nobody in the fraternity. I am not from the orthodox clans or from the unorthodox clans. My name is Han Shaodong."

Another young pugilist said, "That is right. Today, no matter where we are from, we should be friends. Actually for us orthodox clans, it is quite disgraceful for others to know we are fighting over a fraternity treasure…"

Han Shaodong said, "You just tell us that you are from the orthodox clan."

The young pugilist was startled and he looked embarrassed.

Han Shaodong assured him, "Don't worry. We will not force you to tell us your clan of origin. I am sure many of us here are also not using their clan skills too."

The young pugilist said, "You can call me 'Future Sword Saint'. That will be my fraternity name."

Everyone laughed.

Another pugilist said, "Great aspiration! You can call me 'The Invincible Ironfist'!"

Another young pugilist said, "You can call me Tian Kui!"

When all the pugilists had finished introducing themselves, Xiao Shuai said. "Let us form a secret group and do something crazy for a while. We should at least do something that is earthshaking in the fraternity."

Han Shaodong asked, "What do you propose?"

Xiao Shuai said, "We need a leader of course. But if anyone wants to back off now, they can do it now. When the secret group is formed, we must be bound by our agreements. What does everyone think?"

The Invincible Ironfist smiled, "If Sister Xian'Er is in the group, I will join for sure."

Shui Yixian stammered, "When did I become your sister?"

The Invincible Ironfist laughed merrily, "If you are in the group, then you naturally will be our Sister Xian'Er."

The Future Sword Saint added hastily, "If she is in, I will be in the group too."

Han Shaodong said to Shui Yixian solemnly, "What do you think?"

Shui Yixian looked at everyone one by one. She could tell from their passionate eyes that they were all waiting for her to say yes to the idea.

Shui Yixian sighed and said, "Do I even have a choice?"

The idea of a secret group intrigues everyone!

Xiao Shuai said, "Excellent! Now we need to select a leader from among us or else we be a pile of loose sands. We also need to be bound by our holistic agreement on never to reveal our identities and what we have done in this group. Does everyone agree with it?"

The Future Sword Saint said, "We must never kill the innocents too or go against the martial righteousness."

The Invincible Ironfist said, "We should really restraint from harming anyone. But as for martial righteousness, we already broken that protocol or else we wouldn't be here."

Xiao Shuai said, "Agree! Unless someone really wants us dead or else we must not kill anyone needlessly."

Everyone nodded eagerly and was eager to know what exactly Xiao Shuai planned to do.

Han Shaodong said, "It seems that you are our candidate for the group leadership. Anyone else want to be the group leader? I am all for Brother Shuai to be the group leader."

The Invincible Ironfist said, "I nominate Xian'Er of course!"

Everyone looked at the Invincible Ironfist in shocked horror.

Tian Kui said, "What if she wants us to go up to the Heavenly Mountains to pick the Heavenly Mountain Lotus and other trivial things?"

Shui Yixian sighed softly, "Don't you worry about that part. That will be the last thing in my mind."

It seemed that Han Shaodong, Xiao Shuai and Shui Yixian got the most number of votes. In the end, Xiao Shuai was nominated the group leader.

Xiao Shuai said, "We must show great unity in the show of adversity. Only then can our group be the most feared and powerful in the fraternity."

To prove his point, he took out a chopstick and broke it into halve. "If we are individual, our fates will be the same as this lone chopstick and will be easy to break by others."

Next he took out a bunch of chopsticks and passed it to Shui Yixian, "Now try snapping these chopsticks with your fingers."

Shui Yixian took the bunch of chopsticks from him and snapped it into halves effortlessly.

Xiao Shuai and everyone looked at Shui Yixian in stunned silence…

Shui Yixian looked at Xiao Shuai and asked, "Err…I am not supposed to break it?"

The Future Sword Saint asked merrily, "So what the morale of this story?"

Xiao Shuai said after a while, "If we are like a bunch of weak chopsticks, we will be easily be broken by others."

He picked up a thick iron pole-arm from the ground and passed it to Shui Yixian, "But if we are as united as this iron pole-arm, then nothing can ever breaks us!"

Everyone began to shout eagerly and clapping when suddenly the iron-pole arm was snapped into half by Shui Yixian.

Everyone looked at her again in stunned silence.

Shui Yixian protested innocently, "Err…this iron pole-arm is of poor inferior quality…"

Xiao Shuai said, "You know, I totally agree with you that this iron pole-arm is of poor inferior quality…"

The Invincible Ironfist nodded, "Very, very inferior that even a lady can break it…"

Han Shaodong said, "Let's hope that our leadership is not equally inferior too."

Xiao Shuai looked at everyone and smiled bitterly, "You know, even before this leadership has officially started, it is so hard already."

Everyone laughed.

Now that the ice between the various pugilists had been broken, Xiao Shuai suggested. "We will first need a fearsome name for the group. I have already a name in mind."

Han Shaodong asked, "Which is?"

Xiao Shuai smiled mysteriously, "The Celestials from the Celestial Palace!"

Tian Kui said, "We are using the name of the Celestial Palace and slandering them?"

Xiao Shuai laughed, "Indeed. No one really knows if the Celestial Palace actually did exist so it doesn't really matter."

Tian Kui said, "I am from the Western Fraternity. My grand protégé master says it does exist…"

Xiao Shuai said, "Whether it exists or not, it doesn't matter. This is the perfect name for us to spread our havoc!"

The Future Sword Saint asked, "Havoc? What kind of havoc?"

Xiao Shuai smiled mysteriously, "We will raid the various martial clans and sects for their secret manuals and then put it back secretly. We will start with the Infinity Sword Clan."

The Future Sword Saint said hurriedly, "You can't do it. That is something that only an unorthodox clan will do, not us!"

Xiao Shuai laughed, "Remember, we are not aligned to either now. We will put it back as soon as we have finished with it. So why not?"

The Future Sword Saint said, "That is because that is my clan you are talking…"

Everyone turned and looked at the Future Sword Saint, "So you are from the Infinity Sword Clan!"

The Future Sword Saint looked awkward.

In the end, the fake Celestial Palace group was still formed. In less than six months, virtually the entire central plain martial clans were turned upside down by the Celestial Palace. In years to come, the terror effect of the Celestial Palace was still remembered by many of the pugilists.

After six months, the terror of the Celestial Palace mysteriously disappeared from the face of the fraternity as though it had never started.

One of the main reasons was that Shui Yixian was caught finally for sneaking out of the Eternal Ice Palace and was forced to return to the Eternal Ice Palace by her older protégé sister Shui Yichi. After her departure, Xiao Shuai lost interest in maintaining the group and without Shui Yixian to support the group, they begun to lose some of their founding members too.

Xiao Shuai had never expected to find her again after fifty years…

He said, "Why is that you have not aged at all?"

The Celestial Fairy said expressionless, "I had not age at all when I was with everyone and my age then was already twice as old as the majority of you…"

Xiao Shuai muttered, "No wonder, you were always so cold to the whole lot of us except for Han Shaodong. Did he know?"

The Celestial Fairy replied, "No, he doesn't."

Xiao Shuai said, "I don't mind at all, you know…"

The Celestial Fairy interrupted coldly and looked at Ding Yunzi, "Why did you send her to the Heavenly Mountains to kill me?"

Xiao Shuai was startled, "I didn't."

Ding Yunzi said, "I have never been to the Heavenly Mountains."

The Celestial Fairy asked again, "You didn't? Who else knows the Penetrating Hands?"

Xiao Shuai sighed, "I think I know who you are looking for now. My late wife had a feud with the Eternal Ice Palace and my daughter inherited her hatred…"

The Celestial Fairy said coldly, "Where is she now?"

Xiao Shuai said, "I am also looking for her now. She has stolen something very important from me."

The Celestial Fairy said slowly, "I will find her and kill her."

Xiao Shuai looked at her into her eyes, "Xian'Er, you have changed. If you want to kill my daughter, don't blame me. I am now the protégé master of the Virtuous Palace. The martial skills and techniques that I have learnt and known exceeded your imagination. Even though your martial progression was higher than us in the past but you do not fight dirty. Your fighting style is too dead. That is your disadvantage and my advantage."

Chapter 18: Xiao Youxue

The Celestial Fairy looked intently at Xiao Shuai.

She had first taken a liking to him in the past for he was courageous, humorous and full of wiles. He had even warn her to be careful of the Penetrating Hands and similar types of martial arts should she encountered it in the future.

But the more she had spent time with him, the more she realized that he was just a selfish person and there were many things that he had intentional concealed.

In the end, everyone was like a tool to him to be made use of.

That was when she began to distance herself from him and became closer to Han Shaodong.

She asked softly, "Why is that when you have mentioned your daughter, you have such a murderous intent in your eyes? It seems that you want her dead more than I."

Xiao Shuai smiled bitterly, "That is because she dared to hinder my martial progression and dare to break the rules of the Virtuous Palace or else I would have mastered the Divine Virtuous Force by now. I can't allow you to kill her before I do. I will drink her blood and eat her heart when I find her."

The Celestial Fairy said coldly, "You are not a good father…"

She began to turn back as she said softly, "Yu'Er and Mei'Er, let's us go. He is not worth our time to bother with."

Xiao Shuai called out, "Xian'Er, don't go. You have not told me why you want my daughter dead? I am sure with your state of divinity, you will not go around the fraternity just to find a single person even if she had slight you…"

The Celestial Fairy said softly as she disappeared into the darkness with her protégés, "It is because she wants to kill someone dear to my heart…"

Xiao Shuai stood on the same spot for a long time. When he had heard what she had said, his heart became very heavy.

Ding Yunzi called out gently to him, "Master? Are you alright?"

Xiao Shuai clenched his fists as he muttered, "Then I will have to kill that person first. Xian'Er, why can't you understand my difficulties?"

Ding Yunzi asked quietly, "Master, are we letting them off just like that?"

Xiao Shuai stared at Ding Yunzi, "Then you are expecting me to kill her?"

Ding Yunzi kept quiet.

When Ji Lingfeng had escaped from the Gongsun Manor, she had picked an unlikely route to escape her pursuers. If she had gone in the direction of Xiao Shuai, perhaps she could have chance upon Xiao Shuai and the Celestial Fairy…

Ji Lingfeng put her hand over her chest as she coughed out blood! She dropped Yi Ping and immediately collapsed besides a shady tree.

She hoped that her attack would be fatal to Gu Tianle so that she could avenge for her father.

Her breathing was now weak and her vital energies erratic. She was now at a risk of losing her life unless she could restore her vital energy flow.

That was because immediately after using the Asper Horizon Hand earlier in the grand hall of the Gongsun Manor despite her internal injuries, she did not pause to restore her vital breath and to circular the flow of her vital energies to restore its balance.

Instead, she had further stressed her erratic vital energies by forcefully using all her remaining vital energies as she grabbed Yi Ping to escape the Gongsun Manor.

She was even more worried about Yi Ping than herself.

Disregarding her own safety, she placed her left hand on Yi Ping's back and begun to transfer her own vital energies into him while mediating the Divine Revelation at the same time to restore her own vital energy flow.

She was worried for Yi Ping. That was because he had been unconscious for some time and even if he could regain his consciousness, he would be paralyzed for life...

That was why she was not wasting any more precious time.

But as her own vital energy flow had not yet been restored, her efforts took a great toil on her body and she began to feel giddy after some time!

She gritted her teeth and thought, "I mustn't fall asleep... If I fall asleep now, both of us will die here." No matter what happens, she was determined not to lose Yi Ping even at her own expenses!

Even though her resolute was great but her body could not cope and she was now in a half daze state...

All of a sudden, she sniffed a strong fragrant scent from behind her. A beautiful slender hand was on Yi Ping's back as well as her back!

She opened her eyes and saw a lady in a straw veiled hat that was besides her!

The lady in the veiled straw hat said calmly, "Don't you worry; I will do my best to save him. You should try to recuperate for yourself first."

The voice of the lady in the veiled straw hat was young but Ji Lingfeng could feel a soothing transference of vital energy that halts the reversal of her blood flow. This mysterious young lady internal strength was not weak!

She quickly seized the opportunity to lift a vital breath with the Divine Revelation Skill from the energy infusion and began to circulate it throughout her vitality channels, restoring the broken vital energy flow.

After a long while, her breathing had become normal and the feeling of death had departed! She thought, "Lucky!"

She opened her eyes and looked at the mysterious lady in the veiled straw hat. She was still transferring her internal strength into Yi Ping and treating his internal injuries. It was a monument task because Yi Ping had completely lost conscious and the internal injuries sustained by Yi Ping were not light!

Moreover he was also suffering from external wounds and was still bleeding profusely...

Ji Lingfeng had sustained severe internal injuries herself. Even though she had restored her vital energy flow, her martial power would be drastically reduced and it would be a full three months of intensive mediation cultivation before she could fully recovered!

One could imagine how many folds Yi Ping internal injuries had been! He had exerted himself much more severely than anyone could have imagined. It was a miracle that he did not die on the spot!

Who was this mysterious lady? Ji Lingfeng sighed in her heart. She thought that she had finally found the man that she could love and find happiness in. But this was one too many for her young tender heart to take.

A martial practitioner would never give or expended their vital energy strength needlessly, which was also called internal strength to another. It was because vital energy strength once expended was difficult to recuperate back.

Not only would it put the practitioner in danger if interrupted, they would also expose themselves in danger while recuperating. At the same time, while waiting for the lost vital energies to recover, the practitioner could not practice any internal martial arts or else they would only endanger their own lives, hence slowing down their martial progression!

But this mysterious lady was readied to expend her vital energies for Yi Ping. If she was not somewhat related to him or love him enough to make the sacrifice, she would not risk it. Moreover Yi Ping was dying and her efforts would likely to be futile.

She clutched her heart in sorrow as she thought of this. Earlier, she had pushed herself to her very limits and even if she had failed, she would die together with him. But now, watching Yi Ping dying besides her and with another lady was heart-wrenching for her!

After a long time, the mysterious lady said. "I manage to protect his heart. He will live for now but his internal injuries are simply too heavy. I will try to restore his broken vital channels but if that fail, he would be paralyzed for life."

At this, Ji Lingfeng could not resist asking, "Who are you? Why are you sacrificing so much just for him? Do you have any relations with him?" These were the questions that she been asking herself and now, she could not resist asking anymore.

The mysterious lady sighed and said melancholy, "Who I am? I am just a nameless nobody to him."

Ji Lingfeng said, "At least you should have a name…"

The mysterious lady said with a great sorrow, "Xiao Youxue is my name…it is a cursed name."

Ji Lingfeng made a quick guess, "You like him but there is a feud between the two of you?"

Xiao Youxue nodded gently.

Ji Lingfeng sighed, "Can it be resolved?"

Xiao Youxue shook her head, "It is impossible. This is a blood feud."

Ji Lingfeng said, "Yi Ping has a magnanimous heart and is kind. Surely nothing is impossible to resolve."

Xiao Youxue replied coolly, "Will you forgive the killer of your wife? And still likes her?"

Ji Lingfeng gasped. The yellow dressed maiden that Yi Ping had mentioned to her before was her! She was the one that Yi Ping had been searching for. She was also the one that had fought with her brother two years ago!

This revelation shocked her. She had thought that both of them had a blood feud and that both of them would be at odds with each other!

She had never expected that this maiden would also be in love with him…

Ji Lingfeng asked, "Did he know?"

Xiao Youxue shook her head and said, "He don't even know my name and who I am. He only knows that I am the one that he is looking for to avenge his late wife."

Ji Lingfeng said, "You can hide it from him. Perhaps the both of you can be together…"

Xiao Youxue said, "I will never be able to live with that feeling of guilt in my heart. Moreover…"

She paused for a while before looking intently at her, "I can tell that you like him a lot. And maybe both of you are a couple already."

Ji Lingfeng said, "Don't misunderstand! We are not."

Xiao Youxue said, "Is that so? That you are willing to sacrifice yourself for him and you don't like him? I don't believe."

Ji Lingfeng was silence.

Xiao Youxue added, "Even though we are strangers, I have been completely honest with you."

Ji Lingfeng melancholy said, "Indeed you have. I am sorry but we are indeed not a couple and not in any relation. He doesn't like me at all."

Xiao Youxue eyed her intently before she replied, "Surely he is blind!"

Ji Lingfeng smiled, "Yes he is blind!"

But her mood turned somber and she said, "I am from a heretic sect and we are simply from two opposite worlds. There will soon be a battle for supremacy between the orthodox fraternity and the unorthodox fraternity. I don't even know if I can live through this."

Xiao Youxue nodded as she added, "There may be still a way for the two of you to be together. If both of you are willing to quit the martial fraternity, then you can be together."

Ji Lingfeng added, "That is not possible for me. I can never leave my brother in this moment of crisis. There will be a lot of bloodshed and no matter where I go after that, the exponents of the fraternity will follow me."

She smiled and added, "Moreover, like you say. He is blind and he does not like me."

Xiao Youxue was silence. She had seen them in the streets earlier and they were talking like old friends. When she had overheard that they were going to the Honor Manor to settle a score against Gongsun Bai, she had immediately feared for Yi Ping.

Therefore, she took a personal gambit to lure Xiao Shuai and Ding Yunzi who was hot on her heels to the Honor Manor…

All of a sudden, Xiao Youxue said. "I realize that you seem to recover rather quickly. You take only three hours to balance your vital energy flow and I am expecting something like twelve hours or more."

Ji Lingfeng said, "That is why I am able to chat with you!"

Xiao Youxue suddenly turned somber and said, "I hope that you keep our conversation to yourself and not to divulge anything to him. I don't want him to know anything."

Ji Lingfeng said, "I promise you but you must not tell him what I told you too."

Xiao Youxue asked, "Not to tell him what?"

Ji Lingfeng thought she was clever but this maiden was even cleverer. This was the first time that she had been outmaneuvered for words!

She sighed and said unwillingly, "Hmph, you really mustn't tell him that I like him!"

Xiao Youxue chuckled softly, "I promise you then!"

Ji Lingfeng sighed again, "Or else I need to dig myself a hole in the ground and covered my face with dirt!"

All of a sudden Xiao Youxue said, "Weird. Yi Ping seems to have two vital energies in his body. The first one was broken but there is another weaker vital energy that is more intact."

Ji Lingfeng asked hurriedly, "That means he has a hope?"

Xiao Youxue nodded, "I have never seen or heard anything like this. But yes, there is a hope!"

Ji Lingfeng could discreetly see Xiao Youxue tears dripping onto her dress even though she was veiled.

Xiao Youxue said, "The weaker vital energy must be the 'Icy Heavenly Tears Intricate Energy'. It has taken less considerably damage and if I can get it to back to its proper meridian channels…"

Ji Lingfeng heart sunk. She interrupted sadly, "The 'Icy Heavenly Tears Intricate Energy' is different from normal intricate energy. Only the practitioners of the Eternal Ice Palace practiced the 'Icy Heavenly Tears Intricate Energy'. Only a practitioner of the 'Icy Heavenly Tears intricate Energy' can channel to another person with the 'Icy Heavenly Tears Intricate Energy'."

Xiao Youxue said, "I just happen to practice the 'Icy Heavenly Tears Intricate Energy'."

Ji Lingfeng asked startled, "You know the Icy Heavenly Tears!?"

Xiao Youxue said, "That is a long story. My grandmother was the direct protégé of the Protégé Mistress of the Eternal Ice Palace in the past." That was all that she could say for now. That was the start of her tragedy and her family tragedy.

All of a sudden, she gasped again, "What is it? His vital signs seem to be returning so soon! This is indeed extraordinary!"

Ji Lingfeng asked, "What happens?"

Xiao Youxue said, "As soon as I linked the 'Icy Heavenly Tears Intricate Energy', his scattered vital energies seem to increase again. It is as though, it is regenerating on its own accord! But where does the source of the vital energy come from?"

Ji Lingfeng said excitedly, "Could it be that, he has accidentally cleared his Conception Vessel and the Governing Vessel?"

Xiao Youxue was startled. He had cleared his Conception Vessel and the Governing Vessel at such a young age?

Xiao Youxue took out her pouch and took a small golden pill and popped it into Yi Ping mouth as she once again exercised her internal energy into his body.

Ji Lingfeng said, "That golden pill is the great rejuvenation golden pill?"

Xiao Youxue said, "That's right. That is the last one I have. It has the ability to speed healing and added to the martial power growth of the practitioner."

Ji Lingfeng was flabbergasted. The 'Great Rejuvenation Golden Pills' were one of the seven treasures of the martial fraternity. Legends said that three hundred years ago, the Sage King, the top exponent of the entire fraternity only made eight such 'Great Rejuvenation Golden Pills' towards the end of his life. That was because these eight golden pills required him to sacrifice his entire vital energy into making it!

The whereabouts of the 'Great Rejuvenate Golden Pills' remained a beautiful legend.

How did Ji Lingfeng know about it?

That was because when she was only seven year old, she suffered from an illness that almost took her life. Her brother, who was twenty years her senior scouted the entire fraternity for the 'Great Rejuvenate Golden Pill' to save her. The difficulties and sacrifices that he had to pay to obtain it were never mentioned to her but she knew. How could she not know? Her brother had undergone a huge change after that.

That was why she could not abandon her brother even if the entire orthodox martial fraternity decided to battle against him.

When Xiao Youxue popped the last of the 'Great Rejuvenation Golden Pill' to Yi Ping, her eyes had immediately turned watery. It was not because she could not bear to give it to him but it reminded her of her mother's death.

When her mother had failed to merge the Icy Heavenly Tears Intricate Energy together with the Divine Virtuous Force Intricate Energy and was dying, her father Xiao Shuai refused to give her the 'Great Rejuvenation Golden Pills' as a remedy.

He simply said in a cold and calculating manner to everyone in the Virtuous Palace, "This is just a gambit. Whether the 'Great Rejuvenation Golden Pill' will save her or not is not known and we be wasting a precious golden pill. You have no idea how hard it is for me to obtain these 'Great Rejuvenation Golden Pills'. I have already told her of the risks of practicing the Divine Virtuous Force too early but she simply refused to listen."

At that time, Xiao Youxue was only thirteen and she was heart-broken by her father cold calculating attitude.

She could never understand how her father would be so heartless.

Xiao Shuai had obtained it in an underground palace ruins and had almost lost his life for it. When he had formed the secret celestial group, no one else seemed to know how valuable these golden pills were.

He would need as many of those golden pills when he started to practice the Divine Virtuous Force very soon. The Divine Virtuous Force was the most epitome secret martial skill of the Virtuous Palace. In order to practice it, the practitioner's internal strength would need to be as pure and as strong as possible. If the practitioner have less than sixty years of martial power, it was dangerous to even begin it.

That was why the secret skills of the Virtuous Palace focused on secret techniques rather than martial power. It was because they simply could not afford to sustain any injuries as internal injuries would affect their future martial progression by many more years!

The protégés of the Virtuous Palace would seek to end a fight as soon as possible with the least effort and lured their opponents into a false state of security, so that they would strike with complete surprise.

Their Flying Sword Technique was just a decoy for them to approach their opponents and lure them into a false sense of security. Thereafter, they would kill their opponents with the Penetrating Hands, their Flying Scabbard Technique or with their invisible sword!

This invisible sword was actually a foldable blade that all protégés of the Virtuous Palace had around their waist and disguised as a belt!

If their opponents had completely thought that they were weaponless after they had hurled their swords, then they would be making a huge and fatal mistake!

Even though she was his daughter but he had never imparted to her the Flying Sword Techniques. Instead he had imparted to her only the Penetrating Hands.

The Flying Sword Technique was one of the first martial skills that all protégés of the Virtuous Palace should start with. She had never understood why her very own father had forbid her and even forbid others to teach her this secret technique.

She had two older step-brothers who are more than twenty years older than her, Xiao Da the eldest and Xiao Yao who was very distant from her. She supposed to have another older half-sister that she had never seen but who had married off before she was born.

On the other hand, she was very close to Ding Yunzi who was like a close sister to her and Xiao Fei who was her cousin.

Before her mother had passed away, she had secretly instructed her, "Be careful of Yunzi. I always feel that she has an ulterior motive. This is the Golden Impervious Body Divine Skill that I have secretly copied from the martial vault of the Virtuous Palace. You are to practice it as a preventive measure against Yunzi. You mustn't let others know you are in possession of this skill so that they will not be on their guard against it."

Xiao Youxue said, "I have heard from father that if we do not reach the advance stage of the Divine Virtuous Force, it is futile to even practice the Golden Impervious Body Divine Skill."

Her mother nodded, "It is true. That is why you have to steal the golden pills from him. That may accelerate your internal strength for you to begin practicing the Icy Heavenly Tears Skill first. Whether you have the martial willpower and the acumen to comprehend the Golden Impervious Body Divine Skill, it is up to providence. But don't forget to get even with the Eternal Ice Palace…"

Xiao Youxue was afraid, "The Icy Heavenly Tears Skill that we got is incomplete and is only for the first five stages…mother I have no confidence at all…"

Her mother said, "You got to use your wits. The Icy Heavenly Tears Skill at its highest level has a fatal weakness and Shui Yixian will lose her martial power once every thirty-six years. That will be the best time to you to settle our family scores with her."

Her mother smiled bitterly at her on her dying breath. Even though she had never seen Shui Yixian before and had only heard of her name from her mother, her hatred for her was absolute! It was because whenever her husband was drunk, he would mutter her name!

She had a strong suspicious that the 'Yixian and Xian'Er that her husband Xiao Shuai was calling out for was in fact Shui Yixian. When she had questioned him about her, he refused to say anything. Therefore she had also deliberately withhold her suspicious to herself and refused to give Xiao Shuai a glimmer of hope.

That was why she wanted this Shui Yixian to disappear from the face of the earth as well. This Shui Yixian had caused her mother Shui Yisi to be driven out of the Eternal Ice Palace in disgrace and now she had also taken her husband's heart from her.

When the opportunity had arisen three years ago, Xiao Youxue had secretly stolen Xiao Shuai's golden pills when he was in a martial retreat; he was in the crucial stage of reaching the advance level of the Divine Virtuous Force. Without the golden pills, he had to wait another twenty years for the breakthrough.

She had simply walked into his secret chamber while he was in deep mediation and stolen the golden pills right in front of him!

In order to do that, every night for three years, she trained her lightness skill until she could walk in absolute quietness and in time to come, that became her feat!

She had never forgiven her father for indirectly causing her mother's death therefore she had pretended to be docile and stolen all his 'Great Rejuvenation Golden Pills', leaving none for him in his crucial martial level stage.

When he had found out about the theft of his golden pills, he had flown into a maddening rage and had ordered all the protégés of the Virtuous Palace to find her.

She had consumed two of the three golden pills in the past three years. The first time was immediately after she had stolen the golden pill to increase her martial strength and the second time when she was in the final stage of the Golden Impervious Body Divine Skill.

It had been three years since she had left the Virtuous Palace.

During the first year, she was lucky to meet Xiao Fei, her cousin who warned her to be extra careful for her father had mobilized all the clan elders, including her half-brothers to hunt her down.

After that, she was always moving from place to place as she devised a stratagem against Shui Yixian at the same time. She was the one that spread rumor of her death and of the fabulous martial treasures of the Eternal Ice Palace to entice the greedy pugilists.

Why was that when she had killed Shui Yixian, she had not felt happy at all but filled with sorrowful regrets?

Chapter 19: The Divine Dragon Pill

When Yi Ping opened his eyes, he saw Ji Lingfeng.

His entire body was aching painfully but when he saw Ji Lingfeng again, all his pain vanished.

He muttered excitedly, "You…you are well?"

When Yi Ping looked at Ji Lingfeng, he was filled with warm tears and despite his aching pain; he was more alive than ever.

Sometimes Yi Ping feared Ji Lingfeng and did not know when she would suddenly turn against him by hitting him despite her angelic beauty. But from now on, if she were to hit him, he would never complaint anymore…

It was because when he was fighting with Gu Tianle, it was Ji Lingfeng who had taken the most powerful first strike and when they were both severely injured, it was also her that disregard her own life to save him…

Even when she had no strength, she had forced herself to bring him to safety, hence worsening her own injuries.

Even when it was crucial that she could reserve her last vital energy for herself, she had instead used all her vital energies for him…

Even though he was in a daze, he knew that she had endangered her own life four times consecutive for him!

When he remembered how much she had helped him all this while despite being nasty to him at times, he was very guilty.

All of a sudden, he realized that he had fallen in love with her and she was very beautiful, very angelic in his heart…

Ji Lingfeng blinked her eyes as she thought, "Why is he staring at me all of sudden? Usually, he can't even be bothered to look at me…"

But she quickly said, "You should worry for yourself first. Quick, lift your vital breath and circulate it throughout your body. Check if there are any obstructions…"

He did as he was told and after a while he said. "My breathing is smooth."

Just he was about to get up, he saw a lady in a veiled straw hat standing behind Ji Lingfeng. He asked, "There is someone here?"

Ji Lingfeng smiled beautifully, "She is Xiao Youxue and she has saved you."

Yi Ping got up and pay respectfully to her, "Benevolent Senior! I am in your debts. I have no way of thanking you…"

Ji Lingfeng smiled and said, "You don't have to say anything to her. She is a mute and deaf person."

Yi Ping was taken aback, "She can't hear me? Then how do you know her name?"

Ji Lingfeng laughed softly, "You are so stupid! She can write!"

Yi Ping was startled and said, "That is right! I can write to her." And immediately he started to write on the ground with a wooden stick.

He wrote simply, "I am Yi Ping. Thank you for saving me. I am in your debt…"

Xiao Youxue nodded and took away his wooden stick as she shook her hands.

Yi Ping said, "Even though you are saying that it is alright but I can never forget your benevolent kindness. I really thought that I am a goner. But when I am in a coma, I could feel a gentle touch comforting me and that is what brought me back to the mortal realm. Alas, I am so silly. You cannot hear me…"

Yi Ping suddenly thought that this veiled lady must be the most beautiful lady in the world. Her regal appearances and her willingness to expend so much effort in saving him touched him immensely.

He wrote again with his finger on the ground, "Senior, I am but a stranger but you are willing to expend your vital energy for me at your own personal risk. I am wordless and full of gratuities. If there is anything for me to do for you in future, I do anything for you."

Ji Lingfeng sighed sadly, "I saved you so many times yet I have never seen you saying anything like this to me!"

Yi Ping said, "I will also do anything for you as long as it is not against the martial code of righteousness."

Ji Lingfeng pretended to be upset, "You don't have to add that 'as long as'. Humph, why is that I seem to be receiving the lesser gratitude?"

Yi Ping said coolly, "This lady here definitely won't ask me to do anything bad."

Ji Lingfeng said defiantly, "Then I will? How prejudice!"

Yi Ping sighed with a hint of sadness in his eyes, "She is deaf and mute yet she is willing to help me at her own personal risk. Her heart is simply too kind and lack the cunning to harm anyone."

All of a sudden, Ji Lingfeng threw a pebble at him but Yi Ping caught it with his hand. She said angrily, "Hmph, so I am not kind and have the cunning to hurt others!"

Yi Ping quickly said, "That is not what I meant also…"

Ji Lingfeng threw more pebbles at him as she said, "I like to see how many times you can avoid my hits!"

Xiao Youxue took a deep breath. She had expended nearly all her vital energies and her martial power was now weak. It was going to be a long time before she could fully recover. But she was happy that Yi Ping was able to talk and even able to move!

She had been so worried for him. Even though she was able to piece together his vital energy flow, she was not sure if he was able to wake up from the concussion. His injuries had been too severe. So when he opened his eyes, she was instantly glad.

She looked in envy at Ji Lingfeng and Yi Ping. They seemed to be a pair of quarreling couple…

Ji Lingfeng said, "You probably have lost all your martial power. If we were to fight now, you probably be crying and begging me to stop. But even if you have all your strength, I can still beat you. Stop catching my pebbles or I will really imbue my martial power into the pebbles and you'll be hurt!"

Yi Ping hummed coldly, "It seems that my enemies did not kill me but I am already killed by you."

All of a sudden, he dodged a pebble imbued by her martial power by moving his head and exclaimed, "You are for real!"

Ji Lingfeng smiled, "You think I am really joking? This is called, teaching an ungrateful person a lesson! Say sorry to me to make me stop."

Yi Ping said coldly, "Never! You…That time you kicked me in the valley and now you are embarrassing me in front of others."

All of a sudden, Ji Lingfeng stopped and said nothing. She had totally forgotten about Xiao Youxue. She silently scolded herself for being insensitive.

Yi Ping was surprised that Ji Lingfeng had suddenly gone quiet and he was a little worried. Was she seriously injured but kept it to herself?

He asked with concern, "Are…are you…alright?"

Ji Lingfeng averted her alluring eyes as she said softly, "You are just an ungrateful buffalo…" And then she began to ignore him.

Yi Ping turned to Xiao Youxue and wrote with his finger again, "Can I have a look at you so that I can repay Senior in the future?"

Xiao Youxue wrote and shook her head, "I am ugly. You will surely be very disappointed."

Yi Ping wrote, "Looks are secondary. The heart is what matters."

Xiao Youxue wrote, "Don't force me."

Ji Lingfeng said coldly, "You have just opened your eyes and yet you are already lusting for others. Shameful!"

Yi Ping ignored her and wrote again, "Sorry." He removed his white emerald phoenix long sword and wrote again, "This precious long sword may not be worth a lot but if you show me this long sword again the next time, I will do anything for you!"

Xiao Youxue reluctantly took the long sword as Yi Ping had already forcefully placed it into her hands!

Yi Ping had an electrifying feeling in his hands as he held her hands. Her hands were silken smooth and that was not what he had been expecting!

He had been expecting his savior to be an old lady!

If she was not an old lady, how could she possible manage the strong and soothing vital energy flow that he had felt?

All of a sudden, Yi Ping thoughts were interrupted by the sounds of approaching footsteps.

Ji Lingfeng and Xiao Youxue were alarmed too.

They had been discovered?

Yi Ping, Ji Lingfeng and Xiao Youxue were nervous. It was because all three of them had lost most of their martial power and could not even lift sufficient vital strength to fight…

Two old men had appeared from view.

Ji Lingfeng and Yi Ping had immediately recognized them as the Shangguan Qingyun the Protégé Master of the Divine Sword Martial Clan and Yan Nanfei the Protégé Master of the Zen Sect!

Yi Ping put up a defensive posture but because he had not recovered and his wounds had started to bleed again…

Shangguan Qingyun said, "Don't be alarm. We are not here to pursue you."

Ji Lingfeng asked in surprise, "You are not?"

Yan Nanfei said, "There are three of you?"

He had recognized Yi Ping and Ji Lingfeng but not the regal lady that was wearing a veil.

Yan Nanfei said, "We are supposed to hunt you by the orders of the Honor Manor. Right now, almost all the orthodox clans that were at the Honor Manor is searching everywhere for you."

Yi Ping asked, "So that is why you are here?"

Shangguan Qingyun, "Young hero, we admire your courage but we are unable to help you openly. Even though Gongsun Bai had passed away but the Honor Manor remained influential. I will advise you to lie low for a long time with this maiden…"

Yan Nanfei sighed, "I am not sure if we did the right thing as she is from the Holy Hex Sect. A full scale battle between the orthodox and unorthodox clans may start very soon."

Yi Ping was immediately grateful as he said, "Old Seniors, I am truly grateful…"

Yan Nanfei said solemnly, "Don't be too happy yet. You need to be on the move immediately. If we can track you, so will the others and there will be many others very soon. Please take care."

Yi Ping nodded and again his spirit was burning with emotions! There was still martial justice after all!

Even Ji Lingfeng was surprised that they would be willing to let her off even though they knew that she was their enemy.

She immediately asked, "Why are you willing to spare me?"

Shangguan Qingyun said, "If I am not wrong, you must be the Holy Maiden of the Holy Hex Sect."

Ji Lingfeng nodded slowly.

Shangguan Qingyun added, "Who has never done any wrong? Moreover, just because you are from the unorthodox clan, it doesn't mean you are an evil doer. If you truly appreciate our gesture, perhaps you can advise your brother to calm the present situation down. There are too many fights and unrest these days."

Ji Lingfeng sighed, "If the orthodox clans do not provoke us, we will never think of antagonizing them either. But the Honor Manor is leading the entire orthodox fraternity against us…"

Shangguan Qingyun said solemnly, "If your brother had not killed the Old Sword Saint, the Honor Manor would never have the power to mobilize the entire orthodox clans to their banner."

Ji Lingfeng replied sharply, "My brother did not kill the Old Sword Saint. Why don't you muddle heads ask Zuo Tianyi yourself? Isn't it obvious that someone is intently sowing the discord between the unorthodox and the orthodox clans?"

Yan Nanfei asked, "Really?"

Ji Lingfeng was annoyed, "Ask Zuo Tianyi yourself. I don't wish to repeat myself. It doesn't matter if the Old Sword Saint was killed by my brother or not. His death was the perfect excuse for the Honor Manor to assert its domination over the entire fraternity."

Yan Nanfei sighed heavily, "That is true…"

Yan Nanfei took out a pouch and said, "This is our clan 'Prolonging Vital Purity Pill'. It can not only accelerate healing but also improved the purity of one's internal strength…"

Ji Lingfeng was shocked. This 'Prolonging Vital Purity Pill' was the martial treasure of the Zen Sect and was very rare. She had heard of it but she had thought that it was just a legend.

Even Shangguan Qingyun was stunned as he said, "Brother Yan, you can't even bear to consume these precious pills yourself. Why are you giving it to them?"

She took the pouch and looked saw there were two pills inside, "Yi Ping, look. This is the very good stuff."

She looked at Yan Nanfei and was courteous even though she was suspicious, "Why are you giving us this? We are after all completely strangers. Even if you admire us for our courage, there is no need to give us such precious gifts…"

Yan Nanfei said coolly, "You are wrong. We really need more heroes like this young man here who dare to challenge the Honor Manor. When I saw the two of you fighting against Gu Tianle, I suddenly remember the times when I was very young. At that time, I have no fear and plenty of courage. These pills are useless to me or to my protégés. We have all lost our courage a long time ago."

It was said that Yan Nanfei was the prominent Zen Master with a high level of cultivation. For him to give out such valuable pills away so selflessness exhibited his noble state of divinity!

Yi Ping face was wet with hot tears!

He was very touched that Yan Nanfei would offer to give them something so precious and to warn them that he really did not know what to say!

Ji Lingfeng did not hesitate and immediately took one of the pills and swallowed it.

Yi Ping was stunned by her action and thought that she was kind of rude; surely she could wait until they were gone.

Even though Yan Nanfei was a highly cultivated Zen Master but watching his precious pill being swallowed right in front of him was too much for him to bear!

Ji Lingfeng took a gambit. She was highly skilled in poisons and had resistance to poisons. Therefore she took a personal risk and had tasted it first. Finally she said, "It is safe to consume."

It was because the wars between the orthodox and unorthodox clans were not won by pure martial skills. Many times, stratagems played a part too.

Yi Ping said to her, "Lingfeng, you should trust the two seniors…"

Ji Lingfeng looked at him coldly, "You are too trusting and you will find yourself betray by your friends, just like your father."

Her words were like daggers to his heart, causing Yi Ping to be speechless.

Ji Lingfeng did not mean to hurt him but she wanted him to remember the hard rules of survival first. It was because he could not always be so lucky.

Xiao Youxue who was listening by the side was deeply moved by Ji Lingfeng as she thought, "Every single action that she has done is for his own good yet he did not know…"

All of a sudden, Yi Ping had taken the pouch and put it into her hands!

He gestured to her with his hands and pretended to pop it into his mouth to indicate to her that this pill was for her to take!

Everyone was stunned by his action…

Yan Nanfei said hurriedly, "Young hero, this pill is very precious and for you…"

Yi Ping said, "This deaf lady saves my life and has expended almost all her martial strength for my sake. I should return the favor. Without her, I will not be standing here!"

Yan Nanfei was stunned. He thought he had a high level of martial cultivation as a prominent Zen Master but this young man state of divinity was even higher than him! No wonder all these years, he wondered why he could not exceed the Old Sword Saint. Just when he thought that he had finally attained a new level of cultivation by giving away the 'Prolonging Vital Purity Pills', he met another person with an even higher cultivation than himself. And he was just a young man!

Shangguan Qingyun suddenly burst aloud with laughter, "You are all saints here. Everyone is crazy. Only I am sane!"

Everyone looked at him in stunned silence.

When Shangguan Qingyun had calmed down, he took out a pouch with trembling hand. "This is the 'Divine Dragon Pill'. Young man, you are very lucky today. Take it. But let me warn you first, you need at least sixty years of internal strength to consume this 'Divine Dragon Pill' first or you will surely die."

He forced Yi Ping to take the pouch.

Yan Nanfei was startled, "You! When and how did you get the 'Divine Dragon Pill'?"

Even Ji Lingfeng and Xiao Youxue were watching in stunned silence. It was because this 'Divine Dragon Pill' was one of the seven martial treasures that were rumored to still exist…

Xiao Youxue quickly calculated that if Yi Ping were to consume the 'Golden Rejuvenation Pill' and the 'Divine Dragon Pill' at the same time, the strength and pureness of his martial power would be so astounding that it was hard to gauge his future martial progression!

If he had taken the 'Golden Rejuvenation Pill', the 'Divine Dragon Pill' and the 'Prolonging Vital Purity Pill' at the same time…

Shangguan Qingyun suddenly turned slyly as he said, "Fifty years ago at that place…I found it and concealed it from the lot of you. I didn't tell any of you…"

All of a sudden, Yan Nanfei laughed aloud too. "You didn't tell Brother Shuai or me. No wonder you are saying you got a present for Sister Xian'Er that day and behaving like you are the lord of the world. Alas, she just vanished all of a sudden that day…"

Shangguan Qingyun said, "I think we say too much. Let us go now. The sooner they are on their way, the better for them."

When they had walked far, Yan Nanfei began to whisper in a low voice to Shangguan Qingyun, "Old buddy, so Brother Shuai is actually Xiao Shuai and he is from the Virtuous Palace…"

Shangguan Qingyun interrupted with a sigh, "Let's us that hope that the Virtuous Palace does not have the lofty ambition of dominating the fraternity…"

Shangguan Qingyun shook his head as he sighed regretfully, "I can't believe that we have raided even our own clans at that time…"

Yi Ping, Ji Lingfeng and Xiao Youxue watched as Shangguan Qingyun and Yan Nanfei had disappeared from view.

All of a sudden, Ji Lingfeng said melancholy. "Yi Ping, I have to warn and aid my brother."

Yi Ping was startled and asked, "You are going?"

Ji Lingfeng anxiously said, "That is for sure. No matter what happens, I have to go and help my brother."

Yi Ping could sense her worry as he tried to comfort her, "Your brother is now the number one top exponent now. Surely after the Old Sword Saint and Gongsun Bai, there is no one in the entire fraternity that can rival him now."

Ji Lingfeng shook her head, "How can I not be worry? A battle is different from a duel. In a battle, when you are adjusting your footing and vital breath, you can be attacked."

She added, "If you recall your battle with Jue Yuan, Zuo Tianyi and Gu Tianle, if any of the exponents watching the duel decides to attack you while you have lost your footing, you be dead!"

All of a sudden, Yi Ping recalled the situation that Shui Yixian was in as she was being surrounded by dozens of exponents. When he compared the situation he had been when he was battling Jue Yuan, Gu Tianle and Zuo Tianyi, he began to shiver.

If any exponents were to attack him with a secret projectile or behind his back when he lost his footing, he would be dead!

Ji Lingfeng looked melancholy at him with her eyes, "Even as we speak, there are at least a dozen pursuers in this vicinity that is looking for us. Someone have to distract them to another direction. And the only person that has the strength now is me."

Yi Ping said, "I can move now. Surely, we can overcome this together…"

Ji Lingfeng looked into his eyes and said coldly, "You are overestimating your current self and underestimating the pursuers! Moreover, what right do you have to ask me to stay?"

Yi Ping was startled. Indeed, what right did he have over her?

All of a sudden, Ji Lingfeng said gently, "Take care and don't die. I want you to remember me always…"

She raised her right hand slowly…

When Yi Ping saw her raising her right hand, he thought. "Is she going to hit me before she goes?"

He took a deep breath. This time he tried not to struggle even though he was not really afraid of the pain…

The painful blow that he had expected did not come. Instead, he found himself in her embrace as she kissed him gently on his lips…

He was stunned and was flustered. That was the first time he had ever been kissed on his lips by a maiden…

He began to wonder did she forget that that there was another person here…

All of a sudden, Ji Lingfeng broke free of their embrace as she vanished into the shadows, "Good bye and take care…"

No one could see her tears…

Yi Ping stared for a long time at the direction that she had vanished.

Xiao Youxue sighed in her heart, "It is obvious that he likes her…"

Yi Ping was asking himself, "What right do I have? What right do I have?"

Ji Lingfeng cried as she left, "Why doesn't he ask me to stay? Why doesn't he say he likes me? I…will surely stay…"

Chapter 20: The Thousand Year Ice Cavern

Just when Yi Ping was lamenting silently to himself as he clutched his excruciating chest as Ji Lingfeng vanished from his sight, he turned pale immediately!

It was because he had suddenly discovered that the goat skin that contained the Asper Invocations Intricate Recite Manual and the Divine Revelation Skill was missing!

The secret skill had been given to him by his father and was secretly embalmed in a goat skin.

Did he drop it?

Or did Ji Lingfeng steal it from him? She was the only one that knew that the secrets in the goat skin.

Or was it Xiao Youxue?

He turned and looked intently at Xiao Youxue who was standing in a regal manner.

He could tell that Xiao Youxue was a haughty lady and there was a forbidden aura around here but yet there was something else about her that he could not pinpoint yet.

The more he looked at her, he was sure she was not an old lady.

But she could not possibly be the one that stolen his family secret skills because she had just saved his life…

Could it be Ji Lingfeng then? Maybe it was her after all. Maybe she wanted him to go after her…

But he shook his head and said, "No matter if it is Maiden Ji or Xiao Youxue, they are both my saviors. If they really want my family secret skills, so be it. A hero should repay his benefactors with something that is dear to him."

Just when he was about to ask Xiao Youxue by asking her to run in an opposite direction from him, he heard a shout and there seemed to be a group of people that were moving rapidly in their direction.

Panicking, he grabbed Xiao Youxue as they began to move rapidly away from where they were.

Xiao Youxue gasped softly when Yi Ping had suddenly grabbed her hand. She too, had noticed that there were pursuers but was at a loss what to do as she was not supposed to hear anything.

Xiao Youxue wanted to gasp out immediately, "Let go of my hand…" But in the end, she did not say a word and instead, she was blushing as she thought. "He is holding my hand now…"

When Yi Ping had touched her hand, he got the electrifying feeling again as he thought in alarm, "Her hand is so silky and smooth?"

He almost lost his grip on her hand due to her silky hand so he gripped her hand even tighter…

He had no idea why his heart had been beating so fast.

At this time, Yi Ping and Xiao Youxue did not know that besides being pursued by the majority of the orthodox fraternity and the Honor Manor, Xiao Shuai and Shui Yixian were also looking for them at the same time.

It seemed that in this vast fraternity, there were no places for them to hide and seek refuge.

They traveled through the forest in a seeming random direction. Yi Ping had no idea where he was taking Xiao Youxue. He felt sorry for her that she was being forced to be on the run with him. Many times, he stopped to check if she was good as he was worried if she could follow his pace and fearful that she might be too tired.

But the truth was, Yi Ping was also seriously injured and he was slow while Xiao Youxue had intentional kept a slower pace than him so that he would not feel hurried.

Xiao Youxue looked keenly at his back and could not believe that she would one day walk side by side with him…

All of a sudden, Yi Ping spotted a cave along the side of a cliff. That might be a good resting and hidden place. The cave was still far and was concealed by trees but Yi Ping could see it clearly.

So he paused and wrote on the ground quickly with a stick, "Senior, there is a well concealed cave in the direction of that cliff. I think that may be a good place to seek shelter and from our pursuers."

Xiao Youxue paused in her tracks and looked at the direction that Yi Ping was pointing. Even though her translucent veil covered her eyes but she could see through it keenly. But no matter how focus she was, she could not see the concealed cave.

She thought, "His eyesight is that good?"

After Yi Ping had regained conscious, he was suddenly endowed with superior sight, hearing and perception. At first he was startled by it but he was slowly adapting to it.

Xiao Youxue nodded slowly to indicate that she was willing to follow him in that direction.

Yi Ping said to her even though she could not hear him, "Good. I am worried that we may need to do some climbing and you may not have the strength."

Yi Ping began to sweep the words that he had written on the ground quickly with a tree branches and they took off immediately.

They soon reached the cave. When they first entered the cave, Yi Ping and Xiao Youxue was startled by it. It was because the inside of the cave was freezing cold and even had ice in it while the cave outside was warm! It was not yet winter and yet this cave was like an entrance to an ice world!

Yi Ping said, "Alas! Is this the legendary 'Thousand Year Ice Cavern' that never melts even in summer?"

He was now bewildered and unsure if they should enter this cave. It was too cold and that they did not have any winter clothes.

Just as he was hesitating, Xiao Youxue walked into the cave!

Yi Ping called out after her, "Lady Xiao, wait! This cave may be dangerous!"

Then he thought, "She can't hear me. I am so silly!" But still when he ran after her, he was still calling out and waving his hands, "Lady Xiao, wait!"

Even though Xiao Youxue was walking, it took some time for him to catch up with her. He was astonished at her pace. They were now in a huge ice cavern and there was even a stream in the cave. And in the waters, there were even snow white fishes!

Yi Ping was startled at the sight of this huge ice cavern…

Xiao Youxue was astonished too. Even though she had circulated her vital energy to protect herself from the cold, she could still feel the cold. Had she lost too much of her vital strength when she treated Yi Ping or was this cave supernaturally cold?

All of a sudden, a monstrous snow white fish that was at least a hundred times bigger than the other fishes jumped out of the waters and attacked Yi Ping!

Its jaws were so big that it could snap his head.

Even though the fish was startling fast, Yi Ping and Xiao Youxue was even quicker. They reacted with a supernatural speed as both of them struck the forehead of the fish!

The monstrous fish was knocked sideway and crashed onto the floor of the cavern.

Yi Ping was surprised that the Lady Xiao was able to react so fast. If she was not there, the monstrous fish might not be knocked sideway with his strength alone!

He thought, "She has saved my life again. Why am I so unlucky that even a fish thought of bullying me? I almost become the first man to be killed by a fish in this unlikely manner."

They took a look at the monstrous fish that was still flipping on the ground. It was still alive. It seemed that they had afflicted little damage to it.

All of a sudden, Lady Xiao took out the long sword that Yi Ping had given her and slashed the fish on its body!

There was a binding flash of light as the sword hacked across the body of the monstrous fish! But to the surprise of Yi Ping, the sword failed to cut the armor scales of the fish!

Once again, the Lady Xiao hacked at the fish again but this time at its tail.

Yi Ping was already saying, "Wait!" But it was already too late.

This time, she had succeeded in cutting off the tail of the fish!

Yi Ping sighed and said, "We should have release the fish back into the waters. Even though it had tried to harm me but it did not succeed." But he knew that Lady Xiao could not possible hear him. Moreover with her internal strength foundation, she might be much older than him and it was only proper for him to address her as senior and abide by her wishes.

The Lady Xiao cut the monstrous fish expertly with the White Emerald Phoenix sword and skinned the monstrous fish from the inside. Then she took the giant fish scales and put it into a bundle.

Yi Ping was surprised that Lady Xiao was also highly accomplished in swordplay. He had never seen her type of swordplay before. It was swift, precise and beautiful to behold.

He thought, "But why is it when I hold her hand, her hand is so smooth like Yixian and Lingfeng? It is as though she has never been trained with an external weapon…"

When she was done, she wrote onto the ground with the White Emerald Phoenix Sword, "This fish is a thousand year old ice fish. If we eat it, we can resist the cold here and even receive a boast to our internal strength."

When Yi Ping saw that, he immediately knew what he should do. He wrote, "I will go out and collect the firewood."

It was not long that he was back and they were roasting the monstrous fish over the fire that they had made. Lady Xiao had made another fire to boil some water from the stream. She took out a bowl that she had taken out from her bundle and put it onto the fire.

Yi Ping was surprised that this monstrous fish had no fish stink and instead, it gave off a sweet aroma scent. He examined its abdomen and saw that it was virtually empty. This type of fish must have required little food in order to survive.

It was not too long when the fish was fully roasted. No sooner did Yi Ping have started eating the fish that he started to feel the warmth creeping in. In no time, the cold was fully dispelled and he was comfortable.

When they had eaten, Lady Xiao began to pound the bones of the fish and threw it into the boiling water that she had made. After some time, she wrote. "The essence of the fish lies in its bone. Take the soup."

Yi Ping did as he was instructed and drunk from her bowl. As soon as he drunk from the soup, he could feel a surge of renew strength in his body and a surge of vital energy bursting forth. He quickly took a deep breath with the 'Divine Revelation' skill and closed his eyes. Even though he had not said it, he was immensely grateful to her but did not know how to express it.

Xiao Youxue looked at him keenly and thought, "This thousand year old ice fish is a rare catch that the exponents of the martial fraternity can only dream of but is unobtainable except by sheer luck. Miraculous herbs and pills that boast a person vital strength were so rare that its whereabouts can often move the entire martial fraternity to fight over it. Take the 'Great Rejuvenate Golden Pills' and the 'Divine Dragon Pill' for example, imagine the bloodshed that change hands over it."

She asked herself, "Is it too simply a pure coincident? Consuming one miraculous pill is a rare occurrence already. Finding another is simply unheard of. And now, we are feasting upon another. Is he really so lucky?"

She continued to pound the rest of the fish bones into the bowl. After she had finished boiling the soup, she took a sniff before she took consume it. Afterwards, she took a vital breath and began to meditate. Indeed, she could feel her strength recovering slowly.

She could feel her Icy Heavenly Intricate Tears strengthening immediately as her vital energies became more refine than previously! Because the Icy heavenly Intricate Tears was a cold and negative energy skill, this fish was also of the same element and so it was like a powerful tonic! This thousand year old ice fish had saved her probably decades of hard work and wrong turns…

After some time, when she opened her eyes, she saw that Yi Ping was already standing at the corner of the cavern.

When Yi Ping saw the Lady Xiao walking towards him, he began to exclaim, "I found a secret passage! It is really unexpected that this cave has a secret passage and it is man-made!"

Yi Ping sighed. He kept forgetting that the Lady Xiao could not hear him.

All of a sudden, Xiao Youxue cried out panicky…

Yi Ping was stunned. Was she not supposed to be a mute person?

Yi Ping looked at her and she was cowered to a corner at the sight of several rats.

Yi Ping said, "You can talk?"

Xiao Youxue nodded slowly as she removed her straw veiled hat.

All of a sudden, his eyes were wide opened. That was because the old lady that he had imagined had taken off her veiled straw hat and she was in fact, a ravishing young beauty. Her eyes were very beautiful but had a woeful expression.

What really stunned him was that she seemed even younger than him…

Yi Ping stammered, "Senior…Youxue, why did you pretend to be mute and deaf?"

She replied quietly, "No reason at all."

Yi Ping was puzzled, "No reason at all?"

Xiao Youxue averted her eyes, "There must be many maidens that like you. I don't want to be one of them."

Even though this was a lame reason but was also a reasonable one.

Yi Ping could only nod as he said, "If Lingfeng knows you are not an old lady and can even hear, I wonder what she will say."

Xiao Youxue shifted her captivating eyes and said, "You seem to care a lot for her and even mind what she will say."

Yi Ping was speechless. He said, "I only treating her like a sister."

Xiao Youxue said, "But she may not think of you as just a sister."

Yi Ping said with a deep sigh, "A captivating maiden like her will surely have many good suitors for her to choose. Moreover, I am just a poor and out of luck wanderer."

Xiao Youxue asked, "Why are you sighing then. Did you ever ask her?"

Yi Ping said, "I don't have to ask her to know. She has told me she dislike me on many occasions. Moreover, she is like a sister to me."

Yi Ping had only said that because he was shy but when he named Ji Lingfeng as his sister, his heart was actually aching…

Xiao Youxue said, "How do you not know she did not mean the opposite what she is saying? Or else why did a lofty maiden like her talks so much to someone she dislikes?"

Yi Ping muttered, "We are friends…"

Xiao Youxue said, "So now you are calling her your friend instead of sister. How heartless. You are nothing but a flirt."

Yi Ping stammered, "I…I…" He was confused himself.

All of a sudden, Xiao Youxue turned eerily cold and said, "What if I ask you not to see her again?"

She raised the White Emerald Phoenix Sword in front of her as she said coolly, "Don't forget that you have personally told me you will do anything for me. I want you to not to see her ever again."

Yi Ping was speechless. It was true. He had promised her…a hero that went back on his words did not have honor and was to be despised!

But Yi Ping replied firmly, "Anything but that!"

Xiao Youxue said coldly, "What a hero."

All of a sudden, Xiao Youxue smiled and her eyes softened, "Don't you worry. I am only teasing you. I won't ask you not to see Lingfeng. That is because we are friends…"

Yi Ping was confused as he asked, "The two of you are friends?"

Xiao Youxue smiled, "That's right. Therefore you don't have to worry what she will say when she 'discovers' that I am not a deaf and mute person. That is because she already knows."

Yi Ping was startled as he began to rub his nose. That was because he had not expected Ji Lingfeng to lie to him about this as she was the one that told him that Xiao Youxue was a deaf and mute person.

Xiao Youxue looked at him with her mesmerizing eyes and said, "What are you thinking? Didn't you just say that you have found a man-made secret passage? What are we waiting for?"

Yi Ping could only smiled bitterly as he said, "I am still trying to adapt to someone whom I have been addressing as a senior and now becomes my junior."

Xiao Youxue walked past him quickly as she said alluring, "Who…is your junior! Since you have already addressed me as your senior and I have saved your life, you have to listen to me. Let us go now."

Yi Ping was startled. He was not startled by her words but when he saw her walking away, her mannerism and back view looked like the mysterious yellow dressed maiden. Even her voice bears some resemblance.

If she was the mysterious yellow dressed maiden, why would she save him? Surely she would have recognized him and killed him…

But Yi Ping thought, "No. That is not her. I recognized her voice and her mannerism…"

Yi Ping remembered that the mysterious dressed maiden was always very cold and gave off a cold forbidding aura. He could always remember her cold stinging words…but Youxue was affectionate and gave him a comfortable feeling.

Yi Ping did not know how wrong he had been! Xiao Youxue had been suppressing her affections. When it was suddenly released, she became the most gentle, most affectionate and most captivating person. Moreover, after she had killed Shui Yixian, the torments that she had been suppressing was also lifted.

So if Yi Ping thought that he could identify the yellow dressed maiden by her cold forbidding tone and mannerism, he would never find her! But of course, he would never know as he had never seen her face before…

Chapter 21: The Absolute Spirits Intricate Formula

The secret passage led to another larger passage with many winding paths.

Yi Ping led the way with a burning torch and Xiao Youxue followed him.

They walked for some time but there were still no end to it.

Yi Ping expressions were solemn as he said, "We should turn back now. This passage way is too big. We may easily get lost in this passage and never turn to the outside. And the cave is getting colder by the minute."

Xiao Youxue said, "Let us go back then..."

Yi Ping nodded at her and said, "Maybe we shouldn't enter this passageway in the first place."

It was because they were walking too rapidly in the dim cavern. When he looked back and shone the torch at where he had come from, he realized that there were many other passageways.

He sighed, "I think we are lost..."

All of a sudden, Xiao Youxue called out for him, "Yi Ping, take a look at this..."

Startled by her voice, he looked back panicky.

Xiao Youxue was examining a section of the passage wall. There were inscriptions carved onto it. The inscriptions were not too obvious but Xiao Youxue and Yi Ping was able to read every single inscription clearly.

Yi Ping was astonished, "This seems to be a martial intricate formula but is not. What a weird thing. It is a poem?"

Xiao Youxue read it out, "The most powerful act is thought, the highest function is focus, the most positive mind is the absolute will, the universe is beneath the subconscious, nothing is impossible, enable the motivation, inspire the spirits... "

All of a sudden, Xiao Youxue said in utter surprise. "Yi Ping, this is indeed a martial intricate formula. It is the 'Absolute Spirits Intricate Formula', the most powerful mind intricate formula. To think we would have accidentally found it."

Yi Ping was delighted as he said, "I have heard of it too. Among the many famous martial skills, the 'Absolute Spirits Intricate Formula' was said to be created by an elderly priest more than two hundred years ago. It is said that his willpower was so absolute that he was able to resist the Heavenly Temptress and even in the most dire of all situations, he was able to remain absolute calm and was able to overcome obstacles that seemingly impossible to overcome."

Xiao Youxue smiled enthrallingly as she looked at him in his eyes, "You should really learn it. In this way, you won't be tempted anymore."

Yi Ping began to fluster when he noticed that Xiao Youxue was looking at him as she teased him.

Xiao Youxue said, "Yi Ping. Let's spend some time to memorize the 'Absolute Spirits Intricate Formula'. When we use our skills in combination with the 'Absolute Spirits Intricate Formula', we will surely see a marked improvement in our martial progression."

Yi Ping nodded. He could not agree more with her.

When he had committed the 'Absolute Spirits Intricate Formula' into his memory, he noticed that Xiao Youxue was quicker than him and was looking at the surrounding of this cavern keenly so he asked, "Youxue, what is wrong?"

Xiao Youxue said coolly, "Don't you find that it is weird that someone will crave such an epitome intricacy formula in such an isolated place? It is as though it is meant never to be discovered. We can barely read some of the characters too..."

Yi Ping asked, "What do you mean?"

Xiao Youxue said, "Over time, the cravings on the wall will fade or erode. If that person really wants the Absolute Spirits Intricate Formula to be known by future generations, wouldn't he at least try to preserve or hide it carefully first?"

Yi Ping saw what she was trying to say as he said, "So you are saying that this intricacy formula is left by someone hastily?"

Xiao Youxue said, "Very hastily in fact. It was as though he was in his final moments and only wrote it on the walls here so that this skill won't be forgotten by future generations."

Yi Ping too, began to look keenly around. "Alas, I think he was lost in this cavern too and eventually die of starvation."

Xiao Youxue said, "If he had died here, then his corpse will surely be around here..."

All of a sudden, she said. "Yi Ping, there is an opening on top of this cavern and it looks like a dry place. Let's investigate the cave opening."

Yi Ping nodded.

It took them considerable efforts to find a path up the cavern; they had lost much of their internal strength and were not confident to scale the slippery walls of the cavern with their lightness movement skill.

The interior of the cave was much warmer but was still very cold.

What greeted them was another surprise and startled them!

When they had just entered the small cave, they saw a pale looking maiden in a mediating posture.

Yi Ping asked, "Is she still alive?"

Xiao Youxue flew towards the maiden and examined her, she got a shock. It seemed that this dead maiden here was trained in a type of skill that was similar to the Golden Impervious Body that preserved her body.

After a while, she said. "She still has a vital breath in her body but is as good as a dead person."

Yi Ping asked anxiously, "What do you mean?"

Xiao Youxue sighed, "It seems that while she was alive, she had suffered grievous internal and external injuries as evidenced by her scarred body. At her most critical moment, she had slowed down her heartbeat and now she was in a suspended death animation."

Yi Ping nodded and saw her gray skin. Indeed, she had been dead for a very long time.

Besides her was a black sword.

Yi Ping examined the black sword and saw two characters as he read it aloud, "Perpetual Darkness".

Xiao Youxue gasped aloud softly, "This sword is an ancient sword and is famed for its extreme sharpness and craftsmanship. This sword is one of the seven most coveted swords of the martial fraternity!"

Yi Ping said, "Who is this maiden and how come she is in possession of such a precious sword."

She added, "My guess is that she is waiting for someone else to revive her in time but that never happened."

Yi Ping asked, "Can we revive her?"

Xiao Youxue shook her head, "Nothing short of a miracle can revive her now. Even if she could receive a miracle herb now, the odds are so low that it is not even worth trying."

Yi Ping sighed, "What a pity. It seems that the Absolute Spirits Intricate Formula was left behind by her and we have no way to thanks her."

Xiao Youxue looked at him weirdly as she said softly, "We are now lost in this cavern and yet you are thinking of repaying others?"

Suddenly, Yi Ping exclaimed excitedly, "The Divine Dragon Pill! What if we give her the Divine Dragon Pill? I have heard that it has the ability to revive even the dead."

Xiao Youxue was flabbergasted, "That is just hearsay. No one knows if that is the true and there is only one in the world. Surely you are not thinking of giving her something so rare and precious? Do you know how many lives have been spilled over the Divine Dragon Pill?"

Yi Ping said coolly, "This Divine Dragon Pill requires the practitioner to have sixty years of internal strength and it is of no use to me now. Moreover we are all trapped in this ice cavern. Even if we have the Divine Dragon Pill, what good would it be for me if I cannot make out alive?"

Xiao Youxue looked at Yi Ping with a wondrous expression…

The Divine Dragon Pill was a lot far more precious than the Prolonging Vital Purity Pill that he had given her. When he had given to her the Prolonging Vital Pill, she was stunned and extremely touched at the same time.

But this Divine Dragon Pill was so precious that its very whereabouts would spark a furious struggle for it in the martial fraternity. Especially for the super exponents who were all struck at a martial progression level, the power of this pill would create a breakthrough for them and even eradicated some of their training mistakes!

And he thought of nothing about giving it away?

Yi Ping had already decided as he said, "We have already learnt her 'Absolute Spirits Intricate Formula' so even if this attempt fails to revive her, it is still a fair trade off."

Xiao Youxue was about to say more but Yi Ping had already taken out the Divine Dragon Pill, forcibly smashed it into powder as he mixed it with water from his water skin and forced it down the maiden's throat!

She sighed to herself, "That isn't even a fair trade-off. Even a generous person would never give away something so precious without a very good reason. He is so generous…"

But to Yi Ping, that was a good enough reason.

Xiao Youxue liked him more and more as she loathed her selfish father.

She broke into a smile as she exclaimed urgently, "We must immediately transfer our vital energies into her and dispersed the potency of the Divine Dragon Pill into all her vital channels."

Yi Ping nodded immediately and they did not hesitate for a moment longer as they immediately transferred their vital energies into all her vitality channels.

After some time, the 'Dead Maiden' began to cough out and she had actually revived!

Xiao Youxue was astonished as she thought, "This is really a miracle. The Divine Dragon Pill can really revive a person? No wonder so many had fought over it…"

Yi Ping was startled too. There were now some white and pink colors on her face as she started breathing once more!

The 'Dead Maiden' fluttered open her eyes and looked at Yi Ping and Xiao Youxue in complete astonishment.

When Yi Ping and Xiao Youxue saw the pupils of her eyes, they were startled. It was because her eyes colorings were red! They had never seen anyone with such an eye coloring before!

Xiao Youxue said, "She is still far too weak. Just the Divine Dragon Pill alone isn't sufficient to replenish her health. She is in a suspended animation for far long."

Yi Ping nodded and slashed his wrist slightly with the White Emerald Phoenix Sword and dripped his blood into her mouth.

Both Xiao Youxue and the 'Dead Maiden' were caught by surprise by Yi Ping's action.

Yi Ping said, "I hope that my blood can replenish her…"

Xiao Youxue said, "Yi Ping, you are making too much sacrifices for her…"

After some time, the 'Dead Maiden' seemed to be breathing normally as she said weakly, "I…I am still alive?"

Xiao Youxue said, "It all thanks to him that you have swallowed the Divine Dragon Pill that you are now able to talk to us. I didn't expect it to work."

The 'Dead Maiden' was even more startled as she looked at Yi Ping keenly, "You actually have the Divine Dragon Pill?"

Yi Ping smiled gently at her, "I was lucky. A senior gave it to me."

The 'Dead Maiden' still could not believe what she was hearing, "Do you know how precious that Divine Dragon Pill really is?"

Yi Ping said coolly, "It can boast the internal strength of the practitioner and can save lives."

The 'Dead Maiden' sighed, "More than that and you have just given it to me…"

Yi Ping said coolly, "At least it works. I was afraid that it does not work…"

The 'Dead Maiden' nodded slowly as she stared at Yi Ping, "The odds are very low. I…I can't believe that you would seriously try it on me?" She was in tears now and her voice was trembling uncontrollably.

Xiao Youxue looked at the 'Dead Maiden' as she gasped to herself, "Is she…"

The 'Dead Maiden' said to Yi Ping, "I am Lie Qing, what is your name?"

Yi Ping said, "I am Yi Ping and this is Maiden Xiao Youxue."

Lie Qing muttered weakly, "Yi Ping…Xiao Youxue…"

Lie Qing smiled sweetly at Yi Ping and Xiao Youxue, "You are both my benefactors. If you have anything that you require of me in the future, feel to ask of me."

Xiao Youxue was quiet for a moment before she said, "We may have saved your life but your injuries are too severe. I am afraid that much of your former internal strength had been exhausted to maintain this suspended animation."

Lie Qing smiled weakly, "It is alright. I can re-train again. After all, I am alive now and have plenty of time."

Xiao Youxue said, "Why are you here? Who was the one that had injured you?"

Lie Qing smiled weakly, "Good sister, this place is my forbidden ground where I practiced my skills. As for the second question, no one had injured me."

Yi Ping was startled, "No one? Is your enemy so powerful that you are unwilling to tell us?"

Lie Qing sighed softly, "Really no one. I was merely injured by the 'Divine Calamity' and it is much more powerful than I have expected. Out of desperation, I took ten potent pills and entered into a suspended death animation hoping my injuries would recover by the time that I had awakened."

She looked around the cave and said, "This place isn't always this cold. This is the result of the 'Divine Calamity'. In the end, I still couldn't escape from it."

Yi Ping had heard of the 'Divine Calamity' on numerous occasions now but no one was willing to tell him about it.

Xiao Youxue had never heard of the 'Divine Calamity' before. So she asked, "What is that? I have never heard of it."

Lie Qing looked in bewildered at them before she finally said, "You really do not know? How long have I been in suspended animation? No wonder, you can give me the Divine Dragon Pill so freely. If I have the Divine Dragon Pill before I fought with the 'Divine Calamity', then I might have translucent to a higher divinity level. I have failed…"

Yi Ping asked her, "Maiden Lie Qing, what exactly is the 'Divine Calamity'? We really do not know."

Perhaps she would tell him because she looked like an easy-going person…

Lie Qing sighed, "I cannot tell you."

Yi Ping and Xiao Youxue were stunned.

Lie Qing smiled weakly, "Don't be upset. If you ask me what the Divine Calamity is before I have fought with it, then I could tell you. But if I tell you now and prepare you for it, then I would surely die now, at this very instant. Since I cherish my life and I don't want the both of you to die along with me, let's not talk about this, alright?"

Yi Ping could tell that she was a kind hearted maiden and he did not want to force her. Therefore he nodded.

Xiao Youxue took a quick glance at Lie Qing suspiciously as she sighed silently, "Yi Ping, you are really too gullible. Can't you tell that she is only putting on an act? How can you trust anyone so easily in this fraternity? She has the face of an angel but do you really know what really is in her heart?"

Chapter 22: Ambush!

Yi Ping, Xiao Youxue and Lie Qing had recuperated fully for three months before they decided to leave the Ice Cavern.

The three of them led a carefree life during those three months as they recuperated from their injuries and exertions.

Their injuries and depleted internal strength recovered at a much faster rate than they had expected. Perhaps it was due to the freshness and the unique ice fishes that they had fished from the Ice Cavern.

In just three months, Lie Qing had recovered her rosy outlook and Yi Ping was surprised that her real self would be so stunning.

While Xiao Youxue was enthralling, Lie Qing was mesmerizing.

Lie Qing asked Yi Ping, "Brother Yi Ping, who is the richest bachelor in the fraternity now?"

Yi Ping replied, "That honor belongs to Nangong Le, one of the four young masters of the martial fraternity."

Lie Qing asked, "Who is the best young swordsman of the fraternity now?"

Yi Ping said, "Zuo Tianyi. He is barely thirty and his swordsmanship exceeded many who are twice his age. He is also one of the four young masters of the martial fraternity."

Lie Qing could not resist a smile, "Then who do you think is the better man? Zuo Tianyi or Nangong Le?"

Yi Ping smiled weakly. He really did not know how to answer.

When Lie Qing saw that Yi Ping did not answer her, she asked Xiao Youxue. "Sister Youxue, who do you think is the better guy?"

Xiao Youxue smiled faintly, "It really depends if you like a hero or a rich man."

Lie Qing turned to Yi Ping and asked him, "Is there any hero that is also a rich man?"

Yi Ping managed a weak smile, "I do not know..."

Lie Qing asked again, "What about you? Are you famous in the fraternity?"

Yi Ping said, "I am neither a rich man nor a hero in the fraternity. I am just a poor nameless wanderer..."

Lie Qing laughed softly, "That's what you always say. Who knows if that is the truth?"

She looked at Xiao Youxue and asked, "Good sister, what do you say?"

Xiao Youxue smiled, "He is poor but not entirely nameless. He is one of the most hunted men in the entire fraternity now."

Lie Qing expressed surprise, "My heavens! Good sister, you have never told me!"

She began to look at Yi Ping from top to bottom as she exclaimed with horror, "Is he a lecherous bandit or a malicious villain?"

Xiao Youxue laughed softly, "He is just a notorious fool who dare to offend the majority of the orthodox fraternity."

Lie Qing began to sigh, "Then I better keep away from him or else I would never find a good husband at any time soon."

Xiao Youxue asked, "Why are you so eager to find a husband?"

Lie Qing smiled bitterly, "That is because I am not young anymore."

Xiao Youxue asked, "How old are you now?"

Lie Qing looked at Yi Ping and then looked at Xiao Youxue before replying, "This is my secret. I don't want to share with any one of you!"

Xiao Youxue teased, "Not even to your future husband?"

Lie Qing laughed softly, "Naturally not even to my future husband. It is better he does not know either."

Yi Ping rubbed his nose, "I wonder how old Maiden Xiao is?"

Xiao Youxue smiled enthralling as she said, "I don't want to reveal either."

Yi Ping sighed deeply.

Xiao Youxue asked him, "Why are you sighing? Why are you so eager to know our age?"

Yi Ping sighed even deeper, "I just don't understand how you develop your internal strength at such a young age. This is really so unbelievable."

Lie Qing laughed, "Good sister, I have lost all my internal strength. Can you spare me some of your internal strength?"

Xiao Youxue suddenly was tight-lipped and had a moment of irk with Lie Qing. It was because the art of stealing and borrowing one's internal strength was an evil skill in the martial fraternity. It was an action that even the majority of the unorthodox clans condemned except for the vile heretic sects.

Even though Xiao Youxue had been very careful about revealing her true internal strength to Yi Ping, at times she would forget and accidentally displayed it.

Take for example during the first month they were in the forest when all of a sudden, they were attacked by a large wild boar that suddenly charged at them.

If it were not for her sudden reflex and a sudden kick from her that sent the wild boar flying, Yi Ping and Lie Qing would have broken their legs by the charge of the wild boar!

Yi Ping was astonished that her kick was powerful enough to kick a charging wild boar away that even a highly skilled exponent could scarcely be able to accomplish it without breaking their legs first.

Yi Ping asked, "Is that your martial strength or are you using a martial technique?"

She simply ignored him and walked away, leaving Yi Ping mystified and intrigued by her as he sighed, "To think I am almost killed by a pig…"

Even Lie Qing was astonished, "I didn't expect good sister to be so strong despite her gentle outlook."

And now, they had left the Ice Cavern.

Lie Qing asked, "Where are we going?"

Yi Ping said coolly, "I have a few important things that I am going to do first. We should part ways. I so glad that you have almost recovered. The fraternity is dangerous for a maiden. I will escort you to the nearest town or city if you prefer, then we will part ways."

Xiao Youxue secretly stole a glance at Yi Ping. Was it time to part for them? These three months were the happiest day of her life as she got to know Yi Ping better.

Lie Qing asked curiously, "What important things that you have to do?"

Yi Ping was silent for a while as he appeared to be in a daze before he said, "I have to find that Ding Yunzi. Even if she is not the one that killed my wife; surely she knows who the killer identity is."

He paused for a while before saying, "Also, Maiden Ji have stolen my secret manuals. No matter what, I have to find her to get it back." Actually he was more worried if the Honor Manor had already acted against the Holy Hex Sect than retrieving his secret manuals from her but he did not say anything about it.

Lie Qing asked, "Who is Maiden Ji?"

Yi Ping managed a weak smile, "She is an extremely kind hearted maiden that is on the wrong side of the fraternity…"

Xiao Youxue interrupted, "Stealing a secret manual is considered a more heinous crime than killing your wife. In this fraternity, whose hands aren't tainted with blood? You are more eager to avenge a stranger than avenge the theft of your secret manuals?"

Yi Ping answered hesitatingly, "Maiden Ji is a friend…"

Xiao Youxue waved her hand and looked away, "So you are willing to forgive your friends for any heinous crimes that they would commit against you?"

Yi Ping smiled weakly, "That really depends. Some heinous crimes cannot be forgiven. Some can be."

Xiao Youxue asked, "How did you know that your wife killer did not have a justified reason to kill her then?"

Yi Ping did not know what to answer as he looked at her enthralling eyes. For some weird reasons, from her eyes, he seemed to know her for a long time ago.

Lie Qing could sense the cold forbidden aura that was radiating from Xiao Youxue now. She was a little afraid of Xiao Youxue now as she thought, "Lucky I am not interested in Yi Ping or else I would be dead."

Even though she had recovered her some of her internal strength and was confident of her own martial techniques, she was also an experienced exponent in the martial fraternity. She knew that Xiao Youxue may have appeared at ease but her guard was never down. And moreover, she also knew that Xiao Youxue martial levels were actually higher than she willing to display. It was as though she was deliberating suppressing her true martial skills. Even with her experience, she could not tell which sect or clan that Xiao Youxue was from.

Therefore she tried to be friendly towards her and even calling her 'Good Sister' all the time. But no matter what she did in these three months, Xiao Youxue always maintained a cool distance from her.

Yi Ping and Xiao Youxue were the weirdest persons that she had ever met. They did not ask her about her martial background, where she got her 'Perpetual Darkness' precious sword or question her further.

She thought, "Are they trying to put me off my guard so that they can get my martial secrets?"

And the weirdest thing was Yi Ping and Xiao Youxue did not appear to be real friends either even though they were traveling together. There were even certain days that Yi Ping and Xiao Youxue did not even attempt to talk to one another. Instead they spent much of their time mediating and exercising their internal energy.

And this Yi Ping was really a true gentleman, handsome and there was a strong magnetism to him.

Therefore, she was even more confused. "Surely there must be many maidens that have already fallen for him. Why is he in this desolate place? Is he really hunted by the majority of the fraternity?"

She sighed in her heart, "I have never fallen for a man, distrusting them. But now, I really do not know…" She had encountered many pretentious men. Just because they had given her some advantages, they thought that they could get back some advantages too.

Until today, she could not believe that Yi Ping could actually give her the 'Divine Dragon Pill' to save her life. She was now in a dilemma because she had actually lied to him about the 'Divine Calamity'.

"If he knows I lie to him, won't he get a very bad impression of me?" She could not believe that she had actually cared about his opinion of her!

What astonished her most was that Yi Ping actually had more than sixty-years of martial power at his young age!

She had watched him practicing his martial skills and had gauged the depth of his martial power. And his martial power was the type that was very pure and unhindered!

She had almost fainted because of this. It was because attainting sixty years of martial power was almost an impossible feat for the majority of the exponents. Most top fighters in the fraternity, including the old and experienced exponents barely even had twenty years of martial foundation. And if Yi Ping had taken the Divine Dragon Pill, he would have become a superior super exponent instantly! That was because sixty years were the limits and anything above that was almost an impossible feat with too many hindrances. The few exponents that had sixty years of martial power were all super exponents.

Even though the differences between a superior super exponent and a super exponent was not great, any significant breakthrough was important for them to gasp the various superior intricacy skills that would actually prove decisive in a fight.

Of course, Lie Qing did not know that Yi Ping had actually consumed the Golden Rejuvenation Pill , eaten the Thousand Year Old Ice Fish and had also cleared his death and life meridians channels by a freak fighting incident.

It was hard for her not to resist falling for such a promising young man…

Because of the Divine Dragon Pill, her life was actually saved and her internal strength even had a hope for recovery. And Yi Ping had never asked for anything in return and now he wanted to part ways with her…

Xiao Youxue looked coldly at Yi Ping and interrupted Lie Qing's thoughts with a sharp remark, "I will really like to see you avenge the maiden that killed your wife with your cold-blooded hands."

Yi Ping was startled as he sighed, "Alas. It is my own personal affair. I am so sorry. Maybe I have said the wrong words and offend you. I know you are kind and don't wish to see unnecessary bloodshed…"

Xiao Youxue interrupted coldly, "You don't have to be sorry. I am not kind at all. I want to see how you are going to kill someone so cold-heartedly with your own hands."

Yi Ping said, "This doesn't concern you…"

Xiao Youxue raised her white emerald precious sword as she said, "It does now. You have said that you will return me a favor for saving your life. This is what I request from you now. Bring me along so that I can witness your cold-heartlessness."

Yi Ping said, "Youxue, why are you forcing me…."

Xiao Youxue said coolly, "So you are a liar?"

Yi Ping sighed heavily as he said, "My enemy is a very strong foe. I may not be her match. Even today, I am terrified of her martial skills and power. I will put you to danger…"

Xiao Youxue said, "This, you don't have to worry about me. I know how to take care of myself."

Yi Ping walked away as he said, "Up to you. I have nothing more to say anymore."

Lie Qing called out after Yi Ping, "Yi Ping, what about me?"

Yi Ping was startled as he asked, "What about you?"

Lie Qing smiled mysterious at Xiao Youxue as she said, "I would like to see how you are going to avenge for your wife too!"

Yi Ping was stunned, "You too? Do you think of me as a cold-hearted person too?"

Lie Qing smiled as she said, "I am not! Don't forget that my life is saved by Youxue and you. I should help till the very end too."

Yi Ping heaved a sigh of relief as he said, "Silly girl. I have no idea how long this is going to take. If I take twenty-years, don't tell me you are going to follow me for twenty years?"

Lie Qing laughed softly, "Not to mention twenty-years, forty-years I am willing to wait too!"

Xiao Youxue interrupted coldly, "Even if it takes you sixty-years, I will want to see your cold-heartlessness at that moment."

Yi Ping was stunned as he said, "All of you…."

All of a sudden, a piercing quiet demurely voice interrupted Yi Ping. "Maybe you don't have to wait for sixty-years."

Everyone was startled. With their martial levels, who could have walked so quietly without their detection?

They quickly turned in the direction of the intruder and saw a simply dressed demurely dressed maiden who was standing not far away. It was Ding Yunzi!

Ding Yunzi was smiling, "Youxue, have your martial progression actually deteriorated or I have improved? Let me analyze for you, maybe you have spent too much of your time running from us than practicing your martial skills?"

Lie Qing said coolly, "You are here all along by a chance occurrence. You can turn back and try to sneak at us again."

Ding Yunzi looked at Lie Qing carefully. This innocent looking young maiden was actually extremely sharp and quick witted. For her to react and recover her wits so quickly, she must not be an ordinary exponent either. And she got these weird red eyes…

Xiao Youxue was startled when she had appeared as she quickly thought, "How did she find us?"

Yi Ping turned to look at Xiao Youxue as he asked, "Youxue, you know her?"

But Xiao Youxue did not reply to his question and instead threw the white emerald phoenix precious sword to him as she said hurriedly, "Yi Ping and Lie Qing, be very careful. She is an extremely dangerous exponent! Even if the three of us were to fight her at the same time, we may not be able to defeat her!"

Yi Ping nodded as he had personally witnessed her sword skills. He quickly said to Lie Qing, "Qing'Er, you should step back. She is a very frightening opponent!"

When Lie Qing looked at Xiao Youxue and Yi Ping dreadful expressions, she immediately knew that they were not joking with her. And she raised her sword with a defensive stance.

Lie Qing looked at Ding Yunzi carefully. From all appearances, she did not seem to be a threat and there were three of them.

Ding Yunzi raised her thin eyebrows slightly elegantly as she said quietly, "I am so flattered to hear that."

Xiao Youxue said coldly, "How did you find me?"

Ding Yunzi said coolly, "We have seen you entering the Honor Manor but you are not there. It is obvious that you have lured us there for an unknown purpose. Therefore I have concluded that you must still be in the vicinity. I have almost given up on waiting, you know."

Yi Ping interrupted, "Good. I am about to look for you. This saves me sixty years of futile searching."

Ding Yunzi smiled demurely and sighed, "I didn't know you have fallen in love with me and is looking for me."

Yi Ping was caught off-guarded by what she had just said and he stammered, "I…we….I…"

Xiao Youxue warned Yi Ping, "Yi Ping, don't fall into her tricks and her stratagems."

Ding Yunzi could not resist a smile as she asked, "Why are you so eager in looking for me? Actually I should be the one that is looking for you."

Yi Ping asked, "What do you mean?"

While Ding Yunzi was talking to them, she was in fact observing their standing positions and analyzing every slight movement of theirs. How they were going to attack, what were the distances between them and how they could possible react, she had secretly calculated; her winning odds of taking them at the same time was fifty percent. Of the three, Xiao Youxue was the most dangerous.

But of course, the victory was already theirs. It was because her second eldest Protégé Brother Xiao Yuanjia was also here!

Yi Ping asked, "Why are you looking for me?"

Ding Yunzi was looking intently at the white emerald precious sword that Yi Ping was holding as she asked, "Is this precious sword from the Eternal Ice Palace?"

Yi Ping hummed coldly, "That's right!"

Ding Yunzi said, "That is the reason why you must die."

Yi Ping was stunned, "I must die just because of this one sword?"

Ding Yunzi replied quietly, "That is right."

Yi Ping said, "So this is the so call martial justice of the Virtuous Palace!"

At the mention of the Virtuous Palace, Lie Qing shuddered slightly.

Ding Yunzi said, "That is because I have orders from my protégé master Xiao Shuai to exterminate all male protégés of the Eternal Ice Palace and every male that are associated with the Eternal Ice Palace. It is nothing personal."

Xiao Youxue was secretly fuming too. It was because her mother had pleaded with Xiao Shuai to abolish the Eternal Ice Palace and he had refused in the past. And now, he was attacking the Eternal Ice Palace on his own accord.

Yi Ping was enraged as he shouted angrily, "The Virtuous Palace is so reckless with lives." He immediately drew out the white emerald precious sword as he charged towards Ding Yunzi.

Ding Yunzi was surprised that Yi Ping was so easily baited and she took noted of his quick impulsive temper. But she quickly sighed, "After today, he would be dead. What is the point of noting his character?"

All of a sudden, Yi Ping was besides her as he attacked her with the Horizon Swordplay!

Ding Yunzi was stunned at how swift his swordplay was, as mirror images of his sword blades came flashing to and fro in quick successive waves!

But she was not slow to react; she had drawn out her beautiful adored long sword and had swirled around, parrying and blocking Yi Ping's attacks with both her scabbard and long sword at the same time!

As she turned around and wielded ambidextrously, all of a sudden she gave a silent kick and it exploded with a tremendous impact on Yi Ping as he flew backward!

Xiao Youxue and Lie Qing were stunned as they flew towards Yi Ping in an instant!

Less than five seconds after Yi Ping had attacked Ding Yunzi, the fight had ended so quickly when he was caught by surprise by her 'Penetrating Kick' skill!

Yi Ping was stunned that she could distribute her martial power so evenly in both her hands and legs as he fell onto the ground!

When Ding Yunzi saw Xiao Youxue and Lie Qing speeding towards her, she threw her charged scabbard towards Lie Qing! It was because she knew that her projectile attacks would never work against Xiao Youxue, so she decided to eliminate the weaker first!

Xiao Youxue immediately shouted, "Lie Qing, be careful!"

But it was too late as the scabbard flew like lightning past her and there was a tremendous impact!

Ding Yunzi attacking speed was too fast and so silence that few opponents in the fraternity could match her martial skills! But to her surprise, the innocent looking young maiden had suddenly tripped onto the ground as her scabbard missed her narrowly!

Ding Yunzi could not believe the innocent looking maiden extraordinary luck. But before she could analyze further, Xiao Youxue had raised her hand in a downward strike against her.

She immediately retaliated with her sword as Xiao Youxue cancelled her attacks and evaded it.

Ding Yunzi smiled demurely, "Surely you are not thinking of fighting me with your bare hands? That would be to my advantage."

Xiao Youxue hummed coldly as she swirled and evaded Ding Yunzi sword strokes as she brandished the hidden foldable sword around her waist!

Ding Yunzi did the same too with her long sword in her right hand and unfolded the hidden foldable sword from around her waist to her left hand!

Xiao Youxue and Ding Yunzi began to exchange flurries of sword strokes!

Ding Yunzi exclaimed, "You seem to have improved but don't forget that in the past when we have fought, I have won more times than you. And my ambidextrous skills have improved considerably since we have last met."

Xiao Youxue hummed coldly, "As though I care." All of a sudden, her foldable sword was imbued with her martial power as it exploded against Ding Yunzi harder and harder with every single impact!

Ding Yunzi was startled as she exclaimed, "You can actually transfer your Penetrating Hands into your sword techniques!?"

She could not believe at the sudden increase of Xiao Youxue martial power as she took a few steps backward!

Just as Xiao Youxue was about to follow up with more successive attacks, the whirling sound of a flying sword exploded into mid-air and knocked her ten steps backward as she parried in time!

The flying sword rebounded and returned to the hands of a new intruder who was in his forties, Xiao Yuanjia!

Xiao Youxue said coldly, "So it is you…"

Xiao Yuanjia said coolly, "How are you, sister."

Xiao Youxue said, "I am not good of course. It is because you have come to take my life."

Xiao Yuanjia replied coldly, "We have our orders. You are a traitor of the Virtuous Palace. Surrender yourself and the Golden Rejuvenation Pills. Then you may have a chance to live. For the sake of our kinship, I will plead for you at least."

"Youxue, you are from the Virtuous Palace?" It was Yi Ping. He had recovered from the sudden kick and he was besides Xiao Youxue.

But Xiao Youxue was not listening as she was looking intently at Xiao Yuanjia and Ding Yunzi. Any slight distraction and she would be dead!

Ding Yunzi looked at Yi Ping in relief and could not believe that he could actually withstand her Penetrating Kick as she thought, "He is not dead yet?" She estimated that he may have broken several rib bones and was suppressing his pain.

She thought, "You should have pretended to succumb to your injuries and not get up. You are such an idiot."

But why was she relief that Yi Ping was not fatally injured?

Yi Ping was rubbing his chest and exclaiming to himself, "I have been careless." The kick had momentarily stunned him; however it did no lasting damage to him.

"I'm so sorry. I have tripped. Did I miss anything?" It was Lie Qing!

She sighed, "Now I truly believe that you are being hunted, Brother Yi Ping. We should have parted even earlier. But now it is too late."

Yi Ping smiled bitterly. He did not know what to answer.

Xiao Youxue was startled and glad that Lie Qing had somehow survived that flying scabbard. She had not turned her head around and so she did not know what had happened during that intensive moment.

Ding Yunzi re-appraised their strengths and estimated that with Xiao Yuanjia in the fight, their winning odds were still at a hundred percent.

Xiao Youxue shivered at the appearance of Xiao Yuanjia! It was because she knew how powerful he really was. While the other protégés of the Virtuous Palace excelled in surprise attacks and tactics, only Xiao Yuanjia fought with all his true martial strength. Naturally his martial progression was speedy.

If there were anyone that she did not want to see, that was him!

The flying sword that Xiao Yuanjia had thrown was actually a foldable sword. And the large scabbard that he was holding now actually contained five other such foldable swords! In the Virtuous Palace, he was also known as the Swordsman of the Thirteen Swords. But where were his other seven hidden swords?

Chapter 23: The Heavenly Temptress

Xiao Yuanjia said haughtily, "Since you are my sister, I let your group makes the first strike."

Yi Ping was fuming as he said angrily, "You are her brother?! And you want to kill her?" He simply could not believe that he was hearing such an outrageous thing in his life.

Xiao Youxue was secretly touched. She had never experienced kinship other than her mother and even then, her mother had a bitter outlook in life and this caused her to be despised even by her own father.

Her very own father would rather impart the Flying Sword Techniques and other martial skills to Ding Yunzi than to her.

Xiao Yuanjia replied coolly, "She is just my half-sister. In my entire life, I have never exchanged more three sentences with her. Today is the exception."

Yi Ping had already recited the 'Absolute Spirits' intricate formula to calm himself down and to focus all his entire focus to the upcoming fight.

He said, "No matter who you are, I won't allow you to harm Maiden Xiao. I will beat you up so that you will never bully your sister ever again."

Xiao Youxue gasped, "Yi Ping…"

Xiao Yuanjia said, "It seem that you have found a steady but what a pity, he is to die today."

Lie Qing interrupted innocently, "I believe it is a feud between you. Do I have anything to do with it?"

Xiao Yuanjia looked at this attractive and mesmerizing young maiden as he said, "Indeed you don't."

Lie Qing said, "Since I have nothing to do with your feuds, then I have better go and mind my own business."

Even before Yi Ping and Xiao Yuanjia could say a word more, she had already taken great strides and walked off!

Yi Ping was stunned as he muttered, "She didn't even say good bye." But he quickly defended her actions by thinking, "Alas, she had barely recovered from her injuries. Moreover, it is really none of her affairs and we shouldn't drag her into this. Some more I am the one that asks her to step back in the first place."

Ding Yunzi said coolly, "Now there are only four of us. The fight is very obvious now and fair now."

Yi Ping said, "Youxue, let me take care of your brother. I don't wish to see you siblings fighting among yourself."

He said to Xiao Yuanjia, "I am Yi Ping and what is your name?"

Xiao Yuanjia said coldly, "Xiao Yuanjia. Remember my name and tell the King of Hades who has killed you."

Yi Ping said, "I don't want to kill you but I make sure you regret your insolence!"

Xiao Youxue said melancholy, "Yi Ping, you can't fight him. Do you know that he is called the Swordsman of the Thirteen Swords? He has six visible swords and seven invisible swords. Unless you know where his invisible swords are, you can never guard against him."

Yi Ping said, "Youxue, don't say anymore. I won't allow this."

Xiao Youxue interrupted sharply, "I can hold him much longer than you. If you really want to help me, then quickly defeat Ding Yunzi and aid me afterwards."

Xiao Yuanjia interrupted coldly, "You think too highly of yourself, sister. Let me ask you. Where are the golden rejuvenation pills? Surrender it and come back with me to the Virtuous Palace. I will plead with father on your behalf. Don't blame me for being heartless."

Xiao Youxue said, "I have finished it all."

Xiao Yuanjia was infuriated, "You have finished it all? Do you know how precious the remaining three Golden Rejuvenation Pills are for our clan and to father! And you have finished it all?"

Xiao Youxue replied coldly, "That's right. So what?"

Xiao Yuanjia said, "You are very selfish. Very well, don't blame me then. Father says if you really taken the Golden Rejuvenation Pills, then we will drain and drink from your blood!"

Yi Ping exclaimed aloud, "You are barbaric! You actually want to drink your sister's blood? Let me tell you, she has given all the Golden Rejuvenation Pills to me. The blood that you supposed to drink is actually me!"

Yi Ping had already leapt forward and attacked Xiao Yuanjia!

Xiao Youxue called out, "Yi Ping, wait!"

But before Yi Ping could even reach Xiao Yuanjia, Ding Yunzi had intercepted him as she said softly, "Your opponent is me. It is still too early for you to fight my senior protégé brother!"

Yi Ping said, "I was careless just now. I won't allow anyone to harm Youxue. Even if I have to fight you, I won't hesitate!"

Yi Ping and Ding Yunzi began to exchange their sword attacks, attacking faster and faster! And at the very same instant, Ding Yunzi was kicking at Yi Ping!

Yi Ping retaliated with kicks of his own as he exclaimed, "The same technique cannot work twice against me."

Ding Yunzi was startled that Yi Ping strength did not falter and instead he was striking from strength to strength. She had thought that he was injured and it would not be long before he could be defeated by her.

Just when Yi Ping had attacked and was intercepted by Ding Yunzi, Xiao Youxue had also intercepted Xiao Yuanjia!

Yi Ping quickly turned his head around and saw that Xiao Yuanjia had unleashed two powerful spinning flying swords towards Xiao Youxue at the same time!

Just when he was about to disengaged from Ding Yunzi to intercept Xiao Yuanjia again, Ding Yunzi blocked his passage and said coolly to him, "You should pay more attention to our fight. A slight distraction will maim or kill you."

Ding Yunzi had seized a small opening when Yi Ping was distracted to unleash her full martial strength as she attacked Yi Ping with a double sword strike!

One of the strikes missed and cut off the tree truck of a tree with a tremendous impact!

Yi Ping had raised his long sword and he was knocked back three steps by her martial force. He had almost forgotten how powerful her sword strength had been! His sword arm began to tremble slightly!

Even though his martial strength had improved considerably, he found out he could not withstand her true martial strength at close melee range!

Ding Yunzi was slightly startled that Yi Ping could parry her double sword blows. She had deliberated on her attacks and intentionally allowed him to parry her attacks so that he could be intimidated by her and gave up. But from the looks of it, unless he was down, he would not give up.

She sighed to herself, "Why are you forcing me? I don't want to hurt you but swords are blind…"

Yi Ping moved backward as Ding Yunzi took another three steps forward as she lashed left and right in a calm calculating manner.

He was sweating and his sword arm was trembling even harder now. It was because barely after he had parried her long sword attack; her foldable sword would come at the same time! It was like fighting two opponents at the same time!

Yi Ping was sweating and he knew at that instant, their sword techniques differences were simply too vast and he did not know how to deal with such a double fold attacks. Only the sheer strength of his martial power and the Absolute Spirits Intricacy Recite kept him going or else he would have been killed in less than twenty strokes with her if it was three months ago!

No matter which angle he had tried to attack her, he could not get past her double sword defense and she could attack at the same time. This was the first time that he had encountered such a fearsome fighting sword technique!

In the meantime, Xiao Youxue was not getting an easier time too.

Barely had she avoided Xiao Yuanjia multiple flying swords, there was a flash and another short blade appeared in Xiao Yuanjia's hands that aimed at her throat!

But barely when the short blade appeared, Xiao Youxue had immediately evaded it!

Xiao Yuanjia said coldly, "You know where are my invisible swords are?"

Xiao Youxue refused to say anything. Instead, immediately she had evaded his attacks, she retaliated with a flurry of sword thrusts with her foldable sword!

Xiao Fei, her cousin had warned her to be careful of Xiao Yuanjia two years ago and had secretly revealed the positions of his hidden swords. In the entire Virtuous Palace, only Xiao Fei knew his secrets. It was not because Xiao Yuanjia had told him but Xiao Fei was a quiet guy who was particular observant. That was also the reason why Xiao Fei was able to find her first.

All of a sudden, Xiao Yuanjia leapt backward as he threw three flying swords towards her at the same time!

Barely had she parried off and evaded off his three flying swords, Xiao Yuanjia threw his scabbard and that struck her with a thunderous force that sent her backward!

Immediately she gasped with a cry and fell onto the ground!

Xiao Yuanjia smiled coldly, "No one can evade all my successive attacks, no matter how good their swiftness movement skills are."

As he moved to pick her up, Xiao Youxue opened her eyes and attacked him with her Penetrating Hands!

But Xiao Yuanjia was already prepared for such trickery. He avoided her attacks and slashed across her body with his sword!

But instead of the fatal results that he had been expecting, Xiao Youxue ignored his powerful sword slash and instead she struck him six times on his chest!

Xiao Yuanjia was startled as he quickly stepped six to seven steps back as he gasped, "You have mastered the Golden Impervious Body? No, that is impossible. Even the Golden Impervious Body could not possible withstand my martial force!"

He looked intently at Xiao Youxue and looked at her tattered dress which revealed a silvery scale armor! He gasped in surprise, "What type of armor is this that it can withstand my sword strokes?"

Xiao Youxue said coldly, "It is an armor that can absorb your attacks. If you are afraid, you can turn around and run. I won't pursue you."

Xiao Yuanjia laughed aloud, "I am only momentarily careless. There are many ways to kill a person. I can cut off your legs, arms and head for example." He immediately whirled his sword in front of him as he prepared for his next attacks.

He added coldly, "Moreover, no matter how good the armor is, you will surely be afflicted by internal injuries after you took in the full blunt of my martial strength."

It was true. Even if Xiao Youxue's armor could withstand his sword slash, she was still seized by a painful sensation from the attack.

She looked at her surroundings and saw that Yi Ping and Ding Yunzi were now far even though she could still hear the slashing sounds of their long swords.

All of a sudden, Xiao Youxue martial power seemed to have increased.

Xiao Yuanjia could sense a cold wavering force that was radiating from her!

He stared at her, "This is the advance stage of the Divine Virtuous Force?" He too, was a practitioner of the Divine Virtuous Force but he had not got to the advance stage yet.

Xiao Youxue did not say anything and instead she began to take broad strides forward as she kicked the ground with a thunderous impact! It was because she herself was not sure if that was the Divine Virtuous Force or the Icy Heavenly Tears even though she knew that her martial power had suddenly improved by leapt and bounds during these three months!

Through sheer hard work and mediation, especially with the aid of the Absolute Spirits, the Prolonging Vital Force Pill and the thousand year old icy fish, she had broken through the sixth stage of the Icy Heavenly Tears and had even reverted some of her mistakes that she had fatally committed with the Icy Heavenly Tears.

Xiao Yuanjia stared at her martial power in disbelief as he began to take three additional surprise steps backward!

Xiao Yuanjia did not hesitated for long as he attacked her again, because any doubt or hesitation would be fatal! Moreover, he was still very confident of his combat abilities.

Therefore he drew out another two hidden swords and attacked her again!

They had virtually charged towards one another.

As Xiao Yuanjia exchanged blows with Xiao Youxue, his swords shattered as he struck against her!

Xiao Youxue took a step backward as she coughed out blood from the tremendous impact!

As soon as his swords shattered, he had drawn out four additional hidden swords as he slashed against her once more!

His swords torn through her long sleeves and mutilated her hands and arms as her blood shattered in all directions!

But Xiao Youxue exercised her entire martial power and shattered through all his four swords once again with her Penetrating Hands as she struck her brother on his chest!

Xiao Yuanjia fell onto the ground as blood foamed from his mouth! His eyes were still in disbelief as he cursed inaudibly, "You have stolen our clan Golden Rejuvenation Pills and have secretly mastered the Golden Impervious Body..." He could not believe that he had actually lost to Xiao Youxue so narrowly!

Xiao Youxue too, stumbled onto the ground as her entire dress was soaked with her blood. If she was not wearing the fish scales armor and had injured him earlier, she would have lost her life!

After a short while, she got up weakly and began to stagger away as she murmured, "Yi Ping, don't die...I'm coming..." She did not think she would defeat her older brother and would not be so lucky the next time but she had no wish to kill her older brother.

So she just said, "I don't want to ever see you again."

As soon as Xiao Youxue had disappeared from view, Lie Qing walked quietly to the scene as she bended over to Xiao Yuanjia as she smiled innocently, "It seems that my good sister has defeated you. It is a heart-stopping fight. I have thought she may be killed by you."

She seemed to ponder for a while as she said, "So it is the full extent of her martial strength. That's interesting."

The immobilized Xiao Yuanjia was startled at her sudden appearance!

Her footsteps were so light that he did not hear her approaching!

He said coldly as he stared at her, "What do you want?"

Lie Qing smiled softly, "What do I want? You should know. You are haughty and insolent to me earlier. Now you are in my hands."

Xiao Yuanjia said coldly, "I won't beg you for mercy. If that is what you have wished for, you are dreaming! I have lost and I am not afraid of death!"

Lie Qing laughed softly, "I won't let you die so peacefully. I have finally found someone with the Divine Virtuous Force Intricacy Energy."

All of a sudden, she grabbed his wrist hard as Xiao Yuanjia cried out in pain!

Xiao Yuanjia was horrified as his intricacy energy was being drained by Lie Qing! He screamed aloud, "This...is the true Invincible...Divine...Force...just who are...you.....no, that can't be. This skill is supposed...awwww......wiped out...by us...two hundred years...ago..."

Lie Qing smiled coldly, "Just who I am? I am your grand matriarch of course. I am the true mistress of the Virtuous Palace. So you people have found a way to practice the Divine Virtuous Force past the initial stage? The Divine Virtuous Force is just a deviation of the Invincible Divine Force. It is a skill that I have invented to drain the practitioners of the Divine Virtuous Force to enhance my Invincible Divine Force."

That was why she had founded the Virtuous Palace for that very purpose.

The Divine Virtuous Force and the Invincible Divine Force were actually the same skill. When the Divine Virtuous Force reached the intermediate stage, it would become the Invincible Divine Force! That was why Xiao Shuai was desperate for the Golden Rejuvenate Pills to attain that stage!

Xiao Yuanjia was even more confused as he stared in disbelief at her before he expired, "Who are…you…really…"

Lie Qing reached out her hands and closed his eyes as she said softly, "Thank you very much for your intricacy energy. Now I can finally start to practice the Invincible Divine Force again. Who I am? Since you are dead, I can tell you. I am the Heavenly Temptress. It seems that all those that know me are now dead and I can start afresh again…"

She got up and sighed heavily, "But it seems that my clan protégés have stolen many of my secret manuals and even developed several techniques that I have never even seen before. This will make my task of destroying the Virtuous Palace really hard."

All those that had betrayed her, she sworn to make them all pay with their lives!

She could still remember that fateful day vividly! If she had not mastered the Golden Impervious Body, she would have been killed many times over. She took a gambit in a last desperate move to keep alive by entering into a false animated state with the indestructible level of her Golden Impervious Body Divine Skill; that would preserve her body for indefinite period of time until she could recover.

But her internal injuries were too severe and what she had hoped did not materialized until the arrival of Yi Ping…

Chapter 24: The Origin of the Virtuous Palace

Yi Ping continued another flurry of dozens of powerful attacks against Ding Yunzi, who coolly parried all his attacks with just a single left stroke or just a single right stroke.

She smiled with a cool demeanor, it was as though she was the trainer and Yi Ping was the trainee.

Even though Yi Ping was attacking her with all his martial power and strength, he was still forced to take a walk backward with every attack!

He was mystified why even though he had the superior strength and technique, Ding Yunzi could still parry off his attacks effortlessly!

Ding Yunzi had practiced the sword since she was five years old. Her precision and timing was so uncanny and steady that no matter how fast Yi Ping's sword strokes were, she could always strike at the weakest point of his attacks and swerved his attacks to one side with just a sword stroke!

By now, Yi Ping had taken more than forty steps backward and was sweating heavily! Even though his sword arm was aching painfully and his entire body was trembling, he persisted with the Absolute Spirits Intricacy Recite and forced himself to focus on finding a breakthrough!

As long as he did not give up, he believed that he would have a chance to overcome her. It was because he believed that evil cannot triumph over good!

Just when his vision had begun to blur and the last of his strength had faltered, a most unlikely thing happened and stunned him!

Ding Yunzi had suddenly tripped over a soft shriek as she fell on the ground. She had sprained her left ankle as she took a gentle step forward!

Yi Ping quickly halted his attacks in time when he saw her tripping! He refused to take advantage of her in this situation.

He put down his long sword in a downward pose as he said, "I wait for you to get up first."

Ding Yunzi could not believe that she would be so unlucky to have sprained her ankle at the most unlikely of all timing!

Her soft eyes were immediately in tears as she tried to get up awkwardly. She knew that even if she was given a chance of getting up, her combat ability was already affected and she would not be able to fight as well as before.

She supported herself by thrusting her long sword into the ground and pointing the foldable sword at Yi Ping, "You have not won yet. Even if I stay at the same spot, I can still able to kill you. Why don't you try again?"

Yi Ping said to her, "I just want to know who the person that has killed my wife is. Is that you? Or someone else?"

Ding Yunzi asked curiously, "Who…who's your wife? You are married?"

Yi Ping said solemnly, "My wife is Shui Yixian…the one that have killed her knows the Penetrating Hands Skill. Who else knows this skill other than the Virtuous Palace?"

Ding Yunzi was startled, "Shui Yixian is your wife and she has passed away?"

Yi Ping nodded, "That's right."

Ding Yunzi asked, "When did she die?"

Yi Ping said, "Five to six months ago, judging by the seasons…maybe longer…I can't remember, really."

Ding Yunzi was startled. It was because she had just seen her three months ago! She said, "That's impossible. Are you kidding?"

Yi Ping sighed, "I know that all of you refuse to believe that the Celestial Fairy is my wife but…" All of a sudden, he froze. It was because he had seen Maiden Xiao and she was covered with blood!

Xiao Youxue was wounded as she fought her brother in a headlong clash out of desperation. She really had no confident at all. But because she was worried about Yi Ping and had the Absolute Spirits Intricacy Recite to reinforce her fighting spirits, she managed to do the impossible and defeated her brother narrowly.

Of course, this was also because she had also wounded her brother earlier, had the thousand year silvery scale armor and she had also mastered the Golden Impervious Body Divine Skill!

When she saw the man that she liked was talking to Ding Yunzi, there was a great sorrow in her heart immediately and her eyes were fluffy with tears. It was because she had been so worried for him. Instead of finding him in trouble, he was actually talking to Ding Yunzi!

When Yi Ping saw Maiden Xiao, he immediately went to her side and asked gently, "Youxue, are you alright?"

Xiao Youxue was trembling in her blood soaked dress!

Yi Ping tried to give her a helping hand but Xiao Youxue stared coldly at him instead.

For a moment, he did not know what to do.

Ding Yunzi gasped, "Where is Xiao Yuanjia? Did you…?"

Xiao Youxue mustered all her strength as she said, "He has been defeated by me."

Ding Yunzi was stunned. She had defeated Xiao Yuanjia on her own? That was impossible. Was her victory purely due to her resolute or…; she took a look at Yi Ping as she thought, "Youxue mental fortitude comes from this young man? She likes him?"

She thought again, "I know that Youxue have a feud with the Eternal Ice Palace. If this Yi Ping is looking for the person that killed his wife, it has to be Youxue. But the Celestial Fairy is still alive, so how did Youxue kills his wife? And if Youxue did not kills his wife, then why is he looking for Youxue? Maybe he did not even know that Youxue is the one that he is looking for?"

Ding Yunzi looked at Xiao Youxue, "You kill him?"

Xiao Youxue looked coldly at her as she said, "I am not as heartless as you. I treat you as my good sister and you even want to kill me."

Ding Yunzi said gently, "I have my orders and my reasons…"

Xiao Youxue hummed coldly, "So you are saying that my life is not worth your reasons?"

Ding Yunzi was equally cold, "Do you think that in your state of condition you have even the strength to withstand my flying swords? And yet, you can still argue with me."

Xiao Youxue had already noticed that she had sprained her ankle as she said, "You can try but don't let me get close to you."

Ding Yunzi said coolly as she raised her swords, "You really think too highly of yourself."

Yi Ping tried to reason with them, "Since both of you know one another, why don't all of you sit down and talk over first?"

Xiao Youxue looked at Yi Ping, "Did you just forget that she is trying to kill you?"

Ding Yunzi said, "Yi Ping, do you know who she is?"

Yi Ping asked, "Who…"

But before he could ask, he was interrupted by a soft merry laugh.

Yi Ping, Xiao Youxue and Ding Yunzi looked at the direction where Xiao Youxue had just come from and saw Lie Qing!

She was looking rosy and in high spirits. Her air was totally different from a while ago!

As Lie Qing walked towards them, she said. "What about me then? Do you mind if I join in the fun? Three versus one, what do you think of your odds of winning?"

Lie Qing blinked at Xiao Youxue who took a step backward all of a sudden!

Xiao Youxue was startled at Lie Qing's sudden transformation in her aura. It seemed that she had suddenly recovered her internal strength. Moreover, from the looks of it, she had been eavesdropping for some time!

Even Ding Yunzi was startled at her appearances!

Xiao Youxue asked of a sudden, "What did you do with Xiao Yuanjia?"

Lie Qing was puzzled why Xiao Youxue had all of a sudden asked her this question, so she said. "Nothing…"

Xiao Youxue said coldly, "You have killed him? Don't lie to me…"

Lie Qing was immediately guilty as she said, "He tries to kill you earlier. I am just trying to help you…"

Xiao Youxue said coldly, "But I have already defeated him and there is no reason for you to do that."

Lie Qing said, "He may be a threat in the future. Do you think if you let him off this time, you can really win him a second time? He already knows all your tricks in your sleeves!"

Ding Yunzi began to tremble, "Xiao Yuanjia is now dead…?"

Xiao Youxue hummed coldly, "So you have finally admitted to killing him. Not only have you killed him but you have also sucked him dry of any internal energy."

Lie Qing was stunned, "How do you know?"

Ding Yunzi interrupted coldly, "Your red eyes…"

Yi Ping was confused. What were they talking about?

The Virtuous Palace had a deadly legend that was passed down by the elders. In the past, there was a red eye fraction within the Virtuous Palace. They were the masters and they fed upon their slaves. The masters passed down an imperfect skill, the Divine Virtuous Force to their slaves. When their slaves had reached a certain attainment in the Divine Virtuous Force, they would be sacrificed to their masters; their blood and intricate energy would be drained by them.

Eventually, the slaves decided to rebel against their masters. After a hard sought victory over their former masters, the Xiao Clan emerged as the dominant clan within the Virtuous Palace.

Even though this was a legend but this story was part of their martial training and every protégés in the Virtuous Palace knew of this story.

That was why Xiao Youxue was caution of Lie Qing. When she saw her jubilant aura, she had suspected that the worst had fallen to her brother!

The Virtuous Palace, like the majority of the clans in the martial fraternity loathed exponents that practiced evil skills that drained practitioners of their intricate energies. The Virtuous Palace had strict orders to kill anyone that possessed such abilities.

However, it was a legend and over time, this rule had been forgotten. It was only when Xiao Youxue and Ding Yunzi had seen her red eyes did they remember the legends. But they did not suspect that Lie Qing actually had such ability!

Yi Ping looked Lie Qing and asked her, "Did you really practice such an evil skill? And exactly as Youxue has said?"

Lie Qing was annoyed as she pointed at Ding Yunzi with her sword, "Just who are the enemy? That is her! We should be united and fighting against a common enemy, am I not right to say so?"

All of a sudden, Ding Yunzi whirled her foldable sword and threw it as a flying sword against her while she was talking. That was because that was the moment when she had let down her guard and was distracted!

There was a thunderous clashing as the flying sword spins multiple times as it struck against Lie Qing's black sword as she raised it to block against her attacks!

Lie Qing was stunned at the martial power of Ding Yunzi and the ferocity of her flying swords at this distance even though she had secretly observed the duel between Xiao Youxue and Xiao Yuanjia.

She quickly took more than ten steps backward as she tried to deflect the power of the spinning flying sword! But even before she got a respite, Ding Yunzi had raised her other long sword as she leapt forward!

But before she could even took a step forward, Xiao Youxue had raised her long sleeves upward, sending a scurrying of windforce that sent her backward!

Yi Ping quickly intercepted Xiao Youxue as he said hurriedly, "Youxue, she has lost her mobility…"

Xiao Youxue asked him coldly, "Why are you defending her?"

Just when Ding Yunzi had just recovered her footings, Lie Qing had leapt forward and attacked her with a lightning sword arc!

Yi Ping saw the attack and he quickly raised his long sword and deflected Lie Qing's attacks as he said, "Qing'Er, stop. This is all a misunderstanding…"

Xiao Youxue had attacked Lie Qing with her palm and had struck against Lie Qing on her shoulder as she said, "There is no misunderstanding. She is evil!"

Lie Qing was knocked painfully backward as a cracking sound could be heard from her left shoulder!

She hatefully said, "You hit me!?" If she were not protected by her Impervious Golden Body Divine Skill, Xiao Youxue would have fractured her left shoulder!

She immediately attacked Xiao Youxue with her long sword but Yi Ping immediately raised his sword to intercept her as he said, "Qing'Er, Youxue does not have any weapons on her…"

Before Yi Ping had even realized it, he was fighting Lie Qing, Xiao Youxue and Ding Yunzi at the same time, and so were they!

The fights were extremely messy. Yi Ping was trying to stop them from harming one another; the only way to stop them was to fight them and intercept their attacks but at the same time, he was also protecting them at the same time!

None of the maidens really wished to hurt Yi Ping so they stayed their hands. It was because they could tell that Yi Ping was trying to protect them too. But the more Yi Ping defended the other maidens, the more upset they were and the more ruthless their strokes were!

Yi Ping was shouting, "Stop! Stop it!"

But his pleads fell on deaf ears as they continued to fight.

He was parrying, blocking, moving to and forth. This was the most difficult fight in this life; he had never felt so hurried and frantic in his life before!

All of a sudden, Lie Qing gave a soft cry as her black sword become dozens of black blurs that spit out towards Ding Yunzi!

Ding Yunzi gave a startled cry, "What kind of swordplay is this?"

Yi Ping immediately displayed his Horizon Swordplay, the Shadow Horizon Stance and intercepted Lie Qing's attacks!

This stance of his happened to be her swordplay nemesis.

Lie Qing was startled, "How did you know this stance?"

But as she gasped out, Xiao Youxue and Ding Yunzi attacked her at the same time!

Yi Ping turned and parry off Ding Yunzi sword thrust while he intercepted Xiao Youxue's attacks with his left hand!

Xiao Youxue and Lie Qing suddenly blurred out, "Whose side are you on?!"

When Yi Ping heard it, he was momentarily stunned. It was because someone else used to exclaim the same phrase to him; he had remembered Ji Lingfeng all of a sudden.

In this crucial moment, he had actually allowed his mind to wander. If he was fighting others, he would never allow his concentration to lapse. But because he did not really treat Lie Qing, Xiao Youxue or even Ding Yunzi as his enemies; he was distracted when he had suddenly thought of Maiden Ji. Moreover, he was already on his verge of his limits and he could not concentrate further!

Xiao Youxue, Ding Yunzi and Lie Qing were already lenient and careful when they were fighting Yi Ping. But because Yi Ping was suddenly distracted and they had not expected him not to evade their attacks with his current martial progression, they had all slashed and struck him at the same time!

Yi Ping gave a loud cry as he was slashed and was struck by them as he fell onto the ground immediately!

The fighting maidens immediately froze in their tracks at the same time!

Xiao Youxue said melancholy to them, "Why did the two of you slash him for?"

Lie Qing had turned white with ashen as she spoke back and said, "You're the one who struck him the hardest…"

Ding Yunzi shook her head as she smiled bitterly, "You are all his friends..?"

Chapter 25: The New Virtuous Palace

Young Master Qiu Wufeng was breathless. He had narrowly escaped with his life when he was attacked by Ye Lu the Lightning God, Qiao Feng the Shadow Kicker and Lu Baiyun the Heartless Scholar.

He was laughing bitterly now. Ye Lu, Qiao Feng and Lu Baiyun were his former subordinates. Yet they had conspired to betray his clan. Overnight, the Qiu Martial Clan was massacred by these three evil men. More than three hundred of his clan protégés were all killed and the rest had surrendered.

He was fortunate to have escaped.

Gu Tianle was now the Grand Master of the Honor Manor and he had the lofty ambition to dominate the entire fraternity under his leadership.

The Qiu Martial Clan had always opposed the Gongsun Martial Clan and the Honor Manor. Over the years, there had been bad blood between the two major martial clans and many were killed.

It was only in the recent twenty-years that the Gongsun Martial Clan had overshadowed the Qiu Martial Clan. It was more the reasons to resent the Honor Manor.

The Qiu Martial Clan under the leadership of his father Qiu Cang, recruited Ye Lu, Qiao Feng and Lu Baiyun to the Qiu Martial Clan in order to strengthen the fighting strength of the Qiu Martial Clan. They were made the Masters of the White, Black and Yellow Factions.

Ye Lu and Qiao Feng were the ones that had maimed Gu Tianle and there were a bitter feud between them. By taking them in, the feud between the two martial clans deepened.

When Gongsun Bai had died, Gu Tianle took over the helm of the Honor Manor as the new Grandmaster, instead of Gongsun Jing. Gu Tianle proved to be even more ruthless than the late Gongsun Bai and his lofty ambitions were revealed the moment he had become Grandmaster. Many elders and protégés of the Gongsun Clan who had opposed him were killed immediately.

Just when the Qiu Martial Clan was secretly rejoiced over the demise of the once powerful Gongsun Bai, they were also betrayed by their own followers!

Gu Tianle had promised Ye Lu and Qiao Feng that if they could bring the Qiu Martial Clan into the Honor Manor, not only he would forgive them for their past transgressions, he would promise them great wealth and a position as one of the masters of the Honor Manor!

Naturally this offer was extremely tempting to them!

One would have thought that the Honor Manor would have suffered a great blow at the demise of Gongsun Bai. That was not the case.

Over the years, Gu Tianle had carefully nurtured his reputation as a fearsome fighter and his renown was not beneath that of Gongsun Bai; he had already gained fame and renown for killing Ji Yunzhong, the former Protégé Master of the Holy Hex Sect twenty years ago.

Now with the threat of the various unorthodox clans and even the heretic sects in the nervous horizon, there was no other person that was more suitable to lead the orthodox fraternity than Gu Tianle himself.

Because the Gongsun Clan had been oppressing the various orthodox clans for many years, when the Gongsun Clan had met with demise, few pugilists in the fraternity were willing to come to their aid even though what Gu Tianle did was not entirely righteous.

But who could say that Gu Tianle was entirely wrong? He had seized the power and had become the Grandmaster of the Honor Manor. What happened to the Gongsun Clan was their internal affair. The orthodox fraternity had never questioned the internal affairs of the various martial clans. It was because all the martial clans had their own clan rules and internal punishments. It was generally acknowledged that Gu Tianle was now the Grand Master and what was happening now was an act of asserting his authority for the stability of his rule.

Within the first month of assuming the leadership of the Honor Manor, Gu Tianle had established the twelve golden halls of the Honor Manor. Each of the golden halls was to be helm by a master with authority second only to the Grandmaster himself! Criteria to the golden halls were also very strict in the Honor Manor, selecting only the best fighters.

Ye Lu and Qiao Feng naturally did not want to be an enemy of Gu Tianle as they knew of his vengeful nature. Therefore when the Honor Manor had sent them a secret message to bring the Qiu Martial Clan under the influence of the Honor Manor, they had made the decision to accept almost immediately.

Young Master Qiu struck his fist bitterly at a tree truck as he cried out loudly, "Ye Lu, Qiao Feng and Lu Baiyun! You traitors! You have killed so many of my clan members. If I do not cut all of you to pieces, I will not rest!"

All of a sudden, Qiu Wufeng detected the presence of a living person as he said panicky. "Who is that? Who is so sneaky?"

A person jumped down from the tree above him and sighed, "You have not changed at all…"

When Qiu Wufeng saw him, he was startled and said. "Gongsun Jing!"

Indeed, it was Gongsun Jing!

Gongsun Jing smiled bitterly, "I am not a sneaky person. It is just that you are disturbing my rest."

Qiu Wufeng had drawn out his long sword and said, "The Honor Manor is here finally. Gongsun Jing, you're a despicable man. You have killed my kin and many of my followers. If I do not kill you today, I am not a man. Do you dare to fight with me one on one?"

Gongsun Jing drew his long sword as he said, "There are four things that you must know first. First, I am alone. Secondly, I am not from the Honor Manor anymore. Thirdly, I am not the one that has killed your kin. The one that has killed your kin is you!"

Qiu Wufeng interrupted angrily, "I am the one that has killed my kin? What rubbish is that? You are talking crap!"

Gongsun Jing said bitterly, "You may not but that is not what everyone is saying now. Because your affair with your father's mistress is discovered, in your moment of foolhardy, you have killed your father. You have even tried to seize the position of Grand Master of the Qiu Martial Clan but are opposed by your elders. Therefore, your faction and those that oppose you broke into a power struggle. Eventually, evil cannot triumph over good and your wicked deeds are exposed by Ye Lu, Qiao Feng and Lu Baiyun who opposed your wickedness."

Qiu Wufeng was enraged, "This is all lies! I would kill my father!? They are the ones that have killed all my kin!"

Gongsun Jin said coldly, "Do you think that with your puny skills that you can escape from the fraternity three topmost exponents?"

Qiu Wufeng was stunned. He slowly said, "They have intended to make me the scapegoat from the very start?"

Gongsun Jing said, "Now you got it…"

Qiu Wufeng smiled bitterly as he said, "No wonder. But it is my lucky fortune that I have met you alone. I will kill you to vent my frustrations!"

Gongsun Jing said, "Hold! Don't you want to hear my forth reason first?"

Qiu Wufeng said coldly, "You can say it now."

Gongsun Jing said bitterly, "Like you, I am also a fugitive wanted by the Honor Manor and Gu Tianle."

Qiu Wufeng was startled, "You are a fugitive too?"

Gongsun Jing said, "Look at my broken clothes. Do I look like I am lying to you?"

Qiu Wufeng looked carefully at Gongsun Jing. Indeed all his former finery was gone and he looked worn out. He muttered, "What happens?"

Gongsun Jing said, "Gu Tianle is now the Grand Master of the Honor Manor. The mantle should be helmed by me. But because Gu Tianle had become the Grand Master, all my other brothers and elders who had protested were killed by Jue Yuan and him."

He paused before adding, "Like you, I am now a fugitive. My crimes? For killing my brothers…"

Qiu Wufeng lowered his long sword as he said, "To think that both of us who used to be the most powerful young masters of the martial fraternity would be in this plight…"

Gongsun Jing said coolly, "Indeed."

Qiu Wufeng asked, "So what are your plans now?"

Gongsun Jing said, "What else? I have a score to settle with Gu Tianle."

All of a sudden, there was a couple of wicked laughter. "I am afraid you don't have the chance."

Both Qiu Wufeng and Gongsun Jing looked to the direction of the wicked laughter and saw Ye Lu and Qiao Feng!

Ye Lu said, "I have heard that anyone that could capture or kill either Gongsun Jing or Qiu Wufeng would be made one of the Masters of the Golden Halls of the Honor Manor. If we kill the two of them, would we be made the master of two golden halls?"

Qiao Feng laughed, "We cannot let them die until we have what we want."

Gongsun Jing said coldly, "What do you mean?"

Ye Lu said, "Young Master Jing, I have heard that you are always the smart one. If Young Master Wufeng and you are willing to tell us where you hide your clan martial treasures and riches, we will definitely let you go."

Qiu Wufeng shouted angrily, "Never!"

Gongsun Jing said coolly, "I do not know what you mean."

Qiao Feng stepped forward, "There are worst fates that death itself. I would make you regret for not telling us what you know earlier."

Gongsun Jing glanced at Qiu Wufeng as he said, "You are on my side?"

Qiu Wufeng said bitterly, "I hate to say this but yes, I am on your side."

Gongsun Jing said solemnly, "Good. What past is the past. We should put aside our differences and fight on the same side."

The reason that he had said that was because this fight was a critical fight. He did not want to fight against Ye Lu and Qiao Feng at the same time, yet he had to watch his back for Qiu Wufeng.

Qiu Wufeng said, "I agree with you."

Qiu Wufeng was worried about the same thing too. Gongsun Jing words had assured him more or less even though it was hard for them to put aside years of differences and spat.

Qiao Feng said, "Are you done talking? As your seniors, we will let you attack us first."

Gongsun Jing said, "Thank you!" And he immediately thrust his sword at Qiao Feng.

Qiu Wufeng was not slow either as he immediately raised his sword towards Ye Lu!

Gongsun Jing was a renowned swordsman in his own right and he had many martial masters while he was in the Honor Manor. However, no matter how swift or intrigue his swordplay had been, he could not steady his sword against the powerful windforce kicks of Qiao Feng and received a few hard kicks in return!

When swordplay could not be steadied, the openings were many and many of his stances became useless. Therefore he put aside his sword and used his fists instead.

Qiu Wufeng was a superior swordsman. His windless wordplay was renowned in the fraternity. Unfortunately, Ye Lu was his former martial master and was too familiar with his swordplay. In less than a hundred strokes, he had been struck a dozen blows by Ye Lu!

Qiu Wufeng and Gongsun Jing were knocked on the ground at almost the same time. They were haggard and had several external injuries.

Ye Lu said coldly, "Are you convinced now? We will break every single bone in your body and make sure that you are living a worse fate than death. Unless of course, you will tell us what we want to know."

Gongsun Jing laughed aloud as he spat out blood from his mouth, "I would die than tell you anything. Men like you will not keep any promises."

Qiao Feng said, "We promise to let the both of you live and go your way. After all, we have a reputation in the fraternity."

Qiu Wufeng interrupted fiercely, "Promise my foot! You have sworn your fealty to me and now you are after my life!"

Qiao Feng said coldly, "That is because you have murdered your father. That is why!" He raised his leg to kick Qiu Wufeng when all of a sudden, he saw a young man in white appearing quietly.

Qiao Feng and Ye Lu both took a step backward in startled surprise!

They were startled that someone would approach them so quietly until he was in full view of them.

Qiao Feng asked, "Who are you?"

Gongsun Jing and Qiu Wufeng had recognized Yi Ping immediately!

The noble young man in white said coolly, "I am Yi Ping. We have met before."

Qiao Feng looked intently at this young man but he did not remember ever seeing such a dashing young man before. He asked, "We have met before?"

Yi Ping said, "At the Heavenly Mountains, we once had a fight."

Qiao Feng received a jolt in his head, "It is you!" He immediately attacked him with his multiple kicks!

He shouted, "Young man, I'll recognize you!"

Indeed he had. He was still bitter about his defeat by a nobody in the Heavenly Mountains. This had caused him a great loss of face and caused him to be disdained by the Heartless Scholar.

Yi Ping said coldly, "Do you want to be defeated by me again?"

Qiao Feng did not show any mercy as he displayed his most epitome techniques. Yi Ping was startled but composed himself quickly as he unleashed a barrage of kicks in retaliation.

Try as hard as Qiao Feng in attacking him, this young man was like an impenetrable wall. He was astonished that this Yi Ping had progressed so fast in such a short span of time!

After a while, Qiao Feng was surprised at the persistent and strength of the young man's kick that he shouted, "Brother Ye, why are you still standing there? Hurry and help me!"

Ye Lu was startled. Even though they were unorthodox fighters and honor did not mean anything to them but to gang up against a junior…if word get out that they would fight a junior together, they would lose their faces in the eyes of the other exponents in the fraternity!

Qiao Feng was shouting desperately, "Brother Ye, what are you waiting for! Hurry!"

Ye Lu sighed as he reluctantly entered the melee with his famous 'Lighting God Hands', fast as lightning, hit like thunder!

Yi Ping was gaining the upper hand when the Lightning God entered the melee fray. He quickly lifted another vital breath and focused his will with the 'Absolute Spirits Intricate Formula' and used the Divine Horizon Hands against Ye Lu.

Instead of weakening against the combined attacks of Qiao Feng and Ye Lu, Yi Ping was fighting even more furiously than ever!

They were surprised that Yi Ping could use his hands against Ye Lu, legs against Qiao Feng at the same time without breaking into a sweat!

While Yi Ping had been composed, Ye Lu and Qiao Feng was sweating and breathing heavily. They had taken several hits and had used up most of their vital strength and they had still not been able to hit him even once!

Yi Ping had used the 'Resolute Strength Recite' and the 'Unfaltering Recite' from the 'Absolute Spirits Intricate Formulate' to increase his resolute and speed. The stronger his opponents, the stronger he must be!

Ye Lu had never expected this young man to be so strong! Qiao Feng and he was one of the top exponents of the martial fraternity and they had fought untold powerful exponents together, including the Celestial Fairy. Even Gu Tianle was once mortally wounded by them. Yet this young man was able to hold them off effortlessly. It was totally unbelievable!

Ye Lu shouted, "This young man may not be able withstand our martial power at the same time!"

Qiao Feng immediately understood his intentions and he raised the martial power in both his hands. "That is right! No matter how strong he is, he will crack his bones if he tries to withstand our full strength!"

Ye Lu nodded and he too raised all his martial power in his hands as they charged at Yi Ping together! Because they were in close proximity and had suddenly changed their attacking stances, Yi Ping was caught in their midst! He immediately raised his martial power and displayed the Asper Continuum Horizon Hands!

There were a slightly visible blue and yellow flames that seemed to radiate from his shoulders as his hands became dozens of shadow palms as the three of them clashed at each other!

Ye Lu and Qiao Feng could not take the force of this stance which was greater than their martial powers that they were both knocked back onto the ground violently!

Even though the 'Asper Continuum Horizon Hands' was the second stance of the 'Divine Horizon Stances', it was not stronger than the first stance of the 'Asper Horizon Hands'. It was because the second stance actually split the martial power evenly in-between the shadow palms.

Qiao Feng stared in disbelief! He could not believe that he would lose to this young man once again!

Ye Lu was famous for his Lightning God Hands and known for his speed attacks. In that single moment, he had counter-attacked with two dozen quick fists but he was still knocked back and was overwhelmed by more than an extra dozen strikes by Yi Ping!

Together with Qiao Feng, they had unleashed all their martial power as their own attacks split into dozens of shadow punches and kicks. But Yi Ping was still able to block off and counter-attacked with more than a dozen extra attacks more than them!

Yi Ping said coldly, "Now scram!"

Ye Lu and Qiao Feng picked themselves up awkwardly as they stared hatefully at Yi Ping. They were still able to fight and had not used up all their secret techniques.

Qiu Wufeng was stunned as he said, "You are going to let them off? These villains killed my clan protégés. You mustn't let them off!"

Gongsun Jing was silent. He was known as Gongsun Jing the Benevolent but in his heart, he knew these two villains deserved to die.

Ye Lu immediately said to Yi Ping, "Young hero, since you have already said we can go and we are not your enemies, you have to honor what you have just said. Just because we do not fight you, doesn't mean we fear you. We still have several techniques and tricks in our sleeves which we don't want to reveal it yet. So, don't force us."

Qiao Feng warned Yi Ping, "Next time, you won't be so lucky. When I am one of the masters of the Honor Manor, I will surely look for you. But today, you can take them both away. But it is only for today. You can't protect them all the time."

Yi Ping hummed coldly, "I think you are only trying to salvage your honor."

Ye Lu said coldly, "Not at all. We have seen you with the Celestial Fairy. The martial skills of the Eternal Ice Palace are well known throughout the fraternity. Knowing that we are defeated by the Eternal Ice Palace is not a dishonorable thing. Farewell!"

Immediately Ye Lu and Qiao Feng took off. It was as though they had never been here!

Qiu Wufeng and Gongsun Jing bowed with their hands to Yi Ping, "Thank you for saving my life."

Gongsun Jing said, "Why do you come to our aid? Are we not enemies?"

Qiu Wufeng scoffed, "Maybe he saved you just to kill you personally."

Gongsun Jing was startled as he took a step backward.

Yi Ping said, "I am just passing through when I heard the sounds of fighting. Out of curiosity, I have come to take a look. I do recognize you, Young Master Gongsun Jing. My feud is only between your father and I."

Gongsun Jing looked touched as he said hesitatingly, "I am no longer any master. You can call me Gongsun Jing. If you do not mind a down and out friend such as me, I will like to befriend you…"

Qiu Wufeng was startled as he thought, "This Gongsun Jing is really quick to recruit others to his banner. If I am slower than him, then I will lose a lot of prestige and face."

So he quickly interrupted, "Brother Yi Ping, if you don't mind a brother such as me, we can even become sworn brothers."

Gongsun Jing lost his composure as he said coldly, "You call yourself a noble? You just interrupt a conversation between us. I am about to ask Brother Yi Ping if he wants to be my sworn brother first!"

Qiu Wufeng said angrily, "I am the one that suggest it and you are trying to upset me by suggesting the same!"

Yi Ping smiled bitterly as he looked at them before saying, "There is no need to quarrel over this. If Brother Qiu Wufeng and Brother Gongsun Jing do not mind, we can all become sworn brothers. I hope that the two of you will forget past feuds and get along well with one another. I have heard what had happened to you and I do not believe a word of it. At this moment of time, the two of you should unite against a common enemy and find a way to right your wrongs."

Gongsun Jing and Qiu Wufeng were suddenly feeling awkward and were guilty. They lowered their heads in shame…

After some time, Gongsun Jing said. "Brother Yi Ping, you are right. But I have no other friends and with my skills alone, it not possible for me to challenge Gu Tianle or the entire Honor Manor alone."

He turned to Qiu Wufeng and said, "Brother Wufeng, if there are any past offends, I hope that you do not put it into heart."

Qiu Wufeng was stunned that the haughty Gongsun Jing would actually apologize to him. He began to stammer as he said, "Please forgive me for my past transgressions too…"

Yi Ping smiled broadly as he patted their shoulders, "That is the way. From now on, we are brothers…"

All of a sudden, he was interrupted by the terrifying shout of Ye Lu and Qiao Feng who had suddenly returned with fresh injuries!

From the look of that, they had just been attacked when they had just left a few moments ago.

Even Qiu Wufeng and Gongsun Jing were startled at what caused Ye Lu and Qiao Feng to be so terrified. Was there a fighter that was more fearsome than Yi Ping?

An enthralling young maiden in yellow with no weapons had just walked into view.

From Ye Lu and Qiao Feng terrified expressions, it was this young maiden that had caused them to be so terrified!

Qiu Wufeng and Gongsun Jing were moved at her sight.

Qiu Wufeng immediately thought, "It is her? Even though she was veiled at that time at the Heavenly Mountains, I can still recognize her mannerism…She is indeed a wondrous beauty…"

Ye Lu and Qiao Feng both gave a shout as they attacked her at the same time in a desperate bid to escape.

Ye Lu raised all his martial power in his fist as he hurled his fist toward her but she simply raised her palm and there was a thunderous clapping sound as both hands clashed against one another!

Ye Lu was sent flying backward as he yelled aloud in pain!

Qiao Feng had raised his powerful legs and had attacked her with a powerful kick! But she simply raised her foot to retaliate against his kick!

Qiao Feng rolled backward as her kick missed him but there was a loud thunderous impact on the ground as her foot kicked against the ground!

The power of her martial power was startling and frightening!

Yi Ping gasped, "Youxue…"

Just when Qiao Feng had evaded her kick, he had immediately turned into the other direction to flee from her!

But another attractive young maiden had already appeared quietly as she eyed Qiao Feng with her long sword!

Qiu Wufeng and Gongsun Jing immediately turned green with fright as their legs grew soft! It was because they had suddenly recognized this young maiden was none other than Ding Yunzi, whom they had recognized as from the Virtuous Palace!

Gongsun Jing would never forget that it was she that had chopped off his father's head in front of him and it was she that had caused him to be in this miserable state…

Qiao Feng shouted, "Don't you dare to stop me!" He immediately unleashed dozens of secret projectiles at her!

While he was famously known as the Shadow Kicker, few in the martial fraternity knew that his most powerful technique was actually his Shadowless Secret Projectiles! It was a secret that he did not want to reveal unless he had no choice!

Yi Ping was startled as he shouted, "Yunzi, be careful!"

The secret projectiles flew with a loud shrieking sound as it sped like meteor showers towards her!

Ding Yunzi whirled her long sword in front of her. As the secret projectiles struck her sword, it exploded multiple times with a loud clashing sound one after another as thick green fumes were given out!

The secret projectiles had been coated with poison!

Qiao Feng laughed aloud, "Young maiden! You are too inexperienced and belittle me!"

Yi Ping could not see past the thick smoke as he shouted, "You despicable man!"

But before he could take a step forward, the thick smoke had been cleared by Ding Yunzi's whirling sword!

Qiao Feng was startled as he said, "You are unharmed?"

Ding Yunzi said coolly, "Do you think I have not second guessed that wily trick of yours?"

Even before he could recover from his surprise, he saw a flying scabbard that was hurled by her towards him!

The speed of the scabbard was simply unbelievable!

He raised all his martial power and kicked away the flying scabbard just in time. There was a loud cracking sound as he turned pale!

He had not expected this young maiden to have possessed such a great depth in her internal strength. As soon as he kicked the flying scabbard, his foot was fractured with a loud impact!

Ding Yunzi had actually stayed her hand. If she had thrown her flying sword towards him after he had kicked her flying scabbard, he would be too exhausted to avoid her follow up attack.

Ye Lu and Qiao Feng were breathing heavily as they cried out panicky at the same time, "Do we even have a feud?"

"You really want to know?"

Ye Lu and Qiao Feng were startled!

A mesmerizing young maiden in a beautiful pink dress had suddenly appeared behind them!

Yi Ping gasped, "Lie Qing…"

Lie Qing smiled amiably, "I can tell you so that the two of you can die peacefully."

Ye Lu hastily said, "What feud do we have with the Virtuous Palace? We have never offended the Virtuous Palace…"

Lie Qing smiled, "There is no feud in the past but there is now."

Qiao Feng stammered, "What do you mean?"

Lie Qing pointed at Yi Ping as she said, "Who he wants to spare, we will kill. Who he tries to kill, we will let live."

Yi Ping was stammering, "All of you…"

Lie Qing smiled at Qiu Wufeng and Gongsun Jing as she said, "I have heard that the two of you are going to become his sworn brother? Is that so?"

Qiu Wufeng and Gongsun Jing immediately turned white. It was because they had personally witnessed the martial skills of the Virtuous Palace before. And now there were three of them…

Even though they were all enchanting and extremely beautiful, Gongsun Jing and Qiu Wufeng were terrified because they knew they were going to die.

Gongsun Jing looked at Ding Yunzi as he said, "I may not be a hero but I am not afraid of death."

Qiu Wufeng smiled bitterly, "Even though I am afraid of death but I have nothing now. If I can die with my friends, it is at least better than being a coward."

Yi Ping called out panicky, "Lie Qing, why are you threatening my friends?"

Lie Qing swept her crimson eyes at them one by one. Anyone that she swept past with her eyes could feel a cold piercing uneasy feeling that instantly shivered them!

Ye Lu said, "Five of us versus the three of them. If we join hands together, we can win…"

Qiu Wufeng said coldly, "I will rather see you getting killed than join hands with you. Don't forget that I have a vendetta with you!"

Qiao Feng said, "We need to make a decision fast or we won't survive this…"

But before he could finish, Lie Qing had dealt him a blow on his forehead and had moved swiftly past him and struck Ye Lu on his forehead at the same time!

There were two startling loud banging sound as Qiao Feng and Ye Lu fell down dead onto the ground!

Her speed was so startling that Yi Ping, Qiu Wufeng and Gongsun Jing were staring in shock!

Yi Ping shouted angrily, "Why did you kill them for!? They are already injured!"

Lie Qing blinked at him as she smiled, "I am helping you to kill all your enemies so that you can be a righteous hero."

Xiao Youxue said coldly, "These villains deserved their just desserts."

Ding Yunzi asked softly, "Does Young Master Gongsun Jing wants to avenge your father now?"

Gongsun Jing immediately said to Yi Ping, "Brother, since we have agreed to be sworn brothers, you got to help me avenge my father."

At this, Yi Ping was stunned for words.

Chapter 26: Memories

All of a sudden, there was a powerful malevolent aura that seemingly came from another direction.

Yi Ping, Gongsun Jing, Qiu Wufeng, Xiao Youxue, Ding Yunzi and Lie Qing looked towards that direction and saw a man with a sword walking silently towards them!

Yi Ping had recognized him to be Zuo Tianyi!

Zuo Tianyi said coldly, "Whoever tries to lay a hand on Maiden Ding, I will kill him."

Ding Yunzi gasped, "Tianyi…"

Qiu Wufeng spit out, "So it is young master Zuo Tianyi. Are you here to take our lives too? I have great respect for the old sword saint but you are just a lackey of the Honor Manor!"

Zuo Tianyi said coldly, "I don't care what the Honor Manor wants but since you have the intention of killing Maiden Ding, then don't blame me."

He looked at Yi Ping and said, "We seem to have an unfinished duel."

Yi Ping said, "Indeed! But unfortunately I have no wish to fight you and I don't have a sword."

Zuo Tianyi looked at Yi Ping coldly, "You can always borrow one. With or without a sword, I will not hesitate to kill you."

Lie Qing stole a glance at Ding Yunzi before saying to Zuo Tianyi, "I am afraid if you really want to kill Yi Ping, Maiden Ding will never forgive you."

Zuo Tianyi asked, "What do you mean?"

Lie Qing smiled, "That is because Yi Ping is our protégé master now. If you want to kill Yi Ping, then you have to fight the three of us too."

Zuo Tianyi was taken aback, "He is your protégé master now?" He looked at Ding Yunzi for answers. He had always thought that Ding Yunzi was from the Virtuous Palace and that Xiao Shuai was her protégé master!

Ding Yunzi said coolly, "That is so."

Qiu Wufeng immediately knew by now that these three maidens were not his enemies. So he was relieved as he said quickly to the three maidens as he bowed respectfully, "Even though my martial skills are weak, I will gladly fight on your side!"

Lie Qing looked at Qiu Wufeng as she said, "At least you have some courage and willingly to stand by Yi Ping or else I would have killed you instantly earlier."

Qiu Wufeng smiled bitterly at this mesmerizing maiden who was rebuking him fiercely. But he immediately thought, "If I were to be killed by her, it may not be a bad feeling after all. After all, I have lost everything now…"

Gongsun Jing was stunned as he said, "You are all on the same side!?"

Zuo Tianyi stared at Gongsun Jing, "Then I have to kill only you instead."

Gongsun Jing looked at Yi Ping and said, "Brother Yi Ping, you got to help me!"

Yi Ping rubbed his nose as he looked at everyone before he said to Gongsun Jing, "I don't wish to help you because what you want to do is not an entire chivalrous act. Everyone knows that Gongsun Bai had been oppressing the orthodox fraternity for many years…"

Gongsun Jing shifted uneasily.

Yi Ping said, "Even though you have the nick of Gongsun Jing the Benevolent and is different from your father. But that is not what everyone thinks."

Gongsun Jing looked down in guilt. It was true. He had known of his father lofty ambitions for a long time and had even tried to persuade him to take a more benevolent path but his father had scorned at his advice.

Yi Ping looked at Zuo Tianyi as he continued, "Moreover, I don't want to make enemies of Zuo Tianyi. The Zuo and the Yi Clan had been acquaintances for many generations. We are not enemies in the first place and why should it turned into a feud?"

Zuo Tianyi nodded slightly. He knew that was the truth. It was because the Infinity Sword Clan had adjusted its swordplay three generations ago to counteract the Horizon Swordplay. And when they had dueled, he had found Yi Ping to be very familiar as though they had dueled before. The reason that they had fought to a standstill was that both of them knew how to counter one another's swordplay as though they had fought before on numerous times!

That was also why Yi Ping's father, Yi Tianxing knew the Infinity Swordplay so well that he was able to forewarn Yi Ping that the Horizon Swordplay could be broken by the Infinity-First Swordplay.

Finally Yi Ping said to Gongsun Jing as he smiled bitterly, "Your father had courted his own death and refusing to let Xiao Shuai go. It was a fair duel. Even without Maiden Ding interfering, do you think your father would able to win against Xiao Shuai?"

Gongsun Jing said solemnly, "If Maiden Ding had not interfered, the outcome would still be uncertain!"

Zuo Tianyi said coldly, "That was not what I have seen."

Gongsun Jing asked, "What do you mean?"

Zuo Tianyi said coldly, "Even before Maiden Ding had struck your father, Xiao Shuai had already penetrated through his Invincible Divine Force!"

Gongsun Jing said, "That is impossible. There were so many eyes in that hall that day. Xiao Shuai attacks cannot possible penetrates through my father's Invincible Divine Force!"

Yi Ping said, "That is because your eyes are not sharp enough. If Gongsun Bai could even deflect Xiao Shuai's flying sword with his bare hands, do you think that Maiden Ding's flying sword could even cut through his arms at all? That was because at that very instant, his Invincible Divine Force had already been breached!"

Gongsun Jing was stunned. Why he had not thought of that?

He finally said, "You guys have already thought of that?"

Xiao Youxue interrupted as she said, "They didn't and didn't have to. They just witnessed it. Why did you think that Gu Tianle and the rest of the protégé masters of the various major orthodox clans did not bulge at all when Gongsun Bai was killed? It was because their eyes were quick enough to see it themselves."

She knew because she was there too but remained hidden from view! That was why she knew that Yi Ping may be courting his own death and took a gambit to lure Xiao Shuai into the Honor Manor!

She added, "The one that really killed your father is Xiao Shuai. I have heard that even Gu Tianle and Jue Yuan is hunting you. You can't even avenge against Xiao Shuai, Gu Tianle and Jue Yuan yet you are looking to avenge against Maiden Ding? You are really courting your own death!"

Yi Ping said, "Moreover, even if the two of us added up together, do you think we can win against the sword in her hands?"

Yi Ping still shivered when he recalled the battle with her. He had only accidentally won when she had sprained her ankle at the wrong timing!

He did not dare to look into Maiden Ding's eyes directly as he said that. It was because he very well knew that she was toying with him even though he had already used up all the strokes of the Horizon Swordplay! He was now worried that he may hurt her feelings if he was too close to her. The same went for Maiden Xiao Youxue and Maiden Lie Qing too…

Yi Ping said coolly, "You have to decide if you want to avenge against her now or want me as your sworn brother."

Gongsun Jing looked at everyone slowly. It was the hardest decision that he had ever made in his life.

Actually when he first seen Maiden Ding, he had already been attracted by her quiet demeanor and air. When she had stormed into the Honor Manor with Xiao Shuai, he was in fact worried what would happen to her fate. What he had not expected was that Xiao Shuai actually did the impossible and killed his father. And because afterwards, he was persecuted by Gu Tianle, he was filled with a burning hatred for everyone that was involved in the demise of his clan.

When he looked at Maiden Ding's quiet demeanor again, he really could not bring the heart to even lay a finger on her even though he still held her partly responsible.

Gongsun Jing said slowly, "I will still want to be Brother Yi Ping's sworn brother. My real enemies are Xiao Shuai and Gu Tianle."

Yi Ping said, "Then I'll be able to help you. I still have a score to settle with Gu Tianle and Jue Yuan for conspiring with your father to injure my father years ago."

Gongsun Jing said, "You won't hold against me? My father was the one that…"

Yi Ping interrupted, "What your father did is his own business. That has nothing to do with you. Moreover, he is dead now. I hope you can forgive Maiden Ding too. Or else I won't agree to be your sworn brother at all if I bear a grudge against you."

Gongsun Jing was deeply touched as he looked at Yi Ping who seemed to be a giant, surrounded by a strong sense of benevolent and righteousness.

He stammered out, "I don't blame Maiden Ding at all…"

Zuo Tianyi said, "Pity. I have come here for nothing."

Everyone looked at Zuo Tianyi startled. They had almost forgotten that Zuo Tianyi was not on their side yet.

Lie Qing blinked at Zuo Tianyi as she said, "Great Hero, I can tell immediately that you are a master swordsman. What do you mean? Are you here on the behalf of the Honor Manor?" as she took a step forward.

Zuo Tianyi took a step backward as he smiled, "Hold it. Don't come close to me. I have just seen how Qiao Feng and Ye Lu were killed by you."

Lie Qing was offended as she said, "Am I so terrible to behold or too fierce for your taste, Great Hero?"

Zuo Tianyi smiled, "I am not interested in you for sure." He took a quick glance at Ding Yunzi who looked shyly away.

Yi Ping, Qiu Wufeng and Gongsun Jing were clearly amused. It was because even a blind man could tell how mesmerizing Lie Qing was and Zuo Tianyi was telling her how unattractive she was to him!

Lie Qing replied coldly, "So what do you want?"

Zuo Tianyi laughed, "I just want to be a sworn brother to Yi Ping as well and then we find a place to drink or else it will be hard for me to go off just like that."

Yi Ping was surprised too as he quickly said, "It is my honor too! Brother Tianyi!"

Zuo Tianyi said, "Brother Yi Ping!"

Ding Yunzi interrupted softly, "You better go. The further away, the better it is! What we are going to do next will put you in a very difficult position."

Zuo Tianyi said, "Yunzi, why are you so cold towards me? What did I do wrong…"

It was only now that it was apparent that Zuo Tianyi and Ding Yunzi had known of one another! No wonder, when Gongsun Jing had wanted to avenge against Maiden Ding, they could sense a strong killing malevolent intent from him!

Lie Qing muttered with displeasure, "No wonder you are not interested in talking to me. So you already have a sweetheart. You are afraid that she may get jealous…"

Qiu Wufeng quickly said, "If Maiden did not mind, you can always talk to me…"

Lie Qing hummed coldly, "You should practice more on your martial skills first before talking to me."

Qiu Wufeng immediately flushed red with embarrassment.

Ding Yunzi said, "You did nothing wrong. I just don't want to see you."

Zuo Tianyi said, "I know that you are from the Virtuous Palace and that Xiao Shuai may not approve of our marriage in the past. But I am now the protégé master of the Infinity Sword Clan now, surely Xiao Shuai would take that into consideration and…"

Ding Yunzi interrupted coldly, "You think too much. Just go."

Yi Ping said to Zuo Tianyi, "We know that the Honor Manor is raising an expedition to attack the headquarters of the Holy Hex Sect. We are going there to help a friend of mine. If you join us, it is akin to making enemies of all the orthodox clans in the fraternity. I am sure Maiden Ding meant well."

Zuo Tianyi said quickly to Ding Yunzi, "Even if I were to make enemies of the orthodox clans, I will still join you! I don't even care if the Virtuous Palace is now the enemy of the orthodox fraternity. I will still ask for your hands in marriage. "

Ding Yunzi said coldly, "I am no longer in the Virtuous Palace."

Zuo Tianyi was taken aback as he asked, "You are not?"

Ding Yunzi said, "I have betrayed the Virtuous Palace and now, I am being hunted by the Virtuous Palace. In fact, we are all being hunted by the Virtuous Palace or the Honor Manor. Even if you have ten lives, you may not live to survive it. You are so foolish. The Infinity Sword Clan has painstaking took more than three centuries to establish its position in the fraternity. As your cousin, I feel ashamed that you can choose to throw away the repute of the Infinity Sword Clan just like that. How could you face your Zuo Clan ancestors?"

Zuo Tianyi stammered, "I….I…"

Xiao Youxue sighed in her heart melancholy, "Sister Yun is so tragic. Zuo Tianyi is her childhood sweetheart. Because of that incident, she now uses all other means just to reject his overturns…"

A few days ago…

They had reacted with shock as they had fell Yi Ping by mistake.

Xiao Youxue had immediately resuscitated Yi Ping and was relieved all his vital organs were unhurt. She muttered, "He just needs a rest and will recover. But his wounds may be severe…"

Then she looked at Lie Qing with displeasure as she said, "Hand over the antidote. You have applied poison on your sword. How vicious are you!"

Lie Qing quickly took out a small flask as she said, "It is not my intention to hurt him…you have a hand too…"

Ding Yunzi was secretly relieved but all of a sudden, she burst into tears as she ran off.

Lie Qing was startled when she had suddenly run off. She quickly recovered her senses as she asked herself, "Was I in a daze just now? Why was it so? This young man…"

Xiao Youxue said, "Follow her! Don't let her escape…"

When Xiao Youxue and Lie Qing had caught up with her, she was slashing furiously at Xiao Yuanjia instead!

Her act completely caught Xiao Youxue and Lie Qing by surprise!

Ding Yunzi repeatledy slashed and thrust at the dead body of Xiao Yuanjia, mutilating him. There was rage in her eyes as her quiet demeanor disappeared as she wept bitterly.

Lie Qing was startled, "He is already dead. Why are you slashing him so many times for? You can kill a dead man?"

Even though Lie Qing could see her sorrowful expressions but she could not resist adding an intentional remark to goal her into telling her why she hated Xiao Yuanjia so much. But she could guess as much.

Xiao Youxue covered her mouth with her hand as she too, burst into tears.

It was because she knew the real reasons; Ding Yunzi was abused since young by her father and two brothers. Because of that, Ding Yunzi became cold and distant. That was when her visits to the Infinity Sword Clan had ceased as she trained day and night, hoping that one day, she would kill Xiao Shuai, Xiao Yuanjia and Xiao Da.

At first she did not know the real reason and was upset with her. But one night, she witnessed her bestial brother Xiao Yuanjia forcing himself on Ding Yunzi. Even though he did not succeed but she had been horrified by what her brother was trying to do and finally knew the true reason now. That was not the only abuse that Ding Yunzi had faced…

But because she did not want to hurt her further, she pretended not to know anything about it. In fact, so scarring was this memory, she had even forgotten about it as she began to hate Ding Yunzi for siding with her father and brothers.

Only when she saw Ding Yunzi broke down into tears now as she repeatedly slashed at the dead corpse of Xiao Yuanjia, she remembered how tragic she had been through.

Lie Qing looked bewilderedly at Xiao Youxue and Ding Yunzi. She had killed Xiao Yuanjia by draining all his intricate energy.

Earlier, she was a little worried for she had killed Xiao Youxue's brother and she feared that she may take vengeance on her. Even though she feared Xiao Youxue but she was also severely injured so she may not lose. But if Xiao Youxue were to join hands with Ding Yunzi, the outcome would be very unpredictable.

But Ding Yunzi reaction surprised her and led Lei Qing to think, "If Youxue attacks me, should I join hands with this Maiden Ding?"

But to her surprise, the two maidens suddenly embraced each other. They began to pour out their sorrows and wept melancholy together!

This left Lie Qing out again.

She had three options now.

One was to attack them while they were distracted for they were now her enemies due to their association with the Virtuous Palace.

Two was to quietly sneak away while she had the chance.

Lie Qing was a very smart woman so she would naturally picked the third option which was to run into their midst and embraced them together as she wept with them!

For some time, they wept together and poured out their individual grieves!

Finally Lie Qing said, "Our martial skills are not weak but our enemies are far too strong and formidable. If the three of us joined hands together, then we'll be a force to be reckoned with. Anyone that tries to bully us or oppress us, they would have to think twice about it."

Xiao Youxue asked weakly, "Can we fight the Virtuous Palace? There are more than a dozen top fighters…"

Lie Qing said, "As long as we are united, even if we cannot defeat them yet but at least we can keep ourselves alive until we can be stronger than them."

At this moment, even Ding Yunzi's eyes shone with hope. She did not want to return to the darkness again and Lie Qing's words gave her a shimmer of hope to fight back.

Of course at this very moment, Lie Qing was already thinking of draining all the clan protégés of the Virtuous Palace dry of their virtuous intricate energy!

Lie Qing happily clapped her hands, "Since we are all from the Virtuous Palace now, let call ourselves the New Virtuous Palace!"

Ding Yunzi looked at her quietly before saying, "Are we all equals or you will be our leader?"

Xiao Youxue was also looking at Lie Qing intently.

Lie Qing smiled weakly as she thought, "Screw that."

But she replied with a smile, "Of course we are equals! Sister Yunzi and Sister Youxue, your martial level is higher than me. I am so weak. So how can I fit to be your leader?"

Xiao Youxue interrupted coldly, "You may be weaker than the two of us and even the rest of the Virtuous Palace now. But if you are able to drain them of their intricate energy, you will not fear us anymore."

Lie Qing sighed, "Do you know that it is not possible to acquire more intricate energy by draining? I still need to regain my internal energy first."

Ding Yunzi asked, "What do you mean?"

Lie Qing explained, "The purpose of draining intricate energy is to make my own intricate energy as pure as possible so that I can have an easier time to breakthrough to the next level of the Invincible Divine Force."

She sighed, "You have no idea how difficult it is for me to reach my present attainment and the difference between this level and the next is so vast…"

Of course, Xiao Youxue and Ding Yunzi understood it.

Xiao Youxue had to undergo several trials just to master the Golden Impervious Body and the Icy Heavenly Tears. The higher the attainment, the difficulty for the next level progression was many times as frustrating and hard. In fact, advancing through the wrong progression may even cause the martial attainment to deteriorate!

She remembered the fatal mistakes made by her mother that caused her to lose her life. By several coincidences, she had managed to revert some of her old mistakes in training the Icy Heavenly Tears and even attained the level six staging. But that was like the maximum that she could go for the next several decades. It was because she did not have the intricate formula for the next level progression. Even if she had it, she would need at least ten years of dedicated pondering even though she was already highly gifted...

As for Ding Yunzi, she had practiced the Divine Virtuous Force but that was only the basic staging. It was because the elders of the Virtuous Palace had already found a flaw in the intricate formula of the Divine Virtuous Force which was really the Invincible Divine Force and caution practicing it unless the practitioner had sixty years of internal energy foundation.

That was why Xiao Shuai had deliberately experimented with the imperfect Invincible Divine Force and left it in the martial fraternity to see if anyone could really practice it.

By a chance happening, it was found by Gongsun Bai. Xiao Shuai was surprised that Gongsun Bai could actually practice on the original Invincible Divine Force on his own without hindering his martial progression. What he did not know was that decades ago, Shui Yichi had helped Gongsun Bai to correct many of the intricate formula of the Invincible Divine Force.

Ding Yunzi said all of a sudden, "Maiden Lie Qing, so you know the original Invincible Divine Force?"

Lie Qing knew what Ding Yunzi was thinking as she replied, "Who else knows the original Invincible Divine Force other than me? I can teach you the Invincible Divine Force if you want to. After all, we are going to be good sisters soon."

Ding Yunzi was very smart. She did not hesitate at all as she said, "If you are willing to impart to me every single word of the intricate formula, I would be grateful..."

She had purposely stressed "every single word" to emphasis that she meant the entire intricate formula of the Invincible Divine Force.

Lie Qing laughed softly and said, "Then good sister, you must teach me your flying sword techniques. I want to learn it too."

Ding Yunzi smiled and said, "Unfortunately, even if I want to teach you the flying sword technique, it is not possible for you to learn it."

Lie Qing asked in surprise, "Oh?"

Xiao Youxue interrupted gently, "That is because there is no shortcut in acquainting this skill. Not only do you have to know the various different techniques, you need to practice continuous for ten years at the soonest. I know that many protégés in the Virtuous Palace typically take as long as thirty years to even master the basic throwing."

Lie Qing was disappointed immediately as it shown in her expressions. There were many techniques that required sheer hard work and dedication. She knew that it was true. There was simply no shortcut in this type of sword technique. That why it was a martial feat.

In the martial fraternity, no one was truly invincible. The various martial clans were almost famously renowned for one or more exception feats, techniques or martial skills that made the martial clan unique.

Xiao Youxue asked her, "Why do you name us the New Virtuous Palace? Are you trying to create more chaos or just blackening the reputation of the Virtuous Palace? How awkward it is to add a new in front…"

Lie Qing laughed mysteriously, "That is because…I like the name!"

She told a half-truth. That was because she did not want to reveal her sad past, just like Ding Yunzi did not want to tell anyone her past and so did Xiao Youxue.

Digging out the past was the last thing in their minds because they did not want anyone to know about their tragic past.

Xiao Youxue did not want Yi Ping to know that she was the one that had killed his wife.

Ding Yunzi asked, "So who will be our leader? We still haven't settled this yet."

Lie Qing smiled alluring, "Whoever becomes leader, I am sure none of us would be fully in agreement and we can argue whole day. How about Yi Ping?"

Ding Yunzi softened her eyes and muttered something.

Xiao Youxue said, "He is our best option then."

It was because the only person that could keep Lie Qing in check could possibly be Yi Ping since he had saved her life and she could tell that Lie Qing had a lot of respect for him or else she would not talk ceaselessly all the time to him. It was because martial exponents at their advantage staging would prefer more quiet time in mediation and thinking of how to improve their martial progression with whatever little time they had.

All of a sudden, she remembered Yi Ping was still lying on the ground as her sharp ears had picked out the sounds of a wolf pack approaching the forest!

Xiao Youxue immediately gasped, "Oh no! Yi Ping is still there!"

The three maidens immediately rushed to where Yi Ping had fallen and reached there just in time to see a pack of wolves attacking Yi Ping!

Ding Yunzi immediately drawn out her sword and whirled it in a circular motion before she sent her sword flying towards the pack of wolves as it slashed across, killing the wolves in front! The rest of the surviving wolves began to scatter when their wolf pack leader was killed.

Xiao Youxue gasped, "We are just in time. He almost got eaten alive by these wolves!"

Lie Qing heaved a sigh of relief as she said, "He seems to be well like by the animals…"

Xiao Youxue could not resist adding, "Better than killed by a pig…"

Chapter 27: The Terrible Truth

Yi Ping, Gongsun Jing, Zuo Tianyi and Qiu Wufeng were seating at a cozy inn now as they were drinking to their hearts' content.

They had booked a private room for eating and were seating around a large circular table and there were all kinds of food on the table.

Yi Ping looked at everyone before he finally said, "Other than Brother Tianyi, we are all broke and yet we are ordering so much food?"

Zuo Tianyi laughed, "It is alright. Don't be shy and order all you can."

Qiu Wufeng asked, "I didn't know that a secular sect like the Infinity Sword Clan is so rich?"

Zuo Tianyi took out his money pouch and put it on the table.

Gongsun Jing immediately poured the contents out and to their horror; they saw only ten copper coins that spilled out of the money pouch!

Yi Ping said slowly, "This private room and all these food cost at least three silver and we have not considered the rooms that we have booked yet."

Qiu Wufeng looked at Zuo Tianyi as he said, "And you are the one that suggest we come here?"

Zuo Tianyi laughed aloud as he said, "Don't worry. We all can't afford it but someone else will soon come along and pay for all these."

Yi Ping asked, "Who?"

Zuo Tianyi smiled mysteriously, "A rich friend of mine."

Gongsun Jing asked, "Do we know him? His name?"

Zuo Tianyi smiled, "You do know him. His name is Brother Qiang."

Yi Ping, Gongsun Jing and Qiu Wufeng looked at one another in puzzlement. It was because they did not remember having known anyone with that name!

At this moment, Xiao Youxue, Ding Yunzi and Lie Qing had just entered the private room as they stepped through the thinly veiled curtains.

The inn was unusually crowded both inside and outside.

It was because as soon as Xiao Youxue, Ding Yunzi and Lie Qing had entered the Inn, a throng of visitors began to crowd into the place just to admire them. Those who could not get into the inn was standing outside and pointing at the inn!

Lie Qing stroked her long hair as she smiled, "This place is really so crowded. I have not seen so many people in such a long time."

Even as they had entered the private room, Yi Ping, Gongsun Jing, Zuo Tianyi and Qiu Wufeng almost fell out of their seats!

It was because even the simply dressed Ding Yunzi had changed into a long flowing silk dress. They were simply too stunning and moving that Yi Ping, Gongsun Jing, Zuo Tianyi and Qiu Wufeng were staring at them for a long time.

Xiao Youxue was looking shyly because this was the first time that Yi Ping had looked at her in this way.

Yi Ping was the first to react as he said slowly, "Don't forget that we have many enemies. You are all attracting too much attention and moreover, your dresses are all too revealing…"

Silk was a translucent material. During hot summers, it would grow cool and during winter, it would be warm. Naturally, it was also a beautiful but expensive material.

Gongsun Jing gasped at Ding Yunzi as he said, "So beautiful…"

Xiao Youxue said coolly, "Did it really matter? We are already attracting throngs of attention when we have entered the city. It doesn't matter which outfit we are wearing. Why are you guys minding?"

It was true. Even without changing to the silk dresses, they were all absolute stunning.

Qiu Wufeng gulped as he stared at Lie Qing and Xiao Youxue, "I do not mind."

Zuo Tianyi stared at Ding Yunzi as he said, "Yunzi, you are very beautiful…"

Yi Ping sighed as he said, "Somehow I have a very bad feeling tonight. Let's leave the city immediately. The Honor Manor has a presence in this city. It is really unwise that we should be attracting so much attention…"

But before he could finish, a dashing man walked into the private room in an insolent manner as he laughed, "Maidens, can you honor me with your names? I, Nangong Le will be honored to know you."

Indeed it was Nangong Le but he did not seen to have notice that Yi Ping, Zuo Tianyi, Qiu Wufeng and Gongsun Jing was in the room at all even though he was acquainted with them. His attention was entirely focused towards Xiao Youxue, Lie Qing and Ding Yunzi!

In fact, he had even failed to notice that Ding Yunzi was the maiden that had killed Gongsun Bai on that very fateful day!

It was only then that Yi Ping, Qiu Wufeng and Gongsun Jing knows that "Brother Qiang" refers to Nangong Le, a cockroach that could not be killed off and driven away so easily!

Zuo Tianyi had accidentally caught sight of the vain Nangong Le in the city. Knowing what he was like, he had asked Lie Qing to deliberately lure him to this inn!

Nangong Le was in the streets when he caught sight of three stunning beautiful maidens and when they had entered the inn; he began to push rudely through the crowd as he ignored the cursing and swearing.

Lie Qing smiled at Nangong Le, "So you are Nangong Le? I have heard of you."

Nangong Le laughed merrily, "You have heard of me? I didn't know I am so renowned. Hahaha…"

He thought, "I am so lucky today to find three wondrous beauties in this boring city."

Lie Qing thought, "So he is the richest man in the fraternity. He looked more like a lecher to me."

But she smiled as she looked at Yi Ping, "Unfortunately, we are having a meal with some friends here and it may not be convenient for us to talk."

Only then did Nangong Le remember that he had barged into a private dining room. He quickly turned around to apologize when he saw Yi Ping, Qiu Wufeng, Zuo Tianyi and Gongsun Jing staring at him.

Nangong Le was startled as he said, "Brother Yi Ping, why are you here? Do you know you are being wanted by the Honor Manor now? Isn't this Qiu Wufeng? He has killed his father and elders. Gongsun Jing! All of you are wanted by the Honor Manor! Oh mine, even Protégé Master Zuo Tianyi is here. You are from the orthodox clan; surely you know that they are wanted by the majority of the martial fraternity? There is a heft bounty on their heads!"

Zuo Tianyi smiled bitterly, "So what? Are you interested in the bounty too?"

Nangong Le smiled, "Do you think I mind these little bounties?"

Qiu Wufeng sarcastically remarked, "You don't mind those bounty but you want those renown very much. We all know you are a very vain person."

Nangong Le clapped his fan as he said, "Who doesn't want renown? Power, influence, riches, fame and glory, these are the pursuits of everyone."

Lie Qing interrupted with a mesmerizing smile, "And beauties too. You have forgotten to mention it."

Nangong Le laughed, "That is right. And beauties too."

All of a sudden, Xiao Youxue closed the doors of the private room.

Nangong Le was alarmed as he suddenly noticed that the stares of everyone were hostile!

Xiao Youxue said coldly, "What about the honor of killing the richest man in the fraternity. That would be some renown."

Nangong Le smiled bitterly, "Surely maiden you must be joking. You are too beautiful to be a killer…"

All of a sudden, Xiao Youxue drew out her sword and pointed at him. From her expressions, she did not seem to be joking!

Nangong Le immediately looked at Yi Ping to say, "Brother Yi Ping, what is going on? Say something for me."

Yi Ping sighed as he said, "Either we have all heard wrongly or we have misunderstood you. You just suggest that you would betray us for some renown."

Nangong Le protested, "Of course not!"

Zuo Tianyi said, "The Honor Manor has called for an expedition against the Holy Hex Sect. All the heroes of the fraternity are now gathering in force for an attack into the western fraternity. This city is the transit point to the western fraternity. If you are not here to join the westward expedition attack against the Holy Hex Sect, why then are you here?"

Nangong Le said, "I am going there to look for Maiden Lingfeng…"

He turned to Yi Ping and said, "Brother Yi Ping, you know her too. Don't you know that she is actually the Holy Maiden of the Holy Hex Sect?"

Lie Qing was alarmed as she thought, "Who is this Maiden Lingfeng?"

Ding Yunzi thought, "Is she the one that is with him that day in the Honor Manor?"

Yi Ping smiled weakly to Nangong Le, "It seems that you have already forgotten all about her…"

Nangong Le stole a quick glances at the three stunning maiden as he said, "Of course not! But you know, I am just surprise to see all of you…"

Gongsun Jing said, "More like you are surprise to see all the wanted fugitives in the same place."

Qiu Wufeng said, "It seems like we cannot let you go now."

Nangong Le said in alarm, "I know that Gongsun Jing and you do not like me. Both of you are vicious enough to murder your families in order to achieve your aims. I am not like you."

All of a sudden, Yi Ping grabbed Nangong Le to sit down as he said. "Gongsun Jing, Zuo Tianyi and Qiu Wufeng are my brothers now. Let bygones be bygones now. They are only teasing you. After what had happened to their families, they had made light of many things. Surely, you don't mind the past too?"

Gongsun Jing and Qiu Wufeng roared with laughter.

Gongsun Jing smiled, "Surely you don't mind a little joke? We already know what you are like. Would you like to join us?"

Nangong Le the Joyous smiled bitterly, "Do I really have a choice? You are really some friends of mine. Now I am forced to join a company of fugitives."

Yi Ping said, "If you don't want to join us, then you can leave immediately and as soon as possible. It is because our enemies may be here anytime soon!"

Nangong Le took a jar of wine from the table as he gulped it before he said, "Why should I leave? You know I never believe those rubbish that come from the Honor Manor. Many of my other pugilist friends are framed by them too. There are good wines, good food, beauties and my good friends here. As you know, I have never feared the Honor Manor at all…"

Zuo Tianyi laughed as he patted Nangong Le's shoulder, "We know, we know. Even though we have never talked more than a few sentences previously before but I admire your courage. When the Virtuous Palace is here later, we'll be glad to have you on our side."

Nangong Le immediately turned ashen and he almost choked on the wine that he was drinking. He stammered, "Did you just say the Virtuous Palace?"

Yi Ping said, "Somehow, I am wanted by the Virtuous Palace too. This is Maiden Xiao Youxue and this is Maiden Ding Yunzi, they are also wanted by the Virtuous Palace."

Nangong Le broke into a cold sweat as he looked at Maiden Ding as he asked, "She is really the one that was with Xiao Shuai at the Honor Manor that day?"

Yi Ping said, "That is her."

Nangong Le could barely recognize her even though he was looking all the time at her that day. He sighed, "Alas, Nangong alas Le Nangong Le. You are now really in deep trouble."

Lie Qing said unhappily, "Yi Ping, why didn't you introduce me?"

Yi Ping smiled, "Even if I don't introduce you, he will know who you are sooner or later. So why should I introduce you when he will surely ask later."

Nangong Le immediately asked Lie Qing, "May I know Maiden name?"

Lie Qing blinked her eyes at him as she replied, "Lie Qing. That is my name!"

Nangong Le said, "What a beautiful name. I am Nangong Le. You have beautiful eyes too. I have never seen eyes like yours."

Lie Qing smiled mysteriously as she said, "Do you really think my eyes are beautiful?"

Nangong Le said, "Of course!"

Lie Qing asked, "Then you are not afraid of that Maiden Lingfeng would be upset with you for talking to me?"

Nangong Le laughed as he looked at Yi Ping, "I wish she would be upset with me but I can tell that her heart probably belongs to Brother Yi Ping."

Yi Ping stammered, "I…I am married already."

This time, everyone except Xiao Youxue and Ding Yunzi was surprised as Lie Qing asked, "Ping, you are really married? Why didn't you tell us?"

Gongsun Jing said, "I wonder who sister-in-law is. You can introduce her to us in the future!"

Qiu Wufeng asked, "Who is she? Brother Yi Ping's wife must be someone that is extraordinary too."

Yi Ping sighed with sadness, "I wish I could but that not possible. She is no longer in this world."

Lie Qing appeared to be saddened as she said, "I so sorry to hear that…"

Yi Ping looked at Qiu Wufeng as he said, "Actually you know too. She is Shui Yixian the Celestial Fairy."

While the name of Shui Yixian was not familiar to Qiu Wufeng but when he had heard of the name of Celestial Fairy, he was jolted. It was because he was among the group of exponents that had led an attack on the Eternal Ice Palace!

Qiu Wufeng stammered as he asked, "She had died on that fateful day when I had left? Tian Kui killed her?"

Yi Ping shook his head sadly, "It is the veiled yellow dressed maiden that has killed her. No matter where she is, I will never let her off."

Yi Ping looked pleadingly at Ding Yunzi, "Maiden Yunzi, if you know who she is, you must tell me…"

Ding Yunzi interrupted coldly, "I have told you many times, I do not know her."

Qiu Wufeng was bewildered as he said, "You say that Maiden Xiao Youxue is the one that has killed the Celestial Fairy? How is it possible?"

All of a sudden, Yi Ping looked at Qiu Wufeng with a sudden jolt as he stared blankly in the air, "What do you mean? You say that Maiden Xiao Youxue is the veiled yellow dressed maiden?"

Qiu Wufeng was baffled, "Isn't that very obvious? I still recognize her shoes and white jade pendant on her belt…"

All of a sudden, Yi Ping recalled the first time that he had seen the veiled yellow dressed maiden and her terrible kicks that still startled him to this very day. Their shoes were exactly identical!

Yi Ping looked at Xiao Youxue…

There were tears on her face as she had wept silently. She pursed her lips as she said melancholy, "Yes, I have killed your wife. Now you know the truth, are you happy about it?"

This revelation shocked everyone in the room!

Ding Yunzi said, "Sister that is not possible. I have seen the Celestial Fairy only a few months ago…"

Xiao Youxue said melancholy as she took a few steps backward, "Sister Yun, you don't have to console me. I know what I have done is unforgivable but I have no choice back then. You don't have to lie to cover for me. I know that you have meant well…"

Yi Ping got up of his seat as he stared fiercely at Xiao Youxue as he said angrily, "You lie to me! All these months, you are with me. What are your purposes? Are you content just to see me in miserably and never finding you?"

Xiao Youxue wished that this day would never come. This was the day that she had dreaded and feared…

Xiao Youxue threw the white emerald long sword on the table as she said tearfully, "I know you will never forgive me. Even if you want my life, I will never resist."

Yi Ping trembled as he looked at the white emerald long sword as he laughed aloud, "All this while, my enemy is beside me. Yixian! Today I have finally found her! I will avenge for you…."

He trembled as he picked up the white emerald long sword as he said with bloodshot eyes, "You…you…"

Gongsun Jing and Zuo Tianyi immediately tried to step forward to hold him back but Yi Ping waved the white emerald long sword at them as he said angrily, "This is only between the two of us only. The rest of you step back!"

Ding Yunzi stepped in front of Xiao Youxue as she said coldly, "Don't blame me if you want my sister's life!"

Yi Ping said angrily at her, "You know all along that Youxue is the one that I have been looking for. Why do you lie to me as well?"

Ding Yunzi said quietly, "The Celestial Fairy is still alive. I have seen her…"

Yi Ping said angrily, "You are still lying to me. The protégés of the Virtuous Palace are trained in deceptions and bluffs. You are all birds of a same feather flock!"

Lie Qing interrupted unhappily, "Are you saying that I am also a deceptive person?"

Yi Ping said angrily, "Aren't you all birds of the same feather flock?"

Lie Qing raised her enchanting voice, "I dare you to say that aloud again." She had drawn out her black sword!

Yi Ping said angrily, "Fine, fine. You are all in it together. Only you are right and I am wrong."

He stared at Xiao Youxue as he said with trembling voice, "You have saved my life. Now go. Don't let me see you again or else the next time we have met again, it will be a life and death duel!"

Xiao Youxue cried out softly before she stormed out of the room, "I'm so sorry…"

Ding Yunzi looked coldly at Yi Ping, "You will regret this."

And she too left the room.

Lie Qing said to Yi Ping, "Why are you so fierce? Do you think raising your voice aloud proves you are right? Why did you have to say so many hurtful words? Well, enjoy your meal then!" She too stormed angrily out of the private room.

Zuo Tianyi was worried for Ding Yunzi as he said quickly, "I will try to have a talk with them…"

Nangong Le said, "Brother Yi Ping, I am really disappointed in you. You actually raise your voice at them?!"

Zuo Tianyi and Nangong Le left the private dining room at the same time, leaving Yi Ping, Gongsun Jing and Qiu Wufeng alone in the room.

Yi Ping wailed aloud, "Only the three of us are left now…Am I wrong? She is the one that has killed my wife. I shouldn't avenge my wife? Where is the justice then?!"

In the end, he still could not bring himself the heart to kill Xiao Youxue…

Qiu Wufeng was sighing, "I didn't know this will turn out this way…"

Gongsun Jing sighed even heavier as he said, "Maiden Lie Qing is really an interesting maiden. She has actually asked us to enjoy our meals before she left."

Qiu Wufeng asked, "What is so interesting about that?"

Gongsun Jing replied, "You could have seen the wry smile on her face just before she left the room. It seems that she has already anticipated that we have no money to pay for the meals…"

Yi Ping and Qiu Wufeng received a sudden jolt. If they had all left, who would pay for the lodgings and the meals?

Chapter 28: Eternal Ice Palace vs. the Virtuous Palace!

Xiao Youxue had run out of the city in tears, attracting stunned reactions and pitiful sympathies from many.

Those inside the inn may not be able to hear their conversations but they could hear Yi Ping raising his voice. When Xiao Youxue had dashed out of the room, the crowd began to curse the man that had caused such a delicate maiden to be in tears!

When she had reached the outskirt of the city along a river bank, after making sure that there was no one following her, she could not hold back her grief any longer. She collapsed on the grass as she wept bitterly.

She did not know how long she had been crying in the dark.

"Youxue, don't cry please…" It was Ding Yunzi. It took her awhile to find her in the darkness.

Xiao Youxue fell into her embrace as she wept bitterly, "Why must fate torment me just like that? Why must the person that I like, is also the person that hates me the most?"

Ding Yunzi said, "Youxue, don't cry anymore. It is impossible for you to kill the Celestial Fairy for I have seen her on the same day that you have lured us to the Honor Manor."

Xiao Youxue sobbed melancholy, "Sister Yun…you are still trying to comfort me. I have really killed her with my own hands…"

Ding Yunzi was in bewilderment as she asked, "If you have killed the Celestial Fairy, then who is the Celestial Fairy that Xiao Shuai and I have fought against?"

Xiao Youxue looked at Ding Yunzi in her eyes as she asked, "You have really seen the Celestial Fairy? What does she look like?"

Ding Yunzi said, "I will never forget her sight. She is like a heavenly fairy and looked extremely delicate and graceful. Even though her voice is very soft and gentle, I can hear her clearly. Her internal strength is also terrible to behold. With just her sleeve alone, she can deflect Xiao Shuai and my flying scabbards…"

Xiao Youxue gasped, "You have really fought against her? Did my fath…Xiao Shuai and you kill or defeat her in the end?"

She had made that conclusion because if the Celestial Fairy had won against Xiao Shuai and Ding Yunzi, then Ding Yunzi would not be here talking to her!

Ding Yunzi said, "We didn't fight any further. So the fight is inconclusive."

Xiao Youxue asked, "Xiao Shuai let her go, just like that?"

Ding Yunzi nodded as she said, "It seems that Xiao Shuai and the Celestial Fairy are old acquaintances so when she had left, we didn't pursue them. Moreover, we have expended considerable amount of our martial power and need the time to recuperate first."

She began to sigh heavily, "Now I know why Xiao Shuai wants Yi Ping dead."

Xiao Youxue asked, "He wants Yi Ping dead? Why? He didn't even know him!"

Ding Yunzi said coolly, "At first I didn't know the reason. Now I do. It is because Xiao Shuai may have feelings for the Celestial Fairy and that is why we are ordered to kill all the male protégés of the Eternal Ice Palace. Now I have finally understood that he meant to kill only Yi Ping because he is the Celestial Fairy's husband!"

Xiao Youxue was startled, "Shui Yixian is still alive? She is really not dead?"

She was stunned yet she was relieved at the same time.

She said, "If the Celestial Fairy is still alive, why didn't Yi Ping know?"

Ding Yunzi said, "I do not know the exact reason. There are many questions to be asked too. The only way for us to know is to ask the Celestial Fairy herself. But you have to be wary. The Celestial Fairy is looking everywhere for you too…"

Xiao Youxue smiled weakly, "Good. I have tried to kill her. She has every reason to kill me. As long as Yi Ping does not bear a grudge against me, I am content…"

All of a sudden, there were dozens of sparks in front of them as dozens of brilliant needles flew in their direction!

Lie Qing had suddenly appeared in front of them as she deflected the secret projectiles with her dark sword as she cried out alarmingly, "Be careful! There are others here too!"

Lie Qing had arrived just after Ding Yunzi but chosen to remain hidden as she did not want to disturb the emotional moments. After some time, she had suddenly observed two other maidens in black velvet dress had quietly moved towards Xiao Youxue!

If Lie Qing had not seen them with her very own eyes, she could not believe that they could move so rapidly in the darkness like apparitions and it appeared that they were just treading onto the tip of the grass!

Xiao Youxue and Ding Yunzi were alarmed! It was because someone else had not only secretly sneaked within their alert zone without their knowing and had thrown the secret projectiles in such a quiet manner!

Ding Yunzi immediately drawn out her long sword and saw that there were two maidens in front of them!

Ding Yunzi and Xiao Youxue were startled as they took a step backward!

Indeed it was Shui Yujian and Shui Meijian. It was only after the grand congregation in the Honor Manor that they had heard that Yi Ping and the Holy Maiden of the Holy Hex Sect had barged to disrupt the gathering. They had missed Yi Ping only narrowly!

Because Yi Ping was now a fugitive wanted by the majority of the orthodox fraternity, Shui Yixian deducted that since the Honor Manor was planning a western expedition to attack the Holy Hex Sect, then Yi Ping may well be there too since he was associated with the Holy Maiden of the Holy Hex Sect.

A third maiden was standing delicately behind the two beautiful maidens. She was very beautiful as though she was a goddess. All three of them were very fair and were very white. In the darkness, in their dark velvet dresses, they had appeared to be supernatural beings.

Xiao Youxue was shocked. It was because the third maiden that was here was indeed the Celestial Fairy! She thought, "She is really alive. She has really come to kill me…"

Lie Qing was startled too. It was because she was very sure she had seen two maidens but there were now three?! These two maidens that she had seen were identical and it was obvious that they were twins. They had a long precious sword in their hands and the secret projectiles were thrown by them!

Shui Yujian and Shui Meijian were equally startled. They had quietly moved into striking range and were confident they could not miss but their attacks were intercepted by a beautiful maiden with red eyes.

Even Shui Yixian was looking at Lie Qing as she appraised her opponent. All of a sudden, Shui Yixian hurled three silvery needles towards Lie Qing!

Even though the three silvery needles were hurled at the same time, the three silvery needles were moving at different speeds and that was what made it extremely deadly!

The first silvery needle flew with startling speed as it burst with an extraordinary power through the air. Lie Qing's eyes were exceptional sharp as she raised her black sword as she said, "Secret Projectiles are useless against me…"

But to her surprise, the first needle suddenly grew dim and disappeared! Lie Qing was startled as she raised her black sword just in time to parry off the second and third silvery needles one after the other!

The second needle was so powerful that she was forced to take two steps backward and the third needle sent her moving a further three steps backward!

Just when she had just recovered her footings, the first needle reappeared again and flew straight into her body and flew out in the opposite direction with a thunderous impact!

In that single moment, blood spilled out of her body and her dress was tainted red with her blood!

Lie Qing shrieked softly as she was hurled a further five to six steps backward before falling on the ground!

Xiao Youxue and Ding Yunzi immediately flew to her side as they cried out her name!

Ding Yunzi turned and stared sternly at Shui Yixian, "I didn't know that the Eternal Ice Palace has to resort to such despicable means to kill us."

Shui Meijian smiled sweetly, "We just want to teach you a lesson. I still remember we have an unfinished fight with you the last time!"

Ding Yunzi said, "Indeed, we have."

Shui Yujian said coldly, "That old man isn't here today to protect you. Do you think you can escape from our swords tonight?"

Lie Qing trembled as she got up slowly.

Xiao Youxue said, "Lie Qing, you are injured…"

Lie Qing steadied herself as she said to Shui Yixian, "Is this the best that you can do?"

Shui Yixian was startled. This young maiden had actually survived her Soul Seeking Needles? And she had those unusual red eyes…

Lie Qing said, "The same trick won't work against me again. The needle that had struck me is actually a black needle. You have made use of the reflection of the other silver needles and the sudden burst of your martial power to deceive my eyes."

Shui Yixian had noticed that the blood on her dress had also dried and she was not bleeding anymore. She sighed softly as she said, "The Golden Impervious Body Divine Skill. It seems that this fight is not going to be easy. You are so young and yet you have mastered such an extraordinary divine skill."

Lie Qing said coldly, "Do you really think I am as young as you thought?"

All of a sudden, there was a fearsome aura around Lie Qing as she said, "You have dared to injure me. I am going to let you pay for the price!"

Shui Yujian gasped, "That aura is an impervious force?!"

Even Shui Meijian was shaken! That was because even though the Divine Emerald Skill was a type of invisible buffer force, it was extremely draining to use and hard to maintain its focus. This type of impervious force protects the body in its entirety against exterior blows.

Moreover this Lie Qing had mastered the Golden Impervious Body Divine Skill, so she had doubly the protection. An ordinary exponent would never have the chance against her! Needless to say, this type of skill required an extremely strong foundation in internal strength to even use it!

Even if Shui Yixian was startled but she did not shown it. It was because years of practicing the Emotionless Rhythm had made her emotionless.

She just said simply, "Is that the Divine Virtuous Force?"

Lie Qing nodded as she said, "That's right but the original name of this skill is called the Invincible Divine Force."

Xiao Youxue was still looking at Shui Yixian in startled surprise as she muttered, "She really is not dead? I didn't kill her after all…"

Shui Yixian said gently to Xiao Youxue, "We have met again."

Xiao Youxue regained her composure as she said, "Indeed…You have survived."

Shui Yixian was expressionless as she said gently, "Yes, I have survived."

Lie Qing said to herself, "I have heard of the Eternal Ice Palace even during my time. Their most formidable skills are the Divine Emerald Skill and the Icy Heavenly Tears. Even if the three of us join hands, the outcome will be uncertain."

It was because she had suddenly discovered that she could detect no sign of life from this Celestial Fairy. This could only mean one thing, that her internal strength was extremely formidable!

And the fact that her needles had penetrated through her Golden Impervious Divine Skill means that she could also breech her Invincible Divine Skill too…

All of a sudden, she had lost confident in her Invincible Divine Force!

Ding Yunzi was calm as she analyzed, "Youxue, let's us attack the Celestial Fairy at the same time. She is the most formidable opponent of the three. If we split our attention, we may not be able to win. On the other hand, if we join hands and attack her at the same time, she may not be able to guard against all our attacks. After all, she doesn't have a weapon in her hands. So that is to our advantage. Avoid pitting your martial power against her as we wear her out. I have heard from Xiao Shuai that the Divine Emerald Skill may be a formidable skill but it is an extremely draining skill."

Shui Yujian interrupted coldly, "You really think we are invisible?"

All of a sudden, Shui Meijian had attacked Ding Yunzi!

Ding Yunzi immediately slashed her sword towards Shui Meijian but was immediately repulsed by an invisible circular force as soon as she had attacked when Shui Meijian had raised her left fingers in front of her!

Ding Yunzi leapt back a few steps in surprise as she had never fought against the Divine Emerald Skill before. She took out the foldable sword from her belt to her left hand as she thought, "So the direction where her finger is pointing is where the buffer force of the Divine Emerald Skill is centralized. If I slash against the buffer force, I will weaken her martial power or if I attack her from where she is least expecting, I can avoid the Divine Emerald Skill entirely."

So she began to slash from right to left, left to right, as she began her counterattacks, saying to Shui Meijian, "I will like to see how long can you last!"

As soon as her sister Shui Meijian had attacked, Shui Yujian had attacked Lie Qing!

Shui Yujian raised her left finger and her long sword in her hand as she displayed the eerie cold energy wave of the Frosty Icicle Swordplay. But as soon as she found a weak point to strike, she would always be deflected by an outer force similar to the Divine Emerald Skill!

Lie Qing had raised her martial power and display the Invincible Divine Force, merging the Invincible Divine Force into her swordplay as she counter-attacked against Shui Yujian, "You are courting your own death!"

From the initial impact, she could tell that her opponent mastery in the Divine Emerald Skill was not strong enough to withstand the full impact of her Invincible Divine Force. Therefore she had raised her martial power to her zenith.

All of a sudden, Lie Qing sensed that something was not right as she felt her Invincible Divine Force seemed to be faltering when she had struck against the Divine Emerald Force. She gasped. "You are able to neutralize my Invincible Divine Force?"

Shui Yujian replied softly, "This is the exchanging spirit of the Dual Inertness Intricacy, the divinity state of absorbing the essence of heavens and earth as my divinity state, the changes of heavens and earth as my changes, changing the opponent martial power to be used as my own. I am afraid that even before my martial power become exhausted, you would be fallen by my sword instead."

Lie Qing broke into a cold sweat. She had never expected that this young maiden of eighteen would be able to hold against her! This fight was not as easy as it had appeared!

All of a sudden, Ding Yunzi had stepped next to her, startling her!

After Lie Qing took a glance at Ding Yunzi and looked at her opponent again, she was startled! It was because she could not tell which of the twin sisters that she was previously fighting as they moved and attacked at the same time!

Ding Yunzi said panicky, "Lie Qing, be very careful. This seems to be a sword formation!"

In terms of martial strength and techniques, Lie Qing and Ding Yunzi had the advantage. Somehow, to their utter surprises, the twin sisters did not show any sign of fear as they calmly dismantle their strokes one by one!

Lie Qing had displayed one after one another of her mesmerizing sword strokes but the twin sisters were simply unaffected! She thought, "It is impossible…"

Ding Yunzi had rained dozens of her best sword strokes against them. Even a super exponent would have to take a step or two backward but the twin sisters would always find a way to retaliate as though they could see through her feint!

Was that not bewildering?

What they did not know of course was that Shui Yujian and Shui Meijian had combined the Defense Harmony of the Tranquil Spirits with the 'Linking Spirits' progression of the Dual Inertness Intricacy they had just recently learnt. Even before Lie Qing and Ding Yunzi had changed their sword strokes, they had already sensed their intentions through the changes in their intricate energies!

Shui Yixian and Xiao Youxue had also exchanged blows almost immediately!

Shui Yixian raised her fingers as she attacked with her Jade Icy Fingers while Xiao Youxue was attacking furiously and rapidly with her Penetrating Hands Skill!

Both maidens were attacking so fast and furiously that their arms and hands could scarcely be seen! It appeared that their legs were not moving but that was the opposite. As soon as Xiao Youxue raised her foot, Shui Yixian had struck her thigh with her fingers! As soon as Shui Yixian prepared to kick her, she was restrained by another slight kick!

Even though Xiao Youxue's Penetrating Hands were extremely formidable and fast, all her attacks were blocked by the Celestial Fairy and she could feel deadly painful numbness through her hands!

Shui Yixian had raised her Icy Heavenly Tears to the seventh level and was startled that Xiao Youxue would absorb the full impact of her Jade Icy Fingers. Eventually she raised her Icy Heavenly Tears to the eighth and the ninth level but still her opponent persisted!

Xiao Youxue had recited the Absolute Spirits Intricate Formula to fortitude her willpower and there was an outline of faint golden aura around her that only a highly skilled internal martial expert could see!

Shui Yixian muttered softly, "You know the Golden Impervious Body too?"

Xiao Youxue did not reply her. It was because she was focusing all her attention on her opponent! Any slight distraction would be fatal to her!

All of a sudden, Shui Yixian saw a flying sword that spin towards her with startling speed! It was hurled by Ding Yunzi when she saw an opening!

Shui Yixian immediately raised her fingers and swept the flying sword away!

All of a sudden, Lie Qing had flown to Xiao Youxue's side as she shouted, "Attack now!"

Even before the twin sisters could stop Lie Qing, Ding Yunzi had intercepted them by throwing her scabbard and her foldable sword at each of them to buy Lie Qing the precious time!

It was because Lie Qing had quickly discovered the weakness of the Divine Emerald Skill! When the Divine Emerald Skill was activated, it was at its strongest and would wane!

Lie Qing displayed her Mesmerizing Swordplay and had used all her martial power as she leapt upon the Celestial Fairy with a powerful slash.

Lie Qing prayed, "Youxue, keep her engage! Don't let her have the time to use her right hand for the Divine Emerald Skill…"

Xiao Youxue seemed to know Lie Qing's stratagem as she used all her strength to prevent the Celestial Fairy from breaking free of her continuous attacks so that she did not have even a second to use the Divine Emerald Skill!

Lie Qing's sword was the Perpetual Darkness, a sharp precious renowned sword that could cut through metal as though it was like mud! Moreover, her martial power was empowered by her Invincible Divine Force which instead of using it as an impregnable defensive force could also be turned into an unstoppable offensive force too!

Even when Shui Yixian had raised her left fingers to halt Lie Qing's incoming attack, she could feel her Divine Emerald Skill offering minute resistance as Lie Qing's sword slash viciously at her!

Both Shui Meijian and Yujian cried out panicky, "Mistress, watch out!!"

Chapter 29: The Celestial Fairy vs. the Heavenly Temptress

When Ding Yunzi had proposed that they joined hands to attack the Celestial Fairy, she had exchanged glances with Lie Qing and Xiao Youxue. Without exchanging a single word, they had understood that their main opponent was the Celestial Fairy.

Ding Yunzi and Lie Qing had underestimated the twin sisters and that took them off a considerable amount of time before they could time their attacks.

At the first opportunity, Ding Yunzi had thrown her flying sword towards the Celestial Fairy and Lie Qing had quickly seized the initiative to follow up an attack on the Celestial Fairy at the same time!

When Lie Qing had suddenly switched her target to the Celestial Fairy, Ding Yunzi was suddenly attacked furiously by Shui Meijian and Yujian in their bid to get past her!

When the twin sisters had joined hands, their attacks were extremely formidable! In less than five quick strokes, she was forced to step back!

Just when Shui Yujian was about to dash past her, she had suddenly hesitated and took three steps back! It was because Zuo Tianyi had suddenly appeared as he raised his long sword against her!

Nangong Le was right behind Zuo Tianyi as he smiled to the twin sisters, "Hello beauties, we have met again!"

At the same time, Lie Qing had executed her fatal attack upon the Celestial Fairy!

When Xiao Youxue sensed the startled expressions in the Celestial Fairy's eyes, all of a sudden, she was guilty-stricken. It was because she remembered that she had "killed" her once and ever since, she had wished that she could somehow undo that awful deed. Because of that, she was unable to face Yi Ping with an open heart and suppressed her affections for him.

Before Lie Qing and Shui Yujian knew what had happened, Xiao Youxue was suddenly between them!

Xiao Youxue was slashed across by Lie Qing's sword on her back while Shui Yixian had struck her multiple times with her fingers!

Lie Qing's attack was so powerful that her slash cut through Xiao Youxue's silver scale armor that she had worn inside her and even penetrate through her Golden Impervious Body; in that single instant, there was a large gush of blood that spilled from Xiao Youxue's back!

Shui Yixian's strikes were equally lethal! Even though the silver scale armor could protect against external blow, it was useless against internal energy as her Jade Icy Finger injured Xiao Youxue!

Xiao Youxue screamed aloud when she was struck at the same time by the two super exponents as she collapsed on the ground motionlessly!

Shui Yixian and Lie Qing were so stunned at the turn of event that they ceased their attacks at the same time immediately. Lie Qing was trembling and she dropped her sword; all her strength had been snapped away in that instant as her knees grew weak, causing her to collapse on the grass patch!

Xiao Youxue's screams had caught the attention of everyone, who had all stop fighting and were looking in Shui Yixian and Lie Qing direction.

Shui Yixian was bewildered as she said to herself, "Why did she take this fatal attack from me? She has saved me…why?!"

Lie Qing was stunned as she thought, "I have killed her?! No, my target is the Celestial Fairy. She just suddenly comes between us…this is not the plan at all…Yi Ping will hates me forever now…"

Ding Yunzi was the first to react as she reached Xiao Youxue as she cried out to her, "Youxue, Youxue…" She was horrified to see that she was not breathing and the horrifying extend of her wounds as her blood covered the entire ground!

Lie Qing muttered, "It is no use. No one can survive the full impact of the Invincible Divine Force…"

Shui Yixian was expressionless as she said softly, "It is of no use. It is not just external injuries. I have fatally injured several of her vital points too. Even if we have a miraculous herb, in her state, she cannot even consume it…"

Ding Yunzi did not care. She took out a pouch and scattered its content of white powder on Xiao Youxue's wounds but she did not even reacted at all. If a person was conscious, they would surely feel the painful sensational of this 'External Wounds Drug' but Xiao Youxue did not even have a slight reaction at all.

When Nangong Le had turned his head towards Shui Yixian, he was stunned that a maiden of her stunning beauty would actually exist in this world. He had thought that Ji Lingfeng and Xiao Youxue were already very beautiful. In that instant, he was totally mesmerized by her and forgot that he was in the middle of a fight.

If he knew that it was actually her that had caused him to be bedridden for two months, he would be in for a greater surprise.

All of a sudden, Shui Yixian said coolly. "I am going to take her away and give her an honorable burial in the Eternal Ice Palace. She is after all, the daughter of an old friend of mine. She shouldn't be buried in this wayward place."

Lie Qing picked up her black sword again as she said coldly, "No, you can't. She is our friend."

But the Celestial Fairy had already taken a step forward!

Lie Qing mustered all her martial power as she attacked the Celestial Fairy while saying to Ding Yunzi, "Sister Yun, help me!"

But Ding Yunzi was inconsolable. She did not seem to hear her and she was now weeping bitterly as she held a small bloodied doll that had tumbled to the ground…

It was because Xiao Youxue had already stopped breathing. As she wept, she recalled her bitter past and her childhood memories with little Youxue. She was older than her by seven years. She had virtually grown up with Xiao Youxue and she knew her every happiness and sorrows that she had ever experienced for they were really very close sisters.

Because Xiao Youxue's half-brothers were at least twenty years older than her, she was never close to them. There was once, she had wept most bitterly when Xiao Shuai forbid anyone from teaching her the Flying Sword Technique, causing her to miss the best opportune time to pick up the skill. And one of her most joyous times was when Ding Yunzi had given her a ragged doll that she had liked very much too; to this day, Xiao Youxue still had the small rugged doll even though they had fallen out.

Ding Yunzi was staring tearfully at the small bloodied doll now as she sobbed uncontrollably as she held her mouth…

Just when Lie Qing had leapt forward to attack the Celestial Fairy, she could feel a strong irresistible resistance that made every single forward step difficult for her!

She could see the Celestial Fairy putting her right hand behind her back while whirling her left finger tips at her. This was not the Divine Emerald Force that she had experienced earlier but was many times more powerful!

Lie Qing thought, "She was not using her full strength earlier?"

Indeed, Shui Yixian had now raised her martial power for the Divine Emerald Skill to the ninth level!

Lie Qing was determined not to acknowledge defeat. She had raised all her martial power and generated her Invincible Divine Force to its zenith too!

As Lie Qing struck blows after blows at her opponent, Shui Yixian waved her sleeves each time and deflected all her attacks while counter-attacking with her left fingers at the same time!

They were attacking so fast that bursting hot and cold windforce began to generate from them and soon they became a blur! Every strike, every miss that they had made, was so explosive that it was crackled with the raw thunderous impact of their martial powers!

Even though Nangong Le, Zuo Tianyi, Shui Yujian and Mei Meijian were standing quite a distance away, they still could not steady their footings!

Shui Yujian and Meijian immediately extended out their fingers and generated the Divine Emerald Skill to deflect away the powerful windforce that was sweeping malicious all around them!

Zuo Tianyi was stunned. The Infinity-Two Swordplay was an introductory to the principles of sword energy while the Infinity-One was the exact principle of generating sword energies. But this Lie Qing was unleashing shockwaves after shockwaves of deadly cold sword energies. Was that her true strength?

Zuo Tianyi immediately said aloud, "Everyone, muster your internal energies to protect yourself. Don't let the invisible sword energy injure your vital channels!"

Lie Qing said coldly to Shui Yixian, "I would like to see how long you can maintain your internal strength against my sword energies and my martial power!" Even as she had spoken, she had attacked a dozen times in that very instant while evading and counter-attacking against Shui Yixian!

Shui Yixian did not expect Lie Qing was really so formidable and even though she looked so young, she seemed to be an extremely experienced exponent. She had mastered the Icy Heavenly Tears a long time ago and was not affected by Lie Qing's piercing cold sword energies or else her strength would surely be snapped away very quickly.

If she got hit by Lie Qing's sword, even her Icy Heavenly Tears would not stop her deadly sword energy from severing her vital channels. So she did not dare to be careless as she was now using both her hands!

Shui Yixian asked softly, "Just who are you?"

Lie Qing said coldly, "Isn't that too late now to ask who I am? You may be formidable but you have not passed the Divine Calamity tests yet. As for whom I am, after I have drunk your blood, I will tell you!"

Shui Yixian was startled and she was rarely surprised, "You have passed the Divine Calamity?"

Lie Qing replied coldly, "How did you think I got my red eyes then? That is the mark of the Divine Calamity!"

Shui Yixian said, "That…is…impossible. That's an impossible feat."

Lie Qing said, "Others maybe can't but I can!"

Shui Yixian said softly, "You will be my worthy opponent then." As she said, she struck towards Lie Qing with her right fingers but missed her only narrowly, hitting the truck of a large tree behind her. The tree instantly became petrified and cracked under its own weight!

Lie Qing immediately retaliated with a counter-attack but was deflected by the Celestial Fairy sleeve; she struck the ground with her sword and the ground seemingly erupted forcefully with a thunderous impact that sent the soil and dust flying everywhere!

Everywhere they had dueled, everywhere that they had moved on to, it became a dead zone. All the others could only look on in utter disbelief at the sheer ferocity of their martial power!

Even though the duel may looked uneven as Lie Qing had a deadly weapon in her hands but Shui Yixian was no less deadly; when she whirled her sleeves, those sleeves of hers when imbued by her martial power were like deadly spinning blades, disintegrating everything that it hits and could even deflect Lie Qing's sword!

Even Ding Yunzi had returned to her senses as the thunderous impact and the ferocity of the duel shook the very ground as furious hot and cold winds flurried merciless as though a hurricane was in the vicinity!

Lie Qing's martial power was now at her zenith and her entire self was charged with the Invincible Divine Force Intricate Energy! At the zenith of her martial power and at the zenith of her Invincible Divine Force, she could use the 'Pandora Darkness Merciless Strokes'. In that instant, her sword was charged with deadly sword energies as she sent one windforce after one another that sliced through the air in a deadly impact that utterly destroys everything in its path! All in all, she had sent seven deadly slices nonstop towards Shui Yixian!

Lie Qing was really merciless in her attacks as she had immediately used 'Seventh Heavens Strokes' which was also the most powerful stance of the 'Pandora Darkness Merciless Strokes'. It was because she was gambling everything that she got against the Celestial Fairy!

Zuo Tianyi was stunned. These deadly sword energies were real physical sword energies that could destroy everything in its path as a projectile and was the invincible staging of the Infinity-Zero Swordplay! This was a mythical stage that was only rumored to exist and impossible to attain. For her age, it was impossible but he was seeing it with his own eyes now…

Shui Yixian knew that she could not escape fast enough against these energy projectiles. She raised her Icy Heavenly Tears to the tenth level and then raised her martial power again to raise her Divine Emerald Force to the tenth level as her fingers dissipated the incoming energy blades one after another!

Lie Qing simply could not believe that the Celestial Fairy could even dissipate her first energy projectile blades as she came closer to closer to her! By the time, she had unleashed her seventh energy projectiles, her entire body was trembling as her martial power departed away from her, so when the Celestial Fairy was close to her and used the Divine Emerald Skill at the same time, Lie Qing was flung back all the way backward by her opponent's martial power as she coughed out blood!

Lie Qing tried to stand up but she simply did not have the strength anymore and the last blow that she had received may seem to be a simply blow but it was not. If she was not protected by her Golden Impervious Body, all her vital channels would be scattered. She really could not believe that a mortal being could actually survive her 'Seventh Heaven Strokes'.

Shui Yixian did not have the confidence at all to dissipate Lie Qing's deadly attacks. If she did not look for Yi Ping, then she could never have the opportunity to grasp the intricate formula of the Dual Inertness Intricacy. From that intricate formula, she had grasped a breakthrough for the tenth level of the Divine Emerald Skill. If she did not attain the tenth level of the Divine Emerald Skill, then she would never have the martial skill to dissipate her opponent deadly energy attacks.

By the third stroke, Shui Yixian resolute had weakened considerably and she had expended a great deal of her internal strength. It was a lucky thing that Lie Qing's attacks had also weakened by a great deal. Her three most deadly attacks were actually the first three.

Shui Yixian said to Lie Qing, "I have won?"

Lie Qing said weakly as she said defiantly, "You are a monster! In this entire fraternity, there is actually a person such as you. But I will have the last laugh. When the Divine Calamity catches up with you, you will surely die!"

Ding Yunzi had pointed her sword at Shui Yixian as she said coolly, "No need to wait until the Divine Calamity. She will surely die today. She doesn't have much internal strength left. To me, she is just an ordinary exponent now."

Shui Yujian and Meijian were immediately at their protégé mistress' side while Nangong Le and Zuo Tianyi were besides Ding Yunzi.

Shui Yujian said coolly, "Such bold words. Would you like to try?"

Shui Meijian added, "If she is confident at the very least, she would have attacked now."

Zuo Tianyi said, "Yunzi, you still got me to fight besides you. If we join hands, few opponents in the fraternity would be our match."

Nangong Le looked at Lie Qing, looked at Ding Yunzi, looked at the twin sisters and looked at the Celestial Fairy. He seemed to be in a dilemma as he sighed, "It seems that this fight is unavoidable."

Lie Qing shook her head weakly, "We are not her match…we are not her match…Sister Yun, quickly leave while you can. Or else when she has recovered her martial power, there would be no escape. Leave me here, I won't blame you…go tell the others…" All of a sudden, she coughed out more blood; her internal injuries were not light!

Zuo Tianyi said coldly to Nangong Le, "I don't need your help if you are in such a dilemma."

Nangong Le said bitterly, "Why are we fighting one another in the first place? Everyone seems to forget that the Celestial Fairy is our Brother Yi Ping's wife and that we are all Yi Ping's friends. Whoever dies here today, do you think Brother Yi Ping will be happy?"

Lie Qing was stunned. She had totally forgotten that the Celestial Fairy was Yi Ping's wife.

Shui Yixian asked, "You know Yi Ping?!" If he was not Yi Ping's friend, how did he know she was his wife?

Nangong Le said, "Of course, he is my sworn brother too. If you don't believe, you can come with us to look for him."

Shui Yixian pointed at the fallen Xiao Youxue as she said, "Do you know that she is trying to kill Yi Ping?"

Ding Yunzi interrupted, "If Youxue wants to kill Yi Ping, do you really think that Yi Ping will still be alive to this day? If she is really your enemy, will she takes the blow from you earlier?!"

Shui Yixian was stunned as she took a few steps back as she muttered, "Did I make a big blunder? She is also Yi Ping's friend? What is their relationship?"

Chapter 30: A Bitter Lie

Yi Ping had suddenly dropped the wine flask that he was holding. His hand had suddenly trembled all of a sudden. He thought, "Is that an omen?"

Qiu Wufeng said to Yi Ping, "Brother, you must be drunk now."

Yi Ping bitterly said, "I wish I am drunk and never wake up."

It was because he could not believe that Xiao Youxue was the mysterious yellow dressed maiden that had killed his wife. He could not believe that a quiet maiden like her would have the tenacity to travel alone to the Heavenly Mountains with that purpose alone.

He realized that he had known too little of her past even though they had spent three months together, a period that was even longer than Shui Yixian and Ji Lingfeng.

Why was that when she had departed, his heart had been so sorrowful? He had the exact feelings when Ji Lingfeng had departed.

Had he fallen for Xiao Youxue?

He mused, "Yi Ping, Yi Ping. You are either such a rascal or a sentimental person. How could you like a maiden after another maiden? If you have affection for Lingfeng, why are you longing after Youxue? Youxue is the one that killed my wife. You should hate her...I don't want ever to see her again!"

Qiu Wufeng looked at Gongsun Jing as he said, "Yi Ping I can understand but you..."

Gongsun Jing was drinking heavily too. What was he thinking? Like Yi Ping, he was also musing, "Yunzi has a hand in my father's death too. Why is that I am unable to forget her? If we are normal friends, that would be more bearable but I see her every day. If she won't come back anymore, should I be glad? Zuo Tianyi is now your brother and it is obvious that he likes Yunzi. Gongsun Jing, Gongsun Jing, don't forget you are now a down and out person."

Qiu Wufeng shook his head as he said, "It seems that both of you are not even drinking to appreciate wines but are drowning your sorrows."

All of a sudden, he began to pick a flask of wine and poured it into his mouth.

Gongsun Jing asked, "What comes after you?"

Qiu Wufeng said wryly, "If I am the only somber person around, then I be the one who has to pawn my precious sword to pay for the bills."

Gongsun Jing said, "Who would want your scrap metal?"

All of a sudden, Yi Ping said. "Our enemies are here."

All of a sudden, the inn was crowded with more than thirty swordsmen as they charged up the chairs and barged through their private room! Leading the charge was Long Wudi, the Clan Chief of the Six Rivers!

Yi Ping, Gongsun Jing and Qiu Wufeng had recognized him immediately.

Long Wudi said, "What have we here? It seems that the three most wanted men in the fraternity will come to my place."

Gongsun Jing said, "Surely you are not thinking of turning us in for the bounty?"

Long Wudi said, "Even though I may not want to but the Honor Manor is influential. We are just a small martial clan in the fraternity. I hope that the three of you will come with me quietly or don't blame me for being merciless!"

Gongsun Jing said coldly, "So these men are your martial clan best fighters?"

Long Wudi said, "Indeed. In this confine space, don't blame our swords for being blind and merciless! You have better surrender. I will treat you respectfully on behalf of your late father."

Gongsun Jing said, "As soon as my father is gone, all of you have revolted. Have you forgotten that I am still the Master of the Gongsun Martial Clan?"

Long Wudi spat, "I am talking to you in a nice manner and yet you do not appreciate it. The Gongsun Martial Clan is long history. You are the only survivor now!"

Gongsun Jing was startled, "The Gongsun Martial Clan is no more?"

Long Wudi said, "As soon as Gongsun Bai was dead, the enemies of Gongsun Bai began to attack the Gongsun Martial Clan and there were no survivors."

Gongsun Jing was stunned. He began to tremble as he said, "Gu Tianle, Gu Tianle, how vicious are you! First you framed me. Next you redeployed the best fighters of the Honor Manor away or else given the strength of the Gongsun Martial Clan, it is impossible for it to be demolished just like that…"

Qiu Wufeng said coolly, "Surely you have heard of my renown as the Windless Swordsman. If you don't want to die tonight, you have better leave. I don't want to dirty my hands!"

Long Wudi laughed aloud, "Do you think we be so foolish? Ever since you have entered this city, we have been monitoring your movements. It is a little tricky to attack you while Zuo Tianyi is still around. We didn't want to make enemies of the Infinity Sword Clan yet. But I have sent a messenger to the Honor Manor that Zuo Tianyi is in cahoots with you."

Qiu Wufeng said, "The three of us are more than enough to send you all to hell."

Long Wudi laughed, "Don't be too sure. The last few flasks of wines that you have been drinking from contain a slow reacting poison. If you were to exercise your internal strength, the poison will immediately attack your heart, hastening your death!"

Gongsun Jing intercepted, "You….are so despicable!"

Yi Ping looked at Long Wudi and gulped another flask of wine!

Long Wudi looked at Yi Ping and stammered, "You…"

Yi Ping patted Qiu Wufeng and Gongsun Jing on their shoulders as he got up with unsteady steps. Even though, it appeared that he was using their shoulders as a support, it was actually more than meet the eyes!

Qiu Wufeng and Gongsun Jing could feel a strong soothing internal strength flowing through their body as it rejuvenates them. They could feel the enormous stress of the poison effect lifting away and dissolving in their bodies. Indeed, Yi Ping had used the Aspire Invocations internal strength to neutralize all the poisons into nothingness!

The depth of Yi Ping's internal strength astonished even Qiu Wufeng and Gongsun Jing!

Long Wudi smiled, "Now, if you all surrender now, it will save you unnecessary pain and is also good for me. After all, if you are alive when I send you to the Honor Manor, your bounties will worth even more."

"What if I say, they should stay as they are while your men and you should be the one that scram from here?"

Everyone was startled because the enchanting sweet voice did not come from this room!

Long Wudi shouted, "Who is that?"

Yi Ping was stunned. It was because this voice was so familiar even though he had not heard it for a long time...

A maiden of an extraordinary beauty passed through the window and into the middle of the room. Her movements were so graceful and her steps were so light that everyone was startled at her extraordinary display of her lightness swiftness skill!

In just a quick movement, she was already standing serenely in the middle of the room as she looked at everyone with a smile.

When she looked at everyone with a smile, everyone else was thinking of the same time. "Is she looking at me intentional? Can it be that she takes a liking to me?"

Everyone begun to gasped at this heavenly maiden in white that had just appeared. She was stroking her long hair as she said, "Do I need to repeat myself?"

Qiu Wufeng, Gongsun Jing and Long Wudi recognized her immediately as the maiden that had barged into the Honor Manor with Yi Ping!

Yi Ping looked at her with stunned expression as he muttered, "Lingfeng...it is really you. Why are you here?"

Ji Lingfeng sighed softly, "Do I need to explain to you?" She began to pour the wine from a flask to a cup.

Yi Ping quickly gasped out, "Lingfeng, that is poisonous. Don't drink it!"

But before Yi Ping could take a step forward, she had already drunk from the cup as she said, "Good wine. Too bad, it is tainted with the unsavory taste of poison."

She said to Long Wudi, "Since you are the one that adds the poison into the wines, why don't you taste it too if it is savory? Or else you may think I am lying to you."

Long Wudi smiled bitterly, "No need. I believe it."

Ji Lingfeng smiled, "If even you will not drink it, do you think the three of them will really drink it? Of course, unless they are all a bunch of drunkards."

Yi Ping smiled bitterly as he thought, "She has not changed at all after so many months. She is scolding us indirectly as drunkards."

Gongsun Jing and Qiu Wufeng were guilty-stricken. With their experiences, they should have detected that the wines had been tampered with.

Ji Lingfeng said, "If they are not idiots, I am an idiot? If I am not an idiot, why should I drink your tampered wine?"

Long Wudi began to hesitate and had doubts as he thought, "The wines have already been switched? That is impossible..."

Ji Lingfeng smiled at Gongsun Jing and Qiu Wufeng as she said sarcastically, "So what do you think of the feeling of being a fugitive wanted by the majority of the orthodox fraternity?"

Gongsun Jing said coolly, "It isn't a good feeling after all."

Qiu Wufeng smiled bitterly, "You never know if your enemies would appear at any time, even your food and drinks can be poisoned at any time. It is not pleasure at all."

Yi Ping really could not resist withholding anymore as he interrupted, "Lingfeng, why are you here?"

Ji Lingfeng glanced mysteriously at him as she said, "Why? You are suddenly so concern about? I am here to look for my husband of course!"

Many in the room were disappointed at this news and wondered who her husband was.

Yi Ping was stunned as he took a step backward as his entire expressions had changed!

After quickly regaining his composure, he quickly said. "You are married?! Congrats then…"

Ji Lingfeng smiled at him as she said, "You don't sound and look at all pleased?"

Yi Ping said with stoned expressions, "Of course I am happy for you…"

Ji Lingfeng said, "Really? But why is that you don't sound and look too happy?"

Yi Ping replied gloomily, "I am always like this. Surely you know."

Ji Lingfeng said, "I really do not know. I am not the worm in your stomach, how should I know? Don't you want to know who my new husband is?"

Yi Ping said, "You can tell us if you want."

Ji Lingfeng smiled mysteriously, "He is young and handsome. He knows that I am in trouble and have not forgotten about me. He comes all the way to a distant and forsaken place just to look for me. If he's not my husband-to-be, who is he then?"

Yi Ping asked, "Who?"

Ji Lingfeng gave him a gentle kick all of a sudden as she flushes, "Why are you so stupid? He is standing in front of me of course!"

Yi Ping's expressions lit up as he said, "Who…?"

Ji Lingfeng gave him another small kick and tried to slap him but he avoided it.

They seemed to have forgotten that there were others in this room and their little affections were enviable!

Long Wudi coughed and interrupted, "You are the Holy Maiden of the Holy Hex Sect? Almost the entire orthodox clans are attacking the Holy Hex Sect now and you dare to appear here? You are really bold. Good, I am so lucky to take all four of you in one fell scoop!"

Ji Lingfeng said coldly all of a sudden, "Since you know that I am the Holy Maiden of the Holy Hex Sect, surely you must have heard of our 'Consecrated Meteor Shower' and 'Meteor Rain Needles' secret projectile skills. If I am not confident, would I be in this room?"

As her eyes swept from one person to another, she added. "This is a confined room. Do you think my secret projectiles would be faster or your swords would be swifter? Are you willing to take a bet? And how do you know that I am not alone?"

Long Wudi turned ashen immediately. It was because she was right. At this point blank distance, it was almost impossible for them to dodge the 'Consecrated Meteor Shower', a secret projectile technique that was renowned for launching more than one hundred secret projectiles!

Quite a few of the swordsmen and even Long Wudi was looking at the closest exit!

Ji Lingfeng words had already shaken their fighting spirit!

Ji Lingfeng was already saying to Yi Ping, Qiu Wufeng and Gongsun Jing, "Stand behind me."

Yi Ping said, "There is no need for you to be involved. The three of us are more than enough…"

Long Wudi sighed, "Even though it appears that we have the superior numbers but I have seen this Yi Ping's skills in the Honor Manor and the Heavenly Mountains. Moreover there is Young Master Qiu and Young Master Gongsun Jing too. Their martial skills are among the best in the fraternity. As long as they are not poisoned, this attack is doomed to fail. From the looks of it, none of them looked as though they are poisoned…how is it possible? But if I were to retreat now, I will lose a lot of honor and face. If the Holy Maiden is here, then surely there must be clan protégés of the Holy Hex Sect nearby too…"

Ji Lingfeng said, "If you back off now, I will ensure that you can continue to carry on your daily business in this city."

She softened her tone, "I know that the Six Rivers Clan is a neutral clan that did not go on the westward expedition with the Honor Manor or else you won't be here. Even though this is not the Western Fraternity yet, the Holy Hex Sect has a base here. Because we know that your clan had not officially joined the Honor Manor yet but if you were to make an enemy of the Holy Hex Sect today, we will make sure you are in our enemy list and your business will be soured immediately. Surely you have heard of what happened to the Belle Clan that was in this city that had joined hands with the Honor Manor. So choose what you want. Business or destruction?"

Long Wudi bowed his hands respectfully as he said, "Holy Maiden, we will take our leave and we will also give our promise that we will not harass them while they are still here."

He then shouted, "Let's go!"

Ji Lingfeng said, "Hold!"

Long Wudi turned ashen as he asked, "Is there anything else?"

Ji Lingfeng said, "Since these gentlemen are guests in your city and is their first time here, do you think that you should at least buy the tabs for them?"

Long Wudi looked at the private room and the feast on the table. He sighed weakly and put down three silvers on the table.

Three silvers were more than enough.

Ji Lingfeng said coolly, "That is very generous of you. You can go now."

Long Wudi and his men quickly exited the room and the inn!

Qiu Wufeng said wryly, "So we have solved our tabs."

Gongsun Jing said, "I didn't expect that you are really the Holy Maiden of the Holy Hex Sect. How is that you know that we have no money?"

Ji Lingfeng smiled, "I didn't want to know but the three of you were incessantly talking about it."

Yi Ping asked, "You are here for some time?"

Ji Lingfeng said, "Not really. I just arrive too."

Yi Ping said, "You haven't really tell me yet, why are you in this place? You are supposed to be in the Western Fraternity now."

Ji Lingfeng smiled sweetly, "I have told you. I am here to look for my husband."

Yi Ping said, "You can still joke about this. Why are you here in this place?"

Ji Lingfeng said, "I am here to make contacts with a branch of my clan here to strengthen the fighting resolve against the orthodox clans and to find out more information of the other clans activities. I didn't expect to find you here too. Do you know that the Honor Manor and the Virtuous Palace have formed an alliance already?"

Gongsun Jing, Qiu Wufeng and Yi Ping were stunned.

Yi Ping said, "Not counting the dozens of martial clans under the banner of the Honor Manor, just the Virtuous Palace alone is a big headache. Just how did Gu Tianle persuade the Virtuous Palace to join him for the westward expedition?"

Ji Lingfeng said, "Do you think that it is somewhat overkilling? Even though the Holy Hex Sect is the number one unorthodox clan in recent years, we are still unable to compete headlong with the Honor Manor and the various major orthodox clans."

Gongsun Jing asked, "Meaning?"

Ji Lingfeng said, "Someone else must have instigated him or forced him to do so. Someone powerful and we don't know who he is yet that can even persuade the wily Xiao Shuai to join him."

Yi Ping was startled, "I wonder who he is…"

Qiu Wufeng said, "I am afraid his aim isn't about destroying the Holy Hex Sect but to dominate the entire martial fraternity!"

Gongsun Jing said, "Even though my late father wants to destroy the Holy Hex Sect a long time ago, he didn't want to do so yet because such a clash would bring cause a double fatalities and may give his enemies an opportunity to cause havoc or to undermine his strength."

Ji Lingfeng said, "I am afraid his real target is the Celestial Palace."

Yi Ping was startled, "The Celestial Palace?! It does exist?"

Ji Lingfeng said, "Of course it does. It is just that no one has ever survived a trip there. Anyway, we are all just speculating."

She paused for a while before she asked, "Where is Maiden Xiao Youxue? Have you finally found out that she isn't a deaf and mute person?"

Yi Ping was suddenly unhappy, "You already know that she is not a deaf and mute person yet you play such a prank on me before you left. Don't ever mention her again."

Ji Lingfeng was surprised as she continued to smile gleefully, "Why can't I mention her? Is it because you just got rejected by her that you cannot get over it?"

Yi Ping was solemn as he said gravely, "Do you know that she is the one that has killed my wife?"

Ji Lingfeng said calmly, "So what?"

Yi Ping was stunned at her reply as he said slowly, "You…you already know?!"

Ji Lingfeng said coolly, "I have already said, so what."

Yi Ping was really upset at her reply as he said angrily, "I treat you as a friend. You have already known and did not tell me. And you can even tell me so what?!"

Ji Lingfeng blinked at Yi Ping as she repeated again, "So what?"

Yi Ping said, "She is my wife's killer and you know very well, I have been looking for her all this time!"

Ji Lingfeng said, "So what if you know if she is the one that you are looking for? Have you forgotten that she is the one that have saved your life that day? Have you ever asks her what difficulties she has and why did she have to do it? So what if you know who she is? Will you have the heart to kill her? If she really treats you as an enemy, she would have killed you and not saved you!"

All of a sudden, Yi Ping was jolted.

He had suddenly remembered her first encounter with her. She was the very first maiden that he had ever met on the Heavenly Mountains and she had even warned him not to go up there. If he had not disregarded her advice, maybe they would not be foes now.

He had also remembered how he was badly injured after the battle at the Honor Manor with Gu Tianle and it was actually Xiao Youxue who had saved him. She had also saved him from the giant Thousand Year Icy Fish and the wild boar attack. She had also almost got herself killed while trying to fight Xiao Yuanjia while with him…

All of a sudden, he realized how terribly wrong he had been as he muttered, "Youxue, Youxue, I shouldn't have scolded you. I should at least listen to what you have to say first…I am such a heartless person…"

Ji Lingfeng softened her alluring voice, "The reason why I did not tell you is because I owe my life to Xiao Youxue too and I have not yet repaid her this heavy debt. You are a person that knows how to differentiate feuds and debts. So what if Youxue is here now? What will you do?"

Yi Ping muttered, "I do not know. I do not know…"

Ji Lingfeng said to him, "You don't even dare to look at me in the eyes since earlier. That is so unlike you in the past. Have you fallen in love with another maiden?"

Yi Ping was startled by her questioning. He looked panicky at Gongsun Jing and Qiu Wufeng who had kept silent.

While traveling together, everyone could tell that Xiao Youxue was always cold towards all the others except for Ding Yunzi and Yi Ping. Even Lie Qing, who always chatted with her were often left in the cold.

Indeed, he was guilty and that was why he dared not look into Ji Lingfeng's eyes. It was because over the past several months, he had indeed developed affections for Xiao Youxue.

Ji Lingfeng said, "I…do you think that I am a person that can get jealous easily? If you are with Xiao Youxue, I can still accept it but not the others. She has after all, saved my life. The right thing for you to do now is to find her back and apologize to her. Not just a simple sorry, you have to bow down on your knees and begged her for forgiveness."

Actually Yi Ping had already known that Xiao Youxue had taken a liking for him but he dare not reciprocate her affections. How could he not known? He was not entirely stupid but he tried to avoid her whenever he could because he could not forget Ji Lingfeng either.

He said to himself, "Sometimes, it is better for feelings to be buried inside or else you only be hurting her more. Eventually she will get over it and find a more suitable match." Even though that was what he had in mind but that was not what his heart was really feeling.

Finally he had made a decision. Yi Ping regained his spirits again as he said with conviction, "I am going to look for Youxue now."

"You don't have to look for her anymore."

Yi Ping was startled as he saw Ding Yunzi walking into the private room. From her expressions, she looked terribly tired.

Yi Ping went to her, "What happens?"

Ji Lingfeng was startled for she had recognized Ding Yunzi as the super exponent from the Virtuous Palace and she also had an annoying look on her face as she thought, "Yi Ping, Yi Ping, it seems that that you are attracting unwanted attention. I should really help you to chase them all away."

She was even more startled when she saw Zuo Tianyi and Nangong Le walking into the private room.

Nangong Le immediately recognized her as he said, "Maiden Lingfeng! What a pleasant surprise. You are here?"

Ji Lingfeng just smiled weakly.

All of a sudden, Yi Ping saw Shui Yujian and Shui Meijian holding Lie Qing into the room. He was stunned as he said, "Yu'Er and Mei'Er, why are you here?"

All of a sudden, Shui Yujian and Shui Meijian drew their long precious swords when they saw Ji Lingfeng as they gasped together, "It is you!"

Shui Yujian said to Ji Lingfeng, "How vicious are you! You…"

Yi Ping was startled as he looked at Ji Lingfeng, "What did you do?"

Ji Lingfeng said, "I merely teach them a little lesson. They are the ones that had attacked me first that day."

She pointed at Shui Yujian, Shui Meijian and Lie Qing as she said. "Just who are they?"

But Yi Ping did not seem to hear as he reached out for Lie Qing, "Qing'Er, are you alright? Who is the one that has injured you into this state?!"

Lie Qing looked softly into his eyes as she smiled faintly, "I'm really alright. Don't you worry about me, alright?"

Ji Lingfeng nearly fainted from anger. Shui Meijian, Shui Yujian, Lie Qing and Ding Yunzi were all extraordinary beauties, who were all alluring and enchanting in their own ways. Together, they were such a moving sight. But seeing them now was like seeing them as rivals to be eliminated or else it would be so hard to quell her anger!

Lie Qing looked at Ji Lingfeng, "Who are you?"

Ji Lingfeng was indignant as she said, "I am the one that should be asking you who are you. You like a temptress with your vixen looks. I don't like you at all."

Yi Ping was stunned at what she had just said so he quickly said, "They are all my friends. You are all my friends."

Lie Qing smiled weakly as she answered coldly, "Right. I am a temptress. How do you know? I am going to steal your Yi Ping. So what? I don't need you to like me at all."

Yi Ping ignored them all as he turned to Ding Yunzi and asked, "Yunzi, where is Youxue?"

Ding Yunzi suppressed her tears as she said slowly, "She is not coming back anymore."

Yi Ping was startled, "Quickly, let's go and find her again. I…I don't mean what I say…"

Ding Yunzi said coldly, "You have already said that you don't ever wish to see her again and she thinks the same too. She has just one last message for you."

Yi Ping was overcome with emotions as he thought, "She don't ever want to see me again? Maybe that is not a bad thing after all…"

He asked, "What is her message?"

Ding Yunzi said coldly, "She hates you. The next time, she sees you she will surely kill you with her own hands. So don't ever look for her ever again if you value your life."

Ji Lingfeng was startled as she thought, "Xiao Youxue really says that?"

Yi Ping turned ashen immediately as he fell onto the chair as he muttered, "She really hates me so much? I should be the one that hates her but do I?"

Shui Meijian turned around discreetly as she really could not hold back her tears anymore while Shui Yujian did not dare to look into Yi Ping's eyes.

Lie Qing was trembling as though she wanted to say something.

Yi Ping did not notice that everyone had a grim expression. Even Ji Lingfeng, Gongsun Jing and Qiu Wufeng had sensed something was amiss in the atmosphere.

Chapter 31: The Top Exponent from the Virtuous Palace

Just as Yi Ping was sighing sadly, he was suddenly surrounded by Shui Yujian and Shui Meijian who embraced him side by side!

Nangong Le was stunned as he thought, "Yi Ping knows the twin sisters too? Why is that he seems to know all the beauties?"

Shui Meijian exclaimed tearfully, "Master, we have finally found you…!"

Shui Yujian wiped a tear from her eyes as she said gently, "Master, you still have us. Maiden Xiao may not appreciate you but we do."

Ji Lingfeng and Lie Qing were startled at how close they were with Yi Ping.

Ji Lingfeng hummed coldly, "The two of you are so shameless. You are so young yet you are hugging a man so intimately."

Lie Qing wanted to say the same thing too but her injuries were severe and she could not muster her strength. So she was glad that Ji Lingfeng had actually spoken out what was in her mind.

Shui Yujian said coolly, "We are talking to our Master now; you don't have the right to interrupt us."

Ji Lingfeng said coldly, "Oh he is your master? I have never heard of clan protégés behaving so intimately with their master."

Shui Meijian smiled cheekily, "That is because Yi Ping is also our husband!"

Ji Lingfeng almost fainted from anger as she said coldly, "Just who is your husband?!"

Shui Meijian said, "You didn't hear me? Yi Ping is my husband."

Ji Lingfeng said coldly, "How shameless of you to claim Yi Ping as your husband."

Shui Yujian looked at Yi Ping with her eyes full of melody as she said, "It seems that she is hard of hearing. Yi Ping, tell her, you are our husband."

Yi Ping was stunned. When he looked at Shui Yujian's eyes, he began to recall the reason why he had ran away from the Eternal Ice Palace and his cheeks began to flush.

He stammered, "I…I…don't know."

Ji Lingfeng was infuriated, "What do you mean by you do not know? It is either yes or no!"

Even Lie Qing said, "Yi Ping, you…are really their husband?!"

Nangong Le smiled bitterly as he said, "Congratulations for having two lovely wives."

Qiu Wufeng smiled awkwardly as he said, "How many wives do you have, Brother Yi Ping."

Yi Ping replied unhappily, "Now it is not the time for jokes."

Even though Ding Yunzi was expressionless and was quiet but she was stunned by the audaciousness of Ji Lingfeng, Shui Yujian and Shui Meijian in declaring their sentiments as she thought, "Youxue, it is a lucky thing that you did not see this or you will surely be dismayed at this sight. This Yi Ping is nothing but a despicable Playboy! I am so wrong and I thought that he is a good man."

Ji Lingfeng looked at Yi Ping with hurt eyes, "Yi Ping, is that true? You have never told me before…"

Yi Ping really did not know to reply as he thought bitterly, "No one will ever believe what I have said and believe that I did it in a moment of folly. Alas Yi Ping! First you let down Youxue, second you let down Yu'Er and Mei'Er. Now you let down Lingfeng…why must you hurt those that are closest to you?"

Just when he was about to say something, Lei Qing mustered all her strength and gave him a tight slap on his right cheek!

Shui Yujian was startled. She quickly recovered her composure and asked, "Why did…"

Before Yi Ping could even recover from his astonishment and before Shui Yujian could finish her sentence, Ji Lingfeng had slapped him tightly on his left cheek!

Shui Meijian had not even recovered from her initial surprise yet as both slaps happened in a blink of an eye and almost the same time!

Everyone could see how emotional Ji Lingfeng and Lie Qing had been!

Yi Ping could only mutter, "Why did…"

But even before he could finish, Lie Qing had coughed out blood and fainted!

Yi Ping quickly caught hold of her and panicky shouted, "Qing'Er, don't scare me. Wake up…"

When Ji Lingfeng saw that Yi Ping was holding Lie Qing, she was so infuriated that she stormed to the entrance, alarming Yi Ping.

Yi Ping thought, "She is angry? Why shouldn't she? If I were her, I will be angry too…"

Ji Lingfeng had already reached the door but she had stopped short of exiting the door.

Zuo Tianyi said quickly, "Yi Ping, say something to pacify her or she will really leave."

Yi Ping said, "Lingfeng, where are you going? It is dangerous for you to be alone…"

Ji Lingfeng answered coldly, "Hmph, I have been roaming the fraternity alone since I am sixteen. You don't have to worry about me. I probably have more experience in the fraternity than you guys who drink like pigs."

Yi Ping, Qiu Wufeng and Gongsun Jing began to fluster.

Everyone was already anticipating that Maiden Ji would storm off the room as she was getting emotional.

That includes Yi Ping who was still holding onto Lie Qing and he was surrounded left and right by Shui Yujian and Shui Meijian. Yi Ping was really in an awkward position!

Nangong Le and Qiu Wufeng were looking enviably, wishing that they would be in Yi Ping position instead.

Nangong Le thought, "Since Yi Ping is unable to cherish Maiden Lingfeng, when she storms off I will immediately chase after her. Who knows, we may become a couple."

Ji Lingfeng just stood there and was brushing her long flowing hair as she thought, "When Xiao Youxue left the room earlier he did not even go after her. When I have left the last time, he did not even try to make a little effort to stop me. He is really so dumb."

That was why she was still waiting at the door for Yi Ping to ask her to stay or to pacify her.

Ding Yunzi was thinking, "Yi Ping, no maidens will tolerate such a guy that is indecisive. I am afraid today that you are going to hurt another maiden again. You are a good guy Yi Ping, treat others with respect and a sincere person. But sometimes, not everyone can understand you and think you are a fickle minded person. This will cause you to lose favor in the eyes of everyone that do not understand you."

All of a sudden, Ji Lingfeng brushed aside her long flowing hair and walked back to the center of room as she began to sit down, stunning everyone!

Yi Ping was startled, "You are not going?"

Shui Yujian was surprised as she asked, "You are not leaving?"

Shui Meijian asked, "Why did you come back for?"

Ji Lingfeng looked at everyone without batting an eye as she knew that everyone was looking at her for answers.

Even Ding Yunzi who was rarely wrong on her analysis was startled by her sudden reversal as she asked, "What is she thinking?"

Ji Lingfeng said coolly, "Hmph, I am just suddenly curious just exactly how many shameless vixens are there around Yi Ping that lingers around him like nasty flies. They can even claim him as their husband when it is not the truth."

She began to look at her fingernails and looked at Shui Meijian and Shui Yujian.

Shui Yujian said coolly, "It seems that you are trying to pick a fight with us."

Ji Lingfeng replied, "Hmph, so what?"

Shui Meijian looked at Yi Ping with doleful eyes, "We dare not. We are not as bitching as you. We are just eighteen and you are trying to bully us. We are so pitiful…"

Ji Lingfeng was startled at Shui Meijian's reply. This young maiden was smarter than she had appeared to be. Instead of being upset, she was using a soft approach and made it appeared as though she was the bully instead.

All of a sudden, Ji Lingfeng stole a glance at Ding Yunzi and blinked her eyes.

Ding Yunzi was startled but she did not show it. She quickly thought, "This Maiden Ji is not just a pretty doll. Her intellect is not beneath me…"

Yi Ping asked, "Lingfeng, you are not leaving anymore?"

Ji Lingfeng said, "You seem eager for me to leave?"

Yi Ping smiled bitterly, "Of course not."

Ji Lingfeng smiled, "Of course I know you don't wish. All of you have come all the way just for me. If I walk off, you will have to find me again. Therefore I have decided to save you all the trouble from looking for me again."

Yi Ping rubbed his nose as he said, "True, true. If you walk off now, I may not be able to find you again."

Ji Lingfeng said to Shui Yujian and Shui Meijian, "If you are not here to look for me, both of you can leave immediately. Did you just hear that Yi Ping is here to look for me?"

Shui Yujian was exasperated as she said, "You…you…"

Shui Meijian immediately said, "Sister Lingfeng, we are so young. Surely you aren't thinking of bullying us? Yi Ping is indeed our Master and husband. We surely follow him whenever he goes. I'm Mei'Er and this is my sister Yu'Er."

Ji Lingfeng's eyes soften a little and this was not lost on Shui Yujian who had super sensitive sense with her 'Heart Intricacy Skill'.

Shui Yujian melancholy said, "We are orphans. Ever since our Mistress is gone, Yi Ping had been our Master. We are so young and have no one to depend upon. We know we shouldn't call Yi Ping our husband but our chastity…"

Shui Meijian added woefully, "A maiden chastity is important. We know that our Master did it in a matter of folly. We don't blame him and we suffer in silence alone..."

Shui Yujian began to sobbed, "We shouldn't say this in public to disgrace our Master but I hope Sister Lingfeng will take pity on us."

Ding Yunzi was startled and she looked at Yi Ping with a hateful look. Her expressions had suddenly changed and she was trembling.

Ji Lingfeng looked at Yi Ping with woeful expressions as she said coldly to him, "You are a beast in disguise."

Qiu Wufeng and Gongsun Jing began to sigh heavily when they had heard of their tragedies.

Nangong Le, Zuo Tianyi and Ding Yunzi were all thinking at the same time, "We promise to keep their protégé mistress' news from Yi Ping but are we lying to Yi Ping? From the looks of it, these two sisters seem to be expert liars…"

All of a sudden, the twin sisters were crying in Ji Lingfeng's embrace as they said. "We hope that Sister Lingfeng will take care of us and take us in as close sisters…"

Shui Yujian blinked secretly at her sister, Shui Meijian as she thought, "Let this Lingfeng fight it out with Lie Qing and Ding Yunzi first while we wait on the fence. As long as we are coy and amicable, we have Yi Ping's hearts eventually."

Shui Meijian was also thinking the same, "Our protégé mistress have taken Xiao Youxue back to the Eternal Ice Palace and leave us with these strangers. This Maiden Lingfeng can be our ally against them."

Ji Lingfeng began to sympathize with the twin sisters as she said gently, "Yu'Er and Mei'Er, if Yi Ping dares to bully you, I will surely teach him a lesson. Don't be afraid. You are all so young and should be happy. Alas, from now on, we are sisters. If he dares to take in another wife again, I will surely kill him."

Yi Ping smiled bitterly and was relieved that at least Ji Lingfeng was staying so he said, "Lingfeng, I…"

But Ji Lingfeng interrupted him coldly as she said, "I didn't say I want to talk to you. You seem to be enjoying holding this vixen in your arms."

Yi Ping said, "Lie Qing has serious internal injuries. We need to take her to a safe place to recuperate first."

Ji Lingfeng said coldly, "I say I don't wish to talk to you now…"

All of a sudden, Ji Lingfeng, Zuo Tianyi, Ding Yunzi, Shui Yujian, Shui Meijian and Yi Ping froze in fear.

They had sudden sensed a powerful malevolent aura that was silently approaching them!

Zuo Tianyi said, "What a deadly killing malevolent air."

Ding Yunzi had broken into a cold sweat, "That's Yuan Shao. We must quickly leave this place as soon as possible! Hurry!"

Yi Ping asked, "Who is this Yuan Shao? There is only one of him and we have so many? I am not afraid of him."

Qiu Wufeng said, "Why do we need to fear him for?"

Ding Yunzi said, "He is an elder of the Virtuous Palace. He may be ninety-seven year old this year but even our Protégé Master Xiao Shuai is afraid of him. I didn't expect him to be here. We must quickly flee. Meet outside the city at the seven miles pavilion that is on the map."

She began to walk away when all of a sudden Yi Ping caught hold of her while still holding Lie Qing as he asked. "Yunzi, where are you going?"

Ding Yunzi said, "Yuan Shao may not know I have betrayed the Virtuous Palace yet. I will hold him back for a while. Everyone please go now, as fast as possible."

Zuo Tianyi said coldly, "Hey, don't touch her."

Yi Ping flustered as he quickly let go of Ding Yunzi's hand.

Ji Lingfeng was infuriated, "He didn't even try to grab my hand just now…"

Ding Yunzi said, "Yi Ping is now my protégé master. Mind your language, Tianyi."

Zuo Tianyi sighed, "Yunzi, why are you treating me so coldly? Let me go with you."

Gongsun Jing said, "Maiden Ding, I will go with you."

Ding Yunzi drawn out her long sword as she said, "Don't hinder me. You will only cause me to lose my life by tagging along. Yuan Shao kills anyone that is not from the Virtuous Palace and if anyone of you comes with me, he would know that I have betrayed the Virtuous Palace."

She paused solemnly for a while before she adds, "Don't ever think of following me. None of you here except for Lie Qing and Xiao Youxue can even hold thirty strokes from me. Yuan Shao can kill all of you in much less the time. Don't even bother to try."

Then she left the room hastily!

Ji Lingfeng was trembling, "This killing malevolent…we have no hope against it…"

Shui Yujian said, "His malevolent aura can be felt from so far away. Normal opponents cannot stand against him. I cannot imagine if we are near him."

Shui Meijian nodded.

Yi Ping said, "Let's leave quickly before it is too late."

Zuo Tianyi gritted his teeth as he muttered, "She may be right. She may be safer on her own than with us." It was because even he was afraid and shaking now.

Yuan Shao had not reached but his sword and malevolent intentions had already rippled through them! And even top exponents like Yi Ping, Zuo Tianyi, Ji Lingfeng, Gong Jing, Nangong Le, Shui Yujian and Shui Meijian could all feel his startling presence!

They knew that he was very near and time was now essential!

Yi Ping said, "I don't blame her if she returns to the Virtuous Palace. I only hope she is safe. I never expected that the Virtuous Palace would have a super exponent of this caliber."

Zuo Tianyi smiled bitterly, "No wonder my grandfather warned me not to offend the Virtuous Palace in the past. Even Gongsun Bai did not inspire such fear in me…"

Ji Lingfeng said, "Only someone who has killed countless number of people has this type of malevolent aura…"

Nangong Le was smiling wryly as the group left the room, "We are running away from just one old man? It's funny, isn't it?"

Qiu Wufeng said, "You have seen the skills of Xiao Shuai and Maiden Ding? You have not seen real super exponents when they are fighting for real. I can still remember vividly how more than fifty fighters tried to take down the Celestial Fairy and barely even the battle had even start; half of us were already down."

Nangong Le smiled bitterly as he thought, "I have seen the Celestial Fairy earlier and the skills displayed by Lie Qing. Their martial skills are out of the world. I just don't believe an old man from the Virtuous Palace can be as good as them…"

All of a sudden Yi Ping said, "Yu'Er, Mei'Er, help me to carry Lie Qing."

Shui Yujian cried out melancholy, "Master, where are you going?"

Yi Ping simply smiled, "Don't worry. I won't be in trouble and will keep a good distant in case Yunzi is in trouble." And he was gone.

It was only then that the group realized that both Zuo Tianyi and Yi Ping were both missing from the group!

Ji Lingfeng said coldly, "They are foolish, so let them be."

But she was saying silently to herself, "Yi Ping, why are you always meddling into troubles? You must know your limitations."

Shui Meijian said, "I wonder who are more foolish. The Holy Hex Sect or Yi Ping. For the Holy Hex Sect to fight against so many martial clans are more foolish."

Ji Lingfeng smiled mysteriously, "The orthodox clans will soon know that they are courting their own death should they come to the Western Fraternity."

Gongsun Jing asked, "Why is it so? Aren't there a number of powerful orthodox clans in the Western Fraternity too?"

Ji Lingfeng hummed coldly, "However, they all seem to forget that a hidden rule of the Western Fraternity. No matter if they are unorthodox or orthodox martial clans, no clans shall exterminate the other or that will incur the wrath of the other Emei Clans and the Celestial Palace."

There were more than a hundred martial clans in the Western Fraternity and the majority called themselves the Emei Clan when they were outside the Western Fraternity and that included the Holy Hex Sect.

Most martial clans in the western fraternity did not want to reveal their protégé masters and clans openly. While it was understandable for the unorthodox clans, it was mystifying for even the orthodox clans to follow suit as well!

Qiu Wufeng said, "The Celestial Palace is a myth…"

Ji Lingfeng interrupted sharply, "We have all thought it is so too. But perhaps because the ambitious plans of the Honor Manor has even disturbed the Celestial Palace, so this time they are sending a Celestial Envoy to the Holy Hex Sect to help us."

Gongsun Jing was startled, "There is a Celestial Envoy from the Celestial Palace?! The information network of the Honor Manor is the best in the fraternity. Why is that we have not heard anything about the Celestial Palace for the past two hundred years?"

Ji Lingfeng said coldly, "The information network of the Honor Manor is just so and so. You can't even recognize Xiao Shuai that day and you can't even recognize the traitors within your own clan."

Gongsun Jing flustered but he quickly asked again, "How big are the reinforcements of the Celestial Palace?"

Ji Lingfeng said, "Just one."

Everyone was startled, "Just one!?"

Nangong Le quipped, "It seems that we are also courting our own death if we go to the Holy Hex Sect now. Why don't we go to the Tranquil City? I have two great friends and brothers that are from there and one of them is even the Protégé Master of the Tranquil City."

Shui Yujian smiled, "We know Priest Liu Qingcheng too."

Nangong Le laughed, "Of course. We have all met before. I am sure if I was to ask Priest Liu Qingcheng, he would forgive your past transgression and let you take refuge in the Tranquil City where we will be safe for the time being."

Shui Meijian smiled as she added, "No need. He will take us in no matter what you will say."

Nangong Le was puzzled but he continued to smile, "The Tranquil City has very strict rules about entertaining strangers, especially women. Unless I speak for you, it is very unlikely that Liu Qingcheng will take you in."

Shui Meijian said, "He is our Protégé Master too. If your disciples come knocking on your doors, will you reject them?"

Nangong Le was stunned, "Liu Qingcheng is also your protégé master!? He has never told me…"

He made a silent vow to teach Liu Qingcheng a lesson when they had met as he thought, "You have two such beautiful protégés and yet you pretended otherwise. Liu Qingcheng, Liu Qingcheng, you are such a good friend of mine."

Gongsun Jing interrupted Nangong Le, "The Celestial Envoy must be an old martial master. No matter what, it is a good opportunity for us to pay him a visit and to learn some superior epitome skills from him."

Qiu Wufeng nodded, "That is right. Meeting a worthy master will save us a lot of wrongful training in the future. For his daringness to come alone, he must be a top exponent. May I know what the name of this honorable martial master is?"

Ji Lingfeng smiled bitterly, "Hmph, she is not a 'He'. Her fraternity name is the Joyful Goddess and you better don't talk to her or you will surely regret it. She has weird red eyes like this Maiden Lie Qing too. Trust me, you have to be respectful to her at all times as she is highly erratic. On her first day of at the Holy Hex Sect, more than a dozen of our top fighters were killed by her. If I tell you, she is mentally unsound, would you believe?"

Chapter 32: The Joyful Goddess

The streets were dark and void of people as it was already past midnight. Only the moon and the stars were the only visible lights. There was an uneasy feeling in the atmosphere, a feeling of death and despair that caused everyone to avoid this street tonight.

But for Ding Yunzi, these dim lights were more than sufficient for her to move rapidly.

An old man with a white beard was walking quietly in the middle of the streets with a cane. He looked so fragile and harmless but he was the most deadly exponent of the Virtuous Palace, Yuan Shao.

Ding Yunzi walked quietly towards him as she said coolly, "My respects to Protégé Elder."

Yuan Shao looked at her finery and her beautiful dress as he said, "I didn't know that when you do dress up, you will be so beautiful."

Ding Yunzi shifted uncomfortably as she replied, "Protégé Elder, you flatter me too much."

Yuan Shao added, "This is the truth. You seem to have changed. You used to dress simple."

Ding Yunzi was secretly alarmed but she maintained her composure.

Yuan Shao said coldly, "You have been missing for quite a while. Why didn't you report your whereabouts to us? Where are Xiao Yuanjia and Xiao Youxue?"

Ding Yunzi replied coolly, "Both Xiao Yuanjia and Xiao Youxue had been killed. I didn't report my activities because I do not have the chance to do so."

Yuan Shao raised his eyebrows as he asked, "They are dead? Who has the formidable means to kill them? There isn't anyone capable in the fraternity that can kill Xiao Yuanjia as far as I know. What about Xiao Youxue? You have better not lie to me or don't blame for being ruthless."

Ding Yunzi quietly said, "I wouldn't dare, Protégé Elder. We have found Xiao Youxue and she was killed by Xiao Yuanjia."

Yuan Shao nodded, "Indeed, Xiao Youxue isn't Xiao Yuanjia's match. Where is her body? Dead or alive, we must have her body. You shouldn't know it is very important to us."

Ding Yunzi said, "Unfortunately, I am intercepted by a powerful opponent and have to give her the body. It is only feigning to be submissive to her that I am still alive to this day."

Yuan Shao stared sternly at Ding Yunzi causing her to tremble as he said coldly, "You are not weak either. There is hardly anyone in the fraternity that can fight Xiao Yuanjia and you at the same time."

Ding Yunzi shook her head, "Protégé Elder you are wrong. This time round, we have met our match. The powerful opponent that we have met is a young maiden by the name of Lie Qing."

Yuan Shao said coldly, "Xiao Yuanjia and you will lose to a young maiden?"

Ding Yunzi protested softly, "This Lie Qing is no ordinary maiden. She has red eyes and knows the Invincible Divine Force, the most secretive skill of our clan."

Even Yuan Shao was startled, "She really have red eyes and know the Invincible Divine Force?"

Ding Yunzi nodded, "And she has even eaten Xiao Youxue and Xiao Yuanjia while they are still alive. It is very horrible."

Yuan Shao asked, "How did you manage to survive then?"

Ding Yunzi said, "I have asked her why she is sparing me but she simply says that she have no use of my intricate energy yet."

All of a sudden, Yuan Shao raised his cane and swung against her!

Ding Yunzi raised her scabbard to block it. She took five steps backward as the martial force of Yuan Shao was simply too strong for her. She quickly asked, "Protégé Elder, why did you...?"

Yuan Shao said, "I have almost believe you but unfortunately, your story have too many loopholes. You have dared to betray the Virtuous Palace."

Ding Yunzi asked, "Huh?!"

Yuan Shao said, "Firstly, you know very well that I am coming yet you did not attempt to lure them to me. Secondly, if that Lie Qing is as formidable as you have claimed, she would have confronted me. Thirdly, you are not a good liar..."

Before he could finish, Ding Yunzi had already drawn out her long sword quietly and threw it into a flying sword towards him!

But Yuan Shao simply caught her sword with his bare hand and threw it back at her again!

Lie Qing had barely dodged her own sword as it flew past her, smashing through the walls!

All of a sudden, she paralyzed in fear. It was as though Yuan Shao had already pointed his cane at her throat!

To the observers, Yuan Shao was still a good distance from Ding Yunzi but to Ding Yunzi, she knew that she was going to die. It was because even before Yuan Shao had moved towards her, he had already extended his invisible sword intentions at her, paralyzing her!

No matter in which direction that she could move to, she could not escape from his invisible sword intentions!

She broke into a cold sweat.

All of a sudden, she could move again as the invisible sword intentions seemingly disappeared! Ding Yunzi quickly leapt backward to a safer distance!

Yuan Shao mused, "There is another exponent here that can lift my sword intentions here?" He was looking at the other end of the street as a man walked quietly towards him, emitting cold sword energies in all directions.

Ding Yunzi gasped, "Tianyi, why are you here? Leave now! You are not his match!"

Zuo Tianyi said coolly, "Yunzi, are you alright?"

Ding Yunzi nodded as she said, "Quickly leave. I will hold him back. You are not his match."

Yuan Shao said coldly, "Tianyi? So you are the new protégé master of the Infinity Sword Clan? Not bad. At your young age, you have actually attained the divine state of the invisible sword energy. You deserve to be killed by me then."

Zuo Tianyi smirked coldly, "The fight has not even starts and the outcome is uncertain so don't be too sure yet."

Even though he was saying that but the malevolent presence of Yuan Shao was too overpowering and he was extremely nervous. Even walking towards Yuan Shao and speaking in his presence took considerable effort.

Yuan Shao asked, "So you want to challenge me alone or together with Yunzi?"

Zuo Tianyi said, "This is a duel between two swordsmen. Of course it will be just me."

Ding Yunzi said quickly, "No! We will fight you together."

She quickly turned to Zuo Tianyi to say, "Tianyi, don't be foolish. We are not in his league. He has already reached the stage of 'Unison with the Sword' and can use anything as a weapon!"

Zuo Tianyi did not seem to hear as he had already charged towards Yuan Shao with his long sword that was beaming with the blue glow of sword energy!

Ding Yunzi immediately ran after him and threw her scabbard at Yuan Shao while she drew her foldable sword from around her waist!

Yuan Shao simply moved aside slightly as the flying scabbard flew past him! As he evaded the flying scabbard, Zuo Tianyi and Ding Yunzi had already unleashed dozens of sword strokes against him!

As Zuo Tianyi and Ding Yunzi unleashed their barrages of attacks, Yuan Shao simply whirled his cane as a shield in front of him. As he whirled his cane, piercing cold sword energies began to burst through the whirling cane and thrusting at both of them!

Zuo Tianyi was startled as he got stabbed in his shoulder and chest while Ding Yunzi was stabbed in her shoulder too!

Zuo Tianyi was astonished that this old man could defend and attacked at the same time. The weird thing was that he could not see the attack coming and could not guard against it!

Ding Yunzi said quietly, "Tianyi, some of the attacks are Illusions and is formed by his invisible sword intentions. Don't be fooled by it…"

Even as she had said it, Yuan Shao had stabbed the both of them with his left fingers and grievous injured both of them at the same time. Barely a few seconds after they had both attacked, they were now wriggling on the ground in agony!

Yuan Shao said coldly, "This isn't even a duel at all. Beg me for mercy and I will consider sparing you."

Zuo Tianyi broke into cold sweat as he shouted angrily, "Over my dead body!"

Barely had he said that, Yuan Shao had stabbed him with his cane on his right leg and left arm! Zuo Tianyi gritted his teeth but refused to beg for mercy.

Zuo Tianyi was in utter disbelief as he thought, "My Infinity-Two swordplay…unless he has seen my swordplay before, it is impossible for him to break it so fast. How did I get hit by his fingers? That's impossible…"

Ding Yunzi was fatally struck by Yuan Shao's sword finger and she was in a daze. She could only mutter weakly, "Protégé Elder, don't hurt him…He's the protégé master of the Infinity Sword Clan and…"

Yuan Shao interrupted coldly, "Do you think that the Virtuous Palace fears the Infinity Sword Clan or any other martial clans in the fraternity?"

All of a sudden, a young man in white appeared in front of him quietly and lifted both Zuo Tianyi and Ding Yunzi to their feet!

Both Zuo Tianyi and Ding Yunzi gasped at the same time, "Yi Ping!"

Yi Ping said, "Tianyi and Yunzi, your injuries are not light. Meet me at the designated place. I will hold off this Yuan Shao for the time being."

Yuan Shao began to appraise this young man who had appeared so quietly and seemingly displayed no fear whatever so in his presence! In all his years, he had never seen a young man with his righteous air and magnetism.

Ding Yunzi smiled weakly, "Yi Ping, you are also here? Leave us alone. You…are not his match."

Yi Ping said, "Yunzi, don't worry about me. Go now please."

Even though Yi Ping appeared to be composed but he was filled with rage. After losing his temper so many times, he had finally understood the need to control his emotions or he would surely lose even before the fight starts. After learning the Absolute Spirits, he had finally learnt when to suppress his raging emotions even though deep within him, he could not forgive this Yuan Shao for hurting Ding Yunzi and Zuo Tianyi so grievously!

Yuan Shao said coldly, "Do you think that I am invisible?"

Yi Ping hummed coldly, "I'm sure a highly regarded senior with your state of divinity would not attack me first or else you will ruin your practice."

Yuan Shao said, "You are so sure?"

Yi Ping nodded, "I am sure."

Yuan Shao laughed coldly, "Where is your weapon?"

Yi Ping said, "I am afraid that I am not good with weapons and preferring to fight with my bare hands."

Yuan Shao said coldly, "Very good. I will first dispatch you first then I will skin them alive."

Yi Ping raised his hands in a defensive posture as he turned to Zuo Tianyi and Ding Yunzi to say, "Run now or my sacrifice will be in vain."

Ding Yunzi looked at Yi Ping tearfully for a while before she ran off. She did not even say a single good bye to Yi Ping or Zuo Tianyi!

She was in fact crying in her heart as she thought sorrowfully, "Yi Ping, the only way to save you is to revive Lie Qing. The only way to revive her quickly is to let her drain my intricate energy…if you can sacrifice for us, I can also sacrifice for you and will not let you die in vain."

Zuo Tianyi was stunned but he quickly said to Yi Ping, "I will avenge for you in the future. I will never forget you…"

Yi Ping nodded as he watched Zuo Tianyi staggered across the streets until he disappeared from view.

Yuan Shao said to Yi Ping coldly, "Your friends have a head start now. Surely you are not thinking of remaining in that posture until dawn?"

Yi Ping smiled weakly, "You are so smart. How do you know?"

Yuan Shao laughed coldly, "I can tell you that this ruse has been repeated too many times in my presence. I would advise you to make your move now or don't blame me for not giving you a chance to display your techniques."

Yi Ping said, "Junior name is Yi Ping, I make my move then."

As Yi Ping raised his martial power, Yuan Shao did not idle either.

The malevolent aura around Yuan Shao intensified as he sent his invisible sword intentions seemingly like daggers around Yi Ping!

But to the surprise of Yuan Shao, he did not seem to sense any fear in Yi Ping. Instead, he could sense only absolute calmness. Even Zuo Tianyi who had suppressed his malevolent sword intentions with his sword energy was not wholly unaffected.

As Yuan Shao waited, he sent another invisible sword intention with his willpower through Yi Ping. But to his surprise, he sensed another invisible force blocking his invisible sword intention!

He thought, "That's impossible. This young man looks harmless. Unlike Zuo Tianyi, he has either sword energy or my invisible sword intentions, how the heck can he stand there unaffected?"

Yuan Shao did not know that Yi Ping had fortified his fighting spirit with the Absolute Spirits Intricate Recite and even though he had suffered many setbacks but he was a naturally fearless young man. Moreover, protected by the Icy Heavenly Tears, what little remains of the malicious malevolent intentions of Yuan Shao were completed neutralized.

Yuan Shao said slowly, "Why are you waiting for? I am still waiting."

Yi Ping said, "I have already made my move. Now we are even. Senior, you can attack now."

Yuan Shao said, "You have made your move?"

Yi Ping said, "I have raised my martial power. If Senior did not want to attack me, then I will take my leave."

Yuan Shao was secretly startled, "Did he know who I am? Raising his martial power is considered making a move? If he thinks that I am just an old man, then he must be greatly mistaken. Very well then, I will teach him a lesson that he will never forget by cutting off all his limbs."

All of a sudden, Yuan Shao had attacked Yi Ping!

Even though he looked frail and was walking with a cane, when he attacked, he was like barrage of arrows raining blows after blows at Yi Ping.

Yi Ping was astonished. This old man strokes were so fast that he could barely keep up; Yuan Shao strokes were intriguing and formless. It was as though he was fighting against an empty space. He lifted himself with the 'Cloud Evading Skill' and forced to rotate in mid-air as the old man was using a combination of hard and soft stances to neutralize his Divine Horizon Hands!

Yuan Shao was startled as he thought, "Is this the Divine Horizon Hands? I remembered a long time ago I have lost to this skill. Interesting…"

Yi Ping had to use the 'Absolute Spirits Intricate Formula' to follow Yuan Shao strokes; he was defending more and less on attack.

Yuan Shao moves were weird and for every ten strokes that he had unleashed, he could strike Yi Ping with a soft stance that forced Yi Ping to waste even more of his vital breath and energy to neutralize the incoming force.

Yi Ping thought, "This old man, he is forcing me to create an opening for his strokes but I have yet to even land a blow on him or see any opening. This is not going to be good."

Yuan Shao was actually groaning. It was because he was expecting Yi Ping to be onto the ground in no more than twenty strokes! But more than two hundred strokes had passed in a blink of an eye! He was actually thinking, "This young man actually possesses such a deep foundation in martial power, internal strength and mental fortitude…he is such a rare talent…"

Yi Ping lifted another bout of vital breath with the 'Divine Revelation' and lifted his internal strength with the 'Absolute Spirits Intricate Formula' in concert with the Divine Horizon Strokes and the Cloud Evading Skill.

Yuan Shao said, "Weird. It is as though you have seen my kind of attack before?!"

It was because months ago, Xiao Youxue had secretly instructed him against such a martial art.

Xiao Youxue had said to him, "Besides hard and soft aspects of martial arts, there are also formless and energy aspects of the arts. You ought to spar with me to discover a way to break it or to understand it. Then you will not be disadvantage in a real fight with a top exponent."

That was why when Yi Ping sparred with Yuan Shao, he did not give way to panic. Instead he maintained his composure as he moved his hands in a circular movement to guard against his attacks by using the twenty-one stance of the 'Divine Horizon Hand', the 'Circular Defense Stance'; neutralizing the furious thrust of the old man lashing cane or else even if he had ten lives, he could not even deflect the cane without harm.

Yuan Shao said, "So you can still see my movements, am I right? Then how about this?" All of a sudden, he took his cane and poked it towards Yi Ping. The cane attack was so fast that it disappeared!

Yi Ping was startled. He was already concentrating all his focus to follow the old man's movements. He had thought that the old man was almost at his limit and yet he could still increase his attacking speed!

Yi Ping could no longer follow the movements of the cane or the strokes of the old man as he blocked and evade through sheer pure instinct.

In that quick instant, Yi Ping was poked more than ten times and he was suffering from excessive bleeding but he refused to give up as he kept on fighting!

Yuan Shao was secretly startled as he thought, "Is this young man a monster and can feel no pain? Even a good fighter will have fallen by now. However time is on my side."

Indeed, Yi Ping was sweating profusely and was panting heavily. He was now drowsy and exhausted from keeping pace with the movements of the old man attacks and from neutralizing his attacks.

Yuan Shao said, "I want to say to you that conviction alone is not enough to win. Martial skills and techniques that only come with experiences are the only things that are important in a real fight." As he said, he had struck Yi Ping across the face with the cane and thrust it twice into his shoulder at the same time!

Yi Ping was forced to step back but before he could regain his balance, Yuan Shao had struck him with a forceful palm on the chest!

Yi Ping was sent flying across the street in a horrifying crash as he smashed against the street walls!

Yuan Shao asked coldly, "Are you painful? Can you still fight?"

Yi Ping wiped away the blood from his mouth as he mustered all his strength to say, "I…am not…dead yet…"

Yuan Shao laughed, "Very good. I am not yet done yet!"

Yi Ping could barely stand up as he clenched his fists. He knew very well that this old man was toying with him. The differences in their skills were too vast. He tried to muster his martial power but his entire body was trembling hard and he could not muster his strength anymore!

Even though Yuan Shao was jeering at Yi Ping but he was also astonished at his endurance as he thought, "A lesser mortal will have fallen by now and he can still stand? It is a pity to kill such a young man. But if I don't kill him today, he may be a thorn to us in the future…"

"Isn't that enough already? Isn't that too gory already? Why don't you stay your hand and let him go?" A gentle voice said.

Yuan Shao was startled. Someone else was in the vicinity and he did not know?

Yi Ping and Yuan Shao looked up and saw a stunning maiden with long silver hair and dressed in a long red dress walking quietly towards him.

When Yuan Shao saw her eyes, he was startled for her eyes were glowing red!

In her long white slender right hand, she was wielding a long heavy black scythe as though its weight meant nothing to her.

Yuan Shao asked, "Who are you? And where did you come from?"

The mysterious silver hair maiden said coolly, "I am trying to sleep but it is getting really noisy. That is why I am here to take a look."

Yuan Shao smiled bitterly. Even if there were ordinary folks around, his malevolent aura would have caused them to lose their consciousness or develop fearful delusions. The only persons that would dare to come here were those that had extraordinary willpower or superior state of divinity.

Yuan Shao stabbed his cane onto the ground and immediately the ground beneath his cane exploded thunderous as it collapsed three inches underneath!

Yi Ping was stunned at the martial power display of this old man! He thought, "He isn't serious earlier?" All of a sudden, he remembered Xiao Youxue's martial power implosion techniques.

Yuan Shao said, "I have thought that the red-eyes humans are just a mythology. I have never expected to find one today. Just who are you?"

The silver hair maiden smiled at Yi Ping and Yuan Shao as she swung her long scythe in a playful manner, even as she continued to walk towards them.

Yuan Shao was solemn. This silver hair maiden did not seem to fear his martial power. He slowly put his cane in front of him and lifted its lid, revealing a thin razor long sword!

Immediately, the killing malevolent aura in the area intensified and Yi Ping could feel a suffocating presence even as he struggled with his Absolute Spirits! He was forced to step back until his body rested on the wall!

Actually his Absolute Spirits were the most epitome intricate heart formula that could resist the most deadly killing malevolent but in his weakened state, Yi Ping chose to step back to steady himself.

The silver hair maiden smiled, "I should be the one asking who you are first. But anyway, my fraternity name is the Joyful Goddess and from the Celestial Palace. I presume that you are from the Virtuous Palace?"

Yuan Shao said coldly, "Indeed. Yuan Shao is my name."

The Joyful Goddess smiled happily, "That is great. I have heard that the Honor Manor and the Virtuous Palace is attacking the Celestial Palace?"

Yuan Shao nodded slowly, "That's right. We are here to wipe you demons out."

The Joyful Goddess clapped her hands, "Very good. We will be expecting you."

She turned to look at Yi Ping curiously, "Are you Yi Ping?"

Yi Ping was startled as he thought, "She knows me? I do not know her..." But he replied nevertheless, "Yes, I am Yi Ping."

The Joyful Goddess smiled, "Good. I am here just in time. Maiden Ji has asked me to fetch you. There should be two others as well. Alas, I can't be bothered. At least I have found one."

Yi Ping was startled, "You know Lingfeng?"

The Joyful Goddess said, "I do. She is the Holy Maiden of the Celes..."

Yuan Shao interrupted coldly, "Do you think you can leave this place alive?"

The Joyful Goddess said, "Why can't I?"

Yuan Shao said, "It is because my sword has already been drawn. Without tasting your blood, I will not sheathe my sword."

The Joyful Goddess pointed at Yi Ping as she said, "You can stab your sword into him. I don't mind at all. But I am afraid of pain if you do want to stab me..."

Yi Ping was stunned as he thought, "If Yuan Shao stabs me, I'll be dead and she is asking him to do so..."

Before she had even finished speaking, Yuan Shao had leapt towards her!

The Joyful Goddess was not slow to react as she swung her long scythe as dozens of brilliant lights sparkle and shrieked across the mid-air in just an instance!

Yi Ping stared in fascination as their stances and strokes flashed in his eyes as he muttered, "So these are the superior swordplay..."

In three successive instances, they had already exchanged more than one hundred strokes!

Yi Ping's heart began to beat very fast as he immersed in the fascinating sight as he thought, "If I shift my stance in that direction and displayed the Divine Horizon Hands or Swordplay..."

All of a sudden, the Joyful Goddess flew towards him and interrupted his thoughts as she grabbed him, "Come!"

Yuan Shao wanted to chase her but she was simply too swift. He had never seen her type of swiftness movement skill before but it was very similar to the Fairy Breezes swiftness skill of the Holy Hex Sect.

So he could only watch her disappeared from view with Yi Ping even as the Joyful Goddess laughed softly, "Old man, I don't want to fight you yet because I have need of your blood later. And this young man's blood may be even more precious than yours. If you need my help with the Divine Calamity, I can help you."

Yuan Shao was solemn as he thought, "Weird. It seems that she didn't have the Invincible Divine Force and seem reluctant to spar directly with me with her internal strength. If she did, I will be able to use my Intricate Reversal Divine Skill to drain her intricate energy instead..."

Chapter 33: Unexpected Reversals

The Joyful Goddess grasped her abdomen painfully as she broke into a cold sweat as her blood dripped to the ground.

Yi Ping was startled, "You are injured?"

The Joyful Goddess nodded, "That old man is craftier than I have expected. During our clash, he actually had another concealed sword around his waist. In my moment of carelessness, I was slashed by him. It seems that I am out of practice for a long time."

Yi Ping said weakly, "Should we take a rest first? Your wounds are still bleeding..."

The Joyful Goddess smiled weakly, "No need. I am wounded by his sword energy and for the time being, the wound cannot be healed. You have better worry for yourself first. Your bleeding is more excessive than mine."

Even though she was saying so, she had already dropped her long scythe and Yi Ping onto the ground as she collapsed on the ground!

Yi Ping endured his agonizing injuries as he shouted, "Maiden, are you alright!?"

The Joyful Goddess said weakly, "You...are not afraid of me?"

Yi Ping was startled, "Why should I?"

The Joyful Goddess said, "If you are smart enough, you should have run away now lest I decide to kill you."

She added weakly as she looked into Yi Ping's eyes for a reaction, "Most would have run away from my sight. My red eyes and my silvery white hair, don't I look like a monster, a demoness?"

Except for her silvery long hair and her red eyes, even the blind could see that she was a very beautiful maiden. No matter how Yi Ping had looked at her, she did not look like a monster at all. When he had first seen her with her long red dress and long black scythe, she did look terrifying at first sight.

Yi Ping shook his head weakly, "I only know that you have saved my life and you are injured now. No matter the reason, I shouldn't leave you alone."

The Joyful Goddess turned her face away as she said, "How do you know that...I didn't save you only to kill you later?"

Yi Ping said awkwardly, "If it is for later, then I will think of it later."

The Joyful Goddess got up slightly as she breathed gently on him, "I can tell you. I am indeed a demoness and I have to feast on human blood."

She looked intently at Yi Ping as she begun to lick his wounds.

Yi Ping was startled as he said, "You really are a blood drinker?"

The Joyful Goddess smiled weakly, "So you are...afraid now?"

Yi Ping said weakly, "If my blood can help you, by all means take it..."

The Joyful Goddess looked at him, with her eyes beaming. "My name is Huan Le. You can also call me Lele."

Yi Ping said, "My name is Yi Ping..."

She put her fingers on his mouth as she said softly, "I know..."

Earlier…

She had been eavesdropping in the vicinity when she had heard Shui Yujian said melancholy to Ji Lingfeng, "You know that our mission is to protect our Master from harm. We cannot allow him to go there alone even if it meant certain death."

Shui Meijian nodded silently.

Ji Lingfeng immediately rebuked them, "You can sense that person's killing malevolent intent? If you are afraid now, how do you fight him when you are there? You will only be courting your own death."

Nangong Le mused, "I don't think anyone can even have a chance against his state of divinity. Just now, I was so frigging terrified. That Yuan Shao is even older than the Celestial Fairy. He is in the super league in the likes of the Celestial Fairy, Xiao Shuai, Gongsun Bai, Gu Tianle and the Old Sword Saint."

Shui Yujian immediately asked, "Sister Lingfeng, what do we do now?"

Ji Lingfeng said, "Wait for me at the seven mile pavilion. There is only one person that can save Yi Ping and that is the Celestial Envoy."

Gongsun Jing was startled, "She is here?"

Ji Lingfeng nodded, "Indeed. I will look for her now. She may be the only person right now that is able to save Yunzi, Tianyi and Yi Ping. Let's hope that Zuo Tianyi and Yi Ping did not do anything foolish for the time being."

Shui Meijian gasped, "Sister Lingfeng, let us go with you…"

Ji Lingfeng shook her head, "Only I can safely approach her. She is a very dangerous person and highly unpredictable. Protect this Lie Qing or else when Yi Ping is back, he won't be pleased. Wait for me there…"

"No need." A cold eerie voice was heard from the forest.

Everyone began to look around them but could see no one.

Ji Lingfeng turned white with ashen, "The Celestial Envoy is here…"

The Celestial Envoy said coldly while remained hidden from view, "I am only here to protect the Holy Maiden, not the others. And I am not pleased that someone had just criticized me."

Ji Lingfeng thought, "I almost call her a mental…lucky I didn't say it loud!"

Qiu Wufeng, Nangong Le, Gongsun Le and the others immediately looked around them but they could not see where she was.

Ji Lingfeng looked all around her as she said, "No matter what you think, there are three persons that you must bring back. Yi Ping, Zuo Tianyi and Ding Yunzi or else I won't give you what you want anymore."

The Celestial Envoy hummed coldly, "Are you threatening me?"

Ji Lingfeng said, "Think what you want. Don't you want to meet the exponents from the Virtuous Palace too?"

The Celestial Envoy paused for a while before she sighed softly, "You have no respect for the Celestial Palace. But there are three of them. If I can only save one of them, which one would they be?"

Ji Lingfeng smiled weakly, "With your extraordinary martial skills, you cannot save them all?"

The Celestial Envoy said, "There's no need to flatter me. Who is the one that you want to save the most? Quick, I am bored already. I hate to run errands that are none of my business."

Ji Lingfeng hastily said, "Yi Ping. His name is Yi Ping…remember his name…"

Gongsun Jing was solemn for he was more worried about Ding Yunzi…

Shui Meijian said, "Let's hope that the Celestial Envoy is able to bring all of them back or she is really such a disappointment." She had deliberately said it loud.

But no one really knew if the Celestial Envoy was still around….

Unknown to all, in the meantime, Ding Yunzi was making her way back to look for them.

Zuo Tianyi was staggering behind her as he said, "Yunzi, wait for me. Your injuries are not light, wait for me please."

Ding Yunzi said coolly, "There is not a moment time to waste."

All of a sudden, Zuo Tianyi had caught up with her as he grabbed her hand. "Yunzi, why are you so cold to me? Have you forgotten that we are old friends?"

Ding Yunzi said coldly, "That is only what you think. I have never said that. Just because you think you are nice to me, you think I should reciprocate to you?"

She lied. It was because she was fearful of her own past and afraid that it would be discovered. She really did not want to hurt Zuo Tianyi as she secretly sighed, "Tianyi, forgive me…this is for your own good."

Zuo Tianyi was stunned as he asked, "Have you fallen in love with Yi Ping?"

Ding Yunzi said coldly, "That is also what you think."

Just as she had turned around, Zuo Tianyi had suddenly landed a hit behind her neck!

Ding Yunzi was already in a daze and this surprise attack caused her to lose her consciousness almost immediately as she gasped, "You…"

Zuo Tianyi muttered, "I'm so sorry Yunzi…If I cannot have your heart, I will make you mine by force…"

He begun to loosen her silk belt, lifted up her long skirt and pull down her inner garments as he kissed her violently…

Chapter 34: True Friends

As Zuo Tianyi was kissing and holding Ding Yunzi, Ding Yunzi eyes had fluttered as she cried out in tears weakly, "Tianyi, don't! The Infinity Sword Clan is a reputable clan. You will only be degrading you and me as well…"

As Zuo Tianyi was kissing Ding Yunzi violently, an alluring voice shouted at him. "You're a beast! What do you think you are doing!?"

It was Ji Lingfeng and she had attacked him with multiple flying projectiles!

Zuo Tianyi drawn out his long sword deflected all the flying projectiles to one side. But even before he could recover from his initial surprise, two beautiful maidens in black long velvet dresses were attacking him, causing him to take several steps backward!

He recognized them as the twin sisters, Shui Yujian and Meijian!

He was startled as he thought, "Shouldn't they be at the seven miles pavilion?"

At the same time, Lie Qing was besides Ding Yunzi in a flash and had covered her with a cloak as she smiled weakly at her, "Don't shed a tear for this wolf in sheep clothing. I will help you…"

Even as Zuo Tianyi raised his earthshaking swordplay against Shui Yujian, Shui Meijian and Ji Lingfeng, they were joined by Gongsun Jing, Qiu Wufeng and Nangong Le!

Gongsun Jing had a blazing flame in his eyes as he shouted angrily, "After what you did to her, you still have the cheek to beat her. You are worse than a beast!"

Even Nangong Le was clenching his fists as he said, "I may be a playboy but I have never forced myself on anyone."

Zuo Tianyi said coldly, "Is there a difference between the two of us? Just because you are rich, you think of yourself as nobler as me?"

Qiu Wufeng said angrily, "I thought that you have more honor that that. The protégé master of the Infinity Sword Clan is nothing but a beast. When this spreads out in the fraternity, I will like to see how you are going to defend yourself!"

Zuo Tianyi hummed coldly, "No one in the fraternity will believe anyone of you. It is because in their eyes, you are all villains and untrustworthy people."

Ji Lingfeng said coldly, "Humph! I have thought that you are a good guy when we first met. How are you able to face the Old Sword Saint and all your clan ancestors in the netherworld?"

Zuo Tianyi said coldly, "My swordplay is not weak. If you are all thinking that you have a chance against me, think again. The Celestial Fairy isn't here while Yunzi and Lie Qing are injured. Even though I am injured but whom among you other than Yi Ping have a chance against my Infinity-Two Swordplay?"

It was true. Zuo Tianyi's swordplay was indeed frightening!

Shui Yujian said melancholy, "Where is our Master Yi Ping?"

Zuo Tianyi laughed coldly, "I am afraid that he is now a dead man now."

Shui Meijian immediately staggered a step backward and fainted as her precious sword dropped to the ground!

Shui Yujian gasped as she caught hold of her before she fainted on the ground, "Mei'Er, Mei'Er…"

Lie Qing got up and she was trembling as she stared at Zuo Tianyi.

Zuo Tianyi said, "But today I am not in a good mood of killing and because earlier, we are all still drinking together, I decide to spare all your lives instead. But if anyone of you dares to follow me, don't blame me for being merciless."

Without a word more, Zuo Tianyi walked away.

The group could only stare in utter silence as they watched Zuo Tianyi walked off.

It was because they still had something very important in mind and that was to look for Yi Ping immediately!

Lie Qing held onto Ding Yunzi tightly as she comforted her with her eyes.

Ding Yunzi cried tearfully in her embrace, "Why are you all here?"

Ji Lingfeng looked at Lie Qing...

Halfway towards the Seven Mile Pavilion, Lie Qing had regained her consciousness.

The first thing she had asked was, "Where is Yi Ping?"

When everyone explained the situation to her, Lie Qing began to walk towards the city, stunning everyone!

Shui Yujian said, "Where are you going? Master has asked us to wait there for us. You only distract him and hinder him if you are going there."

Ji Lingfeng said, "I have already asked the Celestial Envoy to take a look. Let's go to somewhere safer first."

Lie Qing said coolly, "If Yi Ping dies I don't want to live either. I owe my life to him. Even if I cannot help him, I will want to die besides him."

As she begun to walk off, Shui Meijian was besides her in an instant, "You are Maiden Lie Qing?"

Lie Qing nodded, "We have already been introduced."

Shui Meijian smiled, "Good. I will go with you. If Yi Ping dies, I don't want to live either too. It is good to know a good friend before I die. Can I call you Sister Lie Qing?"

Lie Qing smiled, "Sure, let's us go now..."

But before she had finished, Ji Lingfeng and Shui Yujian were also besides her as they said at the same time, "Sister Lie Qing! We will go with you!"

Even Nangong Le sighed, "I don't mind dying as long as there are beauties accompanying me. I will go too."

Qiu Wufeng laughed aloud, "I may be a coward but tonight I dare to say that I am not!"

Gongsun Jing said poetically, "Living is for a worthy cause. When dying for a worthy case, it is to build an everlasting name for ourselves. Let's us go. Even if he is a top exponent, he would not be unscathed in a fight with us. At most, we will all die with him too!"

In the meantime elsewhere....

Yi Ping carried the Joyful Goddess on his back as he made his way in the dark. He was astonished at the heavy weight of her long black scythe.

Lele was astonished at Yi Ping's endurance and stamina. He had been carrying her for an hour. At first she was reluctant to let him carry her because he was seriously injured too. But Yi Ping was worried that Yuan Shao would catch up with them, so he gritted his teeth and endured his agonizing pain as he carried her on his back.

Lele asked him, "Are you sure you are alright? Your wounds…"

Yi Ping was touched at her gesture as he said, "My wounds have stopped bleeding already."

Lele was startled as she reached out to touch his wounds, "You can heal so fast?"

Yi Ping smiled weakly, "I don't know. I seem to have taken some miracle pills previously."

Lele asked, "Such as?"

Yi Ping said, "The Golden Rejuvenation Pill…"

Lele gasped, "You mean, you have actually consumed it?!"

Yi Ping was puzzled as he said, "That's right."

Lele looked at him in envy as she said, "That is an extremely rare precious divine pill and will be beneficial to me…no wonder your blood tastes so good…"

She could still remember the furious fraternity storm and how countless number of pugilists had perished fighting over the whereabouts of these Golden Rejuvenation Pills…

Yi Ping shivered as he smiled bitterly, "Surely you are not thinking what I am thinking?"

Lele smiled weakly, "If you don't tell me, how I am supposed to know?"

Yi Ping gulped, "Are you thinking of eating me alive?" It was because he had suddenly remembered why Xiao Shuai wanted Xiao Youxue for.

Lele smiled mysteriously, "You are so smart. Do you think I will let you off so easily? Your still beating heart when consumed can boast my internal strength. Perhaps it may alleviate me from my sufferings. So I will definitely not spare you…"

All of a sudden, Lele cried out. "Look out!"

It was because Yi Ping was distracted by her creeping words that he was not looking in front of him and it was also dark. He had missed his footing and to his horror, he had plunged down a bottomless ravine with her!

Lele was horrified as she cried out fearfully, "That old man didn't kill me…you did! I cannot believe that I will die in such an unnatural manner…"

They had both taken down a great plunge down the ravine.

Yi Ping was surprising calm as he thought, "Yixian, I have come to join you now. Youxue, please forgive me. Lingfeng, I hope you can live well. Yunzi, I hope you escape from Yuan Shao…"

Before he could finish, he had plunged into a cold icy lake with Lele!

Yi Ping was startled as he took the cold plunge and he was struggling wildly in the icy waters, grabbing anything he could catch hold of and that included Lele!

Lele cried out, "Stop it. Stop struggling. I will save you…stop struggling! You land tortoise, you don't know how to swim!"

Yi Ping was drowning and he could not really hear what Lele was trying to say to him as he had already given in to panic! He had thought that the more he could struggle; he could keep himself alive…

As Lele swam towards him and caught hold of him, Yi Ping accidentally punched her on her face! She was so stunned and annoyed that she thought she thought of giving him a tight slap when Yi Ping had pulled and torn her dress!

She immediately flustered and at the same time was so infuriated that she actually forgot her agonizing pain as she slapped Yi Ping across his face several times! She did not really count how many times she had slapped him for she was so furious. It was the first time that a man had seen her in the nude.

What little good impression that was left for Yi Ping had totally vanished as her eyes turned murderous.

But when she saw Yi Ping had lost consciousness, her eyes softened and she thought that he was actually cute. She quietly sighed, gathered her clothing and pulled him close to her as she flushed shyly, "I am the Joyful Goddess. I shouldn't lose my temper so quickly. That is so unbecoming of me. When he has awakened, I will put on a happy expression while I slice him alive."

The more she mused on it, the happier she was and the more determined she had decided that was to be that outcome.

Lele took another look at Yi Ping before she sighed again, "I have beaten him up so badly that his face is now almost unrecognizable. Maybe I should wait for him to recover first? He should recover fast enough. Then I shall surprise him by slicing his flesh piece by piece for offending me while luring him into a false sense of security?"

She wrestled with her thoughts for a while before she happily exclaimed, "Haiz, I am the Joyful Goddess and have a reputation to maintain. So count yourself lucky today."

She smiled weakly, "But first I got to pump the water out of his chest first." She clapped his chest with a loud impact as Yi Ping threw out the water before she fainted from exhaustion on the bank of the lake.

Yi Ping had regained his consciousness and was in a daze. He could not remember very much what had happened. He remembered that he was drowning and when he was near his end, Lele appeared in front of him and had pulled him.

Immediately, his heart was filled with gratuity as he thought, "She has saved my life once again. She is a good maiden..."

As he turned around, he was stunned and his eyes almost popped out. Lele was lying just besides him and she was half naked. Yi Ping smiled bitterly as he thought, "Even though I don't know where she comes from but she is a little too liberal."

He quickly looked around and saw her clothing. He quickly got up on his feet as he grabbed her clothing. Just when he had grabbed her clothing and was trying to cover her clumsily as he averted his eyes, he had suddenly sensed a malevolent air.

He hastily turned his eyes around and saw Lele looking at him as she said, "You...lecher! What are you trying to do?!"

Yi Ping immediately dropped her clothing as he stammered, "I...I...I am just trying to cover you..."

Lele's silent tears began to roll down her face as she trembled uncontrollably, "Do you know that a maiden's chastity is her most precious thing? Yet, you did such a despicable thing. If I can muster my strength, I will surely kill you right away."

The thought of being violated by a stranger was too much for her to bear. She began to sob uncontrollably as she could not imagine what Yi Ping had done to her while she had fainted.

She grabbed her clothing with trembling hands and quickly covered herself while staring at Yi Ping with her vacant eyes.

Yi Ping was immediately filled with an utter inconsolable sentiment for her as he quickly said, "I really did not do anything. I just wake up and it is already like this..."

Her tears did not cease at all even as she said melancholy, "What do you mean by it is already like this? You…after taking advantage of me, can still say such lame things? I…will never forgive you, never!"

Yi Ping really did not know what to say. He did not even know what was happening and his mind was still in a complete blank and shock! This time, he was pretty sure that he was not drunk as he thought bitterly, "If she wants to take my life, I am resigned to my fate. I have already seen too much of what I shouldn't have seen. Alas…why am I so unlucky?"

As soon as Lele covered herself, she took a broad stride towards Yi Ping and gave him a tight slap!

Her slap was not light as Yi Ping was sent flying off backward!

She immediately looked around for her long black scythe as she lifted it up expertly with her slender fingers as she looked murderous at Yi Ping.

Just as she took another step, Yi Ping was startled as he said. "Lele, you…"

Lele said coldly, "Do you think you deserve to call me by my name? Call me the Joyful Goddess. So you want to beg for mercy now? Then you shouldn't have begun with what you did."

Yi Ping broke into a cold sweat as he said nervously, "I know I deserve to die but I really do not know what has happened…I really don't know. But you…"

Lele said coldly, "Call me the Joyful Goddess. I do have a name."

Yi Ping smiled bitterly as he said, "Joyful Goddess, you can move now? Your injuries are healed?"

Lele was startled as she immediately touched her abdomen as she thought, "Weird. My wounds have healed."

She turned and looked at Yi Ping and noticed that his injuries on his face had also faded as she thought, "This icy lake is able to treat injuries?"

Once she had composed herself and was glad that her injuries had healed, she begun to look at Yi Ping intently as she thought, "He has violated me. No matter, I have to slice him to pieces or else it is hard to stomach my rage."

But when she looked at Yi Ping benevolent expression and the righteous air around him, her heart beat escalated and her fingers were actually trembling. She thought, "Did I make a mistake?"

She tried hard to remember what had happened. All of a sudden, she gasped as she took a step back as she recalled silently, "I have fainted before I cloth myself…"

Lele was confused as she said silently to herself, "This Yi Ping may be your nemesis. You have never been injured so grievously before. The first time you have met him, you have sustained a terrible wound. Next, you almost die with him when you fall into the deep ravine. Why is your luck so down when you are with him? You hate him but why your heart hesitates to kill him immediately?"

She softened her gaze shyly as she lowered her scythe, "Did you or did you not violate me?"

Yi Ping said, "I really did not. I can swear to the heavens…"

Lele interrupted, "You lie…and you have just sworn to the heavens…"

Yi Ping was startled, "I did? I did not…"

Lele said coldly, "You still dare to deny. You have violated me with your eyes and you have looked at me lustfully…"

Yi Ping smiled bitterly as he thought, "If I violated you with my thoughts, then it is counted too?"

Lele said, "You must be thinking that if you violated me with my thoughts, is it counted too? Of course it does, no matter what forms it takes."

Yi Ping was startled, "You can read my thoughts?!"

Lele said coldly, "So you admit that you have violated me with your thoughts?"

Yi Ping was stunned. The more explanations that he had given, the murkier was the pool!

Lele sighed softly as she said, "From now on, I will follow you and you will follow me. We are a couple now. You have destroyed my honor, surely you are not thinking of shrinking from what you did?"

Yi Ping was startled as he muttered in utter confusion, "I have destroyed her honor…I'm a rascal. But I don't know what is really happening. Why is she not wearing anything earlier?"

He quickly said, "Joyful Goddess, I am not a good man and there are too many entangle romances that are giving me the headache already…"

Lele interrupted, "Lele! You forget that Lele is my name."

Yi Ping smiled bitterly, "Lele then…listen to me…"

Lele smiled at him, "Very well, let settle this then. From now on, you will be my consort. Where I go, you will follow me. As for your troublesome entangle whatever romances, I will help you to severe it. Anyone that tries to get close to you will have to first endure my wrath."

Yi Ping quickly said, "I didn't agree. They are my friends…"

Lele looked at him melancholy as her tears flowed down silently, "You…you…are such a heartless man. I have pledged myself to you and yet you keep rejecting my advances. Am I wrong? You are the one that have violated me and you didn't want to be my consort…"

Yi Ping was startled, "I mean, I don't want you to hurt them and why must I be your consort? I have never heard of a man becoming a consort to a woman…"

Lele looked at him with hurtful eyes, "You don't want to be my consort, very well then I will be your consort!"

Yi Ping was feeling dazed. Somehow she did not seem to understand what he was trying to say or she did not even bother to try to know.

As he tried to protest once again, she had flown into his embrace as she smiled blissfully, "Yi Ping…"

When he looked into her eyes, his vision became a blur as she kissed him gently…

Lele said slowly in an enticing manner, "From now on, your heart belongs to me only. You shall think of no other maidens. You only have me in your heart and you will love me whole-heartedly…"

All of a sudden, Yi Ping sensed that something was amiss as his entire body became weak; his strength had departed from him and he could not focus anymore. He tried to shake his head furiously but his mind was completely blank!

Lele was kissing him nervously and her fingers in his body. The very next thing he could remember was that he was not wearing anything and Lele was shyly removing her own clothes. Before he knew what was happening, he had passed out.

When Yi Ping regained his consciousness with a throbbing headache, he could sniff the sweet fragrance scent of Lele who was lying beside him. She was naked and was saying shyly to him, "You have awakened? From now on, we are a couple. You must love me wholeheartedly or I will be surely heartbroken. We can flee from the Celestial Palace…"

Yi Ping was horrified as he quickly pushed her to a side, stunning Lele.

Yi Ping shockingly asked, "We….you…you and I….I…no…we…did we…!?"

He had realized that they were totally naked and he was embracing Lele in an intimately manner.

Lele was equally stunned at Yi Ping's expressions as she said with utter disbelief, "You…you…no, that is not supposed to happen…aren't you under my…why are you still able to…"

Yi Ping quickly composed himself with the Absolute Spirits as he said nervously, "Lele, why are you not wearing anything?"

Lele was blushing so much that all she could say was, "You…are even worst. You are also not wearing anything!"

Yi Ping was dazzled and his face had turned totally red as he tried to cover himself as much as possible.

Lele had never expected her Bewitching Soul Seizing Skill to fail. It was because she had been extremely confident in her internal strength and her charms. Moreover this type of Bewitching Soul Seizing Skill was the highest order in mesmerizing that requires her to sacrifice her very own chastity. Unless she reversed it, Yi Ping would be totally enthralled by her and be obedient to her. The bad part of this skill was that the enthralled person would lose their free will and would not be their normal self again. The objective of this skill was to cause utter obedient in the target.

So imagine Lele's surprise as she said with shock, "You not supposed to be surprised…"

Lele did not know that there was another person knew the Bewitching Soul Seizing Skill and that was Lie Qing. Lie Qing's mastery of this long lost skill was even more astonishing than her. She had been using her Bewitching Soul Seizing Skill on Yi Ping and Xiao Youxue subtly for months but it would always fail on them.

It was because the both of them had already attained past the stage of 'Indestructible Will' of the Absolute Spirits. Therefore no matter how much efforts Lie Qing tried to bend their wills to her, it would always fail. In the end, she gave up and had really fallen in love with Yi Ping.

Lele was overtly confident and had used the Bewitching Soul Seizing Skill on Yi Ping to capture his heart. It was because she did not really want to kill Yi Ping but was afraid of getting hurt. Therefore she would rather turn Yi Ping into her puppet than being rejected by him.

It was also her overtly confident that caused her to be fatally wounded by Yuan Shao.

In so short a time, her self-confident had suffered a huge plunge. She had never felt so low and vulnerable before, not since the time of the Divine Calamity. She had lost her chastity for nothing…

Yi Ping was even more startled as he had a sudden nose bled, "Lele…you better cover yourself because I am really surprise…"

Lele gasped as she quickly grabbed her clothes as her ears turned really red as she sobbed inconsolably, "I really need to dig a hole to hide myself. Look at what you have done…"

Her sorrows and distresses were so heartbreaking that Yi Ping was feeling extremely awkward and miserable.

Before Yi Ping had realized it, he was already pulling Lele's hands and holding her in his embrace as he comforted her, "Don't cry, Lele…"

Lele looked forlornly for a long time at Yi Ping with brimming eyes as she tightened her grip around him.

Chapter 35: Lost Hopes and Renewal of Faith

Ji Lingfeng, Ding Yunzi, Nangong Le and the rest of the group returned to the small city to search for Yi Ping. However they could find no trace of Yi Ping, the Celestial Envoy or Yuan Shao except for blood strains across the streets.

Among the group, Ji Lingfeng, Shui Meijian and Yujian were the swiftest of the group. They quickly swept the area for Yi Ping, the Celestial Envoy and Yuan Shao.

It was as though Yuan Shao had never appeared.

Gongsun Jing said, "Maybe Yi Ping isn't dead yet. At least we have not found his body yet."

Qiu Wufeng said, "We did not find the Celestial Envoy either. That is worrying…"

Ji Lingfeng was silent. She was now getting anxious as she asked herself, "Where did Yi Ping, the Celestial Envoy and Yuan Shao go to?"

She was naturally not eager to fight Yuan Shao but as long as he was still in the vicinity, they were all in danger.

Unknown to the rest of the group, Ding Yunzi had silently left them.

Her long hair was in disheveled and her tears had long dried up.

Unlike the rest of the group, she did not harbor any illusions that they could be able to find Yi Ping alive. She knew how dangerous Yuan Shao was. In fact, he was Xiao Shuai's benevolent master and it was him that had helped him to become the clan protégé master of the Virtuous Palace thirty years ago.

Deep in her heart, Yi Ping was as good as dead and that he had already sacrificed himself so that Zuo Tianyi and she could make their escape.

She held her dedicate trembling hands to her heart, "Yi Ping, you have saved me but do you know that for me it is a fate that is worse than death? Do you know that I will rather die now? Tianyi, you have shamed me in front of others. I despise you and curse you unto death."

She had even said to Lie Qing, "I know that you need my Divine Virtuous Force to recover fully and that without you, our group cannot hope to even escape from Yuan Shao…"

But Lie Qing simply walked away without saying a word!

This beautiful, appealing and demure young maiden laughed heartily for the last time as she looked at the stars above before she jumped down from the top of the cliff to the bottomless mist below as she said, "Youxue, I have come to join you…Yi Ping, I too have come to join you…"

Ding Yunzi was calm towards her imminent death.

She had fallen through the mist and had plunged into the cold icy waters!

As she began to choke and unable to breathe, a strong hand gripped her and brought her up to the surface!

She opened her eyes and to her utter surprise, it was Yi Ping!

Yi Ping shouted hastily, "Yunzi, are you alright? Who is so vicious as to push you down?"

Ding Yunzi coughed out the swallowed water as she cried sorrowfully in his embrace.

She cried melancholy, "Yi Ping, you are still alive. That's too good to be true. I thought that you are dead…"

Yi Ping said, "Yunzi, you are safe now. I have seen a shadowy figure plunging down and didn't know it is you. Tell me, who push you down? Is Tianyi and the rest safe?"

Ding Yunzi gripped Yi Ping hard and sunk her fingernails into his back, "Yi Ping, please don't mention Tianyi in front of me anymore."

All of a sudden, she was inconsolable and was wailing.

"Are the two of you enjoying a lover's bath together? How shameless! How dare you seduce my man, humph!"

Ding Yunzi was startled and looked out only to see an elegant maiden in red dress looking at her sternly. What was astonishing about her was that she had the same crimson eyes as Lie Qing except for her long silver hair.

Yi Ping said, "Lele, she is Ding Yunzi. She is a friend of mine."

Lele said, "Oh? A friend or a dear friend of yours? Why is she holding so tightly to you then?"

Ding Yunzi was startled for she could feel the maiden's burning jealousy, "Who is she?"

Yi Ping said, "She is Lele. She saved my life…"

Ding Yunzi gasped, "Is she the Celestial Envoy? She is so young…"

Lele raised her eyebrows as she said coolly, "I am older than what you think and see."

Ding Yunzi nodded quietly as she said, "Thank you!"

Lele was startled, "Why are you thanking me for? Did you not hear that I have just scolded you?"

Ding Yunzi said softly, "Thank you for saving Yi Ping. I didn't expect anyone will be able to save Yi Ping from the hands of Yuan Shao. Your martial skills are really impressive. You have defeated Yuan Shao?"

Lele looked away, "No, I am the one that has lost but I swear that I will return him ten times the favor for injuring me."

Yi Ping said gently to Ding Yunzi, "Yunzi, your injuries are not light. Are you painful? Who push you down?"

Ding Yunzi stared blankly for a while before she said, "No one pushes me down. I don't want to live anymore."

Yi Ping was startled, "Yunzi, what has happened?!"

Even Lele was startled as she thought, "What can possibly cause such an attractive maiden to end her life just like this unless the setback that she has suffered is so excessing?"

She looked at Yi Ping and then at Ding Yunzi.

All of a sudden, she had noticed that Ding Yunzi's eyes had never left Yi Ping.

She thought, "Can it be that she jumped down because she thought that Yi Ping is dead?"

Ding Yunzi had noticed that Lele's eyes were filled with jealousy and even her words were stinging. Without a doubt, this Celestial Envoy seemed fond of Yi Ping.

She sighed, "Yi Ping, there are simply too many distinguished maidens around you. Unlike those courageous maidens that dare to profess their intents, I dare not even tell others about my past nor do I dare to share my feelings with them. Is that why I must suffer the same fate as Youxue?"

Ding Yunzi said coldly, "I didn't jump down because I think that Yi Ping is dead. In fact, his life and death means nothing to me so you don't have to worry about us. I jump down because I have lost my will to live…"

She had lied. She had jumped down because she had thought that Yi Ping was no longer in the world.

Lele said coldly, "Do you think that I will believe you so easily? Go on and tell me a good reason or else I will never believe you. If you lie to me, be prepared to lose your tongue…"

Yi Ping said unhappily, "Lele, you are getting ruder. Yunzi is my friend..."

Lele said coldly, "I am your wife now and the two of you are holding one another just now. As your wife, do you think that I do not have the right to ask huh?"

Ding Yunzi was startled as she thought, "She is his wife? They only met for just a few hours…"

But she answered bravely even though she could not hold back her silent tears anymore, "I… I have been almost been violated. Are you happy now?"

Yi Ping and Lele were both stunned.

Yi Ping clenched his fists as he asked angrily, "Yunzi, tell me please. Who did it? I will kill him…"

Ding Yunzi said slowly, "Zuo Tianyi."

Yi Ping was stunned. He did not expected Ding Yunzi to have such a sad past and he did not expect Zuo Tianyi to do such a bestial act. He muttered, "Tianyi, how can you do such a beastly thing?!"

Ding Yunzi burst out in tears, "So all of you know it now. I am too ashamed to live now and I cannot face anyone now."

All of a sudden, Ding Yunzi took out her foldable sword from around her waist to slice her throat. Even though she was extremely quick, both Yi Ping and Lele reacted even faster and knocked the sword from her hands!

Yi Ping caught hold of her hands, "Yunzi, I do not despise you. In fact, I admire your swordplay and your intelligence a lot. I will readdress your honor for you, alright?"

Lele was upset at Ding Yunzi's plight as she had always despised despicable men so she interrupted, "Good sister, if Yi Ping is unable to, I will surely help you! Please don't take your life anymore."

Ding Yunzi sobbed, "It is pointless for me anymore. I have nothing left for me to live on anymore. My life is ruined. The one that I could trust has also betrayed me and hurt me. If you are me, what would you do?"

Lele was stunned.

Yi Ping held Ding Yunzi's hands as he said emotionally, "Yunzi, you still have me. I will take care of you forever. I will not allow anyone to bully you, whether it is now or in the future."

Ding Yunzi shook her head sadly, "You are only taking pity on me. So what if you are willing to take care of me? I am still destined to be alone even when I am old. What happens if you are not around anymore? I won't even have any children to take care of me. Everyone else knows I have been violated and will be scorning me. So what is the point?"

Yi Ping grabbed Ding Yunzi's hand and grabbed Lele's hand at the same time as he said, "Yunzi, I do not despise you. If you are willing, I will take you as my wife. Whoever scorns at you is as good as scorning me. I will take care of you and we will have many children."

Ding Yunzi gasped, "You don't despise me?"

Yi Ping looked earnest at Ding Yunzi, "Never. That day in the Honor Manor, if you did not break the fight between Zuo Tianyi and I, we would have both died. If you have not appeared, Gongsun Bai would have killed me."

He paused for a while, "I should be the one to ask if you are despising me for being such a muddle-headed person. I have let down Lingfeng, Youxue, Mei'Er and Yu'Er. Alas…"

Ding Yunzi said quietly, "You don't need to ask this Maiden Lele here?"

Lele said coolly, "Indeed! Yi Ping, you didn't ask me if I am willing…"

Yi Ping said awkwardly, "You are still in the mood to tease me. I have told you about the rest and you say you do not mind."

Lele smiled, "That is why I am the Joyful Goddess. But you really did not tell me about this Maiden Yunzi here."

She said gently to Ding Yunzi, "Good sister, welcome to the family. I am only making a light joke with Yi Ping. I will avenge your honor for you."

Ding Yunzi gasped, "Both of you…."

She looked at Yi Ping as she said, "I didn't say I like you. I am not as foolish as Youxue and all those lovelorn maidens."

Lele smiled merrily, "So you are saying you are unwilling to marry Yi Ping, am I not wrong to say so? Alas, that is too unfortunately for us. I thought that I am going to have a good sister. That is really so sad. Yi Ping, Maiden Yunzi says she is not willing to marry you…"

Ding Yunzi flustered as she said hastily, "I didn't say I am not going to marry him…"

Lele laughed softly, "So you are willing then?"

Ding Yunzi fell into Lele's embrace as she said shyly, "Good sister!"

Lele held her as she said, "My good sister!"

Ding Yunzi said, "From now on, my name is Ding Yun. Ding Yunzi is now dead."

Yi Ping nodded as he said, "The past is past. Don't dwell on it anymore."

Ding Yun said softly, "Ping, I have something very important to tell you."

Yi Ping said gently, "Take a rest first. You ought to rest first. Come, let me lend you a hand."

Ding Yun shook her head as she said, "It is really very important."

Yi Ping asked, "What can be so important that it cannot wait?"

Ding Yun answered, "We have seen the Celestial Fairy much earlier. She is still alive…"

Even Lele was startled as she thought, "Yi Ping's first wife is still alive?!"

Yi Ping was stunned as he asked emotionally, "Yixian, she is…she is still alive?! How is it possible? I witness her death with my own eyes and it is…Youxue….alas, Youxue kills her…"

Ding Yun said, "It is the truth. We had even fought briefly. Lie Qing and Youxue's injuries are all caused by the Celestial Fairy."

Yi Ping was startled, "Youxue…is she well now? Is Yixian alright?"

He was suddenly terrified. It was because if Shui Yixian had recognized Xiao Youxue as the one that attacked her, then there was bound to be a deadly fight."

Ding Yun replied, "The Celestial Fairy is fine but the same can't be said for Youxue."

Yi Ping was now panicky because Xiao Youxue did not return after she had left. He asked hurriedly, "Youxue, is she well?"

Ding Yun shook her head as she said, "She is gravely injured and in critical condition. I don't even know if she is able to pull through. In her most critical moment, Lie Qing had sacrificed half of her Invincible Divine Force to Youxue to keep her alive…"

Indeed, it was the same Invincible Divine Force that had kept Lie Qing alive while she entered the state of animated dead.

Because Xiao Youxue too had practiced the Golden Impervious Body, at the most crucial moment Lie Qing decided to send her into the state of animated dead by transferring her Invincible Divine Force intricate energy to Xiao Youxue.

It was also at the same time that Shui Yixian decided to bring back Xiao Youxue to the Eternal Ice Palace so that she could find a way to treat and revive her.

Yi Ping was stunned as he muttered, "Youxue, this is all my fault…if we have not quarrel, this could not have happened to you. Lie Qing, you are willing to give up your internal strength…I really owe you so much…"

While Yi Ping and Ding Yun were feeling inconsolable, they had failed to notice that Lele expressions had changed at the mention of Lie Qing and the Invincible Divine Force.

Chapter 36: The Secrets of the Celestial Palace

Ding Yun was already waiting for Yi Ping with two swords in her hands. One was a fine long sword while the other was a soft and thin sword.

Yi Ping was looking flustered as he made his way to her but looking at her right now, made him his heart raced even faster. He tried hard to control his heartbeat through the Divine Revelation Heart Intricacy Skill.

It was because Ding Yun had her hair braided into bun and a long left pony. Even though Ding Yun was not the most beautiful maiden that he had known but her quiet demeanor and her refined mannerism always sent his heart racing very hard.

In the past when he had suspected that she was Yixian's killer, he was obsessed in searching for her to avenge for Yixian. However, he knew now that he was actually attracted to her for his heart never ceases to stop beating fast whenever he was with her. He had actually remembered all her little small gestures and expressions by heart.

He was really afraid to look into her dull expressionless eyes for it seemed to have a magical power that seemed to drawn him to her. He could not believe that he had actually had the tenacity to ask her to be his wife in a moment of anxiety to calm down her suicide tendency.

He sighed in his heart, "Lingfeng, Youxue, I am so sorry...There is still Meijian and Yujian. Alas, Yi Ping, what is wrong with you? You are just a heartless and unfaithful person, unfit to be a hero like your father. How am I going to explain to your father?"

But when he looked at Ding Yun again, his mind became flutter again and he thought, "Yi Ping, you are so lucky to be acquainted with her. As long as she doesn't end her life prematurely and have calmed down in the future, you mustn't hurt her and seriously take her as your wife or you will really be hurting her. Yixian now I know you are alive, I will surely look for you."

Among all the maidens that he had known, only Shui Yixian was the only person that he had really feel strongly for and she was also his sanctioned wife since they had gone through the sacred marriage vows. And he had intended to keep his vows for her and looked for her as soon as possible for he had missed her sorely.

He had not expected that after he had left the Heavenly Mountains, he would have bumped into so many things. He had met Ji Lingfeng, his father and so many others. But his biggest headache was actually Lele. He did not really know how to explain to Yixian. Should he leave Yixian for her own good instead?

Yi Ping sighed again. He did not blame Yixian for hiding her own death from him. After all, she probably had her own difficulties and the Yixian that he had known, was a tender maiden and that she was probably doing it for his own good as well.

But he had instead betrayed her trust in him and had violated Shui Yujian and Meijian in his drunken stupor.

All of a sudden he thought, "What if Yixian knows what I did to Yu'Er and Mei'Er? Maybe that is why she doesn't even want to see me...I am so sinful. Alas! Yixian, what have I done. You will never forgive me now. You have tried to wish me happiness and even appointed me as the protégé leader of the Eternal Ice Palace so that my daily needs can be taken care of. But I have betrayed your trust..."

Ding Yun looked keenly at him before she interrupted quietly, "You are late for practice. Where is Lele?"

Yi Ping stammered, "I…Lele, she is still washing by the pool."

This ravine had many pools and streams.

He added quickly, "She says that the water here is miraculous and she did not want to leave any scar behind she wants to dip in the pool a little longer."

Ding Yun beamed gently, "The two of you seem to be enjoying frolicking in the pools every morning."

Yi Ping turned completed red as he stammered with embarrassment, "She…she…"

Every morning, Lele would secretly grabbed Yi Ping and took him to an isolated spot.

In the wee morning while Yi Ping was still sleeping in the cave, Lele had woke him up by whispering to him, "Ping, I think I have found a way out. Can you come with me quietly?"

Yi Ping asked, "I go wake Yun'Er, wait for me…"

Lele smiled mysteriously, "No need. We just take a quick look first. There a huge rock blocking the path. I need your help to push the boulder aside. Come."

Yi Ping yawned sleepily as he followed her.

Lele took him to an isolated place far from the cave as she eyed him nervously.

Yi Ping looked around the place as he asked, "Where is the boulder?"

Lele said softly, "There is only a pig here."

Yi Ping was startled as he drew his long sword, "Where is the pig? That will make a fine meal."

Lele was so agitated that she scolded him, "You are the pig, silly!"

Yi Ping was startled, "I am a pig?"

Lele said, "If you are not a pig, then who is?"

Yi Ping was surprised as he asked, "Lele, surely you are not asking me to come here just to call me a pig?"

Lele sighed, "You silly piggy. You don't even know what I want?"

Yi Ping blinked his eyes as he exclaimed, "I'm sorry but the way out isn't obvious to me. Yes, I am a pig but can you show me the boulder?"

Lele smiled bitterly as she sighed, "Why you….you are not romantic at all. Have you forgotten what we did last night?"

Yi Ping was flushing red as he stammered, "I…remember…"

Lele suddenly kissed him as she said, "So do you know what I want now?"

Normally Lele would not be so bold. It was because she had used the Bewitching Soul Seizing Skill on Yi Ping. While this skill had a powerful influence on others, this skill was actually a life and death contest between willpowers of the victim and the practitioner. So it was not to be used lightly. Even Lie Qing dared not used it beyond the initial probing.

But Lele had took the skill a step further as she was afraid of losing Yi Ping and letting herself be hurt. She was confident that a young man like Yi Ping would never have the state of divinity to resist the Bewitching Soul Seizing Skill. She was wrong and the skill backfired on her; instead of causing Yi Ping to be hopelessly smitten by her, she was smitten instead.

Of course, the very reason that she had dared to use the Bewitching Soul Seizing Skill to charm Yi Ping was that she genuinely liked Yi Ping in the first place.

Luckily, her state of divinity was strong enough to resist her own skill and the only negative effect was that it weakened her natural resistance, emboldening her fondness for Yi Ping.

Yi Ping was naturally a shy young man. He was electrified when Lele had suddenly kissed him lightly and his heartbeat raced nervously when he touched her soft body. He thought of pushing her away but it seemed that all his strength had departed from him and he was feeling awkwardly hot.

The fact that Lele was an extraordinary beauty weakened his resolute. She was not only glamorous but her dedicated softness caused him to be in a daze. And her fragrance was so delightful that it seemed to have a spell on him.

Yi Ping had never had this sensation and feeling before. He tried very hard to remember if he had this feeling with Yu'Er and Mei'Er before but the memory always eluded him. He had been dead drunk and could not remember a thing!

Before he had even realized it, he had seized Lele as they were kissing, rolling on the ground and undressing one another. He looked at Lele who was now blushing with shyness as he caressed her soft silken body. Her shyness was very obvious for she was very fair, as fair as Yixian, Yu'Er and Mei'Er.

Even though Yi Ping had met many beautiful maidens but this was the first time he had been consumed by lust and for the time being, there was nothing in his mind except for Lele.

Yi Ping was a sentimental person who felt strongly for kinship and friendship with a strong sense of righteousness. He would never take the first initiative to court Lele. But a series of extraordinary encounters and coincidences brought them together.

What they did not know was that they had lost their first time to one another too.

That was why they were now clumsily entangled in each other's embrace as they learnt and experienced new sensations together.

Lele said softly, "You clumsy pig…"

Yi Ping said, "I never done this sort of thing before…"

Lele bit him on his shoulder hard as she said, "You're obviously a liar. You have so many maidens around you. Alas, why must I fall into your hands…"

Yi Ping smiled bitterly, "I should be the one that should say that…"

He was interrupted by another painful bite by Lele as she said softly, "Liar, liar! We should try to do it every day…"

And it was what they had been secretly doing every morning…

However, their actions did not go unnoticed by Maiden Ding Yun as she said in a low whisper, "Both of you are getting too out of hand and getting noisier. Didn't you realize that I can hear your echoes in this valley…"

Yi Ping had suddenly frozen in embarrassment.

Just when Yi Ping did not know what to say, Lele had suddenly appeared as she whispered shyly, "Good sister, let me spar with Yi Ping first!"

Yi Ping was relieved that Lele had arrived in a nick of time to save him from the awkward questioning.

Lele averted her eyes from Ding Yun. She thought shyly, "What a terrible embarrassment! Sister Ding Yun has overheard us. Now I need a hole to hide in…"

Lele raised her dark scythe as she leapt towards Yi Ping, making three rapid thrust in mid-air! This swung technique was her 'Rapid Mirage Bursts'.

Yi Ping mustered his martial power to steady himself even as he raised his white emerald sword as the silence windforce of Lele's attacks threatened to sweep him off his feet!

The most terrifying thing about Lele's attacks was its unbelievable speed. Even though her dark scythe looked unwieldy, many careless opponents were actually fooled to charge headlong into her and hence lost their lives as they lost their footings when the silent windforce caught them by surprise.

Even standing on their ground to exchange strokes with her was not an option for her dark scythe was extremely heavy and it was physical draining to parry it.

Yi Ping's internal strength was not weak. In fact, due to many fortunate coincidences, his internal strength and martial power had increased so tremendously in the past year that most pugilists in their entire lifetime could not even dreamt of.

Even though Yi Ping had parried Lele's 'Rapid Mirage Bursts' umpteen of times with his 'Improved Horizon Swordplay' that was improvised with the aid of Ding Yun, it was still a terrifying and physically draining experience for him. It required his full concentration and he dared not be careless.

The Improved Horizon Swordplay was an improvised new swordplay that was inspired by Maiden Ding Yun to absorb the impact of the opponents' attacks and weakened the opponent strength by using the sword as a shield.

Even as three burst of bright lights and shrieking impact could be seen and heard, Lele had already followed up with another three quick attacks!

Yi Ping immediately followed up with another three strokes to counter her.

In less than a few seconds, they had exchanged more than twenty strokes!

Lele smiled, "Very good. You are improving. You used to unable to even handle even my first ten strokes in the past."

Yi Ping shouted, "Lele, you are not focusing and is careless…"

He had dashed headlong into Lele with his sword when she had just missed him and was talking to him. But to his utter disbelief, Lele had suddenly retracted her dark scythe, turning it aside and crashed it like a heavy pole onto his shoulder!

Yi Ping's reaction was not slow as he had parried with his long sword but the sheer weight and force of her dark scythe was too much for him to bear as he collapsed on the ground!

Yi Ping was stunned as he said, "Lele, what manner of attack is this? You are using your weapon as a pole!?"

Lele laughed softly, "You are dead. I have won again."

She pretended to yawn as she said gently, "No one says my weapon is just a pole-arm. If you exploit the deliberate front opening, then my weapon will be a pole. Do you understand me? In a fight, you ought to be caution and avoid unnecessary gambit. Sometimes the opening that you have seen is just a feint. "

Yi Ping nodded as he sighed, "I have mustered all my martial power with the Aspire Invocations. I just do not understand why I can't block your attack. It is as though your weapon has suddenly become extremely heavy and I can sense a great suffocating weight that crashes on me. Why is that so?"

Lele extended her dark scythe with one hand as she said coolly, "See if you can snatch my weapon from me."

Yi Ping rubbed his palms before he tried to pull the dark scythe from her. But no matter how hard he pulled with both hands, he could not wrestle it from her! It was as though she had cast a spell on it. He simply could not believe that even with two hands, he could not pull the dark scythe one inch from her even though Lele was just gripping it with one hand!

Yi Ping was astonished, "This…this is impossible! This is not just internal strength alone…it is a supernatural feat…"

Ding Yun who was watching the scene, laughed softly. "Yi Ping, this is not a supernatural feat. This is the 'Thousand Weight Feat'. She is able to increase the weight of the weapon and even herself tens of times heavier with her martial power. That is why you do not see her exuding any martial power."

Yi Ping was startled, "There is such a wondrous feat in this fraternity? Lele, can you teach me this skill?"

Lele smiled shyly, "You are my husband. Of course I am willing to teach you. But first you have to start with the basics first. You can try to start by carrying my scythe and climb that tree over there a hundred times daily."

As Yi Ping turned and saw the towering tree, he was stunned for he knew how heavy Lele's scythe was. He secretly thought, "So that is why she always carrying a wicked looking scythe around so that she can practice her internal strength all the time?"

Ding Yun said gently, "Lele is only teasing you. With your present cultivation in internal strength, it will be easy for you. Don't you know?"

Yi Ping smiled bitterly, "I really did not know!"

Lele laughed merrily, "Sister Yun, you should have let him suffer for a while."

Ding Yun smiled shyly, "He…he is my…our…husband. We shouldn't lie to him even if it is a jest."

Yi Ping clapped his hands as he said, "No wonder every time I fight with the both of you and Yuan Shao, I can feel an irresistible overwhelming force…"

Lele said, "That is because you are too focused on martial power and not your internal strength. What if you miss with your martial power, you will only be wasting your physical strength. Even though our weapon techniques looked ordinary, weak and tedious to train, we may not lose to you in a long run."

Yi Ping said, "Lele, you carry such an unwieldy scythe around? Don't you feel it is too inconvenient and tiring?"

Lele smiled mysteriously.

All of a sudden, she unhooked the double wicked blades of the scythe from the dark pole and folded it into a circular shape and inserted it into her straw hat! So expert was her dismantling movements that it took her only a blink of an eye to do so.

Yi Ping was stunned as he muttered, "It becomes a real pole now…"

Lele laughed gently, "That's right."

Yi Ping said, "No wonder, you seem so expert with the pole too."

Ding Yun said, "Not just with the pole, she is an expert swordsman too."

Yi Ping was startled, "Lele, you know how to use the sword? Why don't you use the sword when you are fighting Yuan Shao? You may not lose…"

Lele sighed, "Don't remind me. It is just that I didn't have the opportunity to draw my swords yet."

Yi Ping looked intently at her before he asked, "Where are your swords?"

Lele smiled shyly, "Stop looking at me like this."

She took out the circular double blade from her straw hat and separated it into two sickles as she whirled the sickles ambidextrously in front of her!

Yi Ping could feel the wicked slices of the double sickles as he trembled fearfully even though he was not entirely within reach of Lele's sickles.

He was astonished as he quickly said, "Lele, this is the feeling that I have with Yuan Shao. Quickly, let's us fight again."

Lele laughed shyly, "No way! I have never seen anyone that courts death like the way you do."

Yi Ping said awkwardly, "Of course I fear death but if I let fear overcomes me, how do I hope to defeat the Honor Manor and the Virtuous Palace in the future?"

Ding Yun said coolly, "That is what you say but the truth is, you didn't even bother to think of the consequences."

After spending time with Yi Ping, Ding Yun had realized Yi Ping was a fearless fighter who would not hesitate even if his opponent was many times more powerful than him.

Yi Ping blushed as he stammered, "That's not the point. Lele, let's fight with your swords again."

Lele said firmly, "Unless you can hold at least sixty strokes against my scythe's techniques, it is far too dangerous for us to even try. Even with my state of divinity, it will be hard for me to gauge when to stop."

Yi Ping protested, "But Lele, if I…"

Ding Yun interrupted, "You seem to forget that we have not practiced yet."

Ding Yun had drawn out her precious sword and her foldable sword at the same time.

Against Ding Yun's Virtuous Swordplay, after several days of practice and improving the Horizon Swordplay, he had come up with the Improved Horizon Swordplay that he had picked up from Lele's weapon techniques.

Yi Ping was not discouraged as he said, "I think I have a way to defeat Yuan Shao and you now."

Ding Yun had virtually taught him the entire stances and strokes of the Virtuous Swordplay in the past few days. She said gently, "Even though you know my strokes by now but breaking it is another matter entirely."

Against Ding Yun's Virtuous Swordplay, Yi Ping attacked rapidly and disengaged quickly at the same time!

In an instant, Yi Ping had exchanged dozens of strokes against Maiden Ding Yun's double swords techniques.

No matter how hard he had tried, he just could not breech through her double swords defenses. The feeling that Ding Yun had given him was that of an impregnable defense. She had parried with her long sword and attacked him with her soft long sword at the same time!

Every time, Lele watched their duel, she was still filled with awe. Yi Ping had certainly improved by leap and bounds as he could now hold on his own against Maiden Ding Yun. But Yi Ping had not found a way to break the profound changes of the Virtuous Swordplay yet!

She knew that Maiden Ding Yun was also showing her a way to break Yuan Shao's swordplay too.

All of a sudden, Yi Ping changed his attacking direction from left to right as he kept attacking Ding Yun's left side! The foldable sword that was on her left side was unsuitable to block against his powerful Horizon Swordplay!

Yi Ping shouted, "Yun'Er, I know your weak point now!"

Ding Yun smiled sweetly, "What takes you so long to realize it?"

All of a sudden, she whirled her foldable sword and hurled it into a flying sword at Yi Ping as she shouted, "Watch out!"

Yi Ping immediately raised his sword to block it but he was forced to take several steps backward even as the flying sword spins back into Maiden Ding Yun's hand.

Even before Yi Ping could react, she had dropped her foldable sword to the ground and charged with her long sword against him as she said coolly, "I can do a double flying sword if the soft sword gets back into my hand and charge at you. So what will you do?"

Of course, she did not and was deliberately only extending her long sword at Yi Ping.

Yi Ping recovered in time and he had suddenly discovered that Ding Yun was now on the offensive! Her sword techniques were now similar to Yuan Shao but did not have the fearsome aura that Yuan Shao had possessed!

They were now exchanging sword strokes so fast and rapidly that the entire valley began to echo with their attacks!

Lele held her breath excitedly as she thought, "The two of them are the new generation of the super exponents of the fraternity? How is it possible for them to have such remarkable swordplay at their age?"

It was because swordplay had too many changes. The only way to improve one's swordplay was to keep on using it in a real fight, training the practitioner ability to react and their natural instinct for exploiting openings.

The Horizon Swordplay was a swordplay that utilizes speed and martial power. Combined with Lele's Mirage Speed Technique, Yi Ping had nearly doubled his attacking speed!

The Virtuous Swordplay utilizes speed, internal strength to steady it and was also a counter-attacking swordplay.

No matter how many dozens of Illusional strokes Yi Ping made against her, Ding Yun always lightly parried with a wide arc stroke and counter-attack with a series of fast strokes too.

Lele shouted excitedly, "It is a draw!"

All of a sudden, Ding Yun raised her left hand and stabbed towards Yi Ping!

Yi Ping raised his powerful left palm and blocked it effortlessly.

However, even as Ding Yun stabbed him with her left hand, she had withdrawn instantly and continuous to thrust her left hand at his left palm, causing him to hastily withdraw his palm!

He gasped, "The Penetrating hands?! You know this skill too?"

But before he could ask further, Ding Yun had thrown her long sword and it had landed with thunderous impact between his legs!

She said quietly, "You are dead."

Yi Ping had turned pale immediately as he muttered, "I keep forgetting that the most powerful techniques of the Virtuous Palace are not its swordplay but its extraordinary unarmed techniques…"

Ding Yun said, "Indeed. While swordplay can kill fast without expending much effort but the best martial skills of the Virtuous Palace are actually their Eighteen Unbreakable Hands, Penetrating Hands and the Soul Stealer Finger."

Lele interrupted as she turned pale, "The Soul Stealer Finger and the Eighteen Unbreakable Hands?! The Virtuous Palace actually possesses these two martial skills?"

Ding Yun said, "These are legacy skills inherited when the Xiao Clan takes over the Virtuous Palace from the Red Eye Clan. Xiao Shuai is the only one that knows the Eighteen Unbreakable Hands. As for the Soul Stealer Finger, Xiao Shuai and Yuan Shao are the only ones that know this skill."

Lele asked, "The Red Eye Clan? There are others like me?"

Ding Yun said, "They are dead a long time ago."

Lele sighed, "What a pity. Or else…"

She did not continue.

Yi Ping asked, "Or else what?"

Lele said, "Nothing at all."

Yi Ping asked curiously, "Really nothing at all?"

Lele ignored Yi Ping as she asked Ding Yun, "Good sister, how is that your wounds are able to heal so fast and without a single scar?"

Ding Yun replied, "I have been practicing the Divine Virtuous Force and this skill has a healing effect."

Lele exclaimed in surprise, "What an amazing skill. To think that this divine epitome skill exists. Good sister, will you teach me?"

Ding Yun smiled, "I can teach you but is it risky for you? What if the intricate force of the skill is not compatible with yours?"

Lele laughed softly, "Teach me first and I see about it…"

Yi Ping said solemnly, "Better don't teach her that. It may be far too dangerous. The Divine Virtuous Force, like my Aspire Invocation emphasis on martial power. Lele, your intricate force is similar to the Icy Heavenly Tears that emphasis more on internal energies. It is way too dangerous for you."

Ding Yun said, "I agree. Youxue's mother died because she thought that she can merge the Icy Heavenly Tears and the Divine Virtuous Force together. It ended up in tragedy."

Lele smiled, "I don't believe that my Celestial Force is not able to merge the skills together."

Yi Ping scolded her, "You may end up losing your life and worse still end up with a permanent disability. So what even if you have succeeded? All your martial skills will end up deteriorating and you will end up spending decades to regain it. It is not worth the risk."

Lele was irritated, "I have plenty of time."

Yi Ping was trembling.

Both Ding Yun and Lele were startled to see that his face was tearful.

Lele softened her stance as she said panicky, "Alright then. I promise you I won't try to learn this skill. Don't cry. Real man only shed blood and not tears."

Ding Yun asked Yi Ping, "Ping, what is wrong?"

Yi Ping wiped away his silent tears as he muttered, "Nothing. It is just that…it is just that I am thinking of my mother and Yixian…"

Lele was startled, "What have this have to do with your mother?"

Yi Ping said, "My mother and Yixian are protégé sisters. In order to avert the Divine Calamity, they practiced and meditated endlessly. In the end, they are not able to enjoy life as it should be. I don't think it is worth it…"

Lele rebuked him gently, "It is because you have not reached the proper divinity yet and has not yet received the visions. At the very top, it is a realm that you cannot possibly imagine. Without the Divine Calamity, I…I would never possibly have met you. Do you think that is not destiny?"

Yi Ping asked, "Lele, you have really experienced the Divine Calamity? What is it? Can you help Yixian to overcome the Divine Calamity?"

Lele looked at Ding Yun and Yi Ping slowly before she said slowly, "I really do not want to reveal anything to others for it is the most sacred secret of the Celestial Palace."

Yi Ping was disappointed and it shown on his face.

Lele said, "But you are my husband and Ding Yun is my good sister now. Promise me you won't reveal it to anyone?"

Yi Ping said hastily, "I swear to the Heavens and Earth that I won't reveal to anyone without your permission or else lightning…"

Lele interrupted, "That's enough."

Ding Yun was curious about the Divine Calamity too. She knew from Xiao Shuai that Yuan Shao had been preparing for the Divine Calamity and the Virtuous Palace had been quietly working towards this objective for many decades. That was why the Virtuous Palace had always been reluctant to get involved in the affairs of the martial fraternity and even feared injuries.

So she did not hesitate at all as she said, "Heavens and the Earth is my witness, I swear that I will not reveal what Sister Lele has revealed to me today."

Lele seemed to have lost the glow on her face as her eyes seemed to stare blankly.

She said dispiritedly, "The truth is I don't even know what the Divine Calamity is. It can come in many forms and is a natural phenomenon that is so terrifying that it can kill."

Yi Ping breathed in deeply as he listened attentively.

Lele said, "It occurs when a practitioner reached the highest state of divinity or is nearly immortal when they are nearing a hundred and twenty. After that, the Divine Calamity will give prior warning for seven days before it occur."

Yi Ping asked, "Can't it be avoided or averted?"

Lele shook her head, "It can't but it can be made to prematurely occur."

Yi Ping said, "My father told me that the last stance of the Divine Horizon Hands can trigger the Divine Calamity and warned me never to use the last stance even when I can in the future."

Lele was startled, "The Divine Horizon Hands can trigger the Divine Calamity? It…must be a powerful stance that is beyond human limitations."

Yi Ping smiled bitterly, "And it is also an impossible stance. I have only just started the Divine Revelation and have no time for mediation. I'll be better off practicing the Aspire Invocations instead. At least, I get into a fight daily."

Lele said, "You are just lazy and impatient. Sooner or later, either you will be killed in the martial fraternity or the Divine Calamity will kill you off."

Yi Ping smiled bitterly as he said, "Is the Divine Calamity this simple? What is the secret behind it?"

Lele seemed to hesitate for a while before she finally said, "There is only two persons that I know that had ever succeed in surviving the Divine Calamity. One is the Sage King and the other is the founder of the Celestial Palace, the Jade Emperor."

Yi Ping was startled for he had heard of the Sage King before as he asked, "The Sage King, is he the one that makes the 'Great Rejuvenate Golden Pills?'"

Lele nodded, "You know of his pills? We have been searching for it for a long time too…"

Yi Ping smiled bitterly as he said, "Youxue, she gave it to me when I was once grievously injured."

Lele was stunned as she muttered, "Maybe it is fate…we have been searching for it for centuries…"

Yi Ping was startled, "What do you mean you have been searching for it for centuries? How old are you Lele?"

Lele looked at Yi Ping and looked at Ding Yun as she sighed, "Make a guess…"

Yi Ping said, "Twenty?"

Lele said something but Yi Ping could not hear.

Yi Ping asked again, "Lele, your voice is too soft. I cannot hear."

Lele stared miserably at Yi Ping before she sighed softly, "I…I am four centuries old."

Ding Yun and Yi Ping were both stunned.

Ding Yun asked, "How is it possible? No one can live that long without turning old or dying."

Yi Ping stared at Lele…

Lele averted her eyes as she said softly, "So now you know. You must be despising me now because of my age…"

Yi Ping caught hold of her hands as he said, "No, Lele I am not. I am just surprised that you don't look at all past twenty-five."

Lele said, "That is because I have survived the Divine Calamity at that age and can't age anymore."

Yi Ping asked, "But you just said there are only two persons that have survived the Divine Calamity. You are the Jade Emperor?!"

Lele shook her head as she said, "That is because we have cheated death using an unorthodox means. Because of that, we may have survived the Divine Calamity but we didn't really achieve the new state of divinity and in fact, cannot advance further. My hair turned silver and my eyes turned red overnight…"

All of a sudden, she broke into tears as she begun to tremble. "Once every hundred years, the Divine Calamity revisited us and our numbers began to reduce further. Many of the original survivors are dead now…"

Ding Yun asked, "Why do you need the 'Great Rejuvenated Golden Pills' for?"

Lele nodded slowly, "The Jade Emperor has exhausted his strength fighting the Divine Calamity for us. Without him, we will surely perish. That is why we have been searching for the 'Great Rejuvenated Golden Pills'."

Yi Ping asked, "Since you have all the time in the world, can't you train to fight against the Divine Calamity? Can't the Jade Emperor show you the way to survive it?"

Lele smiled bitterly, "That is what you think? We are supposed to gain the revelation of the Celestial Skill by overcoming the Divine Calamity. Because we have cheated, we are cursed forever and our level of cultivation has to remains as it is before the Divine Calamity. Without advancing to the Jade Emperor level of cultivation, we have no hope whatever so of surviving it."

Yi Ping was bewildered as he asked, "What do you mean? If the level of cultivation is basic, surely it is just so easy to grasp it given the time that you have?"

Lele seemed terrified as she said nervously, "That is the secret of the Divine Calamity! We are supposed to attain a new understanding in our state of divinity first before we can advance. Anyone that forcefully tries to attain a new state of divinity after the Divine Calamity will trigger the deadly Celestial Wrath. No one will be able to survive that."

Yi Ping was startled, "There exists a Celestial Wrath?!"

Lele nodded, "That is our last chance now. If we can survive the Celestial Wrath, we can break away from the curse of the Divine Calamity."

Yi Ping asked, "What curse?"

Lele said, "Each time the Divine Calamity occurs or if we expend our internal energy, we cannot recover it unless we drink the blood of top exponents and eat their hearts…"

Yi Ping was stunned as he asked, "Lele, did you really do that?"

Lele said slowly, "I don't want to lie to you. I have done so on numerous times."

Yi Ping clenched his fists as he begun to walk away.

Lele's eyes were now watery as she thought, "I have lost him forever now. No one will forgive me what I have done…"

Even Ding Yun was gasping, stunned at Lele's revelations as she thought, "She…really is a blood drinker…"

It was because she had suddenly remembered the scary tales of the Red Eye Clan and she had thought that they were stories meant to frighten children.

Yi Ping had walked three steps before he turned back, "According to my father, my great grandfather is killed by the blood drinkers. Are you one of them?"

Lele asked, "Where is your great grandfather at that time?"

Yi Ping said, "I don't know the exact location but it is in the Central Fraternity."

Lele said, "Then it is not me. I have never stepped outside the Western Fraternity."

Yi Ping sighed with relief. He looked stoned. If Lele had the blood of his clan in her hands, would he still have the heart to kill her? Just like if Youxue had the blood of Yixian in her hands, would he still have the heart to kill her? He dare not think of the implications!

Lele said, "Actually you don't have to worry too much. The people that we have killed are all almost at the end of their lives…"

Yi Ping interrupted, "A life is still a life!"

Lele smiled alluring, ignoring his remarks. "Also, most of the time we need to sleep because mere blood alone cannot replenish our strength. Sometimes I need to sleep for decades. In fact, I have just waked up after a span of forty years."

Yi Ping was startled, "You need to sleep for this long?!"

Lele smiled bitterly, "That is why it is our curse. If we do not sleep for extended period of time, our strength will falter and drained away. But even then, when we are awakened, we will still need at least a few years of time to completely regain our martial skills. It is a vicious cycle with no ending."

Yi Ping asked gently, "Is there a way to cure your condition?"

Lele said, "Only a miracle pill like the Great Rejuvenate Golden Pill or something miraculous can alleviate this disorder. That is why we have been searching for it all this while."

Yi Ping said wryly, "It doesn't seem you are making a great deal of effort to look for it, from someone that never left the western fraternity."

Lele chuckled, "We are not that foolish to look for a needle in the ocean. It is just not practicable to look for something that is almost a myth. But should it really exist in the fraternity, there bound to be people fighting over it. When that occurs, we will naturally know."

Yi Ping asked, "How do you know?"

Lele said, "We have secret emissaries that are scattered throughout the fraternity. That is important especially since we are sleeping most of the time."

Ding Yun asked, "How do you ensure their loyalty?"

Lele smiled mysterious, "I am the Joyful Goddess. Naturally, I will promise them eternal joyous life and a chance to gain entry to the Celestial Palace if they serve us well."

Yi Ping growled, "Lele, that is deceiving the ignorant masses. Now I remember. There is a Joyful Cult in the fraternity. Don't tell me you are their leader?"

Lele blinked at him, "It is not that hard to figure it out. So there, you have guessed it. I am the Goddess that they have worshipped."

Yi Ping mocked gently, "It is more like a pathetic Goddess that spends a lot of time sleeping like a pig."

Lele said unhappily, "Yi Ping, are you too weary of living already? In the past, if any one insults me like that, they will be dead in the next instant."

Yi Ping smiled, "So the Joyful Goddess will actually be upset?"

Lele smiled, "You think that I am really upset? I won't fall into your trick. You just want to spar with me. You are such a bully!"

Yi Ping and Ding Yun laughed.

All of a sudden, Yi Ping said excitedly, "Since the Sage King has also survived the Divine Calamity, why don't you look for him to make another 'Great Rejuvenate Golden Pill'?"

Lele smiled bitterly, "That is because he has died centuries ago."

Yi Ping was startled, "I can imagine he is a formidable exponent as well. Who on earth can actually has the means to kill him?"

Lele said, "From what I know, he barely survived his first Divine Calamity and knows that he won't survive his second Divine Calamity. Therefore, he expended all his efforts to create eight wondrous golden rejuvenation pills and hid it in a secret location."

Lele added coldly after a pause, "That is his wickedness and also his stratagem. Because he knew that he was going to die, he wants the majority of the top exponents to die along with him and deliberating spread the news of his creations. Anyone that wants to obtain it had to find his underground palace to locate it first."

Ding Yun asked, "What if the Sage King had lied about the Great Rejuvenation Golden Pills?"

Lele shook her head, "The Sage King won't lie or else he won't reach his level of divinity. He has another purpose of course. At that time he was aware of us too and that our clan requires the hearts of the top exponents. By causing a division and causing them to die prematurely, he had actually caused many of us to succumb to the Divine Calamity."

Lele looked forlornly into the sky and she seemed to be thinking of something.

Yi Ping knew what she had been through. The loss of her kin and friends were a loss that was hard to bear.

Ding Yun said, "It seemed that the Virtuous Palace had eventually located it. Xiao Shuai found it but it was stolen by Xiao Youxue and one of the pills was given to Yi Ping."

Yi Ping asked, "Why didn't he pass it to his descendants?"

Lele smiled, "He is an old priest and did not have any kin. It does seem like that we are the only survivors of the Divine Calamity now."

Ding Yun said quietly, "There is one survivor from the Red Eye Clan, good sister."

Lele was startled, "There is someone else? Thought you have just said earlier that there are none?"

Ding Yun said, "She is supposed to be dead too…"

Yi Ping nodded as he said, "Her name is Lie Qing. When I found her, she is as good as dead. But I had tried to revive her with the Divine Dragon Pill and I had managed to save her life."

Lele looked at Yi Ping in utter disbelief as she took a few unsteady steps backward. After a while, she said with trembling voice, "You actually have the Divine Dragon Pill? Do you know how many times more precious that pill is over the Great Rejuvenation Golden Pill and you give it away just like that?"

Yi Ping scratched his head in puzzlement, "I know that that is one of the seven treasures of the Martial Fraternity…"

Lele interrupted unhappily, "You know nothing at all! That Divine Dragon Pill…alas…that Lie Qing is really so lucky. I…I can't believe that you actually give it away. You should at least keep for yourself."

She wanted to say, "I want to drink her blood and eat her heart." But halfway through, she decided to keep mum.

Lele asked Yi Ping melancholy, "Who is this Lie Qing to you that you can give her something this precious?"

She was alarmed with this Lie Qing. This was the second time that she had heard of her name. The first time her name was mentioned was when Ding Yun had mentioned that she had attempted to save a maiden's life with her Invincible Divine Force.

Somehow, Lie Qing's name sounded all too familiar to her but she could not remember who she was. As for the Invincible Divine Force, she only knew it too well…

She silently thought, "No matter who you are, it will be interesting to fight with you. The Celestial Force and the Invincible Divine Force are the two most epitome martial force in the entire fraternity. If you have really survived the Divine Calamity, then all I have to do is to defeat you and exchange your intricate energy with my Celestial Force, then my state of divinity can be raised…"

Yi Ping smiled bitterly, "I swear I have nothing to do with her…"

Lele said unhappily, "Do you think that I will believe you…"

Ding Yun suddenly said, "I know why the Virtuous Palace is attacking the Holy Hex Sect now."

Yi Ping was startled, "Why?"

Ding Yun said, "That is because Xiao Shuai had once given one Great Rejuvenation Golden Pill to Ji Wuzheng to save his sister life."

Yi Ping immediately turned pale as he said, "Then Lingfeng is in grave danger. Xiao Shuai will really eat her alive just like he wants to eat Youxue alive…"

He hastily said, "We must find a way out immediately! Let's us go now." And Yi Ping had already stormed off in a hurry!

Lele was left grasping her hands to her heart as she muttered melancholy, "Lingfeng…the Holy Maiden…"

Chapter 37: The Deadly Celestial Annihilating Star Formations

It was only a few days later that Yi Ping had managed to find a possible exit. It was a dark cave in the ravine opening.

After exploring the cave for some time, Yi Ping found the cave to be immensely huge. So he had returned to find Ding Yun and Lele.

Yi Ping said solemnly, "I have searched the entire gorge valley and although there are many caves, many are a dead end except for one. I'm going to explore this cave more thoroughly as it is too huge and it may take some time."

Ding Yun said softly, "I will go with you."

Yi Ping sighed, "The cave may be extremely treacherous and it is very slippery. It is better that I go alone."

Lele looked at Yi Ping serenely with an earnest woeful expression, "Yi Ping, even though we have not gone through any marriage rites but…" She looked at Ding Yun who nodded silently, "We should go through woes and joys together. We are now together. If you are to die inside the cave, we will follow you!"

Ding Yun said with equally firm conviction, "That's right!"

Yi Ping was moved as he looked silently at them. Finally after a while, he said. "Let's us go now."

He thought, "Yi Ping, with two such companions that willingly follow you onto death, even death is not to be feared!"

Yi Ping lit a torch as he walked in front when they had entered the dark cave.

When they had entered the cave, Ding Yun began to cling to him closely. It was not out of fear though but she was guided by her natural instinct and being closed to Yi Ping, gave her a feeling of assurance.

The moving light of the torch was not bright in this dark cave. Fortunately, both Yi Ping and Lele had already cleared their eight extraordinary vessels. Even if there were little light, they could see what was in front of them clearly and could avoid the dangerous pitfalls and slippery slopes.

Lele was astonished that Yi Ping could walk so steadily.

She gently asked him, "You can see in the dark?"

Yi Ping nodded awkwardly.

Lele asked again, "You have an owl eyes or have you cleared eight extraordinary vessels?"

Yi Ping said, "I have accidentally cleared my eight extraordinary vessels."

When Ding Yun had heard it, she was astonished and began to look at Yi Ping again with a new light.

Lele smiled, "Really? What about your conception and governing vessels?"

Yi Ping smiled weakly, "I have accidentally cleared my conception and governing vessels due to an incident."

Lele nearly tripped as she almost missed her steps. She was in utter disbelief. It had taken her more than two centuries and with the help of the Jade Emperor to clear her conception and governing vessels!

Her beautiful composure changed as she said, "Do you know what that means? If you have cleared these two vessels which means that you have in control of your life conception and can govern death. These two channels are called the life and death channels. Do you really know how difficult it is to do so?"

Yi Ping smiled even more awkwardly, "Is that so?"

Ding Yun was stunned as she gasped, "You have really cleared your life and death channels?"

For the very first time, she had felt that her martial progress between Yi Ping and hers were so vast.

Lele said, "And you have lost to Yuan Shao, Sister Ding Yun and me?"

Yi Ping asked, "What's wrong with that? You have lost to Yuan Shao too."

Lele gave a soft sigh as she said, "That's different. I am careless and I did not expect to meet an exponent of that caliber."

She quickly added, "That means that you can see all our strokes clearly?"

Yi Ping nodded slowly, "But after exchanging more than two hundred strokes with Yuan Shao, I could not see his attacks too clearly. Then you have come…"

After exchanging more than two hundred strokes with Yuan Shao, Yi Ping was in a daze and hardly maintained his focus. It was only due to his sheer mental fortitude and endurance that he had persisted.

Lele had arrived just after she had seen Yuan Shao stabbing Yi Ping with his cane and fatally wounding him with a blow. Her first thought was that this young man was going to die anyway and why was she even bothering trying to save him?

But the irony happened. Instead of saving him, it ended up it was him saving her.

Lele could only scolded him gently, "You are so pathetic." But she was actually secretly pleased and was proud of him.

Ding Yun said gently to Yi Ping, "You have lost only because Yuan Shao has the superior techniques and he is also more experienced. In time to come, you can certainly defeat him."

Lele said all of a sudden, "Yi Ping, when you are able to defeat Yuan Shao, don't kill him alright?"

Ding Yun and Yi Ping were both startled at her sudden request.

Yi Ping asked, "Yuan Shao has wounded you and you are always threatening to kill those that have slighted you. I am just surprise why."

Lele sighed softly, "Yi Ping, it is better for you to restraint from killing. It won't be good for your progression in the future. As for Yuan Shao, his malevolent air is too heavy and it won't be possible for him to progress further in his state of divinity. Should he encounter the Divine Calamity, he will surely die."

Yi Ping nodded, "Lele, you are too kind…"

Lele smiled mysteriously as she blinked at him as she said to herself, "Yuan Shao's blood is far too precious to be wasted."

Ding Yun said to Lele, "I notice that sister seem to lack the killing intent when you are fighting and it will be your undoing."

Lele sighed incoherently and with great sadness, "I have long forgotten how to fight. Maybe that is why I have survived the Divine Calamities. Or rather, the past Divine Calamities have spared me…"

Ding Yun nodded.

Yi Ping could sense that Lele had suddenly become overwhelming sad so he quickly said, "Let's us be on our way. The torch won't last long."

The cave complex was large and had many paths. After several hours, they were all getting worried and they had already used up two torches. It became apparent that they had lost their way and was too deep.

Lele asked, "So, do we continue or backtrack to the entrance?"

Yi Ping was staring blankly at the surrounding, "This cave is impossibly huge…"

Ding Yun was looking keenly at the surroundings. All of a sudden, she gasped and pointed to a passage, "That passage over there seem to have been used before."

Yi Ping looked at her as he asked, "How do you know?"

Ding Yun said, "Part of the walls is smooth and it looks too unnatural. It is likely to be man-made. Look at the other sections of the passages; do you see that it is rough and uneven?"

It gave Yi Ping hope as he quickly said, "Let's go!"

They soon reached a large cavern and was immediately stunned that that this cavern was actually a large chamber that was constructed by granite and limestone!

Even though it was in disrepair and it seemed that no one had ever been here for a long time, the grandeur and the size of the chamber was astonishing!

At the far end of the chamber, there were three seemingly white statues of three maidens in beautiful poses.

Ding Yun muttered, "It makes no sense to build a chamber here out of nowhere. Unless, there is a possible exit somewhere near here? But shouldn't it be inside the gorge where water is more accessible?"

Lele nodded too but her attention was totally drawn by the objects in this chamber. There was a sense of familiarity and a sense of déjà vu. As she raised her slender fingers to touch and felt the walls of this chamber, she was trembling!

Somehow Yi Ping was drawn to the fading white statues as he seemed to be pulled irresistible to it.

When Yi Ping had walked to the statues, he was totally stunned!

It was not because the statues were so life-like or their workmanship was so exquisite that had stunned Yi Ping!

It was because the white statue that was standing regally in the middle with a noble air was the exact replicate of Shui Yixian and even their standing mannerism was the same!

The other two statues were looking down and had swords in their hands. And the two statues look vaguely similar to Lele and Lie Qing…

Yi Ping simply could not believe his eyes.

Yi Ping said, "Lele, come over here quick…"

Lele snapped out of her trance and with Ding Yun, she quickly walked towards Yi Ping as she smiled, "What's wrong with you? You have never seen life size statues before?"

When she saw her replicate, she was stunned.

Ding Yun was startled too, "Isn't this Lele and Lie Qing?"

Lele smiled weakly, "My statues are all over the fraternity but none of it really looks like me. Maybe it is just a coincidence. I am so upset. I should stand in the middle, right?"

It was only then did she notice that Yi Ping was not heeding her and he was touching the face of the statue in the middle.

Lele interrupted with a soft glee, "What's wrong with you. You actually fallen in love with a statue? Even if you like this statue, you can't move it."

She raised her pole and seemed to threaten to destroy the statues but till Yi Ping paid her no heed and was still looking intently at the statue.

After some time, they could hear Yi Ping muttering, "Yixian, Yixian. How I miss you so. I have finally found you…"

Lele was startled for she knew that Yixian was Yi Ping's rightful wife.

Ding Yun had seen Shui Yixian before and she was many times more moving and beautiful in reality than this statue here. The statue could only capture her likeness but could not capture her unparalleled beauty.

Lele was not pleased as she gave Yi Ping a tug.

Yi Ping woke up from his stupor as he quickly said, "Lele, isn't this statue you?"

Lele smiled, "And what are you touching now? It is just a coincidence. All statues look alike to me."

Yi Ping said, "No, it really look like you and I have never seen such perfect craftsmanship before. Lele, why are you here?"

Lele brushed her silver hair with her fingers. She seemed to be deep in thoughts before she finally laughed softly, "Oh well, I am a Goddess. Someone must be secretly worshipping me here."

All of a sudden, Lele had noticed that Yi Ping and Ding Yun were looking at her intently.

Lele fingered her silver hair as she asked, "What is wrong? Why are the two of you looking at me like that?"

It was because Ding Yun and Yi Ping had suddenly noticed that when she was stroking her hair, she had the exact same mannerism as Lie Qing!

She asked again, "What's wrong?"

Yi Ping was too bewildered as he said, "Nothing…but just wondering what is this place? Who had built it and where are we?"

Lele said softly, "It seems that this place is very ancient and has been abandoned for a long time."

All of a sudden, Ding Yun exclaimed excitedly. "There are inscriptions engraved below the statues!"

Yi Ping quickly shone the torch at the base of the statues. Indeed there were inscriptions engraved on the floor base. He quickly wiped away the soil and dust with his hands.

The words were very ancient and they could barely read it.

Yi Ping stood up as he said miserably, "I can't read it. I don't understand…"

Ding Yun said, "I can read it but I can't really translate the meaning…"

Lele laughed softly, "You uneducated boor. Let me read it. These characters are still in use from my time."

But when Lele began to take a look, she was dumbfounded.

She began to recite as she translated, "Heaven Wrath had descended upon the three realms. My transcendent had been interrupted not by the Divine Crisis but by the most terrible of all the calamities, the Dark Malevolent Star Crisis. In that crisis, all three realms were given acquiescence to destroy in order to transcend. It was a crisis that so woeful that many celestials were slew including my two celestial sisters, Luminous Star and Melody Star."

Lele said, "It makes no sense at all…"

Yi Ping said, "Could the Divine Crisis refer to the Divine Calamity?"

Lele began to ponder, "In that case, she was trying to overcome the Divine Calamity but had encountered the Dark Malevolent Star Crisis? No, that is not right. She had already overcome the Divine Calamity. She was trying to overcome the Celestial Wrath. It was because the next line was more apparent."

Yi Ping said, "Did she succeed?"

Lele continued to translate, "Even though I had a thousand years of divinity and had created a formidable star formation, I was not able to overcome the Divine Crisis. The Ascend failed because the deaths of my sisters had a lasting impact on my attainment and my end was near. In my final moments, my heart still reaches out for my sisters and was not regretful that I did not succeed in my investiture. Even if I take another thousand years, I will do so."

Yi Ping said regretfully, "So she still fails."

Lele said softly, "I didn't know there are others with such high attainment ahead of the Jade Emperor and the Sage King. Apparently, they had either all been killed one after another or had all turned into ashes by the Divine Calamity."

Ding Yun asked, "Why are they forced to kill one another? Don't they have a choice?"

Lele said weakly, "I didn't know that is real…I don't know…"

Yi Ping asked, "Lele?"

Lele said, "The Jade Emperor once told us that there is a deadly calamity that reverse and realign the cosmos. Once that happens, Order can only be restored through an infinitude Chaos when all the Celestials must battle and kill the other Celestials until the cosmos are realigned once again. In the distant past, the Celestials were said to be split into three major fractions as they fight for supremacy. The result of that secret battle is never known. How true that is, even the Jade Emperor does not know."

She added, "Yi Ping, can you smash through the floors of the inscriptions?"

Yi Ping was startled, "For? It is a pity to ruin the inscriptions even if it is not true…"

Lele said coolly, "Just do as I say please. There is something inside the floor."

Yi Ping was startled as he asked, "How do you know?"

Lele said, "This is my guts feeling."

She was looking at him tenderly and she seemed to be pleading with him.

Yi Ping sighed deeply before he mustered all his martial power with his Aspire Invocations and smashed at the inscriptions with his Aspire Horizon Hands!

To his surprise, the floor broke through easily and indeed, it was shallow and had an opening at the bottom!

Ding Yun was startled as she said, "It is really hollow."

Inside the hollow floor, there was a yellow scroll and a long sword. Lele immediately grabbed it and unravel the scroll.

Yi Ping asked, "What it is?"

Lele held it with trembling hands as she gasped startlingly, "This scroll…this scroll actually lists all the state of celestial divinity from start to end. Even the Jade Emperor does not know all the stages and we have been practicing blindly! Genesis, Enlighten, Emotion, Transverse, Seventh Sense, Crisis and Ascend. So she was actually at the last state of divinity when she turned to ashes…"

She continued to read, "Alas, I am actually at the Emotion state of divinity." She looked tenderly at Yi Ping and sighed, "No wonder I am so vulnerable to emotions. The scroll says that every state of divinity have a hidden crisis and the practitioner would get particular vulnerable towards the very end. I didn't know that and did not guard against it…I would die soon?"

Yi Ping immediately turned ashen as he said firmly, "Lele, you won't die. No matter what, I will protect you."

Lele was touched. She looked at Yi Ping shyly as she said, "Actually I know that I won't survive the next Divine Calamity. I won't lie to you. I am…glad to know you, however briefly."

Yi Ping was stunned. He quickly said, "No Lele, you won't. I will help you…"

Lele smiled gently, "You can't and you only get yourself killed. You have no idea how terrifying the Divine Calamity is."

Ding Yun said, "The maiden in the center, she is able to get so far ahead?"

Lele nodded as she browsed through the scroll as she muttered, "There are many intricate heart formulas and methods recorded in this scroll. This scroll is simply too amazing…but it is already too late for me."

All of a sudden, she saw something towards the end of the scroll that startled her. She did not read it aloud.

The end of the scroll wrote, "Dearest Sister, even with my divine cultivation, there is a limit to my divination and it will add on to my calamity. However, it is my last resort already. As you read this, I am no longer in this world. If destiny is willing and fate allows, we will surely meet again in another time. I hope that I may have reached you in time to avert your Divine Calamity. By now, your state of divinity would be high enough to enter the Celestial Annihilating Star Formations. This is the only way to undo your past mistakes. Your sword is the key to the seal."

She kept the scroll and picked the long white sword, unsheathing it.

When she unsheathed it, she was mesmerized by its ringing sound and its brilliant light.

Ding Yun immediately said, "It is a good sword!"

Even Yi Ping who was not good in appraising swords was awestruck by the resounding beauty of the sword. He said, "What a good sword. I wonder what the name of this sword is."

Lele said quietly, "Divine Echo. The name of this sword is Divine Echo. I seem to have wielded this sword before…"

As she held this long sword, it seemed that her fighting spiriting was aroused and a part of her memory was revived.

For no hymn and reason, there were silent tears in her eyes.

Yi Ping said, "Lele?"

Ding Yun said softly, "Sister Le, you are alright?"

But still Lele did not respond. She was completely mesmerized by the long sword!

Yi Ping was worried as he held her and shook her, "Lele, are you alright? Is something amiss?"

It was only then that Lele recovered from her stupor.

Lele asked all of a sudden, "Where am I? How long have I been away?"

Yi Ping and Ding Yun were both startled by her.

Yi Ping said, "You are here all along. You seem to be in a daze for a while."

Lele sighed softly before she sighed gently, "Is that so?"

Her voice seemed to have changed and it had become more gentle and compassionate.

Ding Yun gasped, "Lele, your hair has turned black!"

Lele stroked her hair as she smiled, "Oh really? That's wonderful."

Yi Ping was so astonished. It was because her transformation was so rapid and she was even more stunning than earlier. He could scarcely believe his very eyes that Lele would suddenly be so incredible mesmerizing. It was still the same her but her animus seemed to have changed.

It was a good thing that Yi Ping had the Absolute Spirits or else he would be mesmerizing by her in an instant for at this time, her transformation was at its strongest.

Even Ding Yun was incredulous at her sudden transformation. The other person that had this presence was the Celestial Fairy!

Lele said softly, "Thank you, Yi Ping..."

Yi Ping was startled, "Why are you thanking me?"

Lele said gently, "It is you that brought me to this place. I...I have averted the Divine Calamity and could practice the Celestial Force again."

Yi Ping was startled, "You have averted the Divine Calamity? How?"

Lele said softly, "Just now. I have gone through several tribulations. It may seem like a minute to you but to me, it seem like a hundred years had just passed. I have not only reversed my state of divinity but have also regained it again. I have not only made a breakthrough in my Emotion state of divinity but has even reached the Transverse initiate state of divinity."

Indeed while Lele was in a trance, she was guided by her memories and the Divine Echo as she entered one deadly Celestial Annihilating Star Formation after another that was in her mind. In some of the formations, she was trapped for years and could not escape. It took her considerable efforts to overcome one formation after another.

The Celestial Annihilating Star Formations, the only known Celestial Formations that could stop the Divine Calamity from reacting. This Celestial Formation consisted of sixty-four formations and another eight inner formations. It was a formation within a formation!

What seemed like a minute to Yi Ping and Ding Yun, had actually taken Lele one hundred years to be freed from the Celestial Annihilating Star Formations! That was why Lele had asked, "Where am I? How long have I been away?" That was because she had been away for so long that it took her a while to actually remember!

Because of her high state of divinity, she had averted the Divine Calamity and did not trigger it or else they would all be dead in an instant in this place!

Lele muttered to herself as she trembled slightly, "So I am Melody Star? Then where are Luminous Star and Revelation Star now? Do they have still had their memories? Sister Yun Xiao seems to have found a way to bring us together?"

She immediately extended her hand as she began to move her fingers rapidly. She gasped, "Uh, Luminous Star is in danger and Revelation Star has a forthcoming Divinity Calamity..."

Lele said to Yi Ping and Ding Yun as she took bold strides forward, "Follow me quickly!"

Yi Ping asked, "Where to?"

Lele smiled enchanting, "Out of course. I know the way out."

Yi Ping was startled, "Lele, you know the way out?"

Lele laughed softly, "I think so. This place is created like a celestial formation. How on earth you have managed to find this chamber is pure luck. But luck alone won't get us out as we are already trapped in this formation. But I know how this formation works and may get us out. So, follow me."

Ding Yun nodded, "No wonder this place gives me a weird feeling and seems to be like a huge maze."

Yi Ping smiled bitterly, "The minute I enter this cave, I am already lost."

Lele rebuked him gently, "You should study more, especially on the eight diagrams. Then you won't get lost and it would be good for your martial progression."

Chapter 38: The Honor Manor and the Virtuous Palace

The forest was at the foot of the grandeur Tranquil Mountains.

But Nangong Le was in no mood to enjoy the scenery.

The normally serene forest was filled with the cries of the wounded and an overwhelming malevolent air was everywhere. And dozens of dead and wounded fighters were everywhere!

At this moment, his friends were all in mortal danger and he could only grit his teeth with his Exuberant Divine Skill as he watched them battled and fell!

He had just been wounded by Zuo Tianyi.

As for Gongsun Jing, he was near mortally wounded by Zuo Tianyi and he was battling for his life besides him!

Nangong Le had thought that by bringing his friends to the Tranquil Clan, they would be safe. But a remnant of the Honor Manor, consisting of some of the most powerful fighters in the fraternity was actually lying in wait and stormed the Tranquil Mountains!

Even his friend, Priest Ling Kongquan had just been injured by the Heartless Scholar and was closing his eyes in mediation as he tried to recuperate from his internal injuries!

And now Qiu Wufeng was fighting for his very life against the Lu Baiyun the Heartless Scholar!

Nangong Le said hastily to Priest Ling Kongquan, "Brother Kongquan, I have dragged you and your protégés into this. I'm sorry…"

Priest Ling Kongquan laughed with his eyes closed, "The protégés of the Tranquil Clan are all from an orthodox clan and are all not afraid of death…"

Priest Bai Chongzhen, the protégé leader of the Traverse Clan coughed out blood as he added, "The protégés of the Traverse Clan are not afraid of death too!"

At this, all the protégés of the Traverse were shouting, "The protégés of the Traverse are not afraid of death!"

The Traverse Clan was one of the seven major orthodox clans in the martial fraternity and was situated in the Western Fraternity. When they had received word that the Honor Manor was mounting an invasion to the Western Fraternity, they refused to rally the orthodox fighters.

This action upset the Honor Manor and the Traverse Clan was one of the first clans to be attacked by the powerful Honor Manor and was accused of betraying the righteous martial code of the alliance!

Priest Bai Chongzhen then fled with dozens of his surviving protégés to the Tranquil Clan where they had regrouped.

For a time, the Tranquil and the Traverse Clan had held the Honor Manor back until the fighters from the Virtuous Clan began to join in the assault.

Priest Bai Chongzhen looked sadly at the dozens of protégés from the two clans that had been slain by the Honor Manor as well as the numerous volunteer heroes from the Western Fraternity that had volunteered to fight for their cause.

He muttered sadly, "I have no wine to toast to the fallen heroes."

They were now being surrounded and outnumbered by hundreds of fighters from the Honor Manor. Most of their fighters on their side were wounded or too weak to fight.

The injured and the weak were now forced to watch the ongoing battle as it turned into a several groups of personalize duels!

It was as though an invisible line had been drawn between the combatants and the injured!

Zuo Tianyi who had just fatally stabbed Nangong Le with his long sword was smirking, "Nangong Le, you are not dead yet! Do you dare to fight me again, or do any of you dare to fight with me?"

Nangong Le laughed weakly, "If you want to get me, come over here first! Or else wait for me to take a short breath first and then I will challenge you!"

To Nangong Le and Zuo Tianyi surprise, Gongsun Jing had opened his eyes as he shouted hatefully to Zuo Tianyi, "You vile beast. I will kill you…"

Zuo Tianyi hummed coldly as he cast his eyes at the fights.

Qiu Wufeng was fighting like a berserker against the Heartless Scholar who seemed to be toying with him. The Heartless Scholar was Qiu Wufeng's former mentor, turned enemy who had slain most of his clan and had framed him!

Ji Lingfeng was fighting with Jue Yuan the Merciless Monk.

She was having a hard time against Jue Yuan! It was only her extraordinary swiftness that had prevented Jue Yuan from hitting her but the constant movements had taken a toll on her already faltering strength even as she exchanged blows with Jue Yuan!

Jue Yuan laughed, "Do you still have the strength to use the Aspire Divine Hands? I was caution the last time. But now I know that you are the Holy Maiden of the Holy Hex Sect and could only practice the Holy Amalgamate Skill, I am not afraid of your Aspire Divine Hands anymore. Compared to that foolish young man Yi Ping, your martial power isn't strong enough! Why don't you give up and marry me?"

Ji Lingfeng hummed coldly, "A monk can get married? Shameless!"

Jue Yuan had restrained from using his strength and his deadly stances. It was because part of the condition for the Virtuous Palace to join forces with the Honor Manor was that they had wanted the Holy Maiden Ji Lingfeng alive.

Priest Liu Qingcheng, the protégé master of the Tranquil Clan was fighting with Xiao Fei.

He too, was having a hard time and was fighting for his life. No matter how fast he had switched his stances and strokes, it could not stop Xiao Fei at all.

Xiao Fei had expected to defeat Priest Liu Qingcheng with little efforts but it was proving to take a longer time that he had anticipated. But he was in no hurry. He could tell that Priest Liu Qingcheng was sweating heavily with his physical and mental fortitude being drained away with every stroke that he had made. So he was in no hurry.

The reason why Priest Liu Qingcheng had fared better than what Xiao Fei had expected was that he had advanced in his Dual Inertness Intricacy and being bolstered by the Tranquil Spirits. Moreover his two protégé disciples Yu'Er and Mei'Er were still fighting and no matter what happened, he refused to be defeated first due to face saving measures.

Because of that simple reason, he had fought nonstop for two hours that caused even Xiao Fei's martial strength to falter!

Xiao Fei was now sweating heavily as he said coldly, "You are a worthy opponent and better than a lot of fighters that I have encountered. I am careless."

However, the reason why Xiao Fei and Xiao Da were staying their hands and refused to display their secret techniques were because there were too many people here and Lie Qing was observing them!

Even if they had to use their secret techniques, it would be against the maiden with the crimson eyes who was watching intently at their every fighting strokes and stances!

They were aware of it and part of their attention was also on her.

If their opponent would kill even Xiao Yuanjia, then he or she had to be a super exponent and they were not taking any risks.

The twin sisters of the Eternal Ice Palace, Yu'Er the Jade Sword and Mei'Er the Beautiful Sword were fighting against Xiao Da.

Xiao Da was an extremely formidable foe.

That had caught Yu'Er and Mei'Er by surprise as he could break their Divine Emerald Skill!

Xiao Da was eying them lustfully and he could barely contain his inner lust as he thought, "There are four great beauties here. Father wants the Holy Maiden, alas while the maiden with the crimson eyes who is also the most desirable is our mortal foe. I guess I have to make do with these two maidens then."

It actually would not take much time for Xiao Da to defeat the twin sisters but he had taken much longer than he had expected because they seemed to be able to predict his moves and the cold energies of their swordplay were able to negate his malevolent despair.

Moreover, most of his techniques and strokes were meant for killing. Staying his hand was a much more difficult thing than he had expected.

There were a few times that he had the opportunity to deal them a heavy blow, rather than with his long sword but he had also stayed his hand. It was because he was afraid of Xiao Shuai, his father. Xiao Shuai had warned anyone in the Virtuous Palace not to harm any female protégés from the Eternal Ice Palace or else they would be faced with the harshest of the clan punishments.

And Xiao Shuai was someone who had shown no mercy even to his own kin, including his brothers.

Xiao Da laughed as he flashed his sword from left to right, "Why don't the two of you be my concubines?"

Yu'Er and Mei'Er exclaimed indignantly at the same time, "Dream on!"

There were dozens of pugilists from both sides that were also watching the duels keenly and were awestruck by their extraordinary martial display as they held their breath.

In time to come, Qiu Wufeng would be renowned for his courage and had the fraternity name of the Courageous Windless Swordsman.

Yuan Shao was looking patiently at the fights. It was because victory was inevitable and he was looking intently at a young beautiful maiden on the other side who was stroking her long hair slowly as though she was just a speculator. This enchanting maiden gave him a disturbed feeling, primary because of her red crimson eyes.

Because she did not make her move yet, he had bid his time as well. It was because the other maiden with silvery white hair that he had fought against with many days ago had crimson eyes too and she was an extremely dangerous exponent. Therefore he waited for her to make her first move so that he could gauge her strength.

She was also extremely enchanting and beholden to look at, causing many of the hearts of the fighters to be consumed by lust for her, weakening their resolute.

Yuan Shao thought, "Is she also waiting for me to make my first move and attack me with a surprise attack?"

When he had recalled the terrifying swiftness movement of the young maiden with silver hair, he knew that this amount of distance would not defer his opponent from making an attack in any direction.

Zuo Tianyi had finished his duel and had quietly walked towards him. There were no more fighters from the other side that dared to challenge him anymore.

Zuo Tianyi said, "Master Yuan Shao, it seems like Xiao Da needs some help. Maybe I should help him…"

Yuan Shao stared at him, saying coldly. "With me around, you don't have to be so concerned. If you are to hurt any of the protégés from the Eternal Ice Palace, don't blame me for being merciless even if you have the protection of the Honor Manor."

Zuo Tianyi smiled bitterly, "I dare not!"

Yuan Shao asked, "Who is that maiden with red eyes and a black sword on the other side?"

Zuo Tianyi said, "She is Lie Qing."

Yuan Shao said, "Which protégé clan is she from?"

Zuo Tianyi said, "She claims to be from the New Virtuous Palace. Where she is from previously, I really do not know."

Yuan Shao was startled, "She is from the New Virtuous Palace?"

He quickly regained his composure and asked, "How is her martial level?"

Zuo Tianyi replied coolly, "She is good with the sword but she can't fight now."

Yuan Shao asked, "Why is that so?"

Zuo Tianyi said, "She doesn't have internal strength now, having lost it in a recent fight."

Yuan Shao asked, "Really?!"

Zuo Tianyi smiled, "There is no reason for me to lie to you. We are on the same side now. Even the weakest of the Honor Manor can take her down anytime."

Yuan Shao was alarmed as he cursed venomously!

It was because they had all fallen for her bluff stratagem. The reason why they had hesitated was because of they were caution of the Red Eye Clan!

Yuan Shao immediately raised his cane and had dashed towards Lie Qing!

Lie Qing immediately turned ashen as she cursed Zuo Tianyi silently.

She had used up half of her Invincible Divine Force in an attempt to save Xiao Youxue. It was because Xiao Youxue and Yi Ping were her benefactors. She had unwittingly caused Xiao Youxue to be grievously injured and it was the least that she could do. Of course, most would not even consider giving up their intricate energy for anyone but Lie Qing would do it for Xiao Youxue!

By half of her Invincible Divine Force, it had actually meant all of her internal strength. It was because the other half of her Invincible Divine Force was her inherent life force and could not be given away.

She quietly said to herself, "Lie Qing, you are only living on borrow time. You should be glad instead that to be alive again for these past several months. Yi Ping, Youxue…I am so glad to know you…both of you may not be alive anymore so what there for me to live for now?"

As Yuan Shao dashed across with startling speed, Yu'Er and Mei'Er saw him and tried to intercept him as they raised their long precious swords against him.

Yuan Shao simply raised his fingers as he avoided the furies of their cold beaming swords, striking both Yu'Er and Mei'Er as their Divine Emerald Skills were penetrated by his Soul Stealer Fingers!

Both Yu'Er and Mei'Er crumbled onto the ground in an instant with shrieked cries!

Even as Yuan Shao had struck down the twin sisters, Ji Lingfeng had flew towards him and raised her entire martial power, unleashing the explosive shrieking might of the Aspire Horizon Hand at him!

Yuan Shao immediately switched his Soul Stealer Finger towards the almighty force of the Aspire Horizon Hand as his fingers struck her palm with a thunderous impact!

Ji Lingfeng was sent flying backward as she coughed out blood!

The martial power of Yuan Shao's Divine Virtuous Force and his Soul Stealer Finger was startling!

All of a sudden, a young man in white dashed past and caught hold of Ji Lingfeng in mid-air!

It was Yi Ping!

Ji Lingfeng smiled tearfully as she muttered weakly, "Yi Ping, is that really you? You are still alive?"

Yi Ping nodded, "Lingfeng, it is really me. I am here!"

Just as Yuan Shao had almost flown to Lie Qing, he had suddenly backed off!

It was because an extraordinary beautiful maiden in red dress had suddenly intercepted him in mid-air with her long black scythe!

It was Lele!

Nangong Le and Qiu Wufeng shouted excitedly, "Yi Ping!"

They had also saw a beautiful maiden with extraordinary splendor that they could not recognized but the fact that she could cause Yuan Shao to back off gave them some hope!

Ding Yun had come to the aid of Priest Liu Qingcheng as she caused Xiao Fei to back off at the same time too!

Xiao Fei said coolly, "Yunzi, why are you on their side? Have you forgotten what awaits traitors?"

Ding Yun replied coldly, "Ding Yunzi is dead. From now on, I am just Ding Yun."

Lie Qing covered her mouth in utter disbelief as she burst into tears when she saw Yi Ping!

Yi Ping had quietly helped Yu'Er and Mei'Er up. It was as though Xiao Da was not there.

Xiao Da had hesitated because this young man had a frightening aura and he did not want to take any unnecessary risks.

Yi Ping was trembling even as he checked Yu'Er and Mei'Er for internal injuries.

Yu'Er said weakly, "Master, I'm alright. Don't worry about me. You…are still alive…I am so glad…"

Mei'Er was more emotional as she cried in Yi Ping embrace.

Yi Ping shouted angrily, "Yuan Shao!"

This shout startled everyone by its sheer explosive power and caused everyone except those with strong internal strength to take a few steps backward, causing many of the fighters to cup their ears with their hands!

Yi Ping clenched his fists tightly as he stared angrily at Yuan Shao!

He tried to suppress his bursting rage but when he saw the sorry state that his companions had been and how close they were to death, he had totally lost his cool.

It was because Yi Ping had now returned to a distant past when his mother, Shui Yichi was dying in front of his eyes. At that time, he was just only five but he blamed himself for being so weak. All of a sudden, he could see the dainty sight of his beloved mother moving into his vision, as she displayed one extraordinary stance after the other!

Xiao Da, Xiao Fei, Jue Yuan and Zuo Tianyi had immediately regrouped behind Yuan Shao.

Nangong Le, Lie Qing, Ding Yun, Lele, Yu'Er, Mei'Er, Qiu Wufeng, Ji Lingfeng and Priest Liu Qingcheng had also gathered behind Yi Ping as they supported one another as they all shouting excitedly, "Yi Ping…Yi Ping!"

Lie Qing had quietly walked besides Yi Ping and held his arm as she said gently, "You are here at last…"

Lie Qing touch was electrifying and Yi Ping returned to his senses. He looked at Lie Qing, Ding Yun, Lele, Yu'Er, Mei'Er and Ji Lingfeng as he muttered gently, "Everyone…"

It was the first time that Lele had seen Lie Qing but she had recognized her. Her looks and her crimson eyes were obvious. She wanted to say something to her but Lie Qing seemed to be totally oblivion to anyone except for Yi Ping.

The rest of the fighters that were on the side of the Tranquil Clan were aroused by Yi Ping. It was as though his presence alone could move their fighting spirits by unseen hands and many who had fallen or too weak to move had also got up on their feet, including Priest Bai Chongzhen and even Gongsun Jing!

Even though most of them were now too weak to fight except for Ding Yun and Lele, Yi Ping was like a giant spiritual pillar that was supporting them as they stood defiantly against their foes!

The powerful martial shout displayed by Yi Ping and his righteous air had even caused the fighters on the side of the Honor Manor to be hesitant, affecting their resolute.

Moreover, Yi Ping was being recognized as the young fighter that had dared to challenge Zuo Tianyi, Jue Yuan and Gu Tianle singlehandedly back at the Honor Manor!

There were muttering among the fighters that were on the side of the Honor Manor as they asked, "Is he the one that fight against Master Gu Tianle in the Honor Manor?"

Yuan Shao had never seen someone who could ignite the fighting spirits of the fallen in such a manner. But he was not worried as he had recognized the three newly arrivals. Just not too long ago, he had just defeated them. He was only curious how did their external injuries healed this fast?

Ding Yun he could understand because the Divine Virtuous Force had a healing effect. But as for the young man Yi Ping and the young maiden in red dress? All in all, he had remembered stabbing Yi Ping more than thirty times!

Did Ding Yun secretly teach them the Divine Virtuous Force?

Yuan Shao could only say coldly, "Good! You are all here. It will save us much trouble from eliminating you elsewhere."

Xiao Da laughed aloud, "I have thought who it is. It is just a young man, a young maiden and Yunzi. Yunzi, have you forgotten all about me already?"

Ding Yun's expressions were cold and did not reply. But her fingers were subtly trembling and she was filled with dread and hatred for Xiao Da!

Yuan Shao pointed at Yi Ping as he asked aloud, "He is Yi Ping? And who is this maiden here?"

He was pointing at the young and beautiful maiden in red dress.

It was only then, everyone except Yi Ping and Ding Yun had realized no one knew know who this enchanting maiden was, even though she was too attractive to go unnoticed!

Only Ji Lingfeng had recognized her even though she had never seen the Celestial Envoy without her terrifying mask!

Her red dress, her long black scythe and distinctly mannerism had told her it was the Celestial Envoy but she had thought that the Celestial Envoy was an old woman because of her silvery white hair…

But the fact that she could beat off Yuan Shao, had already raised several eyebrows.

Even Lie Qing was now looking at her and was startled to see that she had the same crimson red eyes as her!

Even Xiao Da and Xiao Fei were intrigued by her. Because she was able to cause Yuan Shao to back off with a single stroke, her martial prowess was not to be underestimated!

Xiao Da was looking lustfully at her and was smiling.

Moreover, they were reminded of the legends of the Red Eye Clan that their elders had always told them to remember. And today, there were two of them!

Lele swung her heavy long black scythe with one hand and thrust it into the ground quietly as she sighed softly, "Who I am?"

It was only then almost everyone who was watching her was caught off-guard by her martial display!

It was because for her to wield the seemingly long black metal scythe weightlessness was a display of her martial prowess upon itself. For her to thrust the blade of the scythe totally into the ground was a seemingly impossible feat!

It was a feat that even Yi Ping and Yuan Shao could not accomplish despite their martial strength!

Yuan Shao was slightly taken aback as was everyone. Her scythe just seemed to go through the ground seemingly like it was tofu. One must know that that the ground was covered only with a thin layer of soil, beneath it was just hardened earth and was filled with rocky debris. Moreover the blade of her scythe was curved, making it even harder.

Yuan Shao, Xiao Da, Xiao Fei, Zuo Tianyi, Jue Yuan and Lu Baiyun immediately knew that her internal strength was at the peak and extremely potent.

They just could not figure out how she was able to do it despite her young age for internal strength unlike martial power, could only be cultivate slowly.

Take Yi Ping for example, his internal strength could be cultivated through the Divine Revelation, an intricate formula to circulate intricate energy but his powerful martial power had come from the Aspire Invocation which enhanced his martial strength.

Internal strength and martial strength was therefore related, however it was not the same. How strong one's martial strength may be dependable on the practitioner's internal strength foundation but it was also somewhat related to the strength of the martial skill too.

Yi Ping's Divine Horizon Hands, the Aspire Horizon Hand required decades of internal strength foundation before he could use this powerful stance. The martial power of the Aspire Horizon Hand had come from the Aspire Invocation which drew its strength from the intricate energies of the practitioner.

Practitioners like Lele and Shui Yixian may seemingly lacked martial strength in their attacks and appeared weaker but that was an illusion. It was because they were the practitioners of the internal martial arts while Yi Ping focused on his martial strength.

Practitioner like Yuan Shao was versatile fighter, switching between martial strength to use sword techniques and internal strength to use the Soul Stealer Fingers while Zuo Tianyi's infinity swordplay at the higher levels actually required a combination of both, especially at the sword energy staging.

While everyone was still taken aback, Yuan Shao, Xiao Da and Xiao Fei had immediately eyed her fingernails, her hair decorations, her long sleeves, her dress, her sword scabbard and her footwear. There was not a single area that they had spared!

It was not because they were lustful but because they were looking for concealed weapons and secret projectiles!

They had observed that she had short fingernails and that would mean that she could be expert in unarmed combat as well!

While Lu Baiyun, Zuo Tianyi, Jue Yuan and many of her opponents were also looking at her, they were quickly mesmerized by her eyes and had forgotten that she was actually their foe!

In no time, Zuo Tianyi, Lu Baiyun and Jue Yuan were filled with lust, just as they were filled with lust for Lie Qing.

Lele exhaled softly, "Who I am? I am the Celestial Envoy."

She purposely waited for her words to be sunk in as she added, "The Celestial Envoy is naturally from the Celestial Palace. I am the Joyful Goddess. Since you are all in my presence, hurry and bow before me with your full condolences!"

At the mention of the Celestial Palace, dozens of fighters from both sides were suddenly paralyzed with fear!

Even though few people in the fraternity could ascertain that the Celestial Palace was even real but there were many dreadful rumors about the Celestial Palace!

No one had ever lived to return from the Celestial Mountains!

Even though the Honor Manor and the Virtuous Palace knew that they were going to attack the Celestial Palace, most had thought that it was just an excuse for a punitive attack to against the unorthodox clans of the Western Fraternity.

It was the fearful invisible hand of the Celestial Palace in the Western Fraternity that had prevented the different orthodox and unorthodox clans in that fraternity to fight openly with one another. That was also the reason why most of the unorthodox clans had also originated from the Western Fraternity!

Even Yuan Shao's face had a twitch at the mere mention of the Celestial Palace!

Just as Lele was secretly feeling gleefully at the startled shock and the uneasiness of her opponents, Yi Ping had stepped forward and said. "She is Lele and she is no Goddess."

This startled Lele and she was secretly scolding him in her heart despite her high state of divinity!

It was because in the fraternity, the pugilists rarely revealed their real names and only use their fraternity names. But Yi Ping obviously did not know that. Maidens like Lele, Ji Lingfeng, Lie Qing, Shui Yixian and Xiao Youxue were willing to tell him their real name only because they had liked him!

Lele had painfully orchestrated an awe striking scene to win the psychology battle so that they could gain an upper hand or at least break even over their deadly foes. It was because there were only three of them who could fight while their enemies numbered in the dozens!

Ji Lingfeng sighed softly. She had almost gave Yi Ping a kick as she sighed silently, "You stupid pig!"

The only person on Yi Ping's side that did not care was Lie Qing as she had already surrendered to her fate and was grateful for the borrowed time. There was only a devoted affection in her eyes for Yi Ping…

Even before Lele could recover from her initial shock, Yi Ping said. "You can all come at me at the same time!"

She nearly fainted from shock, as almost everyone else was also shocked by his bold declaration, including their opponents!

Chapter 39: Melody Star and Luminous Star

Yi Ping of course was not thinking when he had made the bold challenge. He only said that in a moment of anger!!

For a moment, everyone was stunned even as Yi Ping had already stepped forward and had extended his hands in a combat stance!

Ji Lingfeng was the first to recover her wits as she stepped forward besides Yi Ping, saying weakly, "Yi Ping, I am willing to fight alongside with you!"

Yi Ping was touched. Just as he was about to speak, Yu'Er and Mei'Er had also stepped forward as they cried out empathically, "Master, we are also willing to fight alongside with you!"

Ding Yun wanted to step forward too but her modesty held her back…

Lie Qing's heart was wrenched and she was trying extremely hard to hold back her tears because she knew that Yi Ping's very act was suicidal. She wished silently that she had her internal strength back again…

Lele was looking emotionlessly at Yi Ping and was surprised that so many maidens were willing to disregard their lives for him.

The onlookers were envy at the sight.

Gongsun Jing, Nangong Le and Qiu Wufeng may be envy but they were not jealous of Yi Ping. In fact, the maidens were not jealous of one another. They had been through much together in these past few days and had helped to pull one another till this point.

Even Lele who did not go through life and death with them, could see the spark of life in their eyes when they were looking at Yi Ping.

Yi Ping held Ji Lingfeng, Yu'Er and Mei'Er hands one by one as he said, "Everyone…Life and death is predestined. You should treat your internal injuries first lest it worsens."

Ji Lingfeng muttered, "What is the point if you have died?"

Yu'Er said melancholy, "Mast…"

She gulped and said gently, "Yi Ping…I'm so sorry…actually Protégé Mistress, she is still alive…"

Yi Ping smiled gently as he patted her shoulder, "Yu'Er I know. Maiden Ding has told me the truth already."

Mei'Er had already burst into tears as she flew into his embrace, sobbing. "Master Yi Ping, evil cannot triumph over good. Remember it."

Yi Ping turned and said gently to Ding Yun, "Yun, protect them…don't let the flying swords of the Virtuous Palace accidentally hurt them. You are the only one that knows this technique well enough…"

Ding Yun nodded silently as her eyes swelled. It was because she would rather fight alongside with him!

Ding Yun whispered, "Be extra wary of Xiao Da. While most of us only know one stance from the Unbreakable Hands which is the Penetrating Hand, Xiao Shuai has taught him the Breaking Hand and the Eighteen Folds of the Unbreakable Hands."

Yi Ping nodded.

Ding Yun added, "And that Xiao Fei, he is also an extremely formidable fighter. Many fighters that were stronger than him were killed by him in the past."

While Ding Yun was whispering to Yi Ping, Ji Lingfeng looked at Lele with pleading eyes. "The Celestial Envoy, I hope that you can assist Yi Ping."

Lele said coolly, "Are you threatening me again? I have already helped you the last time. Remember your promise to the Celestial Palace."

Ji Lingfeng became quiet.

Actually among all the maidens, Lele was the most intimate to Yi Ping. Only Ding Yun knew about their special relationship. It was just that Lele did not feel comfortable to disclose it.

Lele said coldly, "Since he likes to be a hero, let him be."

Yi Ping sniffed deeply and smiled. Even though Lele appeared to be cold, he was actually glad at heart. It was because he really did not want her to risk her life.

Even though Lele was acting cold but she was actually sighing to herself, "I know that you don't want me to fight but do you think I will watch by the fence and do nothing?"

Jue Yuan interrupted by shouting, "Young rascal, you have thought too highly of yourself! You can't even defeat me and you wanted to challenge the entire lot of us? What a joke!"

Jue Yuan had already stepped forward and had raised his martial power, displaying his famous martial feat, the Merciless Palms!

Yi Ping did not waste a moment more as he quickly dashed forward to meet Jue Yuan headlong!

Because Jue Yuan had underestimated Yi Ping the last time and did not use his full strength, he was determined not to make the same mistake again. Therefore he had raised his martial power to the fullest while shouting to Yi Ping, "Rascal, do you dare to take a blow from my palm?"

Yi Ping did not hesitate at all as he shouted back, "Who is afraid of you?"

Both Yi Ping and Jue Yuan had raised their palms and clashed mightily at one another as everyone held their breath!

There was a thunderous clap that exploded mightily as Yi Ping took three steps backward before he could steady himself!

Jue Yuan took six steps backward dazedly and at the end of the sixth step, he coughed out blood!

Yi Ping took a deep breath and circulated his intricate energy with the Divine Revelation as he calmed his heartbeat down. He was otherwise unharmed!

Lu Baiyun immediately caught Jue Yuan in his arm as he said, "Master Jue Yuan, are you alright?"

Jue Yuan simply could not believe that this young man Yi Ping's martial power had surpassed him by such a wide gap even as he stared furiously at him!

The fighters from the Honor Manor were stunned that Master Jue Yuan, one of the top exponents of the Honor Manor could not take one blow from Yi Ping!

Jue Yuan wiped away his mouthful of blood with his sleeve as he took out his prayer beads as he shouted, "Tianyi and Brother Lu, what are you waiting for? Attack him!"

Lu Baiyun and Zuo Tianyi immediately stepped forward with their long swords.

Xiao Da smirked, "It seems that the Honor Manor may need some help after all."

Xiao Da was the young master of the Virtuous Palace and the only successor to Xiao Shuai now after his brother Xiao Yuanjia had died. It was not wrong to say that he represented the Virtuous Palace in the absence of Xiao Shuai!

At this moment, he was looking intently at Ji Lingfeng. It was because she was the very reason why the Virtuous Palace was here. Upon receiving news that she was sighed in the vicinity, Clan Protégé Master Xiao Shuai immediately dispatched him with the highest urgency to bring her back alive to him.

He was wondering why his father was so eager to have her. After seeing her exquisite alluring beauty, he was gritting his teeth. Even though he was unwilling to hand her over to his father but he was fearful of him.

Moreover, his father had sent Yuan Shao who was also the Elder of the Virtuous Palace to keep watch on him. Therefore he could only secretly sigh.

But he was quickly looking gleefully at Yu'Er, Mei'Er, Ding Yun, Lie Qing and Lele.

This was not gone unnoticed by Nangong Le who had clenched his fist and had wished that he could punch him right into his face!

Jue Yuan, Lu Baiyun and Zuo Tianyi were now encircling Yi Ping!

Zuo Tianyi said to Yi Ping, "Yi Ping, you have better drawn your sword. In the past, we may have fought to a draw but today, you are not my match."

Even as he was saying this, his sword seemed to be shimmering and his frightening sword energy began to spread out in all directions!

Even Yuan Shao and Xiao Da were startled at this phenomenon!

His sword energy was so powerful that it lifted the frightening malevolent air that Yuan Shao had exuded!

Indeed, it was the Infinity-One swordplay!

The Infinity-One swordplay was the highest epitome of the Infinity Swordplay. The Old Sword Saint spent decades pondering over the mysteries of the Infinity-One. While the Infinity-Two was the merging of sword and intricate energy which was called sword energy, the Infinity-One was the act of actually discharging it into deadly sword energies!

The Old Sword Saint had used the later part of his life to research the mythical Infinity-Zero but had failed. Only in his dying days, he had grasped part of the Infinity-Zero. And before he had passed away, he had instructed Zuo Tianyi on the possible intricate formula of the Infinity-First and the Infinity-Zero.

The Old Sword Saint had not expected Zuo Tianyi to grasp the full understanding of the Infinity-Zero for decades to come.

But Zuo Tianyi had.

That was because he had witnessed the duel between two super exponents, Lie Qing and the Celestial Fairy which greatly increased his understanding. Coupled with the near death experiences with Yuan Shao, he had finally grasped the Infinity-First!

Yi Ping could sense the terrifying sword energies that exuded from Zuo Tianyi's sword.

Zuo Tianyi said coldly, "You won't be so lucky this time."

Even as he had said that, he had hacked at Yi Ping with a downward slice.

Even as Yi Ping had parried it with his emerald phoenix sword, he could feel the cold beaming energy that pierced through his sword to his arm!

Yi Ping could sense his sword arm weakening but he quickly raised his martial strength and immediately retaliated with the Divine Horizon Hand with his left hand but Zuo Tianyi avoided it by taking a step back.

All of a sudden, Lu Baiyun the Heartless Scholar had seized the attack opportunity to come from his back, as was Jue Yuan with his prayer beads!

The Heartless Swordsman was a master swordsman and was ranked at one of the top exponents of the martial fraternity.

Lie Qing could not help shouting aloud, "Look out!"

Yi Ping immediately whirled his long sword and displayed the Horizon Swordplay, parrying the attackers.

In an instant, Yi Ping, Lu Baiyun, Jue Yuan and Zuo Tianyi were attacking so fast that there were waves of windforce and cold beaming sword energy everywhere!

In all, they had exchanged more than one hundred strokes in a short while!

The onlookers were amazed as they could sense Zuo Tianyi's sword energies were getting more powerful while Yi Ping's martial power was also increasing!

All of a sudden, Yi Ping gave a loud shout even as a dozen Horizon Sword Strokes were exchanged in the intermediate!

Ji Lingfeng gasped, "The Asper Continuum Horizon Hands!"

But instead of the Asper Continuum Horizon Hands, Yi Ping had merged it with the Horizon Swordplay!

Lele had almost dashed into their midst because she knew how deadly sword energy in its physical form really was. She was startled that this Zuo Tianyi had actually attained such a high state of divinity.

Just as she was about to dash into their midst, Yi Ping had dispelled the seeming impossible to block sword energies with multiple waves of martial power windforce!

She thought, "When did Yi Ping learn how to merge his Divine Horizon Hand with his Horizon Swordplay? And that enemy swordsman, he has actually such a high state of divinity but he will soon trigger the Divine Calamity and will die very soon. At this point, his blood and heart is the most precious to the Celestial Palace…"

But she continued to be nervous. It was because she knew that Yi Ping could not sustain his martial power for long and would eventually be defeated!

All of a sudden, Jue Yuan was forcefully pushed back by the rippling windforce of the Horizon Swordplay and he was torn apart by the cold piercing waves of Zuo Tianyi's sword energies!

Lu Baiyun barely escaped even as he parried dozens of forceful windforce coming from Yi Ping and the sword energy arcs that had circulated from Zuo Tianyi at the same time!

He was struck on his chest by the Asper Continuum Horizon Hands and was mortally wounded by three piercing sword energies!

Even as Lu Baiyun fled back to the safety lines of his camp in startled shock, "Zuo Tianyi, you have dared to kill Master Jue…"

Before he could finish, he was forced to take three additional steps backward as another powerful bout of windforce struck him!

Everyone was gasping at the death duel between Yi Ping and Zuo Tianyi, forcing to move backward even as they watched!

They could only see two dark shadows in the middle, the shrieking clanging of the swords and the thunderous explosive clanking sound of their blows. The windforce that were generated, were unlike any that they had seen before!

Yu'Er and Mei'Er had leapt forward as they raised their fingers as they displayed the Divine Emerald Skill, shielding their companions from the deadly cold energies that had flew in their direction!

The other side was not as fortunately as a dozen of the onlookers were killed instantly even though they were all standing a good distance. This immediately caused a panic and many of the fighters of the Honor Manor began to retreat hastily to a safer position!

Only Xiao Da, Xiao Fei and Yuan Shao remained on their ground and were watching the duel with eager anticipation.

Xiao Fei said, "I didn't know that the Honor Manor has such a highly skillful fighter on their side. I have thought that the young protégé master of the Infinity Sword Clan is just a useless thing. Now, this is interesting."

Xiao Da hummed coldly, "Xiao Fei, let's add something more interesting and create some havoc before I get bored."

Yuan Shao looked sternly at Xiao Da but Xiao Da already thrust four long swords onto the ground!

In split second, he had already drawn up the long sword one by one as he sent it spinning into the other side, displaying the Flying Sword Technique of the Virtuous Palace!

Ding Yun had already anticipated it as she quickly threw her sword into a flying spin as the first sword was deflected!

Yu'Er and Mei'Er had raised their long precious swords and had deflected the second and third flying swords!

The forth flying sword was deflected by Lele.

Xiao Da laughed as he said to Xiao Fei, "What do you think?" Even as he was speaking, he had already thrust a dozen swords in front of him!

Xiao Fei said coolly, "It seems that the other side has only four persons that could handle your flying swords. Of the four, only the Celestial Envoy seems to have the martial level to truly take your blow. The other three are not your match."

Even as Xiao Fei was talking, Xiao Da had thrown more than six flying swords to the other side!

Xiao Da said coolly, "Xiao Fei, come in and join in the fun."

Xiao Fei said, "We may hurt the twin sisters…"

Xiao Da said, "There is nothing to worry. We are not aiming at them. They can choose not to deflect our flying swords and avoid it entirely."

Yu'Er, Mei'Er and Ding Yun had already expended most of their martial strength to deflect the flying swords and had already taken several steps back!

Qiu Wufeng and Nangong Le had tried to deflect one of the flying swords but instead of stopping it, it sent them flying backward!

Ji Lingfeng caught of Qiu Wufeng and Nangong Le as she said hastily, "Everyone back!"

Luckily, the flying sword was deflected in a nick of time by Lele even as it flew past Nangong Le and Qiu Wufeng or else the consequences would be disastrous!

In the meantime, Yi Ping was fighting with his life as he displayed strokes after strokes with both his sword and palm. It was because if he stopped his martial force now, then he could not stop Zuo Tianyi's sword energy from hurting him.

Zuo Tianyi was not having an easy time too. He had thought that he could end Yi Ping's life with his Infinity-Zero with just a few strokes but Yi Ping's martial power was startling.

What Yi Ping lacked in techniques, he made it up with his extraordinary martial power.

Both Yi Ping and Zuo Tianyi were sweating heavily and panting breathlessness. It was because they were both fighting with all their martial powers and executing dozens of strokes at every instant. The first one to stop would lose!

Zuo Tianyi shouted as he displayed a barrage of strokes, "Yi Ping, why don't you give up!"

Yi Ping raised his martial power again with the Divine Revelation as he sent powerful rippling windforce with his sword towards Zuo Tianyi, "It is because I have people to protect. I cannot lose."

Zuo Tianyi hummed coldly, "What a noble mission. Nevertheless, it is still foolishness. You need skill to protect. If you beg me now, I may still let you live!"

Yi Ping raised his sword as he counterattacked with three rippling sword strokes even as he shouted back, "Zuo Tianyi, why are you on their side?! I have thought that you are my friend! Why did you do that to Ding Yun?"

Zuo Tianyi said, "It is because I don't want to die yet. As for Ding Yun, I am really disappointed with her…"

Yi Ping shouted in disappointment, "You don't have the right to criticize her!"

Zuo Tianyi laughed coldly, "I can even tell you this. I am also the one that have led the Honor Manor and the Virtuous Palace here."

In his moment of rage, Yi Ping had a momentary lapse in concentration and his left shoulder was pierced by Zuo Tianyi's Infinity-Five piercing stroke!

Just as Zuo Tianyi was about to attack Yi Ping again with another follow up attack, Lele had flew with startling speed towards them and interrupted his attack, slashing and slightly wounding Zuo Tianyi on his chest who was caught by surprise by her sudden appearance!

Yi Ping was startled as he shouted hastily, "How did you get into here? Get out of here now! It is far too dangerous!"

Lele had shocked and stunned everyone by moving into the death zone of the duel all of a sudden!

Everyone had expected her to be torn apart by the sword energies and the ripping windforce in the middle. But somehow she had made it to the middle unaffected, raising eyebrows from even Yuan Shao, Xiao Fei and Xiao Da.

Lele had reached the Transverse state of divinity of the Celestial Divinity. At this divine state, she could see the invisible waves of the dangerous sword energies. Moreover, the Divine Celestial Force was a defensive martial skill that could neutralize offensive energies. Lele present state of divinity with the Divine Celestial Force was such that she could disregard Zuo Tianyi's sword energies completely.

Lele ignored his warnings and threw the Divine Echo to him, "Yi Ping, use this sword!"

As Yi Ping unsheathed the sword, there was a low hymning sound as it shattered the surrounding sword energies, knocking Zuo Tianyi a few steps backward!

Zuo Tianyi was startled, "What kind of a sword is this?"

Just as Yi Ping was about to seize the opportunity to retaliate against Zuo Tianyi with the emerald phoenix sword and the Divine Echo, a flying sword flew with startling speed in front of him!

Even as he had raised both his swords with all his martial power, he was still knocked back a few steps backward.

Lele swung her long scythe to deflect the flying sword in time as she asked softly, "Yi Ping, are you alright?"

Xiao Fei, Xiao Da and Yuan Shao were now besides Zuo Tianyi!

Even Yuan Shao was asking, "What is this sword?" It was because he had never seen a sword that could hymn by itself and could even dispel sword energies!

Lele said coolly, "It is the Divine Echo."

Yuan Shao was startled. It was because the Divine Echo was a divine sword of legend and legends had stated it was the possession of one of the Divine Star Fairies. Even though Yuan Shao had read of it but it was after all just a beautiful legend and nobody had really seen it.

Even Xiao Fei and Zuo Tianyi were slightly taken aback.

Xiao Fei said coolly, "It is named after a sword of bygone days and is not the original."

Yi Ping said coldly, "Good, all of you have decided to join in the fight. What are we waiting for?"

Yuan Shao said coldly, "This maiden here. She claims she is from the Celestial Palace yet she didn't know the rules of the martial fraternity? Yet she has interrupted the duel."

Lele replied coldly, "This is just a vanity to seek honor and glory for all of you. For me, I intend to just fight alongside with Yi Ping."

Even as Lele was speaking, she had dismantled her long scythe into two sickles in both her hands and dropped the long black metal pole on the ground.

Yi Ping was touched but he stepped in front of Lele as he said, "Lele, step back. These opponents are far too dangerous for you."

Lele said softly, "Even knowing you may die? Why are you so foolish? Why are mortals so foolish and waste their lives in this manner? Why do you insist on being a hero? If we join hands, then we can still have a glimmer of hope."

Yi Ping said quietly, "It is because I want to protect all those that are dear to my heart."

Lele shook her head as she held his arm, sighing melancholy, "I don't understand why you are willing to forsake your precious life. I am an icy divine star from the heavens. Can you hear… the light stirring of my heart, do you know…what stirs my heart…you have awakened my emotions and filled my lonely life. Our hearts have exchanged intricate with each other…can you see the transparent mirror in my heart?"

Even though she was soft spoken but her slow, unhurried words were heard crystal clear by everyone and it was so heart wrenching that many fighters were moved to tears.

At this moment, everyone could sense the emotion stirrings of her heart!

It was because due to her Divine State of Transverse, she had unwittingly affected everyone with her emotions.

Even Zuo Tianyi, Yuan Shao, Xiao Da and Xiao Fei were moved quietly by her and did not interrupt her.

Priest Liu Qingcheng was startled as he looked at Yu'Er and Mei'Er, "Isn't this emotion similar to the highest level of the Dual Heart Intricate? I have…actually witnessed it…"

Lie Qing, Ji Lingfeng, Yu'Er, Mei'Er, Nangong Le, Qiu Wufeng and Gongsun Jing were stunned at the sentiments that the Celestial Envoy was displaying openly for Yi Ping.

Ji Lingfeng was the most bewildered. She had asked the Celestial Envoy to aid Yi Ping and the Celestial Envoy appeared to be the most reluctant to help. When she had seen the way Yi Ping and Lele looked at one another, she knew that their affections were real.

Ding Yun had quietly walked next to Lie Qing...

As Lele looked at Yi Ping, her silent tears dipped onto the Divine Echo as she said. "There is a seal in the Divine Echo. Only the tears of a heavenly fairy can break this seal. The Divine Echo is now yours..."

Yi Ping was trembling as he muttered, "Lele...don't cry...I can feel your heart...I can feel your very heart...the emotions and your heartbreaks...don't cry...we will fight together as one..."

Lele smiled softly, "Really?!"

When she smiled, it was like the arrival of spring and the darkness was dispelled sending gladness into the hearts of everyone!

Yi Ping nodded.

Lele cried softly, "That's wonderful. Even if I am turn to dust and into nothingness, I will always remember you..."

She had silently unblocked all the forbidden celestial channels in her body and had raised her Divine Celestial Force to the highest level as she smiled at Yuan Shao, Xiao Fei, Zuo Tianyi and Xiao Da. To protect Yi Ping, she was willing to sacrifice her own life and even retorted to use the Heavens Earth Sundering Skill of the Divine Celestial Force.

She smiled to herself, "We will become dust together then..."

"Not so fast."

Lie Qing had walked quietly next to Yi Ping!

Yi Ping was startled, "Lie Qing, you have not recovered from your injuries and shouldn't be here. Go back quickly!"

Lele gasped softly, "Luminous Star..."

Lie Qing smiled enchantingly as she swung her long black sword effortlessly, saying gently. "Yi Ping, worry for yourself first. Your wounds are still bleeding now. I am alright now."

Yi Ping was startled, "You have recovered your martial strength?"

Lie Qing smiled, "I have not only recovered my martial strength but my Invincible Divine Force as well."

All of a sudden, there was a burst of marital force that was exuded from around her!

Yuan Shao and Xiao Da said at the same time, "The Invincible Divine Force?!"

They could see seven bouts of circular faint blue light around her!

It was barely noticeable to anyone but the practitioners of the Divine Virtuous Force had recognized what it means!

Yuan Shao had prided himself on his mastery of the Divine Virtuous Force and he could release just five bouts of invisible force around him and that was already extremely powerful.

Xiao Fei and Xiao Da could only managed three and that had already propelled them as the super exponents of the martial fraternity. Just their level of attainment alone was enough to resist the powerful sword energies of the Infinity-Zero!

Yuan Shao asked, "How did you know the Invincible Divine Force?! Who are you exactly?"

Lie Qing said coldly, "Have you heard of the Heavenly Temptress?"

Yuan Shao nodded, "You are related to her?"

Lie Qing said coldly, "What do you think?"

Yuan Shao said coolly, "Very good. Today, we have finally found the successor of the Heavenly Temptress. No wonder you have dared to call yourself the New Virtuous Palace…"

Yi Ping interrupted Yuan Shao, "Are we still fighting or what?"

All of a sudden, Yuan Shao had turned around and began to walk away as he was heard saying coldly. "I don't believe true love exists between the heavens and the earth. Three days. In three days, we will be back to claim your lives. In three days, if you do not hand over the Holy Maiden quietly to us, don't blame us for being ruthless."

Everyone was stunned that Yuan Shao would actually walk away just like that.

There were shouts and cheers from both sides. It was because both sides had been too weary and that too many had died.

Even Xiao Da was startled. He took a lingering look at the Celestial Envoy before he walked hastily after Yuan Shao.

Zuo Tianyi said coldly to Yi Ping before he left, "You got only three days more."

Xiao Fei was looking quietly at the other side. His childhood friend, Ding Yunzi had collapsed in the embrace of the Holy Maiden. He had seen Lie Qing and Yunzi holding hands before she had passed out.

All of a sudden, he had remembered the legends of the Red Eye Clan; the Red Eye Clan had taught the Divine Virtuous Force to the practitioners, only to drain them of their intricate energies at an opportune time to further their Invincible Divine Force. For them to accomplish their vile purposes, they had founded the Virtuous Palace.

He had no doubt that this Lie Qing knew the Invincible Divine Force or else she would not be able to recover her martial strength at such a short notice. He could only say quietly to himself, "Yunzi, do you know what you have done? You may have endangered the Virtuous Palace."

If anyone had though that Yuan Shao really had a change of benevolent heart then they must be greatly mistaken!

It was because Yuan Shao was still his ever cold and calculating self. He was confident of taking Yi Ping and the Celestial Envoy until Lie Qing had stepped in.

There were three main reasons why he had given them three days.

Firstly, the practitioner of the Invincible Divine Force of course may have already mastered the Golden Invincible Body. Therefore he needed time to instruct Xiao Da, Xiao Fei and even Zuo Tianyi on the weakness of the Invincible Divine Force and the Golden Invincible Body.

Secondly, they had a long battle earlier and most of them had already expended most of their martial strength. Therefore they needed the time to recuperate and regained their martial strength to be in their best condition.

However, the above was still not the main point. Thirdly, he needed an opportunity to drain her Invincible Divine Force in order to advance his martial progress. That was his main purpose!

Chapter 40: The Perfect Storm

It was only the first day after the battle with the Honor Manor had just been concluded but everyone was looking at one another nervously while waiting for the Celestial Envoy to be presented.

Priest Bai Chongzhen, Priest Ling Kongquan, Priest Liu Qingcheng, Nangong Le, Yi Ping, Mei'Er, Yu'Er and those that were not bedridden were all presented in the Great Longevity Hall.

Priest Ling Kongquan looked at Nangong Le and Yi Ping as he asked politely, "The Celestial Envoy has instructed us to pay her homage at dawn but more than two hours had passed. Hero Yi Ping, you seem to know the Celestial Envoy quite well, where is she?"

Priest Liu Qingcheng interrupted, "Protégé Brother, don't be rude. No matter how late the Celestial Envoy is, she must have her reasons. It is the honor of the Tranquil Clan for the Celestial Envoy to grace our place."

Priest Bai Chongzhen said, "Indeed! We are all fortunate to witness the divine grace of the Celestial Envoy. The Celestial Envoy must have been pondering throughout the night to draw out a battle plan for our next course of action."

As Yi Ping listened, he began to smile bitterly and thought. "Why is everyone so deferent towards Lele and the Celestial Palace? I have never heard of the Celestial Palace…"

Not only Yi Ping but Nangong Le, Gongsun Jing and Qiu Wufeng had also never heard of the existence of the Celestial Palace. In fact, even most of the pugilists in the Western Fraternity did not even know that it had exactly existed!

The Celestial Palace had existed as an imaginary legendary place and was only hinted by a few. Even those few who had heard of the Celestial Palace quickly dismissed it as a myth.

That was why when the Celestial Envoy had shown up at the Holy Hex Sect, she was immediately attacked as an intruder! It was only through her startling martial display that convinced Ji Wuzheng and Ji Lingfeng that she could be from the Celestial Palace after all.

Nangong Le laughed, "Pardon my ignorant but I have never heard of the Celestial Palace before."

Priest Ling Kongquan whispered, "It is because no one who has ever gone to that place has ever returned alive!"

Nangong Le smiled, "Really? If there are more beauties like the Celestial Envoy there, I will very much like to visit the Celestial Palace!"

Priest Ling Kongquan, Priest Bai Chongzhen and Priest Liu Qingcheng immediately turn white with ashen.

Liu Qingcheng quickly pulled Nangong Le to a side and whispered, "Brother Nangong, listen to me. The walls have ears. Trust me on this. You will not want to go there…did you not see her long black wicked scythe? This type of weapon is meant for torturing and killing. Did you not see her in her red dress? Red symbolizes blood…"

Lie Qing who had overheard it, smiled as she said. "It does seem like she is a horrifying person. I wonder how her martial level is."

Yi Ping said quickly to Lie Qing, "She is not your enemy."

Lie Qing looked at Yi Ping and smiled. She had finally got his attention.

She asked, "Why are you defending her? From the looks of it, she has fallen for you. Why are you so flirty? Maybe you can take my title…my grand protégé mistress' title I mean. You can be the Heavenly Tempter instead."

She purposely took a glance at Ji Lingfeng, who pretended not to hear and then looked at Ding Yun, Yu'Er and Mei'Er.

She added, "You seem to have forgotten us so fast, especially Sister Youxue and the Celestial Fairy."

Yi Ping began to flush and did not know what to say.

He could only sigh in his heart. He had owed Maiden Lingfeng and Maiden Youxue so much. They had risked their lives on many occasions just to save his life. How could he not know their affections by now, especially Maiden Lingfeng?

Lie Qing stroked her braided long hair as she pondered aloud, "Anyway, your affairs have nothing to do with me. You have better find me a rich husband so that I can enjoy life to the fullest." She deliberately took a glance at Nangong Le, who was grinning at her hint.

As she said that, there was a hint of melancholy emotion in her eyes and voice. Even though it was barely noticeable but it was noticed by Lingfeng, Ding Yun, Yu'Er and Mei'Er.

It was because Yu'Er and Mei'Er had already advanced past the 'Linking Spirits' progression of the Dual Inertness Intricacy. If they wanted to and were attentive enough, they would be able to sense the emotions of others. So far, only their Protégé Mistress, Xiao Shuai, Yuan Shao and the Celestial Envoy were unfathomable to their Linking Spirits Skill.

As for Lingfeng, she was exceptional intelligent and quick in wits. Almost nothing escaped her notice. It was only through her brilliant guide that her group was able to reach the Tranquil Mountains while being pursued hotly by the Virtuous Palace and the Honor Manor.

Ding Yun was good in observing and was extremely sharp. It was obvious to her from her earlier actions that Lie Qing had plenty of affections for Yi Ping. However, what she was saying now was obviously a contradiction to her actions. The only person that Lie Qing could fool was Yi Ping.

Lie Qing had mixed feeling about the Celestial Envoy.

It was because the Celestial Envoy seemed to be looking at her more than others and she had even called her Luminous Star. She seemed to know her but Lie Qing had no idea where she had met her before even though she too got a familiar feeling about her.

When Lie Qing first saw the Celestial Envoy, she was startled to see her crimson eyes. It was because it could only mean one thing; she must have survived the Divine Calamity. How could it be even possible?

Even though her martial skills were truly astonishing, it was difficult to imagine what methods and techniques she had used to overcome the Divine Calamity when she herself had failed. She could still remember clearly the horrors of the Divine Calamity as though it had just happened yesterday.

She asked herself, "Is this only a trick to get close to me? Or she has managed to overcome the Divine Calamity by sheer coincidences?"

Even though she would like to ask the Celestial Envoy but she knew that her question would not be answered for the different martial clans guarded their martial secrets only to themselves, just like she had lied to Yi Ping and Xiao Youxue.

The Celestial Envoy would likely to spread misinformation to her so as to teach her a harsh lesson for prying into her affairs. Likewise if the Celestial Envoy asked her about the Divine Calamity, she would not hesitate to lie to her as well.

Lie Qing was worried for Yi Ping. It was because he was really such a gullible young man. The Celestial Envoy must have known about Yi Ping weaknesses and had something in store for him.

At this moment, Lie Qing and Ji Lingfeng were both thinking of the same thing.

All of a sudden, Lie Qing had a frightening thought and was coming close to the answer. "Maiden Lingfeng has promised to exchange her blood with the Celestial Envoy to help Yi Ping. Don't tell me that her true intention is to drain Yi Ping of his blood? That's right! Yi Ping possesses a much stronger internal strength than Maiden Lingfeng…"

In the meantime, Ji Lingfeng was also thinking. "They are all bloodsuckers. Yi Ping, we are surrounded by enemies. How can we get out of here alive? Is it so difficult for us to live a blissful life together? This Lie Qing and that Lele, they all have red eyes and seem to know one another. Alas…what shall we do? I am really at my wits end this time…now I have really regretted helping her. Ding Yun, why did you let her drain you of your internal strength? If I know she knows this type of evil skill, I would never even consider helping her."

Ji Lingfeng had a sudden thought, "Yi Ping had a strong dislike for this type of absorbing skill. If I let him know, maybe he would be upset with both Lie Qing and the Celestial Envoy…The Tranquil Clan and the Traverse Clan are both orthodox clans. Such an absorbing skill is considered to be evil in their eyes…"

Her thoughts were interrupted by Yi Ping who had asked Ding Yun gently, "Yun, you have fainted yesterday. It is better for you to rest more. You have given Lie Qing all your internal strength…I am really worried for you…"

Ding Yun smiled weakly, "I'm alright. Thanks for your concern…"

She stole a glance at Lie Qing, who smiled at her.

Ding Yun did not regret giving up her Divine Virtuous Force intricate energy to Lie Qing. Even though she had lost all her internal strength but she had moved Lie Qing deeply. It was only late last night that Lie Qing had secretly looked for her and revealed a martial secret to her; in order to learn the true form of the Invincible Divine Force, the practitioner must first practiced the Divine Virtuous Force and then let it be drained by the Invincible Divine Force!

Also, Lie Qing had deliberately hid some of the intricate formulas of the Invincible Divine Force from Xiao Youxue and her previously. Lie Qing had apologized with full sincerity and revealed the missing intricate formulas but she had also told her that it was pointless to have the missing intricate without first losing the Divine Virtuous Force. The missing intricate formulas were for the advance Invincible Divine Force and not for their Divine Virtuous Force.

Lie Qing also told her not to worry. In just three days, if there was a practitioner with the Invincible Divine Force to aid her, she would surely regain her internal strength. Not only would her internal strength be purer and stronger than ever, she would have also attain the last staging of the Divine Virtuous Force, which was actually only the initial staging of the Invincible Divine Force. This would give her the martial power to start learning the Golden Impervious Body which was what Xiao Shuai and Yuan Shao had been secretly coveting!

The Invincible Divine Force had five staging altogether, the Virtuous Level, Pious Level, Righteous Level, Holiness Level and the Divine Level.

Lie Qing had told her that she was only on the lower tier of the Righteous Level and the Holiness Level was near impossible to attain but in the past, there were a few that had actually attained it. As for the Divine Level, it was a mythical level and she doubted that it was even possible to attain it.

Ding Yun had asked her, "What happens if we can reach the Divine Level?"

Lie Qing smiled, "Then we are truly invincible and even the Divine Calamity is nothing to be feared. However, no one can reach that staging. Some bored practitioners have speculated of its existence but no one has ever been able to prove that it can actually be attainable."

In the martial fraternity, there were many martial theories and heart intricate formulas. Some martial staging may seem impossible to attain but when the practitioner's state of the divinity was able to advance, so did their martial understanding and the previous impossible martial staging would become possible.

But there were also many intricate formulas that were pure theories and were impossible to attain in actual practice.

Ji Lingfeng glanced at Lie Qing as she walked lightly to Yi Ping, asking. "Yi Ping, don't you feel that it is weird that Maiden Lie Qing is able to recover her internal strength so swiftly? Is there such a miraculous thing in the world? And Maiden Ding Yun has coincidentally lost her internal strength."

Yi Ping clapped his fists as he said aloud, "That's right! Why didn't I think of that?"

Yi Ping happily walked over to Lie Qing as he said excitedly, "Qing'Er, you have really recovered?"

Lie Qing and Ding Yun were startled when Ji Lingfeng had suddenly reminded Yi Ping that Lie Qing was practicing a type of absorbing skill and she had drained Ding Yun of her internal strength!

Lie Qing was scolded harshly by Yi Ping in the past for hinting that she may consider absorbing the internal strength of others.

She tried to retain her composure as she looked at Yi Ping, saying nervously. "Yes…I'm…"

Yi Ping held her hand as he said, "Maiden Yun has sacrificed so much. I hope that you can repay her by teaching her the Invincible Divine Force. I know that martial skills, especially the upper tier martial skills are all forbidden arts and no one will impart to others. Ding Yun, she is really very pitiful. What she did is noble. Qing'Er, I beg you to impart the Invincible Divine Force to her…"

Yi Ping immediately fell upon his knees in front of Lie Qing, much to the astonishment of everyone presented as he continued to say. "I won't get up unless you have agreed. I know that I have no right to ask you to do so…"

Ji Lingfeng and Lie Qing were totally stunned!

Ji Lingfeng was expecting Yi Ping to start rebuking Lie Qing while Lie Qing was expecting an awkward situation, something like asking her to cough out Ding Yun's internal strength which she was unable to and a severe scolding!

Lie Qing took a longing glance at Ding Yun, not knowing what to say. It was because she had already imparted the Invincible Divine Force to Ding Yun. Moreover, Lie Qing, Ding Yun and Xiao Youxue had an agreement that the protégé leader of the New Virtuous Palace would be Yi Ping. But now their protégé leader was actually on his knees and begging her!

If you were Lie Qing, what would you do?

For the first time ever, Lie Qing was completely at her wits' end as she blinked her eyes! Ding Yun winked at her and walked next to her as she smiled shyly, "Sister Qing'Er…" She took Lie Qing's hand and wrote with her fingers on her palm.

All of a sudden, Lie Qing laughed softly.

Priest Liu Qingcheng said to Yi Ping, "Hero Yi Ping, this is an impossible request. You have better get up and forget it. If Maiden Ding Yun does not mind, I will be willing to teach her the Dual Inertia Intricacy Force."

Yu'Er interrupted melancholy, "Protégé Master…you are so prejudice! You have only taught Mei'Er and I the Dual Inertial Intricacy Formula. You have never mentioned to us that there is such a thing as the Inertia Intricacy Force!"

Mei'Er said unhappily as well, "We may as well say goodbye to you!"

Priest Liu Qingcheng was startled as he quickly said, "My good disciples! Wait, hear me out first. The Dual Inertial Intricacy Force can only be learnt at the advance stage of the Dual Inertial Intricacy Formula. Moreover, I only be harming you if I taught you that for it run contradict to your clan's Icy Heavenly Tears intricate energy which is towards cold and negative force."

Mei'Er stomped her foot as she said, "Protégé Master, you are so biased!"

Nangong Le could not help adding, "Brother Liu, you are so biased. You teach Yu'Er and Mei'Er the Dual Inertness Intricacy Formula but not me. You know that I am willing to join your protégé clan anytime. That is why I am here today."

Priest Liu Qingcheng stared at Nangong Le and was amused, "Bullshit! Bullshit! Bullshit! With your jovial character, you will never join the Tranquil Clan quietly. And the last time you want me to teach you the Dual Inertness Intricacy Formula; you are trying to bribe me to be the clan patron saint instead!"

Nangong Le smiled jovially, "Alright then. Let's put Yu'Er and Mei'Er aside first since they are your protégé disciples now. What about Maiden Ding? I doubt she will really join your clan."

Priest Liu Qingcheng rebuked him impatiently, "What do you know? Even if I taught her the Dual Inertness Intricacy Force, I doubt she can really master it. She will need many years of her time to seek an understanding to the advance staging of the Dual Inertness Intricacy Formula first…"

All of a sudden, Priest Liu Qingcheng noticed that everyone was staring at him.

Priest Bai Chongzhen, Gongsun Jing and Qiu Wufeng all said at the same time, "Protégé Master Priest Liu, you have just mouthed vulgarities!"

Priest Ling Kongquan pointed at the white wall in front and said, "Protégé Brother and Protégé Master, the protégé clan rules that are described over there mention no profanities within the Great Longevity Hall. The clan punishments for breaking it, is…"

Priest Liu Qingcheng protested, "It must be this Nangong rascal who has influenced me…"

Priest Ling Kongquan said, "And again…"

Priest Liu Qingcheng ahem aloud, "I am the Protégé Master. I make the rule!"

Priest Ling Kongquan and Nangong Le said at the same time, "Such disrespect for the grandmasters of old…"

Priest Liu Qingcheng said hurriedly, "What is the clan punishment for being disrespectful to the protégé leader?"

Priest Ling Kongquan immediately kept quiet.

Nangong Le laughed aloud, "Luckily I am not your protégé yet."

Priest Liu Qingcheng said, "Not for long. I have decided to take you in now!"

Nangong Le laughed, "Then don't you regret it. You must teach me the Dual Inertia Intricacy Formula then?"

Priest Liu Qingcheng laughed aloud, "You rascal. You want this all along, am I right?"

Nangong Le and Ling Kongquan roared with laughter and their laughter was infectious. Soon everyone was laughing along except for Yi Ping who was still looking at Lie Qing solemnly.

Nangong Le, Priest Liu Qingcheng and Priest Ling Kongquan had always been close friends. That was why they were able to tease one another so openly.

Ding Yun interrupted with a smile, "Priest Liu, you just said that you are willing to teach me the Dual Inertness Intricacy Force. Do you really mean it? As a grandmaster of a repute orthodox clan, do you mean what you have just said?"

Priest Liu Qingcheng sighed, "Today is just not my day. I have gained a useless protégé and now I am going to give away my clan secret martial skill just like that."

Ding Yun smiled, "I take that as a yes then. In return, I will leave the Flying Sword Technique and the Divine Virtuous Force Skill in writing to you."

Priest Liu Qingcheng's eyes began to beam brightly. He had long wanted to look at the intricate formula of the Divine Virtuous Force, even if he could not practice it! It may improve his understanding of the Dual Inertial Intricacy Formula and advanced his state of divinity!

Priest Bai Chongzhen was envy, interrupting. "Maiden Ding, maybe you will be interested in the Traverse Skills. After all, we are one of the seven major orthodox clans in the martial fraternity…"

He was interrupted by Yi Ping, who was now bowing to Lie Qing, "Qing'Er, say something please…"

Lie Qing deliberately sighed, "Get up first."

Yi Ping said, "You have agreed?"

Lie Qing nodded slowly, "But on one condition. Get up first. I don't feel comfortable with you on your knees."

Yi Ping quickly got up as he said excitedly, "Just one condition? Even ten conditions, I will agree!"

Lie Qing smiled mysteriously, "Don't be so hasty first. You may regret it."

Yi Ping said, "As long as it not any wicked things, I won't regret it!"

Lie Qing began to flush as she said softly, "Is that so?"

Yi Ping said, "What is the condition?"

Lie Qing began to stroke her hair as she looked away shyly, "Not yet. I will let you know soon."

Yi Ping said aloud to Lie Qing, "Qing'Er, you are so kind!"

Yi Ping quickly walked to Ding Yun and said, "Yun, you should thank Qing'Er. She has agreed to impart to you the Invincible Divine Force!"

Ding Yun looked tenderly at him, "Yi Ping, you shouldn't have done this for me, especially in front of so many others. Thank you…"

Ding Yun said to Lie Qing, "Thank you!"

Lie Qing and Ding Yun secretly exchange glances, trying extremely hard not to laugh aloud.

Yu'Er, Mei'Er and Ji Lingfeng almost fainted on the spot. How could Yi Ping not know what Lie Qing and Ding Yun were up to?

Ji Lingfeng said to Yi Ping, "Yi Ping, you really shouldn't have done that for her. You are a dense pigheaded hero!"

Yi Ping was startled, "Lingfeng, why are you scolding me? I didn't do anything wrong."

Ji Lingfeng smiled coldly, "You really didn't do anything wrong or just happy to upset my mood?"

Yi Ping protested panicky, "Lingfeng, what actually did I do wrong? If you don't tell me, how do I know what it is that I have done wrong?"

Ji Lingfeng kicked him lightly, "Only you are a hero. You are trying to make me look bad by saying it aloud…"

Yi Ping said weakly, "It hurts you know. My wounds have not recovered yet…"

Ji Lingfeng interrupted, "That's none of my business."

Yi Ping and Ji Lingfeng were protesting and moving in circles. Anyone that had seen it knew immediately that it was not a real quarrel but an enviable sight that only two very close friends could enjoy. They seemed to have forgotten that there were dozens of onlookers in the hall.

Lie Qing, Ding Yun, Yu'Er and Mei'Er sighed secretly and wondered when they would be in a similar position as Maiden Lingfeng.

"Lingfeng, where are my secret manuals?"

"Humph! Come get it if you are capable. This is to teach you for not listening to me!"

"Lingfeng, when did I ever not listen to you? You…ask me to secretly leave the valley, I did. You ask me to go to the Holy Hex Sect to look for you, I did."

"Dense, dense, dense! I didn't ask you to befriend so many…humph young maidens along the way, right? Well, you don't have to go there anymore."

"Why? You are angry with me, Lingfeng?"

"Faint! Because I am here now…you…did that on purpose, am I right?"

"Really, I didn't. You know sometimes I am dense…"

All of a sudden, Ji Lingfeng and Yi Ping had stopped in their tracks. It was because they could sniff the light fragrance of lavender that had suddenly appeared. It came from Lele and she was now standing at the entrance of the hall.

Priest Liu Qingcheng quickly announced, "The Celestial Envoy is here!"

The protégés of the Tranquil and Traverse Clan quickly arranged themselves in neat columns.

Lele was looking at Yi Ping and Ji Lingfeng quietly. Even though she was looking serene but her cold demeanor was unmistaken!

Yi Ping said, "Lele, you are late…"

Lele tone said icily, "You are to address me as the Joyful Goddess, so must everyone here."

Ji Lingfeng looked at her with silent determination. Even though she had said nothing, it was as though her alluring eyes could speak. It was as though she was telling the Joyful Goddess that she would not give in to any threats and give Yi Ping up.

Yi Ping was startled as he thought, "Why is she so cold towards me today? This is so unlike her."

Priest Liu Qingcheng quickly added, "The Joyful Goddess must have stayed quite late to ponder on a stratagem to defeat the Honor Manor. That is why she is late. This is perfectly understandable."

Lele could not resist a soft chuckle. She was trying very hard to be cold towards Yi Ping. It was because she was not entirely pleased to see Yi Ping and Lingfeng on such an amicable term. And moreover, Lingfeng was an extremely alluring maiden and already in the hall, there were many who had already been infatuated by her.

Lele was not called the Joyful Goddess for nothing. She rarely approach things with a heavy heart and acted purely on whims.

When the Jade Emperor wanted to appoint a Celestial Envoy to the Holy Hex Sect to control and understand the situation, Lele had volunteered.

The Jade Emperor had said to her, "You are one of the four Prime Celestials and you have not even fully recovered from your last cycle of sleep. Stay where you are. I will appoint someone else to go."

But Lele was not even listening or paying scant attention and had left the Celestial Palace immediately, much to the amusement of the Jade Emperor. The Jade Emperor had given up on reproaching her over the centuries as he sighed, "Does she even know that I am still talking to her or is her mind already fluttering with the things that she wants to do in the fraternity?"

The Jade Emperor was bemused for a while until he got a sudden jolt, "She doesn't even know the mission at all!"

If anyone thought that Lele was like that, just as the Jade Emperor thought she was; then they must be greatly mistake! That was how astute Lele really was. She had joined the Celestial Palace when she was very young and that was what she wanted others to think of her in this manner. That was her way to shrink away from responsibilities and she was never tasked with bringing super exponents back to the Celestial Palace for no one really trusted her to do any task in a proper manner!

That was how and why Lele had become the Celestial Envoy…

Not only did the Jade Emperor and others thought the same of her, even Yi Ping had felt that she was living in her own world. What Yi Ping did not realize was that Lele was actually very lonely and she cherished every chance to express herself.

Lele stroked her long hair as she laughed softly, "Yi Ping, how do I look today?"

Yi Ping was startled by her question. Yi Ping scratched his nose as he said, "Looking great…"

But he added, "Lele…"

Lele looked annoyed, "Joyful Goddess!"

Yi Ping sighed, "Joyful Goddess then…"

Lele said jovially, "Good. Very good. You can call me Lele now."

This time it was Yi Ping who looked annoyed, "Lele! You!"

Lele laughed softly, "Good boy! Remember only you can call me by my name."

She deliberated swept her eyes at everyone. Her intention was clear. Only Yi Ping could have the privilege of addressing her by her real name.

Lie Qing obviously thought that it was not funny as she gave a soft yawn and fingered her black sword. She had almost raised her sword to point at Lele.

Yi Ping was clearly annoyed as he said, "You are obviously embarrassing me in front of so many others!"

Lele looked at him with her watery eyes, "I am giving you such an esteem honor yet you do not appreciate it. Do you know that you shouldn't have revealed my true name in any circumstances? This is the rule of the fraternity. Most of the exponents in the fraternity use a fraternity name to represent themselves. Unless I have given the permission, you shouldn't have introduced my name to others. I haven't settled this score with you yet. Now everyone knows my name…"

Yi Ping was startled as he looked panicky around him. When he saw Qiu Wufeng and Gongsun Jing nodded at him, he immediately knew that he had committed a terrible blunder.

Yi Ping immediately said, "I'm sorry. I really did not know…please forgive me…"

Lele broke into a smile, "Since you are quick to apologize, I forgive you then! Remember, you are not to call me by my name in the presence of others. Is that understood? You ignorant third tier pugilist who didn't know anything at all."

Yi Ping smiled bitterly, "I got it now."

Even though Lele seemed to be rebuking Yi Ping, she was actually instructing him lightly like a mentor.

It was such an enviable sight that many in the hall wished miserably that they were the ones that were lectured by her instead.

Yi Ping sighed and asked, "Lele…Joyful Goddess. You are late today. Are you working on a plan for us to fight the Honor Manor?"

Lele had a mysterious look in her eyes as she asked softly, "Yi Ping, how do I look today?"

Yi Ping sighed. He really had no idea what was on her mind. This was the second time that she had asked the same question.

But he was patient with her and said, "You are looking great…what about the battle plans? Surely you have asked us to gather so early in the morning for a reason?"

Lele sighed softly, "These are two separate reasons entirely."

Yi Ping was bewildered as he asked, "Huh?"

Lele said, "You have asked me why I am late, am I right?"

Yi Ping nodded and said, "That's right."

Lele said, "The reason why I am late is because I am taking a bath at the Tranquil Pool. I have heard that it is a renowned pool even before I have transcendent as a Celestial. Today, I have finally visited it."

Priest Liu Qingcheng almost fainted on the spot while Priest Ling Kongquan had stumbled weakly backward when they had heard it!

It was because the Tranquil Pool was their most sacred pool and no one had ever bath in its pristine water before. It was considered to be sacrilegious to do so!

Lele continued, "That is the reason why I am asking if you notice anything different about me?"

Yi Ping clapped his hands as he said, "No wonder you are looking so great and had a wonderful fragrant around you. No wonder!"

Yi Ping was looking at Lele intently and he was not aware that Lingfeng had covered her face with her hands in embarrassment, while Yu'Er and Mei'Er were trying very hard not to giggle at him. He was not aware that the protégés of the Tranquil Clan all had a stunned expression on their faces.

Even Lie Qing and Ding Yun sighed silently and wished that they did not know who Yi Ping was for he was embarrassing himself with his ignorance.

The Tranquil Pool was renowned throughout the martial fraternity for its pristine and rumored miraculous water that could clear the mind for mediation.

Gongsun Jing, Nangong Le and Qiu Wufeng were all stunned as well and secretly thought, "Is he really our sworn brother?"

Luckily, Yi Ping was a hero while Lele was the esteem Celestial Envoy so no one dared to say a word.

Priest Bai Chongzhen was thinking, "Someone actually dare to take a bath in the Tranquil Pool and someone who is already a super exponent in the martial fraternity did not know the Tranquil Pool…this is going to the lore of martial fraternity as one of the most unusual events to happen and I have actually witnessed it today. What an honor, what an honor…"

Lele lowered her glance and even her voice softened to almost inaudible, "I have asked all of you here to gather in the morning because I do not want anyone to outrage my modesty when I am taking a relaxing dip."

Yi Ping nodded approvingly, "That's right! All these make sense now. It will be bad if others see you."

All of a sudden, Yi Ping had a sudden jolt. "What about our battle plans?"

Lele said coolly as she looked at everyone, "You have all gathered here since morning, surely you have already discussed the best course of action?"

Yi Ping looked at Lele as he said, "But we are waiting for you!"

Lele asked, "What have all of you been doing since morning?"

Everyone was too embarrassed to say anything and was looking at one another with an awkward expression.

Priest Bai Chongzhen looked at Priest Liu Qingcheng, who was still in a daze before he said to Lele and everyone. "It is still not too late for us to discuss our next course of action."

Qiu Wufeng said, "That's right. Let's fight our way out."

Gongsun Jing smiled bitterly, "Brother Qiu, I think that is the last option. We don't even know if there is an ambush ahead of us."

Lie Qing lifted her long skirt while clutching her black sword as she stepped forward, asking Lele, "So the Joyful Goddess has asked us here just because she wants to enjoy her bath?"

Even though it was obvious to everyone but no one dared to mention it except for Lie Qing.

Lele smiled, "My good sister…we need to talk…"

Lie Qing interrupted coldly, "Who is your good sister? So the Celestial Envoy who has come to aid us has actually asked us to gather since the wee morning so that she can take a bath?…"

Lele sighed softly, "Of course not! I do have another very important reason to ask everyone to be here."

Lie Qing asked, "Which is?"

Lele said, "Tomorrow is Yi Ping and my wedding. It is very important to me and I hope that everyone will be able to attend it."

Everyone, including Yi Ping and Ding Yun were stunned.

Yi Ping asked panicky, "Who is getting married tomorrow? Again?

Lele pointed at Yi Ping, "You are."

Yi Ping asked, "I am? How come I do not know?"

Lele smiled, "Now you do. Due to unforeseeable circumstances, we are getting married tomorrow and these are our guests."

Yi Ping was so stunned by Lele's announcement that he was just staring blankly in thin air!

Nangong Le could not resist adding a sarcastic laughter, "Congratulation for marrying such a beautiful maiden."

Ji Lingfeng smiled bitterly. Her voice was soft but everyone could hear her, "As though we have a choice of not attending. We are all trapped here…"

Lie Qing said coldly, "I protest."

Lele smiled coolly, "Good sister, your protest is invalid."

Lie Qing was stunned at her egocentric behavior that she had raised her fists and had unleashed three quick blows to slap her, saying. "We are all in mortal danger and you still have the mood to celebrate your wedding? That is really too much, even if you are from the Celestial Palace!"

Lie Qing was quick, in a blink of an eye she attacked three times but Lele was composed as she deflected her blows with her sleeve.

Lie Qing was so enraged that she had actually used her martial power when she had missed, as the powerful force of the Invincible Divine Force could be felt!

Lele said coolly, "Luminous Star, you are really serious?!" As she said, there was a thunderous impact when Lele received a blow from Lie Qing with her Celestial Force!

Even Yi Ping was forced to take three steps backward while the weaker pugilists fell onto the ground as they were all in close proximity!

Lie Qing groaned in disbelief that Lele could actually receive the almighty force of the Invincible Divine Force in such short notice. Her achievements in the Invincible Divine Force was so advance that she could muster her martial power anytime that she wanted to and that was really a hard thing to achieve for most exponents. It was because to exponents of the martial fraternity, timing and ability to react were crucial, holding the key to their very own survival!

Lie Qing was so determined to hit Lele that she had used the "Pandora Darkness Fingers', charging five of her Invincible Divine Force intricate energy channels to her fingers as she struck at Lele repeatedly! "I am not any Luminous Star. I am the Darkness."

Lele had raised her internal strength through the Celestial Force as she exchanged blows after blows with Lie Qing, absorbing the powerful impact of Lie Qing's blows with the absorbing martial power of her Celestial Force!

She was secretly startled with Lele's martial power and was panicky, wondering how long she could last in this duel. Every blow that she had absorbed from her, her Celestial Force began to weaken.

Even though they had exchanged just a few words but more than fifty blows had already been exchanged, knocking people down, overturning decorations and destroying furniture from the bursting windforce of their thunderous blows!

Priest Bai Chongzhen said panicky, "Everyone, back!"

Priest Liu Qingcheng was pleading aloud, "Stop fighting. Alas, no fighting in the Longevity Hall…"

Ding Yun, Ji Lingfeng, Yu'Er and Mei'Er quickly went to Yi Ping and shook him hard, "Yi Ping, ask them to stop please before it is too late…they are for real…"

But Yi Ping was completely fascinated by their fights and did not notice…

Yi Ping had thought, "How come I didn't know Qing'Er is so highly skilled? What strokes are they using? I didn't know their strokes can be so intriguing."

Yi Ping had dueled with Lele on numerous occasions so he knew very well how refine her skills were. He had only witness Lie Qing displayed her martial skills only once and that was against the injured Ye Lu and Qiao Feng. So naturally, he was stunned to see her actual martial display!

Just when Yi Ping was about to step forward to plead with them to stop, he was seized by a headache that caused his vision to blur!

As he looked at Lie Qing and Lele again, all of a sudden he had found their movements to be eerily familiar as though he had seen it before!

For no hymn and reason, he was suddenly in a dream. He saw a young man with a noble bearing and three heavenly maidens. The strong rays of the sunset seemed to have turned their eyes red. The weird thing was, he could not see their faces yet that was the impression he had of them.

The young man was suddenly fighting with the three heavenly maidens. The dream seemed to have moved forward and two of the heavenly maidens had succumbed onto the ground. The third heavenly maiden seemed to have lost her fighting spirit and had dropped to her knees on the ground. She was weeping silently and waiting for the young man to end her life.

Somehow, the young man did not seem glad with the victory. There was a hint of sorrow in his eyes. He walked away quietly and found an isolated place to meditate. Many years seemed to have passed as the young man continued to meditate but he did not seem to have aged.

Finally, the young man opened his eyes and looked in the heavens as he saw a bright star in the heavens above that was faltering. His eyes were grayish and seemed void of any light. All of a sudden, the bright star grew extremely dim and seemed to have fallen from the heavens!

The young man said gravely, "Even after three hundred and thirty-three years, you still cannot put this down? You are not going to succeed and this will cost you your Ascend. What right do I have to criticize you? Even after three hundred and thirty-three years, I too am unable to put this down as well."

He began to get up and now was in another place.

The place was like a dangerous underground maze but this young man carefully dismantled all the booty traps before he reached the center of the maze.

The center of the maze was eerily like the stone chamber that Yi Ping had visited before.

Again, the young man saw the heavenly maiden who had survived many years ago.

She said gently, "You have come to stop me? It is already too late. The Celestial Formations are already on the move and without my divine power to unseal it, you cannot stop me now."

She still looked the same but was very weak. As she looked keenly in his eyes, she smiled gently, "You have achieved the Ascend? Why are you still here? After so many years, you still refuse to spare me?"

The young man said calmly, "Why are you so foolish as to give up your precious life? Do you know how many painful years of cultivation and lucky happenstances arranged by the Divine Fate that bring you this far?"

The heavenly maiden said gently, "I am not as heartless as you. That is why you are able to 'Ascend' while I am unable to. Even if I have to do it again, I will do it."

The young man said, "You have not reached enlightenment yet. Your sisters are predestined to die. Only you are able to Ascend. It is not too late now. Stop it before your life force is completely drained."

The heavenly maiden said coldly, "My sisters are killed by you!"

The young man said, "We are on opposite sides and didn't have a choice…"

The heavenly maiden interrupted weakly, "Why don't you leave me to my destiny and complete your Ascend, instead of lingering with lesser mortals like me?"

The young man said, "You won't succeed. There are too many variables involved. And moreover this involves the destinies of three of you. One destiny is already too unpredictable and moreover, you are trying to move three destinies to your wishes."

The heavenly maiden smiled weakly, "Do you think I do not know? I have spent years of my time divining. Only Melody Star will have the best chance to succeed…I'm happy enough to be in her time…We will surely settle our scores with you when the time comes…"

She had now collapsed onto the ground and had turned into sparkling dust!

When she had pulverized into nothingness, the young man had a great sense of loss. He raised his hands and said, "I have reached the highest level of the Emptiness Translucence a long time ago but why I am feeling a sense of great loss?"

He reached out his fingers to touch the still sparkling lights and suddenly remembered that he and the three sisters had been mortal enemies for more than a thousand years, way before they had even embarked on the the path to divinity.

Suddenly he had turned ashen and there were tears in his eyes for the first time in a thousand year. The sparkling light contained the last vestige of Yun Xiao's memories. On their last battle, the three sisters had deliberated lost to him so that he could achieve the Ascend, a rare opportunity that they had all been waiting for many years to come.

"Why…"

He was the very reason why the three sisters had been pushing themselves so hard…

"Yun Xiao's celestial star formation, I can feel it now?"

The young man laughed madly, "I didn't Ascend because I am guilty. Where are the others that had Ascend? Instead of a new state of divinity, they have all turned into ashes and nothingness. Do you know that you have indirectly saved my life? Today, I have finally understood that I am the most foolish one. My enlightenment comes too late…"

The young man too burst into glowing balls of light and into nothingness even as his silent words could be felt saying, "I will help you to Ascend…this is the least that I can do for all of you even if the odds are one in a million."

Yi Ping gave a loud painful yell as Lingfeng pinched him hard and stomped on his foot.

Lingfeng, Ding Yun, Mei'Er and Yu'Er were saying panicky at the same time, "Why are you daydreaming at a time like that! Hurry and stop them before it is too late!"

Yi Ping shouted panicky, "Stop!!!"

Yu'Er shook her head, "It no use. They cannot hear us now. The force inside nullified all other disturbances from the outside…"

Lele and Lie Qing had fought from fast to fighting in slow motion. Even though they looked unhurried as they exchanged blows like a normal exponent but they were leaving deep footprints onto the floor with every step and exuding deadly waves of internal energies!

Exponents like Priest Bai Chongzhen, Priest Liu Qingcheng, Priest Ling Kongquan, Ding Yun and Lingfeng immediately knew that to be struck by anyone of them, would mean instant death!

At this moment, they were surrounded by their martial force as their martial power reached its peak. No one could approach them or they be crushed instantly by the surrounding inertia force. Even metals would bend and wood would crack in their mere presence now!

As Lie Qing clashed repeatedly with Lele, blood tickled from the tip of her pink lips. She had used her entire martial power and yet she could not gain an advantage over Lele. Their fight had degenerate from exchanging blows to a self-punishing contest of pure internal strength. If she had not used her Invincible Divine Force to its fullness, exchanging mere blows with Lele would have killed her!

Lele was not faring too well either. She had just coughed out another bout of blood as she took another blow from Lie Qing! She had exercised her internal strength to its fullness that the very air around her was electrifying. Her Celestial Force may be able to absorb the martial force of the Invincible Divine Force but it was now taking a severe toil on her now!

Lele smiled weakly to Lie Qing, "Why don't you give up now? I let go of your rude offense this time."

Lie Qing said weakly, "I will only stop if you give up first and you must first apologize to everyone for being late…"

Lele interrupted, "You are the one that raise your fist at me first. You are more unreasonable than me…!"

Just as Yi Ping was about to dash into their middle, Ding Yun and Lingfeng held him back panicky!

Yi Ping asked panicky, "Quick! We must stop them. At this rate, they will both die!"

Ding Yun was solemn as she threw her flying sword into their midst!

Yi Ping was stunned as he raised his voice, "Yun, what are you doing!"

But even before the flying sword could reach them, it was deflected by an invisible force around them and flew to the roof of the hall!

Ding Yun said quietly, "You will die if you go in just like that…"

But before Ding Yun had finished, Yi Ping had raised his entire martial power with the Aspire Invocation and had broken free of Ding Yun and Lingfeng's hold, charging into Lele and Lie Qing midst!

Even before Yi Ping reached their midst, his eyes had turned bloodshot and he used the last bout of his martial power to take one blow from Lele and another blow from Lie Qing at the same time!

There was a large explosive force when Yi Ping took their blows as he coughed out blood!

When Lie Qing and Lele saw Yi Ping dashing into their midst, they had already withdrew half of their martial power in panicky but it was still not quick enough!

"Yi Ping!" Both maidens cried out aloud.

Yi Ping coughed out more blood as he collapsed with one knee onto the ground. He smiled weakly, "Good. Now you can hear me…"

Lele rebuked Yi Ping, "Why are you so foolish? Do you know you will die if you barge in just like that?"

Yi Ping said weakly, "There is no other way to get your attention…if your fight goes on, both of you will surely die of internal injuries."

Lie Qing was uneasy as she said, "Yi Ping…"

Yi Ping was right. If it persisted for another minute, both Lie Qing and Lele would surely die of their internal injuries.

Lingfeng was the first to dash to Yi Ping, followed by Ding Yun, Yu'Er and Mei'Er!

Lingfeng immediately felt his pulse and was solemn, "Your intricate energies are erratic now. Even if you can restore it to normal, you won't be in time to use your internal strength. Close your eyes and recuperate first. I will use my internal strength to guide your erratic energy to its proper course. There is no time to lose if you don't want to lose your internal strength permanently."

With that, they sat down.

Lingfeng had wanted to chide Yi Ping but in the end, when she had seen the extent of his internal injuries, her heart was too heartbroken to rebuke him.

Ding Yun held Lie Qing and Lele's hands as she said quietly, "Both of you have sustained terrible internal injuries. Until you have fully recovered, it is best that the two of you sustain from using any internal strength."

Ding Yun added quietly, "Is it worth it? Both of you fighting with your internal strength in this manner just to prove a point?"

Lie Qing and Lele looked at one another sheepishly.

Lie Qing said softly, "I just…I just want to slap her for being so egoistic. She is obviously making a fool out of us."

Lele looked hurt as she quickly said, "I didn't want to fight you, Luminous Star…"

Lie Qing interrupted coldly, "You can address me as Maiden Lie. I am not like someone who dare not use her real name."

She was the opposite of Lele; she had dared to use her own name but not her fraternity name.

Lele said, "I don't want to fight you, Lie Qing but you have left me with no choice."

Lie Qing said coldly, "I am not so close to you that you can address me by my name."

Lele said sadly, "Lie Qing, don't be upset alright? I apologize to you…"

Everyone was stunned that Lele had taken the initiative to apologize to Lie Qing!

Lele looked at Yi Ping sorrowfully before taking a look at Lie Qing again. She turned to everyone and said softly, "I apologize for being late to everyone…"

Lie Qing was startled that she had actually apologized to everyone. It was totally unexpected and out of character for the Joyful Goddess who seemed to look at everyone with disdain to apologize.

Lele repeated softly, "I apologize to everyone again. I hope that everyone will forgive me for being late."

Lie Qing sighed softly as she thought, "Maybe the Joyful Goddess isn't that bad. I should have control my impulse better…"

Priest Liu Qingcheng said solemnly, "Being late is only a small matter. We should plan our next recourse on how to fight the Honor Manor."

He asked, "Joyful Goddess, where are the rest of the people from the Celestial Palace? Will they be arriving soon?"

The Joyful Goddess looked sheepish as she sighed softly, "How far do you think we are from the Holy Hex Sect? The rest of the Celestial Envoys will be going there. I am the only one here…"

Of course Lele did not dare to tell them that she was a fake Celestial Envoy with no mission. She did not even know if there were other Celestial Envoys that were on their way to the Holy Hex Sect.

Mei'Er said melancholy, "It is hopeless. We have better surrender."

Priest Bai Chongzhen asked, "What do you mean? Surrender? Never. We will rather die in battle than surrender dishonorably!"

Mei'Er looked at everyone while Lele and Lie Qing were looking sheepishly, "What are our odds of winning now? The Joyful Goddess, Maiden Lie Qing and Master Yi Ping have all sustained internal injuries and cannot fight in the short term. The rest of us have no hope of winning at all."

All of a sudden, the truth dropped heavily like a thunderous lightning bolt on everyone in the hall!

Lie Qing was feeling so bad now that her eyes turned watery. Mei'Er was right. They had just lost their only hope of survival now…

Lele smiled gently to Lie Qing, "Lie Qing, you don't have to look so depress. Even if we have our internal strength, we stand no hope against the Virtuous Palace."

Everyone was startled.

Lie Qing asked, "What do you mean?"

Lele said, "Why do you think I am holding my wedding tomorrow?"

Just when Lie Qing had started to have a good impression of the Joyful Goddess, she seemed to be back to her own world again. But Lie Qing was too tired to guess or remind her to come to the point directly so she simply said, "Why?"

Lele said softly, "It is because my divination shows that we will all end up in defeat in three days. We are simply not their match at all. That is why I am holding my wedding tomorrow to spend my last days with Yi Ping…"

She swept her glances at Yu'Er, Mei'Er, Ding Yun, Lingfeng and Lie Qing as she looked at them pitifully. It was though she wanted to tell them of the cruel fate that awaits them in three day time.

When everyone had heard that, they could only smile most bitterly.

Even Lie Qing and Ding Yun were stunned at her answer.

Yu'Er smiled bitterly to Lele. "My Joyful Goddess. Your divination is so right. We do not have any chance now!" She was indirectly being sarcastic.

She wanted to say on behalf of everyone, "How can you base our fighting chance on irrational thing like divination. Now it has really come true because of you."

Lie Qing was trembling, "We may not lose if we give our best…but now…"

Mei'Er wanted to cry aloud but she withheld her tears as she said, "If only our protégé mistress is here. Then we have nothing to fear from the Virtuous Palace."

Lele sighed softly, "I am afraid that even if your protégé mistress is here, the result will still be the same!"

Mei'Er said coolly, "Says who? That Xiao Shuai seems to be afraid of our protégé mistress!"

Ding Yun said, "He is not afraid of your protégé mistress. Or rather he gives an order not to hurt the protégés of the Eternal Ice Palace. Or else do you think that even if you have ten lives, you can even survive yesterday battle with Xiao Da?"

Mei'Er asked curiously, "Why did he give such an order?"

Ding Yun shook her head, "I do not know the actual reason but he seems to know the Celestial Fairy."

Yu'Er asked, "Is the Virtuous Palace so formidable? Surely, Master Yi Ping, Maiden Lie Qing and the Joyful Goddess can match their martial skill?"

Lele said softly, "I have already lost to Yuan Shao that night…"

That night, Yi Ping, Ding Yun and Zuo Tianyi had also been defeated by him!

She did not want to reveal to anyone that she was planning to sacrifice herself to bring Yuan Shao down. That was why she had decided to call for a wedding even though she would be inviting ridicule and contempt. But now, she could not even muster the Celestial Force…

Ding Yun said, "If I am not wrong, Yuan Shao must be planning to use the Dark Mono Sword Formation against us."

Lie Qing asked, "What's that?"

Ding Yun said, "If this sword formation is made up of three super exponents, then it is capable of withstanding the strength of nine super exponents. That is how powerful it is."

Lele coughed softly as she asked weakly, "Is there a way to break this sword formation?"

Ding Yun sighed softly, "It is difficult. The changes are profound. And if the formation consists of the three of them, then they are really invincible."

All of a sudden, Yi Ping had coughed out black blood and had opened his eyes!

Everyone that knew Yi Ping was calling his name!

"Yi Ping!"

"Are you much better now?"

"How are you feeling now?"

Lingfeng was startled that he could clear his blocked channels and spat out the bad blood out so fast. Normally, the bad blood would remain in the body until it could dissipate slowly. This process could take anything from weeks, months to years!

She was astonished with his constitution!

Yi Ping was overwhelmed by the concern shown to him as he said, "Brother Nangong, Brother Qiu, Brother Gongsun! Yun, Lele, Qing'Er, Lingfeng, Yu'Er, Mei'Er…"

He got up and said weakly, "Lingfeng, I am alright now. Thanks for helping me…"

Lingfeng was so happy that she began to cling tightly to him as she helped to support him up.

Yi Ping looked at everyone as he said weakly, "I have overheard what Yun has said. No matter, I will surely fight them with my last breath."

Yi Ping asked Ding Yun, "Just how strong Xiao Da and Xiao Fei is when compared to Zuo Tianyi?"

Ding Yun asked him instead, "Just how strong do you think Youxue and the Celestial Fairy really is? Then you will know that Zuo Tianyi is just a small fry."

Yi Ping could not help sighing when he had thought of Xiao Youxue…

But he quickly said, "Why compare Yixian and Youxue with them? Their martial skills are nowhere near Lele…"

Lele interrupted with a smile, "Joyful Goddess."

Yi Ping said weakly, "Does it mean that Xiao Da and Xiao Fei martial skills are weaker than the Joyful Goddess as well?"

Yi Ping answers stunned Ding Yun, Lie Qing and Qiu Wufeng.

Qiu Wufeng said, "You are there at the Heavenly Mountains as well. Surely you have witnessed the Celestial Fairy fighting alone against so many top exponents?"

Yi Ping had suddenly remembered the scene that day…

Qiu Wufeng added, "Do you have any idea how powerful Tian Kui really is? He is considered to be one of the top super exponents in the martial fraternity. Even Gongsun Bai dare not trifle with him!"

The Celestial Fairy and Tian Kui had fought that day in the lofty tops of the Heavenly Mountains! Yixian had known Tian Kui for a long time and had restrained herself. Tian Kui was probably the only person to have dueled with her previously and had survived.

Yi Ping was only seeing Yixian as a vulnerable maiden that needed to be protected and not so much of her martial abilities…

Ding Yun added, "You should have known about this. Youxue almost kill the Celestial Fairy that day…"

Youxue had defeated both Tian Kui and the Celestial Fairy singlehandedly!

Lie Qing continued weakly, "If it isn't for the fear of Youxue, I may have left you a long time ago. Do you know that she has already mastered the 'Golden Impervious Body' at her young age and has reached the peak of her Divine Virtuous Force?"

Ding Yun said, "Why do you think she can steal the Golden Rejuvenation Pills from right under the nose of Xiao Shuai and can evade the Virtuous Palace for so many years? Pure luck? Do you know that Xiao Da is most afraid of whom? He is none other than Xiao Yuanjia and Youxue has already defeated him!"

Lie Qing added, "I have secretly observed their fight from a distance. Xiao Yuanjia is ten times more deadly than even Xiao Da…"

Yi Ping had a sudden jolt as he recalled the first time he had seen Youxue; she was already displaying her extraordinary martial force in an extraordinary manner.

He muttered, "I didn't know that Youxue is this strong…"

He quickly asked, "If Youxue is this strong, how is it possible for Yixian to fatally injure her?"

Lie Qing kept quiet. She dare not tell Yi Ping that she had a hand in injuring Youxue as well.

No one else except for Lie Qing, Ding Yun, Nangong Le and Zuo Tianyi could possible imagined Youxue martial level unless they had witnessed her fight with the Celestial Fairy!

Ding Yun looked at Lie Qing before she said, "The Celestial Fairy is the real monster. The three of us combined cannot even take her down. If you really want to know the martial depth of the Celestial Fairy, I say she is even more formidable than Yuan Shao and the Joyful Goddess. However, the Celestial Fairy may not be able to break the Dark Mono Sword Formation on her own."

Lele interjected, "They have the Dark Mono Sword Formation but we have the Celestial Star Formation. It is a far more formidable formation than any known formations."

Yi Ping looked at Lele, asking enthusiastically. "Will the Joyful Goddess teaches us the Celestial Star Formation then?"

Lele nodded, "The Celestial Star Formation requires a minimum of five and a maximum of nine to complete it."

Lele looked at Lingfeng, Yu'Er, Mei'Er, Ding Yun and Qiu Wufeng.

Qiu Wufeng was astonished and was looking at Yi Ping, "I am to be the hero this time?"

Yi Ping said hurriedly to Lele, "Joyful Goddess. I am alright now. Let me be in this Celestial Star Formation…"

Before Yi Ping could even finish speaking, he was swept off his feet and flung off by Lele who coughed weakly as she muttered. "You can't even take one weak blow from me now. Forget about it."

Qiu Wufeng was gravely solemn as he said, "Leave everything to me."

Gongsun Jing helped Yi Ping up as he said, "At the very least, we have a battle plan now." But he was secretly groaning, "This is terrible. Three of our best fighters just put themselves out of action from infighting. Even the best formation cannot propel any fighter's strength to exceed his potential. A formation is only good for maximizing the effectiveness of the fighter…"

Nangong Le could only smiled bitterly and envied Qiu Wufeng as he thought, "If I am not injured…"

While everyone was looking at the Joyful Goddess, Qiu Wufeng and Yi Ping, no one had noticed that Priest Liu Qingcheng had completed turned ashen as he stumbled backward while muttering to himself. "This is really happening…it happens during my lifetime…"

Chapter 41: The Heavenly Temptress vs. the Joyful Goddess

Just as Priest Liu Qingcheng was about to call Yi Ping hurriedly, the Joyful Goddess had lifted her crimson eyes and said pristinely, "Listen up everyone, I have something to announce."

Lie Qing was slightly startled. It was because the Joyful Goddess looked spirited even though she had just lost her internal strength.

Lie Qing had been secretly relieved that the Joyful Goddess had lost her internal strength and could not harm Yi Ping for the time being. But this was not the result that she had initially wanted. She just wanted to teach the Joyful Goddess a lesson but she had not expected her internal strength to be so profound. In the end, both sustained grave internal injuries and lost the use of their internal strength temporary.

At this time, they would need to muster as many good fighters as possible to resist the advances of the Honor Manor and the Virtuous Palace. Lie Qing knew silently that the Joyful Goddess may be the support that they needed for the forthcoming battle...

She sighed quietly, "The fraternity is full of wiles. A gullible person like Yi Ping will surely fall into their hands sooner or later. The Joyful Goddess may appear to be helping us but who knows her real intention? She may even be in cahoots with the Honor Manor from the very start to draw us into an unsuspecting trap. Good sister Yun, why are you suddenly so close to the Joyful Goddess?"

But Lie Qing was smiling mysteriously as she thought happily, "Yi Ping, in three day time you will see me in totally different light..."

The Joyful Goddess repeated again, "Listen up everyone."

She was looking solemn and her voice seemed to have a mesmerizing hold on everyone!

Lie Qing was startled, "She knows the Bewitching Soul Seizing Skill too? Can it be that Sister Yun is under her mesmerizing influence? But this skill won't work against top exponents..."

All of a sudden, she recalled that Zuo Tianyi had violated Ding Yun and this may cause her will to be broken. At that moment, she was the most vulnerable to the mesmerizing suggestions of the Bewitching Soul Seizing Skill...

Everyone was startled to see the Joyful Goddess addressing them in such a serious manner that the Great Longevity Hall went silent all of a sudden.

The Joyful Goddess hummed softly as she got everyone's attention, saying melody. "Priest Bai and Priest Liu, heed my commands."

Priest Bai Chongzhen and Priest Liu Qingcheng was startled that the Joyful Goddess was actually addressing them. Nevertheless, they replied, "Yes?"

The Joyful Goddess said with a divine voice, "Prime Celestial, Joyful Goddess of the Celestial Palace now officially appoints the Traverse Clan and the Tranquil Clan to be the guardian clans of the Celestial Palace in the Western Fraternity. Anyone clan that infringe on your clan is as good as an enemy of the Celestial Palace."

Priest Liu Qingcheng, Priest Bai Chongzhen and Priest Ling Kongquan were stunned but were also secretly pleased at the same time. It was because even though the Celestial Palace may be an unknown in the fraternity at large, those that knew of it were fearful of it.

But it would not be for long before the entire fraternity would know the existence of the Celestial Palace. When that happens, the Traverse and the Tranquil Clan would gain a resounding renown and recorded in the annuals of the martial fraternity as the guardian clans of the Celestial Palace!

Priest Liu Qingcheng quickly regained his composure and was thinking, "Then it won't be long before the Tranquil Clan will become a first tier martial clan again. Finally a chance to gain esteem honor for the clan and let past venerable grandmasters of the Tranquil Clan be proud! Maybe I will be the most famous grandmaster of all time…"

Priest Bai Chongzhen was also smiling to himself as he was also thinking the same as Priest Liu Qingcheng!

The Joyful Goddess smiled happily before saying, "Do you accept the honor of being the guardian clans of the Celestial Palace?"

Priest Bai Chongzhen and Priest Liu Qingcheng did not hesitate at all and immediately nodded eagerly as both said at the same time, "It is our honor!"

Priest Bai Chongzhen was looking a little awkward as he looked at Priest Liu Qingcheng, "May I know what actually is a guardian clan and what is a Prime Celestial?"

The truth was, Priest Liu Qingcheng did not know either and he was pondering the same too!

Nangong Le and Priest Ling Kongquan sighed as they were thinking of the same, "Both of you didn't know but has accepted the honor so fast. Isn't that too impulsive?"

Lingfeng could only smiled alluring as she thought, "I got a very bad feeling about this…"

The Joyful Goddess patiently said, "The guardian clans will represent the Celestial Palace in the affairs of the fraternity and the leadership will represent the Celestial Palace as the Celestial Messengers."

Priest Bai Chongzhen and Priest Liu Qingcheng were exuberated! The honorific title of the Celestial Messenger seemed grand and they were smiling broadly.

Priest Ling Kongquan who was always a little more daring than his protégé brother and protégé leader asked curiously, "How high is the ranking of the Celestial Messenger in the Celestial Palace?" He had dared to ask because when the Joyful Goddess had lost her internal strength, much of her mystique and his fear of her had been lost.

The Joyful Goddess smiled most alluring, "It is third in the ranking hierarchy!"

Priest Bai Chongzhen, Priest Qingcheng and everyone were gasping in stunned silence. It was something that caught everyone by surprise!

Third in hierarchy! It was beyond their wildest dreams in expectations!

Immediately there were several excited incessant muttering in the Hall as everyone was rushing to speak and talking at the same time!

Priest Qingcheng who had been practicing the Dual Heart Inertia Skill could sense the excitement of his clan protégés and from the others. He was so moved that that he was actually shedding tears as he thought, "Today must be my lucky day. Finally, I am able to bring great honor to the Tranquil Clan!"

Priest Bai Chongzhen stammered, "Who is on the top? At the very least, as Celestial Messengers we should have the right to know?"

The Joyful Goddess smiled alluring, "The Jade Emperor is on the top followed by the Prime Celestials. There are just four of us and I am one of them."

Priest Bai Chongzhen and everyone nodded excitedly.

The buzz and excitement at this revelation did not die down and only increased!

The Joyful Goddess sighed softly to herself, "These are fleeting glories. Why are men always seeking such pursuits and not seek enlightenment?"

She could not resist a jovial smile as she said to herself, "There are just three ranking in the Celestial Palace, the Celestial Emperor, the Prime Celestials and the Celestial Messengers. They are the lowest in ranking!"

But she quickly remembered her main reason why she was addressing Priest Bai Chongzhen and Priest Liu Qingcheng as she said mesmerizing, "Listen, the Celestial Messengers!"

Priest Bai Chongzhen and Priest Liu Qingcheng quickly said at the same time, "Yes!"

The Joyful Goddess laughed softly, "Hurry and prepare for my wedding tomorrow! I almost cannot wait anymore."

Even though Bai Chongzhen and Priest Liu Qingcheng knew that the Joyful Goddess had declared her wedding earlier, they did not know that she was serious and this was their first order that they received as Celestial Messengers! How could they say no?

They could only stammered, "Yes, ye-s...yes."

The Joyful Goddess blinked her eyes as she smiled, "That is good!"

Yi Ping quickly said, "Wait a minute. You are getting married tomorrow? With who?"

The Joyful Goddess laughed softly, "Of course it is you, silly. Who else?"

Yi Ping was startled, "We...we are really getting married tomorrow?"

The Joyful Goddess said, "Yes, of course..."

But before she could finish, Lie Qing, Ji Lingfeng, Yu'Er and Mei'Er all said at the same time. "I protest!"

The Joyful Goddess waved her hand at them, "Protest Invalid. Wedding will continue tomorrow."

Lie Qing was scolding her, "You are too unreasonable!"

Lingfeng said coldly, "Don't you think that you are the Celestial Envoy, I will not slap you. Don't forget, you have lost your internal strength."

Yu'Er said coolly, "Yes, she can't fight anymore. Why don't we teach her a lesson while we can?"

Mei'Er nodded eagerly. She was almost bursting with rage and had already discarded her Emotionless Rhythm to the bottomless abyss when she had heard that Yi Ping and her was going to be wedded tomorrow!

Lie Qing looked at Lingfeng, Yu'Er and Mei'Er and were touched that they were all standing on the same side as she muttered, "Everyone...help me to teach her a lesson then!"

The Joyful Goddess smiled, "Celestial Messengers Bai Chongzhen and Liu Qingcheng, Ding Yun and Yi Ping, protect me!"

Priest Bai Chongzhen and Priest Liu Qingcheng smiled bitterly at her orders. They really got a very bad feeling about this...

Ding Yun hesitated as she muttered, "Uh...hmm..."

The Joyful Goddess said, "Good sister Yun, please come over here!"

Lie Qing quickly said, "Good sister Yun, come over here please!"

Ding Yun was torn between the both of them. It was because she had known Lie Qing first and now she had even imparted the Invincible Divine Force to her!

As for the Joyful Goddess, she was really a good sister to her despite only a short time! The Joyful Goddess said, "Sister Yun, do you want to be linked to Yi Ping?"

Ding Yun asked, "Link?"

The Joyful Goddess smiled, "That means the same as wedded. The Celestials are all incorruptible by mortal desires. So we can only link heart to heart. Sister Yun, come over here."

Ding Yun could only smiled awkwardly as she thought miserably, "Incorruptible? No mortal desires? You are bluffing who? Then why are you getting married tomorrow? You are already not chaste…" She wanted to faint immediately and pretended not to hear anything…

Lingfeng called out, "Yi Ping! Are you listening to me or not? Come over here and resist this witch! You have said that you will listen to me."

Yi Ping was flushing so awkwardly that he wished he could dig a hole and wished that these maidens would not see him but Lingfeng and the Joyful Goddess had.

He did something very smart. He refused to say a word, acting deaf and mute…

Priest Liu Qingcheng said bitterly, "Yu'Er and Mei'Er, come over here. Surely you don't want to fight your protégé master. It is not respectful…"

Mei'Er said tearfully, "You are not our Protégé Master! You are the Celestial Messenger! We are going to beat up all the Celestial Bullies!"

Yu'Er nodded with her beautiful voice saying. "That's right! We don't have a Protégé Master that…that…abandons his own disciples! Don't blame us for not merciful!"

Priest Liu Qingcheng had broken into a sweat as he said, "Am I to be the first Protégé Grandmaster of the Tranquil Clan and the first Celestial Messenger to be killed by my own disciples…alas….I am so pitiful…."

Priest Bai Chongzhen said weakly, "I am still recovering from my injuries…I am also so pitiful…"

The Joyful Goddess laughed softly, "Not at all. It an honor to die for the Celestial Palace!"

Lingfeng said, "It does seem that our side is much stronger. You have no friends and even Yi Ping does not want to stand on your side. If Yi Ping does not stand on your side, then he is actually on our side as the odds are already obvious. Do your math."

At one masterstroke, she had pushed Yi Ping to her side!

Yi Ping was startled.

The Joyful Goddess hummed coldly, "Yi Ping is so gullible and dumb. He don't really think so far ahead. Stop discording us with your lies. Don't forget you are the Holy Maiden."

Lingfeng kept quiet all of a sudden.

The Joyful Goddess said, "Protégés of the Celestial Messengers, stand on my side!"

But no one dared to move. It was because everyone had the common sense to know that it was actually none of their business and it would be disastrous to get involve.

The Joyful Goddess muttered something enchanting.

No one actually knew what she was chanting.

The truth was she was actually cursing out aloud. It was just that no one actually understands it!

The Joyful Goddess said, "Alright then, I grant all of you permission to attend my wedding tomorrow…"

Lingfeng, Yu'Er and Mei'Er was so infuriated that they had raised their hands and fingers, dashing past Priest Bai Chongzhen and Priest Liu Qingcheng, who was powerless to stop them as they stumbled to the side!

They had dashed so sudden that Yi Ping could only shout alarmingly, "Lele! Watch out!"

The Joyful Goddess yawned and raised one hand to block Lingfeng, Yu'Er and Mei'Er but at the same time in rapid succession, she had slapped them on their cheeks! Her speed and martial strength was so astonishing that Lingfeng, Yu'Er and Mei'Er were forced back by her sudden counterattack, even as she reminded Yi Ping. "Remember you are to address me as the Joyful Goddess in the presence of others."

Yi Ping was stunned, "Lele, didn't you lost your internal strength?!"

Lingfeng, Yu'Er and Mei'Er were so startled by the Joyful Goddess sudden counterattack that they got slapped on their faces as they did not anticipated that she would be able to resist their attacks at the same time. Also, they did not use even their full martial strength as they knew that Yi Ping would be upset with them for injuring the Joyful Goddess!

Even Lie Qing was startled as she said, "You...!"

The Joyful Goddess laughed jovially, "I did lose it but I have regained it back already!"

How could anyone regain their internal strength so speedily?

Even though the internal strength of the Joyful Goddess lacked the martial power of Lie Qing's Invincible Divine Force, but the depth of her true internal strength was truly astonishing!

When Ding Yun had inspected her wrist, her meridians were indeed erratic and she had lost half of her internal strength due to internal injuries.

But she had secretly circulated her remaining internal strength through the use of her Celestial Force, dissolving the bad blood within her and restoring the flow of intricate energy in the next instant. Because her internal strength was so profound, she was able to do it secretly without notice as she plunged out the excess bad intricate energies from her invisibly!

In this hall, she was now the most supreme. No one could stop her from doing what she wants and she intended to force Yi Ping to marry her whether he wishes or not.

Originally, she wanted to keep this a secret but when Lingfeng, Yu'Er and Mei'Er had attacked her, she had forgotten about it and had retaliated in self-defense!

Her idea of fun was to torture Qiu Wufeng, Lingfeng, Yu'Er, Mei'Er and Ding Yun mentally with the Celestial Star Formations. She knew that it was impossible for them to learn even the basics in three days. After all, it had taken her one hundred years to fully understand this formation and to break free of it.

Yi Ping said, "Lele, you got your internal strength back? Or some of it?"

The Joyful Goddess suddenly remembered that she was not supposed to exercise her internal strength so she quickly coughed innocently, "They have suddenly attacked me and out of self-defense, I have forcibly mustered my internal injuries. Now my internal injuries have worsened. My days may be numbered..."

Yi Ping was so worried that he quickly walked to her to comfort her, "Lele...!"

Yi Ping turned towards Lingfeng, Yu'Er and Mei'Er, rebuking them. "Look what have you done!"

Lingfeng, Yu'Er and Mei'Er were still stunned by the Joyful Goddess' slaps that they could only hold their cheek and stared tearfully at Yi Ping! It was because the Joyful Goddess' martial strength was so pure that they could not believe that she had lost her internal strength for even a moment. They were also hesitating because they did not want to get another slap so soon!

But before Lingfeng, Yu'Er and Mei'Er could reply to Yi Ping's accusation, Lie Qing said. "Stop putting on an act. Let me expose your lies!" She had suddenly attacked the Joyful Goddess and they were fighting with dozens of blows instantly!

Everyone was stunned that both Maiden Lie Qing and the Joyful Goddess were fighting again!

The Joyful Goddess gasped, "Lie Qing, you didn't lose your internal strength?"

Lie Qing replied coldly, "That is your wishful thinking!"

The Joyful Goddess hastily replied, "No, that's not true. I so happy for you…"

She was suddenly interrupted by an intrigue stroke coming from Lie Qing and she was forced to take two steps back! "Sister, listen to me…we can get marry together…"

Lie Qing hummed coldly, sending forth five more successive attacks on her. "Utter rubbish!"

Yi Ping was startled and so were the rest…

Yi Ping muttered, "Lie Qing, you didn't lose your internal strength too?"

Lie Qing did not reply him as she was focusing all her efforts as she attacked and defended against the Joyful Goddess who was her match in terms of martial techniques.

What the Joyful Goddess lacked in martial power, she had compensated with her stunning agility and swiftness skill!

Lie Qing had temporary lost the strength of her internal strength after the ensuring clash with the Joyful Goddess. However, she had consumed the Divine Dragon Pill, a miracle pill that could rejuvenate her martial power and life force. With her martial foundation, especially the Invincible Divine Force, her internal injuries were healing at a rapid pace.

Moreover, the internal injuries that Lie Qing had suffered were lighter than the Joyful Goddess due to her Golden Impervious Body Skill!

The Golden Impervious Body Skill was a skill that could render most attacks harmless and lessen the damage inflicted. At Lie Qing advance stage of this skill, she could even go into a death trance so that even if she was gravely injured, her body could be able to recover. That was what happened to her when she was sorely defeated by the Divine Calamity!

At that time, Lie Qing had founded Virtuous Palace and was known as the Heavenly Temptress. She had six followers who served as the stewards of the Virtuous Palace, Xiao Boyi, Jing Xing, Ding Jun, Yuan Tieqi, You Nikuang and Qin Siyi.

One day, Lie Qing summoned her stewards and said weakly. "My very end is near. You have seen the deadliness of the Divine Calamity and the destruction that it had caused. It is best that you do not learn of the Invincible Divine Force anymore. That is how most of my martial clan has perished over the years. I have thought that with my martial level, I can actually have a chance…"

Jing Xing said tearfully, "Mistress, your eyes have turned crimson…no you won't die…I don't want this to happen…"

Xiao Boyi said, "You are not imparting the Invincible Divine Force to us anymore?"

Lie Qing said weakly, "It only bring you harm…"

Yuan Tieqi said, "Maybe you have learnt it wrongly. Maybe you can't but others can."

Jing Xing raised her long sword at Yuan Tieqi and Xiao Boyi, "Are you rebelling? How dare you be rude to the Heavenly Temptress!"

Qin Siyi said coldly, "Xiao Boyi, Yuan Tieqi, how dare you be rude to our mistress!"

Jing Xing and Qin Siyi were from the same martial protégé clan as Lie Qing, the Invincible Divine Clan. The Invincible Divine Clan was once the most powerful martial clan in the martial fraternity but its lofty ambitions caused its downfall in a major battle with various other powerful martial clans. Lie Qing was the only solo surviving member of her clan...

You Nikuang laughed, "If you don't impart it to us now, there won't be another time. Why do you think we have followed you even after the Invincible Divine Clan is destroyed? Do you really think we are so free and dare to risk the constant harassment of the other martial clans just for your sake?"

Lie Qing said weakly, "I have taught you many martial skills...how could you betray my trust..."

Ding Jun said, "You taught us all your skills? What a joke. You treat us like dirt and even want to drain our Divine Virtuous Force so that you can have enough martial power to overcome the Divine Calamity."

Lie Qing said, "I have my own reasons..."

But before she could fully explain, You Nikuang, Ding Jun, Xiao Boyi and Yuan Tieqi had attacked her.

That very night, Jing Xing and Qin Siyi had sacrificed their lives for her. She was mortally wounded by the Divine Calamity and from her betrayers...

If it was not for the numerous loyal followers who had shielded her, she could not have escaped from the Virtuous Palace. But even if she could escape, what was the point? She would eventually die.

In her escapade, she had met a young man who seemed to be impervious to her mesmerizing hold with the Absolute Spirits Skill. This young man had not only unconditionally treated her injuries but had even sacrificed himself for her when the Divine Calamity struck again, turning the entire cavern into ice...

At first when she opened her eyes, she had thought Yi Ping was the same young man because they had a familiar look...

Back to the present, Yi Ping was now shouting panicky for Lie Qing and Lele to stop because they were in the midst of a heated confrontation, "Qing'Er, Lele! Stop fighting!"

But all of a sudden, Lele and Lie Qing seemed to have freeze and they were not moving!

Everyone was stunned to see them ceasing their fights all of a sudden!

Yi Ping asked, "What is going on?"

Lie Qing and Lele were trembling as they were looking at the entrance of the hall nervously at the same time and even their fingers were trembling!

It was because they had suddenly noticed that there were two maidens standing at the entrance of the hall quietly!

Everyone followed their glances and was stunned to see two heavenly maidens, one in light blue and one in light yellow standing quietly!

Yi Ping was the most stunned as he looked at the two familiar sights. He was trembling and muttering, "Yixian, Youxue, is that you...?"

Indeed, the one in light blue was the Celestial Fairy. Her sight was so stunning that she seemed so unreal that many in the hall were wondering if they were dreaming!

The sight of Xiao Youxue was also moving, she was always an enthralling young maiden and her air was unmistaken enticing to beholden. That was why Qiu Wufeng had recognized her even when she had veiled herself.

However, they shared the same cold demeanor and cold forbidden aura.

Even Yu'Er and Mei'Er were suddenly frightful, "Protégé Mistress?"

The Celestial Fairy said gently in an unhurriedly manner. "I have heard that someone is planning a wedding tomorrow."

There was a hint of displeasure in her eyes and it was directed at the Joyful Goddess and Yi Ping at the same time!

Chapter 42: Sisters of the Fate

Yi Ping was trembling as he walked weakly towards the Celestial Fairy and Youxue while muttering, "Yixian, Youxue...it is really you! I...I..." He really did not know what to say or noticed the icy coldness of the hall as the maidens were all staring icily at one another.

Yu'Er and Mei'Er knew that their protégé mistress was upset because they had been with her for a long time. Their protégé mistress rarely lost her cool and that only happened when they were just young girls and was playing havoc in the Eternal Ice Palace regardless of the clan rules! It was because they had intentional taken advantage of their mistress easy going nature and broke every single rule frequently!

Lie Qing was awkward as she thought, "Youxue is here and his wife is also here. Why am I in this embarrassing situation? I should go..."

Lingfeng and Ding Yun were also quiet. It was because in the presence of the Celestial Fairy, they knew that they had totally no right. They could not even invoke the rule of the martial fraternity by dueling for their rights. It was because none of them were her martial match except for maybe Lie Qing and the Joyful Goddess.

Yixian and Youxue had hidden themselves from their view because they were too awkward to see Yi Ping. If Yi Ping and his companions could not defeat Yuan Shao in three day time, then they would secretly lend him a helping hand.

Yixian and Youxue divine state of their stealth skill was so startling that they could remain completely invisible even to top exponents. Not even Lie Qing and the Joyful Goddess could detect their presence if they willed it.

But what happened in the Grand Hall of Longevity was simply too much for them to bear, testing even their patience.

The Joyful Goddess was horribly late and that caused them to remain motionless for hours while listening to flirting conversation between Yi Ping and Lingfeng.

And it continued to grow more outrageous when the Joyful Goddess had arrived and they had to listen to her ridiculous excuses and requests.

Not only Lie Qing could not stand her and wanted to teach her some manners, the Celestial Fairy and Youxue were also thinking the same!

The Celestial Fairy and Youxue simply could not believe such an impossible maiden with that kind of an attitude existed in the fraternity. They could only watch in utter disbelief that Lie Qing, the Joyful Goddess and Yi Ping had all lost their martial power from an internal fight!

Were they even aware that they were surrounded by foes?

After they had lost their martial power, the Joyful Goddess was still in a jovial mood to call for a wedding. But because she had lost her martial power, they suppressed their indignation.

Youxue, who was acquainted with Lingfeng, had almost lost her cool when Lingfeng got slapped by the Joyful Goddess.

But still, they continued to endure the antics of the Joyful Goddess till to the very end.

When they realized that they were played by her, they could no longer suppress their wrath for her even with their state of divinity!

As for Yi Ping, he was walking with trembling steps towards them now!

Shui Yixian sighed to herself, "If Yi Ping comes close to me I am going to give him a slap. He has abandoned Yu'Er and Mei'Er. He even wants to get marry to a demoness like the Joyful Goddess. Is he blind or he is consumed by lust for her? I really regret putting Yu'Er and Mei'Er into his hands. I have ruined them..."

Youxue was equally hurt and felt that she had been betrayed by Yi Ping. She sighed silently as her eyes turned melancholy, "We...have barely parted and you have been acquainted with another maiden? Are all men like that? You are...just...like my hateful father!"

And she had raised her hands to slap as soon as he got close.

As soon as Yi Ping got close to them, he was tearful and said excitedly. "Yixian, Youxue! It is really the two of you. I...I miss you. Yixian...I have thought we have been separated by the heavens and the earth...it is really good. Don't leave me anymore..."

Yixian had wanted to slap Yi Ping but when she had seen him again and she was glad that he was now talking to her that her heart calmed down considerably. It was because she knew that Yi Ping had never forgotten her. How would she not know? Xiao Youxue had told her everything...

And then he said to Youxue, "Youxue, I have thought that you are gone for good...please forgive me...I am too impulsive. I shouldn't have said those unkind words to you...alas, I am so dense...I really thought that I would no longer see you anymore..."

Xiao Youxue had wanted to slap Yi Ping too. But what she had wanted to do, her heart did not have the will. She could only mutter, "You...are not taking vendetta for your wife anymore?"

Yi Ping laughed sorrowfully aloud, "I...if I know it is you, I will never have the heart. You have saved me so many times...do you think that I would be so ungrateful?"

Yixian comforted him gently, "She didn't kill me. She had almost killed me but so did I. So now, it is fair. Look at you. Why did you run off from the Eternal Ice Palace? With your mediocre skills and straightforward nature, how many lives do you think you can afford to lose?"

Yi Ping smiled bitterly, "I am still alive..."

Youxue smiled, "You...even a boar had almost killed you! You have better retired from the martial fraternity..."

Yi Ping looked at her gently, "Even a fish could kill me, thanks to you..."

Xiao Youxue had saved Yi Ping from the Thousand Year Ice Fish in the Icy Cavern. After that they had spent more than three months of carefree life together with Lie Qing. That was her happiest period of her life and she had wished that it would never end.

Youxue could not resist a soft chuckle...

Everyone could see suddenly that Yi Ping and the two heavenly maidens were now talking and laughing softly. It was an extremely enviable sight. They seemed to have forgotten about the presence of everyone else in the hall!

Yu'Er and Mei'Er were secretly blinking their eyes and nodding at each other. It was because their protégé mistress was no longer upset. They were smiling at the enviable sight. Even though they had wanted to run to their protégé mistress and to greet her but they were afraid to interrupt this beautiful moment.

Lie Qing was stroking her long hair and had turned away. It was because she knew that she was out of this picturesque scene now that the Celestial Fairy and Youxue were here. Even if she likes Yi Ping, there was nothing left for her to do now...

Lingfeng did not feel uneasy. She was smiling and was teary. She was saying to herself, "Yi Ping has finally found his wife again. That's great…all good things must come to an end. I will never forget you, Yi Ping."

Like Lie Qing, Ding Yun felt out of place.

Of all the timing and of all the people to interrupt, it was the Joyful Goddess.

The Joyful Goddess laughed softly, "Yi Ping, are they your friends? They can attend our wedding too. The more the merrier…"

But she was also playing with her fingers on her chin as she pondered, "The maiden in light blue, she is such a familiar sight?"

All of a sudden, she gasped delightfully. "She is Revelation Star! The statue in the chamber of the Celestial Stars! But her eyes, she has not attained enlightenment yet? Alas, that is troublesome. Oh well…none of my business. She is on her own then…"

The Celestial Fairy and Xiao Youxue had appeared in front of her all of a sudden. Their swiftness movement was not beneath her and was astonishing!

The exponents in the hall were gasping breathlessly. They had never seen someone displaying swiftness movement right in front of them with such startling speed that they did not even notice that they had actually moved from the entrance of the hall to the front of the Joyful Goddess!

The Joyful Goddess was startled but before she could react, they had attacked her.

It was a lucky that that she was agile and she had quickly moved back, "Revelation Star, why are you attacking me?"

The Joyful Goddess had once again provoked them with her incessant arrogance!

The three of them were moving across the hall, flashing to and fro that all the exponents in the hall were rubbing their eyes for they had only seen flashes of shadow!

Yi Ping was gasping, "Speed fighting techniques. Amazing…"

But before he could finish speaking, Lingfeng had appeared in front of him and gave him a knock on his head.

Lingfeng's swiftness movement skill was on par with them!

Yi Ping asked, "Why are you hitting me, Lingfeng?"

Lingfeng said panicky, "You idiot! You are the only one that can stop them now. Stop watching and asks them to stop or there would be casualties!"

Yi Ping was panicky as he quickly shouted, "Yixian, Youxue, Lele! Stop! You are not enemies!"

But his shouts were drowned out by their explosive techniques and blows…

He had lost his martial power and his ordinary shouts could not be heard above the explosive blows that were ringing nonstop…

The Joyful Goddess was shouting panicky, "Two against one, that's despicable!"

Xiao Youxue said coldly, "Aren't you a Prime Celestial? And you are calling for help?"

The Joyful Goddess flew towards Lie Qing and was heard saying, "Qing Qing, help me!"

Yixian and Youxue just wanted to slap the Joyful Goddess but she was proving to be harder than they had expected and extremely good in evading.

Lie Qing hummed coldly, "It seems that we are getting closer to closer each time. Serves you right…"

All of a sudden, a windforce that was created from their rapid fighting sliced past her cheek and scratched her cheek. Lie Qing touched her porcelain face and she looked at the blood that was on her fingers.

Lie Qing had raised her martial power with her Invincible Divine Force as six beaming burst of force exploded from her aura, "How dare you scratch my face!"

And soon, she too was fighting with the Joyful Goddess, the Celestial Fairy and Xiao Youxue!

Lie Qing and Xiao Youxue were friends so they avoided attacking one another.

Xiao Youxue and the Celestial Fairy were friends so they too avoided attacking one another.

The Joyful Goddess had the most disadvantages as she had to fight three super exponents at the same time while Xiao Youxue only need to focused her attention on the Joyful Goddess!

As they fought, their martial power and force increased so rapidly that the entire hall was now shaking and they had already knocked down several pillars!

The Joyful Goddess was now panicking as she had exhausted all her possible strokes against these super exponents; they had seen through all her feints and intrigue moves. It would not be for long before she could be hit by them! She thought, "It is even harder than fighting Yuan Shao…"

But she was also astute shrewd. When she could not take any blows anymore, she would use Lie Qing as her shield by taking evasive action behind her!

If there were a power ranking among these four super exponents however slight it was, the Celestial Fairy Shui Yixian would surely be ranked first, second would be the Heavenly Temptress Lie Qing, Youxue would be third while the Joyful Goddess Huan Le would be last.

But in terms of internal strength, it was the opposite. The Joyful Goddess would outlast them as long as she had the most profound internal strength due to the Celestial Force and her centuries of mediation, provided that she did not get kill first. That was why she was bending attacks with her superior speed against the three of them.

Priest Liu Qingcheng, Gongsun Jing, Nangong Le, Qiu Wufeng, Priest Ling Kongquan and Priest Bai Chongzhen were all shouting to Yi Ping and the rest, "Everyone quickly run! The entire hall is collapsing!"

Yi Ping was reluctant to leave but he was dragged away by Lingfeng and Gongsun Jing.

Gongsun Jing said, "Brother, this place is too dangerous now. The building may collapse anytime. There is nothing we can do except to pray for their safety..."

Lingfeng said, "That's right."

Nangong Le was sighing poetically, "Four heavenly maidens fighting, what a wondrous sight…" But before he could finish, he was knocked onto the ground by a sudden windforce as a shadow dashed past him and he had to be carried away by Qiu Wufeng!

Just as Yi Ping and the last of the group had exited the grand hall, the entire building had suddenly collapsed, leaving the four fighting maidens who were still inside!

The entire structure of the collapsing pillars and walls weighed tons! No one could have possibly survived such a mind blogging heavy crash!

Yi Ping fell upon his knees as he sobbed uncontrollably, "We have just been reunited and now...and now, we have separated again. Why is it that Fate must plays such a cruel trick on me?!"

He began to clench his fists and hit the ground repeatedly until his fists were bloodied...

Lingfeng, Yu'Er and Mei'Er were tearful as they consoled him, "Yi Ping, don't..."

Priest Ling Kongquan said solemnly, "The dead cannot be brought back. We will surely dig up their bodies and give them a grand burial."

Priest Liu Qingcheng was staring at the collapsed Grand Hall of Longevity. It was one of the oldest buildings in the Tranquil Clan with over two thousand years of history.

Priest Bai Chongzhen was sighing to himself, "The Prime Celestial Joyful Goddess is dead...we are still surrounded by our enemies. We are now Celestial Messengers in all but name only..."

Priest Ling Kongquan asked, "How is everyone?"

Gongsun Jing said, "Brother Nangong has fainted earlier. Most of us managed to escape with nothing more than just a few bruises. It is a miracle that we are all able to make it out alive..."

Qiu Wufeng was in tears as he stared at the Grand Hall of Longevity.

Gongsun Jing asked him, "Why are you even more upset than Yi Ping?"

Qiu Wufeng wailed, "I have thought that I would be the hero of the Celestial Star Formation. With the Joyful Goddess dead, who will impart to us the Celestial Star Formation now? We are all as good as dead now. We may as well dig our own graves now."

The hard truth sunk in once again and those who had overheard it were also depressed by the coming outcome!

All of a sudden, Yi Ping got up and he said to everyone. "Priest Liu Qingcheng, I have a request. Let the wedding continues tomorrow. Even if Lele, Lie Qing, Yixian and Youxue are dead, I am going to hold a ceremony for them."

Priest Liu Qingcheng nodded silently.

Ding Yun, Lingfeng, Yu'Er and Mei'Er were now holding hands and were tearful.

When Yi Ping had finished speaking, he had dashed to the collapsed building, picking and throwing away the debris!

Even as Yi Ping had just started picking the debris, Ding Yun, Lingfeng, Yu'Er and Mei'Er were besides him, picking up and clearing the debris with him!

Priest Bai Chongzhen shouted to his clan protégés, "What are you all waiting for? Help them!"

Priest Liu Qingcheng shouted too, "Help them!"

In no time, dozens of protégés from both the Traverse and the Tranquil Clan were also helping to clear the debris!

"What are you doing Yi Ping? Digging dirt like a kid?"

Yi Ping and everyone were startled at this familiar divine voice. It was unmistakably the voice of the Joyful Goddess and he could sniff her lavender scent!

Yi Ping quickly looked up and saw the Joyful Goddess standing in the distance. She was stroking her long luster hair to and fro. Even though she was still quite a distance away but her divine voice could be heard clearly.

Yi Ping muttered, "Lele...are you...human or ghost?"

The Joyful Goddess said, "I am never human. I am a Celestial. When I heard that you are preparing a wedding for me, I have immediately come back from the dead to visit you."

Everyone else was too stunned and fearful to react. It was too supernatural and they were all looking at the Joyful Goddess in utter disbelief.

Yi Ping said sorrowfully, "Lele, I am so sorry. It is my entire fault. I have caused your death indirectly. I shouldn't have asked you to come here in the first place…it is my entire fault…"

The Joyful Goddess sighed melancholy, "Yi Ping, I have only a brief moments left before I vanish. I am so happy that you are going to hold a wedding for my sake. Don't you forget about me, alright?"

Yi Ping was tearful and he was shouting frantically, "Lele, I won't forget you! Don't leave me!"

Ding Yun interrupted, "Yi Ping…Le…the Joyful Goddess isn't a ghost or dead. She has a shadow…"

Lingfeng was startled. She was so seized up by the Joyful Goddess sudden appearance that she was not thinking clearly. If she was not a ghost, then where were the Celestial Fairy, Lie Qing and Youxue?

The Joyful Goddess said melancholy, "I have just died. That…is why I still have a shadow…very soon, even my shadow will vanish and you will never see me ever again…"

Yi Ping cried out, "Le…Lele…."

He had already run with all his might towards her!

But when he had run halfway to her, dashing across the gardens, small pavilions and the stone bridge that was across a small canal, Yi Ping had suddenly paused in his tracks.

He had suddenly turned back and was red-faced.

He began to walk back quietly and there was a shadow in his expressions!

Everyone was stunned!

Lingfeng thought, "Didn't he missed the Joyful Goddess so much that he just ran all the way to her? Why did he suddenly turned back and looking so upset?"

The Joyful Goddess was calling out, "You….you don't miss me anymore?"

Yi Ping turned around and pointed at another direction.

As there were buildings blocking the views, no one except Yi Ping could see what he was actually pointing at.

But Gongsun Jing, Lingfeng, Ding Yun, Yu'Er, Mei'Er, Qiu Wufeng, Priest Bai Chongzhen, Priest Ling Kongquan and Priest Liu Qingcheng hastened to Yi Ping immediately. They were equally stunned at the same time when they saw the Celestial Fairy, Lie Qing and Youxue standing under a pavilion and they were examining a golden scroll together in perfect harmony!

They were all ghosts?

The Joyful Goddess immediately said melancholy, "We have all died…"

Yi Ping said angrily, "Enough! Why did you lie to me, Lele? Do you think it is even in the least funny?"

The Joyful Goddess looked sheepish as she took a glance at the Celestial Fairy, Lie Qing and Youxue before saying, "I just want to know if you are concern for me or not. I…I really had a near miss with death but Revelation Star has grabbed me…"

The Celestial Fairy nodded gently, indicating that it was the truth.

Actually Yi Ping was not really upset with her. He was truly glad that she was alive.

But when he had heard that she really got a near miss with death, his heart immediately softened as he asked gently. "Are you alright?"

The Joyful Goddess nodded slowly.

Yi Ping asked, "What is going on?"

Of course, Lele was not going to tell him now because it was something unorthodox and embarrassing.

When the grand hall was collapsing, they had continued to fight with one another furiously.

At the last crucial moment Yixian had blocked off a falling heavy wooden arc that almost hit Lele with her Divine Emerald Skill as she whispered softly. "We need to get out of here fast or we will all going to die."

Lie Qing agreed with her, "Let's settle the fight outside then."

They were in harmony on that and immediately ceased fighting, using their last ditch efforts to make an escape in the nick of time.

When they were outside and just as they were about to assume their fights, the Joyful Goddess suddenly said. "Sisters look!"

She had took out a golden scroll and rolled it opened in front of their eyes.

Yixian, Youxue and Lie Qing were stunned at the number of intricate formulas that were found in this scroll as they scanned quickly with their eyes. Every single wording of the intricate formulas that were written in this golden scroll was profound!

Because the wordings of the scroll were written in an older text, it took them some time to realize the importance of such a martial treasure!

Youxue asked, "What is this golden scroll?"

Lele said, "These are the various intricate formulas and the paths required to attain divinity. These intricate formulas will aid in your understandings of your martial skills and help you to overcome the Divine Calamity one day depending on your destiny."

Lie Qing was looking at it with trembling eyes for she knew how deadly the Divine Calamity was and she was unsure if she could survive the next Divine Calamity for she had cheated death using an unorthodox method.

Even the Celestial Fairy Yixian was moved by the sight of the golden scroll for past protégé leaders of the Eternal Ice Palace had all perished in the Divine Calamity.

Youxue asked, "Is the intricate formula real?"

Yixian replied, "Appears to be. This and this, are real and even more polish from what I have known. It takes me five years to figure this intricate formula at that staging. If I know of this intricate formula earlier, it can save me four painful years…"

Youxue was amazed of Yixian's ability to read and her mastery of the various intricate formulas.

Lele smiled, knowing that they had been moved by the golden scroll that she had found.

She added, "Clearing the Divine Calamity is just the first step. There are seven stages of divinity at the Celestial Level. They are Genesis, Enlighten, Emotion, Transverse, Seventh Sense, Crisis and Ascend. Each stage of divinity is furthered divided into three tiers, lower, middle and upper. Without this scroll, you can never understand how to clear and survive at each staging."

Lie Qing gasped as she peek at the scroll, "I am only at the Genesis Level. My crisis…"

Lie Qing was the only one that had no difficulty in reading the text but the many of the intricate formula was so profound that she could not grasp the essence of the intricate formula yet.

The contents of the entire golden scroll could probably take centuries to fully grasp and understand!

Yixian was quiet for a moment before she asked softly, "What is it that you want so that you can impart to us the contents of this scroll?"

The Joyful Goddess laughed softly, "Nothing. You are all my sisters. When you have reached the Transverse stage, you will understand. We have a secret destiny waiting for us that even I cannot divine yet. We are once sisters together in a different time. What really happens I really do not know because I do not have those memories too. But if we are to survive until the Divine Wrath, we must be together."

Lie Qing asked, "Is that why you have been calling me Luminous Star?"

Youxue asked in a low whisper, "You…you will help us?"

The Joyful Goddess nodded, "But there are certain things you must know. You must severe all attachments and sentiments until you can reach the Emotion Staging, or else it will be disastrous for all of you. It is a long way before you can even reach the Emotion Staging, perhaps many centuries."

Lie Qing looked at Yixian and Youxue for she knew what they must be thinking. She smiled bitterly, "I don't mind. I am already at the Genesis staging. It not as if I have someone in mind." She had lied of course.

Yixian's reply stunned Lie Qing and Youxue, "This is necessary sacrifices. Yi Ping and I belong to different world. I have already wasted so many empty years and time is running out for me. To overcome the Divine Calamity is not only my past protégé leaders' wishes but is also mine. I…am willing to embark on the path of divinity."

Youxue kept quiet. She was thinking of Yi Ping at the same time and the contents of the golden scroll.

The Joyful Goddess knew that she had successful bribed them and turned them on her side.

For Yixian and Lie Qing's state of divinity, it was not an easy matter to bribe them. No one would surrender an intricate formula without any condition. Each of the intricate formula in the golden scroll was a martial secret and extremely profound. The Joyful Goddess had shown them not one but so many intricate formulas at the same time and so willingly.

How could they not be moved?

She added, "From now on, we are sisters. You still have the time to think over it. I will leave the golden scroll with you for three days.

The Joyful Goddess sighed softly, "But now, I got a bigger headache. I still need your approval for my wedding. I don't want to be slapped or be embarrassed on my wedding date."

Chapter 43: The Emptiness Translucence

The Joyful Goddess was busy preparing her wedding throughout the day. She was virtually everywhere except near Yi Ping because it was considered inauspicious for the bride and the groom to meet before their wedding.

She was jovial regardless if the rest were really sincerely in wishing her the best of wishes.

She had almost driven Lingfeng, Yu'Er, Mei'Er, Lie Qing, Ding Yun, Youxue and even the Celestial Fairy to the point of insanity with her incessant chats.

"Am I beautiful? Is there anything to touch up? I wonder how Yi Ping will feel or think?"

She would ask the same questions to everyone on the same day as though she was intimate with everyone.

Everyone was all thinking if she really knew that they were all envy, upset, scolding or irritated by her?

Obviously the Joyful Goddess did not think the same for her state of divinity was too high.

But for the protégés of the Tranquil Clan and Traverse Clan, it was different. She was a welcoming sight when she had popped up. Her enchanting beautiful presence awed everyone.

She had really sharp ears.

When two protégés of the Tranquil Clan was discussing about the wedding preparation and how lucky Yi Ping was, she had appeared and asked. "Really? Do you think we will be blissful together?"

Even Priest Bai Chongzhen, Priest Ling Kongquan, Priest Liu Qingcheng, Nangong Le, Gongsun Jing, Qiu Wufeng were not spared from her.

She was really treating the Tranquil Clan as her home!

Yixian quietly asked herself and shared with Youxue, "Did we make a mistake?"

Youxue sighed, "I can't even remember if we approve of her wedding and now…"

Technically, Yixian, Youxue and Lie Qing did not say no as they were too engross with the contents of the golden scroll to think clearly. They actually had more questions for her regarding the different methods of cultivation than disagreeing with her.

So before they could even disagree or disapprove, the Joyful Goddess had subtly made all the decisions!

Even Lie Qing was cursing quietly, "And to think we are sisters in the past?! I can't even stand her now…"

Somehow, all the maidens felt that they had just sold Yi Ping away to the Joyful Goddess.

Ding Yun had really no disagreements because she already knew that Lele had already decided that Yi Ping was to be her husband. That included her…

Lingfeng was feeling extremely down. She had wished she was the bride instead…

Yu'Er and Mei'Er were both teary. Their husband-to-be was going to be married and they were not the brides…

Youxue was dejected. It was because she was the first one among all the maidens that had noticed Yi Ping but somehow it seemed that she was always destined not to be with him…

Yixian simply could not believe that the Joyful Goddess would actually be married right under her very nose. It was simply too unbelievable!

Finally, all the maidens had reached a startling conclusion on their very own; they had all fallen into a well-planned but ridiculous scheme that had been elaborately created by the Joyful Goddess!

Lingfeng was the first to have realized that, the more she had thought of that. The more that she had thought of that, the more convinced she was that they were all slowly pushed in the direction that the Joyful Goddess had wanted.

She could not explain it because it was too surreal!

"She really knows divination?"

Lingfeng had already decided that she was going to disrupt the wedding at all costs. It was because she simply could not give up on Yi Ping without a single fight. It did not matter if she lost to the Joyful Goddess. If Yi Ping falls into her hands, then Yi Ping would surely be lost to her forever.

Lie Qing was the second to realize that as she explained suddenly, "She actually has the audacity to woven high level suggestions with the Bewitching Soul Seizing Skill. She was astonished at her state of divinity and courage…

She sigh weakly, "She's not stupid at all. We are the real fools…even though she can't defeat her with her martial skills; she has defeated us with her state of divinity and unsuspecting courage…"

Yi Ping was the most bewildered.

He was getting married tomorrow and he did not even have a choice.

He wanted to go up and approached Yixian, Youxue, Ding Yun and even Lingfeng but he was so afflicted with guilt that he found himself unable to do so.

In the end, he did not get to say a single word to them.

He really had so much to say to Yixian but she seemed to deliberately avoid him.

"Yixian, you have changed or I have changed? You cannot remember me anymore? I have become more rugged while you have become more heavenly. Are we destined to be apart? I don't want to…"

His heart was clearly broken. But he was aware that he could not fault Yixian. It was because he was the one that had promise to take Lele and Ding Yun as his wife.

And there was Youxue.

He muttered, "Youxue…Lingfeng…Yun..."

Just as he had hung up the Divine Echo and the White Emerald Phoenix Sword on the wall in his room, there was a knock outside.

Startled, he opened the door and was surprised to see Priest Liu Qingcheng standing nervously outside.

Yi Ping quickly said, "Priest Liu! What is the matter? It is getting late."

Priest Liu Qingcheng quickly went into the door and closed the door even before Yi Ping could stop him.

Yi Ping asked, "Priest Liu? Yes?"

Priest Liu Qingcheng stammered, "Hero Yi Ping…"

Yi Ping said, "You look troubled. Is there anything I can help? Is it because Lele is causing too much inconveniences and troubles? This wedding thing is too ridiculous, even I am not too happy with it…"

Priest Liu Qingcheng grabbed his hands and said, "Can you decipher this silver scroll?"

He took out a silver scroll and unraveled it in front of Yi Ping.

Yi Ping was really puzzled, asking. "What it is?"

He smiled bitterly in his heart because his level of literacy was really low. He was quite ashamed of that and had been teased a couple of times by Lele and Lingfeng.

The silver scroll was written in a language that was totally out of the world. Yi Ping could recognize that it seemed to be written in the same form as the golden scroll.

Yi Ping said, "Priest Liu, if you want to find someone that can read this scroll why don't you ask the Joyful Goddess? She may be able to help you. I definitely can't."

Priest Liu Qingcheng said, "Don't! Do you know how valuable this silver scroll is?"

Yi Ping shook his head.

Priest Liu Qingcheng said, "This is an intricacy formula that is even more profound than the Dual Inertia Intricacy Formula. It is called the Emptiness Translucence."

Yi Ping was in a sudden daze as his fingers left the silver scroll, "The Emptiness Translucence…" Why was the name of this scroll resounded with such familiarity in his mind?

Priest Liu Qingcheng continued, "Even though we can read its contents but no one understands anything of it."

He sighed softly and began to sit down, "Do you know when the Grand Hall of Longevity was constructed?"

Yi Ping was alarmed as he thought, "Lele, Lie Qing, Youxue and Yixian have destroyed the Grand Hall of Longevity earlier. Is he asking me to pay for the damages? I am too poor to pay…"

He smiled bitterly and shook his head, "I really do not know. But it must be centuries."

Priest Liu Qingcheng nodded and added, "Nearly two thousands year old!"

Yi Ping almost fainted on the spot. He could only say, "I am willing to take responsibility for the damages even if takes me a lifetime to do so."

Priest Liu Qingcheng said, "No need. In fact, I am here to give you this scroll."

Yi Ping was stunned, "You are giving me your clan most precious intricacy formula to me?"

Even though Yi Ping was low in literacy and inexperienced with most rules of the martial fraternity but everyone knew that each clan guarded their martial secrets closely. It was so forbidden that anyone suspected of leaking it or stealing it would be hunted down.

Priest Liu Qingcheng nodded solemnly, "Do you think I am joking with you?"

Yi Ping asked, "But why?"

Priest Liu Qingcheng said, "It is associated with the founding of the Grand Hall of Longevity and the founding of the Tranquil Clan. When the Grand Hall of Longevity was built, our past protégé leader got the Emptiness Translucence Intricacy Formula from an eminent person. We have no records of his name but we refer to him as the White Sage of Emptiness."

He paused for a while before adding, "The White Sage of Emptiness left a copy of his Emptiness Translucence with us. He informed us that in the future, the Tranquil Clan will have an avoidable crisis and a stranger that is not from the Tranquil Clan will appear to aid us. A fight will then break out in the Grand Hall of the Longevity and the stranger that comes to aid us will lose all his internal strength in an act of heroism. Then he is the one that we must pass the Emptiness Translucence to him."

All of a sudden, he looked a little regretful. "Our past protégé leader and elders asked for a further sign so that the precious Emptiness Translucence will not fall into the wrong hands. The White Sage of Emptiness replied that the day the stranger stepped into the Grand Hall of Longevity it will also be the day the Grand Hall of Longevity will be destroyed."

Yi Ping smiled bitterly, "It is based on just a legend. Unfortunately, I can't even read a single word in this silver scroll. No one is able to predict the future."

Just when he was about to reject the silver scroll, Priest Liu Qingcheng recited. "The Boundless Translucence, the Divine Ascendant of the Five Conducts, Spirit, Void…"

Yi Ping muttered, "The Five Conducts of the Divine Ascendants…the Spirit, the Void, the Enigma, the Absolute and the Great Ultimate. The Emptiness of the Spirit, the Emptiness of the Void, the Emptiness of the Enigma, the Emptiness of the Absolute and the Emptiness of the Great Ultimate…"

Priest Liu Qingcheng was stunned. It was because Yi Ping had phrased it in a more concise manner than he had. He quickly asked, "You have seen this before?"

Yi Ping was now looking at the silver scroll quietly. There was a weird sparkle in his eyes as he muttered, "No…but when you start reciting it and when I see this silver scroll, I can visualize the contents…"

He was not bluffing of course. In that single instant, he had fully understood the Emptiness Translucence!

Priest Liu Qingcheng asked excitedly, "You really understand the intricacy formula of the Emptiness Translucence? Is it a supreme martial skill or a supreme heart intricate formula? We been studying it for a long time but none of us really understands it…"

Yi Ping said quietly, "The Emptiness Translucence is not just a martial intricacy formula. It is also a divine state of translucent…"

He could not explain how he knew.

Unknown to even Yi Ping himself, he was already at the Emptiness Translucence of the Enigma and had long attained the Emptiness Translucence of the Void. The Emptiness Translucence of the Enigma which meant worldly attachments was a stumbling block for him.

The purpose of this silver scroll was just to remind him to complete the Emptiness Translucence.

Yi Ping said, "Priest Liu, thank you. You can take back the silver scroll now."

Priest Liu Qingcheng was startled, "You do not need it?"

Yi Ping said quietly, "All this while, the Emptiness Translucence is in my heart. I can't explain it…"

Priest Liu Qingcheng was somehow glad that he could keep the silver scroll so he said, "You don't have to thanks me. You didn't take anything from me."

Yi Ping said solemnly, "Somehow I feel light hearted all of a sudden. I have a heavy heart for a long time. It is like I have reached enlightenment after you have revealed to me the Emptiness Translucence. Priest Liu, can you do me a favor?"

Priest Liu Qingcheng asked, "What it is? If I can help, I will surely do it for you."

Yi Ping sighed softly, "Help me to cancel the wedding."

Priest Liu Qingcheng was startled and he sighed heavily, "I afraid I can't. The wedding plans have already been in preparation. How am I going to account to the Joyful Goddess? This is really putting me into a tight spot…alas…"

Yi Ping comforted him, "I will speak to the Joyful Goddess myself. As for the Grand Hall of Longevity, the damages…"

Priest Liu Qingcheng laughed, "Don't you worry about it, young hero. I just recruit a rich protégé by the name of Nangong Le. I'm sure he will be willing to donate and build a new and grander hall of Longevity."

Yi Ping nodded gratefully.

Priest Liu Qingcheng asked, "I hope young hero that you do not mind me for asking this. Can you enlighten me on the Emptiness Translucence?"

Yi Ping sighed, "The Emptiness Translucence seems to be an intricate heart formula. I can't really explain this but the silver scroll does not contain any intricate formula. That is why no one is able to decipher its mysteries. It seems to be a wordless scroll. Somehow I feel intimate to it. I really wish I can know more."

Priest Liu Qingcheng was startled, "This is the first time that you have heard of the Emptiness Translucent and yet you can recite it…and how does young hero guess that the Emptiness Translucence is an intricate heart formula?"

Yi Ping smiled bitterly, "I really do not…know. But after hearing you reciting it, my heart becomes light and I can feel a bursting renewal in my strength. If it is not a heart intricacy formula, what else can it be?"

Priest Liu Qingcheng was staring blankly and examining him with the Dual Inertia Heart Intricacy. Indeed, Yi Ping mood was heavy when he first entered the room but now his mood was light, unreadable and the air of righteousness around him seemed to have intensified further!

There was a warning about the Seven Heavenly Fairies and that the destined one must avoid them at all costs towards the end of the silver scroll. If the destined one was able to avoid them, then nothing could hinder his enlightenment. Priest Liu Qingcheng was about to mention it when there was a knock on the door.

Yi Ping and Liu Qingcheng were startled that someone else would be knocking late into the night.

Yi Ping quickly opened the door and was startled to see Mei'Er who was carrying a flask in her hands.

Mei'Er was equally startled when she saw her protégé master, Priest Liu Qingcheng. "Why are you here, protégé master?"

Liu Qingcheng smiled bitterly, "I should be the one asking you that. Never mind. I got to go now."

He quickly rolled up the silver scroll and left the room.

Yi Ping asked, "Mei'Er, is something the matter?"

Mei'Er laughed softly, "Master…Nothing really. I know that you can't sleep tonight. That is why I am here."

Yi Ping smiled, "Why do you say that, Mei'Er?"

Mei'Er sighed softly, "Maybe you are too excited to sleep because tomorrow is your wedding day. But I do know that the reason you can't sleep is because…"

She purposely paused for a while before continuing, "You are troubled by matters of the heart. Our protégé mistress is here yet you can't talk to her. You didn't even bother trying to talk to us. Do you know how sad Sister Yu and I are? We have always regarded you as our husband-to-be."

Yi Ping sighed, "I know…I let you all down. It is my entire fault. I…I will do the right thing by canceling the wedding tomorrow."

Mei'Er sighed melancholy, "So you thinks that by doing so, you can settle and forget everything?"

She began to whisper a sorrowful tune…

Yi Ping was greatly troubled by her sorrowful tune as he reluctantly interrupted, "I don't think so at all in fact…"

Mei'Er said sadly, "That is why I am here to bring you this flask of wine. If you can't think of the right way to resolve it, why think about it? Why don't you drown yourself in sorrows?"

Yi Ping was grateful to Mei'Er, "It is something that I need tonight…will you drinks with me tonight?"

Mei'Er smiled quietly, "The last time I drink with you…I…"

She was flushing shyly now.

Even Yi Ping was too embarrassed to look at her.

Mei'Er was dressed in a translucent black silk and he could see through her porcelain white figure clearly. When he looked at her small rosy lips and expressive eyes, he recalled the night that he had awakened from his drunkenness only to find Mei'Er and Yu'Er naked besides him…

All of a sudden Mei'Er kissed him lightly on his lips sending an electrifying sensational into him that caused the lingering Emptiness Translucent to vanish from his heart.

Before he really knew what he was doing, he was holding her and kissing her passionately in return.

But Mei'Er quickly pushed him away and said, "Not tonight…erm…I have something else important to do tonight. Remember… to drink the wine. I got to go now. Bye!"

She seemed to be in a hurry and she was gone in the next instant!

Mei'Er had shyly exited the room. She was thinking, "He does like me after all. I can sense it. I got to run because this concerns our future."

But as soon as she stepped out of the room, she began to deeply regret her decision as she regained her composure. "We…alas! Yi Ping, he…he…did he just kiss me too? He was holding me. Why did I push him away? I just given up an excellent opportunity…I got so caught up with my mission…"

She began to lament regretfully but it was too late and she was too shy to return to the room. "Maybe staying in the room with Yi Ping is the better future…"

Yi Ping was still charmed by her as he shook his head, "Mei'Er…"

He smiled bitterly, "In the end, you are nothing but a lecher. You must have frightened her away so terribly. How can I be thinking of Mei'Er when I should be thinking of Yixian, Youxue, Yun and Lingfeng…"

At the thought of Mei'Er, he was also thinking of Yu'Er and Lie Qing.

At the thought of Lie Qing, he began to think of Lele…

These eight maidens, who had all gone through many adventures and critical situations with him in such a short time, he had affections for all of them.

The truth was that, he had only wanted to be with Yixian. But when Yixian had 'passed away', he was deeply grieved and he was determined to avenge her death against the yellow dressed maiden.

"Yixian…"

But in a moment of folly, he got drunk and had violated the twin sister, Beautiful Sword Mei'Er and Jade Sword Yu'Er. He knew that he did something unforgivable and decided to flee the Eternal Ice Palace to look for his wife's killer first before he surrendered himself to the twin sisters.

"Yu'Er, Mei'Er…"

But along the way, he met Ji Lingfeng, the Holy Maiden of the Holy Hex Sect which was one of the three most powerful unorthodox sects in the martial fraternity…

"Lingfeng…"

Just as Yi Ping was about to drink from the flask directly, he had frozen with a startling thought!

It was because all of a sudden he had recall that on the very night that he was drunk and had slept with the twin sister, Mei'Er had told him the exact words. "Remember…to drink the wine!"

He took a sniff at the flask and immediately he felt sleepy.

Quickly he exercised the Absolute Spirits Heart Intricacy. Immediately after he had expelled the aromatic fumes from his body, he was instantly refreshed.

Yi Ping had turned ashen as he muttered, "This wine has been tampered with. Mei'Er, why are you doing this?"

He was hurt and felt betrayed because he had trusted Mei'Er.

He immediately recalled that night in the Eternal Ice Palace, "The wine that I had drink back then was also tampered with?"

Yi Ping quietly got up and exited the room…

He arrived in a nick of time to see Yu'Er and Mei'Er whispering secretly to each other as they left their room together.

Yi Ping was startled as he asked himself, "What are they up to in the middle of the night?"

Yu'Er and Mei'Er were walking swiftly and quietly. With their level of swiftness movement accomplishments, an ordinary exponent may not be able to catch up with them!

If Yi Ping had lost his internal strength, then he too, would not be able to catch up with them because he could not maintain his pace due to lack of intricate energy circulation.

But after awakened the Emptiness Translucence that was in his heart, his internal strength was revived and his intricate energy could flow once again.

What was astonishing even to him was that his body seemed to be lighter and he could leap twice as far. He was amazed by his new sense of balance and how long he could hold his vital breath through the Divine Revelation!

Yi Ping had no time to ponder over it as he was trying very hard to tail Yu'Er and Mei'Er without being discovered.

Yu'Er paused and looked around her, whispering to Mei'Er. "I got a weird feeling that we are being followed. Are you sure Master Yi Ping is not following you?"

Mei'Er giggled softly, "Sister, you are just being overtly nervous. In this entire fraternity, there are few exponents that can tail us without being discovered by us. Moreover, the Eternal Ice Palace is renowned for the Emotionless Rhyme. If there is anyone in our range of detection, we will surely know. Even if there is someone who can hold their breath, they still have to breathe out when they are moving as rapidly as us. Our Master Yi Ping is still far from that!"

Yi Ping had overheard their talks as his hearing was exceptional sharp. He could only smile bitterly as he thought, "Mei'Er, do you know that I am just behind you?"

Yu'Er laughed softly, "That's true. Our Master is as clumsy as a fat pig. He can't even move properly. I keep forgetting that he was not trained in any swiftness skill and that he has lost all his internal strength. Silly me! If Master Yi Ping is really following you, then I am a real pig!"

Yi Ping rubbed his nose as he sighed silently, "So I am a clumsy pig in everyone's eyes…"

Mei'Er laughed softly, "He is a cute pig. How I wish I can hug him to bed every night."

Yu'Er teased her softly, "Shame on you! You are thinking of a man every night!"

Mei'Er pretended to be upset, "As if I am the only one…I heard you calling Master Yi Ping in your dreams!"

Yu'Er protested softly, "That…that's not true. You're lying!"

Mei'Er teased her back, "Shame! Shame on you!"

Their musical voices were so enchanting, so soul stealing that Yi Ping could now hear his heart beating rapidly!

Yi Ping, who was eavesdropping, began to fluster as he thought. "I shouldn't have followed them and listen to their private conversations…"

All of a sudden, Yu'Er and Mei'Er stopped their conversations as they increased their pace and disappeared behind a canopy of thick undergrowth.

There seemed to be voices behind the thick undergrowth and Yi Ping had in fact recognized quite a number of them!

Yi Ping jumped up a tree and was startled to see Yixian, Lele, Lie Qing, Ding Yun, Mei'Er, Yu'Er, Lingfeng and Youxue!

What were they up to in the middle of the night?

Lele said pitifully, "Seven against one? Even you, Sister Yun?"

Ding Yun said awkwardly, "I really didn't know what it is all about…Sister Lie Qing takes me here…"

Lie Qing said coldly, "We don't want your golden scroll and you are not to marry Yi Ping tomorrow."

Lele stroked her long hair as she hummed coldly, "You have read my scroll for the entire day and now you are retracting from your promise. Isn't that despicable? You are not afraid of being mocked by the heroes of the fraternity? Is there such a thing in this world?"

Lingfeng interrupted, "They have but I did not. You are not going to marry Yi Ping tomorrow!"

Lele asked, "Why? You like him?"

Lingfeng kept quiet immediately.

Lele said coolly, "If you like him, why don't you tell him straight? If you don't want to tell him you like him, then he is mine."

Lingfeng hummed coldly, "Hmph, you are forcing yourself on him. Do you know that his father has already betrothed us?"

Even the Celestial Fairy was startled as everyone asked at the same time, "He has a father?"

Lingfeng said coldly, "All of you don't even know he has a father. Let me tell you. His father is none other than Yi Tianxing, one of the greatest heroes in the martial fraternity twenty years ago. So stop pretending to be close to him when you all are not."

Yixian said gently, "Yi Ping and I are already married. I am his first wife. Whether he is going to marry or not, is no longer for anyone to decide. Tomorrow he will marry Yu'Er, Mei'Er and Youxue."

Lele said coldly, "Really? You have read the contents of my golden scroll and now you are trying to take my man?"

Yixian replied gently, "He is not your man. Moreover, you give your scroll willingly to us and we did not promise you anything."

Lele was alarmed as she said, "When did I give my golden scroll to you? I only lend you for three days!"

Yixian said, "It is in my hands now, isn't it? If you did not give it to me, why is it in my hands?"

Lele was stunned. The Celestial Fairy was even shrewder than she had thought!

She quickly said, "The protégé mistress of the Eternal Ice Palace will actually steal someone else's martial scroll. This is something new."

Yixian replied unhurriedly, "The Prime Celestial of the Celestial Palace will actually steal someone else's husband. This is something new too."

Lele smiled softly as she looked at Lie Qing and Ding Yun, "It does seem that a fight is inevitable. Sister Qing, why don't we join hands together against the Celestial Fairy?"

Lie Qing said coldly, "Why should I join you? I am just too happy to see you getting your just desserts."

Lele said, "Because we are sisters! You know you cannot fight her on your own. If we join hands together, then there is nothing the Celestial Fairy can do to us. And…"

She paused for a while as she blinked at Ding Yun, "Tomorrow, Sister Yun and you can also get marry by my side for we are sisters."

Ding Yun smiled awkwardly as she stole a glance at Youxue who was also looking melancholy at her. They had not expected the both of them to fall in love with the same man.

Lie Qing was almost moved but she was not as shameless as Lele as to force Yi Ping to marry her. It was because love must be mutually or else it would only bring unhappiness. So she replied coldly, "Forget it. This is between the Celestial Fairy and you."

Lie Qing took a look at Youxue and smiled, "I am closer to Sister Youxue than you."

Youxue nodded and said softly, "Thank you!" It was because her life was saved by Lie Qing who gave up her precious internal strength for her!

Lele said quickly to Lingfeng, "You are the Holy Maiden. I have helped you before. You…you must help me!"

Lingfeng smiled coldly, "Help me? I ask you to help Yi Ping and you end up stealing him from me. Even if I want to help you, do you think I'll be able to fight the Celestial Fairy? Forget it."

Lele said, "Yun, you will fight besides me?"

Ding Yun nodded quietly but she quickly added, "Sister, I think there are many things that you have to consider first."

Lele was puzzled, "What is there to consider about?"

Ding Yun said, "You have to consider Yi Ping's feelings first."

Lele smiled alluring, "Of course I did."

Ding Yun said, "As must everyone. The Celestial Fairy is Yi Ping's wife. When he had heard that she was killed by Youxue, he was deeply grieved for he had never forgotten her."

Immediately, Youxue and Yixian lowered their glances.

Ding Yun said, "Isn't it obvious that Yi Ping has a place for them in his heart?"

Lele was upset as she asked, "What about me then?"

Ding Yun broke into a smile, "Of course, he has you in his heart too. If anyone of you is hurt, do you think Yi Ping will be happy? How do you expect Yi Ping to cope?"

Lele said, "Sister Yun, what do you suggest then?"

Ding Yun said calmly, "There are eight of us here. The reason they are confronting you is because each of them has a place for Yi Ping in their hearts too."

None of the maidens protested or said anything. They were all listening attentively.

When Yi Ping had heard it, he sighed. "I don't deserve their affections. It is nothing but trouble. I should sneak away quietly…"

Ding Yun said, "Didn't you say that Sister Lie Qing and the Celestial Fairy is your predestined sisters? Why are you fighting with them in the first place?"

Lele was startled, "That's right. Why am I fighting them? No…they are the ones that try to fight me…"

Ding Yun interrupted, "Now is not the time to find fault but a time to find a possible solution."

Lingfeng smiled bitterly, "There are so many of us. Surely we cannot split Yi Ping into eight pieces, am I right?"

Lie Qing said coldly, "That happens to be a good idea. Let's split Yi Ping into eight pieces then we don't have to fight anymore. It is not like he is the only man in the world."

Yi Ping shivered at the thought.

Yixian, Youxue, Lingfeng, Yu'Er, Mei'Er and Lele all said panicky at the same time, "Don't! If you do that, don't blame me for…"

All of the sudden, all the maidens fell silence again.

Lie Qing smiled coldly as she stroked her long hair, "What better solution is there?"

Ding Yun said, "If we cannot split him, why don't we share him? Since ancient times, it is common for a worthy man to have multiply wives. Yi Ping will surely treat us equally and with fairness."

Yi Ping nearly fell down from the tree when he had heard that.

Lele laughed softly, "Sister Yun…you are so brilliant. Why didn't I think of that?"

Everyone was silently scolding the Joyful Goddess, "Because you are too self-center to think of that…"

Ding Yun looked at everyone, "Anyone has an objection?"

All the maidens were looking shyly at one another. No one raised an objection or protested.

Ding Yun laughed softly, "I assume that everyone is in agreement then. Then the wedding tomorrow will be for all of us."

Yu'Er and Mei'Er were too happy to say anything. They could only nod eagerly.

Lingfeng was grasping her face with her hands as she muttered, "I am getting married tomorrow? I have not prepared yet…"

Youxue walked quietly towards Ding Yun and Lie Qing, holding their hands…

All of a sudden, Lele asked. "Wait a minute! There must be some order for it. I want to be the first wife…"

Yixian interrupted coldly, "No!"

Lele protested, "I am the…"

She did not get to finish it because she had suddenly noticed the cold burning gaze of the seven other maidens. She muttered, "Whatever…"

She smiled again and said, "But…"

"No!"

Before she could finish, there was resounding objections again!

She was startled and thought, "They can all read my thoughts?"

All of a sudden, Yixian and Lie Qing were looking at Yi Ping's direction!

Yi Ping was startled as he thought awkwardly, "I have been detected?"

But before he could react, there was a laughter coming from the undergrowth!

It was Xiao Da!

Xiao Da laughed aloud, "I didn't expect to be detected as soon as I got near. So many beautiful maidens in the same place. It must be my lucky day. Ding Yun, you are also here. Youxue? Is that you Youxue?"

But as soon as he had caught sight of Youxue, he began to lust after his half-sister.

Ding Yun began to tremble when she had seen him.

Youxue quickly said, "Be very careful. In the martial fraternity, he is a super exponent!"

Xiao Da did not wait for the three days to be up before he decided to sneak into the Tranquil Clan in search of pleasure and prey. It was because after he had caught sight of Lingfeng, Lie Qing, Mei'Er, Yu'Er, the Joyful Goddess and Ding Yun, he could not stop thinking about them.

Xiao Da was looking intently at Yixian as he thought, "Who is she? I have never seen such a graceful heavenly maiden in my life before." He had thought that Lie Qing, the Joyful Goddess and Lingfeng were already the most beautiful maidens in the entire fraternity…

He began to laugh, "Why don't all of you just be my women instead? I promise that I won't disappoint you."

All of a sudden, he was in their midst!

His speed was startling!

He had raised his hands and with a single stroke, had broken through Yu'Er and Mei'Er defenses. He tore away their clothes and knocking them unconscious at the same time.

Before Lingfeng could react, Xiao Da had displayed his Unbreakable Hands, knocking her out and brutally tearing her clothing from her!

In just a few mere moments, he had completely disabled three maidens and had stripped them!

Ding Yun and Youxue quickly move in to intercept him but had barely exchanged a few strokes with him before they were forced back by his sheer martial strength, losing their sleeves in the process!

Xiao Da was like a behemoth beast that was unstoppable!

Besides being skillful with profound martial abilities, Xiao Da was also born with a divine strength. In close melee, few exponents could match his raw strength. Coupled with the Divine Virtuous Force, Xiao Da was virtually unstoppable!

Yi Ping was bursting with rage and was about to jump down from the tree to fight Xiao Da when he saw Xiao Da had suddenly fell onto the ground as soon as he had made contact with Lie Qing, Yixian and Lele!

Xiao Da had dashed towards Yixian for she was his primary target!

Yixian began to shiver in secret. It was because she had never met such a brutal and despicable super exponent before. She immediately raised her Divine Emerald Skill to the ninth level and readied her Jade Icy Finger to her fullness as soon as Xiao Da approached her!

Before Xiao Da could grab her, he was repelled by a startling force that was similar to the Divine Emerald Skill. When he had felt a stabbing pain on his chest, he immediately knew he was wrong about this seemingly vulnerable maiden!

Xiao Da could not believe that Yixian, a gentle maiden by all appearances would penetrate through his Divine Virtuous Force with her mere fingers.

With his Divine Virtuous Force and his divine strength, he rarely had to defend himself against any attacks and was fully focus on attack. He had allowed Yixian to hit him because he had looked down on her.

But before he could react in time, Lie Qing had struck him with a sudden bursting martial force on his chest in his moment of carelessness.

But still, it was not enough to bring Xiao Da down and he was now burning with rage but before he could get serious, Lele had flew to his back and gave him an unforgettable powerful kick between his legs!

That proved to be fatal. Even though he was unbelievable strong and bestowed with divine strength, it was nevertheless so painful that he had passed out!

Yixian gasped to Lele, "Did you just…"

Even Lie Qing was stunned, "That is low, isn't it? That's a third tier despicable martial move…"

Lele was sheepish, "The two of you are in front of him and I don't have any space to attack."

Lie Qing said, "His back is exposed to you. Of all places…"

Of course, Lele did it on purpose but she would never admit it. She knew that if they had lost tonight, their fates would be tragic. When she saw how easy Xiao Da had intentionally torn away the clothes of Yu'Er, Mei'Er and Lingfeng while overpowering them at the same time, she was secretly afraid. So her first instinct was to kick his most vulnerable part at the first opportunity rather than giving him the opportunity to recover from his initial shock.

Ding Yun and Youxue had quietly walked next to them.

Ding Yun was teary as she muttered, "We…we have actually…defeat Xiao Da?"

Even Youxue was stunned as she looked at the Joyful Goddess silently, "That unlikely move may have saved all of us. She does it on purpose?"

It was because Ding Yun and Youxue who were behind Xiao Da, were able to see the Joyful Goddess maneuver with startling speed to his back and she did not even hesitated at all when she delivered her kick. It was obviously pre-mediated.

All of a sudden, Ding Yun kicked and stomped on Xiao Da's back!

Yixian said hurriedly, "Don't. He is after all, the son of an old friend of mine. Let him go…"

Ding Yun was teary, "If I let him go, will he let us off? Do you know what he did to me? Do you know what our fates are tonight if we are unable to stop him? Do you know how many wicked things that he has done?"

Yixian was quiet.

All of a sudden, Ding Yun had grabbed Xiao Da's wrist!

Xiao Da immediately opened his eyes as he screamed in agony. But this time he was totally powerless as his body began to dry up!

Youxue turned her head quietly away as she muttered, "Xiao Shuai and Yuan Shao will not let us off…"

Yixian was alarmed, "Energy absorbing skill?!"

Ding Yun had used the Invincible Divine Force that she had learnt from Lie Qing to drain Xiao Da of all his Divine Virtuous Force intricate energy!

But Yixian quickly regained her composure and said gently to the surroundings, "Who is that? It seems that you have been here for a long time."

Lie Qing and Lele were alarmed, "There is someone else in the vicinity?"

Ding Yun and Youxue were also looking keenly at the surroundings.

Yixian said, "For him to conceal his breathing for this long, this person may even be a far stronger exponent than Xiao Da…"

Yi Ping had gasped slightly when he had heard Xiao Da's agonizing scream but however slight it was, Yixian had detected it.

But to her surprise, the intruder that she had just cautioned everyone to be wary was Yi Ping, as he jumped down from the tree top and landed lightly on the grass patch.

Youxue, Lele, Lie Qing, Ding Yun and Yixian were all stunned to see Yi Ping displaying such a superior lightness swiftness skill…

It was because lightness swiftness skill required a lot of hard dedicated work from a young age. No one could acquire it all of a sudden.

Moreover, everyone was under the assumption that Yi Ping had lost his internal strength…

Chapter 44: Surprise Reversals

Below the Tranquil Mountains, inside the main camp of the Honor Manor and Virtuous Palace.

Yuan Shao looked malevolently at Xiao Fei, Lu Baiyun and Zuo Tianyi, "Where is Xiao Da?"

Xiao Fei said briefly, "No one seems to have seen him in camp since morning."

Yuan Shao slammed the table, "Outrageous. He must have gone up the mountains on his own. How dare he disobey my instructions?!"

Lu Baiyun said, "Do we need to send my men to comb the mountains and bring him back?"

Yuan Shao growled, "No need. He will return when he has his fun."

Zuo Tianyi asked, "You are not worried that he has gone up the mountains alone?"

Yuan Shao said coldly, "It not that easy to defeat Xiao Da even if his opponents have the superior martial skills. Even if he could not defeat them, fleeing isn't a problem for him. We don't have to worry for him."

Xiao Fei said quietly, "We need to exercise caution. Even Xiao Yuanjia was killed by them."

Yuan Shao said icily, "Unless I have seen his body, I will not believe hearsay. No one knows the secrets of his thirteen blades. No one can defeat Xiao Yuanjia."

He did not know that Xiao Fei had secretly observed Xiao Yuanjia every single action and had already secretly alerted Youxue.

Zuo Tianyi asked, "All of us are capable fighters here and we still have over a hundred good fighters with us, why are we giving three days to be prepared? We can just overwhelm them with our superior numbers."

Yuan Shao said coldly, "There is no need for us to take unnecessary risk. The longer that our enemies wait in suspense, the more lingering is their doubts and fears. After all, they are young and are afraid of death. When they have too much doubt, killing them is just an effortless thing for us."

He did not know that Yi Ping had never plan more than one step at a time and he was naturally a fearless young man. Even though, Yuan Shao could see that Yi Ping had improved but it was natural for anyone to develop a phobia for the person that almost killed them. He was more interested in trapping Lie Qing and the Joyful Goddess inside the Dark Mono Sword Formation and drained them of their Invincible Divine Force intricate energy.

The "retreat" was just a plan for Yuan Shao to prevent the others from interfering in his diabolic scheme. For that, he had to give specific instructions to Xiao Da and Xiao Fei.

He was already caution of Lie Qing and when the Joyful Goddess had appeared, he was doubly caution but at the same time he was secretly pleased that there were two red eyes maidens.

But no matter how he had analyzed the situation, their enemies were as good as being defeated.

All of a sudden, there was a panicky shout from outside the large tent.

Yuan Shao said coldly, "Who dare to disturb our meeting."

All of a sudden, a few protégés of the Honor Manor began to cart a large coffin into the tent!

Lu Baiyun shouted angrily, "Who ask you to bring a coffin into the tent? Have you all live too long already?"

Zuo Tianyi and Xiao Fei were startled as they looked intently at the large wooden coffin. Yuan Shao said coldly, "Who sends it?"

Yuan Shao had flown to the large coffin and forced it opened with his palm. But when he saw the content of the coffin, he was startled; Xiao Da was lying inside the coffin!

His lips began to tremble as he muttered, "Who...nephew, who kills you?! Is there anyone in the entire fraternity that can kill you?"

Yuan Shao shouted angrily, "Who did it? Who sends it?! I want them to pay with their lives!"

A protégé of the Honor Manor began to tremble, "He says he is Yi Ping and he is now outside the camp..."

Yuan Shao broke his cane and revealed a thin sword from within, shouting. "Yi Ping! I will tear you to pieces!"

He had immediately marched outside the tent with Zuo Tianyi, Lu Baiyun and Xiao Fei at his back.

As soon as Yuan Shao had stepped outside his commanding tent, everyone was startled to see that many of the protégés of the Honor Manor were lying and crawling in pain on the ground outside!

When a protégé of the Honor Manor saw Lu Baiyun and Yuan Shao, he immediately gasped. "We cannot stop them..."

Yuan Shao began to stare furiously at the intruders and there were many of them.

Yi Ping, Shui Yixian, Lele, Lie Qing, Ding Yun, Lingfeng, Yu'Er, Mei'Er, Xiao Youxue, Nangong Le, Qiu Wufeng, Gongsun Jing, Priest Liu Qingcheng, Priest Bai Chongzhen, Priest Ling Kongquan and many others were standing loftily in front of Yuan Shao, Xiao Fei, Zuo Tianyi and Lu Baiyun.

All of a sudden, he was startled.

It was because for the very first time, Yuan Shao could feel that his powerful malevolent aura did not have any effect and was diminished by their presence. He was suddenly hard in breathing...

He could barely recognize Xiao Youxue and besides her, was a beautiful heavenly maiden with an imposing presence. He did not recognize the Celestial Fairy either.

This heavenly maiden had the most compassionate eyes that he had ever seen and her mere presence caused everyone to look at her rigidly.

Only Lu Baiyun knew better. As soon as he had recognized the Celestial Fairy, he had unconsciously begun to stagger backward!

Many of the protégés of the Honor Manor were beginning to be fearful. Even though many of their opponents had not yet fully recovered their strength but the eyes of their opponents were burning with righteous fire and even their fighting spirits were overwhelming; it seemed nothing would stop them today!

Zuo Tianyi shouted, "Yi Ping! You are courting your own death by coming here!"

He had barely lifted his frightening sword energy when Yi Ping had charged into him, drawing the white emerald phoenix sword and brandishing the beaming Divine Echo, instantly neutralizing his sword energies with a low emitting echo!

Zuo Tianyi was surprised that in less than two days, Yi Ping's swordplay seemed to have a marked improvement! It was not only a marked improvement but the speed that Yi Ping had handled the double swords were so quick and lethal that Zuo Tianyi was forced to take one step back now and then!

He thought, "How it is possible? Not only is he unaffected by my sword energies but his speed is quicker than ever before. And where did he pick this double sword technique?"

He quickly executed the Infinity-One, displaying a dozen cutting strokes at Yi Ping.

But Yi Ping swung his twin swords, retaliating more than two dozen strokes in a single instant. His attacking speed was like unstoppable shoot stars, bursting into shades of grey and sparkling lights; his attacks were invisible to all but the keenest exponents!

Xiao Fei laughed softly, "It seems that Young Master Zuo is having some trouble."

All of a sudden, Xiao Fei had flew with startling speed and drawn out his sword, stopping Yi Ping in his track!

Everyone was startled at how fast Xiao Fei's speed, even Yuan Shao!

Yuan Shao thought, "This speed…he has been concealing his true strength all along?!"

In a single instant, Xiao Fei had rained more than a dozen strokes on Yi Ping. Together with Zuo Tianyi, Yi Ping was forced back!

Youxue immediately shouted to Yi Ping, "Yi Ping, be careful. Xiao Fei is known as the Quick Blade Swordsman…"

Xiao Fei laughed softly as he overheard Youxue, "Isn't it too late to warn him already…"

Youxue had already intercepted Xiao Fei, "You dare to hurt him…"

Yi Ping said softly to her, "Youxue, move back. I can still cope…"

Yi Ping had intercepted both Xiao Fei and Zuo Tianyi each with a sword as he retaliated with dozens of flurries of attacks.

Zuo Tianyi burst into a cold sweat as he took several steps back and leaving Xiao Fei alone to tank Yi Ping's sword flurries, thinking. "This…this speed is impossible!"

Even Xiao Fei was startled as he gasped, "You…when did you…"

It was because Yi Ping had used the exact sword technique that he had just displayed, the 'Bursting Light Rays' sword technique and had used it with two swords, something that not even Xiao Fei could accomplish.

Not only was Yi Ping sword techniques more refine than the 'Bursting Light Rays', it also had the traces of the Horizon Swordplay as it sent startling burst of shadows flurrying in all directions! The martial power imbued by Yi Ping was so strong that even Xiao Fei could barely hold him off with his Divine Virtuous Force in full throttle!

Xiao Fei smiled bitterly, "You are a worthy opponent. I have not exhausted my sword techniques yet. Let's have some fun…"

Zuo Tianyi immediately took the opportunity when he was behind Xiao Fei to imbue his sword with beaming cold sword energy. This is the divine state of the Infinity-One, the departing of the sword energy from the sword.

He quickly completed the twelve circulations of his internal intricate energy in less than a minute as he aimed at Yi Ping with a startling burst of deadly sword energy, "You are dead, Yi Ping. Nothing can block the Infinity-One Sword Energy, not even the Divine Emerald Skill."

But to his utter surprise, Yi Ping managed to disengage himself from Xiao Fei, jumping in front and sliced his deadly sword energy projectile into two waves with the Divine Echo, with one of the waves injuring Xiao Fei!

Xiao Fei glanced silently at Zuo Tianyi as he coughed out blood, "He...tries to kill me along with Yi Ping?! It seems that I have to watch my back..."

Xiao Youxue had suddenly raised her sleeves at Xiao Fei while saying to Yi Ping, "Go get that despicable Zuo Tianyi. I will handle Xiao Fei."

Yi Ping took a longing glance at Youxue before he charged towards Zuo Tianyi.

Youxue took a longing glance at Yi Ping...

Xiao Fei said, "You have come to kill me with your own hands?"

Youxue said, "You know I won't. Are you seriously injured?"

Xiao Fei said bitterly, "It is a lucky thing that I am protected by the Divine Virtuous Force and had suffered only a minor internal injury. The bulk of the deadly sword energy has already been dissipated by your sweetheart. I swear I make that Zuo Tianyi pay for this."

Youxue said, "You call that just a minor injury? I think that after you have dissipated your Divine Virtuous Force, you will be lying on the bed for quite a long time. Stop forcing yourself and pretend to be strong."

Xiao Fei laughed softly, "Youxue, Youxue. We are on opposing sides now. To be merciful towards the enemy is to be merciless towards ourselves."

Youxue whispered, "That's what Xiao Shuai and Yuan Shao have taught us, isn't it? I still remember that during my first year on the run, I was caught by you but you have let me go. You...have...even told me where my brother Yuanjia had hidden his thirteen blades. You have saved my life twice."

Xiao Fei whispered, "You have told Yi Ping?"

Youxue nodded.

Xiao Fei smiled bitterly, "No wonder I cannot sense any malevolent air from him when we fought. The only malevolent air seems to be directed at that Zuo Tianyi. I shouldn't have interfered for that rascal Zuo Tianyi. But still, we still have to put on a show first..."

Youxue said coolly, "Why do you think I am here for?"

As Xiao Fei picked himself up and pretended to fight against Youxue, he whispered. "Be wary of the Celestial Palace."

Youxue asked, "Huh?"

Xiao Fei whispered, "The Virtuous Palace, the Honor Manor, the Celestial Palace and the various martial clans are congregating at the Holy Amalgamate Mountains. This you know. But do you know that they are actually contesting for the Heavenly Relic?"

Youxue was startled, "What's that?"

Xiao Fei whispered quickly, "It is a relic from an ancient time, a relic of the immortals! It is said to be able to aid the practitioners to ascend the heavens! The martial intricate formula that is inscribed on the relic hold the secret!"

Youxue asked in astonishment, "How did you know?"

Xiao Fei said, "The seven stars have joined recently and all signs pointed to the Holy Hex Sect. You didn't know about it? The Holy Maiden didn't tell you?"

In the meantime…

Yuan Shao was about to take a step forward with his cane sword when Yixian had intercepted him with her fingers!

He was startled at her attacking speed. As soon as he raised his cane sword to block her, this heavenly maiden had shattered his cane sword into pieces when her fingers landed on it!

Yuan Shao was stunned at her martial power and the cold stabbing sensation of her fingers!

"Icy Jade Finger?! Who are you?"

Yuan Shao did not dare to be careless and he had immediately hacked at her with the hidden waist sword but his sword was immediately deflected by a seemingly invisible force. No doubt, it was the Divine Emerald Skill!

Yixian said gently, "The Celestial Fairy."

Yuan Shao was startled, "You…you are the Celestial Fairy?! Why are you here?"

Yixian hummed icily, "Why can't I be here? And let my protégés be bullied by the Virtuous Palace?"

Meanwhile, Lie Qing was fighting against more than a dozen top fighters and more than a dozen fighters had already been sent wriggling on the ground by her!

Even though these fighters were all experienced top fighters and had surrounded her, they were terrified and dare not be careless. It was because Lie Qing was surrounded by a powerful invisible inertia force that caused their attacks to deflect off her!

Lie Qing was teasing them, "Maybe you should find someone stronger to fight me. It is futile. My Invincible Divine Force is not something that fighters the like of you can breech."

"The Invincible Divine Force!? She knows the Invincible Divine Force! Isn't this Gongsun Bai's skill?"

Just as more fighters were about to join in the attacks against Lie Qing, a flying sword that came from Ding Yun flew with such startling speed that it fell five fighters in an instant, terrifying the other fighters from the Honor Manor!

The Joyful Goddess was sighing in displeasure, "Remember the Celestial Star Formation that I have taught you. Don't break the formation…sigh…no one is even listening…"

Lingfeng laughed softly, "Your so call Celestial Star Formation is too hard to grasp in just a few hours…"

Qiu Wufeng was shouting to Lu Baiyun, "Don't you run. If you are a hero, stand where you are!"

Lu Baiyun smiled bitterly, "Do you think you are worthy to be my opponent yet?"

Gongsun Jing said, "What about me then?"

Nangong Le had also stepped in, "And me!"

Lu Baiyun said coldly, "Three versus one? And you can yourself a hero? But even if there are ten of you, the result will still be the same!"

Gongsun Jing said, "I am no hero. I am a wanted fugitive now."

Nangong Le laughed, "That's right. I didn't know Brother Jing, you can be so humorous!"

Gongsun Jing smiled, "I learnt from you!"

Qiu Wufeng looked at Gongsun Jing and Nangong Le with trembling heart as he said aloud, "My brothers!"

It was because he knew that Gongsun Jing and Nangong Le were grievously injured; they had tried not to show it and had joined the fight besides him!

Gongsun Jing exclaimed, "Brothers!"

Nangong Le laughed, "Let's hope that we don't become dead brothers soon!"

Qiu Wufeng and Gongsun Jing stared at him.

Lu Baiyun had displayed his extraordinary swordplay and had dashed in their midst!

All of a sudden, he was forced back by three additional swords coming from Priest Ling Kongquan, Priest Liu Qingcheng and Priest Bai Chongzhen!

Priest Liu Qingcheng said aloud, "If you want to kill my protégé first, then you have asked me first!"

Nangong Le laughed, "Thank you, thank you."

Priest Ling Kongquan whispered to Nangong Le, "I think he is more afraid of losing his funds to rebuild the Longevity Hall."

All of a sudden, there was a thunderous impact, knocking aside everyone that was around the Celestial Fairy and Yuan Shao.

"Stop fighting." The Celestial Fairy's voice was gentle but it could be heard clearly by everyone.

Yuan Shao had been knocked on the ground and he was coughing nonstop!

The Celestial Fairy said gently, "You can go. Take the coffin away as well."

Yuan Shao was laughing bitterly, "Even with my martial power, I cannot overcome you…"

The Celestial Fairy said softly, "Perhaps if you are able to restraint your rage, the outcome will be different."

Yuan Shao coughed, "Perhaps…perhaps not."

He looked around him and saw that the number of wounded and the dead around him were appalling. It was a complete defeat. He had never expected his side would be nearly annihilated in such a short time. He had never expected the Celestial Fairy to be here and that she would be this formidable…

He closed his eyes and said bitterly, "You may have defeated us today but not the next time…the Virtuous Palace awaits you at the Holy Amalgamate Mountains and we're not the only ones. The Honor Manor and the Seven Major Orthodox Sword Clans awaited you there. This victory is just only a small victory."

Priest Bai Chongzhen interrupted, "You can only count the Six Major Orthodox Sword Clans then. One of the Seven Major Orthodox Sword Clan is on this side."

Yuan Shao ignored him.

Priest Ling Kongquan said, "If the other Six Major Orthodox Sword Clans are as easy to deal with as you, then we won't have such a headache."

Priest Bai Chongzhen stared at Priest Ling Kongquan. It was not funny.

Yi Ping was still staring coldly at Zuo Tianyi, who could barely stand and was looking extremely rugged.

Ding Yun had walked quietly besides Yi Ping, holding him gently on his arm. "Let him go. He is not worth getting your hands dirty…"

Yi Ping said coldly to Zuo Tianyi, "You have betrayed our brotherhood. I don't have a sworn brother like you! Now scram!"

Zuo Tianyi laughed bitterly, "You will regret not killing me today."

He was secretly thinking, "I have lost to you because you seem to have a divine sword that can neutralize my sword energy. I am still not convinced that I will lose to you. In the secret chamber of the Infinity Sword Clan, there is a forbidden sword. I will retrieve that sword and we shall see again."

"Wait a minute!"

It was the Joyful Goddess. She said coldly, "Yi Ping says he will let you go but I have never said I will let you go."

Zuo Tianyi immediately turned ashen because the Joyful Goddess was swinging her wicked scythe expertly in front of him. He had exhausted his martial strength trying to keep himself alive.

The Joyful Goddess said coldly, "I may be the Joyful Goddess but I am also the Harbinger of Death from the Celestial Palace. My duty is to execute all offenders that are disrespectful to the Celestial Palace. And you are no exceptional…."

Zuo Tianyi was instantly terrified and had completely turned white; it was because the Joyful Goddess was suddenly cloaked with a dark malevolent aura and her malevolent air was so suffocating that everyone stopped what they were doing and was looking at her.

Even Yuan Shao was startled at this creepy malevolent air. It was because it was even more powerful than his.

Lele had attained the Transverse State of Divinity. At this state of divinity, she could amplified or diminish her aura. She knew that Zuo Tianyi had violated Ding Yun and she was extremely angry. Combined with her amplifying emotion state of divinity that she had achieved, her malevolent air was so frightening and paralyzing that no one dared to move.

Of course, Lele did not realize that. She was genuinely really very upset even though she did not show it. In her heart, she had already visualized slicing Zuo Tianyi to pieces!

She had not acted yet but her intentions were already materializing in the form of her malevolent intentions! Even though her target was only Zuo Tianyi but everyone could already visualize that they were the ones getting sliced by her!

Ding Yun said, "Don't sister! I am ill-fated as it is already. Don't harm your divinity with reckless killing."

Yi Ping had raised the Divine Echo, dispelling Lele's strong malevolent briefly. "Lele, let them go. There are too many casualties. We have already won."

Lele looked at Yi Ping before she took a look at Ding Yun, sighing melancholy. "You…have not realized the consequences of letting this man off yet…"

Yi Ping saw that Lele's malevolent air had diminished so he quickly said to Zuo Tianyi. "Go now!"

Zuo Tianyi was not the least grateful as he picked himself up and sheathed his long sword in a slow manner. Before he left, he said. "Yi Ping, this is not over yet."

Chapter 45: The Heavenly Relic

It was late in the night and there were cool breezes in all directions.

The peace was disturbed by minute tremors, caused by underground earthquakes.

The Celestial Fairy Shui Yixian was alone with Yi Ping, as they sat on top of a hill, looking at the starry skies and overlooking the majestic Tranquil Mountains.

Besides the Northern Star, there were seven other bright stars in the same constellation.

Yixian muttered softly, "When we had first met, your martial skills were just mediocre. But now, your martial skill has advanced so rapidly in such a short time...."

She added, "The ancients said; one's state of divinity depends on the state of the mind, the will, the heart, the timing of the four seasons and also the divine will of the heavens and the earth. Once all the criteria are met, the state of divinity of one's self is able to overwhelm even the sun and the moon. Everything that you hope to accomplish is within your reach in no time. Even though you are not exposed to any superior heart intricacies but everything about you is just so natural and simple. Do you know that your present state of divinity is not something that others can attain, requiring decades of mediation and cultivation? This is something I do not understand."

Yi Ping looked at her intently and said, "Xian'Er, how long have it been? I...miss you. Do you know how sad I have been when I have thought that you are no longer alive?"

Yixian said quietly, "I will rather you rebuke me...then I will feel much better...Ping'Er, I'm sorry. I am the one that cause you distress. Knowing you is the happiest day of my life."

Yi Ping sighed deeply, "That is mine as well. Why can't you go with me?"

Yixian smiled sadly, "The Divine Calamity is about to descend upon me. Already there are earth and wind changes. In less than one month, when the Celestial Omen appears, the Divine Calamity will strike in seven days."

Yi Ping said defiantly, "Just because of what Lele has said?"

Yixian added melancholy, "That is my destiny. I have only realized it when Lie Qing, Lele and I have fought together against Xiao Da. There is a familiar feeling that I seem to have known them for a long time and it seems that it is not the first time that we have been fighting as a group..."

Yi Ping interrupted, "You can't really believe everything that she is saying. Most of the time, she isn't even serious..."

Yixian put her fingers on his lips as she looked in his eyes gently, "Don't ever think of her in this way. She is right...if I cannot overcome my forthcoming Divine Calamity, then we will really never be able to see each other again. If destiny wills it, we may yet see each other again. Whether what she has said is true, I really do not know. But Lele and Lie Qing are the only ones right now that can guide me through the Divine Calamity."

Yi Ping sighed heavily, "What if we can't see each other again? Why can't we make the full use of our time together?"

Yixian said gently as she held his elbow, "You don't believe in me?"

Yi Ping said, "It is not that...I can help you..."

Yixian smiled as she looked up in the heavens, "No one is able to help me, not even Lele and Lie Qing. If they tried to help me directly, then it will have dire future consequences for all of us..."

She wanted to say, "Even Lele and Lie Qing, with their superior state of divinity and profound martial abilities could not overcome the Divine Calamity on their own. There is nothing you can do to help...do you know that my protégé mistress too was killed by the Divine Calamity and I had personally witnessed how deadly it was?"

She looked at him quietly before saying, "Destiny starts, destiny ends. We have come to the world alone and we will depart alone. Don't put it into your heart. Our destiny may have end but your destiny with many others have not..."

All of a sudden, she began to look at him quietly...

Yi Ping asked, "Is something amiss? Or is there something on my face?"

Yixian was startled by him as she muttered, "Nothing..."

It was because she had suddenly realized something. "Is it too much of a coincidence?"

Lele, Lie Qing and she, all three of them owed their very lives to Yi Ping...

He was like the link that had brought them together...

Yi Ping said quietly, "My mother used to say to me; rather than be troubled by constant worries, it is better to treasure the precious moments..."

Yixian was startled. It was because her older protégé sister Shui Yichi used to tell her the same too. Yi Ping's mother was none other than her older protégé sister Shui Yichi. She still remembered the last time that she had told her that was when she had decided to hand over the leadership of the Eternal Ice Palace to her and had decided to leave with Yi Tianxing.

Till to this day, she could not understand why Shui Yichi could bear to leave her decades of hard wrought state of divinity behind so that she could lead an ordinary life.

It was because they had been practicing a type of internal strength heart intricacy formula in the form of the Emotionless Rhyme. Falling in love or moved by emotions would ruin their decades of cultivation and even cause their internal strength to deteriorate.

Practiced with the Icy Heavenly Tears, the intricacy energy of the Eternal Ice Palace, they would cease to age.

Before Yichi had left, she had said. "I know that you may not necessary understand. Perhaps, in time to come, only you may be the only one that can overcome the Divine Calamity."

She had said, "I have always admired you...my internal strength can never be as pure as you....I should have advanced more carefully in the past. Now it is already too late..."

Yichi had comforted her with a smile, "Little protégé sister. Rather than be troubled by constant worries, it is better to treasure the precious moments. I have already found my true destiny..."

She had said, "I don't understand...you have changed. I have never seen you smile as you do now. Overcoming the Divine Calamity is our protégé mistress wish. Have you forgotten her dying wish for us? Have you forgotten how she had died?"

Yichi just smiled faintly.

Yixian was interrupted by Yi Ping who said to her, "My fate is in my hands and not in the destinies of others."

All of a sudden, Yixian had a spinning headache. This line was so vaguely familiar. It was as though she had heard it somewhere before...

All of a sudden, she began to look at him in a new light.

Her thoughts were interrupted by Yi Ping who was muttering in anguish, "Xian'Er...what exactly is the Divine Calamity? Is there anything I can do to stop it? I don't want it to happen. I don't want you to die..."

Yixian smiled melancholically, "You can't stop it. No one can stop it from happening. As for the Divine Calamity...for us practitioners, we are able to recognize its true form through the many signs and omens..."

She sighed, "When there is life, there must be death. This is the natural law of the cosmos. Martial practitioners like us are sometimes able to prolong our lives through superior mediation techniques and superior heart intricacies, exceeding the limitations of nature. That is when the Divine Calamity will confront us, to curb us, to stop us! It is because it goes against the way of the heavens!"

Just then, another minor quake shook the hill.

Yi Ping was startled, "So these quakes are caused by the Divine Calamity? This is too cruel...why must such a horrible thing exist?"

Yixian said gently, "It is a tribulation and a test. Those who can overcome the Divine Calamity will be able to break free of their current state of divinity and break free of the ills of mortality. This is something to be welcome..."

Yi Ping said bitterly, "I will help you overcome it, I swear. I'll be back and return to help you. Wait for me..."

Yixian just smiled faintly, "Ping'Er...till I have known you, I have finally realized what it is meant to care for someone, to worry for someone and to like someone...If there is a next life...if there is a next life, I want to be with you. No matter how long it would takes..."

Yi Ping's voice was trembling, "Next...life? How long would it be?"

Yixian's eyes were teary and even her voice was shaky, "No matter how long, I will surely wait...no matter how long, I am not afraid...when that time comes, we will be together...alright Ping'Er?"

Yi Ping shook his head, "I don't want. Next life is too long. We're already together..."

He cried aloud, "Xian'Er...let's make an agreement together...you must wait till I am back. Promise me, wait for me! I will come back for you. It won't be too long and we can be together again!"

Yixian looked sadly away as she sighed secretly, "Ping'Er...why must I be from the Eternal Ice Palace...the nemesis of the Emotionless Rhyme is worldly affections and emotions. To overcome the Divine Calamity means I must forget you. Even if I overcome the Divine Calamity, it means that I must continue the divine state of the Emotionless Rhyme...to stop practicing it means I will die as well..."

Yi Ping said with quiet determination, "Our destiny is in our hands and not heavens. Xian'Er, do not be afraid. I will not let you die again."

"We will not let it happen as well!"

Lie Qing had said that and with her were Lele, Youxue and Lingfeng.

It did not take them too long to reach the hill top.

Lingfeng said, "Someone is thinking of leaving secretly, no doubt about it."

Yi Ping smiled bitterly but he refused to say a single word. It seemed that he could never hide his thoughts from Lingfeng.

He called out to Lele as soon as she was near, "Lele…I am about to look for you. Help me to take care of Yixian while I am not around. You and Qing'Er…"

He looked at Lie Qing with pleading eyes.

Lie Qing nodded silently. She stroked her silken long hair with her fingers as she smiled, "Yi Ping, don't worry. With Lele and me around, we will soon find a suitable intricacy formula in the golden scroll that may be useful for Sister Yixian to overcome the Divine Calamity. After all, Lele has already spent centuries looking into the mysteries of the golden scroll."

Yi Ping was startled, "What did you just say, Qing'Er?"

Lie Qing repeated, "I say, don't worry. We can surely help sister to overcome the Divine Calamity."

Yi Ping muttered, "Not that. You said that Lele has already spent centuries looking into the mysteries of the golden scroll?"

Lie Qing said, "That's right. Or else, she won't be able to attain divinity."

Yi Ping was solemn, "That golden scroll…she just found it not long ago. I don't recall her opening that golden scroll even once after we have found it. Lele…"

Lele quickly said, "Erm…that is what they have assumed. I have never said that."

Everyone was looking at Lele in stunned astonishment.

Yixian muttered, "And you just give us the precious golden scroll without first copying it or trying to understand its contents first?"

Lele nodded, "That's right. What is wrong with that?"

Yixian, Youxue, Lie Qing, Yi Ping and Lingfeng were looking at one another and were speechless. It was because intricacy formulas were extremely precious and closely guarded. Even if a person had no use for it, it did not mean that its secrets had to be revealed to others.

Any practitioners would have eagerly pondered over the secret intricate formulas day and night…

But Lele had simply surrendered the golden scroll to them without any second thoughts.

Her true state of divinity was astonishing. It was no wonder that she could advance so quickly in her celestial divinity.

That was only half the truth. The golden scroll originally belongs to Revelation Star and therefore Lele had felt that the golden scroll actually belonged to Yixian. That was why there was no hesitation from her as she handed over the golden scroll to her. If it were others, she would never willingly surrender it. And moreover, after overcoming the Celestial Star Formation that was within the scroll, she knew that many of the intricate formulas in the golden scroll would require Lele and Yixian's help to divine it; in her surreal memories, she was the youngest of the three Sisters of Fate and her state of divinity was also the lowest. It was only through Revelation Star and Luminous Star help that she was able to overcome crisis after crisis.

Lele had another embarrassing reason; she was actually too lazy to think and practiced any intricate formulas at the moment. If anyone was trapped like her in the Star Celestial Formation for a hundred years, exhausting their spiritual and mental strength to escape from it then they would surely understand.

Yixian muttered, "Nothing. There is still time for me…"

Lele comforted her, "That's right. There is still hope. Let's don't give it up. We surely can think of a way. With our state of divinities, we may be able to find a way to overcome the Divine Calamity."

Yixian said gently to Youxue, "Youxue, you have practiced the Icy Heavenly Tears and also know the Emotionless Rhyme. I have already imparted to you all the heart intricacy formulas of these skills. Whether you can advance it depends on your destiny. You…you will take over the leadership of the Eternal Ice Palace from now on."

Youxue was startled, "I…I take over?! Isn't Yi Ping already the protégé leader of the Eternal Ice Palace? And there is Yu'Er and Mei'Er; surely they are more than capable than me to helm the Eternal Ice Palace."

Yixian said gently, "I have made Yi Ping the protégé leader so that I can retain him in the Eternal Ice Palace. However, that does not go as planned. As for Yu'Er and Mei'Er, they have too much worldly affections and it would be difficult for them to advance the martial skills of the Eternal Ice Palace. I really hope that you can do me this favor. I cannot allow the centuries of foundation of the Eternal Ice Palace to be ruined in my hands…"

Youxue looked silently at Yi Ping and then at Yixian.

Yi Ping said to Youxue, "Youxue…don't hesitate, just accept it. It is a good thing."

Lingfeng scolded Yi Ping silently, "You pig head! You have not realized what it means yet!"

Youxue asked softly, "So is there a wedding today or is it cancelled?"

Yi Ping did not know why Youxue was asking him that. He replied seriously, "I…I have overheard your conversation last night…"

Immediately, all the maidens began to flush lightly. Even though they knew that Yi Ping had overheard them last night but it was still a very embarrassing thing to even mention it, especially for Lingfeng. It was because she was almost violated by Xiao Da…

Yi Ping sighed, "I do…understand…"

Lingfeng scolded silently again, "What do you understand…you are making things worse and worse.…"

Yi Ping sighed heavily, "It is better that we cancelled the wedding first or it will be unfair to all of you. I don't even know if I will make it back alive from the Holy Amalgamate Mountains. Also, now that I know that my father is alive, I should at least inform my father. Then it will be proper…"

He had completely misunderstood Youxue.

Xiao Youxue hummed coldly, "Sister Yixian, I accept!"

Yixian nodded gently, "Very good. From now on, you are the thirty-six Emerald Mistress of the Eternal Ice Palace! You are to take care of all clan affairs and to nurture the talents. I…leave everything to your care from now on…"

Xiao Youxue said tearfully, "I…I will…"

Yixian said gently, "This is the Eternal Sealed Ring of the Eternal Ice Palace, the heraldry of the Protégé Leader."

Yi Ping said, "Youxue, congratulations! It is a good thing."

Xiao Youxue looked at him with hurtful eyes…

Yi Ping asked, "Youxue, what's wrong? You must be too happy, am I right?"

Lingfeng sighed, "Yi Ping…you are hopeless…"

Lele interrupted, "Yi Ping, you don't have to worry about the wedding anymore. I'm cancelling it."

Yixian, Lie Qing, Youxue and Lingfeng were startled.

Yi Ping was relieved, "Is that so? I know that it is too hasty. We can postpone it to a better time…"

Lele said coldly, "We are not getting married anymore. Not now, not in the future. Not ever."

Yi Ping was startled, "Lele, is that a joke? You can't…"

Lele said, "Why can't I? I am a Prime Celestial. I have no affections and sentiments whatever so. I…I'm just pulling your leg. Look at you; you are so easy to be baited. You really need more worldly experiences. Have you ever seen a Goddess displaying mortal affections?"

Yi Ping stammered, "But Lele, we…may not have gone through the marriage ritual but we have already through the ritual of man and wife, surely you can't…."

Lele was suddenly flushing, "Wait! You…you….you….don't say it aloud! You…"

Yixian, Lingfeng, Lie Qing and Youxue were suddenly bleary eyes as they thought, "So…they have already advanced so far ahead…"

Even though Yixian was Yi Ping's wife, they had never been intimate before.

Lingfeng and Youxue were trembling…

Lele said coldly, "Our destiny has ended nevertheless. Who you want to get marry to, is your business and not mine anymore. Why don't you go ask your father permission first…you pig head!"

Yi Ping stammered, "I will surely ask my father to approve of it. A marriage blessed by our parents would mean many blissful years ahead. Of course I will ask. Isn't that what I am going to do?"

Lele said icily, "I repeat. I am not to going to be married to you, not ever!"

Yi Ping was bewildered, "Lele, then what about our baby? You can' just…do that…"

All the maidens were startled and staggered backward.

Youxue grasped her hands lightly, "They…are so intimate already…I…"

Lie Qing tried very hard to control her emotions, "Lele has already lost her chastity to Yi Ping. No wonder she tries so hard to hold the wedding. I…I have wronged her and shouldn't have fought so bitterly with her... I have ruined her wedding…"

Lingfeng had almost slapped Yi Ping as she tried hard to restraint herself.

Yixian just muttered gently, "Is that so…"

Lele was startled, "Who say we got a baby?"

Yi Ping was bewildered, "But everyone says so…"

Lele was feeling dizzy, "Who says so?"

Yi Ping said, "Everyone…Everyone says that if two people go to bed together, then they will have baby in no time…"

Lele almost fainted as she smiled weakly, "Yi Ping, you are…a country pumpkin…let me tell you. I am erm…attain divinity a long time ago. It is really impossible for us to have any children, alright? So don't you worry or think too much about it."

This time, it was Yi Ping who was staggering backward. "We…won't have any children? That's impossible…"

But Yi Ping quickly recovered and he said with conviction, "Lele. No matter. I will still take you as my wife…"

Lele looked at Yi Ping tenderly, her voice had softened and her rage dissipated. In that single moment, it seemed that they were the only ones on top of the hill.

Lele muttered shyly, "You...up to you."

Yixian looked at Lie Qing secretly. She could see her sorrowful crimson eyes...

She sighed, "Our fates, our destinies...Ping'Er, I hope that you can forget us eventually...the sooner the better..."

Youxue was thinking, "I have made the right decision to back off..."

Lingfeng was sighing. How would she not know? One by one, they were all giving up on Yi Ping subtly even though they all had a place in their hearts for him. Even she herself was starting to have some doubts. "I may not have much time left too. I may not survive the upcoming battle with the determined Orthodox Clans. We can't even handle one Xiao Da, one Yuan Shao with ease and there are more than thirty major orthodox clans that have already gathered. The number of reclusive super exponents on the opposing sides is just too many..."

Not long ago, she had received word that even the Three Sages of the Orthodox Clans had returned to the martial fraternity and were on the side of the Honor Manor. The Three Sages were the Sword Sage, the Element Sage and the Martial Sage. They were the most powerful fighters of the martial fraternity in their time and did not meddle in the affairs of the martial fraternity for a long time. But for the three of them to retire out of their reclusion at the same time, it was difficult to believe what could possibly move them to do so.

Besides the Three Sages, there were many mysterious old fighters that had suddenly appeared in the Western Fraternity.

The Celestial Fairy, the Joyful Goddess and Lie Qing were not able to help her this time because Yixian the Celestial Fairy had to prepare for the forthcoming Divine Calamity. Her Divine Calamity was prematurely brought forward because she had extended the Icy Heavenly Tears to beyond the forbidden zone of the Tenth Level, a level that no one had ever been able to reach before!

When she had fought with Yuan Shao, the Celestial Fairy was forced to use the Tenth Level of the Icy Heavenly Tears and the Tenth level of the Divine Emerald Skill. And that had brought forward the Divine Calamity.

Lingfeng sighed with a heavy heart.

Youxue suddenly interrupted her, "Lingfeng. What is the Heavenly Relic? Why didn't you tell us about it?"

Lingfeng was startled, "How did you know about the Heavenly Relic. Who...who told you about it?"

Youxue said, "Xiao Fei has told me. He told me the real reason why all the clans in the martial fraternity are on their way to the Holy Amalgamate Mountains is because of the Heavenly Relic."

She stole a glance at Lele before adding, "Even the Celestial Palace is no exception."

Even Lele was startled as she exclaimed, "You all know about the Heavenly Relic too?"

Yixian nodded, "I know..."

Everyone was startled. How did the Celestial Fairy who had spent decades in complete reclusion know about the Heavenly Relic?!

Yi Ping, Lie Qing and Youxue were the most bewildered as they asked, "What exactly is the Heavenly Relic?"

Yixian, Lele and Lingfeng looked hesitating at one another. It was because they were not sure who would start first and whether they should reveal it.

Yixian said gently, "Let me start then and tell what I know. I don't think I know as much as Lingfeng or Lele. I have almost forgotten about it."

She paused for a moment before saying, "This happened a long time ago. There were just three of us, Xiao Shuai, Han…Shaodong…and I…we were at the Holy Hex Sect."

Xiao Youxue was startled, "You really know my fath…Xiao Shuai?"

A thought suddenly crossed her. Then the person that Xiao Shuai was always muttering alone was her?! The person that had caused her parents to quarrel ever so often was the Celestial Fairy?!

Lingfeng was also startled, "You…you know Xiao Shuai! You have been to the Holy Hex Sect?"

Yixian nodded gently, "We are old…friends. Xiao Shuai is the leader of our group in fact."

Youxue and Lingfeng glanced at one another in astonishment!

Yixian sighed softly, "He is the leader of our raiding group. One day, we sneaked into the Holy Hex Sect and entered its forbidden grounds."

Lingfeng was dizzy as she muttered, "No one could have entered the forbidden ground without raising an alarm. That's impossible…"

Yixian smiled gently, "Except for us. In this entire fraternity, nothing could stop the three of us. We had raided numerous martial clans, the unorthodox, the orthodox and the heretic clans. If you had known of the dangers and the close calls that we had with death together, testing our intelligence and limits to the breaking point, then you would eventually understand entering the forbidden ground of the Holy Hex Sect was actually just a simple task for the three of us."

No one had expected Yixian would have such a past. To them, she was the Emerald Mistress of the Eternal Ice Palace and no one would associate her with the Virtuous Palace. And that she had done such an outrageous act. This was a startling revelation!

Outrageous act or not, that was in the past. Yixian was calm when she had said it and was not ashamed.

Her dull beautiful eyes seemed to return to the past as she smiled faintly.

She continued, "Inside the forbidden ground, we chanced upon the Heavenly Relic that the Holy Hex Sect was guarding closely. It was a just clunk of metal in a pit. I saw…the Holy Maiden and the Protégé Leader of the Holy Hex Sect. The Holy Maiden was dripping her blood on the Heavenly Relic. They were saying that once the Seven Stars have joined, it would also be the revival time for the Heavenly Relic. And to do so, it would require the pure negative intricacy energy of the Holy Maiden and her blood. We overheard that this Heavenly Relic is able to aid the practitioner to ascend to the heavens."

She paused for a moment before continuing, "None of us believe any of the nonsense. But Xiao Shuai had wanted to steal the Heavenly Relic. But the clunk of metal was impossibly heavy. Even with the combined strength of Han Shaodong and Xiao Shuai, they could not even bulge it an inch. It was only then we knew that this Heavenly Relic to be something special."

Yi Ping asked, "Xian'Er, you didn't help them to move it? Maybe with the three of you, you can carry the Heavenly Relic away!"

Yixian smiled gently at Yi Ping, "If two men of their internal strength caliber could not carry it, I may not be able to budge it too. You have no idea how profound is their martial skill at that time. Moreover…"

She paused for a while, "Moreover…at that time, I was concealing my true martial skills from them. They didn't know that I was from the Eternal Ice Palace…and they wanted to be the heroes. Even if we could budge it, there was no way for us to take the Heavenly Relic out without detection."

She smiled gently, "I didn't know that Xiao Shuai cannot forget about that Heavenly Relic all these years. That is all I know about the Heavenly Relic."

She looked at Lingfeng quietly. She had purposely withheld a part of what she had known as she did not know whether this was the right time to reveal it.

Lingfeng said, "What the Celestial Fairy has said, is the truth. This is the secret of the Heavenly Relic. Throughout the years, only the blood of the Holy Maiden of the Holy Hex Sect can revive the Heavenly Relic. It is because in order to do so, it will require the Holy Maiden to be chaste and practiced a type of pure negative intricacy heart formula, the Holy Pureness. This has been going on for many centuries. Even my brother does not believe the legends anymore until recently; the Heavenly Relic began to float and had become extremely light…"

She looked at the seven bright stars above, "That is also the time when these seven bright stars have started to appear as well. That is all."

Yi Ping asked, "Lele? What do you know?"

Lele smiled faintly, "Do you really want to know?"

Yi Ping said, "Of course we want to know. Hurry and tell us what you know. Maybe we can even avert this martial disaster."

Lele said uneasy, "This concerns the secrets of the heavens. If I tell you, you may risk shortening your life span and you mustn't tell anyone."

Youxue said coldly, "She's just unwilling to tell us. It is because even the Celestial Palace wants that Heavenly Relic."

Lie Qing glanced at Lele coldly, "Is that so?"

Lele sighed, "If you all insist to know…very well then."

She hesitated for a while before saying, "It is said that when a Celestial managed to become a Sage or when a Sage has successful ascended to the heavens, they will leave behind a Heavenly Relic to aid future generations. The Heavenly Relic is like an ordinary clunk of heavy metal before its true form is revealed and it is said to be able to aid the practitioner to ascend the heavens. From what you have mentioned, it matched the characteristics of the Heavenly Relic alright. I didn't know that the Holy Hex Sect has a Heavenly Relic…"

Lingfeng asked, "You didn't know? Then why did you come to the Holy Hex Sect for?"

Lele was sheepish, "I think I have a mission…"

Yi Ping asked, "You think? What is your mission?"

Lele was trying very hard to recall her mission.

Youxue said, "I hope you be honest with us…"

Lie Qing said, "Don't betray the trust that we have in you…"

Yixian said gently, "We have already welcomed you as our sister…"

Lele said, "It is getting late. I think I am sleepy…"

Yixian said coldly, "You are not going anyway."

Lele smiled bitterly, "If I tell you all, I don't know what my mission is. Would anyone of you believe me?"

Yi Ping looked calmly at her, "Lele, I believe you. I have always believed you."

Yixian, Lie Qing, Youxue and Lingfeng were silently saying, "Only Yi Ping will believe you…"

Lele was touched as she burst into tears, "I…really do not know. I ran out of the Celestial Palace! It is a just a cold and forbidding place. I will never want to go back there again!"

Everyone was startled. They had never expected Lele to burst into tears!

She began to relate what exactly happened.

Everyone was speechless as they heard Lele's account.

Lingfeng shook her head, "It is a lucky thing that Priest Bai Chongzhen and Priest Liu Qingcheng aren't here. They will surely faint on the same spot if they know that you are a fake Celestial Envoy."

Even Lie Qing was so startled that she muttered, "I thought that I am a good liar but you are better. What Celestial Messenger, Celestial Envoy…heavens! You…do I really know you as my sister in the past?"

Lele protested sheepishly, "I didn't actually lie right? At least the Jade Emperor didn't raise any objections. So I am really the Celestial Envoy."

Yixian smiled weakly.

Yi Ping was rubbing his nose because he thought that it was actually funny as he crackled, "Self-appointed Celestial Envoy? That is something new."

Lele looked annoyingly at Yi Ping.

Lele tried to distract them, "There is another Heavenly Relic at the Celestial Palace. Many years ago, the Jade Emperor had found one and he had used it to overcome the Divine Calamity. But ever since then, it had reverted to a clunk of useless metal. I have been trying from time to time to revive the Heavenly Relic. But now…"

She was suddenly frightful, "I have broken the rules of the Celestial Palace and have lost my chastity. Because the Heavenly Relic that the Jade Emperor possessed had already undergone the cleansing of the Divine Calamity, no mere mortals could revive it anymore. In the entire Celestial Palace, only I had the chaste body to attempt the revival ritual. But not anymore now."

Yi Ping clapped his hands, "Lele! Why didn't you tell us earlier?! We can retrieve the Heavenly Relic and help Xian'Er to overcome the Divine Calamity. Quick, let's us go now!"

Lele said quietly, "Things are not as simple or easy as what you have thought. There is a heavy price in using the Heavenly Relic, do you know?"

Yi Ping said solemnly, "I am not afraid of anything. I will do anything to save Xian'Er!"

Lele whispered softly, "If you do that, Lingfeng will die…"

Yi Ping was startled, "Why Lingfeng will die?"

Lele looked at Lingfeng, "Because she is the one that has revived the Heavenly Relic. Her pureness of heart has revived the Heavenly Relic. The Heavenly Relic is an artifact from the heavens. Those who are impure cannot revive the Heavenly Relic."

Yixian kept quiet. It was because she had already known, having overheard it.

Lele said, "I don't know what Lingfeng did to revive the Heavenly Relic. Since it has already been revived by her, if the Heavenly Relic is consumed by the Divine Calamity, she would surely die as well. Nothing is ever free. A life in exchange for a life. This is the order of the heavens' way."

She added, "The Holy Pureness is the correct heart intricacy formula to revive the Heavenly Relic. I know because I know the Holy Pureness too. But that blood part I think is something extra."

Lingfeng almost fainted as she muttered, "Holy crap. I have wasted so much of my blood over the years…"

Lingfeng had remembered that she had visited the secret chamber that housed the Heavenly Relic. At that time, she was very down, having just been separated from Yi Ping. As soon as she had touched the Heavenly Relic, it began to glow lightly and the usual heavy metal cluck suddenly became light…

Yi Ping said to Yixian and Lingfeng, "Xian'Er and Lingfeng, I will not let any of you die. We will always be together. I will not let the Divine Calamity claim Xian'Er and I will not let anyone lay their hands on that Heavenly Relic to claim your life, Lingfeng. Never! We will always be together."

Lingfeng shed a tear as she smiled, "So is that a confession of your declaration of love?"

Yi Ping was stunned, "I…I…"

Lele said, "That is what I have known. Maybe it is just a beautiful legend. No one knows if it is true. So don't take it to heart. But others from the Celestial Palace will not let Lingfeng off so lightly. They are desperate.…"

Yi Ping was startled, "Isn't the Celestial Palace on our side?"

Lele smiled bitterly, "Maybe just the Jade Emperor but he had been very ill for a long time. The Celestial Palace had long fallen into the hands of the more aggressive and bloodthirsty Prime Celestials. None of them want to die after the Jade Emperor is gone and they will want the Heavenly Relic to become a true Celestial. Throughout the years, many of the weaker Celestials of the Celestial Palace had been sacrificed to keep the others alive. The Celestial Palace is not what it is anymore. Even the Jade Emperor can do nothing about it."

Lele took a forlorn look at Yi Ping. If she had not met Yi Ping, then eventually that would be her fate if she were to try to keep herself alive. But a chance happenstance with Yi Ping inside the Celestial Star underground palace, she had become a full Celestial like the Jade Emperor.

Yi Ping said with great determination, "Nevertheless, with the White Phoenix and the Divine Echo in my hands, I will protect all my love ones. I don't care how many they are, how strong they are. I will help Lingfeng's brother and destroyed the Heavenly Relic so that no one can ever harm Lingfeng again. And then I will come back and help Xian'Er to overcome the Divine Calamity."

He added, "There is no time to waste anymore. I…got to go now."

All the maidens were moved to tears, including Yixian.

Yixian sighed silently, "I…I finally understand what Yichi is trying to say to me but it is now too late…"

Lie Qing flew into Yi Ping's embrace suddenly as she sobbed, "Yi Ping! You…must come back alive. How I wish I can lend you a hand…if you can't beat them, you can run. You can just knock that Ji Wuzheng down if he refuses to run with you. You can steal the Heavenly Relic from him if he refused to part with it. Just be smart and don't be a hero…"

Yi Ping was startled by Lie Qing when she had suddenly flown into his embrace. He held her tightly as he sighed heavily.

"Qing'Er, you…"

In the end, the most passionate person in their group was actually Lie Qing who was almost silent the entire night…

Lie Qing sobbed, "Promise me. Till the oceans vanish and the rocks crumble, we will never part. Come back alive! You really don't need to be a hero all the time…"

Yi Ping nodded, "I will…I promise. Qing'Er, I am so sorry. I have never really taken good care of you…"

Lie Qing cried, "What you did for me, are good enough. You already did many, many things for me. Rather, I did nothing for you but caused you endless trouble…I almost kill Youxue. I ruined Lele's wedding…I fought with Yixian, lost my internal strength and ruined Sister Yun. I did so many unwanted things…I am not worthy of you…"

Yi Ping comforted her, "No, it not because of you. Without you, I will never be united with Yixian. Without you, I will never be close to Yun'Er…everything you did, are good. I will be back for you…don't you worry…Qing'Er, help me to take care of Xian'Er…"

Youxue and Lele were weeping silently when they had heard Lie Qing's confession.

All of a sudden, there was a sharp pain in Yi Ping's heart.

Lie Qing gasped, "What's wrong?"

Yi Ping had immediately turned ashen but he said nothing of his discomfort, "The sooner we part, the sooner we will be together again. I promise you, Qing'Er, I'll be back…"

Lie Qing reluctantly let go of Yi Ping…

Lele was thinking silently, "All of you…alas…at this rate, you cannot advance to my state of divinity at any time soon. Lie Qing, you have won yourself a second chance and is a True Celestial now but you are still struck at the lowest staging. Unless you can overcome your emotions, you can never overcome any of the crises. Only Yixian understands it…what do I need to do, so that you can fully understand that we are not meant to be with Yi Ping?"

Lingfeng said, "You're really not saying farewell to Yun, Yu'Er and Mei'Er?"

Yi Ping smiled bitterly as he looked at Youxue, "It is too dangerous for them. Xiao Shuai will never let Yun'Er off. Yu'Er and Mei'Er are too young. I…don't want any of them to be in mortal dangers. Youxue, I rather you stay here instead…"

Youxue said melancholy, "I have already made up my mind. I will follow you to give you a helping hand. You don't have to worry for me. I can take care of myself. In the entire fraternity, there are just a handful that can be considered as my worthy opponent."

She had been so wronged about Yi Ping. She had thought that Yi Ping wanted to cancel the wedding because he could not decide who he really liked. It was because Yi Ping knew that he may not return alive…

And she was greatly moved by Lie Qing…

Yixian sighed softly, "Youxue…"

Youxue smiled as she held her hands, "I know you meant well but I am afraid that this Eternal Sealed Ring you have to hold it a little longer. Things are not as bad as it seems. We promise to return together."

Yi Ping muttered, "Youxue…Lingfeng…Let's us move in haste now!"

Lele reminded them gently, "Yi Ping, Youxue and Lingfeng, remember the Celestial Star Formation that I have taught you. It is also effective with just three people…"

Yi Ping nodded gently before he turned away and walked down the hill.

Yixian, Lie Qing and Lele stood on the hill top for a long time, long after Yi Ping, Lingfeng and Youxue had disappeared from view. They were all thinking of the same thing; if only they could be with Yi Ping, no matter if it was a certain death or not…

All of a sudden, Lele was nausea and she almost lost her footing but she was caught by Yixian.

Yixian asked as she held her wrist, "Are you alright?"

Lele smiled, "I'm alright. It is just that the night is getting cold and I am thinking of something else…"

All of a sudden, Yixian was startled as she said gently. "Weird. There are two heart pulses on your wrist. You…you are pregnant?"

Lele was startled as she quickly said, "That's impossible…"

Lie Qing immediately examined her pulse as she said, "There is no doubt about it…"

Yixian said coolly, "My Joyful Goddess, my good sister Lele. How do you expect us to believe anything that you have ever said?"

Lele sighed softly, "I…I have heard from others too. You must know that there are just only a few Celestials and it is hard to verify things…"

Lie Qing interrupted, "Oh heavens…"

Chapter 46: The Celestial Star Formation

Yi Ping could feel a painful sensation in his heart as he struggled to walk. He had broken into a cold sweat as soon he had walked out of Yixian's sight.

He was thinking of Yixian, Lie Qing and Lele at the same time. He was thinking of Lele's farewell words, "Yi Ping, Youxue and Lingfeng, remember the Celestial Star Formation that I have taught you. It is also effective with just three people…"

Even though he was in pain but he was smiling fondly as he thought, "Lele…and you are telling us a few days ago at the Grand Hall of Longevity that the Celestial Star Formation requires a minimum of five…you can't differentiate three and five? I take it as three then. If it doesn't work, then I come back and settle the score with you. You're like a little girl…"

The Celestial Star Formation indeed required a minimum of three. Lele was trying to drag everyone into practicing her Celestial Star Formation that she had so painstaking learnt in the Celestial Annihilating Star Formation.

What Yi Ping and the others did not know, Lele had overcome the Divinity Calamity when she was very young with the aid of the Jade Emperor. Her time of activity was actually very little. Altogether she was not more than twenty, spending most of her time in a slumber to conserve what little strength she had after the Divine Calamity. She was actually very lonely and had no one to talk to…

He was walking hastily because he did not want Yixian, Lie Qing and Lele to see this sight.

Lingfeng and Youxue were alarmed.

Lingfeng quickly said, "Yi Ping, what's wrong? You…have not totally recovered from your internal injuries yet? Alas, that is an oversight…no one could recover their internal strength so speedily. Don't tell me, you forcible used your internal strength when you shouldn't…"

Youxue helped to support Yi Ping as she looked at him with equal anxiety, "You…are you alright?"

Yi Ping smiled weakly, "I don't know. I'll be fine. I don't have internal injuries. It just that…it just that my heart is experiencing some discomfort…"

Lingfeng checked his pulses as she heaved a sign of relief, "Everything is normal…if it is a heart problem, then there is nothing I can do to help. More likely it is an emotion problem. You're a lecher. Stop thinking of girls and you'll be alright…"

Yi Ping smiled bitterly, "Lingfeng, I'm really alright now. It works!"

Lingfeng was speechless as she rebuked him gently, "Hmph! So you are just pulling my leg. If I don't beat you up, then it will be hard to suppress the anger in my heart…don't you dodge…you such a lecher. I will teach you a lesson. I still can't believe that you and Lele…I don't know what honey tricks you have used to trick the Joyful Goddess but it won't work on me…"

Yi Ping flushed, "No, I didn't Lingfeng…"

She adds, "So you get a reaction from them and not from me?"

Yi Ping quickly said, "Oh no. I still got a slight pain when I think of you but it is not as painful when I am thinking of them."

Lingfeng flushed.

She muttered, "You lecher…shut up."

Yi Ping asked, "Lingfeng, what's wrong? You're….alright? Is it because you are attacked by rage emotions? You shouldn't get upset so easily. It isn't good for you…"

Lingfeng gave Yi Ping a kick as she called to Youxue, "Sister Youxue, what are you waiting for? I can't believe that you can listen to all his rubbish and still be so calm?"

Youxue smiled lightly.

Like Yixian and her mother, she had practiced the Emotionless Rhyme for as long as she could remember. Moreover, the Virtuous Palace was a cold heartless place with little affections for anyone. Her only friends were Ding Yun and Xiao Fei, her cousin who she looked up as her older brother.

By all appearances, Youxue always had a cold demeanor and was forbidden. That did not changed even when she had escaped from the Virtuous Palace.

The real her, was full of affections in her heart. It is just that she did not how to display it.

Her smile may be dainty but that already spoke volumes of her gladness and the happiness in her eyes!

She had already given her heart to Yi Ping and vowed to be with him silently. If Yi Ping could be happy, she would be happy too. By now, she already knew what type of a person Yi Ping was. Many times, she had secretly wished that they would be back to the Ice Cavern where they had spent together for more than three months…

Lie Qing and Ding Yun had shared the secrets of the Invincible Divine Force with her. But it was not possible to dissipate her Divine Virtuous Force and replaced it with the Invincible Divine Force as she had advanced too far ahead. There would be severe consequences if she were to dissipate her martial force; she may even lose her Golden Invincible Skill and her Icy Heavenly Tears that she had so painstakingly mastered.

She had taken a path that no one had ever walked; utilizing two martial forces at the same time and subtly balancing both.

The golden rejuvenation pills that she had consumed were able to grow her Divine Virtuous Force but caused an imbalance to her Icy Heavenly Tears. This caused her martial growth to slow down considerably and unable to advance any further. But a chance happenstance in the Ice Cavern, once again revived the strength of her Icy Heavenly Tears.

When she was grievously injured, Lie Qing had imparted her Invincible Divine Force intricate energy into her, advancing her Divine Virtuous Force to a new level. Moreover, Yixian had also imparted to her all the missing parts of the Icy Heavenly Tears when she was grievously injured and saved her life. This caused a breakthrough to her Icy Heavenly Tears as well!

She may not have known it yet but her present martial progression was nearly on par with Yixian, Lie Qing and Lele! What she lacked was their state of divinity to defeat them. In a real fight, martial skills alone were not the only decisive factor, state of divinities played a big part too in the form of willpower, determination, perception, reflexes, flexibility and how fast a martial practitioner was able to recover their martial strength.

Take Xiao Da as an example, he may be a very a powerful exponent and his martial power was extraordinary. Even against more powerful fighters, Xiao Da could last for a long time but he was unlucky to meet Yixian, Lie Qing and Lele who had quickly exploited his weakness; he was lured into carelessness by the seemingly vulnerable Yixian the Celestial Fairy who could conceal her malevolent air. Lele was even more quick thinking as she knocked him down with one hit in the most unlikely of all places.

That was also why Xiao Shuai and Yuan Shao were such difficult opponents to deal with. Their state of divinity was profound and they would never let themselves be lured into complacency.

All of a sudden, Youxue said. "Be wary. There are people ahead of us."

Yi Ping and Lingfeng stopped in their tracks immediately as they scanned the darkness.

Youxue said quietly, "You don't have to hide anymore. We know you are there."

Two maidens in a black finery dress walked out from the darkness!

It was Mei'Er and Yu'Er!

Mei'Er said, "Youxue, how did you discover us?"

Yu'Er sighed, "We are already trying our best to conceal ourselves yet you can still discover us."

Youxue laughed softly, "Next time…next time…don't use any perfume…maybe I can't sniff you if you don't."

But Youxue was still looking at the darkness. Besides Yu'Er and Mei'Er, there were still others in the darkness.

Mei'Er was startled, "Oh alas, I am so careless…"

Yi Ping was stunned as he stammered, "Mei'Er, Yu'Er…why are you here?"

Yu'Er walked to him and looked gently at him, "Are you thinking of running away just like the last time?"

She began to sigh softly, "I have only heard of the bride running away but never the groom."

Yi Ping sighed, "Yu'Er, go back. Do you know how dangerous the journey can be? We are not going for any sightseeing…"

All of a sudden, Yu'Er held his hands gently. "Mast…Master. You are not only my Master but is also my husband. Surely you are not thinking of abandoning Mei'Er and me?"

Yi Ping smiled bitterly, "Of course I won't…I…never thought of doing so."

Yu'Er said, "Then, shouldn't we go through weal and woes together?"

Mei'Er said, "That's right!"

Yi Ping looked at Yu'Er and Mei'Er, "All of you…"

All of a sudden, Yi Ping was stunned to see Ding Yun, Nangong Le, Qiu Wufeng and Gongsun Jing walking into their sight of view.

Gongsun Jing said, "Maiden Ding is right. You will indeed try to confront the Honor Manor alone. Have you forgotten that we are still brothers? How can we allow you to go alone?"

Yi Ping smiled bitterly, "Because we are brothers, all the more, I shouldn't have involved all of you. It is far too dangerous."

He took a glance at Lingfeng before saying, "Moreover, it is personal."

Qiu Wufeng laughed, "Don't forget, I still have a score to settle with the Heartless Scholar."

Gongsun Jing said, "And I have a score to settle with Gu Tianle and the Honor Manor as well!"

Ding Yun said quietly, "Have you forgotten what you promise me in the valley? As your wife, shouldn't I follow you everywhere?"

Nangong Le laughed aloud, "Right, right. I just cannot stand that Zuo Tianyi for injuring me. I am going to bash him."

Gongsun Jing whispered, "When did Zuo Tianyi injure you? You are taking things too personal, right?"

Nangong Le whispered, "I just can't stand his arrogance and for betraying us."

Even though they were whispering but everyone could hear it loud and clear in the silent night.

Yi Ping sighed, "I guess everyone's minds are already made up. It is pointless to urge further."

Ding Yun smiled, "That's right."

Youxue smiled at Ding Yun, "I know you must be here…"

Ding Yun walked quietly to Youxue, "The Virtuous Palace won't let us off, no matter where we go to and you are like my little sister and my only kin."

Xiao Youxue nodded quietly.

Ding Yun sighed silently, "No matter how bad Xiao Shuai is, I cannot allow the two of you to come to blows. I don't want you to live in regret for the rest of your life…"

All of a sudden, she froze as she noticed that Yi Ping was looking at her.

Ding Yun asked, "Is something wrong?"

Yi Ping flushed, "Nothing…erm…"

Yi Ping quickly tried to change to another topic by saying, "One, two, three…nine. It seems that there are nine of us. It is just nice for us to form the Celestial Star Formation?"

Qiu Wufeng smiled most bitterly, "I have seen many formations but this Celestial Star Formation is too difficult…"

Gongsun Jing nodded. Even though he was listening while Lele was guiding all of them, he could not follow the movements. He was glad that he was injured and was unable to participate in the practice. It was because Lele was gently rebuking everyone incessantly.

Yi Ping said, "Let's decide who is in the Inner Star Formation and who is in the Outer Star Formation…"

But before he could finished, everyone begun to walk rapidly away, leaving a bewildered Yi Ping behind!

The Celestial Star Formation was made up of three groups with each group consisting of three to five participators.

The first group in the Celestial Star Formation, assuming that there were only three, formed the Inner Star Formation. The second group and the third group formed the Outer Celestial Star Formations.

Usually the leader of each of the group was also the better fighter than the other two. This was to ensure that the leader would take care of the other two and forced the opponent to be trapped by the leader.

If the opponents thought that they had a better chance getting rid of the weaker fighters in the formation first, then they were making a terrible mistake. It was because the entire Celestial Star Formation was an enticing sword formation to lure the opponent into attacking the weaker fighters in the formation!

Lele had said, "In the nine circle formation, the Inner Star Formation will ideally consist of Yi Ping as leader, together with Yu'Er and Mei'Er. The second Outer Star Formation will ideally consist of the Celestial Fairy, Lie Qing and me. And of course the leader is me."

Lie Qing and Yixian exchanged glances with each other.

Lele noticed it immediately as she hastily said, "Since I know the entire layout of the Celestial Star Formation, it is naturally that I'll be the leader so that nothing will go wrong."

Yi Ping inhaled lightly as he muttered, "Since I know nothing about the Celestial Star Formation, won't it be a complete disaster if I am a leader?"

All of a sudden, Yi Ping kept quiet because he could sense a killing malevolent intent coming from Lele!

Lele cleared her throat lightly, "The third Outer Star Formation will ideally consist of Youxue, Yun and Lingfeng. Lingfeng should be the leader of the third Outer Star Formation…"

Lingfeng was startled. Her martial skills were beneath that of Youxue and Ding Yun.

Ding Yun was close to Lele and she mustered her courage to ask, "Sister Le, this makes no sense. Shouldn't Youxue be the leader?"

Lele explained, "Lingfeng has the best swiftness skill in the group. Her role is to entice and distract the opponents. Moreover, she is the most intelligent and her reaction is also the swiftness. She will make an excellent leader and tactician for the third Outer Star Formation."

Lingfeng smiled alluring, "I am so honored then."

Youxue secretly smiled. It was because she knew that Lingfeng was being sarcastic.

Other than her, Lie Qing was also trying hard not to laugh aloud for she was thinking. "This is really so funny. I don't think who the leader is, who is in which group really makes that much of a difference. It is the role that is in the formation that makes the difference. But the way she deploying us is really so interesting."

Yi Ping asked, "Isn't the second Outer Star Formation grouping overdoing it? Having the three of you in that group is way too imbalance…"

Lele chuckled softly, "What do you know? Only then will the Celestial Star Formation be perfect!"

She started to draw a circle on the ground and throwing pebbles on it while pointing out, "The standing position of each and every one of us is a triangle formation, overlapping one another. You can see that even though we are in the same group but we are exactly standing in an equivalent distance away from one another at the edge of the circle."

Yi Ping said, "Then that is still considered to be in the same group? Everyone seems to be standing so far away from one another except for the Inner Star Formation…"

Lele giggled, "That is why it is a called a formation so that we won't be identified easily!"

She raised her finger and pointed at the circle that was on the ground, "Now, if group two and group three intersect at one another, what did you see now?"

Yi Ping stared at the intersection for a while.

Lele asked, "So did you see anything?"

Yi Ping smiled bitterly, "I see nothing…"

Lele said, "Of course you shouldn't see anything. I forget to number everyone's position. Let me see…"

Yi Ping groaned and was momentarily speechless…

Yu'Er and Mei'Er were giggling until Yixian gave them a stern discreet look.

Lele exclaimed excitedly, "There! Now do you see? First numbering is me, second numbering is Yixian and third numbering is Lie Qing. Forth numbering is Lingfeng, fifth numbering is Youxue and sixth numbering is Lie Qing. Lingfeng is between Yixian and Lie Qing, Youxue is between Yixian and me while Ding Yun is between Lie Qing and me. Do you see everything perfectly now?"

Yi Ping was startled, "This is…I see it now. Anyone that tries to attack Lingfeng will be in turn attacked by Yixian and Lie Qing…"

Lele said, "That is right. Anyone that tries to attack Lingfeng will be attacked and will be trapped in a pincer attack. And Lingfeng can further lure the attacker into the Inner Star Formation, trapping and cutting the attacker off from his group. We can lure all our opponents inside, restraint all their movements and at the same time support one another!"

Yi Ping clapped his hands, "Lele, that is brilliant! Then we have nothing to fear from the Dark Mono Formation! I have heard that it is a deadly sword formation and I am worried about it. Now I don't have to worry anymore."

Lele beamed excitedly, "Let's practice it immediately then! Let's start with the formation steps first."

Yi Ping nodded eagerly.

Yixian looked at Youxue secretly, Youxue was looking at Ding Yun secretly and Ding Yun was looking at Lie Qing secretly. They could only smile bitterly at Yi Ping's naivety.

It was because they knew how difficult it was to co-ordinate everyone as one in the formation in such a short notice. The bigger a formation was, the more difficult it was. And moreover, the Celestial Star Formation appeared to be a high level formation, requiring nine equally highly skilled practitioners to be truly effective.

Lele said, "Gongsun Jing, Qiu Wufeng and that Nangong whatever, don't idle there and practiced the Star Celestial Formation as well."

Nangong Le smiled bitterly, "But I haven't recovered from my injuries yet…and my name is Nangong Le and not Nangong whatever…"

Lele interrupted, "That's why you are in the reserve and all the more, you should practice twice as hard as the chosen or else how can you lure the opponents into the Celestial Star Formation? Now Nangong whatever, are you listening?"

Nangong Le was stunned, "I lure the opponents into the Celestial Star Formation?"

Lele said, "Since you are not good enough, of course there is a need for someone to distract the opponent and lure them into the Celestial Star Formation. The rest of us got to stick with the formation steps and unless the opponent willingly entered the Celestial Star Formation, there is naturally a need for someone to lure the opponent inside and that someone is you, Nangong whatever."

Nangong Le stammered, "Hold it, why is the way that you are stating it, I seem to be the cannon fodder? And my name is not Nangong whatever."

Lele said, "I don't like someone to share the same name as me. Your protégé master is now my Celestial Messenger and even has to listen to me. Therefore, I have decided to change your name."

Nangong Le was about to protest when Gongsun Jing stepped on his foot!

Qiu Wufeng laughed softly, "Brother Nangong, I will advise you not to protest further. It will only worsen your current predicaments."

Nangong Le sighed, "Now I really regret joining the Tranquil Clan…"

Chapter 47: Penniless

Yi Ping sighed regretfully at the appalling sight that he had seen on the way to the Holy Amalgamate Mountains. There were many fallen clan banners, dead exponents and fighting as they were nearer and nearer to the Holy Amalgamate Mountains.

Exponents from dozens of martial clans in the martial fraternity had fought with one another with appalling results. It was not just a battle between the unorthodox and the orthodox clans. The feud between the Holy Hex Sect and the Honor Manor awakened old hatreds between all the martial clans, who had made used of the unrest to settle old vendettas with one another.

The Unorthodox Clans began to fight with one another openly while the Orthodox Clans began to fight with one another subtly. Even the usual secrecy heretic sects were also surfacing in the martial fraternity, creating more chaos and unrest.

In short, the martial fraternity was now embroiled in a battle for order or supremacy!

Old alliances were broken and new alliances were forged in just a matter of weeks. Altogether, more than a hundred major martial clans fought for supremacy and territories, embroiling hundreds of smaller major clans!

Lingfeng was anxious as she said, "When I left the Holy Amalgamate Mountains, things are not like this. In fact, there are quite a few unorthodox clans that suddenly cut off ties with the Holy Hex Sect, angering my brother. Now it seems that everyone is heading there now."

They had visited one town along the way but did not stay long for there were numerous conflicts and they were afraid of being recognized. They had waited until nightfall to visit the town discreetly for provision and left quickly once they were done.

Nangong Le was downcast after visiting that town. When Nangong Le had entered a merchant bank to take some silver teals, he had discovered that he had been disowned by his father. He was now penniless.

Yi Ping comforted him, "World possessions are just materials. As long as we are alive, we can earn it back."

Nangong Le smiled bitterly, "Brother Yi Ping, you have no idea how long it takes to earn even one silver. Without money, nothing is possible and we will lose plenty of friends and enjoyments."

Yi Ping just smiled coolly, "And you are spending tens of silver every day when you are still the Young Master of the Nangong Clan?"

Nangong Le said, "That's different. Back then, I don't have to earn it."

Yi Ping asked, "You need one silver? That's easy. Maybe I can help you."

Nangong Le was startled, "You look every single bit as penniless as me. If you can really produce one silver in front of me, then it is really a miracle. Money just does not simply drop from the sky."

Yi Ping called to Yujian, "Yu'Er, Brother Nangong needs one silver tael. I don't have any money. I wonder if you can give it to him?"

Lingfeng was surprise, "The sun has risen from the west. You didn't ask me for any money this time."

Yi Ping laughed, "Along the way, all our expenses have been paid by you. I feel bad if I ask you."

Lingfeng smiled alluringly, "Hmph, you still not completely heartless to remember that."

Yi Ping kept quiet immediately.

Yujian laughed softly as she reached into her pouch that was dangling on her belt.

She quickly flashed a silver tael in front of Nangong Le, much to his astonishment.

Nangong Le sighed, "Now I really regret spending all my silvers on entertainment and should have found myself a rich wife instead…"

Yujian laughed softly, "Here is one silver. The interest is one cash every day till you can return the principal sum."

Nangong Le was startled, "Yu'Er, you…I am Yi Ping's brother and you actually charged me interest? You are so shrewd…I am so pitiful…"

Mei'Er interrupted merrily, "You are a high risk debtor. Consider yourself lucky that we didn't ask for any pledges from you. Why do you need so much for?"

Nangong Le looked at everyone, "I just thinking of eating something good in town."

Gongsun Jing smiled bitterly, "You…you are simply too extravagant. One silver tael for a meal! Have you forgotten that we are still on the run and are fugitives?"

Nangong Le said awkwardly, "I used to spend more than ten silver taels on a single meal…"

Qiu Wufeng was in a daze; He was born in a wealth martial clan but the amount of silver that Nangong Le had spent daily was simply too extravagant even for him. He said, "Brother Nangong, do you know that for one silver every month, you can buy the life of a martial exponent to fight for you? The Qiu Clan only pays Lu Baiyun two silver a month."

Gongsun Jing was startled, "That is so pittance! Jue Yuan and Gu Tianle got three silver a month!"

Nangong Le was startled, "You guys…now I know why they have betrayed your clan…even our lowest servants get four silver tael every month!"

Qiu Wufeng said, "That is really too much. Do you know how many mouths we have to feed in our martial clan?"

Nangong Le smiled weakly but he was thinking, "Then you have so many men, why don't put them to good use and get them to do some business and to earn back your investments?"

Gongsun Jing seemed to know what he was thinking for he was saying, "It's a pity that the martial exponents that we have are not good in doing business and can only be bandits…alas…"

Lingfeng had wanted to say she used to spend a hundred silver taels every month but did not say it aloud for it would give Yi Ping and everyone a bad impression of her.

But Yi Ping had already thought of her, "Lingfeng, you carry so much silver taels with you. What are your monthly expenses?"

Lingfeng smiled bitterly, "This is hard to say. Sometimes a lot, sometimes very little. Usually I don't get to spend any money until I met you."

Yi Ping could only smile weakly as he looked at Ding Yun and Youxue, "What about Yun and Youxue?"

Ding Yun smiled gently, "You seem to be checking our finances. Oh well, usually I don't have much money too. The Virtuous Palace isn't a well to do clan. At most I only get like ten to thirty cash a month. Sometimes, the Virtuous Palace does not even give me any allowances on time."

Yi Ping comforted Ding Yun, "Alas…pitiful Yun, don't be sad. I will work hard in future…"

Ding Yun looked at Yi Ping passionately, "I am not sad. Don't worry for me. We will earn our keeps in future…"

Yi Ping was touched as he looked tenderly at Ding Yun until his heart began to give him discomfort again. He quickly recovered as he asked Youxue, "Youxue, what about you? Alas, you must be the poorest…the same as me…you have wandered for three years…leading such a hard life…"

Youxue gave him a shy smile.

She looked adorably at Yi Ping, sighing. "That's right…"

If Yi Ping knew the reality was totally different from what he had thought, he would have fainted on the spot immediately.

Before Youxue had secretly left the Virtuous Palace, she had stolen all of Xiao Shuai's gold taels and nearly causing him to suffer a heart attack! Not only that, through the years, she was constantly causing trouble for all the notorious bandits and fighters in the martial fraternity, using them to practice her martial skills and to lend a hand to their victims.

From these notorious bandits and fighters, she had taken their martial treasures, their unique weapons, their martial secrets and their secret martial manuals. Those that she did not need, she would secretly trade it on the black market for vast amount of silver and gold!

Needless to say, she had already cumulated a vast collection of treasures and riches that exceeded even the Nangong Clan in such a short time!

Yi Ping said gently to Youxue, "Youxue, don't worry. I will work hard to provide for your needs. I will not let you wander in the fraternity again. We will find a serene place with lofty mountains and tranquil rivers to settle. There I will be a farmer and…"

Lingfeng, Youxue, Ding Yun, Meijian and Yujian began to shift uncomfortably. Staying in an isolated place was actually the very last thing on their very minds!

Youxue pretended to nod.

Gongsun Jing clapped, "Brother Yi Ping. I admire your peaceful state of mind. Throughout the ages, there were just only a handful of heroes who could put down everything and retreated to the recess of the mountains. This is really admirable!"

Qiu Wufeng nodded, "If we survive this, maybe I would also retreat to the mountains as well. Maybe I will build a hut besides Brother Yi Ping. Haha…"

Gongsun Jing began to cough lightly.

Of course Qiu Wufeng was not serious. He just wanted everyone to admire his aspirations too. The only person that he could fool was Yi Ping.

Yi Ping nodded approvingly, "That's great Brother Qiu! If we can all survive this, we will do just that!"

Qiu Wufeng grinned but he was already thinking, "With so many martial clans that are gathering at the Holy Amalgamate Mountains, I may win renown for myself…"

Yi Ping asked, "What about you Brother Nangong?"

Nangong Le managed a weak smile, "I don't want any renown. I don't want to be a hero or be a hermit in the mountains. I just want to beg my father for forgiveness…"

Yi Ping patted him on his shoulder, "What a filial son! This is most admirable! The ancients say one of the seven virtues to uphold is filial piety. I didn't expect this from you."

Nangong le laughed, "Thank you, thank you!"

Everyone except Yi Ping was looking at Nangong Le in disgust. It was because they all knew that the last thing Nangong Le had in mind was filial piety but his parents' wealth.

Yi Ping was suddenly sorrowful as he said to Yujian and Meijian, "Both of you are so young…alas…I wonder if it is the right decision for you to follow me…"

Mei'Er was woeful and she was expressed with a hurtful look, "Master, we have accompany protégé mistress since little. Other than her, you are the closest to us. If even you do not want us, there is no point for us to live any longer."

Yi Ping sighed, "The fraternity is so big and there be plenty of hardship with me…"

Yu'Er interrupted with silent determination, "Through weal and woes, we will follow you. We have little possessions and if Master does not despise us and willing to take us in, we…are just too grateful. Yu'Er just wants to sing and play the music for you every day…"

Yi Ping suddenly began to bend forward as a painful agony seized him!

Yu'Er, Mei'Er, Lingfeng, Ding Yun and Youxue were quick to surround him as they displayed their affections and concerns!

"Master…what is wrong!" Mei'Er gasped.

"Yi Ping…are you alright?" Lingfeng asked with great concern.

Yu'Er helped to support Yi Ping while Ding Yun was checking his pulses anxiously.

Youxue was asking softly and showing deep concern, "Yi…Ping…"

Yi Ping smiled weakly and his eyes shone with appreciation as he looked tenderly at all of them, "I don't know why but lately, I have been experiencing some discomfort on my chest…"

While Gongsun Jing and Qiu Wufeng were looking worryingly at Yi Ping, Nangong Le was staring at the translucent jades that were on the twin sister's wrist.

Nangong Le was thinking, "These translucent jades are priceless and worth a huge fortune anywhere…"

He could not resist asking Meijian, "Mei'Er, the jade bangle you're carrying is fragile. You may break them in an ensuring fight. Then it will be terrible, isn't it?"

Mei'Er laughed merrily, "Don't you worry! I have more of these jade bangles at the Eternal Ice Palace."

Nangong Le was secretly startled but he quickly recovered his composure as he thought, "These precious translucent jades were said to have originated from the Heavenly Mountains so it was not entirely surprising for her to have some. But still, translucent jades were still extremely rare find."

All of a sudden, an idea struck him.

Nangong Le laughed, "Well…In that case then, do you mind selling me for one silver tael? There are two good reasons for selling to me…"

Before he could finish, Mei'Er had replied icily. "Dream on!"

He was not someone to give up easily and was about to point out the advantages of selling her translucent jade bangle to him when he noticed that Lingfeng, Youxue, Gongsun Jing, Qiu Wufeng, Yu'Er and Ding Yun were all also looking icily at him.

Lingfeng said icily, "You are desperate, isn't it?"

Nangong Le smiled awkwardly.

He was only saved from further embarrassment when everyone's attention was distracted by a young man in his twenties who was traveling on foot.

The young man was peculiar. He had five swords on his back and he was carrying a martial clan banner. From the characters that were on the banner, it appeared to be that he was from the Five Elements Clan.

Chi Zhengqi, a young man had caught sight of a group of martial exponents walking rapidly along the desolate mountain paths. This group carried no banners and consisted of four men and five maidens. They were all armed with swords except for two of the maidens. He had not used the main road because it was too dangerous in the current martial situation and he had decided to place a gambit on the lesser known paths to the Holy Amalgamate Mountains.

As he was unsure if this group of martial exponents were friends or foes and being outnumbered, he wanted to turn back immediately.

But he soon overcomes his hesitation. He got quite a brave heart or else he would not have dared to go travel to the Holy Amalgamate Mountains alone.

But the only reason that he could muster his courage to approach them was because he had suddenly noticed that the five maidens were all fascinating beautiful even though they had veiled their faces with a veiled straw hat. He had never seen such elegant and graceful maidens…

Also, their glances were investigative and had no malevolent air; that was why he had dared to approach them. Upon seeing that they did not draw their swords when they saw him, he mustered the courage to quicken his steps and to greet them.

As he approached the group, he was already startled; these maidens were indeed extraordinary beauties. He could see their facial features through their thin silken veils!

He was bewildered. What would have caused these maidens to be in these desolate wildernesses?

Chi Zhengqi said respectfully, "I am Chi Zhengqi from the Five Element Clan. I am on my way to the Holy Amalgamate Mountains to witness a battle of the century. May I know your martial clan origin and names if you do not mind sharing?"

He paused for a while to look at each of them before adding, "I really don't see any martial banners…"

Yi Ping immediately bowed with his hands respectfully, "I am Yi Ping. We are from…"

As soon as Yi Ping greeted the stranger, everyone began to be tense and alarmed!

Lingfeng sighed silently, "This pig head is going to divulge all our details to a stranger. He is totally clueless on how treacherous the martial fraternity really is…"

But before she could interrupt Yi Ping, Ding Yun said coolly. "We are from the Righteous Axioms Clan."

Chi Zhengqi was startled as he thought, "I have never heard of it before. Judging by their experienced posture and keen eyes, they must be from a well-known but reclusive martial clan that seldom in the news in the fraternity. The righteous battle between the Honor Manor and the unorthodox clans has revived the interest of many prominent reclusive martial clans back to the fraternity. It is just that I have never heard of their clan before. If I say I do not know their clan, then they will know that my clan is just a small fry in the martial fraternity. I have better pretended otherwise."

Therefore he laughed aloud, "Yes, yes. I have heard of the Righteous Axiom Clan. Judging by the magnificent air displayed by your fellow clan protégés, your clan is sure to rank among the top tier martial clans in the fraternity."

Ding Yun asked, "You are alone? I have never heard of the Five Element Clan."

Chi Zhengqi smiled awkwardly. This maiden was simply too blunt!

It would be the first time that she was traveling in the fraternity and therefore she may not have heard of the Five Element Clan. But it was a good sign that she was talking to him. Maybe she was interested in him?

He said, "The Five Element Clan is just a small clan, occupying a small hill in the Central Fraternity near the Universal Mountains. But hey, surely you have heard of the Universal Truth Clan? Our clans are in close proximity with each other!"

At the mention of the Universal Truth Clan, he was grinning proudly.

Mei'Er said, "I have heard of the Universal Truth Clan alright. It is a leading orthodox martial clan and one of the seven major orthodox sword clans. As far as I know, there are nine other martial clans near the vicinity of the Universal Truth Clan…"

Chi Zhengqi noticed that this maiden who was talking to him had a sweet mesmerizing voice. When she mentioned that there were other martial clans in the vicinity of the Universal Truth Clan, he was secretly pleased as he thought. "This maiden does know the Five Element Clan after all. I didn't know my clan is well-known outside the Universal Mountains as well!"

Mei'Er said coolly, "…however, those nine martial clans are too puny and do not even qualified to be ranked as a third tier martial clan. It is not even worth mentioning the names."

Chi Zhengqi was slight as he thought, "You say my clan is a puny clan and not even worth mentioning? Are you sure? What about your, so call Righteous Axioms Clan? I have never even heard of it before!"

He quickly said, "Maiden, did you see the swords on my back? The Five Element Clan is famous for its five elements swordplay and techniques."

Mei'Er answered coolly, "Five swords may not be able to win one sword. How do you use five swords at the same time? Weird, you have five hands?"

Yu'Er began to giggle.

Yi Ping was feeling awkward. This young man did not seem to have any ill-intention. The way Ding Yun and Mei'Er were confronting him were a little too unfriendly.

Chi Zhengqi turned red as he said, "It is only because you are a maiden or else I will surely challenge you for belittling my clan's martial skills. But I, Chi Zhengqi will let it pass as I just assume that you are still young and have little experience in the fraternity…"

Gongsun Jing and Qiu Wufeng were exchanging humorous glances. It seemed that a fight would soon break out anytime soon. That young man had totally no idea that he was dealing with Beautiful Sword Fairy Shui Meijian, the direct protégé of none other than the Celestial Fairy herself!

But before he could finish, Mei'Er had already drawn out her sword with a sharp ringing sound, the icy aura of her unsheathed long beaming sword could be felt by everyone!

Yi Ping was silently praising her, "Mei'Er, it seems that your sword art has improved! This icy aura was almost similar to the Infinity-Two now!"

The sharp and piercing cold aura of her long sword was so resounding that everyone with the exception of Youxue, Yu'Er and Yi Ping, took a few unwitting steps behind to avoid the direct piercing glare of her cold sword energy!

Chi Zhengqi broke into cold sweat as he stared in utter disbelief that this seeming young maiden could possess such a remarkable high state of divinity in her sword arts and could already merge her intricate energy with the sword to utilize sword energy!

Her cold sword energy was so paralyzing that he could not move and his legs were trembling with fear!

Mei'Er said quietly, "Draw your five swords. I will like to see how you are able to use five swords at the same time!"

Chi Zhengqi found his voice again after a difficult struggle with the paralyzing fear as he said weakly, "Maiden…it is against the martial code of the Five Element Clan to fight with the weaker sex. Even if you have won, it is not a true victory…"

Mei'Er interrupted unhappily, "You…you are just a rascal! Quickly, draw your sword! My sword arm is tired!"

Chi Zhengqi smiled bitterly, "As a man, I won't fight with a lady. It is not only against the martial code of my clan as well as my personal principle…"

Mei'Er pointed at Nangong Le, Qiu Wufeng, Yi Ping and Gongsun Jing as she said coldly, "There are four men here. Have your pick and challenge any of them. If anyone dies, this is the will of the heavens and no one should cast any blame. I want to see your five swords in action."

Gongsun Jing, Nangong Le, Qiu Wufeng and Yi Ping were startled that Mei'Er had pointed at them.

Gongsun Jing, Nangong Le and Qiu Wufeng were smiling confidently. They were after all, one of the Four Young Masters of the Martial Fraternity renown and their martial skills were naturally not weak. In fact, they were a lot better than most exponents in the fraternity.

Chi Zhengqi was panicky as he thought, "What do I do now? I am struck in an awkward situation…"

Yi Ping stepped in front of Mei'Er as he said, "Please pardon Mei'Er. It is not her intention to make things difficult for you…"

Chi Zhengqi was relieved as he thought, "This Yi Ping…he seems amicable…"

Yi Ping said, "…now that Mei'Er has mentioned it, I am also intrigued by your impressive Five Element Swordplay. I wonder if young hero can do me the honor by sparring with me?"

Mei'Er laughed softly, "So even our Master is also curious."

Chi Zhengqi was startled as he thought, "This young man is her Master?! This young maiden is already so formidable then her Master will be even more formidable…how did this turn up like this? Will they kill me?"

In the martial fraternity, age was not used to denote seniority in a martial clan. Rather, direct protégés had a more senior rank and they were usually the ones that were taught the clan's secret skills.

Chi Zhengqi thought miserably, "Now it really becomes the will of the heavens and no one should be blamed if anyone dies. I am the one that fall into this bottomless pit myself…"

Yi Ping had already displayed a fighting stance!

All of a sudden, a thought struck Chi Zhengqi like a deadly thunderbolt!

"Did he say he is Yi Ping? The Honor Manor has branded Yi Ping as a wanted fugitive along with Nangong Le, Gongsun Jing and Qiu Wufeng…"

He began to stare at the three men that were behind men. He had noticed that all of them were inconspicuously touching their undrawn weapons lightly with their fingers except for the two weaponless maidens.

Lingfeng and Youxue were curious that Chi Zhengqi was suddenly looking at them…

Chi Zhengqi quickly thought, "I must stay calm and think of a way. These two maidens must be held hostages by this group of notorious heretics. Come to think of that, I can see their little fingers moving. Maybe they are already giving me so many hints already with their hand gestures. I must be idiot not to notice it much earlier. Maybe they didn't know that I have already known their identities?"

He decided to take a gamble by saying, "I just remember that I have something important to do first. May we meet again…"

Before Yi Ping could say anything, Chi Zhengqi had already turned around and ran in the opposite direction!

Chi Zhengqi was relieved that they did not give chase to him as he thought, "Luckily, I am quick thinking or I will surely die in this desolate mountains. Alas…thanks heavens! The first thing that I am going to the nearest town is to inform the rest of the orthodox clans that the powerful Righteous Axioms Clan is on the way to the Holy Amalgamate Mountains. These notorious villains have also kidnapped innocent maidens along the way…alas…their poor fates. They outnumber me…it is not that dishonorable to run. The most important thing is to keep myself alive so that the righteous orthodox clans can guard against the schemes of the Righteous Axioms Clan. These despicable rapists…"

When Chi Zhengqi had departed, Lingfeng sighed softly. "Why is it that I have such a terrible feeling about all these and that young man?"

Yi Ping was saying, "What a pity. I really will like to see his astonishing Five Element Swordplay…"

Lingfeng said, "Yi Ping, you have better don't report your name so recklessly. We don't know if others are friend or foe. Don't take unnecessary risk, alright?"

Yi Ping clapped his hands, "Alas! I forget that I am a wanted fugitive. Why didn't you remind me earlier, Lingfeng?"

Lingfeng gave Yi Ping a hard kick immediately, "Why don't you go and die first?"

Yi Ping quickly recovered from the hard kick as he said excitedly to everyone, "Lingfeng, your kick just gives me an idea for the Celestial Star Formation. We should stick to Lele's original deployment for the Celestial Star Formation. Yu'Er and Mei'Er will be in the same group as me. Youxue, Yun and you will still be in the same group. Brother Nangong, Brother Gongsun and Brother Qiu will form the third group the Outer Star Formation. I think that Brother Gongsun makes a good leader…"

At the mere mention of the Celestial Star Formation, everyone seemed to have hurried their steps and rapidly walked away.

Yi Ping was bewildered, "What's wrong?"

It was because other than Lele, Yi Ping was the only one that could make sense of the Celestial Star Formation.

Even Lele had praised Yi Ping, "You have learnt the Celestial Star Formation previously? How did you memorize all the moves so quickly?"

Yi Ping had said, "No, this is my first time."

Lele was already thinking, "Can it be?"

She looked at Yi Ping with a curious look. There was something about Yi Ping that she could not pinpoint yet as she thought, "That's impossible. I take a hundred years to grasp it but he only takes a while?"

She was beginning to think that it was no coincident that Yi Ping had led them into the center of the Celestial Star Chamber...

The Celestial Star Chamber where she had found the golden scroll was located in the middle of several deadly Celestial Star Formations. It was almost impossible to find without first having the knowledge of the Celestial Star Formation or having profound knowledge in all the well-known formations...

But before she could ponder further, Lie Qing and Yixian had called out for her; they were also genuinely interested in the Celestial Star Formation and had encountered some difficulty in grasping the intriguing changes of the Celestial Star Formation.

She abandoned her pondering and flew happily to their side, explaining to them with great enthusiasm.

Yi Ping sighed as he recalled that scene back then...

Even though he had just left the Tranquil Mountains not long ago but he was already sorely missing Lele...Lie Qing and Yixian...

He was now clutching his chest again as a sudden pain overwhelmed him...

All of a sudden, there was a loud resounding voice in the mountains.

"Since your sword has already left its scabbard, isn't it a pity not to appease your sword first?"

Yi Ping was alarmed and he immediately sprung ahead.

Mei'Er was looking keenly at the surroundings, checking every single trees, thickets and overgrowths as she said, "Who are you?!"

"Who am I? Ha......Haha...I am the Mountain God." The voice was old and ancient.

Youxue said coldly, "Show yourself. How dare you pull such a roguish ruse on us."

Ding Yun had drew her sword as she said quietly, "God or Demon, you have to question the sword in my hand first."

Lingfeng raised her hands and threw dozens of secret projectiles in the direction of a thick overgrowth as she shouted, "There! He is over there!"

Chapter 48: The Celestial Star Formation vs. the Divine Rejuvenation Force

An old man with a long white beard had jumped out of the shadows of the thick overgrowth. He seemed startled that Lingfeng could actually locate his hiding place even though he had disguised his whereabouts with the Deep Resounding Skill, a skill that can cast out his voice evenly to the surroundings!

They were surprised that it was actually an unarmed old man.

Lingfeng was stunned as she quickly thought, "Where did all my secret projectiles gone to?"

Yi Ping had stepped forward as he shouted, "Who are you..."

The old man ignored Yi Ping; he did not look pleased at all as he pointed his finger at Lingfeng, "What ruthless and deadly secret projectile techniques. How did you guess my location?"

Lingfeng laughed softly, "The birds told me!"

The old man snarled, "Rubbish. Birds can't talk..."

Ding Yun said quietly, "Even though the birds can't talk but the birds can see you. When the birds fly above you, they take a detour. Even though you have tried to conceal your malevolent air but animals are hyper sensitive."

The old man hummed coldly, "It seems that at my old age, I have learnt something new today."

All of a sudden, the old man was enveloped by a powerful killing malevolent intent! His killing malevolent intent was even more deadly and purer than Yuan Shao!

Yi Ping was momentarily startled but he repeated, "Who are you? Why are you acting so secrecy and what do you mean by what you have said earlier?"

The old man pointed at Mei'Er, "Since you have already drawn out your sword, then let's have some fun today."

Mei'Er hummed coldly, "So it is just a lecherous old man!"

She had flown to the old man, displaying the Flying Swallow Slash but the old man raised his hand and knocked her forcefully aside!

Yu'Er gasped, "Mei'Er!"

But before the old man could seize Mei'Er, he was attacked by a flurrying of powerful hazily attacks by Xiao Youxue!

He quietly blocked all her explosive attacks with his left hand and counter-attacked with his right hand aimed at her.

As Youxue took the blow from his right hand, there was a thunderous impact as she was sent flying backward!

She was really startled. This old man had actually parried all her Penetrating Hands when she had quietly appeared and had retaliated against her almost instantaneously!

She warned the others even as she quickly regained her balance, "Be careful! This old man is dangerous! He is a super exponent!"

The old man was also secretly startled at the martial power of this young maiden. Even though this maiden looked weak but when she had suddenly attacked him, every single blow that came from her had so much martial power that it could shatter rocks! He was nearly caught unaware and had quickly retaliated with his remaining martial power on her.

He was astonished that this young maiden could take his blow without suffering any slight ill-effect.

Even as he had pushed Youxue away, he was surprised by a flying sword that was thrown by Ding Yun!

Ding Yun had timed her flying sword at precisely the exact moment when his martial power was retracting so that he could not evade it!

The speed of her flying sword was so startling, imbued by Ding Yun's newly acquired Invincible Divine Force that it was even more deadly than in the past!

But the unbelievable thing happened!

The old man had raised left hand as the surrounding air crackled with the heavy pressure of his martial power. Before Ding Yun's flying sword could even strike him, there was a thunderous explosion in mid-air as the flying sword was deflected to another direction!

The old man said, "This is the Flying Sword Technique of the Virtuous Palace?"

Lingfeng gasped, "Be extra careful! This is the Big Dipper Hands!"

Ding Yun and Youxue were startled. They had heard of this deadly mystifying skill but had never seen it before!

The old man was startled that Lingfeng could actually recognize his secret martial skill.

Just as the old man had deflected Ding Yun's flying sword, Yi Ping had displayed the Divine Horizon Hands fiercely on him!

Once again, the old man was startled as Yi Ping attacks were not only insanely fast but it was also filled with extraordinary pure martial power!

"This is the Divine Horizon Hands?"

After exchanging three dozen extremely fast blows with Yi Ping in less than a blink of an eye, the old man was forced to take a few steps backward when he was confronted by Gongsun Jing, Nangong Le, Qiu Wufeng, Yu'Er, Mei'Er, Lingfeng, Youxue and Ding Yun at the same time!

The old man was beginning to be astonished at their superb martial display. Even though he was the more powerful exponent but these young men and women were not giving him any opportunity to take any breather. Moreover, they were also able to cover one another in perfect harmony!

All of a sudden, he had observed something peculiar about their movements. Judging from their steps and similar circulating movement, it was obviously that they were all trained in the same type of attack formation!

At first, he just wanted to make a fool of these juniors but now he got more than he had bargained for.

Yi Ping had leapt into mid-air as he displayed the Aspire Horizon Hands, shouting angrily, "You have dared to hurt Mei'Er."

The old man knew immediately that the incoming attack was an almighty attack that could shatter rocks and grinding it into dust. He immediately raised both of his hands forward as the flurrying forceful windforce of his Big Dipper Hands exploded around him, sending Nangong Le, Gongsun Jing, Qiu Wufeng and Lingfeng scurrying backward!

Yu'Er and Mei'Er had raised their fingers as they displayed the Divine Emerald Skill to absorb the resultant force but they were unable to press forward their attacks.

Ding Yun raised her left hand forward with the Invincible Divine Force, neutralizing the old man's pressuring windforce as she imbued her foldable sword with the remaining Invincible Divine Force, joining Yi Ping in the attack.

Xiao Youxue had raised her hand in a cutting arc, neutralizing the bulk of the Big Dipper Hand's martial force before she too, attacked at the same time with Yi Ping and Ding Yun!

There was a thunderous impact as the air around him exploded almighty, sending Yi Ping, Youxue, Ding Yun and the old man flying backward.

Except for Youxue, Yi Ping, Ding Yun and the old man were coughing out blood for the resultant backlash of their martial force was enough to cause serious internal injuries!

Like the rest, Youxue was also gasping breathlessly and was desperately trying to circulate and stabilize the flow of her vital energies. She was not as seriously injured as Yi Ping and Ding Yun for she was protected by the Golden Invincible Body and the Icy Heavenly Tears. Moreover Yi Ping and Ding Yun had shared the blunt of the powerful martial force of the Big Dipper Hands, lessening the impact that she had received.

She had barely looked up only to see a startling sight!

The old man was being surrounded by a small inertia force around him. Even though this inertia force was similar to the inertia force of the Invincible Divine Force, Divine Emerald Skill and the Divine Virtuous Force, it was totally different type of inertia force!

The old man had gathered all the martial power around him, wasting none of his vital force and re-absorbing it again.

Xiao Youxue gasped and thought as she saw the slightly visible inertia barrier of the old man, "Isn't that the highest level of vital energy force? Force that can regenerate force. Force that is dissipated and recovered at the same time!" She had thought that it was only a theory and did not think that she would actually witness this today!

The old man was coughing and cursing, "Damn it. You have forced me to display one secret technique after another. If I do not vent my anger fully today, I am not going to leave."

Indeed, he had just displayed the Divine Rejuvenation Force, a secret divine martial skill that could regain his martial power as soon as he had expended it.

Everyone was staring blankly and in disbelief at the fierce martial force that was hovering swiftly around the old man.

Not only was the old man surrounded by a powerful martial force that could constantly replenish his strength, they had just witnessed the unbelievable power of his Big Dipper hands. Even if they could bypass the martial force of his Big Dipper Hands, the resulting martial force that could actually reach the old man would be reduced drastically and not enough to neutralize the inertia force around him. And it had taken the combined force of Yi Ping, Youxue and Ding Yun to injure him.

Moreover, they had already discovered a startling thing about that inertia force; if they fail to injure the old man, then their martial force would be drained to empower the old man's martial power. That was why no one dared to make a false move. Furthermore, the ensuring fight was extremely draining to their martial power as Yi Ping, Youxue, Ding Yun and the rest struggled to quickly stabilize their vital energy flow for the next attack or they would risk internal injuries!

The old man was jeering them as he stroked his long beard, "Young people. All of you together and you can't even handle an old man like me? What a joke! Are you ready for another round? Before I send all of you to your maker, let me tell you that this is the Divine Rejuvenation Force."

He pointed at Yu'Er and Mei'Er, asking them. "Your martial skills are from the Eternal Ice Palace?"

Yu'Er and Mei'Er refused to answer.

The old man said coldly, "I'm not going to berate your clan. At your age, your martial skills are already quite impressive. But what's a pity."

Mei'Er could not resist asking, "But a pity what?"

The old man replied, "But what a pity with five equal attractive rare beauties, I don't know who I should I pick first tonight."

Everyone was moved to teething rage!

Yi Ping clenched his fists in furious rage and helplessness. This old man was the most formidable opponent that he had met until now. All of a sudden, he remembered what his father had said to him, "The Asper Divinity Horizon Hand requires eighty years of solid internal strength to use…if you manage to learn this forbidden skill, in three years' time…you will surely die!"

Yi Ping asked himself, "Do I have eighty years of internal strength now?"

Until now, Yi Ping had never fight against a martial skill with a martial power that exceeded the Asper Horizon Hands till he witnessed the Big Dipper Hands today. If he had to fight on equal footing with the Big Dipper Hand then he had to raise his martial power to his opponent level first!

Ding Yun interrupted his thoughts, "Yi Ping…everyone….stay calm. Even though the Divine Rejuvenation Force is all-powerful, it does have a weakness."

Everyone was startled as they regained some of their lost fighting spirit.

The old man was startled, "Rubbish. My Divine Rejuvenation Force has no weakness whatever so…"

Ding Yun said calmly, "If I am not wrong, maintaining the Divine Rejuvenation Force requires considerable mental effort. It has to be a purely defensive skill. That is why he is not moving forward to attack us or else he risks dissipating the Divine Rejuvenation Force. Or else why didn't he use it much earlier?"

The old man was secretly alarmed as he thought, "She can tell?"

Yi Ping said excitedly, "Yun, you are so brilliant!"

The old man said coldly, "What are you waiting for? Are you waiting for me to get you first?"

Yi Ping had suddenly brandished the White Phoenix and the Divine Echo as he said quietly to everyone, "The Celestial Star Formation. This is our only chance now."

When he had brandished the white beaming blade of the Divine Echo, a resounding echo could be heard ringing from the sword and in the surrounding vicinity!

The old man was startled, "This sword…"

Yi Ping did not want to brandish any weapons against an unarmed foe but this old man was simply too insolent and despicable. Moreover he had expended much of his martial power and could only depend on his swords now.

Yi Ping said aloud, "Yu'Er and Mei'Er, attack with me. Lingfeng, Youxue and Yun attack together. Brother Gongsun, Brother Nangong and Brother Qiu attack together…"

All of a sudden, Lingfeng, Youxue, Yun, Gongsun Jing, Qiu Wufeng and Nangong Le were attacking the old man one after another!

Barely had the old man raised his hands at his attackers, they had retreated and replaced by another! He knew instantly that they were trapping him inside a deadly attacking formation!

Yi Ping had charged at the old man, displaying dozens of furious strokes with his double swords!

The old man was startled at Yi Ping astonishing attacking speed. He had barely raised his Big Dipper Hands to deflect Yi Ping's sword strokes, he was back again with another double strike, again and again!

The old man immediately mustered all his martial power to deal Yi Ping's a crushing blow with the Big Dipper Hand when he was intercepted by Yu'Er and Mei'Er who had stepped in front of Yi Ping as they displayed the Divine Emerald Force at the same time!

Yi Ping seized the opportunity to retaliate against the old man at the same time!

The most astonishing thing had suddenly happened!

Yi Ping had penetrated through the Divine Rejuvenation Force and had slashed the old man twice, on his arm and shoulder, drawing blood!

What startled the old man was not Yi Ping's astonishing speed but the Divine Echo itself. The Divine Echo seemed to have the ability to seemingly cleave through effortlessly through the inertia force that he had created with the Big Dipper Hands and the Divine Rejuvenation Force!

The old man thought alarmingly, "This sword…is made with the metal of the Heavenly Relic? Impossible…other than the Heavenly Relic, there are no swords in the entire world that can dissipate martial force and harken as resounding…"

By the time he had exchanged more than thirty blows with Yi Ping and expecting his martial force to be completely drained by him; his Big Dipper Hands' martial force and his Divine Rejuvenate Force began to falter as the Divine Echo was dissipating his martial force with every strike!

The old man vision began to blur and he could no longer tell the twin sister from each other as they keep swopping places with each other!

He had barely stopped one flying scabbard by Ding Yun with his martial power when she threw another flying scabbard at him with startling speed!

He was now seeing red as the opponents were constantly picking up the fallen scabbards and passing to Ding Yun to hurl at him again and again!

Nangong Le threw his sword scabbard to Ding Yun, "Here!"

Gongsun Jing also threw to Ding Yun his scabbard at the same time, "Here! He can't move from where he is standing. Use my scabbard to exhaust his martial power!"

At the same time, Lingfeng had just threw her Meteor Rain Needles, stopping short of displaying the 'Consecrated Meteor Shower' technique as she did not want this old man to identify her clan of origin; this old man seemed to be a highly experienced exponent that could identify the various martial skills.

When she had attacked the old man, she displayed a varying of martial skills to confuse him.

When the old man tried to retaliate against her, Lingfeng had suddenly displayed the powerful echoing might of the Aspire Horizon Hand, startling the old man. Even though she was forced back with her vital energies in erratic, the old man was genuinely surprised as he thought. "This young maiden, she isn't as weak as I thought she is!"

Yi Ping lifted his spirit with the Absolute Spirits and revitalized his intricate energy with the Divine Revelation again and again as he struggled with his faltering strength to attack the old man, never ceasing his attacks!

Perhaps Yi Ping was trying very hard and was unwilling to allow his martial force to be drained by the Divine Rejuvenation Force or perhaps under the powerful influence of the Divine Rejuvenation Force as he bore the blunt of the old man's main attacks, his Divine Revelation attained a new staging, the Circular Rejuvenation of the Origin!

The Circular Rejuvenation of the Origin was one of the highest states of divinity in martial attainment. At this attainment, as soon as vital energies were used up to maintain martial power, unused martial power could also be revitalized back to vital energies. This attainment was also the nemesis of the Divine Rejuvenation Force, preventing the practitioner's martial force from being drained by external force as well!

The old man was now sweating heavily as he suddenly found his martial power draining at a rapid rate with every renewed attack.

He was already aware by now that he was fighting with three extremely determined strong exponents; the young man with the twin swords, the maiden that could use the Flying Sword Techniques of the Virtuous Palace and the yellow dressed maiden that could move around so quietly that he had to be extremely focus to be wary of her next appearances.

This yellow dressed maiden also seemed to have an inexhaustible martial force as she attacked him again and again with her full martial power. He was also aware that this maiden was protected by a similar inertia force and she also seemed to be trained in a type of internal strength that reduced the effectiveness of his Divine Rejuvenate Force.

Yu'Er said to her sister, "Mei'Er, do you still remember the intricacy heart formula of the Dual Inertia?"

Mei'Er was in a daze as she said weakly, "Sister…you still have the time to think of other matters. I have almost reached my limits!"

Yu'Er reminded her, "The vital energy exchanges but not the body, the divinity exchanges but not the physical, the essence of the heavens and earth as my vitality, the divine state of heavens and earth as my divine state, the changes of heavens and earth as my changes. He tries to steal our martial force, why don't we try to steal from him too? Let's see who is faster and there are two of us here."

Mei'Er laughed softly, "Sister…that's a good idea. Let's do that!"

The old man freaked out when he had heard that and he had decided to do the most dishonorable thing that he had never done before. He ran away like a lightning bolt!

After making sure that the old man was really gone, the nine of them collapsed next to one another on the grass patch, groaning in agony and from sheer exhaustion.

Lingfeng wheezed, "Unbelievable…we really…have won?"

Nangong Le muttered, "This old freak is simply too formidable…no matter how many ingenious strokes that we have used on him, he still lives…"

Mei'Er was muttering unintelligently, "He…is like a cockroach, unkillable!"

Youxue asked Yu'Er, "You can really drain his martial power?"

Yu'Er laughed softly, "Soon...almost...not yet there..."

Youxue smiled faintly, "You...almost have me fooled..."

Yi Ping asked Yu'Er, "That isn't real? Then why did he run?"

Yu'Er smiled tenderly at Yi Ping as she explained, "His resolute was already weakening. I can sense it. I just helping to give him an extra 'push' in that direction."

Yi Ping was grateful to her as he looked at her affectionately, "Yu'Er, lucky for your quick thinking. I don't know if I can last a second longer..."

He paused for a while before saying, "It is also lucky that we have been practicing the Celestial Star Formation. I say, we ought to practice more..."

He was startled that everyone had suddenly become motionless and had fallen completely quiet.

Chapter 49: Guardians of the Holy Chapter

Yi Ping was looking at the stunning view of the Holy Amalgamate Mountains. After an arduous journey, they had all finally reached their destination, encountering only a few minor difficulties along the way.

They had avoided taking the main road and were guided by Lingfeng through the many mountains and valleys.

Lingfeng had explained, "Even though we are near the clan territories of the Holy Hex Clan and her allies, the number of unfriendly clans that were gathering at the foot of the Holy Amalgamate were in the hundreds and their protégés in the thousands. It is best that we totally avoid the main road altogether."

She looked at Yi Ping keenly and asked, "What's wrong, Yi Ping? You seem unhappy. Is it because we are not interested in the Celestial Star Formation?"

Yi Ping was startled, "Lingfeng, you are not interested in the Celestial Star Formation?"

Lingfeng quickly said, "Not that. Why do you look so depress lately? That is so unlike the Yi Ping that I have known who is undaunted by any difficulties."

Yi Ping secretly shared in his worries with her, "Lingfeng, in the past…I lead a simple life and carefree life. I didn't know the fraternity at large and didn't even know what life is in the fraternity. After I have fought with that old man, I have suddenly known fear. It's not that I am really fearful of him but…I don't want to lose anyone of you. I don't want to lose you, Lingfeng. I am really afraid now."

Lingfeng's alluring eyes were watery, "It's alright Yi Ping. You have already done your best. You know you don't have to accompany me back to the Holy Amalgamate Mountains…"

Yi Ping said, "It's not that, Lingfeng. I…want to protect you. I want to become strong now. I…I also can't afford to lose Youxue, Ding Yun, Yu'Er and Mei'Er. If any of you comes to harm, I will be heartbroken. I know that I shouldn't say that but I…really don't even know my heart anymore…"

Lingfeng said softly, "Yi Ping, you don't have to say anymore…I do understand. Just follow your heart…"

Yi Ping smiled bitterly, "I can't even trust my heart anymore. A part of me is telling me to leave clandestinely and forget about the burdens of the heart…maybe it is the Emptiness Translucence that is playing a trick on me…"

Lingfeng said quietly, "Hmph, what Emptiness Translucence…If you do that, I will kill myself in front of you…"

Yi Ping was startled.

Unknown to Yi Ping, Youxue, Yu'Er, Mei'Er and Ding Yun were standing and listening tearfully out of his sight…

Gongsun Jing looked at the breathtaking misty mountains and valleys of the Holy Amalgamate Mountains, he said sadly. "The entire mountain slopes are treacherous. This is really a place that is easy to defend and hard to assault."

He asked Ding Yun, "Maiden Ding, are you alright? You are quiet along the way…"

Ding Yun said demurely, "I have always been quiet. It's not strange."

Gongsun Jing gave a soft sigh, "Is that so?"

Qiu Wufeng said, "I have thought that the Heavenly Mountains are grand enough but this is simply too breathtaking."

Yu'Er disagreed with a soft sigh, "This is not a truly accurate way to say it. For me, I prefer the snow and ice of the Heavenly Mountains."

Qiu Wufeng smiled bitterly, "Yes, yes. You're right." But he was secretly thinking. "The Heavenly Mountains is such a cold and desolate place; I'll never want to go there again…"

Mei'Er added enchanting, "Oh? Why is that what you are saying and what you are thinking seems different?"

Qiu Wufeng protested, "That's not the truth. I swear!"

He quickly tried to divert attention from himself by saying, "How come Brother Nangong is so quiet today?"

Nangong Le smiled dreamily, "I'm admiring the view…"

Yu'Er flushed as she interrupted with a disdain look in her eyes, "He is lying. He is filled with dirty thoughts!"

Nangong Le forced out a weak smile, "That's not true, Yu'Er. You are also so beautiful today. Your astonishing beauty is like a rainbow. I am just appreciating the rainbows here…"

Yi Ping was turning his head as he looked at the surroundings, "Brother Nangong, you really have sharp eyes. I don't see any rainbows…"

Lingfeng almost fainted as she admonished Yi Ping silently, "You are so dense…I give up on you…!"

Nangong Le said to Mei'Er and Yu'Er, "You know. We have so many things in common like music, swordplay, fine appreciation of the arts…"

Mei'Er hummed with an icy tone, "Not again…You can save your efforts, Young Master Nangong."

Nangong Le smiled secretly to himself, "One of these days, I will melt your heart…"

Youxue walked quietly besides Nangong Le, whispering in an almost inaudible voice in his ears. "I will blind you if you dare to take another look at me. And don't think I do not know you have been peeking at us all the time in the quiet along the way."

Nangong Le broke into a cold sweat.

When Yi Ping saw that Lingfeng had put on an annoyed look, he quickly said to her, "Lingfeng! We have finally reached the Holy Amalgamate Mountains. The scenery here is so beautiful. You have grown up here?"

Lingfeng nodded tenderly at Yi Ping, "Yes, I have grown up here."

She pointed at the yellow mountains range in the far horizon, "Do you see those yellow mountains in the horizon?"

Yi Ping said, "It is beautiful, isn't it? Maybe we can stay there in the future…"

Lingfeng smiled weakly, "You…you…don't want to go there! The mountains there are called the Nirvana Mountains. It is said that the Celestial Palace is somewhere in those mountains. No one returns from that place. But we are able to see the Nirvana Mountains from here."

Mei'Er asked her, "Sister Lingfeng, why are your heart filled with sorrow? Shouldn't you be happy that you are now home?"

Lingfeng sighed softly, "I am…"

Yi Ping said, "Lingfeng, don't you worry. I'll protect you no matter how difficult it is."

Lingfeng looked alluringly at Yi Ping.

Yi Ping began to flush.

He quickly turned around and walked hurriedly, "We have better hurry. We're almost there."

All of a sudden, he had frozen in his tracks!

It was because Yi Ping had caught sight of an appalling sight!

The mountain slope on the other side of the mountain was covered with the charred bodies of hundreds of fallen exponents. Their weapons and their martial banners were littered everywhere!

Lingfeng gasped, "The orthodox clans had already made their way to the top?"

Yi Ping said quietly, "So many dead. Is it worth to throw their lives just like that? For what cause?"

Ding Yun calmed Lingfeng, "From the attire and banners of the dead, it seems that they are mostly from the orthodox clans. This could be just a minor skirmish. I see no banners of the major orthodox clans or the Honor Manor."

Youxue said, "I can now understand why it is so difficult to assault the Holy Hex Sect and why the Honor Manor is mustering almost the entire fraternity."

Everyone was looking at Youxue.

Yi Ping asked, "Why?"

Youxue said coolly, "The wind directions are always moving down the slope. It is easy to utilize fire attacks. It does seem that these smaller clans are cannon fodders for the major orthodox clans to exhaust the combustible materials of the Holy Hex Sect before they make their final move."

She paused for a while before she said, "Even as we speak, there are dozens of fighters approaching us from the mountain top…Lingfeng, you have better explained that we are on your side or we be burnt alive."

Ding Yun smiled, "Or be crushed by boulders…"

Yujian had readied her fingers while Mei'Er was waving the Divine Emerald Skill as they giggled, "Or arrows…"

Yi Ping immediately shouted, "Heyyyyyy…we are allies and not foes!!! We are the friends of your Holy Maiden!!!"

His martial shout was extraordinary powerful and immediately there were echoes of his shouts coming back from all directions!

Ding Yun said quietly, "Yi Ping…I don't think you should do that…"

Lingfeng immediately stepped on his foot, "Heavens, they haven't even appeared yet…you don't have to shout like that…you really want the whole world to know…"

Yi Ping said panicky, "Lingfeng, by the time they have seen us…we may have become roasted pigs. It is better that we announce ourselves first…"

Gongsun Jing immediately said, "Brother Yi Ping, brilliant! Well said!"

Qiu Wufeng was equally impressive, "Even I have overlooked it. Brother Yi Ping, you may have saved us from a lot of unnecessary troubles!"

Nangong Le seize the opportunity to flatter Yi Ping, "I am about to praise the wisdom and foresight of Brother Yi Ping but Brother Gongsun, you have snatched my lines first instead."

Yi Ping laughed uncomfortable as he said, "That's nothing. Anyone would have thought of that too. I just happened to be the one who had shouted first."

Nangong Le was laughing, "That's true. Even if Brother Yi Ping did not shout a moment ago, I'm afraid that the next one to shout would be me, Haha."

Qiu Wufeng agreed, "True, true! I would be next too!"

Gongsun Jing smiled, "It is our duty to protect the damsels. Leave this crude shouting to us!"

All of a sudden, more than thirty men in black and with a white blue insignia appeared from all sides of the mountain slope!

In their hands were crossbows, spears and long swords!

Leading them was a refined man with a scholarly look.

As soon as Lingfeng saw him, she said excitedly. "Qian Fan! It is you!"

She turned around and said to her companions, "He is Qian Fan. He's one of the Six Guardians of the Holy Chapters and is also an elder of the Holy Hex Sect."

Qian Fan walked to her excitedly, "Lingfeng! At first when our scouts have reported that they have caught sight of you, I still cannot believe my ears! But then, who else but you knows this secret path? Do you know that we have been waiting for weeks here for your return? Finally, you have returned! Your brother is worried sick for your safety."

He paused for a moment before asking, "These are your friends?"

Lingfeng nodded, "They are all my friends and have come to aid us."

Qian Fan said, "Nowadays we must be extra caution. Friends will betray friends for their own personal ambitions and gains. Even though they claimed to be your friends but their actions may prove otherwise."

He turned and looked at Nangong Le, Gongsun Jing, Yi Ping and Qiu Wufeng before saying, "Who's the idiot that is shouting so loudly just now? Do you want the scouts of the orthodox clans to know that there are other paths up to the Holy Hex Sect?"

Yi Ping had turned completely red while Gongsun Jing, Nangong Le and Qiu Wufeng were looking at one another awkwardly and with great embarrassment.

Yi Ping said, "I…I…"

Lingfeng laughed alluringly, "There are scouts at the top and they can spot us from miles above. That is what Yun is trying to tell you. There is no hole here for you to hide. Why don't you roll down the mountain slope instead? It is way much faster." And she gave Yi Ping a surprise push by displaying the Divine Horizon Hands!

"Lingfeng! You are for real! You…really trying to push me down the mountains!"

"Serve you right for trying to be smart!"

"Lingfeng, I don't remember my father has ever taught you the Divine Horizon Hands. Where are my secret manuals?"

"After I have seen you using it numerous times, I have also picked up some moves. You are joking right? You must have lost it somewhere. Don't try to tell your father that I have stolen it when you have carelessly lost it!"

"Quickly return my secret manuals to me…! You must have stolen it when you…kiss…"

"What…? Shameless! You dare to utter such impudence things in broad daylight! I like to see if your father will help me or you…Hmph!"

Yu'Er and Mei'Er were glancing at one another in subtle embarrassment. It was because before they could praise Yi Ping, the protégés of the Holy Hex Sect had appeared.

Qian Fan was startled. He had never seen Lingfeng this jovial before. She was always careful in maintaining her bearing and adhering to the proper etiquette. As Holy Maiden, her very words were the laws and her very conduct was the symbolic representation of the Holy Hex Sect!

He was jealous and envy of this young man all of a sudden. He asked Lingfeng, "These friends of yours, their names are?"

Lingfeng said coolly, "Yi Ping, Nangong Le, Gongsun Jing, Qiu Wufeng…"

Qian Fan hummed coldly, "I know them alright. They are all wanted by the Honor Manor."

Lingfeng said, "That's right."

Qian Fan had suddenly drawn out his long sword, startling everyone!

Lingfeng chided him, "What are you doing? They are my friends, are you trying to disobey me?"

Qian Fan said, "I dare not. But these men are too notorious and it will be dangerous for the Holy Maiden to be too close to them. I will rather we not have them as allies. We don't need outsiders to meddle in our sect's affairs."

Lingfeng hummed coldly, "Put away your sword. They are framed by the Honor Manor and are good men."

Qian Fan said, "There is no smoke without a fire. Lately, I have heard many bad rumors about them. Everywhere that they have gone to, they have kidnapped innocent maidens and even violated them in the most despicable manner. Their notoriety did not end there. They are even in league with this so call 'Righteous Axioms Clan' and had even killed Xiao Da, the young master of the Virtuous Palace in a despicable and cold hearted ambush. Before Xiao Da died, it seemed that he was put through to a horrifying and agonizing ordeal. I even heard that there is a Maiden Ding Yun from the Virtuous Palace that has been humiliated by that Yi Ping and forced to be with him…"

Youxue was startled as she thought, "We have only used the 'Righteous Axioms Clan' only once and that was in an encounter with a Chi Zhengqi. Don't tell me he is the one that been spreading those rumors?!"

Lingfeng cursed Chi Zhengqi in her heart, "It must be that guy from the Five Element Clan! I'm going to wipe out your entire clan!"

Ding Yun said with a shaking voice, "Shut up…don't say anymore…"

Yi Ping shouted angrily, "Shut up!" He quickly caught hold of Ding Yun's hand and comforted her. "Yun…are you alright? These are just rumors…"

Lingfeng added coldly, "These are all rumors. I repeat. I don't want to hear a word from anyone about these rumors in the Holy Hex Sect. Do you understand me? Or else I will invoke the clan punishment for direct disobedience of my Holy Laws."

Qian Fan sighed, "I obey your wishes, Holy Maiden. But still, Lingfeng you ought to take precautions…"

Lingfeng interrupted with a cold demeanor, "The Holy Maiden."

Qian Fan was startled. His little protégé sister Lingfeng had never spoken to him in this manner before. And she was the one that gave him permission to use her name...

Qian Fan sighed, "I have two things to report. Four of our Elders from the Holy Chapter...they have perished not long ago in a battle with the orthodox martial clans...Elder Wang, Elder Shen, Elder Youlong , Elder Di...alas..."

Lingfeng turned ashen immediately as she quickly asked, "Who...who has the ability to take their lives?"

Qian Fan looked sorrowful, "They are the 'Three Sages' of the orthodox martial clans; Sword Sage of the Aegis Sword Clan, Martial Sage of the Ironclad Clan and the Element Sage of the Five Element Clan."

Yi Ping, Nangong Le, Qiu Wufeng, Gongsun Jing, Youxue, Yu'Er, Mei'Er, Lingfeng and Ding Yun were startled to hear the name of the Five Element Clan being mentioned! Chi Zhengqi was from that martial clan too!

Lingfeng tried hard to hold back her tears as she said softly, putting on a brave front. "Is that so? The Three Sages are all super martial exponents and have lived in solitary for decades. It is not dishonorable to be killed by them."

Only one of the Sages was from the Seven Major Orthodox Sword Clans. The Three Sages had all disappeared from the martial fraternity for the past three to five decades; their legacies became the myth of the martial fraternity and were retold many times till today!

The Ironclad Clan did not attend the congregation held by Gongsun Bai. If it were other clans that dare to reject the invitation of the Honor Clan, then that clan will risk extermination but not the Ironclad Clan. The Ironclad Clan was too influential and the legacy of the Martial Sage was still exerting an invisible hand in the affairs of the martial fraternity!

Yi Ping had been with Lingfeng for a long time. From her subtle expression, he knew that she was dispirited and was grief-stricken.

Qian Fan said quietly, "Holy Maiden, where is the Celestial Envoy that is with you?"

Lingfeng said quietly, "She won't be coming anymore. She has something important to settle."

Qian Fan said, "What's a pity. There is another Celestial Envoy that has just arrived today. He says he is her friend and says that he's a Prime Celestial of the Celestial Palace. If we have two Celestials from the Celestial Palace to aid us, then we have nothing to fear from the Three Sages."

Lingfeng was startled, "What did you say? Quick! Let's hurry back to the Holy Chapter Hall immediately! The Holy Hex Sect is in grave peril!"

Chapter 50: The Celestial Liege

When Yi Ping had seen the anxious expression on Lingfeng, he had totally forgotten about asking her for his secret manuals. It was quite important to him because his martial skills had since progress remarkably. He wanted to attempt some of the harder heart intricacy formulas of the Aspire Invocations that were contained in the Aspire Invocations' secret manual.

It was because without knowing the advance heart intricacy of the Aspire Invocations, he could not even attempt the Asper Divinity Hand. The secret stance of the Asper Divinity Technique was in the Divine Horizon Hands' secret manual.

And both secret writings were now missing.

Together with Lingfeng and Qian Fan, they had stormed into the Holy Chapter Hall of the Holy Hex Sect.

As they made their way noisily into the Holy Chapter Hall, many of the protégés of the Holy Hex Sect were startled as they exclaimed excitedly, "The Holy Maiden is back!"

Lingfeng walked hastily as she asked, "Where is my brother and where is the Celestial Envoy?"

"They are in the inner Holy Chapter Hall. The Holy Sectarian Master says he is not to be disturbed…"

Lingfeng ignored the warnings as she stormed hastily through the many halls of the Holy Chapter Hall. No one dared to stop her.

"Who are these strangers?"

Yi Ping was astonished at the white gold marble walls of the Holy Chapter Hall. He had not expected the Holy Hex Sect to be so magnificent and much grander than the Honor Manor!

He was not the only that were stunned. Youxue, Ding Yun, Nangong Le, Gongsun Jing, Yu'Er, Mei'Er and Qiu Wufeng were all wordless!

Yi Ping asked after Lingfeng, "Lingfeng, these walls are made of gold?"

Lingfeng gave him an annoyed look as she quickly said, "It is only limestone. Only the walls of the Inner Holy Chapter Hall are layered with real gold and the walls inside are craved out of rare white alabaster jadestone."

When Nangong Le heard what Lingfeng had said, he had almost tripped! It was because alabaster jadestones were an extremely rare and costly material. It was worth more than gold itself!

All except Yi Ping was startled.

Yi Ping was not startled because he did not know how rare the 'Rare Alabaster Jadestone' was!

He continued to ask Lingfeng, "Lingfeng, you actually stay here?"

Lingfeng heaved a sigh, "You…you really got nothing better to say, aren't it? Do you know that outsiders are forbidden to enter the Inner Holy Chapter Hall? I am already making an exception for you."

Yi Ping continued to mutter as he was clearly overwhelmed by the beautiful architect of the Holy Chapter Hall, "This is just like a palace and is so big. Are we reaching yet?"

He had noticed that they had passed at least five halls. Each of the halls was so broad and was as long as half a mile!

Lingfeng picked up her pace and displayed her swiftness movements, "We have reached. It is just round the corner of this hallway."

Nangong Le was so in awe of the place that he made a quick mental note to win Lingfeng's heart if the Holy Hex Sect survived this crisis. After all, there was a high probability that Yi Ping would die in the ensuring battle.

He thought, "After all…If my sworn brother dies in battle it is the duty of the sworn brother to take care of his wives. It is really noble of me to make such a grand sacrifice…"

As soon as they had barged into the Inner Holy Chapter Hall, they saw three men.

One was dressed in black attire. He was handsome and had keen eyes. When Lingfeng caught sight of him, she immediately called out. "Brother!"

The man in black attire was indeed Ji Wuzheng and he was extremely displeased to see so many strangers had barged into the inner sanctuary of the Holy Chapter Hall.

Ji Wuzheng immediately reproached Lingfeng, "Outrageous! You are getting more and more outrageous. Do you know that I have given strict instructions to be alone with my sworn brother and the Celestial Envoy?"

The second man who was wearing a fur cloak was obviously the Envoy Celestial. It was because even though he had a young face but his hair was white and his eyes were crimson in color!

The third man was slightly plump and had a red beard. Huo Fu the Flaming Fist was the Sect Leader of the Fire Tablet Sect and he was also the sworn brother of Ji Wuzheng. He had led hundreds of his protégés to the Holy Amalgamate Mountains to reinforce Ji Wuzheng.

When Yi Ping saw him, he had immediately displayed his Divine Horizon Hands as he cried out. "This time, you are not getting away!"

Huo Fu was startled that someone had actually dared to raise his fists at him right in the presence of the Holy Sectarian Master of the Holy Hex Sect and the Celestial Envoy.

Just as he had displayed three counter-attacking strokes, he was overpowered by the Divine Horizon Hand and was struck two times on his chest!

But before Yi Ping could attack again, he was forcibly knocked back by Ji Wuzheng who had just displayed the Dissolution Stance of the Holy Amalgamate Skill!

Yi Ping was startled as he took several steps back in alarm. It was as though his martial power had been dissolved in that instant!

He quickly thought, "What kind of a skill is that?"

Huo Fu shouted angrily, "This rascal. He suddenly attacks me out of the blue. If I don't teach him a lesson, I am not the Flaming Fist!"

Lingfeng cursed softly, "Yi Ping! My goodness! The Celestial Envoy is over there. Are you blind?"

Even Mei'Er gave a startling cry, "Master, that's the wrong person. He's the one with white hair and red eyes!"

Yi Ping quickly said, "There no mistaking! He is Huo Fu! I know him!"

Lingfeng was startled, "You know him? When did you know him? How come you have never told me?"

Yi Ping was startled as he smiled bitterly, "I need to tell you?"

Lingfeng walked silently to him as she secretly pinched him, "What do you think?"

Yi Ping was startled, "You…"

Huo Fu suddenly gave a yell, "I remember you now! You are that young man that tries to seduce that beautiful young maiden in the cave! I haven't look for both of you yet for daring to injure me and you have come knocking on my doors!? Very well, today is just the day for venting my anger..."

The maidens were all gasping one after another, "What beautiful maiden? In a cave together!? Yi Ping, explain yourself!"

Yi Ping quickly stepped forward, "Who is afraid of whom!"

Ji Wuzheng said angrily as he caught hold of Huo Fu, "Hold it brother!"

He stared angrily at Lingfeng and her companions, "What is going on? Lingfeng, take your guests away and stop disgracing yourself in front of the Celestial Envoy."

The Celestial Envoy was looking lustfully at Lingfeng, Youxue, Ding Yun, Yu'Er and Mei'Er as he said, "I don't mind. Your sister is so young and beautiful. This is the unexpected. She is indeed a rare heavenly beauty. I have never seen anyone like her before. She is the Holy Maiden?"

He laughed before introducing himself, "I am the Celestial Liege, the Prime Celestial of the Celestial Palace."

Lingfeng said coldly, "Brother, did he ask for the Heavenly Relic or something?"

Ji Wuzheng said solemnly, "I have already promised to give him the Heavenly Relic and in return, the Celestial Palace will help us to take care of our enemies."

Lingfeng said coldly, "I am afraid that after taking the Heavenly Relic, he will simply disappear and leave us in the lurch."

Ji Wuzheng was startled as he took a glance at the Celestial Liege.

The Celestial Liege lifted his foot and stomp on the ground. Immediately, there was a thunderous impact and the stone slabs beneath his foot cracked into the ground! His internal strength and martial power display was startling!

He said icily, "When the Celestial Palace has heard that the Holy Hex Sect is in trouble, I am sent to specifically aid you. You have no idea how much grace that the Celestial Palace has bestowed upon you."

Ji Wuzheng immediately tried to pacify the Celestial Liege, "Yes, yes."

The Celestial Liege continued, "Don't forget that the Heavenly Relic is originally from the Celestial Palace. We have placed it in the Holy Hex Sect until the day the Seven Stars are aligned. It is just taking back what is rightfully belongs to the Celestial Palace."

Lingfeng hummed coldly, "Hmph...the Joyful Goddess has already told us everything. You are just trying to obtain the Heavenly Relic for your own gain. You are just a half-celestial and depend on the life blood of top martial exponents to sustain yourself. You seem reluctant to mention the Jade Emperor. The Jade Emperor has no use for our Heavenly Relic because it had not undergone the cleansing of the Divine Calamity yet. Only a half-celestial like you will need it to become a full celestial on your next Divine Calamity."

The Celestial Liege was slightly startled, "The Joyful Goddess has told you so much? Where is she? You have killed her?"

Lingfeng said coldly, "We also know that in the Celestial Palace, there is a Jade Emperor and four Prime Celestials."

All of a sudden, there was a fearsome malevolent air from the Celestial Liege that caused even Ji Wuzheng and Huo Fu to take several steps back.

The Celestial Liege smirked, "It seems that the Joyful Goddess is several decades behind time."

Yi Ping interrupted coldly, "What do you mean?"

The Celestial Liege said unhurriedly, "But it is no wonder. She has always been more innocent and purer in heart than us. While we try to prolong our activities by drinking the blood and eating the hearts of top martial exponents, only she chooses to be sleep in suspended animation. She is always in her own world and may not know that that the other two Prime Celestials had long turned to dust a few decades ago."

Ji Wuzheng gasped aloud, "You eat human hearts?!"

The Celestial Liege roared with laughter, "Yes, of course."

He looked at Ji Wuzheng as he smiled, "After you have given me the Heavenly Relic, I have planned to feast on your heart. Your heart is just ripe for my taste and can aid my martial progression. It is just the right feast for my forthcoming Divine Calamity."

Ji Wuzheng said coldly, "But you seem to forget that we are many and you are just one."

The Celestial Liege laughed, "If you think I am in the league of the Joyful Goddess then you must be clearly mistaken. I have never stopped practicing my fighting skills. I can kill all of you with my bare hands and as easy as killing a fly. After that, I will just turn the entire Holy Chapter Hall upside down for the Heavenly Relic. Or maybe, I may just decide to make myself the new Holy Sectarian Master. A little troublesome, yes but the Heavenly Relic will eventually be mine. So why don't you surrender it peacefully. Maybe if I am happy, I may just decide to be merciful."

He looked lustfully at the maidens who were all secretly shivering in fear as he stared at them one by one as he added, "I'm always generous towards those that can please me well."

Yi Ping had stepped forward as he exclaimed angrily, "Let me ask you. Did you kill my grand protégé master?"

The Celestial Liege appraised him before saying, "When you have attacked Huo Fu, you have used the fifth stroke and the ninth stroke of the Divine Horizon Hands, the Flurrying Horizon and the Returning Cloud."

Yi Ping was startled, "You know the Divine Horizon Hands!?"

The Celestial Liege smiled coldly, "I know your grand protégé master. When we have found him, he was preparing for the Divine Calamity. The hearts of such exponents are the best nourishment for us. Unfortunately, exponents of that caliber are really hard to find in the fraternity. Lately all the top exponents have seemingly disappeared or are killed before we can hunt them down. Your grand protégé master is a once in a hundred years meal."

Yi Ping was trembling!

Yu'Er and Mei'Er were so frightful of the Celestial Liege that they were moving back unwittingly. It was because they had practiced the Dual Inertia Intricacy and therefore was hyper sensitive to his killing malevolent intent.

The Celestial Liege laughed coldly, "I have eaten countless number of top exponents and I can't remember most of their names or their faces. But your grand protégé master is an exceptional. It is because my brother the Conqueror Sword who is a Prime Celestial was killed by him."

He laughed depravedly, "In the end…in the end, my brother's heart is also eaten by me…"

Ding Yun, Yu'Er and Mei'Er were nausea from the suffocating despairing aura of the Celestial Liege and after hearing what he had just said; they fell down on their knees and were vomiting.

Lingfeng fell back weakly to the wall and leaned against it...

Nangong Le, Gongsun Jing, Qiu Wufeng and Huo Fu were trembling with a despairing fear that even their limbs could not obey them. They had already seen the outcome and their deaths!

Even though the Celestial Liege was casually talking and waving his hands as he talked, his killing intent had already materialized with his little gestures. Just one stroke, he would kill them!

They could not evaded even one stroke, no matter how hard they tried to!

Before the fight starts, it had already ended for most of them! The differences in their state of divinity was simply too vast!

The Celestial Liege looked at Yi Ping, Ji Wuzheng and Youxue before he laughed, "Very good! Only the three of you are qualified to be my opponent."

Yi Ping, Youxue and Ji Wuzheng could see that the Celestial Liege was now being surrounded by deadly martial energy.

Yi Ping and Youxue had immediately recognized that that this martial energy was the same as Lele when she had fought with Lie Qing; the Celestial Force. Everything around the Celestial Liege would slow down and mere martial strength could not be used against him or risk fatal internal injuries.

In order to fight him, they would have to depend purely on their martial power or the intricate energies of their internal strength.

Any hit by this martial energy was fatal, even if it was blocked.

If not for the timely intervention of Yi Ping, Lele and Lie Qing would have almost killed each other!

But against the Celestial Liege, it was completely one side. His Celestial Force was many times more profound than Lele. He had dared to use the Celestial Force in such an open manner because he was confident.

He seemed to be telling them silently, "This fight is destined to be over as soon as it begins. None of you have the martial skill to even withstand my overwhelming martial energy."

Youxue could barely stand straight. She had forcibly suppressed all her ill-feeling with the Absolute Spirits as she raised her trembling hands. Her most powerful attacking techniques were all frontal techniques. Against a super exponent such as the Celestial Liege, her opportunities were few.

Ji Wuzheng immediately displayed the Dissolution Stance of the Holy Amalgamate Skill even as he muttered, "His internal strength is too unfathomable. We're like eggs smashing against a rock..."

Yi Ping had raised his entire martial power...

All of a sudden, Ding Yun raised her entire martial power too and there were three winks of explosive air burst around her.

The Celestial Liege was genuinely startled, "The Invincible Divine Force..."

All of a sudden, Ding Yun had drawn her long sword so silently and with startling speed; imbuing her entire martial power into her sword and sent it spinning it towards the Celestial Liege!

The Celestial Liege raised his fingers with lightning speed reflexes and knocked the flying sword aside as it shattered into many pieces!

Everyone gasped! Ding Yun's precious sword that could withstand her martial power could actually shatter to bits by the sheer martial energy of the Celestial Liege!

The Celestial Liege muttered, "This Invincible Divine Force is too weak. You almost have me fooled. But then, at your age, it is already an accomplishment."

Ding Yun fell down weakly, having exhausted all her martial power for the flying sword technique, "Do...do...you know that with your present martial progression, you don't even need to parry my flying sword? But because you are too strong, you have acted purely out of instinct."

The Celestial Liege asked her with a curious look, "What is it that you want to say?"

Ding Yun said weakly, "Yi Ping, did you see that? Don't underestimate your opponent. He can still retain his movements while displaying his martial energy. He will be at least twice as fast as any of you!"

Ding Yun had already observed the differences in their martial strength and she was trying to warn them!

Ji Wuzheng broke into a cold sweat, he was about to engage the Celestial Liege and he could now imagine himself lying on the ground!

He took a notable glance at the beautiful demure maiden as he thought, "This maiden...."

Yi Ping said quietly, "Thank you..."

But before anyone could halt Yi Ping, he had charged into Celestial Liege, displaying the shrieking exploding might of the Aspire Horizon Hand as he shouted, "I don't care how strong you are!"

Lingfeng immediately covered her eyes!

There was a thunderous impact as the Celestial Liege caught Yi Ping's thunderous blow, sending burst of flurry heated windforce in all directions and everyone was forced to scurry backward!

As soon as Yi Ping landed his palms on the Celestial Liege, he could feel his intricate energies bursting to its limit and he coughed out blood; such was the irresistible martial energy of the Celestial Liege that the moment that he had exchanged impact with him, his intricate energies begun to reverse upon himself.

Before Yi Ping could react, the Celestial Liege had disengaged and raised his hands with lightning speed and was about to strike him when Xiao Youxue intercepted that blow with her golden beaming hand!

But even then, the Celestial Liege could still react in that single instant as he raised both his hands and sent Yi Ping and Youxue flying backward with two thunderous explosive blows!

The only thing that prevented Youxue and Yi Ping from sustaining even more severe internal injuries was the timely interference of Ji Wuzheng as he suddenly attacked the Celestial Liege with his long sword. This forced the Celestial Liege to divert some of this martial power to counterattack against Ji Wuzheng as he shattered his sword and sending Ji Wuzheng flunking hard against the wall!

Qian Fan shouted panicky as Ji Wuzheng's mouth was foaming with blood, "Holy Sectarian Master!"

He had suffered severe internal injuries and he was coughing blood profusely!

Lingfeng quickly went to her brother side as she cried out, "Brother….!"

Ji Wuzheng smiled bitterly as he panted deeply, "In the end…in the end…with my martial progression, I cannot even take one blow from him…is he not human?"

He had used the 'Great Dissolution Skill' from the Holy Amalgamate Skill to neutralize the electrifying martial energy of the Celestial Liege but it was still not enough!

The Celestial Liege hummed coldly to Ji Wuzheng, "Lesser mortals would have died instantly. Count yourself lucky."

Immediately after the Celestial Liege had knocked back Ji Wuzheng, he saw that Yi Ping and the enticing maiden in yellow were on their feet, helped by their companions!

Yi Ping and Youxue were both coughing blood as they tried to stand weakly! Their internal injuries were not light too when compared to Ji Wuzheng!

Yi Ping gasped for breath as he said defiantly, "I am not down yet!"

Yu'Er was saying inconsolable to him, "Master…don't fight anymore…it is hopeless…we are all not his match…"

Mei'Er was already crying and muttering, "He is only insolent because he hasn't met real opponents yet. If our Protégé Mistress is here and if Sister Qing'Er is here, you'll bet that he can't laugh as it is now."

Everyone's hearts sunk when they had heard Mei'Er. It was because she was right!

They had seen how fast Youxue had recovered after exchanging blows with the Celestial Liege; Lie Qing mastery in her Invincible Divine Force and the Golden Invincible Body was even more startling while the internal strength of the Celestial Fairy in the form of the tenth level of her Icy Heavenly Tears was extremely profound.

Everyone was wishing in their hearts that they were here now.

But the Celestial Liege ignored him and instead looked at Youxue as he said, "That is the Golden Invincible Body?"

Youxue nodded silently.

The Golden Invincible Body was not only a defensive skill. It could also be used to empower attacks after transforming into the Golden Body Halo.

The Celestial Liege said coldly, "So there is another protégé descendant of the Invincible Divine Clan here. Very good. I shall take the opportunity to wipe out the Invincible Divine Clan."

While he was talking to her, Youxue had regained the delicate balance of her intricate energies with the Icy Heavenly Tear.

Her injuries were lighter than Yi Ping; in the meantime Yi Ping was now struggling to stand firm as he tried to renew and stabilize the erratic intricate energies with the Divine Revelation.

Yi Ping was feeling hot as an unnatural heat swelled inside him. He tried to suppress it with his Aspire Invocations but the alien heat refused to be pacified. He could only silently mutter, "When I have exchanged blows with him, I can feel a powerful positive energy force entering my body. Don't tell me I have been afflicted by his Celestial Force?"

But he kept quiet about his condition even though everyone could see that something was not right with Yi Ping as he seemed to have developed a fever and was also flushing red.

Ding Yun quickly diagnosed his condition, "Oh terrible, the Celestial Force has afflicted you…Yi Ping, you mustn't exert your internal strength anymore or it will be fatal…"

Mei'Er asked, "Why aren't Youxue and Ji Wuzheng experiencing the same afflictions?"

Yu'Er said quietly, "The Celestial Force is a pure positive martial force and the Icy Heavenly Tears is its opposite. So both forces are able to negate one another. As for Holy Sectarian Master Ji Wuzheng, his 'Great Dissolution Skill' is able to stop the positive force energy of the Celestial Force from entering his body…"

Youxue asked the Celestial Liege, "You have a feud with the Invincible Divine Clan?"

The Celestial Liege knew that she was buying precious time for Yi Ping and Ji Wuzheng to treat their internal injuries. But he was in no hurry as none of his opponents could really fight him on equal par. And moreover, internal injuries once sustain, could not be treated in just a matter of weeks. At most, he was just allowing them to restore their breathing and heart beat to normal.

However he seemed willing to share it. Perhaps he was too alone or suddenly decided to be merciful. "That was many centuries ago. The Invincible Divine Clan was the most powerful martial clan in the martial fraternity with numerous protégé and followers. Even though the Celestial Clan was a big clan too but we have completely lost in the rivalry. Our clan base was destroyed and a hundred of us left quietly to the mountains…"

He smiled to himself, "In a lucky encounter, we met an old man who we call the Jade Emperor later. He is actually our great grand protégé master who has ascended to be a Celestial a long time ago. We begged him to take us in, to impart to us his skills and the secrets of becoming a Celestial…"

The Jade Emperor had said, "If I help you to ascend to be a Celestial, it will affected my future cultivation and may even incur the wrath of the heavens. Alas, is it divine fate that I will meet my clan protégés in this wilderness? If it is not for the Celestial Clan and Xiaoqie, my little protégé sister who sacrificed her life for me to reawaken the Heavenly Relic, I would never have attained divinity…"

He gave a stern warning, "But you have to bear the consequences! Many of you will die and there is a heavy price to be paid!"

The protégés of the Celestial Clan immediately shouted in unison, "We are not afraid! As long as we can avenge our clan folks and the destruction of our clan from the hands of our enemies, we are not afraid!"

Amidst the shouting, a little girl about seven walked quietly to the Jade Emperor. "Old…man…your heart seemed to be filled with great sadness. What's wrong? Are you thinking of your protégé sister Xiaoqie?"

The Jade Emperor was startled that a little girl like her would actually dare to walk to him boldly given the state of his state of divinity which caused everyone to be in awe of him.

The Jade Emperor had never met a little girl like her before so he asked, "What's your name, little girl?"

The little girl laughed softly as she thought for a moment, "Hmm…My name is Huan Le! And what's your name?"

The Jade Emperor was amused.

The little girl said cheerfully, "Since you are so old… I call you grandpa then…grandpa!"

The Jade Emperor smiled, "Sure…sure…"

A young man walked hurriedly to him and begging his pardon, "Grand Protégé Master, please forgive my little sister rudeness."

After he had dragged her away, he quietly rebuked her. "You have dared to lie even to our Grand Protégé Master…"

The little girl jovially protested, "When I see his eyes, I see great sadness. I am just trying to make him happy. And I didn't lie. Huan Le is going to be my name and I'm going to make grand protégé master happy!"

The young man scolded his little sister, "Hey, you…little brat…"

Ten years later, on the next forthcoming Divine Calamity, the Jade Emperor had helped them to ascend to half-celestials. Many did not make it. Among the survivors were Huan Le, his little sister and him…

The Jade Emperor had imparted to Lele the Holy Pureness, among many other secret skills and techniques, instructing her just like she was his own daughter.

The Celestial Liege seemed to be smiling as he recalled that moment. But he soon grown solemn as he said, "After we have attained divinity, we took our vengeance against the all-powerful Invincible Divine Clan, drink their blood and ate their hearts. Overnight, we totally annihilated them all. More than three thousands of them, men and women…we spared no one…from that point onward, the Invincible Divine Clan is no more. But today, there are actually two survivors…"

Yi Ping clenched his fist as he shouted angrily, "I will not let you lay your despicable hands on Yun and Youxue!"

Yi Ping had already staggered forward even as Youxue pulled him back as she said melancholy, "Yi Ping, stay calm…"

Yi Ping said quietly, "Lele…the Joyful Goddess, she had a hand in it too?"

The Celestial Liege was slightly startled that he knew his little sister's name. He could well imagine that Lele must have been careless and got herself killed when she was dealing with them. She really had too little experience with outsiders and the treacherous martial fraternity. Moreover while his martial progressions were constantly improving, Lele's martial progression seemed to be stagnant as she preferred to sleep in the secret chamber of the Celestial Palace.

He silently vowed to let them pay for their lives in exchange for hers.

But he masked it well and replied coldly, "She is a Prime Celestial. So what do you think? The ranks of the Celestial Palace were denoted by the number of super exponents of the Invincible Divine Clan that were killed."

Yi Ping was trembling as he said aloud, "That's enough!"

All of a sudden, he had drawn out his two beaming white swords and thrust them side by side on the ground in front of him!

As he drew out the Divine Echo and forced it into the ground, there was a flash of brilliant white blue light, followed by a low emitting echo.

This time, the Celestial Liege was genuinely startled as he thought, "This…this sword…is made of the Heavenly Relic!? That is impossible. As far as I know, the Heavenly Relic is indestructible and resistant to all tampering…"

Even more startling was that the White Emerald Phoenix Sword, the White Phoenix was also reverberating as white green light faded in and out of its edges!

The two long swords were vibrating slightly and swaying as the lights of their halo surrounded it. As their halos touched each other, it formed a bigger rainbow halo around it!

Ji Wuzheng was stunned as he muttered, "Lingfeng, did you see that? I have heard that only legendary divine swords are able to resonant…this is the first time I have ever seen it…"

Lingfeng muttered, "These rainbow hues…are so beautiful…"

A tranquil effect overwhelmed her as she looked at the resonating swords and she was no longer fearful.

Huo Fu was stunned, "The reverberating resonant of the divine swords…the reverberating resonant of the divine swords…"

Huo Fu was not only an accomplished martial exponent but a master weapon smith as well. Every dream of a weapon smith was to one day forge a weapon that could resonant. Only a weapon that could resonant could be called a divine weapon; that means the weapon had already successfully absorbed the essence of the heavens and the earth, possessing the ability to overwhelm even the sun and the moon."

Everyone else was also completely fascinated by this unearthly beautiful sight as they could only look on, not knowing when the two swords would stop resonating and when its glaring halo hues would fade away.

Even the Celestial Liege was in a stunned daze as he stared blankly at the two Heavenly Relic Swords. There was not one but two…

Yi Ping was the most astonished. Barely had he thrust the swords into the ground, the strange phenomena had happened, startling him!

Chapter 51: Secrets of the Divine Calamity

The Celestial Liege laughed aloud, "Good, good. It seems that Heavens isn't so unkind to me after all and sends two heavenly swords into my hands."

Yi Ping had already staggered forward, saying weakly. "Heavenly swords or not, I do not know but today I am not going to let you harm any of my friends. I am going to protect them with my own hands. I believe in the righteousness of the Heavens' Way. Evil can never triumph over Good. Good can only falter but not broken."

He had suddenly displayed the opening stance of the Divine Horizon Hands, the Heavens Horizon. His fighting spirit and determination was absolute!

His intentions were all too clear; he intended to fight once more!

Lingfeng could not believe her eyes; Yi Ping had just walked past his swords, leaving his swords behind him! She muttered in utter disbelief, "You...pick up your swords, you idiot!"

Even Youxue and Ji Wuzheng were looking in disbelief.

Youxue gasped, "Yi Ping, your swords..."

Ji Wuzheng called out to him, "Young hero, you seem to forget something..."

Everyone was bewildered. It was because everyone had expected Yi Ping to challenge the Celestial Liege with his swords.

Qian Fan took this opportunity to sneak out of the Inner Holy Chapter even though he was immensely curious to see the battle outcome but reason eventually won over his curiosity. He had thought, "If we let the Celestial Liege takes away the Heaven Relic, then it will be disastrous for the Virtuous Palace. Moreover this is a most excellent opportunity for us to launch an attack, now that Ji Wuzheng is injured."

No one had suspected him to be a spy. He had been planted in the Holy Hex Sect by none other than Xiao Shuai himself when he was little. His real name was Xiao Fan. He knew that this was also the most excellent time to sneak away without notice when everyone attentions were distracted by the wondrous halo of the two swords.

He took a curious look at Youxue and Lingfeng before he sneaked quietly away, "So that is...my little sister Youxue. Lingfeng, you will be mine. There are no other maidens that can rival you in this entire fraternity."

Unknown to Ji Wuzheng and Lingfeng, when Lingfeng had fallen sick when she was little and was dying, it was him that had leaked to Ji Wuzheng that the Virtuous Palace had the Golden Rejuvenation Pill that could save her life. It was also him that forced Xiao Shuai to adhere to his request to give one of his precious Golden Rejuvenate Pill to Ji Wuzheng.

In the meantime, the curiosity of the Celestial Liege was aroused by Yi Ping, "You are not using your swords? You know how vast is the martial difference between the two of us? Maybe if you use your swords, you may still have a little chance of survival."

Yi Ping smiled bitterly, "I have taken down my swords because they are too heavy and hinder my moments. But now you asked me to pick up my swords again? Cast away the meaningless talks and let's fight..."

Lingfeng wanted to faint on the spot as she moaned silently, "Yi Ping, you pig-head! Dense, dense, dense! You lack even basic flexibility. I know you want to use your Divine

Horizon Hands but now your swords are telling you to use them. And you are so dense not to even aware of it…faint!"

Youxue and Ji Wuzheng were besides Yi Ping in an instant…

Yi Ping said to Youxue and Ji Wuzheng with a trembling voice, "Stay back…all of you…this is just between the two of us. This is for my grand protégé master too…also for the thousands of people that are killed…"

Youxue shook her head, "I…don't want to…"

All of a sudden, Yi Ping pushed her forcefully back and at the same time, he had already changed his stance from the Heavens Horizon to the Asper Horizon Hand as he flew to the Celestial Liege, mustering all the martial power that he could gather.

The Celestial Liege laughed aloud, "I forget to tell you. The swords that you have are the only weapons that can counteract my Celestial Force and you didn't realize it…"

Youxue was startled when Yi Ping had suddenly pushed her. When she had recovered her balance, Yi Ping had already charged into the deadly martial energy aura of the Celestial Liege!

Yi Ping's lingering whispering words to her was, "Take everyone and run…!"

Yi Ping had charged into the martial energy of the Celestial Liege with startling speed, enduring the agony pressure of the Celestial Force martial energy as he rained down the fearsome exploding power of the Asper Horizon Hand on the Celestial Liege.

The stone slabs beneath the Celestial Liege shattered and cracked when the Celestial Liege lifted his martial power to take Yi Ping's incoming blow.

There was a thunderous explosive impact as the Celestial Liege received Yi Ping's blow. This time, it was several times more powerful than earlier; there were bursting martial windforce and rocks that were speeding like deadly projectiles that knocked everyone off the ground except for Youxue and Ji Wuzheng who were forced to use their entire martial power to resist the bursting martial force as they slide backward!

Yi Ping had coughed out blood immediately, moving only a step backward!

Even before the first shockwave had ended, the Celestial Liege had displayed the deadly Great Dissolution Skill once again!

Yi Ping willed his entire body with the Absolute Spirits, breaking free of the entangling pressuring force of the Celestial Force and displaying the Asper Horizon Hand once again!

The Celestial Liege was startled that Yi Ping could retaliate against his second Great Dissolution Skill attack in such a short notice. It was because everything around him was like a stasis field, slowing everything down. That was his greatest advantage.

The air around them exploded thunderous, destroying the nearby stone stabs and sending deadly flying projectiles that were filled with deadly martial energy speeding all around them, each one exploding thunderous upon impact!

Yi Ping coughed out blood and began to wobble!

Even before the first thunderous shockwave had died down and the second shockwave had yet to stop, the Celestial Liege raised his martial power with the Great Dissolution Skill again! "This time, I like to see if you can still stand on your feet!"

Just as he had utilized the Great Dissolution Skill again, Yi Ping seemed to have recovered from the wobble as he raised his martial power again.

There were yet another thunderous exploding shockwave!

It was obvious to him that Yi Ping martial power had weakened considerably but he was just astonished that how was it possible for him to take blow after blow of his most powerful Great Dissolution Skill? And how was it possible for Yi Ping to move in the presence of his Celestial Force martial energy?

The Great Dissolution Skill was a powerful divine secret art that could nullify the martial power of the opponents. It was a secret skill that was contained within the intricacy formula of the Celestial Force. The Holy Amalgamate Skill which originated from the Celestial Force also had the Great Dissolution Skill but it was not as pure and as powerful as the one that the Celestial Liege was using.

Yi Ping had already attained the Circular Rejuvenation of the Origin. His martial power could be nullified but not drained. Unused martial power and nullified martial power automatically flowed back as vital energies.

In fact, the Celestial Liege did not know that it had the undesirable effect of protecting Yi Ping against the effect of his Celestial Force as the Great Dissolution Skill caused Yi Ping's martial power to be replenished continuously!

All of a sudden, the Celestial Liege was startled. It was because Yi Ping did not stop there and was now raining blows after blows that were filled with all his martial power upon him!

Even though these blows were weaker than the Asper Horizon Hand, it was nevertheless deadly!

He had immediately recognized that Yi Ping had displayed the Asper Continuum Horizon, the second secret stance of the Divine Horizon Hand!

The second stance of the Divine Horizon Hand was indeed weaker than the first secret stance of the Divine Horizon Hand. But it was rapid, able to display the powerful Divine Horizon Hands one after another! The combined might of the Asper Continuum Horizon Hand was startling when taken as a whole!

Yi Ping of course was not thinking clearly when he had decided to challenge the Celestial Liege. He was angry that such an inhumane beast actually existed in the world and his first thoughts were to bash him. Even though he had experienced firsthand the nullifying effect of the Great Dissolution Skill that caused his martial power to vanish, he was undeterred.

When he had forcefully used the Asper Divine Horizon Hand a second time, he was astonished. It was because the Asper Divine Horizon Hand had an unbroken rule; practitioners were not able to use the Asper Divine Horizon a second time in short notice or risk a backlash; the result would be severe internal injuries. Yi Ping was able to use the Asper Divine Horizon a second time because his Asper Divine Horizon was nullified and he had quickly regained his martial power again!

Of course he did not know. He was just thinking that since he had already been injured by the Celestial Force and may die any soon, he just gave everything he got!

When the Celestial Liege absorbed the blows of his first and second Asper Divine Horizon, Yi Ping was desperate because he had already sustained severe internal injuries and was weakening rapidly. Only sheer willpower aided by the Absolute Spirits prevented him from dropping onto the ground!

Therefore he had decided to gamble using the Asper Continuum Horizon Hand, a much more martial power exhausting technique as he figure out, since the Celestial Liege could attack unhindered and would surely follow up one attack after another, why did he not use the Asper Continuum Horizon Hand to stop him first?

He was astonished when again; he was able to display the Asper Continuum Horizon Hand! He was bewildered as he thought weakly, "I have heard that when one's internal strength reaches its limit, it will also be the death knell. When that moment comes, miraculous feats can be performed and even one's martial power limit can be raised beyond the usual limit. Am I about to die soon?"

As soon as he had thought of it, he coughed out more blood as the severity of his internal injuries seized him but he refused to stop fighting!

And now Yi Ping was now raining the Asper Continuum Horizon Hand upon the Celestial Liege. They were both exchanging blows so fast and were so fatigue that both were actually coughing blood with each exchange as they sent bursting thunderous shockwave after shockwave to their surroundings!

For the first time, the Celestial Liege found his intricate energy reversing; he was coughing blood as the result of his internal injuries. He was alarmed and startled! It was because once his intricate energy began to reverse, that meant that he had reached his limit and had to stop or risk worsening his internal injuries. But he was forced to raise his martial power to use the Great Dissolution Skill again and again; it was because Yi Ping stubbornly refused to back off despite his aggravating internal injuries!

With each use of the Great Dissolution Skill, the Celestial Liege was exhausting his internal strength and aggravating the severity of his internal injuries while replenishing Yi Ping's martial power!

The Celestial Liege was beginning to get fearful and was in alarm, "Is he a monster?"

As he fought with Yi Ping, his vision began to grow more and more hazily, causing him to feel dizzy and even nausea. It was because he had been looking at the bright halo of the Divine Echo and the White Phoenix for quite some time!

Right from the start, the halo of the two swords was causing him discomfort, causing his movements to slow down.

The very instant that he had started to suffer from internal injuries, the rainbow halo of the Divine Echo and the White Phoenix were starting to blind him and causing his vision to be hazy!

As a super exponent, his hearing was exceptional sharp but when he was momentarily blinded, the Divine Echo and the White Phoenix resonant with a piercing ringing and caused his hearings to be falter as well!

The unbelievable thing had happened; the Celestial Liege was suddenly struck by Yi Ping, not once but a dozen times in split second!

When Yi Ping had struck the Celestial Liege with the Asper Continuum Horizon, his martial strength was now exhausted. He coughed out blood and staggered backward!

The Celestial Liege's pupils had turned white, he was coughing blood profusely; his internal injuries was not light! As he staggered backward, he only had just a thought in his mind. "Did he intentionally put those swords there to blind me…no one can defeat me…I am the most powerful exponent in the entire fraternity…"

He was in utter disbelief.

He did not know that if he had not decided to show off his Celestial Force and his unfathomable internal strength, then the result would not be this!

If Yi Ping had really picked up the Divine Echo and the White Phoenix, then the fight would surely be over for him in an instant. It was because with two heavy swords, Yi Ping's movements would surely be more or less hindered. Just a little opening would be enough for him to exploit and defeated Yi Ping with a single strike!

That was what Yi Ping had instinctively discovered. That was why he had put aside both his long swords. That was why the White Phoenix had awakened! It was because even though Yi Ping had no swords in his hands but the spirits of the swords were in his heart! The White Phoenix and the Divine Echo was reverberating and resonating for their true Master!

Yu'Er and Mei'Er had already drawn out their precious swords and displayed the Divine Emerald Skill, circulating the destructive forces away. But still, the flying projectiles that were speeding dangerously in their direction were too many and they had been wounded in several places by it!

Ding Yun had borrowed a solid long sword from Gongsun Jing as she whirled her sword, displaying the Defensive Stance of the Flying Sword Technique as she deflected one flying projectile after another.

Nangong Le, Gongsun Jing, Huo Fu, Qiu Wufeng and Lingfeng were standing behind Yu'Er, Mei'Er, Youxue, Ding Yun and Ji Wuzheng as they evaded, parried and blocked the combine furies of the powerful bursting windforce and the shooting projectiles that were flying in their directions.

They were all bloodied and were all injured by this thunderous raging projectile storm yet none of them had run away and there were a determined look in their eyes!

No one, not even Xiao Youxue and Ji Wuzheng had the martial strength and skill to step forward to aid Yi Ping!

None of them had run away even though this raging projectile storm was too dangerous and there were determined looks in their eyes.

Youxue thought hatefully to herself, "Yi Ping! I wish I can fight alongside with you…do you know that…do you know that…I don't want to live if you are gone…" But her thoughts were suddenly interrupted by a miraculous sight!

Yi Ping had struck the Celestial Liege down!

All of a sudden at the same time, both Yi Ping and the Celestial Liege collapsed on the ground!

Even when they had fallen, they were still trying to move by struggling on the ground. But their internal injuries were simply too severe. They had the will but not the strength. In their mind, this fight had not ended yet and both were still trying to stand up, refusing to admit defeat even though they were filled with agonizing pain and extreme fatigue. Their willpower was simply extraordinary startling!

When they had both fallen at the same time, the fierce bursting projectile winds of their martial contest still had not ended!

Everyone was gasping with startled surprise!

The all-powerful Celestial Liege would actually be defeated by Yi Ping!? What was going on?

Lingfeng, Youxue, Yu'Er, Mei'Er and Ding Yun wished with all their sorrowful hearts that they would be the first one to run to Yi Ping!

Huo Fu was astonished that Yi Ping could defeat the Celestial Liege but he also knew that this fight had no real winners. Both of them had fallen at the same time. Even if they had survived, they would lose all their internal strength or suffer a great deterioration of their martial strength.

He sighed, "I have heard that the divine swords will only resonant when they have found their master and another time when their master is about to die. So the legends are true…" All of a sudden, he stopped because he had noticed that there were hostile stares in all directions!

Huo Fu smiled bitterly, "It's just a legend…"

Just as the fury burst of martial force was slowing down and Youxue, Ding Yun, Lingfeng, Mei'Er and Yu'Er were about to fly to Yi Ping, they witnessed another miraculous sight that caused all of them to halt; Yi Ping and the Celestial Liege were on their feet again!

Their recovery rates were extraordinary startling!

Yi Ping attacked the Celestial Liege again as he muttered weakly, "Asper…Continuum Horizon…Hand…"

The Celestial Liege muttered wobbly, "The…Great Dissolution…Skill…"

They were moving very slowly and weakly, their hands barely touching one another! It was obviously they had lost their all internal strength and were in a bewildering state!

The Celestial Liege muttered coldly, "Asper Continuum…Horizon Hand? Hmph! This…is…fit…to be called…that?!"

Yi Ping replied softly, "Asper…Divinity…Horizon…Hand…then!"

The Celestial Liege gasped as he raised his hand to shield himself, "You know…this secret technique!? Very well, I let you…experience….my …Ultimate…Dissolution…Celestial Force!"

There were only the names of the stances but there were no martial display at all!

Everyone was stunned. Had they turned into madmen?

Mei'Er and Yu'Er had burst into tears at this sight!

Lingfeng was covering her face as her eyes turned teary, "Yi Ping…"

Even Gongsun Jing, Qiu Wufeng and Nangong Le were teary as they witnessed this abysmal sight…their sworn brother Yi Ping had become a madman to protect all their lives…

Youxue and Ding Yun looked at one another quietly…

They walked quietly to Yi Ping.

Ding Yun said softly as she grabbed Yi Ping, "Yi Ping, that's enough…you have won…it's time to rest…"

Youxue was weeping silent tears.

As Ding Yun grabbed Yi Ping gently, Yi Ping began to wobble and fell into her embrace even as he grabbed her tightly around her waist at the same time.

Ding Yun immediately flush shyly.

Yi Ping immediately said in an audible voice in her ears, "Yun, why are you here? You didn't flee while you can?"

Ding Yun was startled as she immediately pushed Yi Ping away, startling Youxue! "You…are still sane?!"

Yi Ping immediately coughed out more blood as he fell onto the ground!

Youxue was immediately besides him and at the same time, everyone was surrounding Yi Ping!

Yi Ping said weakly as he looked at them, "You are all still here?"

One after another, they nodded and smiled, shedding tears of joy!

The Celestial Liege laughed aloud, "He may be alive now but not for long."

All of a sudden, Youxue had raised her hand and slapped him, felling him onto the ground! "Then you are going nowhere as well!"

The Celestial Liege hummed weakly, "Does anyone of you have the right to kill me? I have no personal feud with anyone of you. If you kill me, do you think the Celestial Palace will let this incident pass like this?"

He began to stand up weakly once again as he straightened his fur cloak, "Don't forget I am still the Prime Celestial of the Celestial Palace. Ji Wuzheng, you have dared to keep the Heavenly Relic for your use and even raised your hands against me. Do you think the Celestial Palace will easily forgive this slight?"

Ji Wuzheng said coldly, "The orthodox martial clans are already on their way to the Holy Amalgamate Mountains. There is no need for the Celestial Palace to destroy us first, don't you worry about this. Don't you forget that this is the Holy Hex Sect and all outsiders have to obey the martial Holy Laws of the Holy Hex Sect. The penalty for cannibalism is death!"

The Celestial Liege did not seem afraid as he hummed coldly.

Ji Wuzheng said, "You can go. From now on, the Holy Hex Sect will have nothing to do with the Celestial Palace."

Huo Fu was muttering, "We…really letting him off? He…is too dangerous…"

Ji Wuzheng said, "He had already suffered severe internal injuries and unlikely to recover. Even though the Holy Hex Sect is not an orthodox clan but our founding principles and martial honor demand that we do the right thing. Moreover, he is still our guest. Quickly go before I change my mind!"

Ji Wuzheng stared at Gongsun Jing, Nangong Le, Ding Yun, Xiao Youxue, Lingfeng, Yu'Er and Mei'Er as though he was warning them not to do anything contradicting to his commands or else he would not let them off.

The Celestial Liege smiled coldly as he walked feebly to the entrance.

While the Celestial Liege was talking to Ji Wuzheng, Ding Yun, Youxue and Lingfeng had turn ashen. It was because they had already found something that was amiss!

The Celestial Liege had already normalized his breathing while Yi Ping was still gasping for breathe and was burning with high fever.

They had suddenly recalled that when Lele and Lie Qing had dueled, they too had lost all their internal strength. But to the astonishment of everyone, they quickly fell out again and their seeming 'lost' internal strength had been recovered!

There was a strong reason for the Celestial Force to be one of the strongest inner martial art skills.

It was not that Ding Yun, Youxue and Lingfeng did not want to stop him now. It was because they were unsure if they were able to!

The Celestial Liege took agonizing steps as he reached the entrance. Then he turned back and lifted his thumb at Yi Ping, "Your name is Yi Ping? I have never met anyone like you. It is unlikely that you can survive this battle. When I have recovered, I will come back to retrieve the Heaven Relic and your two heavenly swords."

Ji Wuzheng smirked coldly, "Wait till and see if you can really recover first!"

All of a sudden, Lingfeng said coldly. "Give me the antidote!"

Ding Yun, Youxue, Lingfeng had all stepped in front.

Yu'Er and Mei'Er were too feeble to step forward or else they would surely join them!

Yu'Er was asking Mei'Er, "Are you alright, sister?"

Mei'Er nodded quietly. They had really exhausted too much of their martial power and had been injured by the martial energy force earlier as they tried to protect everyone…

Youxue said, "If you don't hand over the antidote, you are not going anywhere!"

Ding Yun had readied two precious swords that she had borrowed from Mei'Er and Yu'Er in her hands!

The Celestial Liege said unhurriedly, "There is no antidote for the Celestial Force. However, there is still a cure. As long as a hundred chaste maidens are willing to give him their chastity, the positive energy force of the Celestial Force can still be purged. But what's the point? His internal injuries were too severe. He sooner dies first from his internal injuries before he could purge the Celestial Force out."

All of a sudden, he threw a pebble and knocked Youxue down with a startling speed! It was so fast that it completely caught everyone by surprise!

Youxue had seen the little moments in his fingers and had already taken precautions but she was unable to completely evade it!

Youxue coughed weakly as she struggled to stand. That projectile had so much force that it had struck her painfully on her shoulder despite the protection of her Golden Invincible Body! If it was not for her Golden Invincible Body, that pebble would have gone through her shoulder, crippling her!

She turned ashen at that thought!

The Celestial Liege said coldly, "I know that you are protected by the Golden Invincible Body. This is just a small payback for slapping me earlier."

Youxue admonished him icily, "What a grudging man!"

Ji Wuzheng was stunned at the martial display of the Celestial Liege as he took a step back, "He didn't lose his internal strength completely? That's impossible…"

The Celestial Liege said coldly, "If you are having regrets now for not killing me, then it is already too late. It is because with what little internal strength that I have now, I am still capable of protecting myself. Consider this your lucky day today."

Just as Youxue was about to display her startling swiftness attack on the Celestial Liege, Yi Ping had caught hold of her shoulder. "Youxue, life and death is predestined. Let him go."

Yi Ping had stood up on his own!

Yu'Er and Mei'Er immediately flew to support him despite their physical condition as they cried out, "Master…!"

The Celestial Liege was startled as he thought, "He had normalized his intricate breathing so fast?! That's impossible…"

"He is not going anywhere first." A beautiful enchanting voice interrupted his thoughts.

Everyone was startled; it was because this enchanting voice was so familiar!

An enchanting and mesmerizing young maiden was stroking her long braided hair as she stood at the entrance. Her white pink delicate long dress, her black sword, the Perpetual Darkness and her breathtaking astonishing beauty was a familiar sight…it was Lie Qing!

Yi Ping was stunned but overjoyed to see her again as he muttered, "Qing'Er…"

Mei'Er exclaimed happily, "Sister…Lie Qing!"

Ding Yun shed a tear, "Sister Qing'Er…"

Youxue smiled and nodded at her as she saw Lie Qing…

Yu'Er, Lingfeng, Nangong Le, Gongsun Jing and Qiu Wufeng were all smiling broadly when Lie Qing had appeared…

Huo Fu and Ji Wuzheng were startled to see their expressions. It was as though their fighting spirits had suddenly been aroused! Who was this Maiden Lie Qing?

As Lie Qing raised her Perpetual Darkness, there was a sharp ringing echo in mid-air as a halo surrounded her sword. Her sword was exceptional sharp and broke through the air easily!

The dark halo of her sword faded Lie Qing into the shadowy background, merging her with her sword. This darkness merging was actually a profound martial attainment, causing the opponents unable to distinct her actual mode of attacks!

Immediately, the Divine Echo and the White Phoenix began to resonate even more resounding!

When the Celestial Liege saw her, he immediately took several stumbled steps backward!

It was not because he was startled to see three Heavenly Relic swords at the same time!

It was because he had recognized Lie Qing!

The Celestial Liege was trembling and muttering. "That's impossible…Qing'Er, is that really you?!"

Lie Qing sighed softly, "Long time no see…don't you call me Qing'Er. I am not close to you at all. I'm your darkness now… not ever since that night when you have massacred the entire Lie Clan and the entire Invincible Divine Clan. I have said I don't ever want to see you again."

The Celestial Liege was trembling as he saw her crimson eyes and glossy long hair, "Qing'Er, you have become a true Celestial…?"

Everyone was stunned. Lie Qing and the Celestial Liege were acquaintances?!

Lie Qing nodded lightly.

The Celestial Liege hummed coldly, "I know that you have come to take vendetta on me. But if I am not injured, do you think you ever have the chance to kill me?"

Lie Qing said icily, "What makes you think that even if you are not injured, I am unable to kill you?"

The Celestial Liege said, "Your father, the Lord of the Invincible was the top exponent in the fraternity with his seventh invincible force. At that time, we can barely kill him. But now, many years have gone by. My attainment is now on par with his seventh invincible force. In short, I am currently the most powerful exponent in the entire fraternity."

Lie Qing said, "There is no such thing as true invincible and the most powerful or else my father won't be slayed by your clan. Or else…"

She looked at Yi Ping with a loving glance, "Or else…you won't be defeated by Yi Ping!"

The Celestial Liege hummed coldly, "That's because I am careless! If you want to come take my life, do it immediately. But it won't be honorable."

All of a sudden, there were nine burst of faint blue wisp of hovering glow around Lie Qing!

Yu'Er was startled as she began to count excitingly, "One, two, three, four…seven, eight and nine!"

The Celestial Liege was stunned, "That's impossible! The ninth invincible force… you are able to reach the Holiness Level…?"

Lie Qing said coolly, "Even if you are uninjured, you may not be able to defeat me."

The Celestial Liege was silent for a while before he said, "So this is the difference between a Half-Celestial and a true Celestial…"

Lie Qing softened her glances as she said gently, "You are as insolent as ever. Don't think that I do not know that your internal strength is only left with just one tenth and it is impossible for you to recover your original martial strength. You have used the Celestial Origin to forcibly retain what's left of your internal strength. I only pity you!"

The Celestial Liege sighed regretfully, "To think that my centuries of cultivation and martial progression will be ruined today… Very well, come take my life then. You are only able to advance further than me because you are a true Celestial."

Lie Qing said, "Who says I am going to take your life?"

The Celestial Liege was startled, "What do you mean? You want to torture me to a slow death?"

Lie Qing said forlornly, "Who says I am going to avenge for anyone? It has already been so long. Lele asks me to leave a message for you and her beloved."

The Celestial Liege was startled, "My sister has a message for me? She is still alive? Who is her beloved?"

Lie Qing said coolly, "The person that just defeated you earlier is her beloved!"

The Celestial Liege was even more startled as he muttered, "My sister has pledged herself to him?"

Lie Qing continued coldly, "And who says she is dead? She is even more alive than ever. In fact, she is a true Celestial now just like her grandpa."

The Celestial Liege was startled, "She is…a true Celestial now? That's impossible! Her martial levels are way below par. She can't even survive the Divine Calamity alone…don't tell me she has a Heavenly Relic?!"

Lie Qing said coolly, "Martial levels and the Heavenly Relic have nothing to do with her awakening to a true Celestial. She wants me to tell you, even if you got the Heavenly Relic, it is totally useless to you because you have already entered the Dark Asura. Without the state of divinity of the Jade Emperor to calm the malevolent spirits, you will only be courting doom if you try to attempt the Divine Calamity alone. No matter how you try, destruction and death only awaits you"

The Celestial Liege was startled, "I…I don't believe…I don't believe…all my beliefs…"

Lie Qing said melancholy, "The Divine Calamity is a Divine Cleansing of the impure. Long ago, humanity is able to live to a thousand years and has since fallen from grace from the heavens. If you really want to become a Celestial, you must first know how to cultivate as a human sage. That is the only way to become a Celestial. Providence is already so kind to you yet you do not even realize it!"

The Celestial Liege was stunned as he muttered, "If I want to become a Celestial, I must first cultivate as a human sage first…it is that simple?"

The Celestial Liege laughed madly, "Thank you…Qing'Er and Lele…"

He turned around and looked at Yi Ping, who was standing quietly and in great tranquil. He raised his thumb again, "Only you are fit for Qing'Er. I am not worthy. The positive martial energy of the Celestial Force can be purged by a chaste maiden who knows the Holy Pureness, which intricate energy is pure negative. There's no need for me to be too explicit. If you are still alive, then we may one day meet again."

As soon as the Celestial Liege had gone, Lie Qing immediately flew to the embrace of Yi Ping as she wept. "Yi Ping! Are you alright? Where are you hurting at? Let me help you…you have lost all your internal strength…poor thing…"

Yi Ping smiled weakly as his heart began to ache painfully, "Qing'Er, I am so glad to see you…don't worry, I am still live. Losing my internal strength is a small matter as long as…"

Yi Ping looked at everyone, who was smiling at him despite their injuries as he said. "…As long as everyone is safe…"

Lie Qing sobbed silently, "Yi Ping…I hope you don't mind that I let him go…I know I did wrong again…"

Yi Ping comforted her, "No, you did right. You are not wrong…it is a good thing…really."

Lie Qing was almost inaudible as she sobbed, "Really? Sorry…I am late…and cause you to be in such a state…"

Even though Lie Qing was in an enviable embrace with Yi Ping, there was not a single hint of jealousy in these young maidens' eyes. No one dared to disturb their quiet moment because it was also the most romantic moment between the two of them. And moreover, they were only too glad to see Lie Qing who had braved through many dangers with them…

He asked weakly, "Lie Qing, why are you here? Aren't you preparing for the Divine Calamity with Yixian and Lele?"

Lie Qing said, "One day, Lele has suddenly divine that you are in a great mortal danger and because we are all worried for you too, they have decided that I should come to aid you instead."

Yi Ping nodded gently as he stroked her head gently, "How is Yixian?"

Lie Qing looked up gently, "She is attempting a dangerous intricacy heart formula before I have left. But I am sure she will be alright. From the golden scroll, we have discovered many things about the Divine Calamity. While I am away, Lele will be her guardian…"

She was now trembling because she knew how deadly the Divine Calamity was.

Yi Ping held her even tightly because he could sense her fear…

All of a sudden, they were interrupted by three young beautiful maidens that just walked into the Inner Holy Chapter. They all had an appalling looks as they saw the messy state of the Inner Holy Chapter.

These three young maidens were Suxin, Sufeng and Suyue. They were the daughters of Ji Wuzheng.

Suxin immediately said, "Father, you are injured? What's going on? Why is the entire place like that? When we saw the Celestial Envoy a moment ago, he asks us to go the Inner Holy Chapter immediately."

Sufeng was gasping, "Assassins?!"

Ji Wuzheng said, "No big deal. There is no need to be panic."

Suyue flew to Lingfeng, "Aunt! How have you been? I miss you. Who are these people?"

Lingfeng said softly, "These are my friends. There are no assassins. We just have a friendly duel earlier."

Suyue immediately pointed at Yi Ping and looked curiosity at everyone, "A friendly duel?! In this state of awful condition! It looks more like a fight...there are blood everywhere..."

She quickly sighed as she saw Lie Qing in Yi Ping's embrace, "What's a pity. It seems that this handsome young man has already got a beloved."

All of a sudden, she noticed hostile glances from Yu'Er, Mei'Er, Lie Qing, Ding Yun, Youxue and even from her aunt, Lingfeng that caused her to keep quiet.

Suxin was gasping at the Divine Halo and the White Phoenix. "These swords can echo and give out lights...is so beautiful..."

Gongsun Jing was instantly mesmerized by her looks and her voice as he stared blankly at her!

Nangong Le immediately stepped forward, "Lingfeng, I didn't know that you have three such beautiful young nieces that is around your age? Do you mind introducing them to us?"

Lingfeng was born twenty years apart from her brother Ji Wuzheng and her nieces were around her same age.

Lingfeng immediately said, "Suyue, don't talk to this man. He is not a good person!"

Nangong Le smiled bitterly as he thought, "So her name is Suyue..."

When Qiu Wufeng caught sight of Sufeng, for some unknown reason, he was totally captivated by her. As he stepped forward to introduce himself, he stumbled much to his own embarrassment...

Immediately, Sufeng caught hold of him as she asked gently. "Young Master, your injuries are not light. You're alright?"

Qiu Wufeng was surprised that it was Sufeng that had caught hold of him that he was muttering incoherently, "I...I stepped on some debris...nothing...I'm alright..."

Sufeng smiled, "What's your name? I'm Sufeng."

Qiu Wufeng immediately said, "I am Qiu Wufeng." He sounded embarrassed to say his name because he was now a wanted fugitive and got nothing to his name now.

Sufeng gasped, "So you are a mass murderer and one of the monsters from the Righteous Axioms Clan!!!"

Qiu Wufeng immediately denied it with startled horror, "No, no. These are just rumors spread by my enemies...Sufeng...hear me out..."

Suxin immediately pointed at Gongsun Jing, Nangong Le and Yi Ping with an appalled look, "Then these three must be the notorious Gongsun Jing the Dishonorable Playboy, Nangong Le the Flirtatious and Yi Ping the Horrible Torturer!"

She took a spiteful look at Gongsun Jing, "Fancy a fine young man like you would actually be a beast in disguise. If I do not slay you and distribute your flesh as offerings to the innocents today, then my name isn't Suxin!"

Gongsun Jing could only smiled most bitterly as he began to curse that Chi Zhengqi...

He was not the only one thinking of the same thing too. Nangong Le and Qiu Wufeng were already thinking the same!

Huo Fu immediately said as he pointed at Yi Ping, "Young mistresses, I can verify that it is all true. They are indeed the notorious four! I have met this rascal Yi Ping before and he was behaving amorally with a young maiden in a cave."

Ji Wuzheng immediately reacted with shock, "Lingfeng, you didn't tell me that your friends are from the notorious Righteous Axioms Clan! No wonder I find the name of Yi Ping so familiar! Do you know that the four of them are currently the most evil and wanted men in the entire fraternity?!"

Lingfeng got a spinning headache as she said, "These are just false rumors. Listen to my explanations first…" She really wanted to faint. "How did these venomous rumors spread so fast?!"

Suyue immediately said, "Aunt, you just told me that Nangong Le is not a good person! No need to explain, we just feed them to the dogs!"

As Lingfeng moved dazedly backward, she accidentally came into contact with the Divine Echo and the White Phoenix. Immediately the resonating stopped and the halo from the swords ceased.

Just as Lingfeng had calm down and was about to explain, she was interrupted by Yi Ping who said weakly. "Lingfeng, my swords don't seem to like you. They have stopped glowing."

Lingfeng took a fainting look at Yi Ping before saying, "Why don't you go and die first?"

Chapter 52: The Absolute Equilibrium Force

Of course, it was not the truth that the Divine Echo and the White Phoenix dislike Lingfeng. Anyone that accidentally touched the swords at that time except for Yi Ping and Lie Qing would cause the swords to stop resonating as the swords exhausted the spiritual animus that linger on it by its owner.

Yi Ping of course was just teasing Lingfeng because he could feel his life seeping away. That was meant to be his last humorous remark for Lingfeng.

As he collapsed, he was still smiling. It was because when he had taken one last look at Lingfeng; he had remembered how he had first met Lingfeng. How she had saved his life. How she had took him to the valley where he found his father. How she had become his older protégé sister. How they had practiced together. How they had gone against the stern warning of his father and sneaked out of the valley to settle their feud with the Honor Manor. How she had risked disclosing her identity and her life to take him away from the Honor Manor. How he could talk to her about almost anything under the sun. How she had stolen his first kiss and his secret manuals.

Yi Ping was really dying.

He was now in a critical condition. He had not only lost his internal strength, sustained severe internal injuries but had been afflicted by the burning positive energy of the Celestial Force, causing him great agony.

Only his sheer endurance for pain kept him alive till now.

Yu'Er, Mei'Er, Youxue, Ding Yun, Lie Qing and Lingfeng were now eyeing one another intently as they convened.

Yu'Er said melancholy, "The Celestial Liege says that only a chaste maiden that practice negative intricate energy skill can purge the positive energy of the Celestial Force. The Holy Pureness isn't the only negative intricate energy skill that can save master. The Icy Heavenly Tears is also a negative intricate energy skill…"

Lingfeng interrupted softly, "The Icy Heavenly Tears is a cold and negative intricate energy skill. The cold intricate energy will further harm Yi Ping and not purge the Celestial Force out."

Martial intricate energies had many heart intricacy formulas to begin with and extremely complex. Superior internal martial skills that could further develop in strength adhered strictly to the types of intricate energies that were developed.

For example, the Icy Jade Finger of the Eternal Ice Palace depended wholly on the cold and negative intricate energy strength of the practitioner in order to unleash its strength. A practitioner that possessed just the negative intricate energy could not be able to pick up the Icy Jade Finger because they lacked the cold intricate energy to even begin the skill.

Even if the practitioner had the same type of cold and negative intricate energy, it was also not possible to pick up the Icy Jade Finger without knowing the heart intricacy formula of the Ice Heavenly Tears; most superior martial internal martial skills were developed according to the type of heart intricacy formula that the practitioners had already knew so that they could practice it at a lower risk. Heart intricacy skills were often the most risky of all martial skills to begin practice with even for experienced super exponents.

Learning it the wrong way, learning it without a good foundation, learning without adapting the heart intricacies first, learning without understanding would often led to a martial term known as deviation phenomenon, an action that led to death, stroke, paralysis, deterioration of martial strength and many others. It was the most dreadful thing that could happen to a martial practitioner and there were always an emphasis on caution and less haste.

The Celestial Fairy Shui Yixian had progressed too hastily with her Icy Heaven Tears so that she could catch up with her protégé sister Shui Yichi. This resulted in the stunt growth of her future martial progression while Yichi eventually made a breakthrough in the understanding of the Icy Heavenly Tears and at the same time, Yichi's Icy Heavenly Tears was very pure when compared to Yixian, even though they were on the same staging together.

Yichi further developed the cold negative intricate energy to pure cold negative intricate energy, evolving the Jade Icy Finger to Jade Icicle Finger. She did not stop there. Her pure cold negative intricate energy went from pure to extreme cold negative intricate energy as she evolved the Icy Heavenly Tears into another type of internal heart intricacy formula, the Eternal Heavenly Tears.

The Eternal Heavenly Tears was even more astounding than the Icy Heavenly Tears that were developed, improved upon by all her predecessors over many centuries, becoming the first Divine Eternal Mistress of the Eternal Ice Palace to break the stumbling block of the ninth staging of the Icy Heavenly Tears and possibly may even be the first Divine Eternal Mistress of the Eternal Ice Palace to overcome the Divine Calamity. Unfortunately, her martial skills suffered a deterioration after she was injured in a surprise assault by Gongsun Bai, whom she had trusted as her husband's friend and sworn brother.

The many types of intricate energies were classified as positive, negative and equilibrium. Positive intricate energies were the most common in the martial fraternity and can be further define into pure positive, extreme positive and extreme pure positive. The Aspire Invocations was a pure positive martial force while the Celestial Force of the Celestial Liege was an extreme pure positive martial force.

There were actually two versions of the Celestial Force; the Positive Celestial Force and the Negative Celestial Force, making this skill even more complex. The Joyful Goddess was instructed in the Negative Celestial Force because she had to practice another type of heart intricate formula known as Holy Pureness which was pure negative energy.

Equilibrium intricate energies were the most difficult intricate energy to develop, requiring decades. It had only one type of variation, Absolute Equilibrium force. The high level staging of the Invincible Divine Force was one example of the Absolute Equilibrium force, a level of attainment that was almost impossible to reach.

Negative intricate energies were the rarest and also had the most variations. It can be further define into Pure Negative, Extreme Negative, Cold Negative, Pure Cold Negative and Extreme Cold Negative.

Mei'Er said, "But Youxue and you have said earlier that the Icy Heavenly Tears may also be able to treat his internal injuries?"

Yu'Er added, "And yet now you seem unwilling to sacrifice yourself for Yi Ping's sake?"

Mei'Er pointed at Lie Qing, Youxue and Ding Yun, "Why are you all on Lingfeng's side? Only she is right and we are wrong?"

Lingfeng was teary, "Who says I am unwilling? Do you know…do you know…If Yi Ping dies, I am willingly to end my life with him…"

Ding Yun said quietly, "As do I…"

Mei'Er was still doubtful. She whined, "Sister Lingfeng, you say you are willing to lay down for Yi Ping but where is your proof?"

Lingfeng was almost inaudibly as she wept, "Where is my proof? Where are you when I risk my very life for Yi Ping at the Honor Manor? Do you know how close I am to death at that time? If not for Youxue, I might have already lost my life. Do you know that I have risked my life to lure the pursuers away from Youxue and Yi Ping? Do you know that I have barely any internal strength back then? Do you know that as soon as I have recovered my internal strength, I have gone down the Holy Amalgamate Mountains to look for Yi Ping immediately?"

Lingfeng may quarrel with Yi Ping ceaselessly but her love for him was self-sacrificing and noble. Even a dense person like Yi Ping, could feel her alluring attention on him. Moreover, other than the Celestial Fairy, Lingfeng's beauty was almost unparalleled and she had no lack of admirers and suitors. But she was cold towards every single of them except for Yi Ping who had caught her attention with his fearless guts and righteousness air.

Youxue held Lingfeng's hand quietly with trembling hands, "It must really hard on you… I really cannot imagine the hardship and dangers that you have to bear at that time. The pursuers were all experienced exponents of the martial fraternity…"

Lie Qing also comforted Lingfeng, "When we are pursued by Yuan Shao, it is you that guided us to safety. Back then, I was so helpless…"

Mei'Er suddenly remembered what Lingfeng had done for her as well.

She immediately said, "Sister Lingfeng, don't…be upset! Mei'Er is so sorry. I don't mean it. I was just being emotional…"

Yu'Er was also feeling bad as she quickly said, "Sister Lingfeng, Yu'Er is sorry as well. You mustn't blame us. Even our protégé mistress says we are too emotional and ill-suit to learn the Emotionless Rhyme."

She quickly comforted Lingfeng by embracing her.

Lingfeng whispered, "That's alright. I don't blame you. I am just so emotional also…I'm sorry as well."

Youxue walked out of the room, leaving behind her wet silent tears on the floor!

Lie Qing muttered, "Youxue…"

She thought, "Youxue probably needs some quiet time. It's not easy for her to be with Yi Ping and now…"

Like Lingfeng, Youxue had also almost lost her life. But no others carried as much heavy burden as her as she had to struggle with her own guilt and the generation of feuds that she had inherited against the Celestial Fairy who happened to be Yi Ping's wife. Until now, she still could not fulfill her mother's last wish…

Lingfeng sighed, "Maybe we are really too emotional earlier and did not really get the situation correct. Let's explain again."

Yu'Er and Mei'Er nodded, indicating that they would try their best to listen this time.

She said, "Without the Great Dissolution Skill from the Holy Amalgamate Force, it not possible to channel any negative intricate energy to purge the Celestial Force out of Yi Ping's body. I have already tried to channel my Holy Pureness on Yi Ping but it did not work because his internal injuries are too severe and all his channels are broken. Without treating his internal injuries first, all our efforts are in vain and the Celestial Force inside him is preventing us from treating his internal injuries…"

Yu'Er blunt out, "Sister Lingfeng, you seem…unwillingly to sacrifice your chastity for him."

Lingfeng was startled, "What do you mean by sacrifice my chastity for him?"

Yu'Er said shyly, "You didn't hear what the Celestial Liege said, as long as there are a hundred maidens that could give up their chastity for our master or a chaste maiden with the Holy Pureness, the Celestial Force can be purge out?"

Yu'Er rolled up her sleeve on her left forearm and showed them her chastity mark, followed by Mei'Er.

Lie Qing, Ding Yun and Lingfeng were startled.

Lie Qing was exasperated, "I have thought at the inn, you say you have lost your chastity to Yi Ping at the inn…"

Lingfeng and Ding Yun were startled. They were all under that impression too.

Yu'Er sniffed, "Then it is decided. No matter what you have all said, we have already decided to sacrifice ourselves for our master's sake. No matter…if it is going to work or not…"

Mei'Er said melancholy, "There's no other way. Even without the Holy Pureness, we can…we can…hope to help master relieve his pains for a while…"

Lingfeng almost fainted from these two innocent maidens as she covered her mouth, trying hard not to laugh at them.

Ding Yun and Lie Qing were laughing softly.

Yu'Er asked curiously, "This is a critical situation for our master, why are you laughing at us? If you want to, you can…erm…sleep with master too."

Lie Qing turned around, giggling. "Yun, you explain…I really…I really…cannot…stop laughing…"

Ding Yun quickly comforted Yu'Er and Mei'Er, "What the Celestial Liege had said about one hundred maidens sacrificing their chastity is just a figuration of speech. It is just a metaphor, do you understand me? Hmm…" She took a quick look at Lie Qing and Lingfeng who had turned their backs and were trembling hard as they really tried very hard not to laugh aloud. But anyone could see that they were just trying extremely hard to suppress their laughter!

She sighed at them as she thought, "They…all of them are like young girls…"

She quickly recovered from her thoughts as Yu'Er and Mei'Er were still waiting for her to explain, "This negative to positive transference is an exhausting effort and in order to proceed unhindered by intricate energy interferences, it requires both man and woman to remove all their clothes as a precaution. That is what meant by sacrificing the maiden chastity…"

Ding Yun could hear giggling laughers behind her as she continued, "Sister Lingfeng is only unable to proceed further because of the severity in Yi Ping's internal injuries. She can attempt alright but if she fails, she is afraid Yi Ping won't be able to take it. She has already used her Holy Pureness to suppress the Celestial Force in whatever she can. We are thinking what to do first."

Mei'Er was startled, "Really no need…!?"

Ding Yun sighed, "Really no need. From the looks of it, you are both still very chaste maidens. Do you think that with Yi Ping's injuries, he is able to do that kind of a thing?"

Mei'Er asked, "What thing?"

Yu'Er too asked, "Yes, what thing?"

Lie Qing could no longer suppress her laughs anymore, as tears rolled out of her mesmerizing eyes. She gurgled and laughed, "You see…you see…"

She laughed and stole a glance at Lingfeng, who refused to turn her back around. "You see…oh never mind…I don't know what Sister Xian or the Eternal Ice Palace has been teaching the both of you but this is so amusing. I…Sister Lingfeng…you explain…I really don't know how to explain…"

Lingfeng laughed softly, "Don't you drag me into it…"

Youxue had walked out of the resting room and was wandering aimlessly in the premises of the Holy Chapter.

"Maiden, wait a minute!"

It was Ji Wuzheng and he was accompanied by Qian Fan.

She asked, "Yes?"

Ji Wuzheng said solemnly, "I have a question for you."

Youxue said coldly, displaying her usual cold demeanor. "Is there anything I can help you?"

Ji Wuzheng sighed, "I am just wondering if we have met two years ago."

At that time, Youxue had donned her veiled straw hat. She went everywhere in a disguise because she was being pursued by the Virtuous Palace.

Youxue hummed coldly, "Yes, we did. Your sword techniques are really very swift. I was almost killed by you."

Ji Wuzheng laughed aloud, "You are not weak either with your Penetrating Hands of the Virtuous Palace!"

When he mentioned the Virtuous Palace, there was a hostile look in his eyes. He asked, "You have come as a scout for the Virtuous Palace?"

Youxue hummed coldly, "Say whatever you want."

Ji Wuzheng said, "Is it too much of a coincidences? As soon as the Celestial Liege left the Holy Hex Sect, the entire orthodox clans are now charging up the mountains. It is a lucky thing that we have once again halted their advancement even though it is just temporary. But it seems that they know that I am injured? Other than the people that were inside the Inner Holy Chapter who witness our fight with the Celestial Liege, no one else knows that I am injured."

Youxue looked at him coldly, "So you are suspecting me?"

Qian Fan interrupted, "If it is not you, then it is me? What a joke! It is obvious that you are from the Virtuous Palace. We should really take her down and send her corpse to that Xiao Shuai. In this way, we can deal a blow to the morale of the Virtuous Palace. Who knows? She may even be the young mistress of the Virtuous Palace."

Youxue hummed coldly. She had already raised her hand in front of her!

Ji Wuzheng said, "This is the first time that I have seen your face since we had fought two years ago. You look even younger than Lingfeng and maybe even my daughters. Two years ago, you must even be younger."

Youxue said coldly, "That's crap isn't it?"

Ji Wuzheng laughed, "What an interesting maiden. How old are you two years ago?"

Youxue asked, "Why do you want to know so much? Aren't you accusing me?"

Ji Wuzheng was solemn, "Accusing people does need evidence, am I not wrong to say so?"

Youxue nodded slowly.

Ji Wuzheng said, "I don't have any evidence now. In fact, you are free to go freely for now. I am just pointing out some facts. May I know what is maiden name?"

Youxue looked curiously at him before she said coolly, "Xiao Youxue is my name."

She began to take a few steps away when she suddenly turned her head around, adding. "I am seventeen back then. Now I am nineteen." She immediately walked away hurriedly after she had spoken.

Ji Wuzheng was startled as he thought, "She is really so young. To think that I was almost best by a seventeen year old maiden…"

Qian Fan immediately said, "Holy Sectarian Master, you are letting her go just like that? Her surname is Xiao! Xiao is the same surname as the Protégé Master of the Virtuous Palace, Xiao Shuai!"

Ji Wuzheng said coolly, "No, she wouldn't be the spy."

Qian Fan was startled, "How is that so?"

Ji Wuzheng laughed aloud, "If she is a spy, then she must be the worst spy ever. Have you ever seen a spy that is so easily provoked? This young maiden is still the same maiden as two years ago. Moreover there are righteousness in her eyes and the way she is fighting so hard for that Yi Ping. A spy won't even dare to display their secret martial skills in front of me."

Qiao Fan asked, "If she is not a spy? Then who is?"

Ji Wuzheng said, "Maybe it is you."

Qiao Fan was startled, "Holy Sectarian Master, it's not me for sure. I wouldn't dare."

Ji Wuzheng laughed, "Is that so?"

Then he said, "Maybe it is that Nangong Le. But who knows. Everyone is a suspect. Don't you think so?"

Qiao Fan regained his composure as he said, "That's right. Everyone is a suspect."

Ji Wuzheng looked at Qian Fan intently but he did not say a word.

Youxue at this time was walking in despair and was feeling downcast.

All of a sudden, she had discovered that she had walked into Yi Ping's resting as she startled two young maids who were in the room tending to Yi Ping.

She quickly said to them, "It's alright. I am here to see my friend. You can go now. I want to be left alone with him."

The two young waiting maidens nodded hurriedly and left the room.

Yi Ping was lying on a bed and he was in great agony. His face was red and burning with a fever.

Youxue immediately took a wet tower and tenderly wetted his forehead, muttering. "Yi Ping, what can I do to help you relieve of your pain? I wish that the one that is lying in agony is me and the one that is tendering to me, is you."

She was weeping silent tears, "You are burning so hot. It must be really agonizing, am I not wrong to say so?"

She was suddenly reminiscing those happier times when she was in the Ice Cavern with him. The three months that she had with him was the most tranquil thing that she had ever felt. There are no thoughts of vengeance, only quiet romantic thoughts when she was with him. Sometimes it was disrupted by Lie Qing but it was also Lie Qing that allowed her to see Yi Ping's thoughtfulness and unyielding care for a half-dead maiden.

She was smiling to herself when she recalled with horror that Yi Ping had actually decided to give the Divine Dragon Pill to a half-dead Lie Qing. She recalled that together with Lie Qing and Ding Yun, they had accidentally injured Yi Ping. And how they had formed the New Virtuous Palace just for the sake of fun…

She went back even further back in time when she remembered the very first time she had met Yi Ping. She had terrified him then and was amused when he began to dig a grave for the bandit that she had killed. Later on, she was not too happy when she had seen him with the Celestial Fairy and did not know that they had pledged to one another as one…

Suddenly she remembered what the Celestial Liege had said.

"Didn't I also practice the Icy Heavenly Tears? Maybe…maybe I can help Yi Ping to relieve of his pain? Even though my cold negative intricate energy isn't as pure as Yu'Er and Mei'Er but at least I may be able to absorb the heat from his body…"

She began to flush as she loosened her waist belt and let her outer garment dress slipped off her. She poked gently at Yi Ping as she muttered, "Don't you look!"

But she soon sighed, "He is in a feverish state. He can't hear me at all."

She did not dare to take off her white inner garment yet. Instead, she began to shyly slowly remove the light garb from Yi Ping.

She gently said enchantingly, "Do you still remember when you give me the White Phoenix; you have told me that as long as I show you the sword again, you will do anything for me? I…"

She shyly lowered her glances, "I…just want you to be with me…forever." As she said that, she removed her top inner garment, leaving just a piece of lingerie that was strap over her shoulders and tied to the girth seam of her lower back.

Afterward she gently reached out and removed her hairpin one by one, letting down her rolls of dark raven hair that reached to her knee.

Youxue slowly reached out with her cold fingers and touched Yi Ping. She could feel the incessant heat that was from him.

She immediately thought, "So this is losing chastity? Between a man and a woman?" Her heart began to beat rapidly as she flustered shyly. She shyly began to lie down on Yi Ping's chest gently and removing her strap as she felt the warmth of his body…

"Weird. Why I am feeling so warm? Is it because of the positive energy of the Celestial Force?"

But before she could give a second thought, she gasped aloud for she was suddenly seized by Yi Ping who had hugged her tightly as he muttered, "So comfortable…so comfortable…so cool to the touch…"

Youxue gasped shyly, "He…we…I am his now. Yi Ping, you…are hurting me. I can't breathe…I have heard it will hurt…"

Yi Ping had broken into cold dripping sweat as he opened his eyes. It was because he had suddenly realized he was hugging the cold silky body of a fragrant maiden who was muttering incoherent. To his startled horror, it was Xiao Youxue!

His first thought was of course, where was he and why were they holding each other in this intimate position. He dare not move for he was paralyzed with inaction as he thought panicky, "What should I do?"

While Lie Qing was a most mesmerizing maiden and Lingfeng was a most alluring maiden, Youxue was a most enchanting maiden. Even if he wanted to push her away, it was a most difficult thing to do even though they were not doing anything but just embracing. Moreover, they were in such an awkward position,

Youxue was muttering, "Yi Ping...do you feel much better?" as her wet tears dripped down his body.

The resistance of his Absolute Spirits seemed to have melted away and all of a sudden, his heart began to experience an extremely sharp pain. He endured the pain because he was used to the pain. The pain of watching his mother died before his very own eyes were a much agony pain than any pains in the world. But the miracle thing happened, as soon as Youxue's tears dripped on his heart, his pain immediately eased and he was comfortable again. The heart rendering pain that he had endured ever since had totally vanished!

But still he dare not move even as he could sniff the sweet fragrant of her strands of hair that were tickling his nose. In fact, his heart was now beating rapidly as he could feel the electrifying sensation of her smooth back...

Yi Ping asked himself panicky, "What shall I do?"

Unknown to Youxue when she was in the embrace of Yi Ping, he had just completed a titanic struggle with the Celestial Force that was in his body and had just awakened from a deep unconscious sleep.

The powerful Celestial Force of the Celestial Liege overwhelmed his equilibrium intricate force after he had sustained internal injuries in the ensuring conflict, causing it to be imbalance. Without a stable intricate energy force, the Celestial Force could not be purge out from his body with his own effort.

However, the constant agonizing struggle with the Celestial Force reawakened the Eternal Heavenly Tears Intricate Energy that his mother had previously channeled and hidden in his vessel meridian channel. As the extreme pure positive energy of the Celestial Force clashed with the extreme cold negative of the Eternal Heavenly Tears, these two forces neutralized one another and were absorbed into the Aspire Invocation's equilibrium intricate energy force, achieving balance once again.

Not only had Yi Ping now reached the highest level of the Aspire Invocation Force, his internal strength also received a tremendous boast, breaking through several limitations as his equilibrium force grew in strength, evolving into the absolute equilibrium force!

There was a limit to the internal strength that could be gained by internal energy cultivation and that limit was known as the Intricate Energy Limitation or sixty years of internal energy cultivation. Afterwards, it was painfully slow. The only way to cumulative more martial power was through the use of superior martial skills that could boast martial power temporary such as the Asper Horizon Hands and the Invincible Divine Force, which drained the practitioner of their precious internal strength and intricate energy at a rapid rate. This also caused them to be more vulnerable to internal injuries as they lost the use of their naturally defensive martial force.

The absolute equilibrium force was not only a much stronger martial force than the equilibrium force; it could also correct and realign the vital energy forces of the practitioner unconsciously, even healing internal injuries at a rapid rate!

Previously, Yi Ping's Asper Horizon Hands could cause him to be more vulnerable to attacks in exchange for more martial power. The rebound force of the absolute equilibrium force could restore that balance and enabling him to use the Asper Horizon Hand in a much shorter notice without harming his body.

Of course, Yi Ping did not know any of these now. He was more concerned about how to get out of this awkward situation and it was not something he could solve with his martial skills.

Youxue was muttering incoherently and innocently until she had suddenly fallen asleep. It was because she was really too tired and did not sleep the entire time Yi Ping was fighting for his life.

Yi Ping had noticed immediately that Youxue seemed to be sound asleep. It was really a most excellent opportunity for him to get out of this awkward situation by gently moving her aside.

Just as he was about to do so, he heard familiar voices as they entered the room.

Lie Qing said, "We look everywhere but can't find Youxue. Maybe she is here. But then, the three of you is what we needed."

Lingfeng was saying, "It is indeed an oversight. Why didn't we think of that earlier?"

Ding Yun said gently, "It is because we have too many things in our heart and missed the most obvious."

Lie Qing said, "That's because we all thought Yu'Er and Mei'Er is unable to practice the Holy Pureness. That is why we have missed something so obvious. And moreover, Youxue is dual balancing the Icy Heavenly Tears and the Divine Virtuous Force. She obviously cannot learn the Holy Pureness. The risk of a deviation phenomenon is simply too high for her.

Yu'Er said, "Sister Lingfeng, quickly teach Mei'Er and I the Holy Pureness. With the internal strength from the three of us, we surely can plunge the Celestial Force out of master."

Lingfeng laughed softly, "We haven't reached yet. Later we must exercise extreme caution. Remember to listen to all my instructions…"

Mei'Er suddenly gasped with a sudden shock. She was eager to check on Yi Ping and was the first to enter the room.

Her startled cry alarmed Lie Qing, Lingfeng, Yu'Er and Ding Yun as they hastened inside the room with utmost urgency!

They were all thinking of the same thing; had something happened to Yi Ping?!

One by one, they gave a startled gasping shock as they saw Yi Ping and Youxue in a intimating embrace together and moreover, they were not wearing anything.

Yi Ping had turned completely red; his ears, his cheeks and his neck when he saw them.

He immediately said panicky, "This is not what you have all imagine. I do not know what is happening too!"

Youxue was immediately startled by him as she opened her eyes.

She was startled that Yi Ping had awakened and he was holding her body to him. She flushed so deeply that she did not know what to do.

Mei'Er suddenly said to Lingfeng, "Sister Lingfeng, didn't you say that this method does not work?"

Lingfeng was so flustered that she did not know how to reply her.

Yu'Er was muttering incoherently, "Master Yi Ping..."

Youxue was startled. She quickly turned around and gasped. It was because she had saw Lie Qing, Ding Yun, Lingfeng, Yu'Er and Mei'Er; they were all looking at Yi Ping and her in a fluster manner!

Yi Ping stammered, "I...we...it is really not what has happened..."

But before he could finish, Youxue had interrupted shyly with a whisper. "I have already given my chastity to Ping'Er..."

This immediately stunned Yi Ping and everyone else that was in the room, as evidenced by the number of startled gasps and stunned astonishments!

Chapter 53: The Martial Sage

It was late at night and there were four men drinking heavily in the pavilion.

Yi Ping, Gongsun Jing, Nangong Le and Qiu Wufeng were drowning their sorrows with binge after binge of wines. The floor and the table were scattered with flasks and jars of wines. They were just drinking flasks after flasks of wines and none of them had said a single word throughout the night.

Gongsun Jing was drinking alone when Yi Ping popped in with more jars of wine in his hands as he sat down.

He was thinking bitterly, "You have so many ladies as company and you choose to drink with me?"

Even before Yi Ping had sat down, Qiu Wufeng had walked to the pavilion with more jars of wines. Without saying a word, he began to drink from one of the jars of wine that he had brought with him.

Gongsun Jing was startled, "What is wrong with Brother Wufeng?"

Even before his thoughts had settled, Nangong Le had walked to the pavilion in a half-drunk state, "Good, there is more wines here." And he just took a jar of wine that was on the table and began to drink.

After some time, Gongsun Jing could not resist the temptation to ask anymore. "All of you. What is wrong with all of you? I thought that I am the only who is unhappy here. How come everyone is drinking their sorrows?"

Qiu Wufeng smiled bitterly, "You can't be as unhappy as I am."

Yi Ping laughed sadly as he drowned another flask of wine, "Not you I am."

Nangong Le banged the table with his hand, "You? You will be unhappy? There so many extraordinary beautiful maidens around you. Will you be unhappy? Is this a joke?"

Yi Ping sighed, "Precisely it is because of them that it is causing me so much distress now."

Gongsun Jing said quietly, "Brother Yi Ping, do you mind sharing with us what actually is bothering you? Maybe we can help."

Yi Ping sighed sorrowfully, "It is rather embarrassing."

Qiu Wufeng said, "If you don't share, how do you know that you are unhappier than us? Since we are already here and are brothers, is there anything we cannot share?"

Nangong Le rebuked him wobbly, "Wines can be shared and talks can be shared but women, no."

Qiu Wufeng asked, "Which maiden has caused such distress in you?"

Nangong Le was startled, "How do you know?"

Qiu Wufeng smiled awkwardly, "Is there anything else other than women that can cause you to gloom over it?"

Nangong Le said, "There is. Money is one of them."

Qiu Wufeng said, "Obviously it is not now for you."

Gongsun Jing said, "Since we all have a problem, why don't we share it? Maybe it will make us feel better. Brother Yi Ping, will you like to start first? It seems that none of us believe that you can be troubled as much as we do."

Yi Ping hummed coldly, "After I have shared my miseries with you, you will know how troubled I am."

He sighed and his eyes were downcast as he began to relate the source of his sorrows.

When he had just regained conscious, he found himself in a compromising and intimating embrace with a semi-nude Youxue. Before he had realized what was happening, Mei'Er, Yu'Er, Lingfeng, Lie Qing and Ding Yun had walked in with stunned looks at the scene.

Before he could explain, Youxue had said shyly. "I have already given my chastity to Ping'Er…"

Lingfeng recovered from her initial shock as she whimpering tearfully. "Hmph! At first I don't believe what Brother Huo Fu has said about you being alone with a maiden in the cave. But now I do. Now it all makes sense to me. Now I know how the Celestial Fairy and how the Joyful Goddess succumbed to you one by one, one after another!"

She purposely dragged her sentence long because she wanted to let her hurtful feelings sink into Yi Ping's heart so that he would forever remember what she had just said to him!

When she had said everything that was in her heart, she burst into tears and stormed out of the room!

Mei'Er cried out, "You are no longer our Master!"

Immediately after she had made her outcry, she left the room in tears.

Yu'Er stared hatefully at Yi Ping and left without saying a word. Unlike Mei'Er, Yu'Er rarely talk to strangers. When she could not be bothered to say anything to him now; that already spoke volumes of her heartbreak!

Lie Qing said coldly, "So all along, you are just putting on an act in front of us. You have victimized Sister Youxue and yet you refuse to admit what you have done. No wonder, Lele has your…I am really disappointed in you…my heart is cold now and filled with darkness. Like all men, you cannot be trusted!"

Yi Ping quickly said, "Qing'Er, hear me out. This is really not what you have imagined…"

He tried to pull Youxue away from him until he suddenly realized that she was shyly holding onto him tightly…

Lie Qing interrupted him coldly as her tears flowed silently down her cheeks, "Tomorrow at noon, prepare your swords. We will duel in a sword fight and cease only when one of us is dead."

She stormed out angrily.

Youxue comforted Yi Ping, "Don't worry, Ping'Er. Tomorrow I will help you. You need more rest to fully recuperate from your injuries. She suggests a sword duel but must we adhere to a sword duel? If I insist on an intricate strokes martial duel, there is nothing she can protest about."

Yi Ping smiled bitterly, "Youxue, you should know. You have fought with her at the Longevity Hall of the Tranquil Clan before. Even though Qing'Er never left the sight of her sword, her intricate strokes are even more startling than her swordplay."

Youxue muttered, "I won't give her any advantage and knows her disadvantage. I will prolong the fight and drawn her into exhausting her martial power…"

Only Ding Yun was still standing with her usual quiet demeanor in the room. But something in her eyes tell him that something was not right.

Yi Ping panicked said, "Yun, hear me out first. I know that you are the most understanding…"

But Ding Yun ignored Yi Ping as she muttered incoherent, "Youxue, I have ruined you. I…"

Youxue was suddenly cold. She had seen the reactions of Lingfeng, Mei'Er, Yu'Er and Lie Qing as they stormed out one by one.

She said coldly, "This is not Ping'Er fault. Why are you all reacting in such an awful manner? I did it willingly and…and we will eventually be married to each other. It is just a matter of sooner or later!"

Yi Ping was startled to hear this coming from Youxue as he muttered, "Youxue…"

Ding Yun looked at Yi Ping coldly even as she said to Youxue, "I know that by now, nothing that I have said will convince you to change your minds. But do you know why we are so upset?"

Youxue asked coldly, "What else? You must all be jealous to see that I am the one that had resuscitated Ping'Er."

Yi Ping was startled. So it was Youxue that had saved his life and purge out the conflicting Celestial Force from his body. Instantly, he was filled with gratuity for her as he thought silently, "Youxue, you have sacrificed your chastity and yet you have to endure so much humiliation for my sake. It must be hard on you…alas…once again, you have saved my life. Why am I so useless?"

Ding Yun said quietly, "Yi Ping has lied to us all. He can purge the Celestial Force on his own. But he had pretended otherwise. Do you know we have been so worried for him and we did not sleep a wink? Instead…instead of being honest with you, he had taken advantage of you!"

Youxue said coldly, "I don't know what you are saying. That is so unlike you, Sister Yun. This is too irrational isn't it? It is impossible for Ping'Er to fake his injuries with so many sharp eyes around…"

Ding Yun interrupted coldly, "A normal practitioner may not be able to. But a super martial exponent is able to. Don't you find that it is weird that Yi Ping is able to defeat the Celestial Liege but yet he can be afflicted by the Celestial Force? Since he can fight the Celestial Liege on equal terms, the Celestial Force can never overcome his inherent martial force and invade his meridian channels. That's not possible at all. Have you ever thought of that? Is that considered irrational, if you come to think of that? The fact is, he doesn't seem to be afflicted at all and from the looks of it, he looks perfectly vigorous."

Youxue said shyly, "That is because he has…absorbed my cold and negative intricate energy when I sacrificed my chastity for him. It is exactly like what the Celestial Liege has said. Yi Ping is young and he is naturally stronger than most. So it is not surprising that after that one exchange, he has recovered. What's so strange about it? Why are all of you thinks that Ping'Er has taken advantage of me and has lied to all of you, just because…just because…it does not go according to what you have planned? There are always exceptional in many things. What's so astounding and strange about all this?"

Ding Yun said, "Sister, you are too naïve and too innocent. You…I explain to you when you have calmed down first."

She said turned coldly to Yi Ping, "You really disappointed me. Since that day in the valley, I have already pledged my heart to you and I considered myself to be your wife. No matter how bad you are…no matter how despicable you are…if tomorrow Lie Qing kills you; I will take my own life too!"

She left the room in tears!

Yi Ping was startled as he muttered incoherently in bewilderment as he thought, "What did I do actually?!"

Youxue muttered shyly as she embraced him, "Ping'Er, why is that I can sense that your martial force seems to be different now? There seems to be a strong inherent force now. And weird, why is that I cannot feel your Icy Heavenly Tears anymore? Strange, it shouldn't just vanish like this. When you have consumed the Thousand Year Ice Fish, it should be stronger than ever. Don't tell me, don't tell me, your Icy Heavenly Tears has merged with the Celestial Force?!"

However, Yi Ping was not paying attention to her mutterings as he was still looking forlornly at the room entrance.

Gongsun Jing, Qiu Wufeng and Nangong Le were looking at Yi Ping with startled expressions.

Qiu Wufeng muttered with astonishment, "So you are saying, you have fallen out with Yu'Er, Mei'Er, Lie Qing, Ding Yun and Lingfeng?"

Nangong Le was even more startled, "You and Youxue…? You have really taken her chastity?"

Yi Ping drowned another flask of wine as he said bitterly, "So, is anyone of you more unfortunate and more miserable than I am?"

Gongsun Jing who was quiet until now, laughed bitterly. "You think you are miserable? You think you are more miserable than me?"

Nangong Le, Qiu Wufeng and Yi Ping were startled by Gongsun Jing outburst.

Gongsun Jing sighed sorrowfully, "I used to be the Young Master of the renowned Honor Manor which is the most powerful orthodox clan in the entire fraternity, enjoying the admiration and envy of the entire fraternity. But now, I am just a wanted man on the run…"

Yi Ping interrupted, "You blame Ding Yun?"

Gongsun Jing shook his head, "She is really a gentle maiden and a pitiful maiden. I do like her a lot. Alas…she likes you Yi Ping, take good care of her. But you know. Even if she isn't with you, we cannot be together. It is an undeniable fact that that my father is killed by her sword…"

Yi Ping was silent.

Nangong Le muttered incoherently, "That isn't something new at all. Do you need to drink yourself silly over some old memories?"

Gongsun Jing smiled bitterly, "Of course, that's not all. I was scolded as a beast in disguise. This is the first time that I am being so mindful…"

Qiu Wufeng smiled bitterly, "Do you mean Suxin? You like her?"

Gongsun Jing was startled, "You know?"

Qiu Wufeng said, "Actually you don't have to be so bothered about it. Lingfeng has already explained and clear everything. It is just that we don't have any evidence to prove our innocents...alas..."

Gongsun Jing asked, "Why are you sighing? You seem even more eager to find the proof more than I."

Qiu Wufeng made deep sighs, "It's Sufeng...to think that I will like someone from the unorthodox clan. The Qiu Martial Clan has always been reputable in the fraternity...not only have I destroy all my clan repute, I have lost everything now. I don't know what she thinks of me. Alas...is anyone of you more miserable than me?"

Yi Ping and Nangong Le immediately said, "This wine is a toast for you!"

Qiu Wufeng startling halt them, "Don't you finish all the wine and please leave some for me. Both of you sound more like taking advantage of the situation to finish all the wines. You scoundrels...alas...never mind..."

Nangong Le sighed, "Getting disowned by my father is one thing but none of you can be more miserable than I am tonight."

Qiu Wufeng hummed, "I don't believe."

Nangong Le said bitterly, "At least all is not lost with you, Brother Wufeng. The same goes to Brother Jing too. At least Brother Yi Ping can still try his best to explain and at least there is still Youxue who is still willing to listen..."

Yi Ping interrupted, "Tomorrow at noon I am going to get killed by Qing'Er. Is this some kind of a small comfort?"

Gongsun Jing smiled bitterly, "Why don't you come to the point immediately?"

Nangong Le sighed deeply, "I got rejected tonight by Suyue...alas."

Everyone was startled.

Qiu Wufeng stammered, "You actually approach Suyue and make advances to her?"

Nangong Le sighed even deeper, "She says I am Nangong Le the Flirtatious and completely rejected me. My reputation is so bad...why didn't Lingfeng clarify for me..."

Gongsun Jing smiled even more bitterly, "You have been known as Nangong Le the Flirtatious for as long as I can remember. Nothing can change that."

Nangong Le said, "I thought I am known as Nangong Le the Joyous?"

Qiu Wufeng laughed, "That's because they are giving you some face saving measures on accord of the Nangong Clan in the fraternity. But that's what everyone is calling you behind your back."

Nangong Le was stunned, "This is the first time I have known about it. How come none of my friends have ever told me that?"

All of a sudden, everyone had noticed that Yi Ping had frozen and was looking in his opposite direction.

Nangong Le, Gongsun Jing and Qiu Wufeng quickly turned around and were startled to see Xiao Youxue who was just standing quietly. There was a forbidden cold demeanor around her that was terrifying to behold.

From the look of it, she had been standing there for quite some time.

Youxue said coldly, "Ping'Er, how could you tell everyone about us and describing it?"

She hummed coldly before she storm off indignantly!

Yi Ping asked, "Now who is the most miserable?"

"There are so much wines lying around here? It seems that my guests forget that we are under siege and taking the opportunity to empty my wine cellar, leaving none for me?"

It was the Holy Sectarian Master, Ji Wuzheng!

They quickly rose to pay their respects except for Nangong Le who was too drunk to stand.

Ji Wuzheng said, "It seems that none of you are as miserable as me."

Yi Ping was startled, "What makes you say so?"

Gongsun Jing and Qiu Wufeng looked curiously at him.

Ji Wuzheng sighed, "My wines are almost finished up by you guys. The Holy Hex Sect is on the brink of destruction. My sister, Lingfeng is crying tearfully. I have just recently lost four Guardians of the Holy Chapter. My daughters have suddenly gone quiet. Who can be more miserable than I am?"

He sighed, adding. "Do you know that the Orthodox Clans have issued me a challenge in three days' time? I have already accepted it. There are simple too many sacrifices and too many innocents that have perished. Perhaps that is the best course of action. If I am willing to accept their challenge, then they will be willing to spare the Holy Hex Sect from total destruction. Of course, they want my sister Lingfeng the Holy Maiden and our sacred relic the Heavenly Relic as a pledge of peace if we lose the duels."

He hummed coldly, "That is after all, their real objectives. In additional, they want six persons from me; the four of you plus Maiden Youxue and Maiden Yun. The four of you will be handed over to the Honor Manor to be executed and to appease the orthodox fraternity. Maiden Youxue and Maiden Yun will be handed over to the Virtuous Palace. If you are in my shoe, what will you do?"

Everyone was silent. Compared to Holy Sectarian Master Ji Wuzheng's problems, theirs were actually trivial.

Ji Wuzheng said, "The four of you are young and have a bright future. What's there to worry about? A hero will always pick himself up. If there are difficulties, he will overcome it. The four of you have come all the way from the Central Fraternity to aid the Holy Hex Sect to fight the Honor Manor. It is indeed admirable."

Gongsun Jing was blunt, "It is because our feuds with the Honor Manor are not something that we can hope to end alone. We just hope that at least we can fight against a common enemy together and at least stand a better chance to settle our score with the Honor Manor once and for all. Even if we have failed, at least our deaths will not be in vain!"

Ji Wuzheng immediately clapped his hand on the table, "Great aspirations!"

He paused for a while before asking, "Have you heroes thought of joining the Holy Hex Sect instead?"

Qiu Wufeng said, "The Holy Hex Sect is an unorthodox clan. I'm from the orthodox clan…"

Ji Wuzheng said, "What is orthodox and what is unorthodox? Just because the Holy Hex Sect has our own beliefs, we are branded unorthodox? Just because we settle our feuds with the other martial clans in an open manner, we are called the unorthodox sects? The so call righteous orthodox martial clans are the ones that are attacking us. In name, they are avenging the death of the Old Sword Saint. In secret, the Honor Manor and the Virtuous Palace are actually trying to seize our Heavenly Relic. Can their actions be considered orthodox or even righteous?"

Yi Ping said, "Even though my knowledge is limited and maybe you are right but good can only falter for a while and not vanquished. The recognized orthodox clans have fought hard to be recognized as part of the orthodox martial fraternity. Even though these orthodox clans can be misled and even their leadership can be evil for a time, it will soon revert to the orthodox in due time. If an unorthodox clan wants to be an orthodox clan, then it will need to prove itself and take steps to move forward to that direction. That's why these orthodox clans are able to endure for centuries, with many ups and downs. As for the unorthodox clans, how many actually survived for long? If an unorthodox clan is not careful, it may even drift and becomes a secret heretic clan, unable to do things in the open and can only operate in the darkness."

Ji Wuzheng was silent for a while, "I do have the intention to bring the Holy Hex Sect to be part of the orthodox martial fraternity. But prejudice against our sect runs deep in the orthodox martial fraternity or else they won't raise their arms against us and view us as a threat."

Yi Ping said, "Then it has to depend if the ascendency of the Holy Hex Sect in the fraternity is your lofty ambition to dominate others by your strength or be recognized by the fraternity."

Ji Wuzheng asked, "Is there a difference?"

Yi Ping said, "To dominate over others will bring a grudging feeling. To be recognized by others will bring a grudging respect. I don't know what actually happens during the duel between the Old Sword Saint and you. Everyone says that you have caused the death of the Sword Saint and hence, your next step is domination over the martial fraternity."

Ji Wuzheng hummed coldly, "These are mere rumors. With my martial skills and swordplay, I don't have a chance against the Old Sword Saint. Our secret duel is a contest over our sect intricate internal skills, the Holy Amalgamate Skill and the Infinitude Recite. At that time, both of us are seeking a breakthrough. The duel was just an internal strength contest to test our limits. Both of us know the dangerous risk involved but we willingly decide to take this peril to accomplish what we had in mind."

He looked at Yi Ping keenly, "You know. It was in fact a draw between the Old Sword Saint and me. Your father Yi Tianxing has imparted to me the Divine Revelation. When used together with the Holy Amalgamate Skill, the Holy Amalgamate Skill just narrowly won over the Infinitude Recite. The Old Sword Saint acknowledged defeat only because he had thought that would help the Holy Hex Sect regain its standing in the fraternity. He told me if he did not secretly watch the duel between Yi Tianxing and my father, Ji Yunzhong that day, his martial progress would still be hindered. So he is just returning a favor to my father."

Yi Ping was startled, "I didn't...Lingfeng didn't tell me..."

Ji Wuzheng said, "No one else knows the exact details of our secret duel, not even Lingfeng. I survive my internal injuries because I am younger. But the Old Sword Saint eventually crumbles to his injuries. It is not a secret in the fraternity that I have sent an invitation to challenge the Old Sword Saint. When the Old Sword Saint dies, everyone just assumed that the duel we had is not an honorable one."

Gongsun Jing interrupted, "Why didn't you explain? The Honor Manor, my father Gongsun Bai has assumed that your next intention is to challenge his position in the fraternity..."

Ji Wuzheng said, "No one from the orthodox clans will give me a fair hearing. Moreover, it is not something I really cares about. What the orthodox clans likes to think are actually their own business, don't you think so too? Furthermore, your father Gongsun Bai has the lofty ambition to dominate the entire fraternity. This is just an excuse for him to bring the other fraternities forcefully under his control. You should know this more clearly than me."

Gongsun Jing muttered, "That is true…my father's ambitions killed him…"

Yi Ping and Gongsun Jing exchanged looks. Yi Ping had gone to the Honor Manor to seek vendetta for his parents but the irony happened. The son of his enemy would actually become his sworn brother and they now had a common enemy; Gu Tianle and the Honor Manor.

Ji Wuzheng said, "If heroes do not mind, why don't you join the Holy Hex Sect? I won't give you a lowly position. How about becoming the new Guardians of the Holy Chapter? The Guardian position is similar to a deputy clan leader in the Holy Hex Sect."

Qiu Wufeng was startled, "Join the unorthodox clan? That's impossible…"

Ji Wuzheng said, "Orthodox or unorthodox, it is just the action that we do. If you have the righteousness in your heart, why are you fearful of being in an unorthodox clan?"

Qiu Wufeng said, "If we survive this, I hope to restore my clan honor and position in the fraternity. I can't afford to stay in the Holy Hex Sect."

Gongsun Jing nodded, "So am I…"

Yi Ping said, "I am afraid that I may not live that long and moreover, there are many things waiting for me to do…"

All of a sudden, Nangong Le said drunkenly. "I am willing! I have nothing now! If it means I can be close to Suyue, I am willing!"

Ji Wuzheng was startled as he thought, "This rascal is interested in my daughter Suyue? Bringing him into the Holy Hex Sect is like bring a wolf in sheep clothing into the sect. But I have already made known my intentions and can't retract it. Hmmm…if I cannot retract my words, I can force him to quit by making things difficult for him once he is my clan protégé…"

So he smiled at Nangong Le, "Welcome, welcome. You are now the Guardian of the Holy Chapter. How about the Guardian of the Third Holy chapter?"

Nangong Le laughed, "That's good. What are my monthly wages and benefits?"

Ji Wuzheng was startled. In the fraternity, the pugilists did not talk about wages and benefits so bashfully. Rather they would talk about loyalty and clan rules first. Moreover, once he had decided to join, Nangong Le had to respect him as the sect master. He found himself disliking this Nangong Le and decided to make things really difficult for him. It was also to protect his daughter Suyue from him.

But before he could answer Nangong Le, Nangong Le had fallen to the floor in his drunken state.

Gongsun Jing and Qiu Wufeng were secretly thinking, "Brother Nangong is going to be dead very soon if he joins the Holy Hex Sect…"

If Nangong Le were not the self-proclaim sworn brother of Yi Ping; Gongsun Jing and Qiu Wufeng would never become his sworn brothers. It was because Nangong Le had virtually no real friends except for Priest Ling Kongquan and Priest Liu Qingcheng as his insolence and lack of common etiquette in the fraternity basically offended everyone. That explained the hostile stares that he had received from Gongsun Jing and Qiu Wufeng at the Honor Manor when he had arrived late and making a huge scene.

Yi Ping muttered in his half-drunken state and did not noticed that Nangong Le had already been completely knock off, "Congrats to Brother Nangong as the new Guardian of the Holy Chapter…"

Ji Wuzheng said, "Since young heroes do not want to join the Holy Hex Sect, why don't we become sworn brothers instead? If you don't mind having an unorthodox person as a brother…"

Yi Ping said immediately, "I am willing!"

Gongsun Jing said, "If you don't mind a down and trodden person as a brother, I am willing too."

Qiu Wufeng hesitated for a while. It was because the concept of orthodox and unorthodox was too deeply ingrained in him. But when he thought of Sufeng, he immediately said. "I am willing too! So what if I am no longer from the orthodox? I am no longer a member of the orthodox ever since I am forced to be on the run!"

Ji Wuzheng smiled, "Very good. From now on, I am your eldest brother. If you need any help or request, please feel freely to ask from me!"

All of a sudden, Qiu Wufeng got up and was about to walk off when Gongsun Jing caught hold of him, "Brother Wufeng, where are you going?"

Qiu Wufeng smiled bitterly, "I am going to tell Sufeng that I am no longer an exponent of the orthodox martial fraternity. I am going to tell her…she be delighted. She likes me…I can tell…Brothers, talk to you later…"

He broke free of Gongsun Jing and left hastily even as Ji Wuzheng was looking at him with a stunned look.

Ji Wuzheng had not yet recovered from the shock of hearing that Qiu Wufeng was actually interested in his daughter Sufeng when Gongsun Jing hastily got up as he muttered, "That's right. I got to tell Suxin as well…"

Ji Wuzheng was in a complete shock as he muttered incoherently, "Did I do the right thing by becoming their eldest brother? Now I got to help them freely in whatever they have requested. Moreover now it is so late at night and they are so drunk. Oh no!"

All of a sudden, Yi Ping and Ji Wuzheng had heard startled cries. Even though the startled cries were almost inaudible, they were able to pick it up due to their superior hearing.

Yi Ping could even recognize the startle cries as coming from Yu'Er and Mei'Er. Their voices had completely died down almost immediately, leading Yi Ping to fear that the worst had happened to them. The twin sisters were not weak; for anyone to silence them almost immediately indicated that the assailant was a dangerous exponent.

He quickly pulled himself out of the drunken state with the Absolute Spirits as he said gravely, "Yu'Er and Mei'Er are in danger!"

And he had quickly turned around and sped towards their startled cries.

Ji Wuzheng was startled to see Yi Ping displaying his astounding swiftness movement as he caught up with him, "You don't have to worry. The only way up to this place is a narrow ridge and it is guarded by a dozen elite protégés of the sect at all times. Unless the intruder can fly, there is no way he can reach the Holy Chapter. It must be a rat that has startled them."

Yi Ping nodded solemnly but there was no mistaking the anxious looks on his face.

They quickly arrived at the scene only to find an old man trying to silence Yu'Er and Mei'Er as they gasped for breathe!

Yi Ping immediately shouted, "Who are you!"

Ji Wuzheng was startled. How did a stranger get into the premises of the Holy Chapter that was surrounded by sheer mountain walls from all sides?

The old man quickly turned around and whispered, "Not so loud. I am busy."

Yi Ping had immediately attacked the old man, displaying the Divine Horizon Hands! "You lecherous old man! How dare you lay your hands on Yu'Er and Mei'Er!"

The old man hummed coldly, "Young man, you don't know who you fighting…"

He was suddenly startled when Yi Ping unleashed flurrying blows of blows onto him as he shouted, "Good martial strokes! Good martial power! Now this is something I have been expecting. Are you Ji Wuzheng then? No wait, this is the Divine Horizon Hands…"

All of a sudden, the old man had raised his palm and had pushed Yi Ping back with a thunderous blow that exploded loudly!

Yi Ping was stunned at the martial power of this old man even as he quickly recovered his balance!!!

Yu'Er and Mei'Er quickly recovered as they cried tearfully into Yi Ping's embrace.

Yi Ping held them tightly, "Yu'Er, Mei'Er. Don't worry I am here. Don't be afraid. Did he take advantage of you? What happens?"

Yu'Er sniffed, "Master, you are here! You never forget your Yu'Er?"

Yi Ping was startled, "Of course I won't…"

Mei'Er asked tearfully, "You won't forget Mei'Er too?"

Yi Ping smiled bitterly, "Of course I won't…what is going on here?"

Mei'Er looked relieved as she pointed at the old man, "This crazy old man just appears out of the blue, assaulted us and rumbling senseless stuff! He keeps asking where is Xian'Er. We don't know what he is talking about!"

The old man was clearly offended as he clapped his potty belly, "What crazy old man? Young lass, mind your manners. Do you know who I am? I am asking you some questions but not only have you refuse to answer me, you have even tried to attack me. I am only trying to get you to quiet down! Where did you get your swords? Even if these two swords turn to ashes, I can tell that it belongs to Xian'Er!"

Yu'Er interrupted, "We don't know who your Xian'Er is. Fancy an old man like you is still lusting over a maiden. That is a little too outrageous, don't you think so? You dirty filthy old man!"

The old man roared with anger, "You…you! Wait till I get my hands on you! If you don't tell me where you get those swords, don't blame me for being a lot dirtier than you think!"

Yi Ping stepped forward with an angry look as he displayed his opening stance of the Divine Horizon Hand, the Heavens Horizon Stance!

The old man said to Yi Ping, "I recognized the Divine Horizon Hand. So you are that Yi Ping. To think that the Divine Horizon Clan has such a deplorable descendant like you. You have really disgraced the good name of the Divine Horizon Clan!"

Yu'Er immediately said, "Master, be careful. There is a force within a force in his martial force. All in all, there are three continuous forces with each wave growing more powerful than the previous one. That is how he had overpowered us and caught us unaware. I have never seen such a martial force technique before."

Mei'Er nodded as she said, "Be careful Master."

Ji Wuzheng was startled when he had heard Yu'Er describing the details of this old man martial display. He quickly warned Yi Ping, "Be careful! He is one of the superb super exponents of the Martial Fraternity. He's the Martial Sage from the Ironclad Clan, one of the Three Sages. He is also known as the Invincible Ironfist!"

The Martial Sage hummed coldly, "Now you are afraid?"

Ji Wuzheng said angrily to the old man, "I am Ji Wuzheng. How dare did you sneak into the Holy Chapter! Is that how the orthodox exponents go around with their dirty business?"

The Martial Sage hummed coldly, "So you are Ji Wuzheng? I have been looking everywhere for you. So you are the one that have killed Brother Zuo? Good, good. Then we can settle our score here tonight! You want to fight me at the same time or one by one? You can even call all the Guardians of the Holy Chapter and I won't even be afraid. If you don't tell me where is Xian'Er, then I will just have to turn the entire place upside down!"

Ji Wuzheng took out the card that had issued by the Honor Manor and threw it to him, "The Honor Manor has just issued me a challenge that is due to be held in three days and both sides have agreed to observe a truce for the next three days. And now you are attacking the Holy Hex Sect. Is this what the Honor Manor meant by a truce?"

The Martial Sage was startled, "There is a truce? I really did not know."

He really did not know for he had spent many days scaling the sheer cliffs of the Holy Amalgamate Mountains. That was why he could sneak into the Holy Chapter so silently. No one had expected an intruder to come from the back mountains!

He quickly opened the invitation card to read the contents as he muttered, "So it is true…"

By his startled expressions, Ji Wuzheng guessed that the Martial Sage was not aware of it. So he said, "Respected old senior, you can leave now. If you want to take vendetta on me, then you have to wait for three more days! Even if you are a legend of the martial fraternity, you still have to adhere to the rules of the martial fraternity!"

The Martial Sage said, "Not so easy. I have to take back these two maidens away first."

Yu'Er immediately said, "You…can you consider yourself to be a legend of the martial fraternity and a hero? Why don't you fight someone that is in the same seniority as you? If my protégé mistress is here, she will surely kick your ass!"

The Martial Sage laughed aloud, "Young lass, even if you ask your protégé mistress to come, even your protégé mistress's protégés mistress and even your protégé mistress's grand protégé mistress to come, they are all not my match!"

Mei'Er interrupted coldly, "What's an insolent old man!"

Yi Ping said, "Then what about me then? I happen to be their protégé master. Let me teach you a lesson!"

The Martial Sage laughed, "You! Young man! You are so young and are their protégé master? What's a joke! From their lingering and affectionate eyes that are on you, they are more like your little sweethearts!"

Yu'Er and Mei'Er immediately flushed.

The Martial Sage had suddenly attacked Yi Ping with a powerful forward blow, "Let me test your martial foundation first!"

Yi Ping immediately reacted and retaliated with the Asper Horizon Hand!

There were a thunderous blow and the impact created such a bursting windforce that it immediately sent Ji Wuzheng, Yu'Er and Mei'Er scurrying backward!

Just as Yi Ping had caught the Martial Sage's blow, all of a sudden, there was a second stronger martial force pushing through his Asper Horizon Hand!

Yi Ping quickly muster all his martial power and managed to suppress this second martial force but no sooner had he stopped the second martial force, a third martial force made its way through his palm, knocking him backward!

Yi Ping slide backward before he was took several forced steps to steady his balance!

Yu'Er and Mei'Er were panicky as they cried out, "Master, are you alright? Are you hurt? Where are you hurting?"

Yi Ping coughed, "I'm alright…don't worry…"

The Martial Sage was astonished too. He did not expect Yi Ping to have such strong rebounding martial force as they clashed. This did not reached the result that he was hoping for so he said, "Young man, let's fight again!"

Ji Wuzheng had quickly stepped in front of the Martial Sage, "Old Senior. Everything ought to have a limit. You are in my premises now. Surely you know the rules of the martial fraternity? You have already vented your frustration. Surely that is enough?"

All of a sudden, Mei'Er had unsheathed her long precious sword. The cold piercing sword energy of her sword could be felt by everyone as she displayed the Swallow Slash on the Martial Sage!

The Martial Sage quickly turned his palm into a fist as he caught the tip of her long sword between the fingers of his fist! He yawned, "Young lass, you are tens of years too early to even challenge me yet. I will look for you in three days' time after the stupid truce."

Mei'Er was flabbergasted, "You dirty old man!"

Yi Ping had once again displayed the Divine Horizon Hands as he charged at the Martial Sage even as Ji Wuzheng shouted to him, "Brother, that's enough for tonight!"

The Martial Sage hummed coldly, "Persistent young man!"

All of a sudden, he raised both his fists together to receive the Divine Horizon Hands. When they were near, the Martial Sage suddenly displayed dozens of fists as he rained upon Yi Ping!

Yi Ping was in utter disbelief as the martial power of the Martial Sage scattered the martial power of his Divine Horizon Hands and knocked him flat onto the ground with a smashing thunderous impact!

Yu'Er and Mei'Er were besides Yi Ping immediately as they cried and comforted him.

Yi Ping was struggling weakly on the ground and his entire body was trembling! He simply could not believe that his Divine Horizon Hands could fall apart in an instant as he stared blankly in bewilderment!"

The Martial Sage said coldly, "This is just a small lesson for you before I go. If it isn't for an old friend of mine, I would have hit you even harder."

And he was gone in an instant!

Ji Wuzheng was stunned and was shivering. The martial display of the Martial Sage was too profound and difficult to deal with as he muttered, "The Invincible Ironfist…the Invincible Ironfist…"

Yu'Er comforted Yi Ping, "Master, are you…alright?"

Yi Ping was trembling and muttering, "Yu'Er, don't worry about me. I am really alright. I just surprised that he seems to know the weakness of my Divine Horizon Hands so well…"

As Mei'Er and Yu'Er were helping Yi Ping to stand, Mei'Er suddenly said. "Alas! I suddenly remember something!"

Yu'Er asked, "What is it?"

Mei'Er whispered, "Xian'Er? Isn't that also our protégé mistress namesake?"

Yu'Er smiled, "Our protégé mistress wouldn't know such a dirty old man and won't be bothered to even know him. It is just a coincident."

All of a sudden, there was a startled cry in the darkness. And it seemed to be from the Martial Sage!

Yi Ping, Yu'Er, Mei'Er and Ji Wuzheng were alarmed as they quickly dashed towards the direction of his cry.

As they turned to a smaller courtyard, they saw Lie Qing, Youxue, Lingfeng and Ding Yun. They were all looking awkwardly at Yi Ping, Ji Wuzheng, Yu'Er and Mei'Er!

Yi Ping was startled to see them together.

Even more startling, the Martial Sage was now lying on the ground in a bloody condition!

Ji Wuzheng asked in alarm, "What's happen? Do you know that we have a truce with the Orthodox Clans at this moment and I have just allowed him to go back to his side?!"

Lie Qing was stroking her long hair as she looked sheepish, "He is not dead yet. We have already restraint ourselves."

She added, "This dirty old man has intentional knocked into us without apologizing. After I have tried to ask for an apology from him, he keeps saying he is the legend of the martial fraternity and there is no need for him to apologize to anyone. And he even tries to grab me. Out of self-defense, I hit too hard and he is now lying like this."

Youxue said almost inaudibly, "I only hit him just a few times…"

Yi Ping said weakly, "Not many people can survive a direct hit from your Penetrating Hands…"

Ding Yun smiled weakly, "I…only hit him once with my scabbard…"

Yi Ping muttered, "Your martial power imbued scabbard can kill almost anyone…"

Lingfeng said, "I only hit him once with the Asper Horizon Hand…and once with the Great Dissolution Skill…his martial power is so terrifying. I didn't know that Sister Lie Qing has already subdued him…"

Yi Ping muttered, "Two of the most powerful divine skills in the martial fraternity, used at the same time and doing a direct hit…"

Ji Wuzheng said, "Do you know who he is?"

All of them shook their heads.

Ji Wuzheng smiled bitterly, "He is the Martial Sage, one of the Three Sages and also the grand protégé master of the Ironclad Clan. He didn't lie to you. He is indeed the legend of the martial fraternity. Now can anyone tell me, what I am supposed to do now?"

Chapter 54: Reciprocate of the Hearts

Six extraordinary and beautiful breathtaking maidens were standing in the silent night. Any man who caught sight of them would surely be captivated by them and thought they were heavenly maidens that had just descended upon the mortal realm.

Ji Wuzheng was only a mortal man and he was not an exception.

Since that day when his sister Lingfeng had brought these maidens into the Inner Holy Chapter, he had been astonished that in the entire fraternity, there were other such beauties that could rival Lingfeng in her peerless beauty.

What really startled him were not their great beauties but the level of their martial proficiencies which immediately ranked them among the top echelon exponents in the martial fraternity.

And just how good were their martial proficiencies?

He was now staring in complete astonishment at the Martial Sage who was rumbling incoherently on the ground, "Dirty…rematch…don't count…Xian'Er…why did you hit me…"

Ji Wuzheng was astonished at the seemingly iron strength of the Martial Sage as he thought, "This is his Iron Vest Aegis Skill? He can take so much punishment…"

He was not the only person that was stunned at the sight of the Martial Sage lying on the ground.

Yi Ping was also stunned at the sight.

It was because he had just been bashed by the Martial Sage and the martial strength of the Martial Sage still filled him with awe, "It is Qing'Er that knocks him down?"

He had suddenly realized that he knew very little about her and her martial origin. To him, Qing'Er was the vulnerable maiden that always needed his protection. The few times that she had used her Invincible Divine Force were just a demonstration of her martial force and not an indication of her actual fighting techniques. The only time that he had actually seen her in a real action was her fight with Lele. But that was not an indication of her true skills for he could see that she was just trying to slap Lele and there was no killing intent.

Yi Ping was beginning to lament his fate tomorrow.

As the Martial Sage lay on the ground, he was dreamily calling out for Xian'Er once more and he began to recall the events in the last few days…

The Martial Sage had vented some of his frustrations and was secretly cursing the truce for happening at the wrong timing. He had spent days climbing the dangerous sheer mountain cliffs of the Holy Amalgamate Mountains, replying on his iron will and physical endurance so that he could surprise and avenge the death of the Old Sword Saint on Ji Wuzheng directly. He simply could not understand why Xiao Shuai was delaying an all-out attack on the Holy Hex Sect even though they had been camping for more than two weeks at the foot of the mountains.

Many of the martial clans were not pleased with the lack of action and decided to assault the Holy Amalgamate Mountains on their own; none succeed and with a great appalling loss of lives.

Even when the Three Sages had succeeded in killing four of the Holy Chapter Guardians of the Holy Hex Sect, the Honor Manor and the Virtuous Palace continued to take no action.

He had confronted Xiao Shuai and Han Shaodong, who was actually Gu Tianle's protégé master and he was also the new grandmaster of the Honor Manor.

Han Shaodong said, "Be patient. The big fish has not yet arrived."

"What big fish, small fish? Ji Wuzheng is the one that has killed our brother. We only need to kill him and our brother's death can be avenged!" He had said.

They were referring to the Holy Maiden and of course, they did not reveal their real plans to the Martial Sage.

Xiao Shuai was reluctant to tell him more so he merely said, "We are waiting for all the fraternity Notorious Four to show up first. They would surely come to the aid of the Holy Hex Sect. This expedition is not only to address martial justice for the Old Sword Saint and to foil the ambitions of the Holy Hex Sect; it is also to lure the Notorious Four from hiding."

The Martial Sage was not as tolerant as them and decided to take the course of action into his own hands as he was hopping mad, "Brother Xiao Shuai and Brother Han Shaodong seem to have become another person…"

He could still remember fifty years ago, there was a rumor of a lost martial treasure trove in an underground city in the great desolate desert. Accordingly, it was the martial treasure of the legendary Sage King. At that time, hundreds of martial exponents were also traveling to the desert in search of this underground city; no one wants to be the last. Against the knowledge of his protégé master and elders, he had secretly arrived at the desert even though they had warned him that it was highly possible that it was a conspiracy to cause infighting among the martial exponents. But the prospects of meeting exponents from different fraternities and different martial clans excited him more than any dangers.

It was then at that time, he met the changing point of his life!

He had seen a maiden like no other and she was Xian'Er!

She was at the inn, stunning everyone with her extraordinary beauty. From the exquisite scabbards and the exquisite adorn on the sword hilts, it was obvious that she had with her two precious long swords. Other than that, there were no other clues to her identity.

Besides him, dozens of daring exponents had tried to make advances to her without success. No matter how repute the exponent was, orthodox or unorthodox; none of them succeed in getting her name or her martial origin.

Pretty soon, it became quite hilarious as he watched scores of exponents getting beaten up by her at different intervals, one group after another!

If the exponents could not overcome her using hard methods, they would try all kinds of underhand soft methods like offering her spiked drinks, bribing the innkeepers, pretending to be waiters to ambush her, faking their life stories and hoping to get her sympathies.

None of the methods worked!

A group of bulky exponents had just entered tavern and it was obviously they were looking for her for they were staring at her lustfully. The leader of their group said, "So this is the young beauty that injured our brothers? If you will company us for a week then we can forgive you for the slight…"

Barely had he had spoken, the young beautiful maiden had thrown several chopsticks that were in a bamboo container with a startling speed!

Immediately all the bulky men were lying and crawling on the floor, screaming in agonies as the chopsticks pierced into their bodies like piercing daggers!

As the young beautiful maiden raised more chopsticks in her fingers, those big bulky men were immediately filled with terror and they left as fast as they had come, hastily stumbling out of the tavern!

At that time, another stranger was sharing the table with him. He was the Future Sword Saint which later became the Sword Saint.

The Future Sword Saint said to him with a conceit look, "Look, let's have a bet with you. With just two moves, I can get her name."

The young Martial Sage was startled, "What is the bet and how are you planning to do it? So many have already failed."

The Future Sword Saint said, "I bet my only sword with you. You can surely tell my sword is no ordinary sword as well. If you lose, you must pay my tab and lodgings. As how I am going to do it, you will soon know."

The young Martial Sage asked, "Just two moves?"

The Future Sword Saint laughed, "No more, no less!"

The young Martial Sage thought, "This young stranger sure like to boast. Very well, let me bet with him then. At most I only lose my coins but at least I may get to know her name."

So he laughed aloud, "That will do it then!"

The Future Sword Saint smiled mysteriously as he tapped his head with his fingers, "Watch me then. Sometimes we got to use our intellect. I am going to use a clever ruse to trick her."

The Future Sword Saint walked unhurried to the beautiful young maiden. He had purposely slowed down his steps and walked heavily so that everyone's attention would fall upon him.

He seemed to be enjoying the moment immensely!

There were a low rumblings as the crowd whispered, "There's another challenger. Wonder if he will succeed…"

The Future Sword Saint said, "Maiden, may I know your name?"

The beautiful young maiden continue to sit quietly and refusing to answer him.

The Future Sword Saint laughed, "Maiden, watch out!"

All of a sudden, the Future Sword Saint swung his scabbard at her. But because he had already warned her, she dodged his swinging scabbard effortlessly.

Instead of attacking her with a follow up attack, the Future Sword Saint had seized the two swords that had belonged to her which were carelessly place on the table with his other hand!

The Future Sword Saint laughed, "Maiden, if you want to get back your swords, you must at least tell me your maiden name…"

But before he could finish, the beautiful young maiden had seized back her swords from his hands and had kicked him, causing him to lose his footing!

And before he could even recover from his footing, the beautiful young maiden had gave him another vicious kick and sent him flying across the floor!

The onlookers immediately moaned and laughed, "Another one…"

The Future Sword Saint struggled weakly to his seat and said to the young Martial Sage, "If you are a hero, then it is your turn."

The young Martial Sage smiled at the Future Sword Saint, "Give me your sword first."

That was how the Martial Sage had met Xian'Er and the Old Sword Saint Zuo.

A fine looking young man who was seating next to them had heard their wager. He laughed aloud, "If I can get that young beauty to drink with me, the two of you will pay for all my tabs here?"

The Future Sword Saint laughed coldly, "You? Don't make me laugh! If you can, we will surely pay for your tab!"

The young Martial Sage laughed, "If you can, we will pay for all your tabs. But I think it is better to admire her from afar. She is a flower with real painful thorns."

The fine looking young man smiled, "Deal! If I can get her to drink with me, then the two of you will pay for my entire tab in this tavern!"

As he got up with a flask of wine and a cup in his hands, he smiled at the Future Sword Saint and the young Martial Sage.

He went to the beautiful young maiden as he toasted her, "Maiden, will you honor me by allowing me to toast you with a drink?"

The beautiful young maiden smiled gently and lifted her cup to return his toast.

The Future Sword Saint and the young Martial Sage was instantly stunned…

The young Martial Sage was secretly startled, "She likes man with refine looks?"

The fine looking young man then walked back with a broad grin to the Future Sword Saint and the young Martial Sage, "My tabs are on you guys!"

The young Martial Sage stammered, "How…how did you do that? You know magic?"

The Future Sword Saint was astonished, "How the hell did you manage to get her to return a toast to you? You know her?"

The fine looking young man smiled and calmly explained, "She is aware that I have been paying for her tabs and lodgings for several days now. Now she is merely returning me a small appreciation by returning a toast with me. You guys have lost and my tabs are all yours now."

The young Martial Sage was startled, "I am paying for her tab and yours now?!"

The Future Sword Saint was even more startled, "Darn! Why didn't I think of that?!"

The fine looking young man was Han Shaodong!

Not long after, there was news that the underground desert city in the desert had been found. All the exponents in the small desert town began to trek into the great desert!

However, the great desert and the underground desert city proved to be too perilous. Many perished in the trek across the great desert. Those who had survived found the traps of the underground desert city to be even perilous than the great desert itself!

Almost all the surviving exponents that survived the trek across the great desert perished in the underground desert city. Among the fallen, were scores of renowned exponents and quite a few were even the super exponents of the fraternity!

Many had either fallen to the deadly traps of the underground desert city or fallen to infighting between the martial exponents hoping to be the first one to reach the lowest level for the martial treasure trove.

Eventually for those that persisted in the underground city, there were just twelve survivors. They either have plenty of luck, extraordinary intelligence or exceptional skill in order to survive to the lowest level of the underground desert city palace. In short, these twelve were also the most talented of their generation.

Among the twelve, there was the young beautiful maiden and her name was Xian'Er!

The Martial Sage had never forgotten that she had accidentally let it slipped out that her name was Yixian!

The twelve survivors decided to band together to form a secret group and to do something really outrageous together while keeping their identities a secret.

The new group of course had to have a leader to lead them.

Naturally, the young Martial Sage had dominated Xian'Er to be the group leader. However, the group leadership was eventually led by Xiao Shuai who had the most votes and this new group was later known as the Celestial Palace Group.

Under Xiao Shuai's leadership, the secret Celestial Palace Group infiltrated the various martial clans of the fraternity and secretly read their secret manuals when they got their hands on it. After that, they would put the secret manuals back after copying it.

What was astonishing was not how startling the martial skills of the major orthodox clans were but the number of secret skills and secrets that the smaller martial clans had possessed. Due to generations of decline, most of the epitome skills could not be practiced.

They quickly unravel many secrets and secret histories of the various martial clans, even from their own clans!

The young Martial Sage and many of the group were left cursing after they had realized that their protégé masters and elders had hidden many intricate strokes and techniques from them even though it was actually a fairly common practice to do so in the martial fraternity; the master would always held back a few hidden techniques to protect themselves.

But of course, they were not always successful. Most of the real forbidden secrets of the various clans like heart intricacy formulas were still off limits to them. Without the intricate heart formulas to understand the intricate strokes, the true quintessence and the embodiment of the martial skill could not be unraveled!

They were all simply testing their limits and stealth skills.

Despite several constraints, in a short time they had collected dozens of martial skills and used the knowledge to improvise their own martial skills and to fix several shortcomings.

Everyone except Xian'Er was overcome by the intrigues and madness of stealing and peeking at the secret manuals of the other martial clans.

But when Xian'Er had disappeared one day, the young Martial Sage was almost driven to desperation as he searched the entire fraternity for her but to no avail. It was because the fraternity was so large and he really had no idea which martial clan she had come from!

With Xian'Er missing and no longer in the secret Celestial Group, the thrill of being part of the secret group was gone and many eventually left quietly, causing the secret Celestial Group to be disbanded.

Imagine his jovial happiness when he caught sight of Yu'Er and Mei'Er swords! He had recognized these swords as belonging to Xian'Er! He did not care how old Xian'Er was now. In his heart, he had to know her whereabouts for he had been searching for her for as long as he could remember!

But before he could get any information from them, he was interrupted rudely by Ji Wuzheng and Yi Ping.

But before he could settle his feud with Ji Wuzheng, he was told that there was a short armistice between the Honor Manor and the Holy Hex Sect, which left him fuming mad.

As one of the Three Sages and as an exponent of the righteous orthodox martial clan, he was bounded by honor to follow the truce.

So when an angry Yi Ping attacked him, he decided to teach him a hard lesson or two. Given Yi Ping's notorious reputation, he would have gladly killed him on the spot. Again, it was his honor that prevented him from dealing justice on the spot.

The 'hard' lesson was not what he had expected!

He was expecting Yi Ping to be completely overwhelmed by his martial technique, the Hundred Invincible Iron Fists.

His old heart skipped a beat when Yi Ping changed his attacking stance to a defensive one as he took all his Hundred Invincible Iron Fists. Even though it appeared that he had plummeted Yi Ping onto the ground with a thunderous crashing impact, Yi Ping had in fact neutralized most of his powerful Hundred Invincible Iron Fists with his Divine Horizon Hands.

Other than temporary draining Yi Ping of his physical strength and causing him some discomfort, there seemed to be no other external injuries!

"This young man…how is it possible?" He was secretly startled!

If word got out that he could not even handle a young man with his famous Hundred Invincible Iron Fists, he would surely be the laughing stock of the martial fraternity!

So just before he had gone on his way, he had put on some face saving measures as he said coldly. "This is just a small lesson for you before I go. If it isn't for an old friend of mine, I would have hit you even harder."

As he left and made several winding turns in the maze-like Inner Holy Chapter premises, he had suddenly dumped into four extraordinary beautiful maidens!

He was astonished by their extraordinary beauties!

He immediately grabbed them as he stammered excitedly, "Xian'Er, is that you? No you're not. You have her features and you have her eyes…"

Lie Qing was startled as the Martial Sage grabbed her waist, "Outrageous, dirty old man! Take your hands off me and apologize or else I will be nasty! What do you think you are doing?! Who are you?"

She tried to push him away but this old man was too simply overwhelming strong.

He began to grab Lingfeng, Youxue and Ding Yun at the same time!

Lie Qing immediately asked Lingfeng, "Sister Lingfeng, who is he?"

Lingfeng panicky exclaimed, "I don't know! He is an intruder!"

The Martial Sage quickly said, "I am a good guy…"

But before he could finish explaining his intentions, the four maidens had displayed some of their most intricate techniques and struck him at the same time!

Lie Qing gave a soft sigh, "I told you we have already restrained ourselves. It is just a small punishment for laying his hand on us. This dirty old man is really infuriating."

Youxue said coldly, "That's right!"

Ji Wuzheng was secretly startled, "What has actually happened? Did they join hands to knock the Martial Sage on the ground? Or is it just this Maiden Lie Qing?"

He had suspected that it was Maiden Lie Qing because in recent years, Gongsun Bai seemed to have found a deadly divine martial skill called the Invincible Divine Force and with that, he had begun to dominate over the fraternity, causing the influential power of the Honor Manor to increase from day to day!

And the Celestial Liege had also made scant mention of it.

Ji Wuzheng shook his head as he lifted the rumbling Martial Sage with his arms as he walked away.

Yi Ping asked panicky, "Big Brother, you are leaving me alone?"

Ji Wuzheng turned around and said, "Junior Brother, I got to go first and tend to the injuries of the Martial Sage."

And he was gone in a hurry, leaving Yi Ping alone with the six maidens.

Lingfeng asked, "Big Brother? Junior Brother? When did my brother and you become dear brothers?"

Yi Ping smiled bitterly as he scratched his nose.

The six maidens were all looking at Yi Ping with great shyness and their eyes were filled with a hundred affections for him.

Yi Ping was startled when Lie Qing blinked her mesmerizing eyes at him.

He was even more startled when she started walking towards him, causing him to take a step or two back until he dumped into Yu'Er and Mei'Er.

He thought, "She is going to hit me?"

Lie Qing immediately flew into him as she said with utmost affections, "Yi Ping, do you still remember we have a pledge to be with each other till the oceans vanish and the rocks crumble on the night that you have left the Great Tranquil Mountains?"

Lingfeng was also besides him, looking alluring at him. "You have said that we will always be together that night too…"

Youxue said shyly, "I promise you. I will always be there when your heart is filled with sorrow and despair…"

Ding Yun shyly enquired, "Ping'Er, How are your injuries? I hope you are recovering good…"

Yi Ping was totally bewildered as he asked secretly, "What is going on? Aren't they going to hit me like that Martial Sage to a pulp?"

That night when Lingfeng walked out of Yi Ping's resting room in anger, she was joined immediately by Lie Qing, Yu'Er, Mei'Er and Ding Yun.

Ding Yun asked quietly, "Sister Qing'Er, you are really going to duel Ping'Er tomorrow?"

Lie Qing said in a teary emotion, "If I don't kill him, it will be hard to vent my anger!"

Even though that was what she had said but that was just in a moment of anger. Unknown to the other maidens, Lie Qing was not really seriously upset with Yi Ping but had pretended to be otherwise. She just did not want to be isolated by these sisters and got caught in an awkward situation. One of the reasons why she got the fraternity name of the Heavenly Temptress was that she was also an excellent actress as well. But even for the Heavenly

Temptress, her feelings towards Yi Ping were more real than anything else; she had struggled with her true feelings for many months until she realized that would only bring herself immense suffering and she had never met a more righteous and selfless person like Yi Ping in her entire life.

Until now, when she had remembered how Yi Ping had saved her life and offered her the Divine Dragon Pill, she would still secretly smile with silent appreciation.

Yu'Er pleaded, "Don't kill Master. Just beat him into a pulp will do…"

Mei'Er hummed, "Turn him black, green, blue, red and purple! Don't you agree, Sister Lingfeng?"

Lingfeng had calmed down considerably and she appeared alarmed.

Ding Yun asked, "What's wrong, Sister Lingfeng?"

Lingfeng said almost inaudibly, "Maybe…maybe we have all wronged Yi Ping."

The rest of the maidens were immediately startled!

Mei'Er quickly asked, "What do you mean?"

Lingfeng sighed softly, "I just remembered that the last time Youxue and I were treating Yi Ping's injuries, there was an extremely cold and negative intricate energy in his body. Even though it was barely noticeable, Youxue and I had noticed it immediately."

Ding Yun was startled, "No wonder when I had checked Yi Ping's pulses many times in the past, I could feel a cold and negative intricate energy. I didn't dare to say anything because I am unsure if my diagnosis is correct. But when he was in a feverish state, that cold and negative intricate was barely visible."

Lie Qing was startled, "So that means, the cold, negative intricate energy in his body and the positive, extreme intricate energy of the Celestial Force may have neutralized each other, creating a counterbalance…"

Lingfeng nodded.

Ding Yun gasped, "Then we may have made a terrible mistake and was so harsh towards Ping'Er and Youxue. What shall we do now?"

Yu'Er was miserable, "We can't go in now. We just come out. It will be so embarrassing…"

Lie Qing said melancholy, "Lingfeng, Lingfeng…why didn't you tell us earlier? You just destroy whatever good impressions Yi Ping has for me…"

Mei'Er sniffed, "Mine as well…what can we do now to salvage the situation?"

Lingfeng smiled bitterly, "Erm, after I have calmed down…I have thought of that…instead of stopping me from over-reacting, all of you seem to encourage me. Sister Yun, why didn't you stop us instead? You are the most rational in our group."

Ding Yun was startled, "Me? I am supposed to be the nanny? I can't be irrational sometimes?"

Yu'Er said, "What shall we do now? Let's go in and apologize?"

Lie Qing laughed softly, "We don't have to apologize. He probably won't put it into his heart. Let's just pretend nothing has happened…"

Lingfeng smiled weakly, "Somehow I got a bad feeling about this…"

Ding Yun nodded slightly, "I agree…"

Mei'Er immediately hugged Lie Qing, "Sister Qing'Er, Mei'Er goes along with your plan!"

Yu'Er inhaled a soft sigh, "Master, please forgive us…"

And just a while ago, they had dumped into Youxue who was wandering forlornly and confirming their suspicious…

The real reason why Youxue was unhappy was because Yi Ping did not share his problems with her or look for her for companionship. Instead, he was drinking despondently with his sworn brothers.

It was no wonder that Yi Ping was bewildered when the six maidens had suddenly displayed their affections for him!

Mei'Er laughed jovially, "Master, you have been drinking? There is a strong whiff of alcohol all over you."

Yi Ping smiled weakly, "I was unhappy."

Yu'Er smiled, "And now?"

Yi Ping sighed gently at the jovial, smiling and the hundred affections around him as they pulled him to and fro. "I really miss all of you. I thought…I thought that all of you are too upset with me to talk to me anymore. Erm…can anyone tells me what is going on here?"

Mei'Er quickly said, "Master, let's have a drink together first. Mei'Er wants to drink…"

Yi Ping got a jolt as he suddenly recalled something so he quickly asked, "Mei'Er and Yu'Er, why did you spike my wine back at the Tranquil Clan? At the Eternal Ice Palace, did you do the same thing too?"

Yu'Er and Mei'Er were so flustered now that their usual white complexion had deep flushes of pink!

Lingfeng quickly interrupted with an alluring soft laugh, "This is not the time to ask such questions. We should really talk about something more romantic…"

Yi Ping got another jolt as he quickly asked Lingfeng, "Lingfeng, why did you take my father's secret manuals? Quickly return it to me!"

Lingfeng stepped hard on his foot, "Did you just hear what I have just said? I say we should talk about something more romantic. Why are you so unromantic? You are such a miser. I am merely taking your secret manuals for a closer look. It is all your father's fault. He didn't want to teach me the Divine Horizon Hands and show me the advance intricate heart formula of the Aspire Invocations. And how do I know your father didn't lie to me about the intricate heart formula of the Asper Horizon Hand that he had tricked me to learn?"

Lingfeng was suddenly flushing, "And this is the only way to let you remember me and to come to the Holy Amalgamate Mountains for me…"

Yi Ping said, "Lingfeng, my father won't lie to you and moreover, I will surely look for you. Aren't I here now?"

Lingfeng said coolly, "Only Heavens know what you are thinking. You are just looking for me because you are looking for your secret manuals, humph!"

Yi Ping said, "No, that's not the truth. You…you…surely know what I am thinking…"

Lingfeng flushed, "No, if you don't say it aloud, I surely don't know what you are thinking. I am not the curly worm in your stomach. Why don't you say what's in your mind?"

Yi Ping asked, "Says what Lingfeng?"

Lingfeng said coldly, "You can start with your beautiful encounter with that beautiful maiden in the cave first."

Lie Qing interrupted with a smile, "Sister Lingfeng, don't bother with this pig head. Let's go and drink first, alright?"

Yi Ping suddenly asked Lie Qing, "Qing'Er, are we still going to fight tomorrow? Can you show me your extraordinary intricate martial strokes? I really am curious on the strokes that you have used on the Martial Sage…"

Youxue was gasping as she gently tugged Yi Ping's clothing. It was because she had seen the sudden change in Lie Qing and Lingfeng expressions!

Ding Yun quickly tapped Yi Ping with the hilt of her long sword, causing Yi Ping to turn around and ask. "Yun, what's wrong…"

Ding Yun hinted him by whispering, "Say no more…you're going to be seriously injured pretty soon."

Lie Qing and Lingfeng said almost at the same time, "You are really courting your own death."

Lie Qing said coolly, "You don't have to wait until tomorrow. I can show you now."

Chapter 55: The Rise of the Heretic Sect

The Inner Holy Chapter was the inner sanctuary of the Holy Sectarian Master and the Holy Maiden. Unless special permission was given, no one was allowed to enter the Inner Holy Chapter. But today, it was unusually crowded.

Ji Wuzheng was sitting in the middle of the hall. Besides him were two young maidens in white. They were his personal attendants as well as his swordsmaidens. Sitting beside him was Ji Lingfeng, the Holy Maiden and a beautiful refine lady.

Standing at the exits of the Hall were a dozen exponents in black.

Ji Wuzheng was unusually solemn today.

Yi Ping would later found out that the beautiful refine lady was actually Ji Wuzheng's wife, Dugu Zhen. She was not only the proud mother of three beautiful daughters Suxin, Suyue and Sufeng but she was also one of the First Guardian of the Holy Guardian.

When Yi Ping stepped into the Inner Holy Chapter, he simply could not believe his eyes as he caught sight of Lingfeng. She was radically very different from last night; her countenance was absolutely stunning in her Holy Maiden ceremony garb and light blue jewelries as he secretly thought, "Is she really Lingfeng? She looks like a totally different person and she seems so cold today."

But as soon as he had thought of that, Lingfeng had secretly blinked and smile at him before she reverted to her cold and forbidden self again. He sighed softly with relief, "She is still the same old self."

Ding Yun noticed it immediately and whispered to him, "You didn't realize Lingfeng is actually a peerless alluring beauty until today, didn't you? You keep staring at her."

Yi Ping was immediately flustered as he quickly stammered, "She is so different from last night. I am just a little startled…"

Even though Ding Yun appeared to be smiling, Yi Ping failed to notice the sorrows and melancholy in her eyes. He had also failed to notice that Dugu Zhen was looking at Ding Yun with unusual eyes.

Youxue quickly whispered to Yi Ping, "Sister Lingfeng looks so enthralling today. You look like you have never seen her appearance before?"

Yi Ping managed a weak smile, "Of course I have. But…I have never seen her this quiet…"

Lie Qing whispered with an enchanting smile, "Then does you like her to be quiet or friendly?"

Yi Ping dare not answer her. It was because even though Lie Qing's whispers were almost inaudible, he had suddenly noticed that Lingfeng's alluring eyes were looking and questioning him!

Gongsun Jing, Nangong Le, Qiu Wufeng and Qian Fan were also looking intently at Lingfeng…

But Gongsun Jing, Nangong Le and Qiu Wufeng were quickly distracted by Suxin, Suyue and Sufeng as they entered the hall.

Even though Lingfeng had been in their company for quite some time, she had rarely removed her thinly disguised veil in their presence.

Huo Fu was looking in stunned appraisal at Ding Yun, Youxue, Lie Qing, Youxue, Yu'Er and Mei'Er. It was because they were all smiling and whispering jovially with one another in intimate exchanges.

When Ji Wuzheng saw everyone that was supposed to be here had reached, he stood up and announced with a deep resounding voice. "I have two important matters to announce today." Immediately the hall fell into silent as everyone listened attentively.

Nangong Le was grinning as he thought, "Is he going to announce my appointment as the Third Guardian of the Holy Chapter and maybe even betrothed Suyue to me?"

Ji Wuzheng said almost immediately, "Firstly, due to the unfortunate demise of our four Holy Chapter Guardians, the Holy Hex Sect has suffered a huge blow to our strength and morale. Therefore there is an urgent need to appoint capable leaders as new Guardians to restore the holy sect's diminishing strength."

Nangong Le knew that Ji Wuzheng was about to appoint him as the new Holy Chapter Guardian and he was delighted. He immediately stole at glance at Suyue who was listening attentively.

Ji Wuzheng nodded at him before he said aloud, "Nangong Le, step forward to receive my commands!"

Nangong Le stepped forward proudly as he stole a glance at Suyue who was startled. "Looking at her expressions, she must be so surprised! It is my chance to impress her! I was worried that my sworn brothers would be the first one to be called out. Haha, it must be because I was the first one to agree to join the Holy Hex Sect so Ji Wuzheng has subtly given me the honor to be called out first!"

Immediately there were several low murmurings in the background!

Nangong Le grinned broadly as he thought, "They must be so startled and wish that they can be in the limelight first. That honor is now mine."

Ji Wuzheng said, "Nangong Le will be appointed the Third Guardian of the Holy Chapter. All holy protégés of the Third Chapter will be under his command and leadership."

Nangong Le was immensely pleased as he grinned. He could not help asking, "Who is the currently the First and Second Holy Chapter Guardians?"

Ji Suyue stepped forward, interrupting him. "My mother Dugu Zhen is the First Guardian of the Holy Chapter. There is currently no Second Guardian."

Nangong Le was startled when Suyue stepped in to talk to him. "Is she impressed by me now? There is no Second Guardian? Does it mean that I am currently the second most important Guardian? No wait. Brother Yi Ping had defeated the Celestial Liege. Surely he will be the one who will be appointed the Second Guardian. Still, as Third Guardian, my rank is way superior to Gongsun Jing, Qiu Wufeng and that Qian Fan."

He laughed jovially while asking Suyue, "Qian Fan is also a Guardian. Which number in rank is he?"

Suyue stole a glance at Qian Fan as she said coolly, "He is our Sixth Holy Chapter Guardian."

Nangong Le was secretly pleased as he thought, "I am in the upper Guardian Ranks…"

Suyue smiled gently at him, "Congratulations!"

Nangong Le muttered out, "Suyue, I so glad to have your appreciation…"

Suyue flushed as she quickly interrupted him with an icy tone, "The Third Guardian isn't more important than the First or Sixth. Each of the Guardians has a different role. The First Guardian is in charge of protecting the Holy Chapter while the Sixth Guardian is in charge of protecting the Holy Hex Sect. As for…"

Qian Fan chipped in, as he could no longer bear to see the insolent smiles on Nangong Le's face. "The Second to Forth Holy Chapter Guardians are in charge of repulsing the foes. Congratulations on your new appointment as the Third Holy Chapter Guardian. Our survival now depends on your brilliant leadership and tactics now to repulse the over hundred martial clans that are at the foot of the mountains!"

While Qian Fan was explaining to Nangong Le, Suyue secretly heaved a sigh of relief. "That idiot. He dares to make such a bold advance on me and even call my name in front of so many." Even though she was scolding him in her heart but she was secretly pleased…

Nangong Le was startled but he tried to put on a brave front, "Brother Yi Ping, Brother Qiu Wufeng, Brother Gongsun Jing and I will do our best as Guardians to protect the Holy Hex Sect, there's no doubt about it."

Ji Wuzheng said, "They will not be appointed as Guardians. Only you will have the honor of serving the Holy Hex Sect as a Guardian."

Nangong Le was stunned, "They…they are not going to be appointed as Guardians?!"

Ji Wuzheng said, "No, they are not. That is the second announcement that I am going to make. I am honor that I am going to have three more sworn brothers now. They are Yi Ping, Gongsun Jing and Qiu Wufeng!"

Nangong Le was startled, "What about me?"

Ji Wuzheng grinned, "You are just my Guardian."

Nangong Le was stunned…

Ji Wuzheng said to Yi Ping, Gongsun Jing and Qiu Wufeng. "This is Huo Fu, my sworn brother. If you don't mind, Huo Fu can be your Second Brother while I am your Big Brother. What do you think?"

Yi Ping said, "I don't mind! Brother Fu and Brother Wuzheng, your younger brother pays my respect to you!"

Huo Fu was taken by surprise, "You are not upset with me and even acknowledge me as your Second Brother?"

Yi Ping said, "I really don't mind. Maybe if it isn't for you back then, the Celestial Fairy and I would not be together as a couple. Alas, maybe that is all predestined. Maybe I should thank you instead."

Huo Fu was startled, "That beautiful young maiden that was with you was the Celestial Fairy?!" He was shocked because the Celestial Fairy was rumored to have led the Eternal Ice Palace for some twenty years before she passed away from old age!

Yi Ping was curious, "That's right. Is something wrong?"

Huo Fu murmured, "Nothing…"

But he was already thinking, "No wonder her martial skills are so profound for a young maiden. But how is it possible?" Till today, he had been thinking of her. It was because she was not someone that could be easily forgotten…

Even Ji Wuzheng was slightly startled, "I didn't expect the Celestial Fairy of the Eternal Ice Palace to be just a young maiden. The rumors of the fraternity are many and most are exaggerated and not to be believed recklessly."

Lingfeng said, "I have seen the Celestial Fairy. She is younger than me. Come to think of that, Yu'Er and Mei'Er, how is that your protégé mistress is so young? Yet, her martial skills surpass you by a large gap?"

Yu'Er and Mei'Er exchanged nervous glances.

Yu'Er quickly recovered from her senses and smiled, "That is why she is our protégé mistress!"

Youxue was silently thinking, "Only Yu'Er, Mei'Er and I know her true age. Maybe even Sister Lie Qing and the rest did not suspect…"

Yi Ping said, "Brother Gongsun Jing and Brother Qiu Wufeng and I have an agreement to address one another as equal brothers. So if you don't mind, the three of us can be your Third Brothers!"

Ji Wuzheng and Huo Fu laughed as they said together, "We don't mind! We are brothers now!"

Gongsun Jing stepped forward and bowed with his hands, "My respect to Big Brother and Second Brother!"

Qiu Wufeng too stepped forward and offered his respects, "My respect to Big Brother and Second Brother!"

Nangong Le sighed bitterly, "How I wish I can join them in this brotherhood. I don't want to be a Holy Chapter Guardian anymore…"

Suxin and Sufeng were giggling as they said, "So we got three more Uncles now? They are not so much older than us. We really have to call them Uncles?"

Suyue sighed softly, "I hope that they are not as mean as our father."

Ji Wuzheng stared sternly at Suyue, "Look at you…"

Dugu Zhen smiled gently to Ji Wuzheng, "Suyue is just teasing her new Uncles. Let her enjoy the moment instead."

Ji Wuzheng sighed, "You are just spoiling her too much. Now she doesn't even respect her father anymore. I have told her many times that in this Holy Chapter, I am her Holy Sectarian Master. At all times, she must remember that she is the same as the other protégés…"

Suyue immediately said to Yi Ping, "Uncle Yi Ping, you look like a nice guy. My father is bullying me! Help me!"

Yi Ping smiled bitterly at her.

But he quickly said, "If Big Brother does not mind, can you take in Brother Nangong Le as your Third Brother too? After all, he is with us and is our brother too."

Ji Wuzheng nodded and glanced sternly at Nangong Le, "Since Third Brother Yi Ping has interceded on your behalf, you can join our brotherhood. But I must warn you, brother or not brother, I am always very strict with the clan rules."

Nangong Le smiled bitterly as he said uneasily, "Thank you…Big Brother!"

Suyue laughed softly, "Now I have another Uncle! Uncle Nangong Le!"

All of a sudden, Nangong Le was jolted as he quickly thought. "If I am her Uncle, then can we still be together in a proper relationship?"

But just as he was about to protest, Ji Wuzheng proclaimed aloud. "From now on we are sworn brothers. If anyone of us betray this brotherhood, may he be cursed and be struck by the thunderbolts of heavens. He also will have no descendants. May we share through weal and woes together!"

Nangong Le smiled most bitterly as he sighed deeply, "Brother Yi Ping, do you know that your goodwill has screwed up my happiness…"

Ji Wuzheng said, "Today, I am going to make an exception and bring the lot of you to the forbidden ground of the Inner Holy Chapter."

Dugu Zhen was startled, "Is that a good idea? They are all strangers."

Ji Wuzheng said solemnly, "They have all saved our Holy Sect from annihilation. There is no doubt about it. They are either all my brothers now or Lingfeng's sisters. Maybe with their help, I may be able to understand more about the Heavenly Relic and its secrets."

Dugu Zhen nodded gently, "Then Qian Fan and our daughters will take our leave first."

Ji Wuzheng said gently to his wife, "Don't worry. Nothing will go wrong. I trust them too."

Dugu Zhen said, "You can trust them now but can you trust them ten, twenty years later? People do change over time. I hope you know. I take my leave now."

She stood up and said, "Qian Fan, Suxin, Sufeng and Suyue. Follow me."

Suxin sighed, "I have never been to the forbidden ground before and is curious what the Heavenly Relic looks like."

Dugu Zhen said sternly, "Don't say I didn't warn you. You have better don't say anymore."

Suxin looked unhappy, "Yes mother."

Sufeng whispered to her, "The time Suyue and I try to enter the forbidden ground; we are nearly beaten to death by our father…"

Suyue nodded and there was a hint of tear in her eyes.

Ji Wuzheng hummed coldly to indicate his displeasure.

After Dugu Zhen, Qian Fan, Sufeng, Suxin and Suyue had left the hall, Ji Wuzheng said, "Come with me."

Ji Wuzheng began to lead them into the inner sanctum.

After a few winding turns along the passage way, Ji Wuzheng pushed down a hanging torch and revealed another secret passage.

Very soon, they come to a concealed door.

Ji Wuzheng turned a secret mechanism and gave the concealed door a push , revealing a dark passageway.

Youxue said softly, "So we are going to see the forbidden ground of the Holy Hex Sect? I have heard that members of the Ji Clan are the only ones that are allowed into the forbidden ground."

Lingfeng said, "That's right. Not even Dugu Zhen, my brother's wife is allowed inside. Even Suxin, Sufeng and Suyue as well."

Yu'Er was startled, "Aren't Suxin, Sufeng and Suyue from the Ji Clan too?"

Lingfeng looked at her brother who nodded gently before she said, "Only the male descendants of the Ji Clan and the Holy Maiden are allowed inside. It is because the Holy Maiden must always remain with the Holy Hex Sect."

Mei'Er said, "But we are strangers too…even sworn brothers and sisters are not as close as one's wife…"

She took a quick look at Yi Ping.

Yi Ping saw her glance and he stammered out irrelevantly, "Don't worry, Lingfeng. I will take you away…"

Lingfeng sighed, "You really have nothing better to say to me…"

Lie Qing said humorlessly, "In the Virtuous Palace and the Invincible Divine Clan, there is a forbidden ground too."

She looked at Ji Wuzheng and Lingfeng with a weird expression, "The only times strangers are allowed inside are also the last time that they could leave alive too."

Ding Yun quietly said, "That is right."

Yi Ping said, "We don't have to make wild guesses. Brother Ji Wuzheng is after all Lingfeng's brother. I trust him completely."

Lie Qing looked at him and sighed softly, "You have never been betrayed by your closest friend. I have been betrayed on a number of times by people that are close to me until to the point I have lost faith in anyone until I have met you…"

She quietly held Yi Ping's hands…

Yi Ping said, "Qing'Er, I will never forsake you. I promise you. We will always be together."

Lie Qing nodded as she said, "Somehow, today I have an uneasy feeling. It is like…it is like…this will be the last time that I will see you…"

Yi Ping said with a quick smile, "That is unfounded. You are just worrying for nothing."

Lingfeng said, "There is a great hero here who can protect anyone, am I right Great Hero Yi Ping?"

Yi Ping said, "Lingfeng, you don't have to be so sarcastic. Besides Big Brother and Second Brother, there are so many of us around."

Ji Wuzheng said, "We have reached."

He had reached out another secret mechanism at the end of this passage and when he moved it, the wall slowly opened up and revealed an underground stair!

Ji Wuzheng said, "Let's go in."

Gongsun Jing muttered, "This is even more complex than the secret passages of the Honor Manor."

Qiu Wufeng said, "The Holy Hex Sect has always been secretive in its affair."

They were now in a large airy stone chamber as they walked down the stairs.

Ji Wuzheng said, "There are many secret chambers in the Inner Holy Chapter. This is where the Heavenly Relic is."

The chamber was quite empty saved for two peculiar large statues at the end of the chamber. In the middle of the statues was a small levitating silver metallic rock, the size of a large fist. Enveloped around the Heavenly Relic was a rainbow halo.

Everyone knew instantly that this must be the Heavenly Relic and was gasping at it in astonishment except for Yi Ping and Ding Yun.

Nangong Le and Huo Fu were astonished as they said at the same time, "This is the Heavenly Relic?"

Huo Fu muttered, "How is it possible for it to defy gravity and levitate in midair?"

While most of them were looking at the Heavenly Relic, Ji Wuzheng and Lingfeng were secretly observing everyone's expressions.

Except for Yi Ping and Ding Yun, everyone else had broken into thrilling murmurings as they tried to touch and asked curious questions!

Yu'Er was saying, "It is so beautiful."

Huo Fu laughed, "Brother Wuzheng didn't say we can touch it."

Mei'Er said coolly, "Well, he didn't say anything."

Nangong Le said, "I wonder what the selling price for this in the fraternity…"

Lie Qing laughed softly, "I feel like stealing it already…"

Amidst the excitement generated by everyone, Ding Yun did not seem to be interested.

Ji Wuzheng noticed that Yi Ping was looking at the two peculiar statues instead.

He had rarely taken notice of these two life size statues in the past. But when Yi Ping was looking curiously at it, he too began to take a closer look.

The two statues depicted two identical maidens with large feathery wings on their back as they faced one another, reaching their hands and crossing their long swords together.

When Yi Ping had first entered this chamber, he had immediately visualized himself battling with two beautiful angelic maidens. It took him a while to see past their glowing visage and he was immediately stunned when he found himself looking at Yu'Er and Mei'Er!

This was not the most startling!

In his hazy vision, he had cut them down with his sword and they had died tearfully in each other's embrace!

What were even more startling than that was that before they had closed their eyes, they seemed to look at him with a lingering look and their smiles were tranquil!

All of a sudden, another angelic beautiful maiden in black had appeared. She had a long black sword in her hand. Somehow, he seemed that he had already known her given name; the Dark Enchantress of the West!

Lingfeng asked gently, "What's wrong, Yi Ping? What are you looking at?"

Yi Ping was startled by her and that caused his vision to vanish.

He murmured, "I don't know. These two statues seem to have come alive and are visually beautiful."

Lingfeng was obviously unhappy, "Hmph! Fancy you lusting over two statues! You haven't got enough of last night's beating, didn't you?"

Yi Ping asked, "These statues, what are those?"

Lingfeng said, "I don't know. I have heard that these statues were already here even before the founding of the Holy Hex Sect. But who cares, am I right?"

Yi Ping smiled bitterly as he secretly glanced at Yu'Er and Mei'Er who were laughing jovially with the others.

Yi Ping was now looking at his hands, which was trembling uncontrollably!

Ji Wuzheng hummed aloud to get everyone's attention, "This is the awakened Heavenly Relic. How it is able to levitate on its own, I do not know. According to one of the legends, the Heavenly Relic is able to aid the practitioner to ascend to the heavens."

Huo Fu said solemnly, "It is indeed a heavenly metal. According to my sect own legends, if the heavenly metal can be made into a divine sword…" he stole a glance at Yi Ping. "Then, if the practitioner has also attained the merging with the sword spirit, one with the sword and the merging of self with the heavens and the earth, then the practitioner will be able to use it as a celestial flying sword to ascend to the heavens!"

Lie Qing said coldly, "I don't mean to pour cold water on you. How do you know it is true? You have a Celestial in your sect?"

Huo Fu said solemnly, "According to my sect history, there were three Celestials in my sect in the past."

Lie Qing hummed coldly, "Oh really? Where are they now?"

Huo Fu laughed, "That was a long, long time ago. Three thousand years ago to be exact. Maybe they have already ascended to beyond the Ninth Heavens. Haha!"

Yi Ping suddenly said, "Or maybe they have all perished in a bloody killing with one another…"

All of a sudden, there was a purple vapor hissing into the chamber!

Ji Wuzheng immediately shouted, "Everyone hold your breath! This vapor is poisonous!"

Yi Ping and Lie Qing immediately displayed several stances as they sent flurries of windforce all around the ground, rolling back the purple fumes!

Youxue said coldly, "It seems that we have quite a lot of uninvited visitors!"

Ji Wuzheng shouted angrily, "Who is that? How dare you barge into the…"

Everyone was stunned when they saw Dugu Zhen walked into view as the purple fumes scattered.

Ji Wuzheng asked, "Why are you here? Do you know that this place is off-limits to you?"

Dugu Zhen was dragging a bloodied and unconscious Qian Fan on the ground. Instead of replying him, she threw him in front of her and said coldly. "His true identity is Xiao Fan and not Qian Fan. He may think he is smart for fooling us but he is not. He is also the one that causes the death of four of our Holy Chapter Guardians."

Xiao Youxue was startled as she thought, "He is my brother?"

Ji Wuzheng did not ask how Dugu Zhen knew about Qian Fan. Instead he said coldly, "Who are the three people behind you?"

Three old men immediate walked calmly into view.

Lingfeng was startled as she gasped softly.

Even Ji Wuzheng was startled.

Huo Fu was baffled so he asked, "You know these old men?"

Lingfeng said, "These three old men are old stewards of the Holy Hex Sect. I only know today that they are actually no ordinary stewards but are actually martial exponents!"

Youxue was startled as well, "These three men are also no ordinary martial exponents. Aren't they the Three Evils of the West? They are the Moon Heretic, the Blade Heretic and the Blood Heretic!"

Immediately, everyone was stunned including Ji Wuzheng and Huo Fu. It was because the Three Evils of the West were super exponents that were greatly feared by all as they rampaged throughout the martial fraternity with their super martial skills!

It was rumored that they had passed away decades ago. But why were they here? And how did Youxue recognize them?

The old man with the shorter white beard said, "I am the Moon Heretic. Young lass, how did you know who we are?"

Youxue said coolly, "I saw your portraits in the Virtuous Palace."

She pointed at the old man with white whiskers, "You are the Blade Heretic."

Next she pointed at the old man with a pale face, "And you are the Blood Heretic."

Dugu Zhen laughed gently, "Excellent! So the Virtuous Palace has already known that the Three Evils are hiding in the Holy Hex Sect."

She turned and looked at Qian Fan who was lying on the ground, "So this spy has already known but why didn't he expose us?"

Huo Fu said angrily, "So you are all from the heretic sect?"

Everyone was startled. The heretic sect had actually infiltrated the Holy Hex Sect!

Dugu Zhen said, "Yes, we are if you want to. We actually prefer to call ourselves the Sacred Divine Clan."

Ji Wuzheng said, "Zhen, you are really from the heretic sect? Come back to me, there is still hope. Our daughters, are they in the heretic sect too?"

Dugu Zhen said, "You don't have to worry. They do not know anything at all. If you smart enough, you will hand over the Heavenly Relic to us on your own free will or else, don't blame me."

Huo Fu said, "There are so many of us here. Do you think we will fear just the four of you?"

Dugu Zhen said coldly, "Do you really think there are just four of us here only?"

All of a sudden, Ding Yun had stabbed Lie Qing with a dagger with her right hand and dealt her a heavy crushing blow on her heart with her left hand using the Penetrating Hand!

Even as everyone was still reacting with shock, Ding Yun had unsheathed her long sword and had displayed a barrage of sword slashes on Lie Qing!

Lie Qing was taken completely by surprise even as she parried off the attacks weakly

Yi Ping immediately raised his hands at Ding Yun! "Yun! What are you doing!? Why did you…"

Ding Yun immediately stepped aside to Dugu Zhen's side even as Youxue, Mei'Er, Yu'Er, Lingfeng, Ji Wuzheng, Huo Fu, Gongsun Jing, Nangong Le and Qiu Wufeng attacked her at the same time!

Youxue said tearfully, "Sister Yun! Why did you do that to Lie Qing? I have thought that we are sisters? Why did you attack Lie Qing?!"

Yi Ping was now holding the blood-soaked Lie Qing in his arms as he lamented loudly, "Qing'Er, wake up. Don't sleep…"

Lie Qing smiled weakly, "I told you…I really…have an uneasy…feeling today. I have been betrayed again…I think my destiny is finally coming to an end…Yi Ping, I am so happy to know you during this short time…"

Yi Ping drawn her close to him as he transferred his vital energies into her, "Qing'Er, don't talk anymore. Try to hold on…"

Lie Qing said weakly as she looked at Yi Ping with silent tears, "Don't waste your precious internal strength on me…it is no use…my heart pulse is broken…save your strength to fight your foes instead…"

Yi Ping cried out, "If I stop now, you will die! Qing'Er, I can't let you die…"

Lie Qing was murmuring weakly, "…till oceans vanish and rocks crumbled to dust…together…"

Lingfeng was trembling as she stole a glance at Lie Qing while trying to hold back her tears, "Sister Yun, you…are really from the heretic sect?"

Ding Yun said quietly, "That's right. You have better surrendered. None of you are our match in skill."

Ji Wuzheng said coldly, "I only got a question. Why did you wait for twenty years?"

Dugu Zhen said, "It does take us this long for us to steal your Holy Amalgamate Skill and to practice it. Without the Holy Amalgamate Force, our holy sect is unable to fight the Divine Calamity and ascend to be Celestials."

Ji Wuzheng said, "You marry me because you want to steal the Holy Amalgamate Skill?"

Dugu Zhen said, "Is there any other reason? I also know that now you are injured and are unable to display the full martial power of the Holy Amalgamate Skill. However, I am different. I have been secretly practicing the Holy Amalgamate Skill for a long time. I am afraid that even if you are not injured, you may not be able to defeat me."

Ji Wuzheng was silent, "Is that so? Even if you have defeated us and taken the Heavenly Relic away, do you think the Orthodox Martial Clans will simply let you off just like that?"

Dugu Zhen hummed coldly, "This, you don't have to worry. At this moment, I am afraid that the Orthodox Clans are too busy fighting among themselves."

Ji Wuzheng said, "What do you mean?"

Dugu Zhen said, "Do you think that we have only infiltrated just the Holy Hex Sect?"

Ji Wuzheng was taken aback as he looked at Ding Yun. Even the Virtuous Palace had long been infiltrated…

Yi Ping was inconsolable and he was wailing aloud, not caring if others were watching or staring at him.

Youxue stepped forward as she shouted icily, "Ding Yun! Ding Yunzi! Why did you betray us?! Don't you know that Yi Ping, he loves you and I have always regarded you as my dearest sister? Why did you betray us?"

Ding Yun's eyes were sorrowful as she said quietly, "Do you know that those in the Sacred Divine Clan have to take a terrible blood oath? Once we in the Sacred Divine Clan, we are forever in the Sacred Divine Clan. Other than obeying, I don't have any other choices."

She looked at Dugu Zhen as she said, "Even for her, she has no other choice. We are all manipulated by fate."

She looked at Youxue, "But I can tell you this. You may have wronged your father, Xiao Shuai."

Xiao Youxue was startled, "What do you mean?"

Ding Yun said, "Your father didn't want to teach you any skills because he is actually trying to protect you. Should he dies, at least his enemies won't think of you as a real threat. It is because he already suspects of our presence in the Virtuous Palace."

She lowered her glances, "I am sorry Youxue. I have always regarded you as my dearest sister too and Lie Qing too…"

Youxue said icily, "And now because of you, she is now in a critical condition and this is what you mean by dearest sister?"

Ding Yun refused to answer her directly. Instead she said, "My role in the Virtuous Palace is to sow discord between your two brothers, causing them to fight with one another."

Youxue said coldly, "You don't have to explain your role and your part to me. My brothers aren't close to me. I only want to ask, how you can be so vicious as to lay your hands on Sister Lie Qing!"

Ding Yun refused to say anymore as she thought, "Forgive me, everyone. Yi Ping, how I wish you have allowed me to take my own life in the valley…"

Yu'Er was weeping for Lie Qing but when she looked into Ding Yun's eyes, she could feel an unspeakable sadness…

Even Mei'Er could feel it.

Dugu Zhen looked at Gongsun Jing, "Gongsun Jing, do you know that your father Gongsun Bai is actually one of us?"

Gongsun Jing was startled, "That's impossible! My father is a great hero…"

Dugu Zhen said coolly, "That is just an identity given to him by us. In order to become the Master of the Honor Manor, he has to betray his sworn brother which is Yi Ping's father, Yi Tianxing. Unfortunate, we made a fatal mistake and this resulted in a terrible loss for us."

Gongsun Jing asked, "What mistake?"

Dugu Zhen sighed, "Our mistake is to give Gongsun Bai the incomplete Invincible Divine Force that Xiao Shuai had deliberately circulated in the martial fraternity. Only someone who knows the intricate heart formula of the Divine Virtuous Force can truly mastered that incomplete Invincible Divine Force. That is as good as telling Xiao Shuai and Gu Tianle that we have infiltrated the Honor Manor. That is why, your entire Gongsun Clan is exterminated by Gu Tianle. That is something very regrettable on our side."

Gongsun Jing stammered, "I don't believe…my father will never be a heretic member…"

Dugu Zhen said, "Whether, you want to believe or not, is up to you. However, we do welcome you to join us, just like your father has joined us."

Gongsun Jing shouted angrily as he drawn out his long sword, "Never! Never! I rather die than join the heretic sect!"

Dugu Zhen said coldly, "Then, all of you will have to die today."

Ji Wuzheng said regretfully, "Zhen, I already know you are from the heretic sect twenty years ago."

Dugu Zhen said, "Stop bluffing. If you know who I am, will you still let me live to this day?"

Ji Wuzheng said, "That is the truth."

Lingfeng said quietly, "My brother already knows twenty years ago…"

Dugu Zhen was startled but she quickly said, "I won't fall into your ruse. Surrender the Heavenly Relic now or else we won't be merciful anymore."

Ji Wuzheng asked, "At least before we die, shouldn't you at least tell us who is the grandmaster of your heretic sect is, am I right?"

Chapter 56: The Universal Force

Many years ago, Ding Jun was one of the followers of the Heavenly Temptress. He had pretended to join Xiao Boyi, Yuan Tieqi and You Nikuang in a rebellion against the Heavenly Temptress. Unknown to everyone, Jing Xing who had died in defense of the Heavenly Temptress had actually pledged herself to Ding Jun and they were actually a loving secret couple.

So when Xiao Boyi, Yuan Tieqi and You Nikuang had killed Jing Xing in the ensuring rebellion, Ding Jun secretly sworn to avenge her and founded the Sacred Divine Sect to continue the legacy of the Invincible Divine Clan.

Dugu Zhen said coldly, "So you want to know who is our Holy leader is? Only the elders of the Sacred Divine Clan know who the Holy Leader really is. Not even the likes of Gongsun Bai have that knowledge."

Lingfeng interrupted coldly, "The heretic sect can claim to be holy? What a joke! Your leader is nothing but a coward who hides in the darkness."

Dugu Zhen hummed coldly as she looked at Ding Yun.

Ding Yun gazed at everyone intently before she said, "Look no further. I am the Holy Leader of the Sacred Divine Clan."

Ji Wuzheng was in disbelief that the Holy Leader would actually be a young maiden, "You…you are the Holy Leader of the Sacred Divine Clan?"

Gongsun Jing, Nangong Le, Qiu Wufeng, Yu'Er, Mei'Er, Lingfeng and Huo Fu were equally startled!

Ding Yun said with quiet demeanor, "You only have this one chance to kill me."

Xiao Youxue had already raised her hands and her fingers were surrounded by a golden halo as she said melancholy, "Sister Yun, forgive me. What you did to Sister Lie Qing is deplorable and unforgivable. I really have no choice but to fight you today."

Ding Yun clapped her hands gently and immediately, the Three Evils of the West had sped forward and were standing beside her! "But you must also know that the Holy Leader of the Sacred Divine Clan cannot be so easily killed."

Dugu Zhen added coldly, "No one can stop us from ascending to be Celestials today!"

The Blood Heretic hummed coldly in his old voice, "What a pity, what a pity that we have to kill so many beauties today."

The Moon Heretic said, "Remember, don't kill them so fast. We need their blood and hearts after we have ascended to be Celestials in order to recuperate. Just disable them will do."

The Blade Heretic sighed, "You know that each time I draw my blade, I have to feed it with the lifeblood of its victims? This is really too hard for me…"

The Blood Heretic laughed wickedly, "You can kill the weaker ones. We have no use for them. Remember, our next opponent is the Celestial Palace. So we need to recuperate fast."

Ji Wuzheng interrupted quickly, "Zhen, listen to me. It is not as easy to ascend to be a Celestial as you think. What you intending to do is the unorthodox way and will result in divine retribution. It will turn you into bloodthirsty monsters and many will be sacrificed. Do you really want that to happen?"

Dugu Zhen smile coldly, "As long as I can be a Celestial and have an immortal life, does it really matter? What does the life of others matter to me?"

Ji Wuzheng was startled! "Zhen, you have changed..."

Dugu Zhen hummed coldly, "You're wrong. It just that you have never really understands me. How much time have you been with me? You just too busy for your martial cultivations. Even if I don't want to take the Heavenly Relic from you, do you know that Xiao Shuai and his conspirators are all eyeing the Heavenly Relic as well? It is because they too, want to be a Celestial and have been planning for decades. They are all waiting for the Seven Stars to be aligned, a Celestial Omen that could make their ascendant much easier."

She walked gently to Ding Yun and tapped lightly, "Do you know that before I have married you, I have already another daughter? Dugu Yunzi, today you can finally use the Dugu clan name."

Ji Wuzheng, Lingfeng, Youxue and the others were stunned...

Ji Wuzheng stammered, "Maiden Ding Yun is actually...your daughter?"

Dugu Yunzi was trembling lightly as she said softly, "That's right. She is my mother and I am Dugu Yunzi. When the Ding clan found the Sacred Divine Clan, we have since taken Dugu as our secret clan name even though we are still known as the Ding Clan while in the Virtuous Palace."

The Moon Heretic had suddenly raised his hands with a mighty flurrying of windforce as he attacked Ji Wuzheng, "That's enough talk already. No one can stop us from becoming Celestials today. The Heavenly Relic must be seized today and the Holy Maiden must be the blood sacrifice!"

Immediately after the Moon Heretic had displayed his martial force forward, Ji Wuzheng had immediately reacted with a counter blow. As both clashed with their palms, there were a thunderous impact. Almost immediately Ji Wuzheng had coughed out blood as he was forced to slide five steps backward!

The Moon Heretic was his superior in internal strength and martial power!

But before the Moon Heretic could continue on his advantage, Youxue and Lingfeng had immediately attacked him!

The Moon Heretic laughed coldly, "I am in luck. I have two beauties here that are interested in me."

Lingfeng interrupted coldly, "Shameless!"

Xiao Youxue and Lingfeng were experts in swiftness agility and movement skills as they immediately unleashed dozens of shadowy flurries on the Moon Heretic. However to their astonishment, the Moon Heretic had matched their blows with equal fast shadowy attacks as he laughed coldly. "Is that what you got? I am expecting better!"

Lingfeng was now displaying the Sacred Heart Skill as she made dozens of flurry strokes in front of the Moon Heretic. It was a deadly skill that was part of the Holy Hex martial skills that could break the pulses of her target. Now that she was back to the Holy Hex Sect, there was now no need for her to conceal her true skills. Her attacking speed, her swiftness skill and even her martial power were greatly augmented when she imbued herself with the Holy Amalgamate Force!

Lingfeng said coldly to the Moon Heretic, "You don't dare to kill me, am I right? Then it may be a costly mistake for you and you will never be able to ascend!"

The Moon Heretic said coldly as he looked at her lustfully, "There is worst fate than death itself. I can let you have a taste of that."

Even as she changed her stances rapidly, executing deadly secret martial techniques like the neutralizing martial power of the Great Dissolution Skill and the bursting power of the Asper Horizon Hand, she still could not scratched the Moon Heretic even though Youxue was also fighting besides her and were using all her best techniques as well!

Just as Ji Wuzheng had recovered from the blow that he had just received from the Moon Heretic, Dugu Zhen had attacked him as she executed the Swallow Slash movement by dashing towards him and displaying the third and fifth stance of her Cherry Blossoms techniques, the Windchaser Slide and the Mirror Reflection Splitting Images!

Huo Fu immediately intercepted as he shouted, "Brother, watch out!"

At the same time that Dugu Zhen had made her move, the Blade Heretic had already drawn his sword and had leapt towards the Heavenly Relic!

Ji Wuzheng shouted, "Don't let them seize the Heavenly Relic!"

Gongsun Jing, Nangong Le and Qiu Wufeng had immediately displayed their best swordplay techniques at the Blade Heretic!

The Blade Heretic immediately slashed at Gongsun Jing, Nangong Le and Qiu Wufeng with lightning speed, slashing them and spilling their blood! "If you want to stop me, I am afraid that you are still early by tens of decades!"

If it were not for Yu'Er and Mei'Er who had also made their moves and displayed their swordplay at the Blade Heretic; Gongsun Jing, Nangong Le and Qiu Wufeng would have been killed in an instant!

The Blade Heretic was startled to see such an astonishing sword display from the twin sisters. Even as he slashed his sword at them with pin-point accuracy, he was met with a sudden resistant. "The Divine Emerald Skill? You are from the Eternal Ice Palace?"

Yu'Er said coldly, "That's right! Prepare to…"

But before she could finish, the Blade Heretic had imbued his sword with strong deadly sword energy and broke her Divine Emerald Force, sending her scurrying backward!

Mei'Er immediately blocked the second stroke of the Blade Heretic with her cold sword energy, preventing the Blade Heretic from moving forward as she cried panicky. "Sister, watch out…"

Yu'Er gasped as she quickly recovered from the attack and she had flew to Mei'Er again, "The Shifting Stellar Duo Sword Formation, sister! Two in one, one into two!"

The Shifting Stellar Duo Sword Formation and the Shifting Stellar Trio Sword Formation was an intricate formation created to confuse and to utilize the speed techniques and defense techniques of the Eternal Ice Palace.

The Shifting Stellar Duo Sword Formation was even more deadly when it was used by Yu'Er and Mei'Er, precisely because they were splitting images of each other!

This was their last critical death strike technique for them to use now as they made a desperate stand. Even against so many powerful foes, they did not use it as they did not want to disclose their secret martial techniques to anyone.

Yu'Er was now attacking and Mei'Er had vanished behind her, taking the Blade Heretic by surprise!

As soon as he had attacked Yu'Er, she had deflected his attack with a flurrying of sword strokes and displaying the Divine Emerald Force. All of a sudden, Mei'Er had reappeared from behind her and slashed at the Blade Heretic, taking him by surprise.

Just as he had parried the attacks that were from Mei'Er, she had switched to the Divine Emerald Force and Yu'Er was attacking him again!

Because these two sisters were splitting images of each other, the Blade Heretic was momentarily confused which of the sister would be the attacker and which one was drawing him into making an opening!

Gongsun Jing was clutching his blood soaked chest as he got up weakly, "Brothers, are you alright?"

Qiu Wufeng was trembling as he struggled to get on his knee. He had never expected to be defeated by a mere stroke despite his expertise in swordplay! When the sword stroke of the Blade Heretic had slashed across his body, he was also injured by a deadly sword energy as well. But he said weakly, "I am alright. I can still fight…"

Nangong Le's swordplay was the weakest but he was less affected by the sword energy due to his Exuberant Divine Skill. But his wound was also the heaviest. He smiled weakly, "I am not defeated yet. Yu'Er and Mei'Er need our help. The three of us can still display the Celestial Star Formation. Let's fight him again."

Gongsun Jing nodded as his warm tears streamed from his eyes, "Today, we are going to die for a worthy cause to stop the heretic sect. I am going to wash away all the sins of my clan!" With that, he charged towards the Blade Heretic!

Qiu Wufeng too, had mustered all his remaining strength as he charged at the Blade Heretic at almost the same time as Gongsun Jing!

The Blood Heretic had displayed his hands into claws as he smirked with great disdain at the resistances even as he sped towards the Heavenly Relic, "They didn't know how futile it is to oppose us."

But before he could seize the Heavenly Relic, Yi Ping had intercepted him and there was a mighty thunderous thunderclap that shook the chamber aloud as the Blood Heretic retaliated with a blow!

Immediately, the fighting around them paused for a moment as everyone saw Yi Ping and the Blood Heretic had both taken several steps backward!

Yi Ping was carrying the motionless Lie Qing's who was leaning on him with his left hand and had beaten off the Blood Heretic with his right palm!

Yi Ping said with a solemn heartbreak, "Qing'Er, even though you are not with us anymore but your spirit will lives on.

Everyone was startled.

Yu'Er and Mei'Er broke into tears as they muttered, "Sister Qing'Er isn't with us anymore."

Yu'Er stared at the Blade Heretic and Ding Yun with cold hatred as she said, "It is either you die or I die today!"

When she had finished speaking, she had immediately attacked the Blade Heretic with a startled speed but her stroke was immediately countered by the Heretic Blade!

The Blade Heretic hummed coldly even as Yu'Er, Mei'Er, Gongsun Jing, Nangong Le and Qiu Wufeng raised their long swords at the same time as they attacked him from all sides.

The Blade Heretic said coldly, "It is only a matter of time before I can break your sword formation. Already all of you are panting with exhaustion while I have barely even used any strength."

At the same time, when the Blood Heretic was being forced back, he was secretly startled. "This young man can actually have the martial strength to force me back using only one hand? Is that possible?"

The reason he was startled was because with his combination of martial power and internal strength, there was not many exponents in the fraternity that could stop him anymore. Moreover, his opponent was but a young man!

Dugu Yunzi was looking at the heartbroken Yi Ping. She had never seen him with this type of expression before.

Yi Ping glanced at the Blood Heretic and Ding Yun as he coarsely said, "Yun, I don't believe you will betray us. There must be a reason for you to do so. No matter what you do, I am willing to listen…"

Dugu Yunzi interrupted, "Forget it Yi Ping. You are still in denial. It is an undeniable fact that I am the Holy Leader of the Sacred Divine Clan. Moreover, I have killed Lie Qing…"

Yi Ping smiled weakly, "I…I don't know how to explain this but the last time, the last time…in my dreams…I seem to have made many terrible mistakes. Sometimes the truth isn't so straightforward…"

Youxue had broken free of the Moon Heretic as she sped towards Ding Yun, "Yi Ping, stop saying so much to her!"

Yi Ping said, "Youxue don't attack her, I almost lost you the last time. I don't want the same thing to happen again. Yun, please come back. Surely we can talk over…"

Dugu Yunzi simply interrupted Youxue's charge as she raised her scabbard that had been imbued by her martial force and threw it towards her, forcing her to evade it and back to the entanglement of the Moon Heretic again who hummed coldly as he dealt her a direct blow on her back, "Not so fast, young beauty. Do you think I am non-existent?"

Youxue had immediately coughed out blood! The blow that she had received was simply too heavy even for her Golden Invincible Body!

Yi Ping was about to dash to aid Youxue when the Blood Heretic had attacked him with multiple waves of powerful windforce that had been directed at him!

He was forced to halt and retaliated with his Divine Horizon Hands!

The Blood Heretic had sent blows after blows of shadow claws, displaying intrigue strokes one after another with thunderous impact, stirring up windforce in all directions!

Even though Yi Ping was sweating now but he still refused to put down Lie Qing and fight back blow for blow, stroke for stroke and counter for counter!

The Blood Heretic was now startled. It was because he had already used all his martial power and was using both hands while Yi Ping fighting with just one hand. Even though he knew that the fight would eventually turn on his favor as his opponent got more and more tired, he was not happy. It was because with his present state of divinity and martial strength, he could not bring a young man down.

The Moon Heretic, the Blade Heretic and even Dugu Zhen were all having an easier time than him even though they were fighting multiple opponents. They were so overwhelming in their martial differences with their opponents that they did not even need to use all their strength. Their mere strokes could cause their opponents to evade, parry, block or retaliate hence wearing down their physical strength and internal strength.

Lingfeng quickly gasped to Yi Ping panicky, "Yi Ping, put down Lie Qing. She is dead now. You are only endangering yourself!"

Yi Ping refused to heed her and instead he willed himself with the Absolute Spirits as he displayed several stances of the Divine Horizon Hands once again!

Yi Ping muttered, "Qing'Er…Yun…why…"

The reason why Yi Ping was sweating profusely was not because he was reaching his limit and was hard pressed by the Blood Heretic as everyone had thought, since sweating was a good indication of one's limitation had been reached and current state of physical conditioning.

The real reason why he was sweating profusely was because he was still transferring his internal strength into Lie Qing's lifeless body and that action was snapping his stamina at a rapid rate!

All of a sudden, Yi Ping experienced a great discomfort in his heart and his strokes faltered.

The Blood Heretic immediately sensed a moment of weakness and seized the faltering speed of Yi Ping by increasing his own martial power all of a sudden, breaking through his Divine Horizon Hand and sent a thunderous cracking impact on Yi Ping!

Yi Ping immediately coughed out blood as this thunderous impact could grind even stones into dust as he was sent flying through the air!

But the weird thing was the Blood Heretic was also thrown back by a rebounding force that was so almighty that even with the full execution of his martial power, he was not able to stop it!

Yu'Er gasped, "Master!"

In her moment of distraction, the Blade Heretic had slashed her on her shoulder. Even Mei'Er was slashed as she tried to parry for her sister!

Within just a few seconds that saw Yi Ping flew backward with a thunderous impact and with blood spilling in mid-air, Ji Wuzheng, Huo Fu, Nangong Le, Qiu Wufeng, Gongsun Jing, Yu'Er and Mei'Er, with the exception of Lingfeng and Youxue were all rolling in agony from their injuries on the ground!

The Blade Heretic and the Blood Heretic had immediately joined the Moon Heretic as they joined hands to attack Lingfeng and Youxue, who were already faltering from attacks from all sides!

Dugu Zhen said, "In the end, there are just two capable fighters standing. Ji Wuzheng, you call yourself the Holy Sectarian Master, yet you can't even hold a candle to your sister."

Ji Wuzheng smiled coldly as he struggled to stand, "If I am not injured, do you think you can really defeat me? If you are not my wife, do you think I will hold back?"

Dugu Zhen hummed coldly, "Why is that all men likes some face saving measures? A win is a win and a loss is a loss."

Ji Wuzheng replied, "Don't underestimate the Holy Hex Sect and my sister. She has after all, taken the Golden Rejuvenation Pill. Her internal strength is a match for the Three Evils!"

Even though he was saying so, Lingfeng was reaching her limited as evidenced by the sweat on her face. Youxue was also sweating profusely while the Three Evils had not even broke into a sweat yet!

Youxue and Lingfeng knew that in terms of internal strength, martial power, martial skills and technique, they were being outclassed! What kept them going was sheer willpower and determination not to be defeated by these vile heretics!

Just as Lingfeng took a step back and was about to seized by the Moon Heretic, Yi Ping had displayed the Asper Horizon Hand with a mighty flurrying windforce that sent the Moon Heretic moving backward!

The Blood Heretic was startled, "You are not dead yet?"

The crashing blow that had landed on Yi Ping was a hit with all his martial power. Even a super exponent may not survive such a direct hit!

Yi Ping staggered weakly with Lie Qing in his embrace as he raised his right hand, "So this is the Heavenly Relic that you want?"

He was clutching the Heavenly Relic in his right hand!

He had picked it up when he was flung back.

Ji Wuzheng was startled as he thought, "Without the Great Dissolution Skill, he can grab the Heavenly Relic?" But he got no further time to ponder more as he quickly shouted panicky, "Third Brother Yi Ping, don't give them the Heavenly Relic!"

Youxue and Lingfeng staggered weakly besides Yi Ping even as the Moon Heretic, Blood Heretic and the Blade Heretic stopped in their tracks.

Yi Ping shouted angrily as he raised the Heavenly Relic in front of them, "So this is the Heavenly Relic that you want, am I right?!"

All of a sudden, there was a cracking sound as Yi Ping crushed the Heavenly Relic in front of them!

Everyone could see heat and dust vaporizing as Yi Ping crushed the Heavenly Relic with his hand!

Dugu Zhen, Dugu Yunzi, the Moon Heretic, the Blood Heretic and the Blade Heretic was startled and were in disbelief as they muttered, "The Heavenly Relic can be crushed by mortal hand!?"

Even Ji Wuzheng was astonished and was staring in disbelief!

Yi Ping had used all his martial power, augmented by the Aspire Invocation Force as he broke the Heavenly Relic into five smaller pieces in a fit of rage! He scarcely even knows what he had been doing. He was just preparing his martial power for the next attack but because he had not attacked yet and he had the Heavenly Relic in his hand, he vented all his anger and martial power onto the Heavenly Relic instead!

By the time, he had realized that he had accidentally caused the Heavenly Relic to be broken into five pieces as it dropped onto the ground, he himself was stunned!

When Yi Ping had suffered a heartbreaking pain in his heart earlier, it was not because his sentimental emotions had once again triggered the side effect of the Emptiness Translucence. It was because his undying devotion to Lie Qing and his undying forgiveness for Dugu Yunzi had caused his Emptiness Translucence to achieve a stunning breakthrough from the Enigma Divine Ascendant to the Absolute Divine Ascendant!

Besides devoid of all worldly attachments, there was actually another way for a practitioner to achieve a breakthrough in the Emptiness Translucence. But it was almost impossible to attain; the practitioner had to be devoid of hatred and also had undying love for the one that he loves. It was either hate or love; both conditions could not be possible to exist at the same time! How could one prove his forgiveness and his undying love for someone at the same time?

Yi Ping had refused to put down Lie Qing, refusing to believe that she had died and even transferred his internal injuries to her dead body even though he was facing a terrible powerful foe at the same time. That was undying devoted love!

Even though he had witnessed Dugu Yunzi injuring and mortally wounding Lie Qing with his very own eyes, he was in great denial. He believed firmly that she must have a strong reason for doing so and that he would be willing to believe her even though he was in great grief! That was undying faith and true forgiveness!

In that very instant when Yi Ping had suffered a heartbreaking pain in his heart, he had actually killed off the doubt emotions in his heart forever, hence attaining the Absolute Divine Ascendant of the Emptiness Translucence!

At the same moment, the divine force power release of the Emptiness Translucence was also at its strongest. So when the Blood Heretic had struck Yi Ping fatally on his chest, instead of causing Yi Ping a fatal wound, he had unwittingly helped Yi Ping by distributing the powerful divine force throughout all his meridian channels. This had the unknowing effect of propelling Yi Ping's internal strength and martial power to an unsurpassed height!

Before the divine force power release of the Emptiness Translucence had yet to completely merged with his Aspire Invocation Force to form the Boundless Divine Force, Yi Ping had unwittingly use the only force in the entire universe that was capable of breaking or molding the Heavenly Relic, which was actually called the Universal Force by the Celestials as he crushed the Heavenly Relic with his bare hands!

The Universal Force was a rare occurrence that only happened at the creation or destruction of a new state of celestial divinity, enabling the Celestials to create Celestial Weapons and to divine the mysteries of the Ninth Heavens. Certain Celestial Weapons were so powerful that they could create the Universal Force on impact with one another; however the result was not benevolent Creation Universal force but the Destructive Universal Force that brought forth chaos and mayhems.

Lingfeng smiled weakly, "Just nice. You can now distribute these five pieces to them and everyone can have a share."

Even though she was in a precaution situation, Lingfeng's humor did not go away.

Dugu Zhen was so stunned that she stammered, "You…you….you…actually broke it!"

The Moon Heretic stammered as well, "Is this Heavenly Relic a fake?"

The Blade Heretic was shouting angrily, "Who wants this broken Heavenly Relic now! Now you have really enraged me!"

The Moon Heretic, the Blood Heretic and the Blade Heretic were obviously extremely enraged as their killing malevolent aura had suddenly intensified!

All of a sudden, there were six bursts of visible blue glow around them as they mustered their martial power!

Youxue gasped, "The Divine Virtuous Force!?"

Dugu Yunzi said coolly, "That's right. The three elders have not only mastered the epitome levels of the Divine Virtuous Force but they had also successfully merged the Holy Amalgamate Force with it. So what you are seeing now is their true strength."

Lingfeng broke into cold sweat. This combination of martial force was extremely deadly and had no weakness! The dissolution force of the Holy Amalgamate Force weakened their opponents' martial power and strength at close melee and the seemingly impenetrable force of the Divine Virtuous Force that could only be penetrated by superior martial power would make them invincible!

No wonder, they seemed to have the confidence of overcoming the Divine Calamity!

Even Ji Wuzheng was dismayed when he had seen their martial display. He knew instantly that even if he was not injured, he could not even be able to defeat one of them, let alone there were three of them now!

Everyone seemed to have given up hope now and their eyes were downcast.

Even Youxue's will to fight was faltering; she had forced herself with the Absolute Spirits to stand up against their overwhelming martial strength! The results were just plain obvious...

Yi Ping said stubbornly as he displayed the Horizon Heavens, the opening stance of the Divine Horizon Hand. "Life and death is predestined. I will fight you and bring Yun back to my side!"

Dugu Yunzi looked up at him and eyed him with a curious look...

Even Youxue and Lingfeng were startled at his stubbornness. Until this point, he had not given up on Dugu Yunzi! But did he know that he was facing an impossible odds and he had only one hand that was free?

Lingfeng signed with a soft resignation as she muttered, "That is why I like him. Yi Ping, I will fight with you to bring Sister Yun back to us!"

Youxue nodded too, "Ping'Er, we...will bring her back even if we were to die fighting!"

Yi Ping was deeply moved as he nodded in appreciation at them.

Even Yu'Er and Mei'Er were sobbing, "Yes, bring Sister Yun back..."

They had all been moved by Yi Ping's undying determination and devotion!

Dugu Yunzi put her slender fingers to her back because she did not want others to see her trembling fingers even as she said coldly, "Don't waste your efforts. It is all meaningless and you only be throwing your lives. Just quietly surrender the Heavenly Relic."

Yi Ping said quietly, "Youxue, Lingfeng. Step aside please..."

Youxue and Lingfeng both shook their heads in protest!

Yi Ping said with a heartbreaking voice, "Even though you have tried to hide it but I know that both of you have already sustained grievous internal injuries."

He had already seen the blood tickling down from their lips and knew that they were forcing themselves to fight!

All of a sudden, Lingfeng gasped weakly as she pointed to the five broken pieces of the Heavenly Relic that were on the ground!

The five broken pieces of Heavenly Relic were hissing with vapor and were melted to a reddish coloring as intensive heat melted its outer metal shells rapidly to reveal five yellow pearls!

Everyone was baffled at this curious sight and not knowing how to react, including the Three Evils, Dugu Zhen and Dugu Yunzi!

Lingfeng had gasped with a startled cry, "The Divine Dragon Pills!!!"

Yi Ping quickly said as he recalled that it looked exactly like the Divine Dragon Pill that he previously had, "That's right...looks like it."

Xiao Youxue had also recognized the Divine Dragon Pills! But her reaction was even swifter as she shouted quickly, "Yi Ping! Grab the pills and don't let them have it!"

The Three Evils were astonished as well and were not slow to react as they mustered all their martial power and charged towards Yi Ping, Xiao Youxue and Ji Lingfeng!

Everyone other than Yi Ping, Lingfeng and Youxue had heard of the Divine Dragon Pill before and they had thought that it was just a legend! The Dragon Divine Pill was said to possess the ability to increase the martial power of the practitioner tremendously, raising the state of divinity of the practitioner or even have miraculous healing power to bring the dead back to life!

The Moon Heretic shouted, "Don't let them seize it! These Divine Dragon Pills are even more precious than the Heavenly Relic!"

Lingfeng immediately executed the movement of the Swallow Slash as she dashed past Yi Ping as she substituted the stroke of the Swallow Slash with the invocating martial burst of the Asper Horizon Hand as she clashed against the Moon Heretic, "Didn't you guys just said you didn't want these broken Heavenly Relic earlier..."

But before she could finish, the mighty palm power of the Moon Heretic had knocked her flying backward!

Yu'Er and Mei'Er used their last strength to leap and caught hold of Lingfeng as they heard her muttering, "I...sorry...I no longer have any strength to fight beside you, Ping'Er..."

Even as Lingfeng had sped past Yi Ping, Youxue had picked up all the Dragon Divine Pills and displayed her Golden Invincible Stance as she parried the blades of the Blade Heretic with her martial imbued sleeves that were now as hard as iron!

Youxue immediately threw one Divine Dragon Pill to the back as she exclaimed urgently, "Give it to Lingfeng and don't let her die! Transfer your internal energies and diffuse the vital energies of the Divine Dragon Pill throughout her body!"

Yu'Er immediately caught hold of the Divine Dragon Pill and popped it into Lingfeng's mouth, inviting angry stares from the Three Evils who could only watch as one of the five precious Divine Dragon Pills got swallowed by Lingfeng as they were caught in a desperate defense put up by Youxue and Yi Ping at the same time!

Almost immediately after Yu'Er had given the Divine Dragon Pill to Lingfeng, she was showing signs of revival!

Yi Ping was not slow to react as he had already displayed the Asper Continuum Horizon Hand as he displayed dozens of shadowy flurry of windforce at the Blade Heretic, Blood Heretic and the Moon Heretic at the same time!

After knocking back Lingfeng, the Moon Heretic turned his target towards Xiao Youxue who had the Dragon Divine Pills but he was being blocked by Yi Ping. He mustered a flurrying of martial power that echo thunderous as he shouted angrily, "Your strokes are still not powerful enough to stop me!"

The Blood Heretic had dissolved the Asper Continuum Horizon Hand as he raised all his martial power on Yi Ping, "I let you have a taste of my blood techniques!"

As the Moon Heretic and Blood Heretic raised their martial power with the blue wisps of the Invincible Divine Force speeding and fading in all directions, the entire floor exploded and was being destroyed at the extraordinary display of their destructive martial power! This immediately sent dust, windforce and pebbles flying in all direction!

Yi Ping still refused to let Lie Qing down as he muttered, "Qing'Er, wait me. I come and join you soon!"

Suddenly he gave a mighty shout as he mustered all his martial power, deflecting the speeding projectiles of the debris as he raised his right hand. "The Asper…Divinity…Horizon Hand!"

When Yi Ping had shouted the skill name of the Asper Divinity Horizon Hand, his surroundings immediately exploded into a ring of bursting martial power, knocking Youxue back and the Blade Heretic back even as he stood on his ground to receive the crushing force of the Moon Heretic and the Blood Heretic at the same time!

In that split second and at the same time, Dugu Yunzi had silently drawn out her long sword and was whirling it one wave after another as barely visible blue wisps was swallowed into her sword!

As soon as she had released her flying sword, she said coldly. "The Invincible Divine Flying Sword!"

In that instant, she had sent her flying sword with an extraordinary tremendous speed as it went through the body of the Blade Heretic, splitting him into half, stunning everyone at the same time!

At the same time, Yi Ping martial force had clashed against the martial force of the Moon Heretic and the Blood Heretic with a huge thunderous impact, it sent an exploding ripple of shockwaves around them in a burning fury that caused the three of them to cough out blood!

Even as Yi Ping's Boundless Force was being consumed by the power release of the Asper Divinity Horizon Hand, he had coughed out blood and was knocked back by the powerful combined martial power of the Moon Heretic and the Blood Heretic; he heard a familiar gentle voice saying. "The Invincible Divine Pandora Darkness Merciless Stokes!"

There were loud wailing screams that came from the Moon Heretic and the Blood Heretic as Lie Qing cut them down with two beaming bluish slashes from her Perpetual Darkness with the reflective halo of her darkness merging display as soon as she drawn her precious long sword!

No one had expected a dead Lie Qing to move!

Yi Ping was stunned that he muttered weakly, "I must be hallucinating. Is this an effect of the deviation phenomena after I have used the Asper Divinity for the very first time?"

Lie Qing was stroking her long hair as she said shyly, "What do you think then? Why didn't you let go of me? Do you know that you have almost disrupted Sister Yun and my plans to foil the heretic sect? Do you know that I am trying very hard not to laugh at you?"

But before she could finish, Yi Ping had hugged her tightly as he cried aloud, "Qing'Er, Qing'Er! You are still alive! I am so happy…"

Lie Qing shyly said, "Of course I am still alive, silly!"

Yi Ping muttered tearfully, "But I saw you die right in front of me and your heart had even stopped beating…"

It was true that Dugu Yunzi had stabbed Lie Qing. But because Lie Qing had already perfected her Golden Impervious Body, her wounds were able to close and heal rapidly. That was the effect that they had wanted to fool the eyes of their enemies!

It was true that Dugu Yunzi had strike the defenseless Lie Qing fatally on her heart pulse with the Penetrating Hand. But again, she was protected by her Golden Impervious Body and the inherent force of the Invincible Divine Force. And moreover, Yunzi had also restrained herself!

It was also true that Lie Qing's heart had also stopped beating but it was only because Lie Qing had intentional gone into the state of animated dead on her own accord to hasten her recovery!

Lie Qing whispered almost inaudible as she echoed in Yi Ping's ears with the Great Whispering Skill, "You know that I am dead, yet you refuse to keep your hands off my breasts…I know you are trying to transfer your internal strength to my heart pulse but you seem to be enjoying taking advantage of me. How am I going to get marry in the future, huh?"

Even though it appeared that Lie Qing was rebuking him but she was in fact, extremely touched by Yi Ping undying devotion for her as she continued, "Today, I finally know how deep your love for me is. I don't want to be a Celestial anymore…"

Lingfeng, Youxue, Yu'Er and Mei'Er had overcome their initial shock as they flew towards Yi Ping and Lie Qing with utter elation as they cried out, "Sister Qing'Er! You are still alive!"

Even Gongsun Jing, Nangong Le, Qiu Wufeng, Huo Fu and Ji Wuzheng were teary as they suppressed the rush to give Lie Qing a welcoming hug!

Dugu Yunzi's eyes were in tears as she walked silently besides Yi Ping and Qing'Er.

Yi Ping immediately embraced Dugu Yunzi at the same time as he cried out tearfully, "Yun, I know you will not betray us. I know…I just know…I miss you…do you know how hurt I was when you turn your back on me…"

Dugu Yunzi was trembling as she covered her mouth as she wept, "Even if I am cursed, I will never, never betray you Ping'Er. I would rather die in your stead than allowing you to die."

Lingfeng cried as she held Yunzi's hands, "I am sorry. I have wronged you…"

Youxue was crying as she said, "So am I…Sister Yun, please forgive us! You are the one that saved all of us!"

Even though Yu'Er and Mei'Er were blood soaked, they were so happy to see Lie Qing and Dugu Yunzi on their side again that they were shedding tears of joy and forgetting their agonizing pain!

Dugu Zhen was so startled by the new happenings that she staggered backward even as she looked at Dugu Yunzi hatefully, "My daughter, do you know what you have done? Have you forgotten about the blood curse of the Sacred Divine Clan and the blood oath that you have made?!"

Dugu Yunzi glanced quietly at Lie Qing before she pointed out, "Do you know who she is?"

Dugu Zhen said bitterly, "I don't care who she is. I only want to know, why did you betrayed your oaths, your clan and your mother!"

Dugu Yunzi sighed softly as she said quietly, "Dearest mother, all these years I have never disobey you. It is all over now…"

Lie Qing broke freed of Yi Ping reluctantly. She raised her long black precious sword at Dugu Zhen as she looked at her keenly with her crimson eyes, "Dugu Zhen, from now on. I am your Holy Leader. My commands are absolute and I am above your oaths!"

Dugu Zhen was startled as she asked, "What do you mean?"

Lie Qing answered, "Let me tell you then…"

A day ago in the late of the night…

Lie Qing and Dugu Yunzi were both sitting on the roof of the Holy Chapter as they viewed the lofty Holy Amalgamate Mountains from afar.

Lie Qing said coolly as she stroked her long hair in the cool windy breezes, "You don't have to lie to me. I know from your eyes that you are hiding something from us."

Dugu Yunzi replied quietly, "I have…nothing to hide…"

Lie Qing sighed softly, "Really? Why is that when we walk past that Dugu Zhen, both of you averted your glances with each other and pretending not to know each other? That Dugu Zhen is really a shrewd lady, keenly observing everyone except for you. Isn't that a little too weird?"

When Lie Qing had pointed this out, Dugu Yunzi appeared to be jolted!

Lie Qing continued unhurriedly, "And moreover, I see betrayal in your eyes. I have seen this cold expressionless emotion in the eyes too many times."

She sighed as her tears swelled in her eyes, "In my entire life, I have been betrayed too many times by the people that I have placed my trust in. Moreover, you know that I am a Celestial now and have the ability to divine."

Dugu Yunzi was startled, "You really have the ability to divine?!"

Lie Qing smiled at her, "That is right. All Celestials have the ability to divine. Why do you think Lele sends me here? She knows that you are in trouble and I am the only one that can help you."

Dugu Yunzi was silent for a while as she averted her teary eyes, "I am not as good as what all of you thinks. I am also not as chaste and innocent as the other maidens. Do you know that I am actually from a known heretic sect with an infamous reputation in the martial fraternity?"

She looked teary at Lie Qing with her voice trembling in extreme grief, "Do you know that that I am now being forced by my mother, Dugu Zhen to betray the man that I truly loves? Do you know how heartbreaking my innermost is? Do you know that I am also the Holy Leader of the Sacred Divine Clan and I have to bear the burdens that are placed upon me by the clan elders?"

Her voice grew even melancholy as her tears fell silently, "I only wish to be with Ping'Er but my blood oaths prevented me from betraying my holy sect. Those that betray the Sacred Clan even if they have descendants, the males would be slaves while the females would be prostitutes. They would never enjoy a full life and be cursed for all generations to die of horrible mishap. Anyone that took them in would be met with the same fate too. That is how deadly my blood oaths are!"

Lie Qing was startled.

Dugu Yunzi lamented, "And tomorrow, I have to betray everyone. You have better warn the others and ask them to flee as far as they can. It is because if you stay, all of you will surely die!"

Lie Qing looked at her into her eyes before she said slowly, "Good sister, you are not leaving with us?"

Dugu Yunzi's voice was one of great despair, "By telling you all this, I have already broken my oaths and have betrayed my clan. By going with all of you, I will only be harming Yi Ping and everyone! Please, please leave me alone!"

Lie Qing said quietly, "Good sister, I truly understands what you have been through."

She looked up the skies and at the seven beaming celestial stars above as she said softly, "The Invincible Divine Clan used to be the most powerful heretic sect in the fraternity and we have achieved domination over all the other major martial clans. I am the Heavenly Temptress of the Invincible Divine Clan. After the Invincible Divine Clan had been annihilated by the Celestial Palace, I have founded the Virtuous Palace in the Far East as a remnant of the Invincible Divine Clan to avoid pursues by the enemies of the Invincible Divine Clan. But it was not before long that I was betrayed by my own followers, including your ancestor Ding Jun…"

Dugu Yunzi was startled as she quickly interrupted, "What do you mean by you have founded the Virtuous Palace? Aren't you just a descendant of the Invincible Divine Clan? And what do you mean by, you are the Heavenly Temptress?!"

Lie Qing averted her glances, "I lie. I didn't want anyone to know my true age. Don't you find it weird that the Celestial Liege knows me? The Invincible Divine Clan that he had destroyed is not a recent happening but one that happened a long time ago, before the founding of the Virtuous Palace. That is why I have named our group the New Virtuous Palace so that I can seek vengeance on the present descendants of the Virtuous Palace."

Dugu Yunzi stammered, "How is it possible for you to live this long…it is impossible…then are you really a true Celestial?"

She suddenly gasped, "That means that Celestial Liege was not just stating things metaphorically when he talks about the feud the Celestial Palace had with the Invincible Divine Clan many centuries ago. He was actually there! So my mother and clan elders are not chasing a mad dream but they actually found a way to ascend as a Celestial. Are you really the Heavenly Temptress?!"

Lie Qing nodded as she covered her face with her hands, "I am indeed the Heavenly Temptress and please don't go around telling anyone or I will surely faint. The last time I go to town, my fraternity name seems to be even more notorious than ever before."

She lamented as she cursed softly, "Don't let me catch those rumor spreaders that added to my notoriety or I surely skin them alive! And from what Youxue and you have shared with me, there is also a legend of the red eyes in the Virtuous Palace. It seems that the red eyes of the Celestial Palace that massacred my other clan, the Invincible Divine Clan now become the oppressors of the Virtuous Palace. I was betrayed by your ancestors and they had covered that betrayal with another tale. Those traitors did not want to let their descendants know their evil deeds and had covered everything up."

Dugu Yunzi said, "My ancestor Ding Jun did not betray you. In fact, he had secretly founded the Sacred Divine Clan to honor you and to remind us to destroy the Virtuous Palace one day. But the Virtuous Palace that you have founded has too many super exponents. Moreover the Xiao Clan kept many martial secrets like the Dark Mono Sword Formation to only descendants of the Yuan and Xiao Clan. There are also the secret martial skills of the Eighteen Unbreakable Hands, the three killing techniques of the extinct Southern Isle Clan and others."

All of a sudden, Dugu Yunzi bowed down on her knees, "My respect to the First Grand Protégé Mistress!"

Lie Qing was taken aback but she quickly recovered from her surprise as she smiled mysteriously, "Good sister, don't ever bow to me. I will surely feel very bad. Please get up first. Let me ask you; that mean if the Sacred Divine Clan is created in my name, does it also mean that I can also void all the blood oaths too?"

Dugu Yunzi was startled as she quickly replied, "That's right…in all our ceremonies and oaths; we will always invoke the name of the Heavenly Temptress to be our witness…and her dead spirit to execute the oaths…"

Lie Qing laughed softly, "Oh Heavens! I have become a dead spirit now. That's great. Then, I shall release you from all your oaths. You have never betrayed the Sacred Divine Clan because you have never betrayed me! Then can I just avert this crisis of yours by announcing my presence?"

Dugu Yunzi said quietly, "I am afraid that it is not possible. Many sect elders that had protested against the 'Celestial Pan' as a dangerous gambit that may destroy the clan had all been killed by the Three Evils. Even if you are the Heavenly Temptress, the 'Celestial Plan' cannot be stopped now because the entire Sacred Divine Clan is now so close to becoming Celestials. Moreover, would anyone believe you and believe someone that had never led the clan for even one day of her life? They would rather kill you than believe in you."

Lie Qing smiled bitterly, "I ought to remember this as another betrayal. So much for using my name to unite the scattering protégés into the Sacred Divine Clan and then forgotten about my real person. Oh Heavens!"

Dugu Yunzi, "We should flee on this very night…but for Ji Wuzheng and Sister Lingfeng, would they believe us?

Lie Qing asked, "What if we choose to stay behind and make a stand?"

Dugu Yunzi sighed melancholy, "Sister Qing'Er, you do not know who your opponents are or else you won't think about it. I know very well how powerful the Three Evils of the West are. Moreover they have already merged the Holy Amalgamate Force with the Divine Virtuous Force into a Super Virtuous Amalgamate Force. Any one of them is already considered to be a superior super exponent and moreover there are three of them. Even if Yi Ping and you can defeat them, you may not survive your injuries too. The odds of winning against one of them are fifty-fifty for both sides. But if they joined hands, no one in the martial fraternity will be able to stop them except for the Dark Mono Sword Formation of the Virtuous Palace."

Lie Qing smiled mysteriously, "What if we fight evil with evil?"

Dugu Yunzi asked, "What do you mean, sister?"

Lie Qing turned extremely solemn, "However, this will be very risky for you and you may even be killed by Yi Ping and the rest."

Dugu Yunzi said with quiet determination, "I am not afraid of sacrificing my life for Ping'Er and for the rest of my good sisters, as long as everyone can have a chance of surviving. I am willing to do that!"

Lie Qing said, "This will requires extreme acting skills on our side. I just hope that Yi Ping doesn't make it so hilarious in an otherwise serious situation or the entire plan will come to a futile end. Sometimes you know, like Lingfeng, I cannot resist giving him a hard kick for saying or doing stupid things at the wrong time. Luckily, Sister Lingfeng always gives him a timely hard knock for that or else I surely will be the next to kick him hard!"

Dugu Yunzi laughed softly, "Actually me too…"

But she quickly asked, "What is the plan? Can you divine it first?"

Lie Qing sighed softly, "There is no such thing as divination."

Dugu Yunzi was startled, "But you just say Celestials have the ability to divine and you can see the betrayal in my eyes? You have also said that Lele has sent you here because she has divined that we are in danger?"

Lie Qing smiled weakly, "Good sister, I am sorry. I lie again."

Dugu Yunzi was startled.

Lie Qing said shyly, "Lele don't have any ability to divine. She lies too. It doesn't take a genius to know that all of you are going to be in danger. Because all of us are worry for Yi Ping, it just a convenient excuse to use divination as an excuse for me to come to your aid. She may think I can't tell but somehow I can tell all from her sheepish and subtle expressions. As for the betrayal in your eyes, it is based on my personal experience and not a result of any divination."

Dugu Yunzi was stunned, "Sister Lele and you are really so alike…in many ways. I am beginning to feel that the two of you may be twins in your previous life. Even your mannerism is the same…"

Lie Qing laughed softly, "Is that so? Sometimes I think so as well."

She looked at Dugu Yunzi for a while before she said, "Sometimes I feel that I have known you, Lingfeng, Yu'Er, Mei'Er, Lele, Yixian, Youxue and even Yi Ping from a long time ago too. But that's not important. So here is the plan…the code for action will be Invincible Divine…"

Dugu Zhen laughed coldly as she looked at Ji Wuzheng, Yi Ping, Lie Qing and Dugu Yunzi one by one, "So, that is the plan…what a good plan. We all have been fooled. The three elders are dead now. The Celestial Plan is no more. I have lost everything now."

Ji Wuzheng said quietly, "You have not lost everything. You still have me and you are still the proud mother of our three daughters."

Dugu Yunzi nodded as she cried out, "Dearest mother, you still have your Yunzi!"

Dugu Zhen was stunned as she looked tearfully at Ji Wuzheng, "After all that I did, after you have known that I am from the heretic sect, you are still willing to forgive me?"

Ji Wuzheng reached out for his hands and immediately Dugu Zhen fell into his embrace as he said, "No matter what you did, I am willing to forgive! I can't do with you. I know that throughout the years, you have also done an excellent work in the Holy Hex Sect. No one will need to disclose that you are from the Sacred Divine Clan. It is almost no more now."

Dugu Zhen muttered, "You have no idea how influential is the Sacred Divine Clan. There are still three powerful elders that know my identity that are undercover on the orthodox clans' side."

Ji Wuzheng said, "It doesn't matter. I will protect you even if it means that I have to give up my life for you."

Dugu Zhen sighed tearfully, "You…"

She turned and looked at Lie Qing as she stammered, "Are you really the Heavenly Temptress?"

Lie Qing nodded quietly.

Dugu Zhen fell on her knees as she said, "May Grand Protégé Mistress forgive me for any transgression that I have made. I am also willing to atone for my terrible mistakes!"

Lie Qing said awkwardly as she fingered her long hair in front of her face, "Rise please. Your daughter, Yun is my good sister. How would I have the heart to punish her dearest mother? You just need to reveal to us the further plans of the Sacred Divine Clan as atonement. Then we can prevent a martial calamity from happening."

Dugu Zhen nodded even as Dugu Yunzi and Ji Wuzheng helped her up at the same time while Yunzi said shyly, "Stepfather!"

Ji Wuzheng was very happy, "I have got another daughter now. It is something worth celebrating and I should open my precious wine cellar!"

Huo Fu was rubbing his bloodied face that was mixed with his tears. He had never seen such a moving scene in his entire life before and was quiet the entire time…

All of a sudden, Yi Ping clapped his hands as he said excitedly. "So this is all part of a plan! I almost got fooled by it."

Lingfeng gave Yi Ping a weak kick as she laughed softly, "You are slow, aren't you? And it is not almost. You really got fooled by it."

Yi Ping smiled bitterly, "I almost thought that I have lost Qing'Er and Yun'Er. Qing'Er, Yun'Er, why didn't you tell us your plans beforehand? At least I won't be so panicky!"

He took a quick look around him and nodded silently to Nangong Le, Gongsun Jing and Qiu Wufeng who all gave him a thumb up from afar. "At least we are lucky to have all survived. This is one of the hardest fights that I have ever fought…"

Lie Qing said shyly as her eyes displayed a thousand affections for him, "If we tell you and the sisters first, we will not get the result that we want. You have such bad acting skills, if we tell you first; the plan would be doomed from very start. Also, or else I won't know how much you really care for me."

Dugu Yunzi nodded affectionately at him, "Ping'Er, now I also know how you feel for me…"

Mei'Er exclaimed with a mischievous look in her eyes, "I also want to know how much Master have for me in his heart. Prove to me, Master!"

Yi Ping could only smile bitterly at Mei'Er.

Yu'Er had covered her face at her sister open declaration of her heart. That was really so bold of her sister and she was startled!

Mei'Er said, "Master, I want you to prove it now! Did you not see my injuries and wounds? All these are for you!"

Yu'Er quickly said, "Mei'Er, you are asking Master to prove his love for you and not the other way round!"

Mei'Er protested softly, "Is there a difference?"

Yi Ping bowed to Ji Wuzheng as he glanced at Lingfeng, "Big Brother, I have a favor to ask from you."

Lingfeng was startled as she quickly thought, "Is he asking for my hand? I won't say no if he really asks…"

Yi Ping said, "There are now five Divine Dragon Pills now. One of the Divine Dragon Pills has been taken by Lingfeng and there are only four left. I have two friends of mine who may need the Divine Dragon Pills urgently. Can I have two of the Divine Dragon Pills?"

Ji Wuzheng laughed, "We are brothers. Of course you can have it. Even if you want all of it, I will surely give it all to you!"

Yi Ping said, "That's alright. I don't need more."

Ji Wuzheng said solemnly, "Alas, you should take one for yourself too. These Divine Dragon Pills are actually created from your own hands and I really have no more right to them. What I own is actually the Heavenly Relic and not these Divine Dragon Pills."

Dugu Zhen smiled gently. She was now at peace with herself and did not hunger to be a Celestial anymore. It did not matter even if her husband wanted to give all the precious Divine Dragon Pills away! All she wanted now, was to spend time with Ji Wuzheng…

Yi Ping said to Youxue, "Youxue, can I have two of the Divine Dragon Pills and return two of the Divine Dragon Pills to Brother Wuzheng?"

Youxue quietly opened her hand and revealed only one Divine Dragon Pill as she said sheepishly, "There is only one left now."

Everyone was stunned.

Yi Ping was in a daze as he asked her, "What happened to the other three?!"

Youxue averted her enthralling glances as she said sheepishly, "I have consumed one earlier while you are all talking."

Everyone was stunned.

Youxue explained sheepishly, "I am also seriously injured so I have taken one of the Divine Dragon Pills."

Yi Ping muttered, "I have thought that you have actually consumed three at the same time. You have taken one and where are the other two?"

Youxue pointed at Yu'Er and Mei'Er, "It in their stomachs now."

Yu'Er and Mei'Er too, were sheepish as they said at the same time, "We are injured and we almost die too…"

Mei'Er said, "Or else you won't see me talking to you now. I will be lying there. Is that what you really want to see huh?"

Yi Ping smiled weakly as he sighed, "The Divine Dragon Pills cannot be consumed by practitioners that have less than sixty years of internal strength or it does more harm than good. Youxue has the martial foundation already but the two of you… "

Yu'Er was suddenly afraid and was sorrowful, "Master, will we die?"

Mei'Er said panicky, "But we are feeling a lot better than earlier…"

Lingfeng said anxiously, "I don't have sixty years of internal strength too…"

Youxue quickly said, "There is no need to worry. The Divine Dragon Pill does not necessary need to be used to increase the practitioner's martial strength. It can also be used to save lives. Much of the potency of the Divine Dragon Pill will be consumed during the process of treating your injuries and wounds."

The truth was that Youxue was not confident of what she had said but she withheld her worries.

Yi Ping was a little relieved to hear that.

Huo Fu, Ji Wuzheng, Dugu Zhen, Lie Qing, Dugu Yunzi, Lingfeng, Gongsun Jing, Nangong Le and Qiu Wufeng were all stunned that four out of five of the Divine Dragon Pills had all been consumed at such a rapid rate!

Yi Ping murmured bitterly, "One Divine Dragon Pill is now left. Should I give it to Yixian or Lele?"

When Youxue saw that Lingfeng had really revived so suddenly, she knew instantly that these Divine Dragon Pills were not fakes. All of a sudden, a thought crossed her mind. Lingfeng martial progression would surely advance much faster after consuming the Divine Dragon Pill. If that happened, then Yi Ping would surely trust her more and more. With that thought in mind, she immediately popped in one of the Divine Dragon Pills secretly!

After consuming it, she was overwhelmed with guilt. She had thought that if she could find one or two others to take it too, then she would not feel so awkward later. So she gave one each to Yu'Er and Mei'Er who had also immediately taken it!

Yi Ping said to Youxue, "Do you know that it is improper to take others' stuff first without asking? Didn't your parents or elders teach you that?"

Youxue said coolly, "My father and elders, including my mother just told me that anything that I can lay my hands on, it is mine. It is the responsibility of others to protect what they want. If they can't protect it, then finder is keeper."

Yi Ping was stunned, "Did your parents really teach you that?!"

Dugu Yunzi giggled, "That's right. That is the rule of the Virtuous Palace!"

Yi Ping, Ji Wuzheng, Huo Fu, Gongsun Jing, Nangong Le and Qiu Wufeng were stunned at this revelation.

Yi Ping said to Yu'Er and Mei'Er, "Is that a rule of the Eternal Ice Palace too?"

Yu'Er said shyly, "We have no such rules. But if a good sister offers us something good to eat, it is considered disrespectful not to take it."

There was nothing Yi Ping could do now except to smile bitterly.

Ji Wuzheng laughed, "It seemed that you have a lot of troubles in your hands in future with these maidens. Don't worry too much about the Divine Dragon Pills. You can have them all."

Yi Ping bowed respectfully, "Thank you Brother…"

Youxue, Yu'Er and Mei'Er said at the same time, "Thank you!"

The only person that was sore about the Divine Dragon Pills was actually Lie Qing. She was actually counting the number of state of divinities that she could actually reach with each of the Divine Dragon Pill that had gone up in smoke! "They have no idea how precious the Divine Dragon Pills are…consuming them so recklessly…faint! These Divine Dragon Pills can only be obtainable by the sheer arrangement of destiny and cannot be sought…"

All of a sudden, Yi Ping said to her, interrupting her thoughts. "Qing'Er, I found the name of the Heavenly Temptress to be so familiar. Did you mention that you are a protégé in the Heavenly Temptress Clan? Why have you become the Heavenly Temptress now?"

Lie Qing looked at him as she pretended to be upset, "I don't want to explain to someone as stupid as you. Go figure out yourself!"

Yi Ping was left in bewilderment as he thought, "Did I say something wrong?"

While he was still pondering why, Youxue had quietly fallen into his embrace as she said quietly, "Sometimes it is better not to know too much, as long as everyone can be together…"

When Youxue had fallen into Yi Ping's embrace, Lingfeng, Yu'Er, Mei'Er, Yunzi and Lie Qing had also fallen blissfully into his arms.

The sight was enviable and it seemed that time had stopped for them.

Indeed, for a long time, no one dare to disturb their tranquil gathering!

Nangong Le, Gongsun Jing and Qiu Wufeng were exchanging enviable glances with one another even as they sat on the floor. Their injuries were too heavy for them to move, especially Gongsun Jing who had been fatally slashed by the Blade Heretic on his leg.

Youxue suddenly whispered, "Ping'Er, who does you really like the most? Is it me? Have you already forgotten what we have been through that night?"

Yi Ping was stunned by her question and all of a sudden, he noticed all the other maidens were looking at him with an equally hostile look at each other as they waited for him to answer this question!

Lingfeng warned him gently, "You have better answer correctly or else you will be dead very soon."

Yi Ping smiled most bitterly.

Chapter 57: The Fiery Phoenix and the Blue Heavens Divine Sword

The camps of the orthodox clans were burning furiously and there were chaotic fighting everywhere!

Thousands of exponents from over two hundred martial clans were fighting against one another in great confusion!

Everywhere, there were fallen exponents, the thunderous impact of fists and the shrieking clanging of weapons as martial clan fought against one another.

Everyone was accusing one another to be a heretic exponent as they fought against one another. Most of the accusations were actually false as the martial clans took advantage of the confusion to settle old feuds and realign their alliances.

When the heretic sects had descended upon the camps of the orthodox clans, there were no prior warnings. It was because most of the sentries had already been killed or had been infiltrated by the heretic sects!

Indeed, the extent of the infiltration of the heretic sects were so widespread that the entire orthodox exponents found themselves in great confusion as they fought the heretic exponents and other orthodox exponents at the same time!

Six of the more prominent heretic sects, the Ancient Relic Sect, the Salvation Palace, the Three Swords Clan, the Episode Sect, and the Rhapsody Sect were led by the elders of the Sacred Divine Clan in a sudden attack on the orthodox clans in the dead of the night!

Panic quickly spread throughout the camps of the orthodox clans!

"They are…the heretic exponents! There are so many of them!?"

Among the more than one hundred martial clans, there were more than a dozen martial clans that were secretly aligned with the major unorthodox clans and had infiltrated the camps of the orthodox clans.

Adding to the number of heretic clans and unorthodox clans that were already on the opposing sides, were their infiltrators in the various orthodox clans that deliberately created more confusion and chaos during the attack by misleading the others that the clans that they were in were actually the enemies!

Three immediately factions were fighting for supremacy in the chaos, the Evil Heretic Clans, the Unrighteous Unorthodox Clans and the Righteous Orthodox Clans!

Assembled inside the large tent of the Virtuous Palace were the leaders of the three major Sword Clans; Yan Nanfei the Protégé Master of the Zen Sect, Zuo Tianyi the Protégé Master of the Infinity Sword Clan, and Shangguan Qingyun the Protégé Master of the Divine Sword Martial Clan.

The Honor Manor led by Han Shaodong, Gu Tianle the Protégé Master and the Heartless Scholar who had just assumed the new leadership of the Twelve Golden Halls of the Honor Manor were also presented.

Also presented were the Sword Sage of the Aegis Sword Clan, the Element Sage and his protégé grand-nephew Chi Zhengqi of the Five Element Clan.

Besides Xiao Shuai were Yuan Shao, Xiao Fei and Xiao Ao.

Xiao Ao was the son of Xiao Da. He was casting long glances at Han Xingyue, who was the granddaughter of Han Shaodong. And it was pretty much obvious.

Han Xingyue did not seem to mind the attention given to her. Even though she was no more than twenty and had an innocent and angelic look, Zuo Tianyi and the Lu Baiyun the Heartless Scholar were secretly fearful of her!

When her mysterious gray eyes looked at them, they were immediately seized with fear!

It was because despite her angelic and innocent look, she had seized Zuo Tianyi's divine sword, the Blue Heavens just a few days ago and had severely injured them!

Her real name was actually not Han Xingyue but was Shen Xingyue the Fiery Phoenix. Even though she had been introduced as Han Shaodong's granddaughter, she was actually Han Shaodong protégé mistress!

As a matter of fact, Han Shaodong's Divine Rejuvenation Force was imparted to him by her!

A few days ago…

Lu Baiyun was saying to Zuo Tianyi, "I see that you have a good sword in your hands."

Zuo Tianyi said, "The sword is not unsheathed yet, how do you know that it is a good sword?"

Lu Baiyun said, "I am also an accomplished swordsman myself. The sword isn't unsheathed yet but already I can sense its killing intent. It is a good sword but it is a pity that it is a malevolent sword. If I am not wrong, this sword is a calamity sword and would bring harm only to its master. A swordsman should be in control of the sword and not let the sword controlled him, don't you think so?"

Zuo Tianyi said coldly, "Don't you worry about it. As long as this sword is able to help me to kill my enemies, this is a good sword. With my present attainment, no matter how malevolent this Blue Heavens is, its sword energy won't be able to harm me."

Lu Baiyun laughed, "I am really curious about this sword. May I have a look at it?"

Zuo Tianyi hummed coldly, "If the sword is unsheathed, then it must draw blood. Do you want your blood to be upon this sword? Moreover, the mere sword energy of this sword will only harm you. This is something that you won't be wishing or else the Honor Manor would soon lose one of its most capable fighters."

"What if I want to look at it?" An angelic voice said alluringly.

It was Han Xingyue.

She was always cold and kept to herself. Today was the first time that she had spoken to them.

Zuo Tianyi hummed coldly, "If anything happens to you, how would we answer to Master Han Shaodong. You have better forgotten about it."

Han Xingyue smiled. Her smiles were beautiful and really enticing to behold as she sighed softly, "Is that so?"

Lu Baiyun was looking lustfully at her as he said, "If maiden you are interested in swords and swordplay, you can come to the tents of the Honor Manor and I would be pleased to show you our precious swords."

Han Xingyue had already seized the scabbard from Zuo Tianyi with a startling speed, as she broke the harness of the sword scabbard with her fingers!

Zuo Tianyi was stunned to see this display. Even though he had seen her making her move and was about to stop her; his scabbard was seized right in front of his very eyes! What was even scary about her was that she seemed to have deliberately hinted that she was coming forward and when Zuo Tianyi had raised his hands to stop her, she had simply seized it.

Beautiful or not, whether she was angelic or not and whether she was from the Virtuous Palace or not, Zuo Tianyi's malevolent killing intent was aroused and he raised his sword fingers to stab her. It was because taking and stealing a swordsman's sword was considered to be an act of great sacrilegious. In the fraternity, it was an act that was punishment by death duels on the spot!

Even Lu Baiyun was shocked!

But just as Zuo Tianyi had just raised his sword finger, Han Xingyue had already unsheathed the blue beaming cold blade of the divine sword. When the Blue Heavens was unsheathed, a sudden burst of cold bluish burst of sword energy burst in all directions, fatally wounding Zuo Tianyi and Lu Baiyun as the shockwave of the sword energy sent them flying backward and rolling on the ground in agonizing pain!

Zuo Tianyi was stunned!

It was because even for his state of divinity, he had to be careful about unsheathing this sword and had to use his sword energy attainment to suppress the sword energy of this sword. Even though the Blue Heavens was radiating a powerful sword energy force in his hand, he had never seen this type of sword burst before!

This sword energy display was already the attainment of the Infinity-Zero!

What was even more startling was that Han Xingyue was still standing in the same spot and was not affected by the sword energy burst as she said, "Lucky I am able to have to release the cumulating sword energies of this naughty sword with my Rejuvenate Divine Force or else the backlash would be great. Oh well, it does seem this is a calamity sword. When it is unsheathed, it must draw blood. Luckily, it is not mine."

As she raised the divine sword in her hands, the light of the sun was diffused by the sword and a golden halo formed glaringly on its blade, "So the name of this name is the Blue Heavens."

She sheathed the sword and carelessly threw it down on Zuo Tianyi's feet as she hummed coldly and said disappointing, "It is a pity that this sword has been tainted by a malevolent force that has yet to be dissipated. If you continue to use this sword, you will only be harming yourself."

She looked at Zuo Tianyi and Lu Baiyun as she said, "See, I didn't lie to you am I right? The both of you are now fatally injured by the sword. Unfortunately even if I want to help, I am helpless for your internal injuries are really too severe. You have better rest in bed for the next three months if you value your life."

Zuo Tianyi and Lu Baiyun had turned ashen with agonizing pain as they broke out in cold sweat even as they stared at her with shock.

Han Xingyue said, "I forget to add. Even if you can recover from your internal injuries, your internal strength will be lost forever. But then consider yourselves lucky, lesser mortals will have died immediately."

She appeared to sigh as she talked to herself.

Zuo Tianyi and Lu Baiyun were trembling uncontrollably as they stared at her with burning hatred! They were using all their strength to suppress their agonizing pain and were gagging in pain on the ground. Whenever they mustered the strength to interrupt her, they found no words and instead of words, they had coughed out blood!

Han Xingyue sighed again; she picked up the Blue Heavens again as she kicked it into her hands, saying. "Come to think of that, I guess such a precious sword isn't safe in your hands. What if it would to fall into the wrong hands? Let me keep for you until you are able to handle this sword safely."

She looked at Zuo Tianyi and Lu Baiyun curiously, "Are you trying to say something? I can't hear anything. Maybe you want to cough out all the blood first before you say anything to me? Or maybe you want to beg me to save your lives? Oh very well, even though it is none of my business, I guess I will try to help. I just can't stand emotion distress."

She took out two pills from her pouch as she threw it carelessly onto the ground, "This is the Heavenly Dreams Divine Pills. If you consume it, your internal strength will be protected. After your internal injuries have recovered, it may even receive a significant boast for you! But of course, the side effect is that you must consume one Heavenly Dreams Divine Pill every month or else…"

She appeared to be sad but quickly recovered her angelic composure, "Since I have saved your lives, you must address me as your benevolent mistress when you see me and do my biddings. Or else…"

She looked at Zuo Tianyi, "You know, when a person has saved your lives, even if it takes you an entire life to repay your benefactor, it is never enough. If you are willing, I just take your Blue Heavens as a gift. I take it as a yes then since you didn't protest."

She blinked at them before walking away; leaving Zuo Tianyi and Lu Baiyun alone on the ground as they could only stared bitterly at her with their bloody tears!

That was why they had been so terrified of her when they had seen her standing angelically besides Han Shaodong!

Xiao Shuai was laughing inside the commanding tent of the Virtuous Palace as the chaos outside ensured, "So the heretic sects have finally taken their action."

Yuan Shao nodded, "This is exactly as you have predicted. The heretic sects have seized the three days armistice lull to attack us."

Xiao Shuai said coldly, "The heretic sects are baiting their time for us to annihilate each other as we assaulted the fortress of the Holy Hex Sect and their allies. By announcing a ceasefire and an ultimatum in three days' time, the heretic sects know that the Heavenly Relic and the Holy Maiden would be ours when that time comes."

Han Shaodong added wryly, "When they have taken action against us, we can take this opportunity to weed up all the infiltrators and collaborators as well. In a masterful move, we would get rid of the dangers of the heretic sects."

Xiao Shuai nodded, "Once we get rid of the heretic sects then we will immediately charge up the mountains with our full force and we can accuse the Holy Hex Sect for conspiring with the heretics and breaking the truce."

The Element Sage said solemnly, "There will be many dead and the price will be heavy."

Han Shaodong said, "The fraternity has been too peaceful, producing weaker and weaker exponents every generation. This fight may be costly but it will be helpful for the experiences of the survivors. Our real objective is to ascend to be Celestials and fight the deplorable Celestial Palace. We must not let the Celestial Palace knows that we are already aware of their manipulative influence in the fraternity."

Chi Zhengqi whispered to the Element Sage, "Grandpa, I don't understand. What Celestial Palace and what this ascension means?"

Element Sage whispered, "Keep quiet and listen. You have no right to talk here."

Han Shandong laughed, "Child. Your name is Zhengqi? You don't have to worry. It is something beneficial and good for you."

Chi Zhengqi mustered the courage and said, "The others are fighting with their lives outside. Why are we here and not helping?"

Gu Tianle laughed, "Young man. Five hundred fighters from the Honor Manor are fighting outside already. It is more than enough. We are conserving our strength and waiting for the Three Evils of the West to appear first. If they are not killed, then all our plans will not come into fruition!"

Chi Zhengqi was stunned as he stammered, "The Three Evils of the West! I have heard many terrifying tales of their rampage in the martial fraternity. They will be here tonight?"

Gu Tianle said, "With my protégé master here, the Three Sages, the Virtuous Palace and the protégé leaders of the three major sword clans here, there is nothing for you to fear. However, to lure them out, we must not appear to be prepared first and when they think they can influence the fight with their presence, they will naturally appeared."

Xiao Fei added, "Even though it appeared chaotic outside, there is a perimeter of death around this camp. Our best fighters are lying in ambush for them."

Chi Zhengqi nodded, "So it is actually a plan. But after this fight, do we have the strength to assault the Holy Hex Sect? Most of our fighters would be in need of rest and for their wounds to be tended. I really don't know how we are able to fight the notorious Holy Sectarian Master."

Xiao Shuai was amused by this young man. He had actually smiled and said, "Don't you worry. I have news from my informant that Ji Wuzheng and most of the top exponents of the Holy Hex Sect are injured. This is really the best time for us to attack them. Heavens is really on our side."

Chi Zhengqi looked reassured, "Then I am really relieved. The Holy Sectarian Master and the Righteous Axioms Clan are all vile people. It is really a blessing of the fraternity if we can get rid of them."

Han Shaodong was the old man that day. He had recognized the banner of the Five Element on Chi Zhengqi that day. Suspecting that Chi Zhengqi had been bullied by the Righteous Axioms Clan, he decided to teach those young exponents a lesson. But in the end, he was forced to beat a humiliating retreat.

As this was meant to teach those young exponents a lesson, he had actually restrained himself on them but these young exponents had retaliated with all their skills and he got more than he had bargained for. That was so much for teaching them a 'lesson'.

But now, he knew that they were the notorious Righteous Axioms Clan, he would not restraint himself anymore and moreover, he had to avenge his humiliating defeat and silence them or else his reputation in the annals of the martial fraternity would be tainted.

No matter, he must not let Xiao Shuai know of it or he will be a laughing stock.

So Han Shaodong said, "I didn't know that they are the notorious Righteous Axioms or I really will teach them a harder lesson."

Xiao Shuai said, "It is a lucky thing you did not. I have heard the Holy Maiden is travelling with them. You should have brought her back that day..."

Han Shaodong smiled bitterly when he had recalled that battle that night but he said, "I told you I didn't know they were the Righteous Axioms Clan. Their skills are really mediocre and not a threat to us at all. I got tired of playing with them after a while."

The Sword Sage interrupted, "I am a little worry for the Martial Sage. He has been gone for one week. I suspected that he has gone to the Holy Hex Sect to seek vendetta for the Old Sword Saint."

Xiao Shuai said coldly, "Indeed he has."

The Element Sage interrupted as he asked anxiously, "You know?"

Xiao Shuai said, "Don't worry. He is still alive. He is now a guest of Holy Hex Sect. He is lucky to be still alive after barging into the Holy Hex Sect and has almost screwed up our plans. I hope it is a lesson that he can remember well."

"What lesson?"

An old man with a ruby complexion and a portly tummy was standing at the entrance of the tent. He was the Martial Sage!

Everyone was stunned.

Xiao Shuai asked, "Aren't you being held prisoner in the Holy Hex Sect?"

The Martial Sage laughed, "They are lax and thought that I am too seriously injure to move. They didn't know that I am called the Invincible Ironfist while I was younger. Haha. There are fighting outside and why are all you chatting so leisurely here? Come out quickly. We got a good fight waiting for us!"

He patted his hard body and laughed.

Xiao Shuai was silent for a while before he asked solemnly, "How did you come here? Didn't you see any sentries? Why didn't anyone inform us?"

The Martial Sage laughed merrily, "Oh those? I thought they are on the heretic sects' side when they suddenly attacked me. Don't worry, after a few knocks, they did recognize me and let me through...Haha. I told them not to inform anyone of you. I want to give you all a surprise!"

Han Shaodong said coldly, "Great, great. For a moment, I thought that you almost disable our defenses. Do you know how much effort I have put in that Golden Blades Formation and you have actually survived through it?"

The Martial Sage laughed again, "I recognize how tricky that formation is. After playing with it for a while, I began to shout that I am the Martial Sage. Luckily, there were a few that had already recognized me!"

He had lied of course. All his thoughts were into the breaking of the Golden Blades Formation. It only stopped when the protégés of the Honor Manor were able to immediately recognize him.

The Sword Sage said coldly, "Have you forgotten the real reason why we have come out of our recluse? It is to escape the eyes of the Celestial Palace and eventually ascend as Celestials."

The Martial Sage did not seem to be pleased as he said rudely, "I only know I have here to avenge my brother the Old Sword Saint. This ascension thing is more like a wishful thing. I admit I don't know as much as all of you and never seen a Celestial before. But I know something that all of you don't! Haha!"

The Sword Sage hummed coldly, "Stop beating around the bush and tell us. You will actually know something that we don't?"

The Martial Sage walked into the center of the tent with a jovial expression as he looked at everyone, "I know where Xian'Er is now!"

Almost immediately, the Sword Sage, the Element Sage, Xiao Shuai, Han Shaodong, Yan Nanfei and Shangguan Qingyun were startled.

Yan Nanfei who had been keeping quiet all along stammered, "You know where Xian'Er is now?"

Shangguan Qingyun quickly caught hold of him with trembling hands, "Old fellow, quickly tell me! You have really seen her?"

Besides the Martial Sage, Shangguan Qingyun was also infatuated with Xian'Er. Once he had found a priceless martial treasure, the Divine Dragon Pill. Without a second thought, he had wanted to give it to Xian'Er.

After many years of martial cultivation and mediation, he still could not put down Xian'Er from his heart. He wanted to see her for the last time before he died and was always wondering where she was!

Those that did not know who Xian'Er was had started to wonder who she was now!

Even Shen Xingyue was intrigued for she could see from the startled expressions of these old men that they were familiar with this Xian'Er!

The Martial Sage said, "Even though I have not really seen her but I do recognize the twin swords that she used to carry with her all the time. I say, she must be related to the Holy Hex Sect. Therefore we must not attack the Holy Hex Sect anymore. I see a couple of maidens and they have some of her resemblances!"

Yan Nanfei said, "Let's don't attack the Holy Hex Sect then. If the Holy Maiden is related to Xian'Er, then we are doing her a great disservice. Surely we can find another way to defeat the Celestial Palace and to ascend into Celestials."

Han Shaodong was trembling as he muttered, "Xian'Er, are you still alive after all these years? How long have it been? I really miss you…"

Even the haughty Sword Sage was muttering incoherently now!

The Element Sage asked, "Xian'Er, she is really from the Holy Hex Sect? That is the last place that I have been expecting from."

Xiao Shuai interrupted coldly, "Don't worry so much. Xian'Er isn't at the Holy Hex Sect nor is she related to the Holy Hex Sect. Therefore our plans must continue."

The Martial Sage shouted angrily, "What do you know? I owe my life to Xian'Er in that accursed underground palace ruin. Just because you say she is not there or related to the Holy Hex Sect, do you expect us to believe you?"

Xiao Shuai noted the angry glances and smiled bitterly. At this point of time, he must not allow his plans to come to naught. Even though he was not willing to share with them where Xian'Er was, he found himself left with no choice. "I know where Xian'Er is."

Everyone was stunned.

Han Shaodong shouted at him, "You know where Xian'Er is? And you didn't tell us?! Where is she now?"

The Martial Sage was also shouting, "Xiao Shuai, you old scoundrel. Do you still consider us as your brothers?!"

The Sword Sage was staring coldly at Xiao Shuai.

Xiao Shuai said coldly, "I have originally intended to tell all of you after we have vanquished the Holy Hex Sect so that none of us will be distracted by the forthcoming battles."

Han Shaodong hummed coldly, "So you are saying, only you can be distracted and not us? What a joke? Stop beating around the bush and tell us where Xian'Er is now. Is she well?"

Xiao Shuai said, "She is well. I have seen her. You may have heard of the name of the Celestial Fairy in the fraternity. That is her."

Shangguan Qingyun was shocked, "Xian'Er is the Celestial Fairy? But I have heard that the Celestial Fairy passed away last year…"

Xiao Shuai said, "That is the rumor of the fraternity. She still lives and in fact…"

He pointed at Yuan Shao who was coughing weakly, "…Xian'Er has even injured my benevolent teacher."

Han Shaodong was suspicious, "Xian'Er has the martial skill to injure Yuan Shao? Is that possible?"

Xiao Shuai said, "You have better believe it. Until now, Yuan Shao has not recovered from his injuries and yet to expulse the deadly Icy Heavenly Tears intricate energy from his body."

Yan Nanfei said, "How do we know if you are telling the truth? I trust the Martial Sage more than you. The Eternal Ice Palace is so far away from the fraternity and moreover the Eternal Ice Palace has never entertained any strangers. How do we know you are telling us the truth?"

Xiao Shuai pointed at Zuo Tianyi, Lu Baiyun and Xiao Fei as he sighed. "They have seen her too. If you still don't believe, you can ask them!"

Han Shaodong turned and asked Lu Baiyun, "Is that true?"

Lu Baiyun stammered, "Is true. We have seen the Celestial Fairy and her sight was simply out of the world. I have never any maiden as beautiful as she is."

Han Shaodong slapped Lu Baiyun, "Rubbish! Do you know how old the Celestial Fairy is rumored to be in the fraternity! Beautiful my foot. You don't even know how to flatter us!"

Lu Baiyun was startled as he stammered, "But the Celestial Fairy we have seen is really very young and she is like a goddess…"

Xiao Shuai interrupted with a soft sigh, "That is the truth. I have seen Xian'Er a few months ago. She didn't age at all since we have last seen her and she has even become more elegant in her beauty."

Han Shaodong was startled as he secretly looked at Shen Xingyue before he asked, "Is that possible?"

Xiao Shuai said, "It is only possible if that someone has extreme cold negative internal strength. It happens that the Eternal Ice Palace's practitioners are all cold negative internal strength practitioners."

The Martial Sage said, "Alright, let's say you are right but how do you explain Xian'Er swords that I have seen that were in the Holy Hex Sect?"

Xiao Shuai said, "They are Yujian the Jade Sword Fairy and Meijian the Beautiful Sword Fairy. They are the protégés of the Celestial Fairy."

The Martial Sage was startled. Indeed, he had heard them calling themselves Yu'Er and Mei'Er.

Han Shaodong was stunned. He had fought with Yujian and Meijian before but he had failed to notice the swords that they were wielding hence missing an opportunity to find Xian'Er. He thought, "Is that why Xian'Er has left me? Because I am not as attentive as the Martial Sage?"

The Martial Sage asked aloud, "Is Xian'Er at the Holy Hex Sect now?"

Xiao Shuai shook his head, "Where she is now, even I do not know. But one thing is for sure, Xian'Er seemed to be under the spell of that Yi Ping. Unless we can kill him, we can't save her from his evil clutches."

Chapter 58: The Ascension Sect

It was late at night and Yi Ping had gone down the Holy Amalgamate Mountains alone without a word. He had saw flames rising from the foot of the mountains and knew immediately that something was amiss.

Not even a full day had passed after he had fought with the Three Evils of the West.

He was astonished how light his body had been after he had looked into the Emptiness Translucent silver scroll at the Tranquil Clan. His entire body was energized with rejuvenating vigor that even he could find no words for that. He was now more alert and did not even feel sleepy. The amount of sleep that he required was drastically reduced and even a short nap could rejuvenate him like a full rest.

Upon reaching a sheer cliff below, he mustered his Boundless Divine Force which used to be his Aspire Invocation Force as he jumped down to the ground below. Somehow he knew he could make it through the jump. Indeed, he landed lightly and he heaved a sigh, "I can actually jump from this height? In no time I will be able to reach the mountains below."

He muttered, "Qing'Er, Youxue…Lingfeng, Yunzi…Yu'Er, Mei'Er…forgive me. I don't want to endanger any one of you anymore. Besides Xiao Shuai, Gu Tianle, Zuo Tianyi, Yuan Shao, there are still many more powerful exponents on the opposing side. That old man that we fight on the mountainside is also really deadly. I really don't want to see anyone of you getting injured or even died in front of me anymore."

Something that he could not explain seemed to be drawing him into the camps of the orthodox clans. Somehow he had an uneasy feeling that the truce was not what it seemed to be. He muttered, "Brother Wuzheng, if I enter the orthodox clan camps alone, then it won't constituted as a breach of the truce?"

Just as he had begun to whistle a tune, he sniffed a light familiar fragrant as he looked around him with a startled expression!

Two beautiful maiden with long raven hair, in black velvet had just walked enchantingly into view. They were identical and were laughing softly in the windy darkness.

Yi Ping's heart was beating very fast when he had caught sight of them as he stammered, "Yu'Er and Mei'Er, why are you here? You have not recovered from your wounds yet…quickly turn back!"

Yu'Er flew to him immediately as she looked up to him, "Master, our injuries are almost healed. The Divine Dragon Pill may be a little hard to swallow but it is quite effective in treating our injuries. Other than feeling just a little weird, we are really alright."

Mei'Er was also besides Yi Ping in an instant as she sighed softly on his neck, "Master, you are thinking of abandoning Mei'Er and goes down the mountains alone? I want to fight besides you, no matter how difficulty the road in front is. You are not going anywhere without us and we are not allowing that to happen."

Yi Ping smiled bitterly, "It is too dangerous, Yu'Er and Mei'Er. Go back, I command you…"

Yu'Er interrupted, "Look over there first."

Yi Ping turned and saw four extremely beautiful maidens were standing near the edge of the mountain slope below and they were casting forlorn glances at him; indeed they were Lie

Qing in her elegant pink dress, Yunzi in her gray robe, Lingfeng in her white garb and Youxue in her light yellow long dress.

Yi Ping was stunned, "They are also here?!"

Mei'Er laughed softly, "We have been waiting for you for quite some time. So what's take you so long to be here?"

Yu'Er added, "It is either you go back, let us come with you or…"

Mei'Er continued, "Or…you just have to follow us to protect us!"

Yi Ping signed in resignation as he held their hands, saying aloud in a clear audible voice. "Let's go!"

Lie Qing, Youxue, Lingfeng and Yunzi had heard him and they were smiling and had immediately turned around and were hopping down the mountains in advance!

When Yi Ping and his companions reached the camps of the orthodox clans, it was already daybreak and the mayhem that they had seen were simply too appalling!

Thousands of exponents were lying on the ground and several hundreds were still fighting and there were also many individual duels!

But when Yi Ping had hopped into their midst, the fighting between the exponents ceased all of a sudden!

Whether the exponents were the orthodox exponents, the unorthodox exponents or the heretic exponents, they had all paused in their tracks!

Yi Ping was startled for everyone was now staring in his direction, causing him to be extremely awkward!

His original intention was to muster a martial shout to get all the fighting exponents' attention but as soon as he had flew into the camp, the fighting had totally ceased!

While the exponents were fighting, their sixth sense alerted them to the presence of a righteous air that had suddenly descended upon them!

This was totally different from the usual killing malevolent air and in each of every single exponent's heart; a weird throbbing feeling had suddenly seized them!

When they had all turned around, they were stunned to see that the righteous air had come from a young handsome man in white who had with him two sword scabbards by his side. Somehow this insignificant young man was the very source of their attentions and there was a mystifying magnetism around him!

They were further stunned when almost immediately after the young man had arrived, six extraordinary beautiful maidens had also appeared into view next to him. Awed by their unbelievable beauty and their elegance expressions, all the exponents began to lower their weapons or soften their combat stances!

Quite a few exponents had already recognized Yi Ping as the young hero that had dared to come on his own to challenge Gu Tianle, Jue Yuan and Zuo Tianyi as they muttered among themselves, "I recognize him. He is Yi Ping…"

Yi Ping shouted aloud as he mustered his martial power, "Everyone! Stop fighting…"

The martial power of his shout was so pure that his shouts could be heard clearly throughout the entire camp and even resonated a few times. Immediate, even the doubtful exponents were immediately in awe of his internal strength!

Mei'Er was giggling to Lingfeng in an almost inaudible whisper, "They have already stopped fighting!"

Yi Ping had overheard Mei'Er as he hummed softly before he shouted again, "Everyone, listen to me. Go back to where you have come from! This fight is meaningless!"

Some exponents were muttering, "Even if we want to retreat, would the heretic exponents spare us?"

Dugu Yunzi stepped out as she eyed the heretic exponents. She knew that they were unwilling to reveal their names and she had no intention of letting the others know that some of the surviving heretic exponents that were looking at them now were actually her clan elders and protégés!

So she said, "I am the Holy Leader of the Sacred Divine Leader. My holy will is the holy execution."

She raised her long sword elegantly and said demurely, "Sacred Divine of the Heavenly Temptress Will, I command all the Sacred Divine protégés to go now!"

If she had come earlier, the elders of the Sacred Divine Clan may not want to listen to her as they were waiting for the Three Evils to reinforce them. But they had not turned up and most of their numbers were either dead, wounded or suffered from extreme fatigue from the fighting throughout the night. Upon seeing righteous air of Yi Ping and the extraordinary air of their Holy Leader, the elders of the heretic sects shouted, "Go!"

Immediately hundreds of exponents began to pull out of the vicinity, carrying their dead and wounded with them!

The orthodox exponents did not stop them and were only too relieved.

Lingfeng said coolly, "I am the Holy Maiden of the Holy Hex Sect. Those who are weary and did not want to fight anymore can just leave. The Holy Hex Sect does not have the desire to dominate the martial fraternity. The death of the Old Saint was just the result of a friendly duel between my brother and the Old Sword Saint. Whether you believe or not, it is up to you."

It was mostly the exponents from infiltrators and those clans that had suffered a crushing defeat at the hands of the other clans that had heeded her advice and began to withdraw. But the vast majority of the clans remained!

Lingfeng had no sympathy for these unorthodox clans for they did not fight on the same side as the Holy Hex Sect. Most of the unorthodox clans presented were actually on the side of the Honor Manor and had raised the pretentious banner of righteousness!

This was the martial fraternity, where the lines between orthodox and unorthodox clans were sometimes extremely blurred. If an unorthodox clan joins the orthodox clan, then it gained fame and was considered to be an orthodox clan by the heroes of the fraternity. But if an unorthodox clan joined the Holy Hex Sect, then it was considered to be an evil sect and was branded as an unorthodox clan or a heretic sect!

Even the majority of the orthodox clans were not spared the clan struggles within the orthodox martial fraternity. To be just an orthodox clan required a proven action. It was because an orthodox clan was not yet a righteous orthodox clan and not yet a major orthodox clan!

That was why there were over two hundred martial clans, big and small that flocked to the righteous banners of the Honor Manor, which was leading martial clan in the fraternity. Through the success of the Honor Manor, all the clans presented would be able to gain renowned for their clans!

Youxue said coldly, "They are consumed by their lust for the martial secrets of the Holy Hex Sect. Now that the heretic sects have retreated, they are all thinking that they may stand a chance to storm the Holy Chapter Citadel. Even if most of them are injured, they will crawl up the mountains for a chance for glory."

There was a cold laughter that shook the surrounding!

It was Xiao Shuai!

Behind him were Yuan Shao, Han Shaodong, the Sword Sage, the Element Sage and many others!

Five hundred fresh elite exponents from the Twelve Golden Halls of the Honor Manor had also appeared as they quickly surrounding Yi Ping and his companions!

But it was not Xiao Shuai or the five hundred fighters that had surrounded them that had startled Yi Ping. It was because he had caught sight of an angelic young maiden that had walked into view. Immediately they had exchanged glances as the angelic young maiden was also looking at him at the same time. Even though this was the first time that Yi Ping had caught sight of her but he immediately murmured, "The Dark Enchantress of the West…"

Lie Qing had also noticed her and had heard him as she whispered, "You know her?"

Yi Ping shook his head even as all the maidens were secretly annoyed with him. They were all curious who this angelic maiden was and what was her relationship with Yi Ping!

Lie Qing asked, "Then how did you know her name? Don't you tell me, you know her name in a dream?"

Yi Ping smiled bitterly.

Lie Qing whispered softly, "Be wary of her. She may be a difficult exponent to handle. If I am not wrong, she is already a Celestial and one with extremely high attainment. When a Celestial has reached past a certain attainment, the eyes will turn to gray. That means that she has already got past to the Celestial Divine Stage of Crisis and soon about to Ascend. That's why she could disguise her crimson eyes."

Yi Ping smiled weakly, "Indeed she has gray eyes. But isn't that a strange thing? Only blind people have gray eyes. Don't tell me she is blind?"

Lie Qing stomped on his foot hard as she rebuked him lightly, "Does she look like a blind maiden to you?"

Yi Ping shook his head as he said, "No…"

Lie Qing said, "This is the sign of a Celestial Ascend. It is called the darkness before the light. When she has ascended successful, then her eyes will turn golden! At that point of time, even if all of us joined hands together, we may not be able to defeat her. Unless, of course we are all Celestials and with at least one of us beyond the Crisis level."

Lie Qing did not continued anymore because Xiao Shuai had approached within their hearing range!

When Yi Ping had looked intently at the exponents that had surrounded them, he had recognized Yan Nanfei and Shangguan Qingyun among them. He immediately bowed silently with his hands politely when he saw them!

Xiao Shuai had walked in front of Yi Ping but he had maintained a considerable distant away from Yi Ping as he laughed, "What do we have here? The Holy Leader of the leading heretic sect and the Holy Maiden of the leading unorthodox sect are both here? It seems that I do not need to expend any efforts and you have already fallen into my hands. So Yunzi, you are actually the Holy Leader of the Sacred Divine Clan. This is really a surprise. Even though I have suspected the Ding Clan to be associated with the heretic sect but I have never expected the Ding Clan to be the famous Dugu Clan."

Dugu Yunzi interrupted coldly, "That's right. I am Dugu Yunzi, the Holy Leader of the Sacred Divine. Let me introduced you to my grand protégé mistress the Heavenly Temptress. She is the founder of the Sacred Divine Clan and the Virtuous Palace."

Lie Qing stroked her long hair as she smiled mesmerizing, "Alas, my grand protégé descendants. Why didn't you greet your grand protégé mistress?"

Xiao Shuai laughed coldly and eyed her with scorn, "You are the Heavenly Temptress? I am afraid that you are several centuries too late! Don't make me laugh. You are nothing but a pretty face. Not only will the Virtuous Palace not let you off but the rest of the martial clans will also do the same too. You are the descendant of the red eyes clan and we all know that you live by feasting on human blood and hearts!"

After he had coolly rebuked the young and mesmerizing Lie Qing who had claimed to be the Heavenly Temptress, he had expected thunderous shouts and cheers from his side but instead there were total silence!

He turned around and was startled to see Xiao Fei and Xiao Ao were smiling in idiocy at Lie Qing, Youxue, Lingfeng, Yu'Er, Mei'Er and Dugu Yunzi.

There were not the only ones; the Element Sage and his grand protégé nephew Chi Zhengqi were both staring dreamily at them. There were also Shangguan Qingyun, the Martial Sage, Yan Nanfei, the Sword Sage and even Han Shaodong!

For a moment he was too speechless to continue until Yi Ping interrupted him, "You are as stupid as me. I didn't figure out the last time but now I finally do. The Heavenly Temptress is but a hereditary title. That is why Qing'Er is the Heavenly Temptress. Now you got it?"

Immediately, Lie Qing and the other maidens had burst out in soft laughter as they chuckled softly.

Lingfeng was laughing so much till her eyes had turned watery as she said to Yi Ping, "You are… (chuckle)…so smart (chuckle)…now!"

If the maidens did not laugh, then it would not be that bad for Xiao Shuai's side. Once they had started laughing unwillingly, their every single gesture had melted the hearts of all the onlookers, as they had never seen such a mesmerizing carefree natural laughter. Immediately, the fighting spirits of the exponents seemed to drop drastically. Even the evil exponents that were looking lustfully at them could not find the heart to hurt them.

Even Zuo Tianyi was muttering, "Yunzi…if I want you to come back to me now, is that possible?"

Yi Ping was startled by the maidens reactions as he thought, "This is a serious moment. Why are they laughing at Xiao Shuai?"

From Yi Ping's blank expression, Lingfeng knew that Yi Ping did not know that they were laughing at him. When she had finally thought she could stop laughing, Yi Ping's blank expression made her laughed jovially again.

Even Youxue, who usually would not laugh easily, was smiling jovially.

Xiao Shuai did not know why they were laughing too…

He turned to stare fiercely at Youxue as he appraised her, "My daughter. Do you know that I have been looking everywhere for you? It has been three, four years now? You have grown up now and have grown into a true beauty. How old are you when you left the Virtuous Palace? Sixteen?"

Youxue laughed softly, "If you want to know how many Golden Rejuvenation Pills I have left now, I can tell you. I have finished all of it."

Xiao Shuai was stunned as he thought miserably, "My precious…Golden Rejuvenation Pills…"

When Youxue saw his disappointed expressions, she added cheekily. "If you are looking for the Heavenly Relic to ascend as a Celestial, you can also forget about it. That is because Yi Ping has destroyed it during the battle with the Three Evils."

Xiao Shuai was stunned.

After some time, he asked. "Where are the Three Evils now?"

Youxue said coldly, "They have already ascended as the Three Celestials of the West and have gone to the Blissful Realm of the Western Paradise now. They are one step earlier than any one of you!"

Xiao Shuai was even more startled when he had heard that, as he muttered. "Xiao Fan didn't say a word to me…those bastards…they have already ascended…all our plans for nothing now…"

Youxue said, "You don't have to worry for Xiao Fan. He has been enlightened by the Three Celestials of the West and has gone to become a monk now."

Xiao Shuai nearly suffered a heart-attack after hearing bad news after bad news.

Xiao Youxue was not telling the truth. She just enjoyed tormenting Xiao Shuai.

Xiao Shuai said coldly, "Do you know how precious these Golden Rejuvenation Pills are and how much effort that I have put to obtain it? Do you know that with these Golden Rejuvenation Pills, I would have perfected the Divine Virtuous Force and learnt the Golden Impervious Body? Do you know that the Virtuous Palace depends on these Golden Rejuvenation Pills to help us to ascend as Celestials and saved our lives later?"

Xiao Youxue said melancholy and her eyes had turned teary, "Do you know that I am your daughter and not your tool? You really want to drink my blood then you will be content?"

Xiao Shuai was a little startled when he saw her tears.

Just as Yi Ping was about to step forward to clarify, Lingfeng had immediately jabbed him and took a quick telling glance at him. He could only smile bitterly and kept quiet.

Xiao Shuai beamed with anger, "My two sons, Xiao Yuanjia and Xiao Da, who among you have killed them!"

Yi Ping immediately said coldly, "I am the one! I am Yi Ping, son of Yi Tianxing!"

There were a sudden mutterings among the older exponents who seemed to recognized Yi Tianxing's name!

Lie Qing and Dugu Yunzi gasped secretly. It was because Yi Ping was taking all the blame for them upon himself!

Xiao Shuai stared at Yi Ping coldly, "So it is you! I promise you that you won't be able to leave this place alive!"

Xiao Shuai said to Han Shaodong and Gu Tianle, "Order your men to attack them at once!"

Yu'Er interrupted, "You are not fighting us yourself? You are the one that is talking so much!"

Xiao Shuai hummed coldly, "Young lass, if it isn't for your protégé mistress I would have taught you a lesson now for being disrespectful to me. Even your protégé mistress dares not be disrespectful to me and you have the cheek to give me a lecture. I am not teaching this young man a lesson personally because I am his senior. I don't want the heroes of the fraternity to laugh at me for bullying a young man!"

Yu'Er and Mei'Er hummed coldly.

Yi Ping had already stepped forward as he raised his hands with the Heavens Horizon Stance!

He whispered to his companions, "Step aside. Remember what you have promised me earlier while we are coming down. Only when I am in trouble, you can aid me or else I won't allow any one of you to follow me."

All the maidens sighed softly and looked affectionately at Yi Ping. Even though they were not willing to let Yi Ping fight alone but they knew that at this moment, they must support him quietly so that he would not be distracted in this crucial battle. They could only nod reluctantly...

Yunzi sighed secretly, "It is obvious that they are trying to force him into exhausting his strength."

These five hundred exponents that had surrounded Yi Ping were the best fighters that were selected from the Honor Manor, the Infinity Sword Clan, the Divine Sword Martial Clan and many more!

And these five hundred fighters were placed under the alliance leadership of the Honor Manor!

Han Shaodong took a glance at Shen Xingyue for further instructions.

She nodded slightly.

Earlier, Shen Xingyue was startled to hear the powerful echoing of martial force that had swept throughout the vicinity and was amused that someone was actually expending his martial power even before the battle had begun.

The entire contingency led by Xiao Shuai were alarmed that the fighting had suddenly stopped. When Yi Ping had displayed his martial force shout, Xiao Shuai had led them outside to confront the intruder. This intruder turned out to be just a handsome young man with a righteous air, surrounded by six heavenly maidens!

When Shen Xingyue had caught of Yi Ping, Lie Qing, Yu'Er and Mei'Er, she almost gasped in disbelief! It was because she had recognized the four of them!

Even though they were all slightly different now but due to her superior state of divinity, she could recognize them as a previous incarnation of a former Celestial that she had known!

The young maiden who was wielding the divine sword Perpetual Darkness, was in fact Luminous Star, one of the Three Star Sisters of Fate. She had recognized the Perpetual Darkness because that was originally her divine sword but she had lost it during a deadly fight.

But now, when she had reached out to her aura sense towards the Perpetual Darkness, she was met with rejection from her very own sword!

She immediately thought with a sense of loss, "Don't tell me, she has successfully merged into one with the Perpetual Darkness?"

But she quickly got over the loss as she remembered that she had found another divine sword, the Blue Heavens that could also aid her in her ascension. The Perpetual Darkness was a true sword of calamity and was a sword of great darkness. Unless the practitioner had entered the darkness itself and found the light within, then it would be disastrous for the practitioner eventually.

Many years ago, an old Ascended Sage had given her first artifact, the Divine Sword Perpetual Darkness. Even though he had warned her not to pry too deep into the mysteries of the Perpetual Darkness as she could ruin her state of divinity, she did not heed his advice as artifacts of any kinds was simply too rare even for the Celestials.

Because she wanted to ascend as soon as possible and to reach new stages of divinity, she could not resist the temptations of the Perpetual Darkness and started practicing the divine stages of the Perpetual Darkness. In time to come, among the Celestials, she was to be known as the Dark Enchantress of the West.

Because in the realm of the Celestials, those who possessed a Heavenly Relic were rare enough, she was soon known as a First Celestial. The difference between a First Celestial and a normal Celestial indicated the difference in actual supremacy between the two.

At that time, the Celestial Realm were divided into three main fractions, the Ascension Sect which she belonged to, the Great Quiescent Sect and the Melody Palace. There were other Celestials that did not belong to the three main fractions and were known as the Autonomous Celestials.

Luminous Star was from the Melody Palace while this young man who called himself Yi Ping was known as the White Sage of Emptiness and he was from the Great Quiescent Sect.

She was also known as an Ascendant as she was from the Ascension Sect, so were the twin maidens who were in the same sect as her. The twin maidens were then known as the Eclipse Heaven Goddess and the Axis Heaven Goddess. They were two of the most supreme Ascendants in the Ascension Sect, able to divine all the celestial signs and constellations.

Even though she was a First Celestial herself, the Eclipse and Axis Heaven Goddesses were still supreme. Even in the Ascension Sect, they were a mystery. But one thing was for sure, they had already reached the Ascend Level as evidenced by their golden eyes! It was rumored that that the Eclipse and Axis Heaven Goddess had already survived through a cycle of the Calamity Star in the past. Even though they were in the same sect but they hardly knew one another; all the Celestials lived in isolation from one another.

When the Calamity Star had suddenly descended one day, panic quickly spread throughout the Celestial Realm. It was because most of the Celestials had never experienced the cruel realities of the event known as the Divine Descendant in their life before, which was the opposite of the Divine Ascendant. This was also the only time that the Celestials were allowed to kill other Celestials without incurring the Divine Calamity and the Divine Wrath.

When the Celestial Descendent happened, every year for the next seven years the Celestials must kill another Celestial and absorbed their celestial force to avert the calamity of the Divine Descendant. This virtually forced the weaker Celestials to fight for their own survival.

There were many stronger Celestials that refused to partake in the killing but after experiencing the deadly calamity effect of the Divine Descendant during the first year, most were too scared or too seriously injured to experience the Divine Descendant a second time and one year was not enough for them to fully recover!

In their weaken state, most of the stronger Celestials who were still recovering from the Divine Descendant were killed by the weaker Celestials who took the opportunity to kill the weaken First Celestials and seized their artifacts!

By the second year, the terrible reality had sunk into the hearts of all the Celestials. No one wanted to destroy their years of cultivation and be killed. A full scale terrible Celestial war began. Many Celestials were killed, including Celestials that were Crisis Level and Ascend Level!

The Ascension Sect was the biggest and most powerful celestial sect, with many Celestials of Crisis Level (gray eyes) and Ascend Level (golden eyes). It was plain obvious that the other Celestials were being outclass by the more numerous and powerful Ascendant Celestials.

Maybe it was precisely the Ascendant Celestials were too powerful; many of them had actually belittle their opponents and were careless. In the end, they paid the price for being careless with their lives!

She could still remember that day vividly. She had arrived too late to lend the Eclipse and Axis Heaven Goddesses a helping hand. To her horror, they had already fallen on the ground and their eyes seemed to be pleading at the White Sage of Emptiness for mercy.

A fierce fight broke out between the two of them.

If the White Sage of Emptiness had not fought with the Eclipse Heaven Goddess and the Axis Heaven Goddess, she might not be his match. She had recently heard that he had even defeated the Three Star Sisters of Fate. She shuddered to think that what kind of a person he was and what was his level of attainment that even the deadly Celestial Star Formation could not stop him? It was because the Three Star Sisters of Fate was feared for their deadly Celestial Star Formations and few Celestials dared to trifle with them on account of that.

Maybe it was because the White Sage of Emptiness had exhausted himself during the epic fight with the Eclipse Heaven Goddess and the Axis Heaven Goddess, she soon found herself gaining the upper hand!

Just when she was about to kill the White Sage of Emptiness, she was startled to be attacked by the Eclipse and Axis Heaven Goddesses at the same time. Injured by the sudden attack, she had slipped and fell down to the mountain gorges below!

She survived the fall but had lost all her celestial force. It was a lucky thing that she had practiced a type of divine martial art called the Divine Rejuvenation Force. But maybe it was because she had lost all her celestial force, she was also spared the visitation of the Divine Descendant.

Because she had lost her divine sword during the fall and had survived, she gave herself a new celestial name, the Fiery Phoenix! The phoenix was a sign of rebirth. After she had lost her Perpetual Darkness, she forced herself to relearn the Divine Rejuvenation Force again. To her surprise, she made several breakthroughs with the Divine Rejuvenation Force and in her celestial levels after spending more than a thousand years in quiet recluse!

Without the Perpetual Darkness and with a thousand years of quiet time, she had by now broken through the Crisis Level and was now a Supreme Celestial!

To her stunning surprise, when she had visited all the old haunts of the Celestials, she had discovered that she was the only one left. What had exactly happened in the aftermath of the Divine Descendant? Had all the surviving Celestials ascended to the ninth heavens already?

Even though the Divine Descendant was harmful, it had the effect of shortening the Ascend period and returned an auspicious omen when it was time for the Celestial to face the Ultimate Divine Wrath. Once a Celestial reached the Ascend Level, they still had to face one major tribulation in the form of an Ultimate Divine Wrath in order to ascend successfully. Because the Ultimate Divine Wrath was so deadly, an auspicious omen was much needed to lessen its malevolent power for the Celestial to overcome it.

Even though the betrayal had helped her instead of harming her but to this day, she was still bitter about it. Imagine if you were her, having come all the way to lend her fellow Ascendants a helping hand and moreover they were the Supreme Celestials of the Ascension Sect. In the end, instead of appreciating her, they had attacker her!

All of a sudden, her thoughts were distracted by the cries of five hundred exponents that had charged and had surrounded Yi Ping!

Yi Ping had displayed a flurrying of blows and immediately the windforce of his Divine Horizon Hands caused a dozen exponents to fall and roll on the ground with cries of pain!

Barely had a dozen exponents fall onto the ground, Yi Ping had displayed the Asper Continuum Horizon Hand in a desperate bid to deal with the more capable fighters that were all displaying their best killing techniques on him!

Immediately, more than two dozen exponents were rolling on the ground after they were struck by the irresistible martial force of the Asper Continuum Horizon Hand!

Even before the confusion had ended, Yi Ping had dashed through the hundreds of exponents as he displayed his Divine Horizon Hands, felling dozens with every change of stance as he displayed strokes after strokes!

All the exponents were astonished!

It was because they had never seen anyone who could move so fast, while changing stances with such lighting speed at the same time!

Even Lie Qing was stunned.

It was because the Divine Horizon Hands and the Asper Continuum Horizon Hand was a type of martial art that consumed a lot of martial power and strength. That was why it had to be displayed while stationary to conserve as much martial strength as possible. After displaying it, the practitioner would be tired and continuous display of the same stance would only cause the stances to be weakened and hence become an exploit for the opponents!

But Yi Ping was just displaying his Divine Horizon Hands as he walked swiftly in all directions, knocking one powerful exponent after another!

Even Xiao Shuai was taken aback as he secretly muttered, "He still have so much strength? I barely even step back to relax and one hundred expert exponents are now lying on the ground!?"

Han Shaodong was shouting, "Readied the sword formations and don't panic! Fight martial power with martial power."

Gu Tianle was enraged as he shouted, "Are you guys all lambs? Use all your strength and don't underestimate your opponent."

He was so enraged that he mustered his martial power and leapt towards Yi Ping as he shouted angrily, "Young man, do you dare to accept my Ultrapowerful Force!!!"

Immediately the surrounding air around Gu Tianle was busting with his martial power and the harnessing of his windforce. Everyone knew that this was the moment that they were all waiting for; the clash between the Ultrapowerful Force and the Asper Horizon Hand!

Xiao Shuai, Han Shaodong, the Martial Sage, the Sword Sage and the Element Sage were both humming coldly to themselves as they thought, "Your grandfather is an old friend of ours. We all know the weakness of the secret techniques of the Divine Horizon Hands and the weakness of the Divine Horizon Hands itself. You can only use it at most just a few times. Then you will be overcome by exhaustion and will eventually succumb!"

Yi Ping was still sweeping and fighting the exponents with the Divine Horizon Hands when Gu Tianle had leapt upon him with the Ultrapowerful Force. But he simple raised his hand up with a simple movement and there were a thunderous explosive impact as he sent Gu Tianle flying in the opposite direction, as he crushed and landed with a huge thunderous impact!

Lingfeng, Yunzi, Yu'Er, Mei'Er, Youxue and Lie Qing were so worried when Gu Tianle had suddenly interfered in the battle and had started the battle with his famous technique, the Ultrapowerful Force!

When Gu Tianle was sent flying in the opposite direction, all the maidens were baffled as they secretly gasped, "What is this martial force?! How did his martial power improved so tremendous? He wasn't this strong when he was fighting against the Three Evils. Did he secretly consume the Divine Dragon Pill?"

That was actually Yi Ping newly acquainted Boundless Divine Force. When used together with his absolute equilibrium martial force and with the Circular Rejuvenation of the Origin, Yi Ping martial power had not only increased tremendous but he was also regaining back his martial strength rapidly if his opponents were not on par with him, allowing his unconsumed martial power to be converted back to his martial strength again!

The maidens were not the only one that were surprised, Xiao Shuai and most of the exponents were all stunned that Gu Tianle, a super exponent could be flung off so effortless!

While they were stunned and were looking at Gu Tianle who was struggling to get up again, Yi Ping had fell another fifty exponents onto the ground!

Shen Xingyue inhaled deeply as she calmed down. She was startled when Gu Tianle had suddenly jumped into the battle. "I am worried for him? No…I just want to kill him myself…"

Zuo Tianyi had a burning hatred for Yi Ping as he stepped forward while saying coolly, "Let me take care of him. I just happen to know his fatal weakness."

Chapter 59: The Number One Swordsman in the Fraternity

Yi Ping's arms and hands were now trembling as he deliver blow after blow.

Even though it appeared that he had the upper hand but there were simply too many exponents; out of five hundred, only a hundred odds had actually fallen. The rest of the exponents were the best of their generation and they were now encircling Yi Ping as they looked for a weakness to deal him a death blow!

These exponents were not weak. Among them were several exponents that were even more skillful than the Four Young Masters of the Martial Fraternity. These exponents also consisted of many experienced elders of the various martial clans!

Many of the exponents were at first taken by surprise by Yi Ping's tremendous martial force. Even though many had fallen to the ground with one hit, they soon picked themselves up and adjusted their fighting strategies accordingly. This was because Yi Ping did not really used all his entire martial force to deal any fatal blows; he was just content to knock the attacking exponents aside as he moved on to fight the other standing exponents!

The protégés of the Zen Sect had organized themselves into their Seven Stars Illusionary Sword Formation, with each formation consisting of seven protégés and they had formed seven waves of the Seven Stars Illusional Sword Formation as they descended upon Yi Ping on all sides!

The Seven Stars Illusionary Sword Formation emphasized on feigns and sudden attack movements to trap and assault the opponent. The effectiveness of this type of sword formation was especially deadly against a lone opponent!

The Infinity Sword Clan was also executing the massive attacking movement of the Infinitude Sword Formation now. This type of formation was dependable on the changes of the Infinity Swordplay. Each of the fighters in this formation was an individual as well as a part of the Infinitude group.

Yi Ping was dazzled by the wavering display of the Infinity Swordplay in all directions. It was a lucky thing that he was quite familiar with the Infinity Swordplay as he had fought with Zuo Tianyi on a number of occasions and had the Absolute Spirits to fortify his willpower or else he would have panicked and had been killed by now!

As the five hundred exponents were all from different martial clans, there were also many other formations and extraordinary martial skills that were being displayed at the same time against him.

In additional to these five hundred exponents, an additional two hundred exponents that could still fight could not resist the temptation to join in the fight against Yi Ping as well!

All the onlookers were gasping and muttering among themselves as they watched some of the most intrigue strokes that they had ever seen being displayed right before their eyes!

Lingfeng, Lie Qing, Yunzi, Yu'Er, Mei'Er and Youxue were watching the fight keenly as they were concerned for Yi Ping's safety.

Gu Tianle had just coughed out a mouthful of blood and was struggling to stand when Zuo Tianyi had said suddenly, "Let me take care of him. I just happen to know his fatal weakness."

Xiao Shuai, Han Shaodong, the Martial Sage, Shen Xingyue and all the exponents that were on the side of the Honor Manor had overheard Zuo Tianyi was intrigued by his statement and their curiosity were aroused.

Gu Tianle was muttering, "I didn't use my full strength because that Yi Ping is my junior. Now I am not going to show any mercy…"

Han Shaodong raised his hand in front of him as he whispered, "Don't be hasty first. Let see what this Zuo Tianyi can do. He seems to have a vendetta with this Yi Ping."

Gu Tianle sighed as he stared fiercely at Yi Ping. He was the Master of the Honor Manor. For him to suffer such a humiliating defeat in the presence of his protégés and the heroes of the fraternity was a great loss of honor.

Shen Xingyue was also startled by the claims of Zuo Tianyi and she was looking curiously at him now.

Chi Zhengqi had noticed that she was eyeing Zuo Tianyi and he was overcome with envy so he said to her, "He sure knows how to boast. I say, my martial skills are even better than him!"

Xiao Ao who was also pursuing Shen Xingyue said quickly, "When we are alone, I will show you the intrigue swordplay of the Virtuous Palace and you will know that the Virtuous Swordplay is the best in the entire martial fraternity!"

Xiao Fei was rubbing his nose as he looked inquisitively at Shen Xingyue. It was because he was also interested in her but was too shy to say so. When he knew that his nephew Xiao Ao was interested in her, he was at a loss! It was something that he had never experienced before!

He found himself turning red in front of her and he was even stammering in front of her. Somehow he knew that this Shen Xingyue was a very special maiden but he had no way to prove it nor was he interested to do so. Her extreme calmness and brilliant eyes impressed him greatly. Earlier when everyone was startled by Yi Ping's martial shout and had rushed out in alarm to investigate, she walked unhurriedly and was not even startled. It was as though she was not afraid of death or dangers…

In the Virtuous Palace, Xiao Fei was renowned for his keen perception. That was why he could figure out where Xiao Yuanjia had hidden his thirteen secret swords and could warn Youxue!

When he noticed that she had Zuo Tianyi's sword, he was secretly alarmed and thought that it could be Zuo Tianyi betrothal gift to her. That very night, he had drunk himself silly…

Shen Xingyue nodded gently but did say anything. She knew that they were just trying to get her attention and that they had been doing so ever since the first day that they had met.

She patiently tolerated their incessant talks because she did not want anyone to know her true martial levels. So far, she had only revealed herself to Zuo Tianyi and Lu Baiyun because she had recognized the Blue Heavens as a divine sword of the Ascension Sect and it was her duty to retrieve it back.

The Blue Heavens was actually a heavenly sword that was owned by the Lord Almighty who was the Celestial Leader of the Ascension Sect. This heavenly sword was also the foundation artifact of the Ascension Sect!

The Lord Almighty and dozens of Celestials from the Ascension Sect were killed by the deadly Celestial Annihilation Star Formation created by the Three Star Sisters of Fate when they had attacked the Melody Palace.

No one had known how deadly the Celestial Annihilation Star Formation was when they first confront it. The Lord Almighty and several of the Supreme Celestials had seen many kinds of celestial formations and by the time they had become Supreme Celestials, formations of any kinds were useless against them.

No one was also expecting a strong resistance from the Melody Palace. When the Melody Palace was on the verge of defeat, the timely arrival of the dozen Star Celestials from the Melody Palace and their sacrifices saved it from total annihilation.

In the end, they were deterred by the legendary Celestial Annihilating Star Formation which was put up by the Three Star Sisters of Fate. However the Lord Almighty was not willing to withdraw without putting a good fight and he did not believe that with the intellect of so many Celestials, they could not destroy the Celestial Annihilating Star Formation.

The Celestial Annihilating Star Formation was a defensive formation that was created by the Ascended Star Celestials long ago. Even before the Divine Descendent event, it was already a well-known Celestial Formation in the Celestial Realm. It had only one purpose, to kill all the Celestials that were trapped inside!

The Lord Almighty knew that the Celestial Annihilating Star Formation was held into place by nine Heavenly Relics in its outer formation and the inner formation was held by three divine swords as its pillars. If they could break the Celestial Annihilating Star Formation, then they could obtain the three divine swords and the nine Heavenly Relics. One of the divine swords was the much coveted Heavenly Earth Sword that exuded the Universal Force!

And so driven by their greed, they had entered the formation to confront the surviving Celestials of the Melody Palace. In the end, more than eighty Celestials, including the Lord Almighty could not escape the formation and they were all killed by the Universal Force of the Celestial Annihilating Star Formation.

That event marked the beginning of the end for both the Celestial Ascension Sect and the Celestial Melody Palace.

That was how the Blue Heavens had been lost until now!

Shen Xingyue's thoughts were interrupted by Zuo Tianyi who was now shouting, "Everyone move back first! I will challenge this villainous Yi Ping!"

Immediately all the exponents made a hasty withdrawal.

Dugu Yunzi hummed coldly as she said with cold demeanor, "Don't you slander Yi Ping. You know what you did."

Zuo Tianyi said, "Yunzi, you know my feelings for you. But you have strayed on the wrong path and even collaborated with the heretic sects. Even though in my heart, I have sympathies for you but I am also the protégé master of the Infinity Sword Clan. The Infinity Sword Clan is one of the major righteous orthodox clan in the fraternity…"

Dugu Yunzi interrupted, "You are right to say that the Infinity Sword Clan is a righteous orthodox clan but you are definitely not. You are just a wolf in sheep clothing, despicable and evil!"

Zuo Tianyi had imbued his sword with his sword energy and he was exuding fearsome burst of piercing cold sword energies in all directions as he walked in front of Yi Ping, "Yi Ping, do you dare to duel with me?"

Yi Ping had immediately displayed the Heavens Horizon in a defensive stance as he said, "Why will I not dare?"

Zuo Tianyi said, "But you know, I am a swordsman and my honor requires that I shall not fight an unarmed person. Moreover against an unarmed foe, I am restrained and cannot give my very best. Even if you have won, there is nothing for you to be proud of for it is not a true victory."

By now, everyone knew what Zuo Tianyi was hinting at. Swordplay was Zuo Tianyi's expertise but to Yi Ping, he was more familiar with the Divine Horizon Hands than the Horizon Swordplay.

Yi Ping and Zuo Tianyi had crossed swords previously but Zuo Tianyi had since progressed greatly in his swordplay. He could now imbue his internal intricate energies to his sword and releasing it as killing sword energy. That was the energy form of the Infinity-First Swordplay, the ability to kill invisibly from afar; sword energy could be sense but it was invisible and could not be block!

Even though Yi Ping possessed extraordinary martial power but he could not transfer the extraordinary martial power to his swords! It was because he was not trained in utilizing internal strength as a pure form. The very act of harnessing it was called sword energy and that required decades of hard work and constant practice. Even for the Old Sword Saint, it took him some four decades before he could attain the level of the Infinity-Two to finally transfer his internal intricate energies into sword energy!

Also as a purest form of intricate energy, sword energies could dissipate the martial power of even the strongest opponents and went right through their bodies!

Zuo Tianyi was a prodigy and had reached the Infinity-Two when he was in his twenties. When he had witnessed the fight between the Celestial Fairy and the Heavenly Temptress, he was inspired and finally figured out a way to reach the Infinity-One, which was the Old Sword Saint level!

Moreover, the Heavenly Divine Dreams Pill that Shen Xingyue had given to him actually had the effect of boasting his internal strength and had helped him to refine the pureness of his sword energy!

Zuo Tianyi was secretly thinking, "After I have killed Yi Ping, I will make Shen Xingyue my woman. This is to a lesson for you for messing with me. I will let you know how a man will treat a woman. After that, I want you to quietly hand over your clan two divine skills to me, the Big Dipper Hands and the Divine Rejuvenation Force. And of course the secrets of your Heavenly Divine Pills will also be mine. I will use it for a better use for the domination of the entire fraternity!"

When he had thought of that, he secretly took a lustful look at the beautiful angelic Shen Xingyue and imagined her begging him for mercy on the bed…

Lingfeng was secretly sighing in her heart but she had interrupted, "Strange, then for you to defeat Yi Ping, it is considered a true victory?"

Zuo Tianyi replied coldly, "The Horizon Swordplay is also renowned in the martial fraternity. Yi Ping can choose not to accept the challenge though."

Yi Ping said, "I will accept the challenge but…"

Zuo Tianyi laughed, "But? Swords are blind. If you want to surrender during a battle, I can try my best to grant you your request. You only need to say the word 'surrender' and I will stop. But your friends will have to make to surrender as well."

Yi Ping eyed Zuo Tianyi coldly, "I have no intention to surrender or use my companions' life to exchange for my own. I have yet to settle my feud with you for your despicable act. I have only one request and that is to fight Lu Baiyun, Gu Tianle and you at the same time!"

Lingfeng, Yu'Er and Mei'Er gasped.

Lingfeng was rebuking Yi Ping quietly in her heart, "One Zuo Tianyi is more than what you can handle and you want to fight these three super exponents at the same time?"

Yu'Er was muttering, "Master…"

Youxue whispered coldly, "If he wants to be a hero, let him be…"

Even though her voice was cold but she was actually extremely worried for him!

Shen Xingyue's fingers were trembling!

When he had declared that he would challenge Zuo Tianyi, Gu Tianyi and the Lu Baiyun at the same time, her heart skipped a beat; there was an air of righteousness around him when he made the challenge. It was not arrogance but a demand for justice for the wrongs that had been given through injustice. It was because as a Celestial that had already attained past the Emotion State of Divinity, she could sense the burning righteousness in his heart!

She was secretly startled. It was because the White Sage of Emptiness that she had known was a Celestial with a high attainment. There were many times that she had secretly wished that she could sense his emotions and know what he was thinking…

From his righteous eyes and burning heart, she could sense that he wanted to protect these maidens. But it caused her to be even more confused as she secretly thought, "These maidens are previous incarnations of the Celestials that are all killed by him. They should hate him and shouldn't be together with him. Even if they have no memories of their previous self but the memories of their hatred for their killer would never vanish and this instinct would become a natural mistrust."

There was a hint of a tear in her angelic eyes as she secretly sighed, "So whether it is the White Sage of the Emptiness or you now, you really can't remember who I am or because you never have me in your heart?"

Lu Baiyun was heard laughing, "Do I have a feud with you?"

Yi Ping said, "That is for my sworn brother Qiu Wufeng and all those that you have tried to harm weeks ago at the Tranquil Mountains."

Yuan Shao interrupted hummed coldly, "You seem to forget about me. I was there at the Tranquil Mountains too."

Yi Ping said solemnly, "I can tell that you have not recovered from your injuries. I can wait until you have recovered before we can settle our feud."

Yuan Shao hummed coldly but he gave no indication whatever so of what he was thinking.

Lu Baiyun was secretly thinking, "If Gu Tianle, Zuo Tianyi and I are to fight this Yi Ping together, our odds of winning are high. This is my chance of gaining even more fame and impressed Shen Xingyue. If I can win her hand, then I will not only gain myself a rare beauty as a wife, I will also gain the Big Dipper Hand Divine Skill and the Divine Rejuvenation Force. With the powerful Master Hao Shaodong as my backer, the entire Honor Manor and even the martial fraternity will soon be mine!"

So he smiled and said to Gu Tianle, "What do you think?"

Gu Tianle said, "Even though all of you will be fighting with your swords, I will stick to my fist. After all, I am a senior pugilist and the Master of the Honor Manor. I don't mind giving this young man a handicap."

Yi Ping said, "Good! No matter who is the winner of this duel, no one in the fraternity must pursue Gongsun Jing, Qiu Wufeng and Nangong Le ever again! I will settle their feuds with the martial fraternity on their behalf."

Gu Tianle took a hurried glance at Han Shaodong who nodded silently at him.

Gu Tianle laughed, "The crimes that they have committed are simply too heinous to be forgiven. But on account for your bravery, I will promise you that the Honor Manor would not pursue their heinous crimes. But only if you are able to win the three of us at the same time!"

Many of the martial exponents on the side of the Honor Manor were now incessantly muttering that this Yi Ping was simply too insolent and arrogant to challenge Gu Tianle, Zuo Tianyi and Lu Baiyun at the same time and they were debating the outcome of the fight even before it had begun! But of course, the end result of the debate was that which one of the three would be the first one to take Yi Ping's head!

All of a sudden, an angelic voice interrupted Gu Tianle. "Master Tianle, is it alright for you to show some restraint?"

It was Shen Xingyue!

Lie Qing, Lingfeng and the rest of the maidens that were on Yi Ping's side were startled to hear her interceding for Yi Ping!

When she had spoken, everyone was instantly seized by her angelic voice even though she was soft spoken. It was as though her quiet angelic voice could immediately sent their hearts to pace rapidly!

But Shen Xingyue quickly laughed softly, "He is so insolent that even I feel like dueling him as well. If you killed him, then I have no one to test the new sword that Master Tianyi has given to me, am I right Master Tianyi and Master Baiyun?"

Gu Tianle nodded and said, "I won't be too hard on him then."

Zuo Tianyi laughed, "On Maiden Xingyue's account, I will definitely show him some mercy!"

Lu Baiyun laughed as well, "Don't worry, he won't die."

Even though they had all given Shen Xingyue's their assurances, their smiles were full of malevolent. It was obvious that they had no intention of showing any mercy!

Zuo Tianyi was secretly pissed off and his heart was burning with jealousy. He had already noticed that Shen Xingyue seemed to have given Yi Ping a great deal of attention from her alluring eyes!

He thought, "Why is it that all the maidens seem to like this nameless and poor Yi Ping? What is so good about him?"

All of a sudden, he raised his sword and pointed malevolently at Yi Ping.

Immediately there was a cold and terrifying piercing aura that could be felt by everyone!

Even Yuan Shao and Xiao Shuai were startled. They had never seen such terrifying sword energies before!

Even Yi Ping was startled as he took a step backward and his hands were trembling; the cold piercing sword energy waves had already penetrated through his body even before Zuo Tianyi had attacked!

Lingfeng whispered in alarm, "Oh dear! Yi Ping had lost the protection of his Icy Heavenly Tears internal force. At that close proximity, Zuo Tianyi's sword energies have already enveloped him and restrained him…"

Xiao Youxue, Yu'Er and Mei'Er who had been practicing the Icy Heavenly Tears were alarmed at the piercing cold waves that were emitting from Zuo Tianyi. Even though they were standing far away but the paralyzing sword energy waves had already paralyzed them and caused numbness to them!

Lie Qing was solemnly as she looked at Yi Ping with watery eyes. She was clutching her long sword now. It was obvious that she had no intention to just standing at the back anymore as she said in a low voice, "After displaying five hundred and sixty strokes, Yi Ping's fingers can no longer hold his swords steadily. That Tianyi, I am sure is aware of it."

Dugu Yunzi said quietly, "That's five hundred and sixty-one strokes. There is an extra stroke that he had used to stabilized himself after he had beaten off Gu Tianle. That is the Thousand Weight Fall skill that Lele has taught to him while we are in the valley."

Youxue said coolly, "I have actually lost count after the four hundred strokes. I was distracted by that young maiden on the other side. Did you notice that she is looking at us from time to time? It is definitely not a friendly look. Did you see her fingering the long sword besides her? It is obvious that she has the intention to draw that sword into battle anytime."

Lingfeng, Mei'Er and Yu'Er were all startled that Lie Qing, Youxue and Yunzi were able to keep track of every single movements made by Yi Ping while keeping themselves alert!

Lie Qing whispered, "Sisters, if I die in battle. Please flee with Ping'Er as fast as possible…"

Lingfeng was startled. For Lie Qing to say that, that maiden must be really a formidable opponent!

Dugu Yunzi looked quietly at Lie Qing and said, "Sister Qing'Er, I have no intention of fleeing. I will fight on your side, whether you like it or not."

Youxue said coolly as she arranged her sleeves, "I don't have that intention too. You seem to have forgotten that we are all from the New Virtuous Palace."

Lie Qing sighed softly as she looked at Yunzi and Youxue, "All of you…"

Lingfeng whispered with an alluring smile, "Didn't we defeat the Celestial Liege together? Didn't we overcome many difficult fights together? Do you think we can flee with so many exponents around us?"

Yu'Er said with a determinate look, "That's right! We have no intention of going back alive anyway. I am willing to lay down my life for Yi Ping!"

Mei'Er nodded as she said melancholy, "If protégé mistress is here, these men would not dare to bully us!"

Lie Qing laughed softly, "Even if your protégé mistress is here, these men would still dare to bully us."

Mei'Er protested indignantly, "Then my protégé mistress will kill every single one of them!"

Lie Qing whispered sadly, "It is precisely because your protégé mistress has killed too many exponents, her Divine Calamity will be extremely difficult…"

Yu'Er was startled as she said, "What did you just say and what do you mean?"

Lie Qing sighed softly, "I don't want to hide it anymore from any one of you now. It is because I may not survive this battle and after all, we have been through a lot together. I shall tell you then. The Divine Calamity of the Celestial Fairy will be one of the most malevolent Divine Calamity ever. It is because she has simply killed too many exponents in the past. Even though we have helped her find a most spiritual spot to prepare her but most likely it is futile. That is why your protégé mistress wants me to be here to help Yi Ping because she knows that she is going to die soon."

Yu'Er and Mei'Er were startled and their eyes were teary.

Mei'Er cried out, "No, that is not the true. Our protégé mistress will never leave us alone…"

Lingfeng interrupted, "The fight is beginning soon…"

Indeed, Yi Ping was clutching the hilt of his two swords with trembling fingers as he said aloud to Zuo Tianyi, "What are you waiting for?"

Zuo Tianyi smiled bitterly, "You can't even pull your swords now. Are you so scared now that even your fingers are trembling? Don't tell me you lack the strength now to pull your swords from your scabbard? Or are you thinking of using your fists and forgot about the duel condition?"

Yi Ping clutched the hilts of his swords even tighter when Zuo Tianyi pointed it out. He quickly said, "Enough say already. Are you fighting or not?"

Lu Baiyun was already swinging his sword strokes, "You have not yet drawn your weapons."

Yi Ping hummed coldly as he explained, "I know that my swordplay isn't as good as the both of you. So I will wait for an appropriate time to draw my swords so that the drag of my swords would not slow down after I have executed my swiftness movement…"

Gu Tianle laughed aloud, "You mean your evading movement skill? What an idiot. Now we all know your strategy!"

Lu Baiyun whispered to Zuo Tianyi, "He is trying to weaken the strength of your sword energies so that he can display his Horizon Swordplay. Don't waste any more time with him anymore!"

Lu Baiyun had immediately displayed his Heartless Strike Technique. This secret technique had three killing technique, each one more powerful than the previous execution!

Gu Tianle was not slow to react either. He quickly move to Yi Ping's back and displayed his Ultrapowerful Force!

Zuo Tianyi had broken through the air with his long sword with a startling burst of speed, sending waves of cold piercing sword energies upon Yi Ping!

Yi Ping knew that he was trapped by the superior air of the Infinity-First swordplay and his steps had suddenly become extremely heavy. He raised his fighting spirit with the Absolute Spirits and drew the Divine Echo and the White Phoenix at the same time!

At that single point of time, Yi Ping had a new awakening in his perception of the Absolute Spirits and had merged the heart intricate formula of the Absolute Attack, Absolute Speed and Absolute Reflexes of the Absolute Spirits into one, becoming one with his swords!

There was two brilliant flash of light and a low humming echo as Yi Ping drawn the Divine Echo and White Phoenix. All of a sudden, the cold bursting sword energies that were formed from the Infinity-First sword stance had dissipated and Zuo Tianyi, Gu Tianyi and Lu

Baiyun were lying on the ground in great agonizing pain; their abdomen had all been sliced by Yi Ping at precisely the same time!

Everyone was startled!

The speed of Yi Ping quick draw technique was too fast that the moment that Yi Ping had drawn out his swords, only a few exponents could actually see what had actually happened!

Xiao Shuai was not happy as he muttered, "Yunzi, you have actually taught him our secret quick draw technique?"

Yi Ping himself was startled that he could actually be faster than the Infinity-One swordplay, the Heartless Strike Technique and the Ultrapowerful Force combined. He did not want think of anything except that in order to survive, he had to be even faster than them!

But that was not what everyone had seen that had caused them to be in awe!

The moment that Yi Ping had drawn out the Divine Echo and the White Phoenix, there was a resounding echoes from the two swords that pierced everyone and removing the paralyzing effect of the deadly sword energy aura of the Infinity-One. At the same time that Yi Ping had swung his two swords in a slash at the same time, two beaming halo of lights enveloped his two swords, dazzling everyone!

Shen Xingyue was startled as she gasped secretly, "Isn't that the Divine Echo and the White Phoenix divine swords, the divine swords of the Star Sisters of the Fate? He can actually use both swords at the same time? No one can use two divine swords at the same time, not even the Celestials…"

After the spiritual awakening of the divine swords, the mental strength of the practitioner would also be consumed by the divine swords, causing extreme fatigue with every use! Using two divine swords at once, even if it did not awakened yet, were already mentally and physically draining enough!

Moreover, a divine sword had its own self-awareness and would reject the other divine sword.

From the halos of the two swords, she could also tell that Yi Ping had already become one with the swords and were in full control of the two divine swords!

There was a sudden confusion among the exponents!

It was because no one actually knew what had happened. Were Zuo Tianyi, Lu Baiyun and Gu Tianle defeated by the divine swords as the swords lifted the cold piercing sword energy aura or did Yi Ping really defeat them with his own skill?

Yi Ping muttered to the fallen Gu Tianle, Zuo Tianyi and Lu Baiyun who were still wriggling on the ground. "Remember to keep your promises."

Lie Qing smiled happily as she thought, "He is a good man. He didn't kill them."

Unless Yi Ping had no other choice, he would never take a life unnecessary. That was his principle.

Han Shaodong quickly commanded his protégés, "Take them away and take good care of them."

Immediately, several exponents from the Honor Manor and the Infinity Sword Clan took Gu Tianle, Zuo Tianyi and Lu Baiyun away.

Yi Ping said, "So who is going to be next and if there are no more challengers, I hope everyone would go back to their own clans peacefully!"

Xiao Shuai asked, "What do you all think of his skills?"

The Martial Sage said, "He is nothing. I have just defeated him a few days ago and he was crawling on the ground as a matter of fact."

Xiao Shuai said coldly, "Then why don't you fight him now?"

The Martial Sage said with a straight face, "I don't have a weapon and his swords look terribly sharp. I am afraid that my iron fists will hurt."

Xiao Shuai hummed coldly.

The Martial Sage said, "Don't be angry. I am just waiting to see your famous Dark Mono Sword Formation."

Xiao Shuai said, "This is not the time yet."

The Sword Sage dashed past them as he croaked in his old voice, "Young man! How about fighting against me?"

Immediately, the Sword Sage had unsheathed his heavy broad sword and he had leapt above Yi Ping in a flash and had hacked down towards him!

The sword of the Sword Sage was made of chromium alloy, an extremely rare metal in the martial fraternity. The process of making chromium alloy was lost after the warring states period and the few swords that were made of chromium alloy were highly regarded as precious swords in the martial fraternity!

Besides the Sword Sage's sword, which was called the Brave Frontier Precious Sword, the swords held by Beautiful Sword Fairy and Jade Sword Fairy were also made of chromium alloy.

As the Sword Sage came crushing down onto Yi Ping with his heavy sword that was imbued by his martial power, it had the added effect of causing the weight of the sword to increase by many manifold!

Yi Ping was startled that the Sword Sage could wield such a heavy sword in such an agile manner!

He immediately raised the Divine Echo and the White Phoenix in a cross shape above him as he received the blunt of the Sword Sage's attack!

Immediately the ground around Yi Ping exploded into a thunderous circular shape as the full impact of the Brave Frontier came crushing onto Yi Ping!

The Sword Sage was surprised that Yi Ping could take his direct hit and in that split second, rebounded by the martial force from the clashes between them, he had somersault in mid-air again and hacked at Yi Ping again with a series of sword strokes as he shouted, "The Three Strokes of the Dragon Descending!"

All in all, the Sword Sage had unleashed three strokes upon Yi Ping, with each stroke even heavier and more powerful than the previous!

Immediately after the first stroke had exploded thunderous above him, Yi Ping had coughed out blood while a dust storm began to fly in all directions!

Before the second stroke of the Dragon Descending had landed, Yi Ping had raised his martial power as he shouted. "Asper Divinity!" But instead of displaying the Asper Divinity Horizon Hand, he had mustered the tremendous martial power of this forbidden technique to receive the incoming sword blow!

Immediately after Yi Ping had used the Asper Divinity, a blue ring of white fire burst out in all directions with such tremendous force that all the exponents were struck by a burning forceful windforce that caused them to move back unsteadily that was made worst by the dust storm!

But even before all the exponents had recovered, the Sword Sage had already executed the second and third strokes of his Dragon Descending, which immediately exploded thunderous in mid-air as Yi Ping parried with his two divine swords, sending martial shockwaves so powerful that the weaker exponents that were too near or those that were unable to resist the martial energies, to sustain serious internal injuries or were killed on the spot!

Yu'Er and Mei'Er had immediately displayed the Divine Emerald Skills with their swords in front of Lingfeng, Youxue, Yunzi and Lie Qing!

Lie Qing had immediately thrust her sword scabbard onto the ground in front of her, creating another shockwave that deflect the multiple forceful incoming shockwaves that trembled in all directions!

Chi Zhengqi, Xiao Fei and Xiao Ao immediately drawn out their swords in front of Shen Xingyue and parried with all their strength to defend her from harm!

Shen Xingyue said nonchalantly, "Thank you all!"

Barely had the dust storm and windforce had died down, Yi Ping was swinging his swords ambidextrous at the Sword Sage who responded equally as fast!

Their attacking movements were so fast that their swords were now shades of grey as they stirred up the dust in the surrounding into walls of wavering windforce!

In every split second, they had exchange more than a dozen strokes with seeming no advantage!

It was only then the exponents of the fraternity knew that the exploits of the Sword Sage were not something that was made up even though he was not seen for many decades in the martial fraternity!

All of a sudden as Yi Ping and the Sword Sage had dash past one another in another attack, both had suddenly halted and were coughing out mouthful of blood!

They had used so much martial power that their blood had reversed itself and they were both coughing out their bad blood!

Yi Ping had already been injured at the onset of the first stroke of the Dragon Descending and he had forcefully used the Asper Divinity, causing his internal injuries to worsen!

The Sword Sage sighed and walked back to where he had first come from as he said, "Young man, you have won!"

Yi Ping bowed respectfully with his swords still in his hands as he said humbly, "Senior, thank you for showing mercy to me!"

Xiao Shuai said coldly to the Sword Sage, "You have not lost yet, so why are you staying your hand? If you have persisted longer, you would have won."

The Sword Sage laughed as he began to sit down on the ground to meditate as he said aloud, "Win or lose, is there a need to be so clear about it? This young hero has broken the invincibility of the Infinity-One Swordplay and fights me to a standstill. At first I thought Zuo Tianyi has been defeated by him is because the sword that he is holding could dissipate the sword energy of the Infinity-One. But this is not the case. He is really a remarkable swordsman. I like him."

Xiao Shuai turned and said to the Element Sage, Shangguan Qingyun, Han Shaodong and Yan Nanfei, "What are you waiting for?"

Yan Nanfei smiled coldly, "I have long neglected my martial progression in pursue of martial attainment. I am afraid I am not his match."

Shangguan Qingyun said aloud, "The Divine Sword Martial Clan will not be an enemy of this young hero."

Xiao Shuai had already raised his long sword, "Yan Nanfei and Shangguan, have you forgotten about our brotherhood?"

Yan Nanfei said, "We didn't but our honor refuses to let us take advantage of this young hero at this moment."

Han Shaodong said coldly, "So you are all honorable heroes while we are not?"

While they were talking, Yi Ping had thrust the Divine Echo and the White Phoenix onto the ground as he coughed another bout of blood!

Han Shaodong had raised his martial power as he prepared to step forward when there was a sudden flash in front of Yi Ping!

It was Lie Qing and as she raised her Perpetual Darkness, there was a black halo around her and no one can see her clearly except for a black figure!

She said coldly, "I don't care for honor. If anyone wants to take Yi Ping's life, then they have to fight me first!"

Yi Ping caught hold of Lie Qing's hand as he muttered, "Qing'Er, go back please. There are too many of them…"

All of a sudden, Yi Ping was startled! It was because there were tears on his hands; it was Lie Qing's silent tears!

She said woefully in his ears, "If you have died, I would not want to live either…do you understand?"

Han Shaodong shouted, "Step aside if you value your life. My target is only the young man. We have an agreement. If he can triumph over us, then all of you are free to go. But if he would to lose, then all of you have to come with us!"

All of a sudden, he had leapt into battle and the air around him exploded thunderously as he raised the extraordinary power of his Great Dipper Hands as a powerful gravity force attempted to crush onto Yi Ping and Lie Qing!

All of a sudden, there was a shadow flash as Youxue and Lingfeng had displayed their extraordinary swiftness movement skill in mid-air as they raised all their martial power at the same time to display the Penetrating Hands and the Asper Horizon Hand at Han Shaodong!

There were a thunderous explosion as Xiao Youxue and Lingfeng coughed out blood as they fell onto the ground!

Han Shaodong was knocked back but he was otherwise unharmed but he was startled that the combined martial power of these two maiden could actually halt his Great Dipper Hands!

Xiao Shuai was expecting Youxue to be killed on the same spot when Lingfeng and she held one another up, even as Yunzi, Yu'Er and Mei'Er flew to their side to support them!

Han Shaodong was secretly startled, "How is it possible for them to be still alive? If any practitioner fails to take the full impact of the Great Dipper Hand, the backlash of martial power will cause them to be killed instantly!"

Yi Ping was shouting, "Youxue and Lingfeng! Please go back…"

Yi Ping had already raised his divine swords and was taking dragged steps forward!

Xiao Shuai knew very well how deadly the Big Dipper Hands was. Even for him, he dare not risk facing the full impact of the Big Dipper Hands in such an open manner. He could not resist asking, "Child, are you well? Quickly turn back now and recuperate. Your injuries are not light!"

Youxue hummed coldly as she said weakly, "You don't have to worry for us. We won't die so easily. After all, Sister Lingfeng and I have consumed the Divine Dragon Pills."

This immediately created uproar among the exponents at the mere mention of the Divine Dragon Pills!

Even Xiao Shuai was so startled that he was muttering, "You have actually consumed the Divine Dragon Pill and the Golden Rejuvenation Pills…"

Yuan Shao whispered to him, "If you were to eat her heart, it is as good as consuming the Divine Dragon Pill and the Golden Rejuvenation Pill too. Your internal strength will receive a tremendous boast and mastery of the Divine Virtuous Force is also a piece of cake. Maybe that Yi Ping has also consumed the Divine Dragon Pill, that is why his martial progress has been so speedy and his martial force so unfathomable."

Xiao Shuai's eyes had suddenly turned murderous.

Han Shaodong, Xiao Shuai and the Element Sage had stepped forward at the same time!

The Element Sage said, "Surrender the Divine Dragon Pill or don't blame me for being nasty!"

Xiao Shuai said, "I am tired of toying with you already, young man."

Han Shaodong said to Lie Qing, "Step aside maiden or don't me for being nasty."

Lie Qing said melancholy and her voice was sorrowful, "You know very well that he cannot win. You know very well that you are all the top exponents of the martial fraternity and each one of you is his equal in martial strength. Very well, I shall be your opponent and be your darkness. Even if I have used up my last breath, I will fight all of you to a bitter end!"

Xiao Shuai hummed coldly, "Foolish girl! Then don't blame me for not showing any mercy and seize your divine sword!"

Shen Xingyue smiled softly, "Is that so?"

She had already stepped forward as she adjusted her violet red feathery dress.

Xiao Shuai said, "Young lass, step aside. You don't have to take any risk. We can handle this troublesome girl ourselves."

Xiao Ao and Chi Zhengqi had both surrounded her as they said, "Maiden Xingyue, it is far too dangerous for you to be out there."

Xiao Fei stammered, "Maiden Xingyue…I think…you have…better stay put…"

Xiao Shuai said to Han Shaodong, "Ask your granddaughter to step back now. I won't be responsible if anything happens to her."

Shen Xingyue smiled modestly, "Young lass? Is that so? Too dangerous for me? Seems so."

All of a sudden, she had vanished from sight right in front of everyone!

The only telling sign where she had disappeared to next was a brilliant blue halo when she had drawn out the Blue Heavens as she exchanged a dozen resonating sword strokes with Lie Qing!

The black halo and the blue halo were zapping and hovering around each other so fast that the onlookers were dazzled with near blindness!

But as soon as they had exchanged the sword strokes, Shen Xingyue was standing with the blue glow of the Blue Heavens beside Chi Zhengqi, Xiao Fei and Xiao Ao again. All these took place in just a blink of an eye!

Xiao Fei was totally stunned. He was sure that no one else knew how fast his speed technique skills were. Even that Yi Ping may not be able to surpass him. But when he had just seen Shen Xingyue and Lie Qing's speed attacks, he was completely in shock!

Lie Qing had broken into a cold sweat; she was stunned at the attacking and movement speed of this young maiden. If she had been slower, she would have been killed by her! But she quickly composed herself as she thought, "Very well, then I shall remain stationary and I would like to see how you can break down my defense with your speed. I shall overcome you with motionless versus your motion, countering you with my prepared martial power versus your weakened martial power as you move!"

Even Yunzi, Youxue, Yu'Er, Mei'Er and Lingfeng was gasping in astonishment at the astonishing speed of the young maiden! Indeed, they had never seen anyone moving with such startling speed except for the Celestial Fairy and the Joyful Goddess. Even then, this young maiden's speed was simply out of the world and was superior to them!

Yi Ping was also startled that this young maiden could turn up to be such a difficult opponent! But he soon calmed himself down as he raised his two divine swords besides Lie Qing as he muttered, "Qing'Er, this is my battle. Don't you worry for me, alright? Take a rest first. I can still fight."

Shen Xingyue looked at everyone before she gave a bemused soft sigh, "Look at me. I must be getting old. I have forgotten to introduce myself first. I am Shen Xingyue the Fiery Phoenix and also the Supreme Celestial of the Celestial Ascension Sect."

Even before Xiao Ao, Xiao Fei and Chi Zhengqi could recover from their initial surprise, they were again stunned at her revelations!

Xiao Shuai looked at Han Shaodong as he muttered in shock, "Isn't she your granddaughter, Han Xingyue?"

Han Shaodong stunned everyone when he replied with a deep sigh, "She is actually my protégé mistress. Don't look at me with those eyes. I didn't know my protégé mistress is a Celestial either and that her martial skills are this stunning."

While they were talking, they had overheard Shen Xingyue saying to Lie Qing, "You must be Luminous Star, am I right to say so? What is your name now?"

Lie Qing said coldly as her crimson eyes flared up, "If you say so, then I am. You can address me as Lie Qing if you want to."

Shen Xingyue said, "Maiden Lie Qing then, why are you on his side? Do you know that that he had killed you in the past? Do you know that he is actually a cold and heartless man? You should join me instead. It is not easy for you to become a Celestial again. Do you really know the odds of surviving the Divine Calamity and becoming a Celestial is so remote that I am really astonished to see you as a Celestial again?"

All the other exponents were startled once again!

This Maiden Lie Qing was also a Celestial!

Yi Ping said firmly once again, "Your opponent is me and not Qing'Er!"

Somehow, he seemed to be ignored by Shen Xingyue once again as she asked Lie Qing, "Prepare yourself. I am coming for you!"

Lie Qing was perplexed. It was because this Shen Xingyue had chosen to interfere at exactly the wrong timing when victory was almost theirs to take; she had stopped Han Shaodong, Xiao Shuai and the Element Sage to challenge her. It was almost as though she was deliberately giving Yi Ping a chance to recuperate and to regulate his vitality energy flow?

Yi Ping was shouting at Shen Xingyue, "You can come after me first!"

Shen Xingyue pretended not to see Yi Ping or to hear him.

Instead she said to Lie Qing, "Since you have refused to join me and is my opponent, then I have to mention this to you first. Your sisters and you have the blood of eighty of my fellow Ascendant Celestials in your hands so I have no other choice but to seek vengeance on their behalf to appease their angry spirits. So don't blame me for not showing you any mercy."

Chapter 60: The White Sage of Emptiness

Xiao Fei stammered, "Maiden Xingyue, you are really a Celestial Being?"

Chi Zhengqi and Xiao Ao were in awe of her to even move or speak!

It was because when she had manifested her divine aura, there was a weak yellow hue around her that caused everyone to be in awe of her.

Shen Xingyue did not reply Xiao Fei and instead, she had walked unhurriedly towards Lie Qing with her long fluttering feather dress flying gently around her. It seemed that her loose feathery cloak was lifted by a powerful inertia force that was surrounding her; the Divine Rejuvenation Force!

As Chi Zhengqi broke free of his awe and ran towards her, he fainted before he could even come within reach of her!

The Element Sage scolded Chi Zhengqi aloud, "Foolish!" as he grabbed him to safety! It was because this Divine Rejuvenation Force was constantly replenishing her own martial power by draining the martial power of the weaker opponents around her!

Lie Qing was stroking her long hair even as nine wisps of blue hue hovered around her!

Shen Xingyue was swinging the Blue Heavens while Lie Qing had raised the Perpetual Darkness in front of her as they now began to encircle each other with extreme caution!

Yi Ping was standing awkwardly in their middle as they encircled him and he was shouting, "Qing'Er, back off. Maiden Xingyue, your opponent should be me!"

Shen Xingyue took a quick glance at Yi Ping with a curious look before she turned to say to Lie Qing coolly, "It seems that my speed techniques are useless against you."

Lie Qing smiled mesmerizingly, "If you attempt that one more time, I am afraid you would already been killed by my Pandora Merciless Strike. You really missed a good opportunity to take me by surprise. Now it is already too late for regrets."

Shen Xingyue nodded, "And it seems that both of you are not affected by my Divine Rejuvenation Force? Nevertheless, we shall see who has the last laugh."

She was deliberately displaying her startling swiftness skill to gauge the strength of her opponents and was astonished that Lie Qing was the only one among all the maidens that could follow her speed movements and even retaliate against her. And this Maiden Lie Qing had assumed correctly that if she would attempt another speed attack against her, she would be killed. It was because speed attacks would leave her vulnerable to retaliation against a skillful and powerful non-moving opponent if it failed to draw blood on the first try.

Yi Ping did not notice that while they were talking, many of the exponents had suddenly fainted on the ground one by one and at the same time! The rest of the exponents were all scurrying as far as possible from the gravitating martial force pull of the Divine Rejuvenate Force; her Divine Rejuvenate Force was tens of times more powerful than Han Shaodong and it was also capable of moving along with her, something that Han Shaodong was not capable of doing!

At the same time, Xiao Shuai, Xiao Fei, Yuan Shao had mustered their martial force with their Divine Virtuous Force as they seek to protect themselves from the draining effect of the Divine Rejuvenation Force as they observed the forthcoming battle in close melee!

Han Shaodong had raised his Divine Rejuvenation Force around him!

Yu'Er and Mei'Er were swinging their swords slowly in front of them as they displayed the Divine Emerald Skill.

Yunzi had displayed her Invincible Divine Force while Youxue had fortified herself with the Golden Impervious Body.

Lingfeng had mustered her martial power and had used the Great Dissolution Skill to neutralize the draining pull of Shen Xingyue's Divine Rejuvenation Force.

But none of them had the martial power to even come close to Yi Ping, Lie Qing or Shen Xingyue to render any help or to intervene!

Yi Ping was protected by his Divine Boundless Force and his Circular Rejuvenation of the Origin prevented his martial force from being drained away by the Divine Rejuvenation Force. That was why he could stand in close proximity next to Shen Xingyue!

Shen Xingyue sighed softly as she was secretly alarmed, "He is not affected by my Divine Rejuvenation Force? I have already lowered the effect of my Divine Rejuvenation Force and subtly tried to intimidate him off. He is still his same old self…"

She began to sigh…

The White Sage of Emptiness that everyone had known was a Celestial with a high accomplishment in martial and spiritual attainment. He was also a refine and young looking man, having becoming a Celestial early.

Normally, by the time most men and women could have the necessary attainment to become a Celestial; they would be almost a hundred years old and had aged. It was because becoming a Celestial did not mean that they could restore their youth. However the Celestials' countenance and complexion was different from ordinary people and were like a well-nourished baby despite their aged appearances.

As a highly eligible Celestial, the White Sage of Emptiness was the focus of quite a number of beautiful but haughty Celestial Maidens that were disdainful to the aged Celestials or did not find them to be a good match to be their celestial companions, not that there were many beautiful Celestial Maidens in the first place. Most of these beautiful Celestial Maidens may not be that young either but because they had based their martial foundation on a certain type of internal negative energy, they were able to retain their youthful appearances.

However, the White Sage of Emptiness was unmoved by the pursuits and temptations of the beautiful Celestial Maidens. It was because he had been practicing the Great Emptiness Translucence and he spurned their advances.

Back then, almost all the Celestials had lived in isolation from one another. Even though they had all belonged to different fractions but duels between the Celestials when they had met usually did not result in death unless for the most extremely cases; since killing a Celestial were detrimental to their celestial advancement.

She could still remember vividly how she had met the White Sage.

That day, she was on the way to the Ascension Palace to attend an important event that only happened once every one hundred years. When she was near the Great Tranquil Mountains, she saw an auspicious rainbow halo and an auspicious rainbow cloud. She was immediately startled!

It was because auspicious celestial omens were a rarity in the Celestial Realm and only seen when a celestial event had happened. When she had reached the scene, she was just in time to see a handsome young man struggling to stand straight after overcoming the Divine Calamity!

She immediately thought, "Who is this young man? Why is that he is so fortunate to have two celestial omens to aid him to ascend as a Celestial?"

She deliberately observed for a while and was stunned. This young man was clearly alone and there were no other Celestials in sight to serve as his protectors, nor did he have any Heavenly Relics with him. How did he manage to ascend as a Celestial when he was so young and moreover the occurrence of two celestial omens that happened at the same time was also an oddity itself!

She had never seen or heard of any Celestials that had two accompanying celestial omens that appeared at the same time. For most Celestials, the appearance of a celestial omen was an extremely rare event; for most of them, it only appeared when most of them were not prepared or had no divine crisis to overcome. It was more of a celestial sign for things to come...

As for her, even though she had received the indirect aid of the other Celestials and given the Perpetual Darkness, she could still remember how she had nearly lost her life in her ensuring Divine Calamity.

She secretly sighed, "Talk about bad timing for myself and good timing for him...I have become a Celestial not long ago and I have to suffer so much."

She was immediately intrigued by him and had flown with startling speed next to him, causing him to react with a surprise expression as she asked, "Are you alright?"

She had no idea how a simple 'Are you alright' would affect the two of them later!

The young man had just overcome the Divine Calamity and his eyes had just turned crimson. When he had thought that he would die in the aftermath of the Divine Calamity, a beautiful angelic heavenly maiden had appeared next to him and comforted him with soft words!

Because he had practiced the Great Emptiness Translucence, he was not interested in the physical appearances of any beautiful maidens nor could he be moved by any temptations easily. But somehow, at his lowest ebb in life and just when he had experienced the Celestial Awakening, his emotion awakening was also the most easy to be shaken; as he had not got used to his new awakening senses yet.

The young man appeared to be extremely touched and his eyes were bleary as he quickly said, "I'm alright. I guess I have ascended as a Celestial and maiden you must be a heavenly maiden that have comes to receive me to the Celestial Realm?"

Shen Xingyue was a little amused as she laughed softly, "You are indeed a Celestial now but I am not here to receive you. In fact, I am a little busy and in a rush. It is only my curiosity that has brought me here. Well then, good luck on being a Celestial and good bye!"

She had already turned around and had leapt away!

"Heavenly Maiden Sister! Please wait awhile!"

It was the young man again and he had leapt next to her in a startling flash!

But because he was still very weak, as soon as he had leapt next to her, he stumbled and had fallen right into her!

Shen Xingyue was startled and she began to flush shyly as she quickly pushed him away, "You, watch your steps! I have never seen a Celestial that is as clumsy as you!"

The young man apologized most profusely as he quickly said, "Usually I am not that clumsy…"

Shen Xingyue was amused again as she laughed softly, "So you are intentional?"

The young man apologized again as he quickly said, "I feel a little weak after overcoming the Divine Calamity…"

Shen Xingyue whispered shyly, "You don't have to explain! I understand! I am only teasing you!"

All of a sudden, she had found herself talking to this young man more than she was willing at first.

She asked patiently, "What do you want? I am really in a hurry!"

The young man said with a sudden loss, "I am new as a Celestial. I really do not know the rules of the Celestial and how to proceed further. I wonder…"

The young man seemed embarrassed and he was now flushing. He had never flush as red as now, "Heavenly Maiden Sister, erm…I just wondering if I can come with you? Maybe I can train as a Celestial with you?"

Shen Xingyue laughed softly, "So you are thinking of Dual Celestial with me?"

The young man asked curiously, "What is a Dual Celestial?"

Shen Xingyue explained with a soft amused grin, "You really do not know?"

The young man had a stunned expression in his eyes.

Shen Xingyue said quickly, "Oh well, I can tell you but don't tell anyone I say this to you, alright? My reputation in the Celestial Realm will be ruined if you tell anyone of it."

The young man nodded eagerly.

Shen Xingyue said, "The Dual Celestial Progression is between two Celestials that pledge themselves as a pair, something like earthly couples. Now you got it? But it is considered to be more like a hindrance to the Celestials and not many are willing to practice it as our celestial progression will slow down. And moreover the two celestial couple must be able to progress at the same time or else their divine crisis will be extremely difficult. Until now, I have never heard of any Celestials that had successful ascended to the Ninth Heavens via the Dual Celestial Progression."

The young man asked, "Heavenly Maiden Sister, then can I Dual Celestial with you?"

Shen Xingyue was amused as she laughed softly, "I am afraid that you are still many celestial years too early for that. First you must overcome the Emotion Celestial State of Divinity or else it will be too dangerous for you."

The young man seemed to be stunned as he asked, "What is the Emotion Celestial State of Divinity?"

Shen Xingyue sighed softly, "I guess I help you all the way then. You really don't know anything about being a Celestial… I wonder how you overcome your Divine Calamity in the first place. (Sigh), let me give you a quick crash course then. There are seven celestial divinities to overcome before you can finally ascend to the Heavens above. They are Genesis, Enlighten, Emotion, Transverse, Seventh Sense, Crisis and Ascend. Got it?"

The young man was in awe, "I didn't know that there are so many states of divinities. It seems that being a Celestial is harder than being a human."

At that, Shen Xingyue sighed too as she said. "That's right…it is much more difficult and we can die at any moment…on the whims of the Heavens. That is why we need to trend carefully with every step forward."

The young man asked, "Heavenly Maiden Sister, can you explain to me what are the functions of each of the state of divinity?"

Shen Xingyue smiled bitterly, "I am really too busy to explain in depth to you but very well on account that I am your first celestial friend…"

The young man nodded happily, "My first celestial friend…"

Shen Xingyue continued, "The divinity state of each staging is a crisis that has to be overcome before the next celestial advancement and it is furthered divided into a lower tier, intermediate tier and an upper tier. Genesis is the awakening state which you are currently at now when you first become a Celestial. The Enlighten state is the awakened state when you survived to become a full Celestial and you will have achieved near immortality. Most Celestials actually stagnated after they become a Celestial. They are unable to achieve a breakthrough to the Enlighten state as they fall victim to their inner demons. Maybe it was because their Divine Calamities are too fearsome. Speaking of that, what is your Divine Calamity? Maybe I can give you some extra advice."

The young man sighed deeply as his eyes become bleary again. "It is my worst nightmare come true. My Divine Calamity is so terrible that I have no words for it and I will never want to experience it again…"

Shen Xingyue comforted him, "Have no fear. This is something you must overcome. The worse Divine Calamities are the heavenly lightning bolts and fireballs. Surely, yours can't be worse than that? I see no blackened marks around you. Don't worry; your Divine Calamity isn't as bad as you think."

She looked at him with a sympathizing look as she tried to comfort him, "If you are willing, you can share with me."

The young man nodded uncomfortably as he began to tremble, "I saw seven spiritual heavenly maidens dancing around me and trying to seduce me. It is lucky that I have a tremendous willpower and…just as I thought I have almost overcome my nightmare, a rainbow cloud and a rainbow halo increases the glory of these seven heavenly maidens…"

Shen Xingyue was totally stunned as she could not believe what she was hearing; a non-malevolent Divine Calamity was totally unheard of…

Shen Xingyue was still staring blankly at him when the young man asked her, "Heavenly Maiden Sister, what about the third state of divinity, the Emotion Divine State?"

She recovered her wits as she sighed softly, "The Emotion Divine State is also the Emotional State and is the period when a Celestial is most vulnerable. So you must be extra vigilant when you have reached this staging. If you can overcome this crisis, then you are able to enhance all your heart intricacy skills. The Transverse State is also the Reflex State. If you can overcome it, then you will gain enhance speed. The Seventh Sense is also called the Visualization State. It will enhance all your senses and unlock the Divine Sense. The Crisis State is also called the Calamity State, overcoming it will unlock your highest potential and your eyes will become gray. The Ascend State is the hardest and it is also called the Celestial State. It is the unison of the Heaven and Self. Your eyes will turn golden and you will live as long as the earth and the heavens last."

The young man was clearly extremely impressed and his eyes were glowing, "Thank you so much. Now at least I have an idea!"

Shen Xingyue smiled as she said politely, "Good luck then and good bye!"

She was reluctantly to part with him but she knew that their destinies had only crossed briefly.

The young man seemed reluctantly to part with her too as he asked, "Heavenly Maiden Sister, can I come with you?"

Shen Xingyue smiled patiently, "That is impossible. My protégé masters and protégé grandmasters won't be too pleased to see me bring an unknown Celestial to the Ascension Palace."

The young man seemed disappointed but he asked, "Celestials have protégé masters and protégé grandmasters too? And what is this Ascension Palace?"

Shen Xingyue explained with a soft laugh, "You will soon find the rules of the Celestial Realm to be even more rigid than the martial fraternity. I belong to the Celestial Ascension Sect, one of the three major celestial fractions in the Celestial Realm. There are many others of course. The Ascension Palace naturally refers to the location of the Celestial Ascension Sect."

The young man was impressed as he asked, "Then can I join the Ascension Sect? I really want to learn and advance my celestial progression with the celestial masters."

Shen Xingyue shook her head, "To be honest, I am just a low ranking Celestial and I have also ascended as a Celestial not long ago. Only the First and Supreme Celestials have the right to invite another Celestial to the Ascension Sect. The criteria are strict and most of us are handpicked even before we become a full Celestial. Maybe you have a better destiny elsewhere and you shouldn't force your destiny. There is nothing I can do to help you to gain entry to the Ascension Sect."

The young man was clearly disappointed as he sighed, "The Celestials always believe in the providence of heavens. Maybe it is really not my destiny to join the Ascension Sect then…"

Shen Xingyue said, "Don't worry too much and best of luck. Goodbye!"

The young man seemed reluctantly to say goodbye as he asked again, "I haven't know your name yet…"

Shen Xingyue laughed softly, "That's right. But I won't tell you my real name. It is because all Celestials have to use a Celestial Name and our old name is best forgotten. My Celestial Name is the Dark Enchantress of the West."

The young man listened attentively as he said, "What a beautiful and cool name! Since you are the Dark Enchantress, then I will be the White Sage then!"

Shen Xingyue smiled gently at him, "You are doing that on purpose, am I right? I…won't Dual Celestial with you, not ever."

The young man mustered the courage to ask, "Why?"

Shen Xingyue found herself confiding in him, "I have a sad past. I don't want to be engaged to anyone anymore. Anyway, that is the past."

The young man was saddened to hear that. It was because he really had a very good impression of her and he knew that she was friendly enough to explain so much to him. But he tried to cheer her up, "Let the past be the past. By the way, where do you stay before you have become a Celestial?"

Shen Xingyue chorus softly, "I stay near the scenery West Translucent Lake!"

The young man laughed, "What a coincidence! I have actually stayed near the West Translucent Lake, at the East City Gate. I am the eldest son of the protégé master of the Translucent City. But that is not important. It is all in the past and I have been disowned…"

Shen Xingyue had turned away and she was trembling!

Without a word more, she had left hurriedly and she was weeping silently tears!

The young man failed to notice her expressions as she had left too hastily!

He was still thinking of her very first words to him…

Shen Xingyue did not know how long she had been running before she finally stopped and collapsed on the ground as she cried inconsolably.

It was because that young man that she had seen earlier was her heartless fiancé that she could not get over with and one that broke her heart!

Their parents had betrothed them when they were still little.

One day when she had turned sixteen and soon to be married into his clan, she had received word that he had run away from home with a priest to pursue enlightenment.

Even though they had never met, she was shamed and heartbroken at this cold heartless lad who had run off just like that. It was because she was eagerly anticipating the wedding and what it meant to have a family!

When he had left so suddenly, her world came stumbling down!

In a spur of a moment in excessing grief, she ran away from home and decided to travel to the various holy mountains to seek enlightenment. She was really fortunate and a Supreme Celestial from the Ascension Sect was touched by her sincerity and potential; she was then picked to be his direct protégé. Five years later, she had successful overcome the Divine Calamity and had become a Celestial. The speed of her celestial ascension was said to be the fastest in the entire known history of the Ascension Sect!

She had never expected to meet him after she had become a Celestial…

Many years later after they had met, the White Sage of Emptiness had joined the Great Quiescent Sect and had actually progress rapidly. Soon, his level of attainment, his righteous air and compassionate heart caught the imaginations and attentions of many beautiful Celestial Maidens. However, he did not seem to be interested in their advances but that did not stop many Celestial Maidens from secretly falling in love with him.

In a blink of an eye, hundreds of years had passed. The White Sage of Emptiness was known for his compassion and quiet chivalrous acts, impressing many, including the Celestials from different fractions. It was said that he had often traveled the fraternity in search of a maiden but he had never found her.

It was because Shen Xingyue simply refused to see him!

She wanted to be more cold-heartedly than him…

When the Divine Descendant happened, quite a few of the Celestial Maidens were worried that the White Sage could not survive the Divine Descendant due to his compassionate nature. Therefore they secretly traveled to the Great Tranquil Mountains to secretly protect him or to sacrifice themselves for him so that he might live.

That included Shen Xingyue…

When she had arrived at the Great Tranquil Mountains, she was startled to find the Eclipse Heaven Goddess and the Axis Heaven Goddess lying on the ground and they were injured.

She simply could not believe that the White Sage could harm her protégé sisters or even capable of hurting two Supreme Celestials.

But the White Sage of Emptiness had said to her, "It is a good thing that you have arrived or you may be too late to save them. You don't have to ask. It is I who has injured them. If you do not kill me, I will kill you because I do want to survive the Divine Descendant."

Without waiting for her to respond, he had attacked her!

She had retaliated but when she had gained the upper hand, the Eclipse Heaven Goddess and the Axis Heaven Goddess had mustered their remaining strength to stand, not to attack the White Sage but her!

Their surprised attacks had caused her to fall down a deep chasm.

That was how she had lost her celestial force and had survived the Divine Descendant!

And now she was facing the White Sage again who was Yi Ping and Luminous Star who was now called Lie Qing. On his side, was also the Eclipse Heaven Goddess and the Axis Heaven Goddess.

Shen Xingyue of course knows that Yi Ping was not the White Sage even though he may look like him. The real White Sage may have already been killed by the other Celestials or had ascended to the Ninth Heavens after the Divine Descendant. He was the one that she had secretly loved and no one could ever replace him in her heart. It was because she hated him as much as she loved him.

She did not even know why she had been so irrational and had chosen to intervene to save this Yi Ping from the Honor Manor. Perhaps, in her heart the Divine Descendant had never ended and this was a thousand year battle that was still continuing.

All of a sudden, Yi Ping was wiping his tears with his sleeves as he said in a trembling voice to her. "You are the Dark Enchantress of the West…I know you. You are Shen Xingyue and you stay near the West Translucent Lake…"

When Shen Xingyue had heard that, she was so stunned that she had actually dropped the Blue Heavens as she gasped, "You remember…?"

Chapter 61: The White Sage and the Three Star Sisters of Fate

Yi Ping countenance was emotional as he cried aloud and his entire body was trembling, "How is it possible for me to forget you? You are the one that I have been searching for all along. You are my fiancée…it is only when we have parted that I have realized who you are and your real name from another Celestial but no matter how hard I have searched, I cannot find you…"

Shen Xingyue was trembling, "Is that why you have purposely said all those cruel words to me that day so that I would kill you?"

Yi Ping was weeping emotionally, "I am really so happy to see you that day but there are two other maidens that day that have also decided to sacrifice themselves for me. I know that you are planning the same or else why of all times, you have to decide to come during the Divine Descendant?"

The Eclipse Heaven Goddess and the Axis Heaven Goddess were not the only ones. The Three Star Sisters of Fate, the Celestial Ocean Heavenly Maiden and the Endor Fairy Vixen did the same as well.

Shen Xingyue muttered as she sobbed in his embrace, "Maybe I have come to take your life as well…"

Yi Ping had walked quietly to her and had brought her into his embrace as he placed his arms around her tightly, "No, you won't. Your eyes have betrayed you. If you hate me, you won't look at me with such concern. That day when you have left, your eyes have the same expression. If you really hate me, then you would have rebuked me or beat me up that day and not left in sorrows…"

Shen Xingyue was weeping inconsolably, "I have thought that I would never see you again…" She was suddenly startled as she looked up curiously at him, "How did you know…are you really him? No, that can't be…"

She began to break free of him and took a step back as she stared at him with a shocked realization. It was because it was impossible for anyone to carry memories of their past incarnations. Moreover, Yi Ping was not the White Sage.

But Yi Ping said, "I am the White Sage. It is a long story…"

He turned and looked at Lie Qing, who was staring at Shen Xingyue and him with utter disbelief and shock.

Lie Qing could not believe what she was seeing when Yi Ping and Shen Xingyue had suddenly embraced each other. She had lowered her long sword and her eyes were bleary.

She was not the only one.

Everyone was stunned and bewildered.

But as the windforce and martial shockwaves of Lie Qing and Shen Xingyue were still continuing unabated, everyone continued to adopt a wait and see attitude, not that they could do anything at the moment.

Han Shandong was shouting, "Mistress, don't believe this Yi Ping. Don't forget we still have a greater enemy to face…"

Shen Xingyue was only paying scant attention to Han Shandong as Yi Ping had already pulled Lie Qing close to him as he put their hands together. He sighed deeply as he muttered, "We only have Qing'Er and her sisters to thanks for it…"

Lie Qing broke into a soft laugh, "Tell me about it then."

She looked at Shen Xingyue with tendering eyes as she smiled, "Shall I call you dear Sister Xingyue then?"

Shen Xingyue was startled at the sudden change in Lie Qing's attitude; the sudden animosity that was displayed by her was replaced with an approachable and receptive friendliness!

She did not know that Lie Qing was also a smart maiden that did not like to go hard against a more powerful opponent unless she had no other choice. That was why she could turn Xiao Youxue and Dugu Yunzi on her side eventually, proving that she was worthy of their trust with her sincerity.

Others who did not know Lie Qing may think of her as an opportunist but that was not true.

She could tell that Yi Ping and Shen Xingyue already had something going on between them. She knew that if she wanted to be with Yi Ping, she must ready to be accommodating. After all, it was common for many men to have many consorts and it was not a too big issue to her; her father, uncles and brothers too had many consorts.

Shen Xingyue nodded slightly and smiled gently at her but she did not let down her guard, maintaining her Divine Rejuvenation Force.

She was secretly glancing at her surroundings and looking secretly at Xiao Shuai, Yuan Shao, Han Shaodong and the Three Sages. She was in an awkward situation and was thinking how to resolve it for she knew very well that the Virtuous Palace and the Honor Manor were determined to gain the secrets of immortality.

The irony was that even Han Shaodong was not aware that his protégé mistress was a Celestial; it was because she had deliberately hidden this knowledge from him. She did not know that he had conspired with Xiao Shuai to make an attack on the Celestial Palace and the Holy Hex Sect so that he would be a Celestial himself. He had revealed his plans to her recently because he had hoped that his protégé mistress would retire out of her reclusion to lend him a helping hand.

Alarmed and intrigued by the prospects that there were other Celestials, she had agreed.

When Lie Qing saw that Shen Xingyue had nodded, she took it as a hint of silent approval and greeted her happily. "Dear Sister Xingyue! You can call me your Sister Qing'Er!"

Shen Xingyue said softly, "Sister Qing'Er, sorry for giving you a scare."

Lie Qing whispered, "That's alright, Sister Xingyue. But we are being surrounded by our enemies and we need a plan fast."

Yi Ping said quietly as he held their hands, "Qing'Er, Yue'Er…hold my hands and look into my heart…"

Earlier when Yi Ping looked into Shen Xingyue in her eyes, his Emptiness Translucence had suddenly overwhelmed him and he could remember his past vividly!

In that one single instant, his Emptiness of the Absolute broke freed of his present state of divinity and reached the highest level of the Emptiness Translucence, the Emptiness of the Great Ultimate, transforming his Emptiness Translucence to the Great Emptiness Translucence!

Because Yi Ping previous self was the White Sage and the Great Emptiness Translucence was also a divine skill that could transverse as a mirror, keeping precious memories until he could finally reawakened once more as he progressed through it once again. This of course was not enough for a theoretical divine skill to really happen but at his moment of death, a divine coincidence happened to him as he collided with the Divine Universal Force that was presented in the Celestial Annihilating Star Formation, blurring time and space as he gave up his divine life force into the Celestial Annihilating Star Formation!

Lie Qing and Shen Xingyue were startled as they seemed to enter a dream.

Yi Ping had now remembered vividly that that day when he had first met the Three Star Sisters of Fate…

He had blundered into their Celestial Annihilation Star Formation in the mountains by a mistake when he saw a series of intriguing celestial lights in these desolation mountains.

Intrigued by it, he moved to investigate and it was then that he had chanced upon three beautiful heavenly maidens in white.

He was astonished at the intriguing and moving sight of Revelation Star (Yixian) when he first caught sight of her though it was not exactly a friendly welcome. It was because he could sense a great tranquil peace within her and instantly knew that she must be a highly attained Celestial Maiden!

She had said coolly, "There is an intruder and he must be after our divine swords. Activate the Celestial Star Formations and let the formation deal with him!"

The White Sage was startled as he quickly said, "I am not a thief. Are you all Celestials too?"

Revelation Star smiled gently, "Isn't it obvious?"

The White Sage said, "That's great! I am a Celestial too…"

Revelation Star interrupted gently, "We know. Or else, you will not have the ability to break into the sealing circle that we have setup and talk to us now."

Luminous Star (Lie Qing) was smiling at him, "Such a cute young man. Do we really want to kill him?"

The White Sage quickly apologized, "Erm…I will leave immediately. I didn't know that this is a Celestial Formation setup and didn't mean to intrude. I am just looking for a celestial sect to join…"

Luminous Star laughed softly, "Then you are looking at the wrong place. The Celestial Melody Palace only permits celestial maidens and you are obviously not."

Revelation Star added gently, "It is already too late. The formation has already been activated." And she had faded into the Celestial Star Formation!

The White Sage stammered out after her, "Isn't it forbidden for Celestials to kill one another?"

But it was already too late to call after her; walls of dust, sand and flying stones had whirled around him as his surroundings erupted into thunderous hovering burst of flying projectiles!

Luminous Star laughed softly as she answered him, "That's not true and there are several exceptions."

The White Sage broke into a cold sweat, "Killing a Celestial will be detrimental to your divine progression, isn't it?"

Melody Star (Lele) winked at him and laughed jovially, "So we have an ignorant Celestial in our midst right now. Judging from his expression, he must be a new Celestial. Let me tell you then. You will soon be killed by the renowned Celestial Annihilation Star Formation and not by us so therefore it doesn't affect our divine progression at all."

The White Sage asked gently, "Is there a difference? Getting killed by your Celestial Annihilation Star Formation that you have created and getting killed by you directly?"

Melody Star was laughing softly, "Actually there is no difference at all."

The White Sage was startled, "And then?"

Melody Star replied with an amusing soft laugh, "We have the celestial right to kill anyone that attempts to break into the Celestial Annihilation Star Formation and we have already killed quite a number of Celestials already. Do you know why this is called the Celestial Annihilation Star Formation? It has only one purpose, to kill all intruding Celestials!"

The White Sage laughed softly, "Now I see. May I ask how do I get out of here?"

Melody Star winked at him, "Shameless! You suppose to figure out yourself!"

Luminous Star quickly said, "Sister Melody, that's enough talks already. We don't know if he is alone or there are still many others."

Melody Star nodded and she quickly turned around and faded into a wall of hovering projectiles!

Luminous Star smiled at the White Sage, "So you are afraid now?"

The White Sage rubbed his nose and replied, "Not really."

Luminous Star was startled, "You are not?"

The White Sage said, "This is the first time that you are setting up this Celestial Star Annihilation Formation?"

Luminous Star was startled, "How did you know?"

The White Sage said coolly, "I saw nine celestial lights and a hint of the Universal Force in the mountains aligning constantly. If I am not wrong, you are experimenting with this Celestial Star Annihilation Formation for the very first time. I am plain unlucky to blunder into your Celestial Star Formation so you have decided to use me as a live subject to test your Celestial Formation?"

Luminous Star laughed softly, "It seems that you have guessed correctly but that doesn't help you in your predicaments. But no matter what happens, don't try to break into the inner formation or you will surely die. Just get out as soon as you can.

After warning him, she faded into a wall of furious sandstorm!

The White Sage immediately leapt forward to where she had disappeared and instead of fading into the wall of sandstorm, he was knocked back onto the ground by a powerful rebounding force and was badly bruise by it!

Even though he was badly bruised by it and sustained a minor internal injury, he was smiling. "So she is just waiting for the wall to move into her position so that she can fade into the other side. As I made the leapt a few seconds later than her, I have encountered a solid force blocking me. This small amount of force can injure me? If I am not wrong, this entire celestial formation is held into place by the Universal Force. But how is it possible?"

He began to look at his surroundings for a way out…

Revelation Star was touching the Heavenly Earth Sword, the White Phoenix Sword and the Divine Echo that were thrust in the middle of the Celestial Annihilation Star Formation gently as she had a melancholy look in her eyes.

Melody Star was stroking her long hair, "Don't tell me that our aloof sister will actually take a liking to him?"

Revelation Star was startled, "Rubbish!"

Melody Star laughed, "He is cute and fine looking isn't he? I can't believe he is a Celestial. It will be a pity to kill him then."

Revelation Star hummed coldly, "It seems that you are the one that likes him."

Melody Star winked with a playful expression, "If Sister does not like him then he is mine then?"

Luminous Star sighed, "Why are you only asking Eldest Sister? I didn't even say I don't like him. Why didn't you ask me instead? Don't forget I am your Second Sister."

Melody Star was woeful, "You…like him?"

Luminous Star laughed softly, "Why not? He looks like a fine looking young man and I am unattached."

Revelation Star was solemn, "Sisters, we don't know his background. There are many treacherous Celestials around that wants obtain the Heavenly Relics and secrets of the Celestial Annihilation Star Formation. The Melody Palace has entrusted us to protect these three divine swords from falling into the wrong hands. In the wrong hands, a celestial calamity could happen."

She looked woefully at the golden halo of the Heavenly Earth Sword as she said, "This celestial sword is the only sword in the entire universe that contain vestiges of the Universal Force. The only place that it can be used without disrupting the order of the universe is in this Celestial Annihilation Star Formation. We must not give the Dark Celestials any opportunities to bring chaos into the world…"

Melody Star was sorrowful too at the mention of the Dark Celestials, "During the last battle with the Dark Celestials, many of the protégés of the Melody Palace had perished and we had almost lost the Heavenly Earth Celestial Sword."

Luminous Star said to Revelation Star, "Earlier when we had lost control of the three divine swords, it was his sudden appearance that had stabilized the Celestial Annihilations Star Formation or else given our predicament earlier, we would have almost all been killed. Are we really too harsh with him?"

It was their first attempt in trying to recreate the deadly Celestial Annihilation Star Formation after their protégé mistress the Stellar Heaven Fairy had ascended. Just before she had attempted the divine sojourn, she had revealed the secrets of the Celestial Annihilation Star Formation to them, warning them that the first attempt was always the most difficult as they may not be able to control the celestial force within this huge celestial formation. That was why there were nine others celestial maidens watching nearby and ready to take their place should they failed in their attempt!

Revelation Star smiled gently, "Don't worry. The killing celestial force of the Celestial Annihilation Star Formation is not activated and no real harm will happen to him. I just want to warn him off so that he will be mindful to get out of here as soon as possible."

Luminous Star was relieved, "Thank you Eldest Sister!"

Revelation Star asked, "Thanks me for what?"

Luminous Star giggled, "You obviously know…"

Melody Star laughed lightly, "But you know it is pretty scary that we have almost turned to star dust earlier and now we are making light of our situations."

Revelation Star was once again solemn as she said, "We need to recollect what has gone wrong and what we ought to do so that we will not cause a repeat of what had happened earlier."

Luminous Star was solemn too as this concerned their life and death destiny as she sighed sadly, "We may not have the celestial attainment to control the divine swords and the Celestial Annihilation Star Formation yet. There are many who are chosen but they were all killed during the confrontation with the Dark Celestial Sects not long ago. We are one of the youngest…alas…"

Revelation Star was quiet, "It is too late now for regrets. We need to regain control of these divine swords before the more powerful celestials took notice of us. We can't just leave these three divine swords, especially the Heavenly Earth Sword here."

Melody Star was muttering, "What has actually gone wrong? There are at least twenty-one parameters that can have gone wrong or waiting to break apart earlier. Without our protégé mistress to guide us, I am really afraid of attempting the Celestial Annihilation Star Formation again."

Revelation Star sighed, "Is it the end of our destiny today?"

All of a sudden, there was a startled expression on her face, followed by Melody Star and Luminous Star!

It was because the young man that they had encountered earlier had just popped into the innermost of the Inner Formation of the Celestial Annihilation Star Formation while they were all talking!

It was not possible for anyone to enter the innermost inner formation without any one of them knowing!

The White Sage was sweating profusely as he said excitedly, "I have finally found the three of you!"

Melody Star stammered as she had raised her long sword in front of her, "What do you want? If you are thinking of seizing the three divine swords, then you have better forget it!"

Revelation Star and Luminous Star were too stunned for words as they muttered unintelligently…

The White Sage said, "I forget to introduce myself. My name is the White Sage. That's my celestial name now. I forget to ask for maidens' names and the directions to a reputable celestial sect so that I will be able to advance in my divine progression. Erm, I am new to the Celestial Realm."

Melody Star was asking, "You are really just asking for directions?"

Revelation Star looked at him curiously as she asked, "I am Revelation Star Maiden. You can call me Revelation Star. How did you come here?"

Melody Star quickly interrupted, "I am Melody Star Maiden. You can call me Melody Star and this is my other sister the Luminous Star Maiden!"

Luminous Star was looking at Revelation Star. Both of them were thinking of the same thing!

This young man did not barge into the Celestial Annihilation Star Celestial and stabilize the formation by accident. He actually knew what he was doing!

Revelation Star smiled gently at him, "We believe you then. I actually know the Celestial Ocean Heavenly Maiden from the Great Quiescent Sect. I am sure that if I were to recommend you to her; she may make an exception for you to join the Great Quiescent Sect. But first you need to tell us how you circumvented this Celestial Annihilation Star Formation."

The White Sage was still panting breathlessly, "It is not an easy thing to do. If I am not wrong, this Celestial Formation consists of eighty-one star formations on the outside and nine more on the inside. But the deadliest part of this Celestial Annihilation Star Formation is actually on the inside. I nearly died of sheer exhaustion as I made my way through."

Revelation Star immediately took out her handkerchief as she helped him to wipe away his sweat on his forehead as she said gently, "It is a lucky thing that we have not activated the Celestial Star Formation fully or else you won't be able to make your way here."

Not to be outdone by Revelation Star, Melody Star and Luminous Star also took out their handkerchiefs as they helped him to wipe away the beads of sweat on his forehead!

Melody Star was coy as she said, "How did you enter the Celestial Annihilation Star Formation in the first place? Do you know that it is dangerous for you in the first place?"

The White Sage explained, "There were plenty of mysterious inertia forces around. When I first enter this celestial formation, I was profound by its astonishing changes. However, I was curious at the same time. I also took the liberty of channeling part of the misalign forces away with my Mirror Reflection of the Emptiness Translucence. I hope that I didn't cause any damage?"

The three Revelation Star Sisters were startled and they were exchanging knowing glances at one another!

Revelation Star laughed gently, "On the contrary, you have been a great help and even save our lives. You can really detect the motion of the changes of the Celestial Star Formation? How did you do that?"

The White Sage nodded as he said, "If I focus hard enough, then my Emptiness Translucence is like a clear crystal lake on top. Any outside disturbances will create ripples on it. That is how I can sense the flow of the inertia forces."

Luminous Star laughed softly, "We are forming this Celestial Annihilation Star Formation for the very first time. I hope that you can guide us as we lay the changes of the Celestial Annihilating Star Formation one by one, telling us which area of the Celestial Star Formation is imbalanced."

Melody Star looked at him with pleading eyes, "It may take a long time but I hope that you can stay to help us…"

The White Sage said, "I guess I can. I am free anyway. But I hope that after this formation is completed, it won't be used to kill anyone."

Revelation Star laughed softly, "This is a defensive formation. Usually it is formed to protect an area. There is no way we can use it to harm anyone if they don't want to harm us in the first place. Moreover we are from the Celestial Melody Palace, one of three most orthodox celestial clans in the Celestial Realm."

The White Sage was startled as he said, "Oh really! I didn't know. That's great to know. What about that Great Quiescent Sect then?"

Luminous Star laughed softly, "The Melody Palace, the Great Quiescent and the Ascension Sect are three of the most powerful celestial clans."

The White Sage was clearly impressed as he said, "I have heard of the Ascension Sect before. Melody Palace and the Great Quiescent Sect…I guess I am in luck…"

That was how they had met and remained as friends for centuries.

The White Sage did not know that since then, the Three Star Sisters of Fate had already fallen in love with him. Throughout the centuries, they had all tried to give him several hints but it was obvious that the White Sage had only one thing in mind, overcoming through the various divine progressions and eventually ascended as a Celestial Sage.

The three normally dormant and slacking Three Star Sisters of Fate were all astonished at his divine progression every time that they had met him that they began to spend more and more of their time in their divine progression; they did not want to lose to him. Also as the White Sage progressed further and further, he was attracting plenty of unwanted attentions from the other celestial maidens, causing panic among the Three Star Sisters of Fate yet they did not have the courage to profess their likes for him openly as the Melody Palace had strict rules on celibacy.

When the Divine Descendant had struck, the Three Star Sisters of Fate had already made great advancements in their divine progression and had joined the ranks of the First Celestial, including the White Sage and Shen Xingyue.

The Divine Descendant was a major celestial catastrophe that pitted the celestials among one another. Because the Three Star Sisters of Fate had caused the deaths of too many Celestials, they were beginning to feel guilty and somehow knew that their ascension as Celestial Sagess were doomed in the first place.

And so they had decided sacrifice themselves for the White Sage.

It was because Revelation Star had stumbled upon the secrets of the Divine Descendant by accident; most of the Celestials did not know that they were actually dooming themselves after the seven years period of the Divine Descendant. That was when the Greater Divine Calamity would occur!

The Greater Divine Calamity would fall on those that had the bloods of the other Celestials in their hands. It was an even worse calamity than the Divine Descendant itself, seven folds of all the Divine Descendant combined, with virtually no survivors except the pure hearts.

In the end, Revelation Star and the White Sage seemed to be only survivors in the dawn of the new celestial realm.

As much as the White Sage and Revelation Star had secretly liked each other since then but their hearts were heavy with the deaths of Luminous Star, Melody Star and the other Celestials. Since then, they had silently gone on their separate ways as they tried to seek atonements for their sins.

Revelation Star did not attempt to ascend as a Celestial Sagess as the White Sage had secretly hoped. Instead, after she had overcome the Crisis state of divinity, she had spent much of her time pulling the threads of fate into the Celestial Star Formation so that one day, she would finally be united with her other close sisters and they would start all over again.

Her celestial plans were flaw from start as no one was able to accomplish what she was going to do. Even if she gives up her entire celestial life force, this was not going to help.

The White Sage was reawakened once again and he immediately came to the aid of Revelation Star. But it was too late. In that last moment, he could see her tears and her innermost feelings for him. It was only then he realized that all along, the Three Star Sisters of Fate was only trying to provoke him to kill them so that he may live, just like all the other celestial maidens!

His heart was in great agony and he felt that as a Celestial, he had actually lost much. He was the one and only Celestial Sage. But that was pointless to him. In that single instant, he too sacrificed himself and reworked the balance of Revelation Star's imperfect Celestial Star Formation with his Great Emptiness Translucence. No matter how small the odds were, how vain his sacrifices were, he had decided to extinguish his life for this gamble!

Lie Qing was trembling and she was crying. She did not know that they had such a past together! No wonder Lele was always calling her Luminous Star and dear sister. She did not lie to her and to think she had actually fought with both Lele and Yixian…

She took a quick glance at Yunzi, Lingfeng, Yu'Er and Mei'Er…

Lie Qing said quickly, "Yi Ping, let's go and help Sister Yixian now. She is in mortal danger…"

Xiao Shuai, Yuan Shao, Han Shaodong and the Element Sage had suddenly encircle them as they shouted, "You are not going anyway!"

They had seized the opportunity to attack them when they were all distracted!

Xiao Shuai had already thrown his flying sword at Yi Ping even as he was shouting!

Yunzi had already seen it coming as she readied her own flying sword against Xiao Shuai's flying sword but her flying sword was no match for Xiao Shuai's martial power; it got deflected while Xiao Shuai's flying sword went through into Yi Ping's body!

Immediately Yi Ping fell down onto the ground, startling Shen Xingyue and Lie Qing!

"Yi Ping!" all the maidens almost cried out at the same time!

Without waiting for Lie Qing and Shen Xingyue to react, Yuan Shao had thrown his flying sword sped towards Lie Qing, striking her with a thunderous and forceful impact! As she was still being protected by her nine hovering Invincible Divine Force, the flying sword was deflected and she was knocked slightly off balance.

In that split second when Yuan Shao's flying sword had temporary broke through the martial force of Shen Xingyue's Divine Rejuvenation Force, the Element Sage had struck Shen Xingyue's on her right shoulder with a thunderous impact even as she tried to avoid it!

Shen Xingyue coughed out a mouthful of blood even as she muttered, "Despicable!"

She had barely knocked the Element Sage backward when the crushing force of Han Shaodong's Big Dipper Hands came weighing and crushing onto them as he shouted, "You are not going anyway. Surrender your divine swords!"

Shen Xingyue said weakly, "Do you know that I am your grand protégés mistress?!"

Han Shaodong shouted coldly as his martial force came crushing down onto her, "Step aside, Protégé Mistress if you are still on our side!"

Even as Shen Xingyue and Lie Qing raised their swords in defense of this tremendous force that were raining upon them, Xiao Shuai, Yuan Shao and the Element Sage had immediately regrouped behind Han Shaodong with their raising swords glowing in purple hues!

The Martial Sage, Shangguan Qingyun, Yan Nanfei, the Sword Sage, Xiao Fei, Xiao Ao and Chi Zhengqi were shocked that Xiao Shuai, Han Shaodong, the Element Sage and Yuan Shao would actually launched a secret attack at Yi Ping, Lie Qing and Shen Xingyue!

Dugu Yunzi was startled that the Element Sage was also displaying the Dark Mono Swordplay as she shouted out panicky, "Be careful! That is the Dark Mono Sword Formation!"

Chapter 62: The Celestial Ocean Heavenly Maiden and the Endor Vixen Fairy

Lie Qing immediately displayed the full force of her Invincible Divine Force as she extended out her left hand to accept the incoming force of Han Shaodong's Big Dipper Hand while merging into the recess of the dark halo of her Perpetual Darkness Sword.

Shen Xingyue spoke out softly but her words could be heard loud and clear in everyone's ears, "I am not going to forgive any one of you!" She too, extended out her left hand. But instead of the Big Dipper Hand, she had displayed a finger stance of the Starlight Divine Fingers!

Almost immediately, there was a thunderous explosive impact as Lie Qing and Shen Xingyue clashed with the Big Dipper Hands at the same time, the resulting impact immediately created three additional ringing burst of shockwave as it broke the advance of Xiao Shuai, Yuan Shao and the Element Sage!

Han Shaodong immediately coughed out a furious bout of blood as he was thrown back in disbelief as he could not believe that their combined martial power would exceed his own!

Even before Lie Qing could press forward with her advantage, she was being surrounded by Xiao Shuai, Yuan Shao and the Element Sage as she parried their attacks aloud with a series of bright clash!

As Han Shaodong landed with a large crash behind, he shouted. "What are you all waiting for? Seize the heretics! And you, Sword Sage and Martial Sage, what are the two of you waiting for? This is a fight between good and evil!"

Immediately, more than a hundred exponents began to draw their swords as they charged forward!

But the Sword Sage, Shangguan Qingyun, Yan Nanfei and the Martial Sage refused to bulge!

They were in fact trembling!

Han Shaodong reminded them, "Have you forgotten our oaths?!"

Shangguan Qingyun lamented aloud as he laughed to the heavens, "The binding oath…"

All of a sudden, he took out his long sword and sliced off the thumb from his sword arm as he cried out in agony!

Yan Nanfei immediately said, "Brother! Why are you doing this?!"

Shangguan Qingyun laughed aloud, "Now I can't fight anymore. Do I need to be bind by the oath?"

Yan Nanfei was trembling, "Right, right. Now you can't even use a sword anymore and can't fight anymore…"

Immediately, Yan Nanfei unsheathed his long sword with a lightning speed and sliced off the thumb of his sword arm! "Now I can't fight too…"

The Martial Sage sighed, "Is that necessary? Do you know that we still have a greater foe to fight later?"

Han Shaodong reminded them, "Don't forget that maiden over there is the bane of the martial fraternity. The Invincible Divine Force and her crimson eyes! She is a blood sucking Celestial. If we let her escape today, the consequence will be disastrous! The Invincible Divine Clan wiped out numerous martial clans centuries ago. There are also hundreds of respected exponents from numerous martial clans that were sucked of their blood and their hearts eaten by the red eyes clan. Don't forget how they have died and so many of us are forced to go into hiding!"

The Sword Sage began to tremble as he raised his huge sword and charged into battle, while muttering. "I didn't forget how my protégé master had died..."

The Martial Sage marched into the battle with his fists!

Han Shaodong smirked at the sight as he unsheathed his long sword. Immediately, there was a purple glow in his sword as he imbued his sword energy into his long sword. "Xiao Ao, Xiao Fei, what are you waiting for? Execute the Dark Mono Swordplay immediately!"

Xiao Fei was startled. Judging from the energetic sword energy on Han Shaodong's sword, he could tell that Han Shaodong had been practicing the Dark Mono Swordplay for a long time and his level even exceeded him! He asked with a bewildered look, "You know the Dark Mono Swordplay of the Virtuous Palace too?"

Han Shaodong said coldly, "Not only me. The Martial Sage, the Sword Sage, Shangguan Qingyun and even Yan Nanfei know it as well. We been preparing for this day for a long time."

In the meantime, Shen Xingyue was not slow to react either. After she had countered the Big Dipper Hands with the Starlight Divine Fingers, she clasped her right shoulder with a cracking sound as she restored her dislodged shoulder. Immediately, she had picked up the Blue Heavens with her left hand and had swept the blue rippling shrieking shockwaves of her martial force all around her, knocking dozens of skilled exponents aside!

Shen Xingyue and Lie Qing were being surrounded by Xiao Shuai, Yuan Shao and the Element Sage as they sped across them from different directions with the Dark Mono Swordplay. They had displayed the purplish burst of energies in rapid succession at the same time!

The Dark Mono Formation was actually a deadly sword energy swordplay that emphasized on the swiftness speed of the practitioners as they whizzed across a target from three different directions at the same time and at the opponents' blind spot; this disabled the opponents' ability to defend themselves!

Lesser opponents would be instantly killed by them instantly!

The onlookers were stunned as they were forced to scurry by the powerful scattering sword bursts that were flickering in all directions!

Most of the exponents were watching in stunned silence as their movements and attacks were simply too fast for them to follow; they could only see shadowy figures and each time the shadow figures intercepted one another, there were more than a dozen of loud impact sound and flashes of light in that split second. It was the only indication that in a blink of an eye, these super opponents had actually exchanged more than a dozen sword strokes!

Lie Qing broke into a cold sweat as she parried swiftly in all directions!

Even though they were slower than Shen Xingyue but fighting them at the same time in three different directions was physical demanding and also, she had to deal with the dozens of exponents that had joined in the battle against her at the same time!

They seemed to have noticed that she was not as agile as Shen Xingyue and seemed to be focused more on her.

Just as Xiao Shuai and Yuan Shao had sped past her and were about to make a U-turn towards her, Lie Qing had suddenly raised her Perpetual Darkness towards them as she had just deflected an attack from the Element Sage; she had displayed the Pandora Merciless Strikes as she sent two arc of sword energies bursting with instantaneous speed in two different directions, one towards Xiao Shuai and one towards Yuan Shao!

They were immediately startled for they did not expected that she would be capable of imbuing her martial power into projectile sword energies and sending it homing towards them with such deadly power!

It was because the art of releasing sword energies as energy projectiles was already in the league of the Old Sword Saint Infinity-One! Other than the Old Sword Saint and Zuo Tianyi, this young maiden could actually reach this level of attainment that all the swordsmen in the martial fraternity dreamed of day and night!

And judging from her skillful display and precision aiming, she seemed to have reached this level of attainment for a long time!

Moreover, even the Old Sword Saint and Zuo Tianyi was unable to display two sword energy bursts at the same time!

They did not know of course that Lie Qing was conserving her martial power for a perfect timing and she was actually capable of unleashing up to seven bursts of sword energies but that feat would drain her powerless.

Xiao Shuai immediately raised his entire martial power and deflected the sword energy arc with his sword. There was a large impact even as he was forced to take several steps backward!

Almost immediately, two exponents near to Xiao Shuai had become his human shields and were killed by the deflected sword energy!

Yuan Shao was taken by surprise when Lie Qing had released a speeding sword energy at him. As he had just attacked Lie Qing several times when he dash past her and had used his remaining martial power to make a speedy escape, he was struck by her cold piercing sword energy!

It was not enough to bring Yuan Shao down as he was protected by the Divine Virtuous Force but he was coughed out a bout of blood as he cursed, "If I am not injured by the Celestial Fairy that day, this attack would never be able to hurt me…"

Actually Shen Xingyue was not faring too well either!

She had not recovered the use of her sword arm and was parrying the whizzing sword energy bursts of Xiao Shuai, Yuan Shao and the Element Sage at the same time when the Martial Sage, the Sword Sage and Han Shaodong too had joined in the battle!

This time, she was furious!

Immediately, she had displayed the 'Bursting Phoenix Dance' after Yuan Shao when he had narrowly missed her and his attacks were parried.

At her sudden burst of martial power, her Divine Rejuvenation Force intensified and exploded tremendous around her, instantly killing a dozen exponents who could not escaped in time!

Yuan Shao had barely escaped from the shockwave when Shen Xingyue had appeared with a startling speed on top of him as she brought her Blue Heavens down on him, pinning him forcefully onto the ground and breaking the powerful inertia force of his Divine Virtuous Force!

In that single instant, her swiftness speed and martial power had exceeded that of Yuan Shao!

Yuan Shao gave a loud dying cry as his chest was pieced. He discarded his sword and grabbed hold of Shen Xingyue's hands, pulling her down with him as he shouted. "My sacrifice will not be in vain!"

The Sword Sage, Xiao Fei, Han Shaodong, the Martial Sage and Xiao Ao who had also joined in the battle with the Dark Mono Swordplay noticed an opening against Shen Xingyue immediately!

As Shen Xingyue pinned down Yuan Shao, Han Shaodong and the Sword Sage took the opportunity to go after her and were already descending on top of her!

But before Han Shaodong and Sword Sage could land their swords on Shen Xingyue, they were intercepted by Ji Lingfeng, Xiao Youxue, Dugu Yunzi, Yu'Er and Mei'Er!

Yu'Er and Mei'Er had immediately displayed the Divine Emerald Skill with their swords as they intercepted Han Shaodong and the Sword Sage at the same time!

But Han Shaodong and the Sword Sage was simply too powerful and the martial power that were imbued on their swords were simply too overwhelming; Yu'Er and Mei'Er Divine Emerald Skills were broken in just an instant as they fell next to Shen Xingyue!

Just as they had fallen, Ji Lingfeng had displayed the Aspire Divine Hands with her right hand and the Great Dissolution Skill with her left hand!

At the same time, Youxue's hands had turn into a golden halo as she displayed her entire martial power at the two crushing force!

Yunzi had also attempted to intercept Han Shaodong and the Sword Sage at the same time by raising her two swords at them!

A ring of mighty force exploded in mid-air as Yunzi, Lingfeng and Youxue were all swept aside!

This gave Shen Xingyue ample time to turn around as she parried the combined attacks of Han Shaodong and the Sword Sage as the crashing blow from them exploded thunderous as they clashed with their swords!

This immediately caused her to slide several steps backward!

This entanglement was noticed by Xiao Shuai as he zapped towards Shen Xingyue at the same time but before he could thrust his purplish sword energy into her, two beaming bright halo knocked him, the Sword Sage and Han Shaodong aside at the same time!

Shen Xingyue was the first to gasp, followed by the rest of the maidens!

It was Yi Ping!

He was wielding the Divine Echo and the White Phoenix!

The two divine swords were surrounded by a bright blue and white halo, as they began to resonate loudly, startling everyone!

He was bleeding profusely from his body and he was foaming a great deal of blood from his mouth!

Shen Xingyue was in tears as she gasped, "Yi Ping...don't move anymore. Your wounds are still bleeding..."

Yi Ping muttered weakly, "I am really alright, don't you worry..."

All the maidens had grouped around Yi Ping one by one as they eyed their foes with burning hatred!

Yunzi and Youxue had quietly supported him as they looked tenderly in his eyes.

As they held him, Yi Ping had a sudden revelation suddenly who they were!

The first time that he had met the Celestial Ocean Heavenly Maiden (Yunzi) was when the Three Star Sisters of Fate brought him to the Great Quiescent Sect.

His first impression of her was one of awe and reverence!

Her quiet demeanor and her quiescent aura were so imposing that he was looking at her in stunned silence. She was not tall but she appeared to tower over him and there seemed to be a golden halo around her as he stared into her gray eyes!

Revelation Star smiled gently at him, "You are a Celestial and yet you are looking lustfully at the Celestial Ocean Heavenly Maiden? Isn't that rude?"

The White Sage woke up from his stupor as he panicky said, "I didn't. I just…find her to be so imposing. Sigh, I don't know how to explain it…"

Luminous Star and Melody Star burst into soft laughter.

Luminous Star laughed, "Don't worry. We are only teasing you. Most low attainment Celestials would have immediately bowed down on her knees. Sister Celestial Ocean's attainment is really very high. She is about to reach the final stage of Ascend soon."

The Celestial Ocean Heavenly Maiden asked gently, "Who is he?"

Revelation Star smiled, "Sister, he is a newly attained Celestial. You won't believe this. Not only did he save our lives, he has even helped us to complete the Celestial Annihilation Star Formation. As his wish is to find a reputable Celestial Sect to join, we decide to approach you."

The Celestial Ocean Heavenly Maiden was slightly startled as she asked, "A newly attained Celestial actually has the ability to help you complete the Celestial Annihilation Star Formation? That is quite unbelievable."

Melody Star laughed softly, "That's right. We find it so hard to believe too. But it is the truth. We hope that sister do us a favor by taking him in as your protégé."

The Celestial Ocean Heavenly Maiden expressed her concern calmly, "You know the celestial rules? This applies to all the other major celestial sects too. A celestial protégé has to be observed over a period of time for good character or it will be disastrous for the celestial clan. In the past, there are many Dark Celestial Infiltrators. They may appear to be good nature on the outside but they are actually wolves in sheep clothing. The last battle with the Dark Celestials were costly for both the Celestial Melody Palace and the Celestial Great Quiescent Sect. Our opponent was the Celestial Supreme Sect, having been infiltrated and corrupted by the Dark Celestials. I don't wish for the Great Quiescent Sect to suffer the same fate as the Celestial Supreme Sect. It is actually not a bad idea to be an Autonomous Celestial. At least, he can be carefree and led a happier life. When it is time for him to face a celestial crisis, he can look for me anytime for guidance."

The White Sage was stunned as he protested weakly, "I am not a Dark Celestial."

Even though she was soft spoken but she had finished said everything explicitly, leaving no room for arguments!

Revelation Star looked at the Celestial Ocean Heavenly Maiden with a pleading eyes and it was noticed by her.

The Celestial Ocean Heavenly Maiden said quietly, "Unless you can tell me who your Celestial Protégé Master is, there is no other evidence to prove otherwise."

The White Sage was solemn for a while before he said, "I don't know if my protégé master is a Celestial or if my grand protégé mistress is a Celestial but I have sworn never to reveal who they are. I'm so sorry."

The Celestial Ocean Heavenly Maiden hummed coldly, "They sound like Dark Celestials to me to have this type of secrecy. Judging from your celestial aura, you don't seem to be a half-Celestial but it doesn't prove to me that you are not a Dark Celestial either. You can go now."

Luminous Star and Melody Star both pleaded at the same time, "Sister, please consider. We come from afar and you are simply too cruel to turn us away! Have you forgotten how we used to fight side by side?"

The Celestial Ocean Heavenly Maiden was quiet for a while before she finally sighed softly, "This concerns the future of the Great Quiescent Sect. We cannot be hasty…"

Revelation Star turned her head away as she said gently but her tone was firm, "Then this is the end of our sisterhood. You can forget that we have ever met and we have ever been sisters!"

The Celestial Ocean Heavenly Maiden sighed softly, "Sister Revelation, how is it possible for me to forget that we are sisters and you have even saved my life before? Very well then, if he really wants to join the Great Quiescent Sect, he still has to pass a test to prove that he is worthy. What do you say?"

Revelation Star, Melody Star and Luminous Star had immediately cheered up and there were smiles on their faces as they hugged the Celestial Ocean Heavenly Maiden!

Even the White Sage was delighted even though he did not know what the test was about and he was uncertain if he could pass it.

The Celestial Ocean Heavenly Maiden said, "Don't be too happy yet. It is not an easy test and he has to overcome it himself and no one must help him."

The White Sage bowed respectfully with his hands as he said, "Thank you! I am willing to take the test anytime!"

The Celestial Ocean Heavenly Maiden turned around quietly as she thought, "Why is it that with my attainment, I feel an attraction to him? That is not right."

But she quickly recovered her composure as she said, "Follow me. Sisters, please wait here for a while."

The White Sage walked behind her respectfully.

As he looked up to her long flowing hair that reached almost down to her shoes, his heart was pounding hard. He could not explain the reason why he was feeling in this manner. But somehow, he knew that if she could accept him as her celestial protégé, he would be able to advance quickly. From what the Dark Enchantress had said to him, the Celestial Ocean Heavenly Maiden was a highly attained Celestial and her quietness moved him. Maybe it was because his Great Emptiness Translucence was aligned with the heart intricacies that she was practicing and that was what causing his heartbeat to accelerate!

After they had made several turning in the dark passageways, the Celestial Ocean Heavenly Maiden said, "We have reached."

She took out a bell and rung it before she opened a door politely as she said, "You can go in now."

The White Sage noticed that she was still staying outside so he asked, "You are not coming in?"

The Celestial Ocean Heavenly Maiden said, "No need. This is your test and not mine."

The White Sage asked, "What is the test about?"

The Celestial Ocean Heavenly Maiden said, "You will find out when you are inside." And she closed the door immediately after she had spoken.

However, the White Sage could still see her shadow outside and knew that she was waiting for him to complete the test. Not wanting to disappoint her and eager to complete the test, he took great strides into the chamber and got a shock of his life!

In front of him, he was looking at a most desirable maiden in an explicit sitting meditation pose; she was resting her head with her right hand on her forehead and her legs were spread casually.

She was dressed in light transparent purple silk and her skirt was really very short.

The White Sage gulped and swallowed hard as he thought panicky, "Is this the test?"

The extremely beautiful and desirable maiden opened her crimson eyes and smiled enchantingly at him, "Who are you and why are here?"

The White Sage averted his eyes because her silk dress was really too thin and he could see that she was not wearing anything underneath!

He said hesitatingly, "I am the White Sage. I am send here by the Celestial Ocean Heavenly Maiden here to take a test so that I can join the Great Quiescent Sect. May I know what the subject of the test is?"

The extremely beautiful and desirable maiden sighed softly, "The test may be too cruel for you. You can choose to give it up now before it is too late."

The White Sage said with great determination, "I won't give it up, no matter what it takes!"

The extremely beautiful and desirable maiden said enchantingly, "But if you don't look at me, how do you take the test?"

The White Sage was startled as he looked at her, "What do you mean?"

The extremely beautiful and desirable maiden smiled, "I am the test. You must open your eyes and look at me. If you don't, then you will fail your test. Do you understand me?"

The White Sage was startled, "What so difficult about it? That is also considered to be a test?"

The extremely beautiful and desirable maiden laughed softly, "That's right. It is a very easy test as a matter of fact. But you can only look and can't move, is that understood?"

The White Sage nodded, "I am ready any time."

The extremely beautiful and desirable maiden smiled enchantingly and with a mystique look with her eyes, "Good. My celestial name is the Endor Vixen Fairy. Nice to meet you. It is rare enough to encounter such a young looking Celestial. I hope that this won't be your disadvantage after all, young men are hot blooded usually."

She got up and walked towards him shyly.

The White Sage was already flustering!

If she had not got up, then it was still alright to him. But when she had got up and walked to him, she was like the most moving heavenly maiden that was alive and was extremely desirable to look at, no matter from which angle!

She began to loosen her belt shyly and in that instant her silken dress was loosened!

The White Sage was stunned as he stared at her tempting figure…

The Endor Vixen Fairy reminded him gently, "Remember, you must not move from your position or close your eyes."

The White Sage swallowed hard as he began to exercise his Great Emptiness Translucence as he muttered its heart intricacy formula, "See no evil, the great emptiness translucence is the absolute emptiness above all material temptations…"

All of a sudden, he got a nose bled when the Endor Vixen Fairy stripped herself in front of him shyly as she asked, "Am I beautiful?"

The White Sage muttered, "Very beautiful…"

The Endor Vixen Fairy laughed softly, "Am I desirable?"

The White Sage muttered as his nose began to bleed, "You are the most desirable of the desirables…"

The Endor Vixen Fairy asked, "Am I fragrant?"

The White Sage could sniff her delightful fragrance as he replied softly, "Very mesmerizing fragrance…"

The Endor Vixen Fairy whispered enchantingly as she breathed down on him, "You know, this may be a test to test your willpower but you have to be absolute serious about it."

The White Sage was startled, "I am serious."

The Endor Vixen Fairy laughed softly she gave him an enchanting mesmerizing wink, "Oh really?"

She had reached out and loosened his belt!

The White Sage was alarmed, "Maiden, what are you doing!"

The Endor Vixen Fairy whispered softly as she flustered, "This is a test remember? And moreover, you have seen my everything and I have not. Is that fair?"

The White Sage was stunned.

The Endor Vixen Fairy said, "From this moment, you mustn't say a word more. This is part of the test. Is that understood?"

The White Sage nodded.

The Endor Vixen Fairy smiled softly as she took off his clothing piece by piece, "Good. Let me ask you, are you married?"

The White Sage shook his head, bewildered at her questions but he did not think much of it. It was because his nose was bleeding nonstop as he continued to stare at her. He began to rub his nose but that did not stop his nosebleeds.

The Endor Vixen Fairy asked again, "Are you a virgin?"

The White Sage nodded in embarrassment.

The Endor Vixen Fairy gasped in delight as she said shyly, "You know, I am also as well. I have found no Celestials to be worthy of me. My role is just to tempt them and made them fail the celestial test. However, I can help you to pass your celestial test…"

All of a sudden, she was in his embrace and she was kissing him lightly!

And soon, they were rolling on the ground!

She said with a soft murmur as her eyes turned watery, "Don't you forget about me. Remember that I have put my tear in your heart for all eternality…"

Soon after there were several sounds of moaning and there were heavy breathing…

The Celestial Ocean Heavenly Maiden, who was standing and listening outside, was trembling and her quiet composure was disturbed!

After some time, the Endor Vixen Fairy walked out of the door and saw that she was still trembling. She smiled enchantingly and said, "He has a tremendous willpower and has passed the test but I am afraid that he has passed out. He lost too much blood from his nosebleed."

The Celestial Ocean Heavenly Maiden hummed coldly, "What are the two of you doing inside? Did you forget your duty? How can you do such a disgraceful and shameless thing! He has failed the test and he has to go immediately!"

The Endor Vixen Fairy said coldly, "Do you think I enjoy it each time you send those flirty old men to me? Don't forget that I am the assessor and if I say he passes, then he surely passes. It is not up to you to declare that he fails. If you are not going to take him in as your protégé, then I am going to!"

The Celestial Ocean Heavenly Maiden said in tremble voice, "You dare!"

The Endor Vixen Fairy smiled, "Why shouldn't I dare not? But really, why are you trembling? Do you have the mortal urges as well? If you are willing, I don't mind sharing him with you."

The Celestial Ocean Heavenly Maiden rebuked her, "Outrageous! He...he can join the Great Quiescent Sect but I am to be his protégé mistress and I not letting him see you ever again!"

The Endor Vixen Fairy was upset as she gasped in rage, "You....you...!"

That was how the White Sage had joined the Great Quiescent Sect. He was also extremely guilty thereafter. After that, he spent decades inventing and perfecting a new heart intricacy formula, the Absolute Spirits Intricacy Formula to strength the resolve of the heart!

Unknown to the White Sage, the supposedly invincible Absolute Spirits failed to work centuries later because of her one tear that was embedded deep in his heart and that resulted in a new awakening of his Emptiness Translucence!

After Yi Ping had remembered who Youxue was previously, his nose started to bleed as he looked at her in a new light!

The maidens were all gasping with concern when they saw the blood tickling out of his nose.

Lingfeng quickly popped in a pill into his mouth as she said with concern, "Swallow this. This may help you a little and stop the bleedings. But you should not move at all..."

Yi Ping muttered, "Lingfeng...thank you..."

Lingfeng smiled alluring at him, "Not at all...let's hope it is not too hard to swallow..."

Youxue and Yunzi, who were standing behind Yi Ping, had covered their mouths in shock for they had seen Lingfeng reaching into Yi Ping's pouch and what she had just given him was the Divine Dragon Pill!

Immediately after Yi Ping had swallowed the pill that Lingfeng had given him, he felt energetic and his wounds were not as painful as before. He clasped his chest and was stunned to find that his bleedings had stopped...

He thought in wonder, "What is it that Lingfeng has given me?"

Xiao Shuai interrupted his thoughts coldly, "You are now surrounded by the formidable Dark Mono Formation. If we all attacked at the same time, surely you know of the consequences. So be smart and dropped your weapons!"

Indeed, the Sword Sage, the Element Sage, the Martial Sage, Han Shaodong, Xiao Fei and Xiao Ao had surrounded them in six other different directions!

Yuan Shao had stood up weakly as he walked towards Xiao Shuai, "Good…my sacrifice is not in vain…"

But he could only take three steps forward before he stumbled onto the ground!

Xiao Shuai muttered, "My benevolent teacher, I will not let you die in vain."

He stared coldly at Shen Xingyue as he said to her, "You have killed my protégé master. Do you know what this means and what are the consequences will be!?"

Shen Xingyue began to tremble!

It was because with her extra sensory senses, she could feel the cold malevolent air of Xiao Shuai as he stripped her naked with his stares!

It was because no matter how Xiao Shuai had looked at her, she was an extremely beautiful maiden and Xiao Shuai was not going to let her die in such an easy manner and he was projecting his lustful thoughts at her, not knowing that she could actually sense it!

Yi Ping shouted weakly, "Remember, unless I am down you are not to take actions against any of them! If you have a score to settle, you can come after me first!"

Xiao Shuai hummed coldly, "That agreement is now voided!"

Shen Xingyue looked tenderly into Yi Ping's eyes, "Unless they have what they want today, they are not going to let any of us off. If only I…"

She wanted to say, "If only I am alone, I will be able to deal with them…" But her heart was unable to say it aloud. It was because after these maidens had intervened to help her, she could not bear to use her Divine Rejuvenation Force at such close proximity!

But Han Shaodong knew what she was thinking as he said coldly to Yi Ping, "What a joke. She can't even use her most powerful divine skill, the Divine Rejuvenation Force because she did not want to hurt anyone of you. With her swiftness speed, she can probably abandon you and yet you are trying to protect her!"

Mei'Er said, "What are you waiting for? We are not afraid of you. If our protégé mistress the Celestial Fairy is here, you will be the ones that are begging us for mercy!"

The Martial Sage interrupted, "Is Xian'Er well?"

Yu'Er said coldly, "She isn't happy that you are fighting against her two protégés now!"

The Element Sage said to the Martial Sage as he reminded him, "Don't get distract and get careless. She is just taunting you."

Xiao Shuai shouted aloud, "Youxue, I want you to come over here right now. Or don't blame your father for being ruthless later."

Xiao Youxue hummed coldly, "You have always been ruthless. That's doesn't concern me."

Xiao Shuai said, "Very well, don't blame me then. I will take care of you personally and kill you by my own hands."

He was in fact indirectly trying to warn the others not to touch her. In this way, he could protect her from the others.

Xiao Shuai had now waved his left fingers forward as he gave the signal for the Dark Mono Formation to take effect!

The rest of the exponents who could still stand were all holding their breath in nervous anticipation. Unless they were in their martial class, they could only watch now…

Chapter 63: The Birth of the Two Celestial Swords

Even as Xiao Shuai had raised his hand for his side to prepare to attack, Ji Lingfeng had whispered to Yi Ping and her group. "Execute the Celestial Star Formation. Yi Ping, Yu'Er and Mei'Er will be in the inner perimeter while Yunzi, Youxue and I will be in the outer perimeter. Lie Qing and Shen Xingyue try to hold as much as you can and fall back to us…"

Yi Ping and the rest of the group nodded.

Shen Xingyue had already visualized the entire battle in a blink of an eye now that she got the time to refocus, grasping the attacking and movement speed of all her opponents!

She was already channeling her intricate energies through to her right fingers as she made a full recovery from her earlier disability. Her Divine Rejuvenation Force had an accelerated healing recovery effect. With her present attainment, this was just a slight injury similar to a short momentum knock!

She had decided that when Han Shaodong had moved forward, she would use her Big Dipper Hands to attack him and to force him back. At the same time, when the Sword Sage, the Element Sage and the Martial Sage had leapt forward, she would do a turnaround speed attack and displayed the Starlight Swordplay with the Blue Heavens to blind and disable them. As for Xiao Shuai, as soon as he had attacked her or anyone, she would move to intercept him and striking him with her Starlight Fingers!

All of her main opponents would either be injured or lying on the ground in a blink of a second!

But her plan had a flaw. That would leave her vulnerable to the rest of her opponents. But she did not care less as long as she would injure these main opponents, then Yi Ping, Lie Qing and the rest would eventually find an opening to overcome them!

Lie Qing was also thinking of the same thing.

She had already observed that Xiao Shuai, Han Shaodong, the Sword Sage and the others were already panting or breathing heavily after using the Dark Mono Swordplay.

If her guess was not wrong, even though the Dark Mono Swordplay and Formation were formidable, it was a physically demanding swordplay to display and required a great deal of physical stamina to execute the precision strikes. That was why even though it was formidable, if the practitioners of this Dark Mono Swordplay could not defeat their opponent in a timely manner, then the risk would be on them instead!

The Heavenly Temptress Lie Qing was protected by her defensive Invincible Divine Force. She soon discovered that although the Dark Mono Swordplay was extremely deadly, she had succeeded in exhausting their martial power with her impregnable defense and skill.

Therefore she had decided to take a gambit and lowered the martial power of her Invincible Divine Force and transferred it to her sword as she prepared for her ultimate sword technique, the Pandora Merciless Seven Strikes!

She was wondering, "I am going to treat Xiao Shuai and that arrogant Han Shaodong some of my Pandora Candies. Since the two of you are the leaders of this group, my targets will naturally be you!"

Like Shen Xingyue, Lie Qing's plans had the same flaw. She would be exposed to several openings and put herself at risk. However, she too was prepared to sacrifice herself so that Yi Ping and the rest of her sisters would live…

In the meantime, Yi Ping was looking intently at his opponents as he raised the Divine Halo and the White Phoenix. He had already seen how powerful the Dark Mono Sword Formation was and with the maidens caught in the midst of this deadly sword formation, he was extremely worried.

He said in a low voice, "Yu'Er, Mei'Er, Lingfeng, Youxue, Yunzi…stay behind me. Their sword energies are formidable and you lack Qing'Er and Xingyue sword skills…"

Lingfeng smiled alluringly, "I guess, we may all die today…"

Yi Ping looked at her and smiled weakly, "We will not die…"

All of a sudden, he froze when he was looking at her. He had actually regained some of his most precious memories from his previous incarnation and was startled to know that all these maidens were all in one way or another acquainted with him in the past except for Lingfeng…

But now, he had suddenly remembered who Lingfeng was and he was startled!

The Heaveness was Lingfeng's previous incarnation. She was also the one that had taught him the Emptiness Translucence!

She was also the protégé mistress of the Universal Old Man, the old priest that had coerced him to abandon worldly desire to be a Celestial Sage. In short, she was actually his grand protégé mistress!

When he had first met her, he was in awe of her for he was only sixteen. He had expected the protégé mistress of his protégé master to be an old lady but instead, she turned out to be the most beautiful lady that he had ever seen…

The Universal Old Man had laughed at him then, "You didn't expect this, am I right?"

The Heaveness smiled alluring at him, "You look like a bright young man. Alright then, I will accept you into the clan and impart to you the most forbidden divine skill of our clan the Great Emptiness Translucence. Whether you can become a Celestial and overcome the Divine Calamity is up to Providence. But you must swear never to reveal our names to anyone, alright?"

He had nodded eagerly and he was totally overwhelmed by her smile that reached into his heart…

The Heaveness looked at him alluringly, "You can address me as the Heaveness and I am your grand protégé mistress, the protégé mistress of your protégé master who is the Universal Old Man."

He looked at his protégé master, the Universal Old Man as he thought. "So he is the Universal Old Man. He only allows me to address him as Old Priest Master when there are others around and I can't even call him my protégé master…"

He stammered as he mustered his courage, "Protégé Master never reveals the name of our clan, telling me that it is forbidden. Even his name and your name are under wraps. Did I accidentally join a cult or something? Why can't I tell others my clan and yours?"

The Heaveness laughed softly as she explained patiently, "We are not exactly a Celestial Clan or a Martial Clan. So there isn't any official name for us yet. Moreover, there are just three of us only."

He was startled as he stammered, "There are only the three of us? What is the unofficial name of clan then?"

The Heaveness said with an alluring and mystifying look, "It-Is-Forbidden."

He was disappointed that the Heaveness did not reveal the name of the clan to him and his disappointment was showed on his face.

The Heaveness rebuked him gently, "Why are you feeling so downcast? Just because you cannot know the name of the clan? Names are but an illusion. How are you going to overcome all the mysteries of the divine state to become a Celestial in the future when you can't even handle a small disappointment? Let me tell you, the name of our clan is called 'It-Is-Forbidden'."

He was stunned as he stammered, "That is our clan name?"

The Heaveness laughed softly, "Precisely. In state of divinities, there will be many things to ponder and many obstacles to overcome. Sometimes the texts of the heart intricacy formulas will mislead you and took you to the wrong deviation when you are confused. The name of the heart intricacy formulas have never changed in the first place, so never deviate from your exact purposes. You just need to know that the Great Emptiness Translucence is to teach you to be absolute peaceful and still, only then can you see through the illusions of things."

He was very much enlightened as he bowed down hastily on the ground, "Grand Protégé Mistress has indeed enlightened me!"

The Heaveness gave an alluring smile at him as she helped him up.

The Universal Old Man took a curious look at the Heaveness and was slightly startled. It was because he had never seen the Heaveness smiled before. When she smiling, it was as though the entire atmosphere had been changed to a gentle and moving alluring scene!

He had asked again, "What about your name? Is there any reason why you do not want others to know?"

The Heaveness sighed deeply, "Actually by knowing our names, in the future you will surely know a little about us. I will tell you a little more in the future but not today, alright?"

He nodded and did not argue. It was because he could sense the sorrows that were within her.

The Heaveness smiled again, "I am sensitive to others calling me by my name whether good or bad. So don't do that, alright? It is because in my time, names are sacred and that is the original language."

He looked at her in awe again as he said, "I won't call you or tell others that you are the Heaveness…"

Immediately, there was a tinged in her eyes as she quickly said. "Don't!"

He immediately kept quiet as he flustered with embarrassment at the gentle rebuke.

Time passed…

The Universal Old Man taught him the Emptiness Translucence patiently as he explained, "There are five stages to the Emptiness Translucence, which is called the Five Conducts of the Divine Ascendants which is the Spirit, the Void, the Enigma, the Absolute and the Great Ultimate. These are the stages of the Absolute Tranquil and beyond these five staging is the Great Emptiness Translucence. The Great Emptiness Translucence is a divine state that we may never possible reached…other than the Heaveness…"

The Universal Old Man taught him for a whole year while the Heaveness would occasionally appear but only at night to give him some guidance.

Even though the Heaveness had never appeared to him except at night but there were times he would encounter her in the most unexplained situation in nearby cities and towns; she would be a maiden that was selling textiles and clothes as she stood alluringly in the shop, a beautiful humble weaver attracting a great deal of attention, a singer with a beautiful voice and quite a few other roles. But each time when he tried to approach her, she would shake her head in a subtle hint and refused to talk to him!

But the Heaveness was secret startled. The numbers of coincidences were too many. There were many cities and towns in this region; something unexplained was drawing them together.

The Heaveness was sighing to herself, "This will be your undoing in the future. Perhaps it is better than you leave this place altogether…"

One year later, the Universal Old Man had suddenly disappeared and left him a note, giving him some advises and encouraged him to continue pursuing his attainment.

That was the last time that he had ever seen the Universal Old Man and the Heaveness again…

Years later after he had overcome the Divine Calamity, he would return to the Great Tranquil Mountains and had visited the Tranquil Clan which he had secretly founded. Among the intricacy heart formulas that he had left behind were the Emptiness Translucence and a description of the Divine Calamity that he had faced!

But Priest Liu Qingcheng had actually misunderstood the message in the Silver Scroll and had warned him to be wary of the Seven Maidens!

Back to the present, Yi Ping had unconsciously recalled this scattering fragment of his memories. As he looked at Lingfeng, he muttered in an almost inaudible voice. "Heaveness…"

All of a suddenly, Lingfeng's eyes began to twitch and there were beaming tears in her eyes as she muttered softly. "Look at me, I am feeling emotional again…"

At this moment, Xiao Shuai had finally turned his left flickering fingers into a forward fist!

It was because he had been waiting for the majority to recover their regular breathing first and the bright halos of Yi Ping, Shen Xingyue and Lie Qing swords were also causing their visions to blur as well as a feeling of nausea, slowing the pace of their recovery!

Immediately, Xiao Shuai, Han Shaodong, the Three Sages, Xiao Fei and Xiao Ao, altogether there were seven of them. They began to dash forward at the same time and their swords were colored with a purplish color!

They had only three targets; Yi Ping, Lie Qing or Shen Xingyue!

It was because even though they did not say it loud, they had known that their swords were not just any ordinary precious swords. Judging by the resonating vibrations and the halos of their swords, it had to be divine swords!

They were determined to seize their swords at the same time and to prevent others from seizing it. The most obvious target was Yi Ping and he looked to be an easy target!

Lie Qing and Shen Xingyue had immediately raised their divine swords and lifted their martial power as they braced for the incoming attack. They had already visualized all the possible outcomes and were just waiting!

Yi Ping too, had raised the Divine Echo and the White Phoenix as seven beams of purple sped towards him!

Yu'Er and Mei'Er were already secretly nodding at each other when the seven beams of purple light sped towards Yi Ping! They had already made up their minds to sacrifice themselves for Yi Ping as they bade him a silence goodbye. They had already figured out that the outcome would be unpredictable with their Dual Inertness Intricacy Skill.

Therefore, they had already decided that before Lie Qing, Shen Xingyue, Yunzi, Lingfeng and Youxue had a chance to intervene and possibly sacrificing themselves in the process, they were determined to intercept their opponents first and slowed down their speed attacks, sacrificing themselves first so that the others would find an opening.

So when the seven purple beaming of light had flashed towards Yi Ping, they had made the first move and had deliberately blocked Lie Qing and Shen Xingyue as they raised their precious long swords towards the seven purple beaming lights!

Shen Xingyue gasped as they sped past her all of a sudden as she called out loud, "Don't! It is too dangerous!"

It was already too late to stop them as seven beams of light clashed with two golden lights as it quickly developed into dozens of purple lights as it hovered around one another!

But when the purple and golden lights made contact with one another, the air around them exploded thunderous in a large blinding flash as the deadly martial force exploded into a wave of deadly pure energies, knocking and sweeping everyone aside!

Almost instantaneous, everyone including the onlookers was rolling and crying out aloud on the ground as the entire ground trembled continuously as though an earthquake had just struck!

The explosive martial wave was so deadly that scores of onlookers including those that were watching at the furthest end were killed in that single moment!

And immediately, cries of agonies were heard everywhere!

It was as though they had just been visited by the infernos of hell!

Shen Xingyue had raised her Blue Heavens and wrapped the Divine Rejuvenation Force around her when the extraordinary martial force struck her. She was stunned that the martial force had simply rippled through her and tearing her Divine Rejuvenation Force apart. Immediately, she coughed out blood in disbelief as she gasped, "No, this can't be. This martial force is the energies of the Divine Calamity…why am I so unlucky whenever I see these two sisters…"

Lie Qing was also coughing weakly as she used up half of her martial power to counter the extraordinary martial force!

When Yi Ping had seen the rippling effect of the extraordinary martial force that were ripping towards him, he gave a mighty martial shout as he raised the Divine Echo and the White Phoenix, executing the martial power of the Asper Divinity as a white burst of white light wisped around him!

At the same time, this white burst of light that was formed from his Boundless Divine Force created a wall of buffer as the extraordinary powerful martial force swept across him!

Yi Ping was startled secretly!

It was because it seemed that the martial power of his Asper Divinity had increased several folds in strength all of a sudden!

However, although the newly attained Asper Divinity was extraordinary and he had already buffered much of this deadly martial force, he was still swept backward!

Lingfeng had mustered her entire martial power as she displayed the Great Dissolution Skill to deflect the bursting energies of the weakened deadly martial force!

At the same time, Yunzi had mustered her Invincible Divine Force while Youxue had displayed the Golden Invincible Body and also the Divine Emerald Skill, startling Yunzi and Lingfeng as they gasped. "When did you learn the Divine Emerald Skill?!"

Youxue did not reply them as she was training her entire focus to maintain the circular motion of the Divine Emerald Skill!

She had of course learnt it from the Celestial Fairy who had already decided that she would be her successor. However, the Celestial Fairy had also told her not to use this secret technique unless she had no other choices for overtly dependent on it would be detrimental to her martial progression and using it too early against a dangerous foe would lose the element of surprise for her.

But now, she had no other choice!

She gasped softly, "Sisters, get behind me immediately!"

As soon as Yi Ping had coughed out a bout of darken blood, he picked himself up weakly as he turned around panicky to take a look at Yunzi, Lingfeng and Youxue who had all gave a startled cry when they were struck by the deadly energy of the sweeping martial force!

He was somewhat relieved when he saw Yunzi, Lingfeng, Youxue, Lie Qing and Shen Xingyue were all already on their feet and struggling to stand feebly.

Shen Xingyue angelic voice was already warning them, "Everyone don't stand up first. Quickly meditate and try to put the erratic energies into order first. Don't try to exercise any martial power for the time being. You are injured by the Universal Force. Unless you can purge it out of your body, you will soon lose your life and your martial skills!"

Xiao Shuai, Han Shaodong, the Three Sages and many others were already sitting in a mediation pose as they coughed out bouts of bad blood. From the look of it, their internal injuries were extremely serious!

At the same time, everyone was staring at Yu'Er and Mei'Er in complete disbelief as they stood in the middle of the carnage and the pandemonium!

Yu'Er and Mei'Er were now surrounded by two bright golden halos as bright as the sun that were radiating from their golden swords!

It was because as they had intercepted the sword strokes of the Dark Mono Sword Formation and when their long precious swords had struck against each other in their attempt to overcome their opponents' martial strength by combining their swordplay together, their swords had suddenly turned into a golden hue permanently and a bursting burst of light that were created from the impact of their swords exploded into all directions!

As unbelievable as it could sound, in that instant, Yu'Er and Mei'Er had brought all the exponents to their knees!

No one had an idea what had happened except for Shen Xingyue!

The Sword Sage had just thrown out another bout of black colored blood as he struggled to speak in trembling fear, "What kind of combine swordplay is that? In my entire life, I have never seen such a destructive swordplay…"

Even Xiao Shuai had a look of fear in his eyes for he had never seen anything like that. His Divine Virtuous Force was scattered instantaneous and his martial power was completed drained by the blinding unstoppable force!

He stared blankly at Xiao Ao who had been knocked unconscious for he was caught in the direct blast.

Han Shaodong was not faring too well either. His powerful Divine Rejuvenation Force was completed drained by the extraordinary martial force and it was only his sheer fortitude that had preserved his martial skills.

He was now looking at the surrounding carnage in stunned horror; he had estimated that at least two thousand exponents from all the martial clans were instantly killed and several hundred had lost their martial skills permanently. It was like a nightmare scene and extremely appalling!

The Sword Sage, the Element Sage and the Martial Sage had closed their eyes and were already trying to treat their internal injuries as much as possible.

Almost immediately at the same time, they had popped in a pill that was made by the Element Sage to speed up their recovery.

Xiao Fei was seriously injured and he was barely conscious…

There were also hundreds of loud wailing and moaning that came from the hundreds of exponents all around…

A number of surviving exponents were exclaiming in great shock as they queried weakly, "What is that martial skill that is displayed earlier? If I die, at least I ought to know the name of this epitome divine skill that has brought me to my grave…"

Xiao Shuai muttered solemnly, "You have won. We admit defeat. What is the name of this divine skill?"

Han Shaodong laughed weakly, "That's right. We are totally defeated. Our dream of ascending as a Celestial is now completely shattered. If we can't even defeat two maidens here, what hope have we got to defeat the Celestial Palace?"

The Sword Sage had opened his eyes as he muttered, "If Maidens can enlighten us to the divine skill that has defeated us, I will be gratuitous to you when I go down under the earth!"

Even though they were all admitting defeat but it was actually a delaying tactic so that they would have enough time to calm down the erratic energies in their bodies!

Yu'Er and Mei'Er were sobbing inconsolably as they looked at the terrible carnage that they had caused. They did not know even know what was going on at all!

They were still looking at Yi Ping, Shen Xingyue, Lie Qing, Xiao Shuai, Han Shaodong and everyone in bewilderment and in shock.

It was because Yi Ping, Xiao Shuai, Han Shaodong, Lie Qing and Shen Xingyue were the main characters of this battle and now when the twin sisters were suddenly cast as the main characters, they felt lost and was terrified!

Shen Xingyue was muttering, "This is the first time that I have heard of and witnessed the birth of two divine swords through the use of the Universal Force. And these two golden swords are as potent as the Heavenly Earth Celestial Sword that is said to be created at the beginning of time…how is it possible…"

Yu'Er and Mei'Er did not know that they had just generated the creation energies of the Universal Force by sheer coincidences!

It was because they had consumed the Divine Dragon Pills but because they lacked the internal strength to digest it and that they were not even seriously injured in the first place, the potency of the Divine Dragon Pills remained in their bodies. If they had not learnt the Dual Inertness Intricacy Formulas and suppressing their discomfort by using the vital energy exchanges but not the body and exchanging it with the essence of heavens and earth as their vitality, they would have been engulfed by the burning potency of the Divine Dragon Pills!

However, they could only delay the potency of the Dragon Divine Pills from reacting, delaying the harmful effect through a slow and painful process that was detrimental to their health.

The Dragon Divine Pills happened to be created from the meltdown of the power release of Yi Ping's Emptiness Translucence as it transformed his Aspire Invocations to the Boundless Divine Force (See Chapter 56), creating the Divine Dragon Pills from the broken pieces of the Heavenly Relic as a spark of the accidentally generated Universal Force was created and was stored in it.

The Dual Inertness Intricacy Divine Skill was a skill that balanced the vital energies of the inner force and the outer force in a delicate manner. In short because the twin sisters were unable to digest the Universal Force of the Divine Dragon Pills and at the same time, they were unable to purge it out, the Universal Force remained in equilibrium in their bodies for the time being.

So when they had cross swords with one another by channeling all their martial power, they had unconsciously power released the Universal Force that were in their bodies by exchanging the Universal Force with each other via the concept of the divine state of heavens and earth as their divine state!

As the Universal Force revived and clashed with each other, the power release was exactly that of the Creation Universal Force. It immediately tampered its way through their precious long swords, transforming it into two celestial weapons that were capable of absorbing the Universal Force as these two Universal Forces clashed against each other in total equilibrium!

As the creations of the two celestial weapons were completed, the remaining Universal Force shattered its force all around them, exploding all around with a huge big bang!

In that single moment, everyone was knocked or swept aside as the Universal Force was the ultimate force in the entire universe, killing or injuring everyone in the vicinity!

Yu'Er and Mei'Er were still looking at each other when a rainbow halo had descended around them; they were like celestial fairies that had visited the mortal realm and were extremely beautiful to beholden.

Shen Xingyue coughed weakly as she walked towards them as she said, "This is a celestial omen, indicating the creation of these two celestial weapons. Congrats!"

Yu'Er and Mei'Er were still teary and they looked at Shen Xingyue curiously.

Mei'Er asked in a frightened voice, "What has just happened? We seem to be surrounded by a glowing light…"

Yu'Er was still staring appalling at the numerous dead and injured.

They seemed to be glowing with a soft white light as they held onto their golden long swords.

Shen Xingyue smiled mysteriously, "Don't worry. Only Celestials and those that have attained a high level in their state of divinity can see it. Right now, you should give a name to your celestial swords."

Yu'Er suddenly gasped, "Mei'Er, your eyes! Your eyes have turned crimson! What is going on?"

Mei'Er was startled but when she saw her sister's eyes as well, she was gasping aloud too. "Sister, your eyes are red too!"

"Yu'Er and Mei'Er, are you alright?"

It was Yi Ping and he was being supported by Yunzi, Youxue and Lie Qing.

Yu'Er and Mei'Er had immediately flown to his embrace as they cried aloud.

Yi Ping comforted them weakly, "It is alright now. Everything is alright now. Let's leave this place immediately…"

Lie Qing asked quietly, "What has exactly happened?"

Shen Xingyue sighed softly as she looked at the appalling carnage all around her, "It seems that somehow these two maidens have just released the Universal Force that only exists from Beyond. I can't explain it too but what we are witnessing today are the rare occurrences of the birth of two celestial weapons. And they have also just been elevated as Celestials too."

Lie Qing was stunned as she quickly asked, "They can be elevated as a Celestial without experiencing the Divine Calamity?"

Shen Xingyue muttered, "I find it hard to believe too but that is what has exactly happened. What did they actually do…"

She had immediately raised and moved her right fingers rapidly as she seemed to be deep in thoughts!

Yi Ping muttered as he embraced Yu'Er and Mei'Er, "The big bang that has just struck us is indeed the Universal Force. It is a lucky thing that it is the benevolent Universal Force or else all of us would have perished just now."

Shen Xingyue nodded lightly as she looked tenderly into Yi Ping's eyes.

She was not the only one doing the same. All the maidens except Lingfeng were all looking tenderly in his direction.

Yi Ping looked at them one by one with an uneasy feeling and a feeling of guilt overwhelmed him. When he looked into Xiao Youxue's eyes, all of a sudden his nose began to bleed again. It was because he could not shake the image of the Endor Vixen Fairy from his mind and the scene when Youxue had 'given' him her chastity.

Immediately the maidens seemed to forget that they were still in the middle of a battle and were all panicky when Yi Ping had started to nose bleed; they began to take out their handkerchiefs to help him wipe his blood and sweat as they murmured all manners of concern for him!

It was such an enviable sight. All of a sudden, the surviving exponents felt a great sense of loss and they were all reminiscing to a point of time when they were with their loves ones or when they were in happier times…

Yi Ping said, "Somehow it seems that Yu'Er and Mei'Er have exchanged and absorbed the Universal Force as their own vitality energies. That act alone would have killed them but it didn't and instead they are elevated as Celestials…"

Shen Xingyue smiled softly, "It seems that there are moments that the White Sage can be wrong. The Divine Calamity did happen but it only appeared very briefly before it got extinguished by the Universal Force. The shockwaves that we have all experienced were the result of the clash between the Divine Calamity and the Universal Force. These two maidens have a heart of gold and that is why the Divine Calamity didn't last too long for them. This must be the shortest Divine Calamity that I have ever seen and also one that had arrived without any prior warning. If I am not wrong, creations of divine and celestial weapons can also brought forth the Divine Calamity. If they fail their Divine Calamity, not only would they die but their celestial weapons would also be destroyed."

Yi Ping smiled, "You are right…"

Ji Lingfeng had walked quietly to their side. No one seemed to have noticed her quiet expressions.

When the Universal Force had struck her, she had experienced a headache and was feeling nauseous. The Universal Force had reawakened a familiar feeling within her…

All of a sudden, there were hundreds of black ironclad fighters that that had appeared in the horizon.

Yi Ping had recognized that the man leading these fighters was Ji Wuzheng and the lady next to him was the Lady Dugu Zhen!

Yunzi was delighted as she said with a smile, "Mother is here!"

The orthodox fighters were alarmed that the Holy Hex Clan had arrived with their reinforcements and they were grim. It was because none of them had the strength to fight with the unorthodox fighters now. Out of five thousands orthodox fighters, only less than five hundred had remained.

Ji Wuzheng was appalled at the sight as he walked towards Yi Ping as he muttered, "What is going on here?"

As Ji Wuzheng turned and looked at Xiao Shuai, Han Shaodong and the Three Sages, they pretended not to see him as they focused on regaining their martial strength.

Xiao Shuai was startled when Xiao Fan walked silently besides him and said, "Father, forget it. It is all over. We should go back peacefully. Ji Wuzheng has promised me that they will not be pursuing any vendetta. Let bygones be bygones."

Xiao Shuai was startled, "Son, you are still alive? Who beat you up in this horrid manner?"

He was comforted that Xiao Fan was alive because among all his sons and daughters, he was his favorite.

Xiao Fan grinned as he looked at Dugu Zhen, Dugu Yunzi and Lingfeng, "This is the work of the heretic sects. We have all fallen into the stratagems of the heretic sects. It is Ji Wuzheng and that Yi Ping who has actually saved my life."

Xiao Shuai was startled.

Xiao Shuai said grimly, "Even then, have you forgotten that we are all so close to becoming a Celestial?"

Xiao Fan sighed, "Father, look around you. So many lives have already been lost. Is it worth it?"

Xiao Shuai said with a cold determination as he got up as he spat out the last bout of bad blood, "It is worth it, my son!"

His recovery rate was startling!

At the same time, Han Shaodong and the Three Sages had also recovered as they all stood up one by one!

Han Shaodong said aloud, "This is not over yet. I have thought that this two maidens have learnt some epitome divine Skills. So it is just a freak celestial manifestation. But if you are all willing to surrender your swords, you can leave here immediately. I will give you my honor for that!"

Shen Xingyue said softly, "Han Shaodong, Han Shaodong. I have thought you are a good man and that is why I take you in as my protégé disciple and even imparted to you the Divine Rejuvenation Force and the Big Dipper Hands. Why are you acting so malicious?"

Han Shaodong said solemnly, "It is because the Celestial Palace left us with no other choices! Do you know how many exponents were killed by the Celestial Palace over the years? If we miss this Seven Star Alignment, goodness know how long must we wait again for another favorable sign to ascend as Celestials?"

Yi Ping interrupted, "You can never overcome the Divine Calamity because…"

"Who wants to challenge the Celestial Palace?" A beautiful and mesmerizing voice was heard.

Yi Ping was startled. It was because he had recognized her distinctive voice!

Even Lie Qing was smiling, "I didn't think I am beginning to miss her at any moment but now I do."

Shen Xingyue was the first to catch sight of her as an extremely beautiful maiden appeared in their midst via her traverse speed, brandishing her wicked long black scythe!

She was slightly startled because she not only resembled Melody Star; her swiftness speed was also comparable to her!

Indeed, it was Lele as she laughed softly. "I am the Joyful Goddess, Prime Celestial of the Celestial Palace. Who is looking for a fight with the Celestial Palace? I am here now."

Xiao Shuai, Han Shaodong and the Three Sages were startled at her sudden appearance and when they saw her crimson eyes, they were alarmed and knew immediately that she was a Celestial!

All of a sudden, the Joyful Goddess had noticed Shen Xingyue and gasped. "Aren't you a Celestial too? Your eyes are gray…"

Shen Xingyue nodded and said, "Yes, I am a Celestial too…"

The Joyful Goddess began to encircle around her rapidly as she seemed to be pondering something, "Why is that I find your scent so familiar? Have we met before?"

Shen Xingyue refused to answer her but smiled angelically.

Han Shaodong was stunned as he thought, "My protégé mistress is a Celestial?!"

Xiao Shuai interrupted coldly, "There are five of us now. Pick five of you to be our challengers…"

A soft gentle voice said, "I will be your first challenger then."

Everyone turned and saw an extremely beautiful maiden in light blue long dress walking silently into view. When she had appeared, she was like a beautiful goddess whose beauty had no comparison!

It was Shui Yixian the Celestial Fairy!

Even though her cold demeanor was colder than ice as she gazed at everyone but the hearts of everyone was warm!

Yi Ping was trembling as he muttered, "Xian'Er…you are still alive?"

Xiao Shuai was startled, "Xian'Er…"

Han Shaodong was muttering, "Xian'Er, is that you? I have grown old but you have not changed at all…"

The Martial Sage was in tears as he ran towards her, "Xian'Er, is that really you? I didn't expect to see you after so many years!"

Even Shangguan Qingyun and Yan Nanfei who were not interested in the outcome of the battle were trembling with excitement as they ran towards her with joyful tears, "Xian'Er, is that really you? You have not changed at all!"

Chapter 64: A Heroic Fight!

Shui Yixian was a little teary and a little emotional when she saw her old friends again!

She was being surrounded by Xiao Shuai, Han Shaodong, the Three Sages, Shangguan Qingyun and Yan Nanfei.

That was something that was unexpected for her. It was because she was a high level practitioner of the Emotionless Rhyme. The last time that she had lost control of her emotions was when she had first met Yi Ping...

She said gently, "Yes, I am Xian'Er."

The Martial Sage was actually crying as he said, "Xian'Er, do you know that I have been looking for you everywhere?"

Han Shaodong stammered, "Xian'Er, it is really you?"

Shangguan Qingyun laughed heartily, "Xian'Er, I didn't expect to see you again. I am so happy. How have you been? When Xiao Shuai had said that you are still alive and you are actually the Celestial Fairy and the Divine Eternal Mistress of the Eternal Ice Palace, I didn't really believe him...you are really in the Eternal Ice Palace all along?"

Yixian nodded gently at him, "Yes, I am the Celestial Fairy and I have been in the Eternal Ice Palace all this while."

Yan Nanfei sighed, "I should have guessed a long time ago..."

Shangguan Qingyun stared at him, "You always saying this same old line. Can't you change to something else? Why Xian'Er had disappeared, you had said the same time too."

Yan Nanfei laughed aloud, "You know that is my favorite line."

The Martial Sage interrupted, "You always try to pretend to be wiser than anyone of us. But the fact is you are not."

Yan Nanfei said, "I know that you are now one of the Three Sages but I am after all, the protégé leader of the Zen Sect. You should at least give me a little face saving measures in front of Xian'Er."

Xian'Er smiled gently as she probed, "You are now the protégé leader of the Zen Sect?"

Shangguan Qingyun quickly interrupted, "I am the protégé master of the Divine Sword Martial Clan too."

Yan Nanfei was looking immensely proud of himself when the Element Sage interrupted, "With a protégé leader like him that pretended to be wise, no wonder the Zen Sect seems like a cult to me. Xian'Er, do you know that he didn't stick to our sacred covenant and even refuse to fight alongside with us. He has even cut off his thumb. What a loser, humph!"

Yixian had already noticed that Yan Nanfei and Shangguan Qingyun had cut their thumbs. She could already guess what had happened as she secretly stole a glance at Yi Ping, who was looking at her with a sense of loss...

Xiao Shuai and Han Shaodong were muttering, "Xian'Er..."

But Yixian seemed to give them the cold shoulder as she said gently to Yan Nanfei and Shangguan Qingyun, "It is really hard on you to do this."

Yan Nanfei and Shangguan Qingyun were extremely comforted by Yixian's words as tears swelled in their eyes...

Shangguan Qingyun stammered, "It is worth it..."

The Martial Sage interrupted, "Xian'Er, how have you been? Do you know I have been waiting for this day when I can see you again…"

Yixian interrupted coldly, "If you still regard me as your friend, why are you attacking my husband?"

Han Shaodong was taken aback, "Xian'Er, you are married? Who is your husband?"

Xiao Shuai kept quiet. He had already guessed that it would be Yi Ping and that was why he was trying to get rid of him.

Yixian said gently as she smiled at Yi Ping, pointing towards him. "He is my husband!"

Everyone presented was startled except for Xiao Shuai.

The Martial Sage stammered, "That young man is your husband? How can it be?"

The Element Sage, the Sword Sage and Han Shaodong, Shangguan Qingyun and Yan Nanfei took a step back in shock and stared at Yi Ping…

Yixian said, "If he is not my husband, who else would it be? It is every maiden's dream to find a good husband and I have found mine."

Xiao Shuai said coldly, "Yixian wake up from your senses. Did you not see there are so many beautiful maidens around him? He is nothing but a flirt and a lecherous man!"

Yixian interrupted coldly, "Anyone that wants to challenge my husband will have challenged me first."

The Martial Sage said, "Xian'Er, you are obviously putting us in a spot. You know that we won't fight you…"

Even Xiao Shuai agreed, "That's right…"

Han Shaodong said, "Xian'Er, it doesn't matter if you married to him. I am willing to accept you…"

The Element Sage said, "Let me teach that rascal a lesson for you…"

Yixian did not reply them but instead she walked past them and walked towards Yi Ping.

As Yixian walked towards him, Yi Ping too had walked towards her. Behind him, followed the rest of the maidens!

As Yixian and Yi Ping smiled blissfully to each other, they reached out and held each other's hands.

Yixian said gently with great politeness, "My husband…"

Yi Ping said, "My wife…"

Shen Xingyue was slightly startled but she was not entirely surprised for she could tell that all these maidens were all affectionately attached to him but she asked nevertheless, "You are married to Revelation Star?"

Just as Yi Ping was about to answer her, Yixian smiled gently at Shen Xingyue and said politely, "Hello. I am Shui Yixian the Celestial Fairy, from the Eternal Ice Palace and you are?"

Shen Xingyue was startled that Revelation Star would be this amicable and even though she was not a Celestial, she had an air of tranquil that marked her no differently from a Celestial. Therefore she smiled angelically, "I am Fiery Phoenix. In the past, I am known as the Dark Enchantress. You can call me Shen Xingyue!"

Yixian nodded gently as she said, "Really nice to know you."

She Xingyue smiled delightfully, "The same goes for me."

Lele said coolly to Yixian and for everyone within earshot, "We ought to be careful of her. She is a highly attained Celestial and we don't really know her dark purposes. With a name such as the Dark Enchantress, she is hardly worthy of trust…"

Lie Qing laughed softly, "Lele, you think too much. She is…really on our side."

Lele sighed, "I guess she can be the concubine then. I am alright with it…"

Just as Shen Xingyue protested, "I don't think so…"

Lele suddenly embraced her, "Alright then, welcome to the big family!"

Shen Xingyue was momentarily stunned and did not know what to say except for, "I suppose to say thank you?"

Lele did not seem to hear her, she just exclaimed happily. "Sister Xingyue!"

Shen Xingyue sighed to herself, "It seems that this Lele is going to be hard to deal with."

She did not know she was not the only that found Lele to be extremely hard to handle; she could even test the patience of the Celestial Fairy with her unpredictable actions!

All the maidens except for Yunzi had found her almost impossible to handle. It was because Yunzi did something smart. She had pretended to be deaf and mute when she was handling Lele when things went out of her predictions!

Lie Qing had shared the same vision with Shen Xingyue and therefore she knew that she had a long entwined destiny with Yi Ping.

Yixian was immediately surrounded by her two protégés Yu'Er and Mei'Er who delightfully surrounded her and exclaimed joyously, "Protégé Mistress, look what we got!"

Yu'Er and Mei'Er had showed her their two golden swords!

Yixian smiled gently and said, "I see that both of you are Celestials now. I am always worried if the two of you are able to overcome the Divine Calamity when I am not around one day. It seems my worries are unfounded and I should worry for myself first. These two divine swords will be able to help you in your future progression. Have you given a name to the swords yet?"

Yu'Er pondered for a while before she said quietly, "I like to call this sword Harp Whisperer."

Mei'Er laughed softly, "I am going to call my sword the Lyrical Whisperer."

As they named their celestial swords, their swords resonate in response and its golden light encircled brightly along its edges!

As Yixian and Yi Ping were looking at each other tenderly, Xiao Shuai obviously was not happy to see it. So he interrupted by shouting, "Xian'Er, step aside. We have not finished our fight yet."

Han Shaodong said, "Step aside Xian'Er. I am going to teach this insolent young man a lesson. He is nothing but a lecherous man and incompatible for you."

Yixian looked at them with an unsympathetic look, "If he is incompatible for me, then who is? I have said that if you want to challenge my husband you have to fight me first."

Yi Ping coughed weakly, "Xian'Er, they won't give up unless they can get what they want."

The Element Sage said as he stared at Lie Qing, Lele, Yu'Er, Mei'Er and Shen Xingyue, "We are only interested to rid the Martial Fraternity of the evils of the Celestial Palace and avenge the dead."

Lele was annoyed as she rebuked him, "So you are saying I am the one that kills them?"

The Element Sage retorted, "Young maiden, the deeds of the Celestial Palace is not a secret. Even though you have a pretty face but I will not show my mercy toward you."

Lele laughed softly, "Oh really? It should be the opposite..."

Yi Ping knew that if this continued, an irritated Lele was bound to come into conflict with the Element Sage so he quickly said. "I am the one that you are looking for. You are a martial elder and aren't you ashamed to pick on a young maiden?"

The Element Sage was speechless.

Yi Ping looked solemnly at Xiao Shuai, Han Shaodong and the Three Sages as he said. "Does our earlier agreement still stand? If I am able to win all of you, you will let us go and retreat peacefully?"

Xiao Shuai hummed coldly, "You want to challenge all five of us?"

Yi Ping said, "That's right!"

Immediately, all the maidens crowded around him except for Yixian as they disagreed with his decision.

Lie Qing said, "You are injured and you have been in too many fights. This is really too forceful..."

Shen Xingyue said, "We have just met and you are going to leave me again?"

Even Lingfeng was saying, "You...we should all fight together. We may not lose to them now..."

Yunzi said, "At least allow me to fight alongside you..."

Youxue said, "Let me fight besides you..."

Yu'Er said melancholy, "They just say, it is a five versus five fights..."

Mei'Er said, "Master, their hearts are filled with killing intent and it not wise for you to fight them alone..."

But Yi Ping looked tenderly at them one by one as he said, "I can't afford to lose any one of you. Moreover, we have an agreement with them and I hope that they can stick to that agreement..."

He was determined to help his sworn brothers so that they would not be hunted or attacked by the pugilists of the martial fraternity anymore.

Han Shaodong shouted, "If you are able to win against the five of us, then we will let all of you go and we will not pursue your past deeds. But only if you really are able to win the five of us!"

Yi Ping gripped his two divine swords tightly as he stepped forward, "So shall that be!"

Lele said to Yixian, "Sister, why didn't you stop him?"

Yixian said gently as she looked at Yi Ping with utmost affections, "Let him try. I have faith in him. Moreover, he has the White Phoenix Sword and the Divine Echo."

Yi Ping looked at Yixian as he said, "Thank you...I will not lose."

The Martial Sage had interrupted, "Xian'Er knows you will surely lose to us, that why she don't care if you have died in battle. Let me be the first one to send you to your maker first!"

Yi Ping had already displayed the opening stance of the Horizon Swordplay when Xiao Shuai said coldly, "Do you think that it is fair that you have two divine swords in your hand?"

Xiao Shuai had already noticed that Yi Ping swords and his skills in swordplay were not as weak as what Zuo Tianyi had described and he was silently cursing him!

Yi Ping was startled, "We are not contesting swordplay now?"

Han Shaodong said, "Naturally it is not. The Martial Sage and I are actually better with our hand to hand fighting techniques…"

Lingfeng said coldly, "How despicable! It is already five against one and you want to fight a weaponless man?!"

Han Shaodong hummed coldly, "Not at all. Do you think that the blood of all the dead can be settled in such an easy manner? Then how do you expect us to be answerable to their clans and their families?"

Lingfeng said coldly, "So you mean to say that Yi Ping must die today?"

Yi Ping said gently to Lingfeng, "Lingfeng, do you know that you are…alas never mind about that first. I know your concern for me but…if I can settle this with them; we can prevent further bloodshed from happening…"

Ji Wuzheng said, "Sworn Brother, be careful. I know that you are doing this to help me as well. But like what my sister has said, we may not lose if we fight them together…"

Yi Ping smiled and said, "There are hundreds of martial clans and if we cause more bloodshed today, these martial clans will surely come to the Holy Amalgamate Mountains again with greater vendetta. Even those exponents that are neutral may decide to join them. In the end, the entire martial fraternity will be covered in bloodshed. I really don't want that to happen."

Lingfeng reluctantly nodded.

Han Shaodong interrupted, "Not only must he be dealt with today; the Celestial Palace must also be taken care of today!"

Lele hummed coldly as she stole a glance at Shui Yixian and Shen Xingyue. They were surprising calm and she wondered what they were thinking about, "We shall see about that. All these are just brags."

As she said, she took a look at Lie Qing who was brushing her long hair and blinked at her. "I wonder what Sister Lie Qing is thinking?"

Lele too, began to stroke her long hair as she lowered her long black scythe as she pondered. "Don't tell me they are all planning to rescue Ping'Er when he is in trouble so that their standing in front of him will increase? I mustn't lose to them then…no wonder they are all so quiet. They just pretending to be docile and submissive in front of Yi Ping and by trying to dissuade him, I am already losing my own position. Not so easy, I am not allowing that…"

Lie Qing, Youxue, Yunzi and Yixian were secretly smiling.

It was because they were all waiting for Lele to screw the battle for them and were secretly thinking what she would do later. The more mysterious and quiet they appeared to be, the more Lele would suspect something was amiss. Knowing Lele, she would probably break every single martial rules and conventions, intervening in whatever manner she liked. That was why they were secretly smiling!

Yi Ping had sheathed his two divine swords behind his back and had displayed the Heavens Horizon with his hands as he said aloud, "I am ready!"

Yu'Er and Mei'Er said at the same time, "Master, be careful!"

Yi Ping coughed weakly but his eyes were gentle as he looked at them and said, "I will."

Lingfeng sighed as she knew that she could not persuade Yi Ping anymore. Even though she was unwilling to allow this to happen but she knew that at this point of time, she must not allow herself to distract Yi Ping anymore. She took a look at the other maidens who had all fallen into silence as she stepped aside most reluctantly!

Xiao Shuai, Han Shaodong, the Sword Sage, the Martial Sage and the Element Sage exchanged malevolent looks at one another and nodded at the same time…

Even though they were all thinking of different thing, they had the same objective; to kill this young man!

The Martial Sage was thinking, "Just any one of us is a match and more than enough for this young man to deal with. I have to be tactically careful not to be the one that kill this young man so Xian'Er won't hate me thereafter. I must be so brilliant to think of that!"

While the Martial Sage was praising himself, the other four were actually thinking of the same thing; they were pretty sure that with the reckless and stubborn nature of the Martial Sage that once the battle had begun, the one that could dirty his hands to kill this young man would be the Invincible Ironfist who was now known as the Martial Sage!

Xiao Shuai was actually thinking, "Once you have killed him, I will purposely fall out with you and declares that my intention was actually to just punish him and have no intention to kill him. Therefore even though my Unbreakable Hands is formidable, I am not going to use my full martial strength and skill. It is to allow Xian'Er to notice that from the very start, I have deliberately shown mercy towards him!"

Han Shaodong was also thinking, "Xiao Shuai, Xiao Shuai. You didn't treasure Xian'Er in the past and has always been too engrossed with your schemes. Once the Martial Sage has killed this young man, I will mobilize the Honor Manor to give the young man that is killed by you a good honorable name. Not only will Xian'Er be touched by my gesture, she will also fall into my arms on her own accord…"

The Element Sage was the first to attack Yi Ping as he shouted, "Young man, how about taking my Five Element Fists?"

Immediately he was upon Yi Ping as he rained dozens of powerful blows upon Yi Ping!

Yi Ping immediately retaliated with the Divine Horizon Hands as he counter-attacked with equally lightning fast attacks!

Immediately, a burst of circular dust storm whirled around them and began to spread out even as the thunderous blows of their impacts could be heard!

Shen Xingyue had immediately lifted her martial power by tapping lightly with her foot as she sent an invisible globe of buffering light windforce that encircled Ji Wuzheng, Dugu Zhen and the rest of the maidens!

At the same time, Yixian had lightly lifted her left fingers and there was also a buffering refreshing icy windforce around them!

Lie Qing, Lele, Ji Wuzheng, Dugu Zhen, Youxue, Lingfeng, Yunzi, Yu'Er, Mei'Er and the rest of the onlookers were startled at their martial display!

Ji Wuzheng muttered, "Such a wide extending arc of martial force yet so gentle…"

Shen Xingyue smiled amicably at him, "You don't want to get dirty right?"

Yixian smiled gently at Ji Wuzheng for an instant but her attention had returned immediately to the fighting…

Yi Ping was now being surrounded by Xiao Shuai, the Martial Sage, Han Shaodong, the Element Sage and the Sword Sage at the same time!

They were all now fighting so fast and so furiously that all the onlookers were in awe of their strikes and speed, hardly believing that it was even possible!

The orthodox and unorthodox exponents were all muttering, "So these are the martial skills of the legendary Three Sages…."

But regardless on whose side the exponents were, they were all astonished that Yi Ping, a young man was able to tank them all at the same time…

Yi Ping was forced to use the Asper Continuum Hands, a secret technique that required all his martial strength to execute as he attacked and parried against his opponents with startling speed!

Han Shaodong was stunned that Yi Ping was tougher to defeat than the last time that he had fought with him. As he lifted his martial power and displayed the deadly Divine Rejuvenate Force around him, he had also displayed the pressurizing force of the Big Dipper Hands against him!

But Yi Ping switched towards him with an instantaneous speed, shouting aloud as he displayed the Asper Horizon Hands with a mighty force and knocked him five steps backward, forcing him to cough out a bout of blood!

Han Shaodong could not believe that the martial power of the almighty Big Dipper Hands would actually lose to the Asper Divine Hands!

But this ensuring distraction allowed the Sword Sage to leap upon Yi Ping as he displayed his sword finger, stabbing him on his back!

Yi Ping staggered forward and coughed out a bout of blood even as he knocked the Sword Sage aside!

Xiao Shuai was immediately upon him with his Eighteen Unbreakable Hands, enveloped by his Divine Virtuous Force in its entire martial power!

One thing for sure, the easy fight that they were expecting did not turn out to be easy and they were now fighting with all their strength even as they took multiple hits from Yi Ping!

Yi Ping too had received multiple hits but he had tanked the powerful hits, retaliating with all his strength!

The hits that Yi Ping had received were no ordinary hits and each one was capable of shattering rocks and grinding it into powder.

Lingfeng, Youxue and Yunzi were teary and they could not bear to watch anymore as they turned their heads away.

Yu'Er and Mei'Er had already cast their Emotionless Rhyme away and were already in tears.

Yi Ping and his opponents were now all sweating heavily. They were now at the peak of their martial powers and everyone was holding their breath for the fight.

Xiao Shuai shouted, "Now!"

Immediately, Han Shaodong had once used all his martial power to display the Big Dipper Hands and the Martial Sage had displayed his Hundred Invincible Ironfist secret technique!

The Sword Sage, the Element Sage and Xiao Shuai had displayed their martial techniques as well as they attacked Yi Ping once again from all sides!

Yi Ping gave a great martial shout as he displayed the Asper Divinity Horizon Hands, as a white ring of bursting fire exploded thunderous around him, not once but five times!

There were five bursting loud thunderclaps and five ripples of powerful windforce that immediately swept across the onlookers, knocking many onlookers to the ground!

The Asper Divinity was an extremely powerful martial technique that could equal the martial power of any martial technique, including the Big Dipper Hands. When it was displayed, a ring of white fire would burst around the practitioner and exploded the air around him at the same time as the martial power that went into displaying the Asper Divinity was so powerful and tremendous that before the Asper Divinity had struck its opponent, the resultant force was lethal enough to kill or maimed most opponents!

Therefore the five Asper Divinities that were displayed at the same time was comparable to Yi Ping's opponents being struck five times continuously with a force that was equivalent to the first secret technique of the Divine Horizon Hands, the Asper Horizon Hands!

Everyone was gasping.

Yi Ping had been desperate and he was fighting five equally powerful opponents therefore he decided to use all his remaining martial power to use the Asper Divinity five times in quick successive, directed at each of his opponent, knocking them all back with such thunderous impact that they were all flung backward!

Xiao Shuai tried to muster all his martial strength to block the Asper Divinity but it was too late as the powerful martial power of the Asper Divinity shrieked and swept his martial force aside and he was hit with a thunderous cracking impact!

Xiao Shuai, Han Shaodong, the Three Sages had all turned white; they simply could not believe that this young man had actually bested their combine martial skills at the same time!

Even as Xiao Shuai, Han Shaodong and the Martial Sage struggled weakly to get up, they were coughing out blood. The flow of their blood was reversing and they had lost all their martial strength to continue the fight!

As for the Sword Sage and the Element Sage, they had been knocked unconscious and they were now lying unmoving on the ground!

Yan Nanfei and Shangguan Qingyun immediately lifted them to a sitting position as they hit their vital channels on their back several times; they were attempting to clear their erratic vital energies and attempting to save their lives!

Yi Ping was standing in the middle and he had turned completely white!

The second Asper Divinity had been used quite forcibly by Yi Ping. But because he had just swallowed the Divine Dragon Pill, the Asper Divinity could still be forcibly attempted for a second time. But when he used the Asper Divinity for the third time without a break, his blood had reversed and he had coughed out blood, indicating that he had reached his limit!

But when he had tried to use the Asper Divinity for the fourth time, even his heart was not able to take it and he was knocked into a daze, snapping several meridian channels at the same time. If he had not cleared his life and death channels, he would have died immediately on the spot!

Even though he was in a daze but his subconscious was bent on defeating every single opponent that was fighting against him so that he could liberate his friends. Theoretically he had already expended all his entire strength and could not muster any martial power, even for the Asper Horizon Hand. But because he had already reached his limit and was on his death knell, he had reached into his reserve life force and had executed the Asper Divinity; only a person that had reached this limit could muster their life force but the result of using up this reserve would only mean that the person was going to die…

Yixian, Shen Xingyue, Lingfeng, Lele, Lie Qing, Youxue, Yu'Er, Mei'Er, Youxue and Yunzi were immediately besides Yi Ping as they called out to him frantically but he was not responding; he was just standing on the same spot unmoving with his eyes straight, either hearing or responding to anyone of them!

Yixian, Lele and Lie Qing had immediately hit him on his life channels in an attempt to revive him!

Shen Xingyue had transferred the life reviving force of her Divine Rejuvenate Force onto him in an attempt to revive him but she was soon shaking her head, "It is no use. Even if we used up all our internal strength, we are losing him too fast. His meridian channels and his intricate life force energies are either not intact or in complete disarrays…"

Chapter 65: The Heaveness

Hundreds of orthodox exponents and unorthodox exponents were now watching in stunned silence; none dared to move and were looking at one another for instructions and signs.

All nine maidens were now furiously striking Yi Ping's body lightly with their internal strength in an attempt to keep him alive. Ji Wuzheng and Dugu Zhen could only look on with an unspeakable grief in their eyes…

Ji Wuzheng could only said coldly to Xiao Shuai and Han Shaodong as he stared at them, "My sworn brother Yi Ping has won. So quickly turn back and never let me see you again!"

But Xiao Shuai laughed aloud, "Look who is dead now? He has won? We are the ones that have won the fight!"

The Martial Sage said weakly, "That's right! We are the ones that have won!"

Han Shaodong said, "From now on, nothing can stop us, not even the Celestial Palace…"

As Lele and Lie Qing were hitting Yi Ping to revive him by transferring bursts of their internal strength in an attempt to clear his blocked channels and stemmed the flow of his blood, they were also staring with a murderous intent towards Xiao Shuai, Han Shaodong and the Martial Sage!

Yixian was muttering, "It is no use. His body has already turned rigid. Not even a Celestial and any divine pills can save him now…"

Shen Xingyue was trembling as she stared at Han Shaodong…

When Han Shaodong caught her piercing glare, it was like a piercing arrow that had already pierced his heart and he was shivering from fear!

He had never seen his protégé mistress with this type of malevolent aura and saw her losing her angelic smiles. His impression of her was that she did not care for anything that had happened in the fraternity and it took him considerable effort to persuade her to join in the western expedition against the Holy Hex Sect and the Celestial Palace!

Shen Xingyue replied softly to Yixian even as she looked malevolently at Han Shaodong, "Unless the Celestial Heaveness is here, no one will be able to save him…"

Youxue was trembling as she cried out, "Who is the Heaveness, why don't you get her now…"

She knew in her heart that it was impossible to find anyone in such a short notice and was totally irrational to ask that question but nevertheless she still asked; it was because she had totally lose her rational self now!

Even Yu'Er, Mei'Er, Lingfeng were asking, "Where is the Heaveness and who is she?"

Shen Xingyue said melancholy, "She is just a mythical figure. No one has ever seen her. Some says that she is the first among all the Celestials. Some others say that she is never a human and has always been a Celestial and is the creator of all. Some others also say, she is able to travel between Beyond and here at will. It is said that she is the only Celestial that the Divine Calamity is unable to affect. There were times when she had revealed herself to some of the other Celestials but these Celestials were always reluctant to say a word. If there is a Celestial that can actually do the impossible, then it must be the Heaveness…"

Yunzi said with a heavy heart even as she continued to hit Yi Ping's body with her internal strength, "What is the point of telling us about the Heaveness when it is obviously that she doesn't exist? This will only give us a false sense of hope!"

Yixian looked coldly at Xiao Shuai, the Martial Sage and Han Shaodong. "You have won? Look around you. There are so many people that have died because of your ambitions! Is it worth it?"

But before they could even reply her, Lele had already flown to Han Shaodong with a startling speed as she raised her long black scythe high into the air, which immediately exploded the air around her with a terrifying booming sound!

She had appeared in front of Han Shaodong in the next instant as she said coldly, "Did you just say that nothing can stop you? The Celestial Palace or from ascending as a Celestial? You are just a muddle headed old man. Let me wake you from your senses!"

Before Han Shaodong could react in time, Lele had slapped Han Shaodong on his face even as he tried to raise his hands feebly to block her!

She then proceeded to give him a high kick that sent the defenseless Han Shaodong into the air!

Han Shaodong could only call out panicky as he landed with a stump on the ground as he coughed out more blood, "Help me!"

But the protégés of the Honor Manor was all looking at the ground and not one of them made a slight move to help him!

It was because the malevolent aura of Shen Xingyue and Lele was everywhere, striking fear in their hearts!

Xiao Shuai said weakly, "Despicable…"

But just as he had muttered out a word, Lele had already descended upon him as she gave him a kick across his face!

She cursed softly, "You say you have won the fight. You say you want to fight the Celestial Palace? I am from the Celestial Palace so your opponent should be me instead!"

Even as Xiao Shuai had landed backward with a loud heavy crash, Lele had already picked up the Martial Sage and had flung him towards Xiao Shuai and Han Shaodong. She was already upon the three of them again as she gave them several kicks and slaps in a blink of an eye!

The kicks and slaps that they had received were so brutal that they were quickly covered in bruises as they pleaded, "Heroine, please have mercy, no more please…"

Yixian and Youxue were already besides Lele as they intercepted her!

Yixian said gently, "That's enough already…"

Lele said spitefully, "Sisters! Do you know that they have just killed our husband?! Are we letting them off just like that?"

Youxue cried out, "He…he…no matter how bad he is, he is after all my father. I can't bear to see him in this state…"

Yixian was also teary, "Sister, as much as I hate them but this fight is fair. If we really want to make Ping'Er happy, we should at least persuade them to declare Yi Ping as the victor. Don't forget, you are now a Celestial. Do you want to suffer the same fate as me?"

She added with a forlorn sorrow as she looked at the numerous dead and the number of wounded people around her, "There are simply too many dead today…"

Lele sighed sorrowful, "You are right…"

She quickly withdrew her long black scythe as she swung it backward.

As she swung it backward, the backend of the metal scythe dealt accidentally hit Xiao Shuai, Han Shaodong and Martial Sage, smashing against their faces at the same time!

Immediately, they cried out in agony and pain as the blow was not light!

Lele quickly turned around panicky as she quickly apologized, "Awwww, I am so sorry. That is an accident…" But as soon as she had turned around, once again she had accidentally swung her long heavy scythe and broke Xiao Shuai's nose, struck the head of Han Shaodong and sent the Martial Sage flying upward and landing with a hard stump!

The Martial Sage was muttering miserable, "Maiden, you…you did that on purpose!"

Yixian and Youxue were stunned!

It was because Lele had left them in a worst condition before they had intervened!

Lele seemed to be able to read their thoughts as she quickly said in panic, "That is totally an accident! I didn't do that on purpose!" As she said that, she stepped on Xiao Shuai who was lying on the ground; there was a loud cracking sound as she stepped on his hands and legs!

Lele was astonished as she gently rebuked Xiao Shuai, "Why are you lying on the ground and getting in my way?" She proceeded to lift him up with care.

By now Xiao Shuai was too terrified of this extremely beautiful maiden as he mustered all his strength weakly to speak, "Don't…don't….touch…me…" But he was too weak now to even resist her!

Before Xiao Shuai could even reply her, Lele had turned around to Han Shaodong to ask him. "So Master Han Shaodong, who had won this fight?"

There was a loud cracking as Xiao Shuai was hit again by her long scythe as she turned around!

Xiao Shuai immediately fell down flat on the ground!

Once again, Lele turned around to check on Xiao Shuai who was accidentally hit by her as she fingered her long scythe clumsily around and Han Shaodong was hit in the face by the metal end of her long scythe!

Lele's long scythe was made of steel. Even if it was made of wood, the force that was hitting Xiao Shuai and Han Shaodong was enough to send most exponents bedridden for months. Moreover they had been struck so many times…

The Martial Sage was staring weakly at Xiao Shuai and Han Shaodong as he thought miserably to himself, "This young maiden has the face of a heavenly maiden but she is no saint…"

The Martial Sage was also badly injured but not as severe as Xiao Shuai and Han Shaodong. Moreover, he was renowned for his Invincible Iron Shroud Skill but this young maiden was still able to kick through his martial protection and injured him…

He could only sighed weakly to himself, "If we are not injured by the twin sisters and lost half of our internal strength and martial power, that Yi Ping may not be able to injure us especially with the five of us joining hands together. Now we are at the mercy of this young maiden…this is so disgraceful…"

Yixian had intercepted by reaching out and caught hold of Lele's long black scythe as she said, "That's enough already sister. They are already half-dead…"

Lele said unhappily, "I didn't say I want them dead. I am just asking them the outcome of the fight."

But Xiao Shuai and Han Shaodong were unable to answer her anymore. They were covered with blood and were muttering incoherently on the ground!

Lele stroked her long silken long hair as she said, "Weird, they are looking so refresh a while ago and now, they are half-dead. Oh well since they didn't answer me, I declare Ping'Er to be the victor then!"

Xiao Shuai was muttering, "I…this fight…"

Lele stepped forward as she asked, "What did you say? I can't hear you…"

All of a sudden, Xiao Fan had dashed in front of her and was bowing his head on the ground as he pleaded to her. "Maiden! Please have mercy on my father…"

Even Youxue had also fallen on her knees in front of her as she pleaded tearfully, "He is after all my father. Good sister…"

Even Xiao Fei had also fallen on his knees besides Youxue…

Lele said softly to Youxue, "Please get up sister…"

But Xiao Youxue shook her head with a quiet determination to plead for her to let her father off.

Lele's eyes softened but she did not say anything.

Xiao Shuai was stunned to see Xiao Fan, Xiao Fei and Xiao Youxue kneeing in front of the Joyful Goddess and pleading for his life…

For the very first time, he was sincerely touched as he muttered almost inaudible, "The wrongs that I have done, is it too late to seek amends? Can I hope for any forgiveness?"

Xiao Shuai got up weakly and he was trembling in his blood soaked sweat, "I…I admit defeat. The young hero Yi Ping has won this fight. From now on…the Virtuous Palace will wash our hands from the martial fraternity…"

He looked at Yixian, "Xian'Er, will you…forgive me?"

Yixian looked quietly away. It was because while she was appearing emotionless on the surface but her heart was in grieving pain!

At the same time, Shen Xingyue had silently appeared besides Han Shaodong and all of a sudden she had given him a thunderous blow on his chest!

Immediately Han Shaodong threw out a bout of blood as he sunk into the ground in an awkward position!

Shen Xingyue said emotionlessly, "You have disgraced me and betray your protégé mistress. Your skills are imparted by me and now I am taking it back!"

Just as she was about to disable his skills, Yixian had intercepted her with a counter-strike!

Shen Xingyue said in a mono tone, "I am sparing his life but I am going disable his martial skills. This is just a light punishment for him!"

Shui Yixian sighed softly as she looked at Han Shaodong who was coughing weakly, "He…is my friend and I believe that they have learnt a hard lesson…"

Han Shaodong looked at Yixian feebly and he was actually teary!

He muttered weakly, "Xian'Er, you still treat me as your friend?"

Yixian nodded gently as she said, "In my heart, always."

Han Shaodong laughed aloud as he wept, "Good…good!"

He rose up weakly and bowed on his knees at Shen Xingyue as he wept aloud, "Protégé Mistress! Your protégé disciple is undeserving of your forgiveness and grace…"

Shen Xingyue sighed softly as she looked around her; thousands of exponents had set off for this expedition and now only less than a thousand had remained…

All of a sudden, there was a large implosion as Lie Qing thrust her long black sword into the ground in a moment of anguish and frustration!

Everyone began to look into her direction.

She was covering her face with her hands as she cried tearfully and had broken down emotionally!

Who would have expected that the Heavenly Temptress Lie Qing would be the first to have broken down?

Among all the maidens, she had the strongest will and was rarely affected by anything. But she had really fallen in love and was emotionally attached to Yi Ping. He was everything to her and she could not afford to lose him. It took her a long time to find someone that she could finally trust; that day when Yi Ping had refused to put her down despite fighting against the odds. This touched her greatly. This was not the only thing that Yi Ping had done for him. She had long pledged her heart to him.

Her silent tears flowed down her porcelain cheeks as she contemplated suicide as she said silently to herself, "Ping'Er, I have said to you that I want to be with you till the earth disintegrate, the rocks turned to dust and the oceans dried up. Now that you are gone, do you really think that I will want to live on my own? You are so heartless, how can you bear to leave me alone…"

Her thoughts were back again in the Icy Cavern with him when she had first known him…

In the meantime, Lingfeng too was overcome by grief as she continued to rejuvenate Yi Ping's dead channels with her Great Dissolution Skill by striking him again and again.

And besides her were Yu'Er, Mei'Er and Yunzi who were also doing the same and did not stop trying even though Yi Ping body had become rigid and his skin color had turned gray!

They had ignored their surroundings and were exhausting all their internal strength just to create a shimmer of hope.

Even Lie Qing had given up hope as she threw her sword with a thunderous impact into the earth as she wept bitterly.

Yixian, Lele, Shen Xingyue and Youxue were all internal martial experts and were among the first to realize that they had already lost Yi Ping and that was why they had stopped trying to resuscitate him.

Lingfeng muttered softly, her hands were trembling as she held his face, "Yi Ping…"

Earlier, Lingfeng had experienced a severe headache. She rarely had migraine but after she was struck by the Universal Force that was generated by Yu'Er and Mei'Er, she had experienced the discomforts.

At first, she had thought that she was seriously injured by the Universal Force. But she soon realized that she was the only that seemed unaffected by it.

The Universal Force had awakened her true self, giving her a weird sense of familiarity which she could not point her finger at. As she looked at everyone, there was a strange feeling of quiescent. It was as though she was just a speculator and not part of the scene. This peculiar feeling stunned her for quite some time as she looked quietly at her surroundings.

But when it was obvious that she was losing Yi Ping and when Lie Qing had suddenly threw her long black sword into the ground, she was jolted; she had suddenly realized who she was!

Lingfeng sighed softly as she stroke Yi Ping's face gently and arranged his long hair aside before she said delicately, "Yu'Er, Mei'Er, Yunzi…please step aside first. I can save him."

Yunzi, Mei'Er and Yu'Er were startled as they examined her but from the look of it, it did not seem to be a casual remark.

Even Lie Qing was looking at Lingfeng curiously as she quickly said, "You…really have a way?" But as soon as she lifted her eyes to ask her, she was startled!

Ji Wuzheng and Dugu Zhen were also looking at Lingfeng with a startled expression!

It was not because of her casual remark that had startled them but as they turned to look at her, she had tiptoed and kissed the petrified Yi Ping on his lip in everyone's presence!

Yu'Er and Mei'Er were blushing as they lowered their heads.

There were gasps and muttering from hundreds of onlookers.

Even Shen Xingyue, Yixian and Lele were also looking in Lingfeng's direction!

Many were sighing secretly regretfully that this young alluring maiden had received too much of a shock and was emotional distress. Quite a number of exponents from both sides of the martial fraternity wanted to go to her and to comfort her but they lacked the courage.

But to everyone astonishments, the young hero Yi Ping was now trembling as color returned to his skin and face!

Perhaps the greatest astonishment comes from Yi Ping when he opened his eyes and found himself kissing Lingfeng…

His first thought was, "I am not dead? Or is it a dream? I can't even feel the excruciating pain in my heart now…"

Not only did his excruciating pain vanish, his strength was also slowly recovering and the aching pain of his injuries was also slowly relieving!

"Breathe in and out gently first. You are not dead and this is not a dream. I am trying to treat your injuries so don't move for the time being alright or you will undo all my efforts. I can only attempt this only once." It was Lingfeng's voice in his head!

Yi Ping was startled as he thought, "I can hear you inside my mind?"

"This is the linking spirits of my Great Emptiness Translucence. While we are physically linked, we can exchange our spirits. Therefore you can hear me and I can hear your thoughts."

Yi Ping said to her, "Lingfeng, you know the Emptiness Translucence too?!"

Lingfeng did not reply him.

Yi Ping suddenly said quietly, "You are the Heaveness?!"

Lingfeng trembled slightly, "Don't say my name! You have promised to keep it to yourself!"

Yi Ping was startled, "You are really the Heaveness!"

This time it was Lingfeng who was startled in his thoughts, "How…did you know who I am?!"

Yi Ping was not sure how he knew so he said, "I don't know either. I have seen you as the Heaveness through a vision with the Emptiness Translucence…"

He could hear her gasping with astonishment, "You know the Emptiness Translucence too?"

Yi Ping said to her, "I don't know how I know this heart intricate skill. It was rekindled in my heart when Priest Liu Qingcheng had shown me a silver scroll and had recited to me…"

Lingfeng interrupted melancholy, "But still when a person dies, all memories should vanish as well. Even if you could learn the Emptiness Translucence again, it is not possible for you to retain any memories of old self. Unless…"

She seemed to pause for a while…

When Yi Ping noticed that Lingfeng was silent, he asked. "Unless…?"

He could hear her sighs as she said, "Even though the Great Emptiness Translucence is able to retain some vestige of a person memory but at the time of that person's death, he has to think of her strongly…there exist a small possibility but that is impossible…unless…"

She paused for a while before she quickly changed to another topic, "No one should remember anything for sure. Maybe at most, you only get a vision of two…"

Yi Ping said gently, "You are the Heaveness and my grand protégé mistress. Why did you suddenly disappear that day? Where did you go?"

She gasped aloud and her surprise was evident in his mind!

"You…remember…?" She asked.

She was embarrassed to say it to him but she had forgotten that at this moment, they were linked spirit to spirit with each other. Even if she wanted to conceal her thoughts from him, it was impossible!

When he had mentioned that he was previously her grand protégé and had asked her whereabouts, she had unwittingly refreshed her memories!

That day, she had met him once again in the streets.

This time, he had mustered his courage to ask her when there was no one else around, "Grand Protégé Mistress, why are you here? It seems that we keep bumping into each other everywhere. This time, you are a songstress. I am surprise that you can sing so well but the song is too melancholy…"

The Heaveness said softly, "Yes, we keep bumping into each other everywhere…"

He mustered the courage to ask, "I have thought that grand protégé mistress is an eminent Sagess but why is that whenever I see you, you are always in such humble roles?"

The Heaveness sighed softly, "In a sense, I am trying to experience the emotions of others."

He asked curiously, "Have you succeeded?"

The Heaveness smiled at him with her alluded eyes, "I may never be able to experience their emotions. Their happiness, their sadness, I can never experience. Nothing that they do or feel excites me."

He was startled, "Is that the highest level of the Great Emptiness Translucence? To be completely freed from all emotions? That is a state of divinity that I hope to attain one day."

The Heaveness looked away, "What if I tell you I am born with the Great Emptiness Translucence and have never feel any emotions for anyone?"

He said, "I may be young and ignorant but I hope grand protégé mistress pardon me for saying this, surely you will have felt a sense of loss when you lose someone or joy when you have learnt something new? I have seen protégé mistress in so many different roles and I am really impressed by your talents."

He paused to catch his breath, "Surely, grand protégé mistress will have some affection towards me or else you won't instruct me so patiently?"

The Heaveness was quiet.

Curious that she had suddenly turned quiet, he asked, "Am I not right to say so?"

The Heaveness said, "You are wrong. I have never felt anything toward you. I only know that you are the protégé of the Universal Old Man and I should instruct you accordingly. Other than that, I do not treat you any differently from the others. The so call humble roles that you have mentioned are just my way of expressing my disilusions with the people. Why am I being treat differently from the others? Just because I have a pretty face and I am able to attract people to patronize for me?"

Even now, there were many people who were looking at her in the streets and they were holding their breath at her alluring beauty and wondered who she was...

Just as he was pondering what she had just said, a little girl had accidentally bumped into him, causing him to trip as he fell into the Heaveness and accidentally kissing her on her lips!

The Heaveness was stunned. However, she quickly recovered her composure and pushed him lightly away but because she had utilized her martial force, he was sent flying away and tumbled onto a stall!

The Heaveness gasped to him, "I...sorry..."

An elderly old man who was tendering the stall quickly said aloud, "Hey young man, watch out!"

As he picked himself up, he quickly apologized profusely to the elderly old man many times.

But when the sleepy elderly old man had saw the alluring and refined Heaveness standing next to him, he appeared to be somewhat startled as he said again. "It is a couple that is quarreling?"

He was flustered as he quickly said, "She...alas, she's not. In fact, she is my..."

The Heaveness interrupted him with a soft hum and he suddenly remembered that he was not supposed to tell anyone about her so he quickly said, "She's a friend..."

The elderly old man laughed merrily, "One is a young maiden and one is a young man. It is only natural to be together. There is nothing to be shy at. Do you want to get your fortunes told?" He pointed at his banner that read 'The Divine Teller, Never Missing a Telling'.

The elderly old man laughed merrily, "Are you impress now? Let me tell you, if I am not accurate then I won't charge you a single cent. So what do you want to divine? Marriage, status or fortune?"

He was startled and he quickly shook his hands as he said, "That won't be necessary. I am really sorry for knocking into your stall..."

The elderly old man laughed, "Don't be shy. If you don't know your eight birth characters, I can still be able to help you divine your destiny. All you need to do is to show me your palm or write a character on my table. How about that?"

He smiled bitterly at the elderly old man, "To be frank with you, I am a young priest. There is nothing that I desire to ask of…"

The elderly old man said with a smile. "Don't be hasty first. Maybe you don't want to know your destinies but your female companion may want to?"

He quickly replied to the elderly old man, "She isn't someone who is interested in this sort of things…"

The Heaveness said softly, "Don't make my decision for me. This won't be good for your future attainment. Remember this."

She smiled alluringly at the elderly old man and said, "Old Senior, you won't charge a cent if you are not accurate?"

The elderly old man laughed merrily, "Naturally I won't! So far, I have never been proven to be wrong."

The Heaveness pointed at her grand protégé and said, "Why don't you try on him first. I like to know his destiny."

The elderly old man smiled and turned to ask him, "Young man, do you want to divine through your palm or your character?"

He reluctantly placed his palm on the table.

The elderly old man smiled and said, "What are you most interested in?"

He was hesitating for he really did not know, "I…anything?"

The Heaveness looked at him before she said, "Old Senior, help him to divine his marriage. How about that?"

When the elderly old man saw that the young man did not object, he laughed softly and said. "Marriage so be it!"

The Heaveness smiled alluringly, "Thank you."

So the elderly old man took the young man's palm and fingered it. But he was soon bewildered as he muttered while staring at the lines of the young man's palm, "Weird. Your palm lines are straight. I have never seen anything like this."

The elderly old man had broken into beads of perspiration on his forehead as he said, "I can't read your destiny but you don't have any marriage lines. There will be plenty of missed opportunities though…"

He tried to comfort the elderly old man as he said, "Don't worry Old Senior. I am a priest, remember? So don't worry. I really do not mind at all."

The elderly old man sighed heavily and said to the alluring young maiden, "Maiden, do you want to get your destiny foretold as well?"

The Heaveness nodded and said, "That will be interesting, isn't it?"

She proceeded to take a brush and wrote the character 'Heaven' on a piece of white paper.

The elderly old man stared at the character 'Heaven' as he muttered, "In my entire life, I have never seen anyone write the character 'Heaven' in such a perfect manner. Every stroke, every line is in such perfect harmony…"

The Heaveness asked, "So what are my marriage lines?"

The elderly old man was quiet for a while before he said, "If it is not offensive to maiden, may I take a look at your palm?"

The Heaveness nodded and took out both her tender palms at the same time for him to read.

Just when the elderly old man had said, "Just the right palm will do…" as he looked at her palm, he had suddenly staggered backward!

Both her palm lines seemed to have the same 'Heaven' character that she had just written!

Even the young man was startled for it was the first time that he had seen her palms and he had never seen anything like this before!

The elderly old man had immediately bowed down on his knees and kowtowed repeatedly on the ground!

The Heaveness said, "Please rise, old senior. You haven't foretold my marriage destiny yet."

The elderly old man cried out miserly, "Maiden, please forgive me. Even if I know, I dare not divulge it. Moreover maiden, your destiny is in your own hands. If you are willing, everything is yours to will!"

The Heaveness said gently, "Is that so?"

She turned to say to her grand protégé, "I need to be alone for a while. Can you leave me for now?"

He nodded and bade his grand protégé mistress farewell, "Then I take my leave first…"

He seemed to have more things to ask of her but he could sense that the Heaveness was not in a good mood and moreover, he was still feeling guilty that he had just outrage the modesty of his grand protégé mistress. Therefore, he quickly left.

However, he did not know that that was actually the very last time that he would ever see the Heaveness again!

As the elderly old man watched them as they left, he was muttering. "Such tragic fates, such tragic couple…"

After they had parted, the Heaveness had walked quietly to the outskirt of the town, toward the mountains. Along the way, she had attracted the attention of many men who had tried to tail her. Even though she appeared to be walking leisurely and casually, her pace was astonishing and her admirers could not catch up with her; one by one, they fell behind from fatigue as they tailed her up and down the mountain paths.

In a short while time, she was deep in the mountains and had soon reached a waterfall.

She waved her hand with her inertia martial force as she caused the waters of the waterfall to part to the side, revealing a hidden cave behind the waterfall!

Immediately, she walked into the hidden cave and into what seemed to be a tunnel.

It was not long before she had reached the other side of the mountains and was in what seemed to be a beautiful adorned garden where there were all kinds of fruit trees and flowers.

As she stepped into the garden, the songbirds that were in the garden which came in a rainbow variety of colors began to sing jovially at the sight of her!

The Heaveness raised her hands as she whistled, mimicking their songs.

These songbirds instead of shying from her were all around her, flying and hopping around her!

The Heaveness said with a soft sigh, "My friends…"

"You are finally back. I am a little worry for you." The Universal Old Man had walked quietly to her.

The Heaveness nodded gently, "I have met him earlier…"

The Universal Old Man asked, "Our protégé?"

She nodded gently.

The Universal Old Man said, "Does he know that we are leaving? I have left him a note at the usual place and he should be able to know it tonight."

The Heaveness shook her head, "I didn't tell him. You are his protégé master. That's your duty, not mine."

The Universal Old Man laughed jovially, "I want to imagine his expressions when he has learnt that his protégé master and grand protégé mistress have both abandoned him."

But he had suddenly turned solemn, "If we do not hurry to the Firmament Mountains and transmigrate to Beyond, we will have to wait for a long time before another opportunity arises. I don't want to be struck here for too long and continue to address you as my protégé mistress."

The Heaveness said with an alluring smile, "What's so bad about being my protégé?"

The Universal Old Man said, "You and I are equal. Just because I lost a bet to you and you have found him first, I have to pretend to be your protégé."

The Heaveness said, "If we switch our roles, he may not necessary want to follow us. You have the look of a wise old sage and is convincing as a highly attained priest. If you don't want to be his protégé master, then you are asking me to be his protégé mistress? He will end up being distracted by me and ruin his attainment. This is something that I am trying to avoid."

The Universal Old Man sighed, "It is a lucky thing that we are able to find him just before we go but one year is really too short to impart to him anything. Hopefully, he will be able to survive the Divine Descendant in the future. But if we don't leave now and when the Celestial Wrath descends upon us, countless lives will be lost. It is not something that we want to see. The question is; is he the one we are looking for?"

The Heaveness looked up to the cloudy heavens as she sighed melancholy, "To be able to ascend to Beyond, is the dream of every aspiring Celestials. But it is a place that I do not want to return; that vast expanse of empty spaces, that eternal loneliness. After I have returned from Beyond, I really do not wish to go back again. While they are all aspiring to ascend as a Celestial and transmigrated to Beyond, they didn't know that a greater tribulation actually awaits them there and the Celestial Wrath in Beyond is even more deadly than the Divine Calamity here."

The Universal Old Man said solemnly, "Time is running out for us. We are already at the last staging where we can finally transmigrated to the Gods' Realm but that is something that have always eluded us. The longer we delay the celestial transmigration, the more powerful the Celestial Wrath is. Already so many of us have perished at the Astronomic Stellar Formation or at the Stellar Sanctuary in an attempt to locate the last mystery. Do you still remember that the reason we have come back here is to look for the last clue for the final ascension?"

The Heaveness nodded, "It is said that the Stellar Sanctuary is created by the first person that has ever ascended as an immortal being and the Astronomic Stellar Formation is the only place that is possible to transmigrate to the Gods' Realm. The clues that we have found indicated that the immortal being had actually returned to the lower world to accomplish something and take something from here so that he could ascend. But what is it that exist here but did not exist in Beyond?"

The Universal Old Man added solemnly, "We have already incurred Heavens' Wrath by trying to divine the secrets of heaven and returning here. The best of our divinations indicated that our protégé may hold the key to that clue. But while he can still take his own sweet time to become a Celestial, we really don't have any time left. This time when I am back to Beyond, I am going to the Stellar Sanctuary again. It is better to die attempting to transmigrate than to be killed by the Celestial Wrath. I hope that you can accompany me to the Stellar Sanctuary again."

But the Heaveness did not reply to his request, instead she muttered, "Do you think we can come back here again?"

The Universal Old Man said, "That is impossible. Do you still remember how many celestial artifacts we have to sacrifice in order to return here? All that for nothing! Even though I am a highly attained Celestial and no longer have any worldly desire over material things but I still feel a terrible ache in my heart over the loss of so many artifacts that made our descend here possible. Our next Celestial Wrath would not be easy to overcome and could well be our last without those celestial artifacts to ward us."

The Heaveness smiled, "Highly attained Celestial? I am astonished that you can make it so far as a Celestial. You are always grudging over every little things, even trying to take my pomegranate fruits, mulberries and honey peaches."

The Universal Old Man said grumbly, "You must know that I have been in Beyond for a long time and my nourishments come from those divine fruits. There aren't any here except for those rare occasions. You will go with me to the Stellar Sanctuary?"

The Heaveness looked away quietly, "Since the great separation of the Heavens and the Earth, before the Great Inundation and when mortals could live to a thousand years, we have known each other. We have survived countless number of cycles of Celestial Wrath and have fought against terrible foes together. We are also the first among the Celestials but now only just a few of the original Celestials are left…"

The Universal Old Man was puzzled that she was suddenly melancholy and did not reply to his request but he said, "Your heart is sorrowful? You shouldn't have those emotions because you are never a mortal in the first place!"

The Heaveness said, "Maybe I have already decided to be a mortal. I will not leave with you."

The Universal Old Man was startled, "Do you know what you are saying? If the Celestial Wrath descends while you are here, nothing will survive!"

The Heaveness was without any emotions but her countenance was piercing sharp as she tossed a pearl with a rainbow halo on the ground, "This is my Heaveness Pearl. You may need this in the future. I am not going with you because I have already decided to transmigrate as a mortal instead. My greatest mistake in my entire life is to transmigrate from here to Beyond in the first place."

The Universal Old Man was stunned and was left speechless!

The Heaveness said almost inaudible, "I want to be able to sing sentimental songs. I want to know what it is meant to love someone…"

Even when the Heaveness had walked away, he was still rooted on the same spot as he continued to mutter the same thing over and over again. "You are really going to give up all your hard earned attainment…"

Chapter 66: The Dark Celestials

When Lingfeng realized that Yi Ping was reading her thoughts, she was immediately flustered and rebuked him gently in his thoughts, "How dare you read my thoughts…"

She quickly willed her Great Emptiness Translucence into a formless mirror that deny her thoughts from him.

Immediate, Yi Ping could no longer see or share in her memories.

Lingfeng laughed softly, "You are just a peeping tom."

Yi Ping was silent.

Lingfeng asked, "You are upset?"

Yi Ping quickly recollect his thoughts, "I am not. It is just that I have been thinking, why should you give up being a Celestial and instead choose to be a mortal? Today, I have finally realized that only the Universal Old Man and you are the real Celestials and you shouldn't be in the lower world. You and I, our gap suddenly seems so vast and…"

Lingfeng said convivially, "I used to be your grand protégé mistress and now I am just your older protégé sister. Our gap has closed down considerably already! Why, you are jealous of me?"

Yi Ping said, "That is not what I mean…"

Lingfeng interrupted, "I know…I hope we can be like before again."

Yi Ping was silent for a while before he said, "I hope so too. Lingfeng, I thought that I am a goner. Why is that I am still alive?"

Lingfeng said, "I am now invigorating your meridian channels with the Divine Invigorate Skill and is transferring the essence of the Divine Dragon Pill that I have consumed earlier to you."

Yi Ping was startled, "Lingfeng, if you give me the Divine Dragon Pill, that will be detrimental to your future attainment. Even though I may be stupid, I know for a fact that extracting the essence of the consumed Divine Dragon Pill from your body is harmful and your martial skills will surely deteriorate! Let go of me now!"

Lingfeng said, "It is already too late. Stop struggling. If you distract me, not only will you die, I will suffer serious internal injuries and may die too. I hope you know what I mean…"

She was taking too long to heal his injuries. In the past when she was the Heaveness, this was just an easy matter to her. Even though she had recalled her Divine Invigorate Skill but her mortal body was not strong enough to co-ordinate with her efforts. It seemed that from now on, she had to relearn and started her divine practice from scratch again…

Yi Ping sighed, "Your sacrifice is too great. I am not the White Sage. You should know this. I am just an illiterate person that knows just a few necessary words and I am not interested to be a Celestial or follow in the footsteps of the White Sage. I may know these maidens in previous incarnations but that is in the past. I should cherish what I have now. I am not the one that you are looking for…"

Lingfeng said softly, "That is true. When I come into contact with your Great Emptiness Translucence, I can already feel that it is different from him. It is full of love and affections, devoid of materialism. But how do you know that this is not the staging that I have always been yearning for? Maybe that is why I choose to be transmigrated as a mortal. Maybe you are the one that I have been waiting for and not the White Sage that you have mentioned?"

Yi Ping was startled, "That is quite improbable. Even though I have some visions of the White Sage through the Emptiness Translucence but I am not him. Like I say, I wish to lead an ordinary life."

Lingfeng said almost inaudible in his mind, "You have misunderstood me. I don't wish to ascend as a Celestial Being either. I just want to lead an ordinary life. Why do you think I have transmigrated as a mortal? I want to be with you, do you understand?"

Yi Ping was stunned at her bluntness.

He asked, "Are you Lingfeng or the Heaveness?"

Lingfeng said, "Even you can't tell the difference?"

Yi Ping answered with a deep sigh, "I can't. Can you enlighten me?"

Lingfeng said melancholy, "Whether I am the Heaveness or Lingfeng, is it important to you? I am still the Lingfeng you have known. I don't even want to recall the past."

Yi Ping said quietly, "But I know that you have changed. Your air has totally changed. You have exactly the same air as the Heaveness in my visions. You have tried to conceal it but somehow I know that you are no longer the Lingfeng sister that I have known."

Lingfeng said nonchalantly, "Since you have known, why did you ask?"

Yi Ping was quiet again but he mustered his courage to ask, "Will you leave?"

Lingfeng asked instead, "Do you hope that I can stay?"

Yi Ping sighed, "I don't know…"

Lingfeng asked, "You don't know?"

Yi Ping said, "If I ask you to stay, is it selfish of me?"

Lingfeng sighed melancholy, "So you want me to stay? Why don't you say to me directly then?"

Yi Ping was startled, "I am afraid…"

He could hear her soft laughs as she said, "You are really so dense. What are you afraid of? I have already given you so many hints. I am willing to stay. Whether I am the Heaveness or not, I am still the Lingfeng that you have known."

Yi Ping was relieved, "Lingfeng…"

"Yi Ping…"

Yi Ping was suddenly jolted, "Since you have transmigrated as a mortal, you shouldn't remember anything. How did you recall the Great Emptiness Translucence and remember everything? It is as if, you have never passed on…"

Lingfeng was silent for a while before she said, "You…you are right! This time you are so brilliant!"

Yi Ping was startled to hear her praising him for the first time and he was momentarily confounded.

Lingfeng pondered, "I have regained my memories when I am struck by the Universal Force…"

All of a sudden, she said excitedly, "That's right! The clues to the final transmigration! Why didn't I think of that previously? The immortal being that left the clue in the Stellar Sanctuary was looking for the Universal Force in the lower realm! There are no Universal Force in Beyond! The lower realm is the closest place that is near to the source of the Universal Force!"

She was suddenly saddened, "But what the point of knowing that now? I am no longer a Celestial. This knowledge has come too late…"

Yi Ping said, "Lingfeng, don't be sad."

She replied, "I am not."

Yi Ping said, "That is good…"

All of a sudden, he had thought of Yixian and he knew that she was facing the Divine Calamity very soon. So he asked, "Lingfeng, Heaveness…"

She was suddenly solemn, "Promise me not to call me by my celestial name. I am really sensitive to it. And don't tell others that I am the Heaveness previously, especially to Shen Xingyue and the Celestial Fairy."

Yi Ping said, "I promise but I hope that you can use your past experience as a Celestial to help them to overcome the Divine Calamity…"

Lingfeng said, "I can't and I will end up doing more harm than good."

Yi Ping was clearly disappointed at her downright rejection.

She added gently, "It is not that I won't try to help. But I have never experienced the Divine Calamity in the first place."

Yi Ping was stunned, "You have never experienced the Divine Calamity before?"

She said, "Do I sound like I am lying to you? During my time, there is no Divine Calamity and things aren't as hard as now. It is only when I have transmigrated to the Ninth Heavens to a place we call Beyond, we are forced to experience the Divine Wrath. Ninth Heavens may sound like a beautiful place but to us, it is actually a terrifying place where we have to undergo what is known as the 'Nine Great Heavenly Tribulations' and eighty-one minor crises in order to reach the final ascension level."

Yi Ping asked out of curiosity, "Which level are you at previously?"

Lingfeng replied coldly, "I am already at the final ascension level."

Yi Ping asked, "Is it hard to reach that final ascension level?"

Lingfeng explained patiently, "Extremely difficult. Even though I have not experienced the Divine Calamity before but I do know that after overcoming the first Divine Calamity, a Celestial Seeker has to first overcome the 'Three Divine Calamities' in order to transmigrate to the Ninth Heavens. After that, they have to face multiple Divine Wraths. Many don't even survive on their first attempt. When a Celestial has overcome the 'Nine Great Heavenly Tribulations', they have to face what is known as the Celestial Wrath which is even more terrifying than a Divine Wrath. Altogether, it is said that there are just seven Celestials that can attain to that level. The Universal Old Man and I are one of them."

Yi Ping was stunned and he could not imagine how arduous that journey was and how long it had taken her to reach the final ascension level.

He muttered, "I cannot imagine the difficulties that you have faced in the past. For you to give up all your hard earned attainment must be very hard on you…"

Lingfeng said casually, "It is precisely because I have reached the highest state in the Great Emptiness Translucence that I cannot feel any sense of loss or regrets. So you really do not have to feel pitiful for me."

Yi Ping muttered, "Where is this Beyond that everyone wants to transmigrate to?"

Lingfeng said patiently, "Above the region of death."

Yi Ping asked again, "Where is the region of death?"

Lingfeng said enigmatic, "You are really curious. Isn't that for you to find out yourself so that you can attain to a higher level in the future?"

Yi Ping teased her, "I don't really want to be a Celestial. I am asking my grand protégé mistress and older protégé sister for the answer."

Lingfeng laughed softly, "I can tell you but you must not reveal it to anyone. Or else your life span will surely be reduced drastically and even your descendants will suffer."

Yi Ping reluctantly agreed, "That is so serious?"

Lingfeng said, "So do you still want to know?"

Yi Ping said, "Will I affect you?"

Lingfeng said, "A little."

Yi Ping said, "Then better not."

But Lingfeng said, "The region of death is at 9000 meters above where no humans can survive. The Ninth Heaven can be entered at that point only. Not higher, not lower!"

Yi Ping was startled, "Lingfeng, why did you tell me..."

Lingfeng said, "Because that is my business and I like to do so."

Yi Ping was stunned.

Lingfeng said, "You can find the highest mountain when it is time for you to ascend. But you better be prepared to build an altar of heaven first and figure out a way. Because there are no mountains in the entire world that can take you to the region of death."

Yi Ping was stunned again, "Then how do I reach the Ninth Heavens?"

Lingfeng said, "If you can move the Heavens, the Ninth Heavens will descend to you. That is all I can tell you. Wait for the changing winds. That is all I can reveal to you."

Yi Ping tried to change the conversation, "That's good enough already. There must be many highly attained and admirable Celestials in the Ninth Heavens. How I wish I can meet them..."

Lingfeng was heard sighing, "Maybe when you have met the Dark Celestials, then you won't find them so admirable after all."

Yi Ping was startled, "There are Dark Celestials in the Ninth Heavens?"

Lingfeng nodded, "You may think that is improbable but there are many of them actually."

Yi Ping was somewhat stunned as he asked quietly, "Won't the Divine Calamity dealt with them?"

Lingfeng said, "Yes and no. There are always highly attained Celestials that strayed from the path and walked on the dark side. Most Dark Celestials are hard to identify. That is why the Celestials in Beyond do not trust one another easily."

She paused for a while before saying, "There are three types of Dark Celestials. First is the Ancient Dark Celestials. In the time before the Intermediate Era, there was no Divine Calamity in the lower world. Those who can ascend and transmigrated are able to reach the Ninth Heavens. Such is the grace of the Heavens upon all the mortals. In those years, mortals aged gradually and many could live to almost a thousand years. Six hundred years of age was just the beginning for the mortals, similar to a twenty year mortal!"

Yi Ping was startled, "Mortals can live that long?"

Lingfeng said, "If you read your classics, most Sages are able to live hundreds of years. Never mind, I know you don't read."

Yi Ping thoughts were full of awkwardness but Lingfeng seemed to have changed and did not try to tease him.

She patiently explained, "But something else had happened that caused their mortality to reduce to just a hundred and twenty. The reduced life-span became a trial to overcome the tribulations of eventually ascension. The Dark Celestials that overcome the Divine Calamity was able to transmigrate to Beyond are the second type of Dark Celestial."

Yi Ping asked, "These Dark Celestials can overcome the Divine Calamity?"

He was also curious to know of the event that had caused mortality to reduce so drastically but he decided not to ask for the time being.

Lingfeng said, "That's right! Either they are very powerful or they have actually taken advantage of the Divine Descendant to transmigrate to the Ninth Heavens during that time."

Yi Ping sighed, "Why must Heavens allow the Dark Celestials to exist?"

Lingfeng said, "Because Heavens is merciful and no matter how harsh things are, there are always a way out."

Her voice became almost inaudible, "We have been looking for a way out of Beyond for a long time too…"

She quickly said, "The third type of Dark Celestials is those that have joined the dark side willingly after they had ascended as a Virtuous Celestial."

Yi Ping asked curiously, "But once they are in Beyond, isn't there such a thing as the Divine Wrath to deal with them?"

She paused for a while and appeared to be melancholy, "Once they have reached Beyond, good and evil no longer exists. What is good, what is evil? The Divine Wrath won't deal with them as they have already ascended as a full Celestial. But killing another Celestial directly is forbidden and detrimental to the practitioner's progress."

Yi Ping said, "That is a relief to hear that. At least there is no more killing in Beyond…"

Lingfeng hummed coldly, "No more killing? That when you are wrong. There are many ways to kill a Celestial. For example, the most often used method is to injure the Celestial while not killing directly. In this way, the weakened Celestial would be killed by the Divine Wrath or spent too much recuperating rather than actually making progression in their state of divinity and eventually be killed."

Yi Ping said, "I didn't expect that the Ninth Heavens to be exactly the same here. I wonder how powerful a Dark Celestial is…"

Lingfeng laughed softly, "You! You…are just a martial idiot! You really think that martial skills can get you everywhere? Let me tell you this. Not all Celestials can fight."

Yi Ping was somewhat startled, "They can't fight then how do they reach the Ninth Heavens?"

Lingfeng said, "Your previous incarnation can't fight at all. He is just a scholar. The Divine Calamity is a Divine Calamity that tests one's limit. In order to ascend as a Celestial, you have to overcome yourself first. Sometimes it may be easier for a non-martial exponent to ascend but it is no less dangerous. In Beyond, the martial Celestials are the majority since those Celestials that couldn't protect themselves can't really survive on their own."

Yi Ping was not paying attention anymore. He was extremely worried. "Yixian had learnt the Divine Emerald Skill to the tenth level. Does it mean that her Divine Calamity will test her to the very limits?"

Lingfeng said coolly, "Unfortunately yes. If she had stopped at the ninth level, things may be easier for her. The tenth level of her Divine Emerald Skill is said to be the ultimate and also an absolute defense martial force field. But the Divine Calamity will breech her Divine Emerald Skill for sure. Pity, there is no eleventh level in the Divine Emerald Skill. Even if it exists, she doesn't have the time to divine that understanding."

Yi Ping sighed softly.

While Yi Ping was sighing to himself, Lingfeng was startled!

It was because Yi Ping was now absorbing the essence of the Divine Dragon Pill at an alarming pace!

She was taking all necessary precaution to slowly transfer the essence of the Divine Dragon Pill to him because the Divine Dragon Pill itself was an extremely potent miracle pill. Even if an internal martial expert would to take one, it was not without its own risks. Taking two Divine Dragon Pills out of greed at the same time would kill anyone, including the Celestials.

But now, Yi Ping seemed to be absorbing the essence of the Divine Dragon Pill rapidly from her as though there was a vacuum in his body!

Lingfeng was very much perplexed for she had never seen anything like that before. She began to analyze and had come out with a conclusion; he could have reached the physical limit break and had undergone a startling physical transfiguration!

No matter if a person was a mortal or a celestial being, the physical limit would never change. The most adept mortals could be capable of utilizing a tenth of their physical limit while the most powerful celestials may be able to utilize up to one third of it. There were no exceptions for both mortals and celestials; none was able to reach the physical limit break!

But somehow, Yi Ping had reached beyond his physical limit break after he had used the Asper Divinity five times in a row. Now that she had recalled it, she had a startling thought all of a sudden; how did he even manage to unleash the Asper Divinity more than two times continuously in the first place?

Was it even possible for a mere mortal to achieve a physical transfiguration without becoming a Celestial Being in the first place?

But because she had no answers for that, her thoughts quickly shifted to her new awareness as she thought. "So I am the Heaveness. I am now able to feel despair, love, hurt, joy, the seven emotions and the six desires of a mortal. This is a wonderful feeling…"

Just as she was deep in thoughts, she could sense that Yi Ping had awakened and had gently stepped backward awkwardly…

Yi Ping was looking at her with embarrassment but he had also felt a deep sense of appreciation for her.

When the other maidens saw that Yi Ping had opened his eyes and had recovered his countenance, they quickly surrounded him in amazement!

At this distance, they were slightly taken back. When Yi Ping had opened his eyes, his eyes were golden but it quickly grew dim and normalized it in an instant.

All the maidens except Shen Xingyue did not think much of it, thinking that it came from the reflections of the Twin Sisters' golden swords which were still glowing with a brilliant golden light!

Yu'Er and Mei'Er quickly sheathed their divine swords into their scabbards as they were afraid that its brilliant light would cause Yi Ping to feel discomfort.

As soon as they had sheathed their golden swords, many of the onlookers were feeling much better, their nausea had somewhat eased slightly.

Shen Xingyue was thinking, "Did I just see his eye pupils turned golden?"

Youxue quickly asked, "Ping'Er, are you alright?"

Lie Qing asked in surprise, "How did you recover…"

She looked suspiciously at Lingfeng…

Lingfeng pretended to be startled, "I don't know either…"

Yu'Er and Mei'Er did not care to know the reasons. They were simply too overwhelmed with joy as they embraced cuddly around him as they cried joyfully, "Master, we are so worried for you…"

Yi Ping sighed weakly as he looked at them with heartfelt emotions for he was deeply touched by their concerns for him.

The first thing that he had awakened and said was, "Have we won?"

Yunzi smiled and said, "Yes, we have won! Xiao Shuai and Han Shaodong have admitted defeat!"

Lele said coolly, "That's only because of me. I should be given some credits."

Yixian, Lie Qing and Shen Xingyue were exchanging knowing glances at each other. They simply could not believe what they were seeing and they were eyeing Lingfeng with some suspicious.

Even Ji Wuzheng, Dugu Zhen, Xiao Shuai, Han Shaodong, the Martial Sage and many others were incredulous!

Xiao Shuai was stunned, "Is he human?"

He was saddened for he knew that it was over for them. Their lofty ambitions of ascending as Celestials were shattered; they had completely lost!

Han Shaodong and the Martial Sage had walked quietly next to him as they said, "Brother, this time we have completely lost."

Xiao Shuai nodded slowly as he looked at the direction where Yi Ping was.

After he had lost in such complete manner, he had finally realized that certain things could not be forced. He had already lost two of his sons and his mentor master Yuan Shao. If he persisted further, he may lost even his other son, Xiao Fan, his daughter Xiao Youxue, his nephew Xiao Fei and even his grandson Xiao Ao.

When he saw Xiao Fan, Xiao Youxue and Xiao Fei discarding their prides and pleading for his life, he was extremely touched and he knew that he had erred horrendously.

It was because the protégés of the Virtuous Palace was all trained by him and he knew that they all carried a strong sense of pride. He knew that they would never beg anyone for anything. That was what he had taught them and he had ensured that it was the unwritten rule; for a swordsman to lose their pride, they would lose their honor and fighting spirits!

He had only himself to blame for his sons' death. Actually, he did not feel any remorse over the death of his two sons' death. It was because he knew them to be as scheming as him. He had the intention to appoint Xiao Fan, his illegitimate son as his successor but he was wary that his other two sons might harm him. He knew for sure that Xiao Yuanjia and Xiao Da would definitely scheme to get rid of Xiao Fan just as they had always schemed against each other.

His injuries were not light and practitioners of the Divine Virtuous Force were fearful of getting internal injuries. Even though the Divine Virtuous Force was a powerful martial force skill, any internal injuries that were sustained were extremely difficult to treat and could even cause a deterioration of their martial skills!

When he had forced himself to fight Yi Ping again after sustaining internal injuries from the Twin Sisters, he knew that he was already hovering on death's door and could not sustain any more serious internal injuries. But pride kept him going.

That was also the same for Han Shaodong, the Martial Sage, the Sword Sage and the Element Sage.

He was now looking at Yan Nanfei and Shangguan Qingyun who had managed to revive the Sword Sage and the Element Sage…

He was not someone who valued brotherhood or friends. But somehow, he was being sentimental about it. Maybe it was because they used to fight alongside one another and they had been fighting for the same cause as him even though they all had their differences.

All of a sudden, he seemed to have enlightened as he stared into the blank air.

Yixian had quietly approached him as she said gently, "It seems that you have finally seen through the illusions of life. The oppressing aura in your eyes is gone now."

Han Shaodong and the Martial Sage were also sighing weakly as they looked at Yixian.

Han Shaodong said weakly, "I don't think we can live for long and is just sustaining ourselves through our internal strength. Xian'Er, it is good to see you again. But it is a pity, we cannot be a Celestial anymore…"

Yixian expressions were full of sorrows as she said gently to them. "I am about to experience the Divine Calamity soon. If you are interested, you are invited to witness it."

Xiao Shuai, Han Shaodong and the Martial Sage were stunned.

Xiao Shuai began to tremble as he muttered, "If my Golden Rejuvenate Pills are not stolen and if this plan of ours had succeeded, we may invoke the Divine Calamity and ascend as a Celestial under the auspicious seven stars…alas…"

Han Shaodong said regretfully, "We are so close to the Heavenly Relic for ourselves and becoming a Celestial. So close yet so far now."

Yixian asked, "Why do you want to become a Celestial?"

They went silent. It was because they all had their own selfish reasons for it.

The Martial Sage was the first one to find an excuse, "Xian'Er, you may not know this. The Celestial Palace is our common enemy. Do you know how many martial exponents have been killed over the years by them? Why do you think that with the martial skills of the Three Sages, we are still being forced to go into hiding? If we can be Celestials, then we can join you as a Celestial too. Isn't that a good thing?"

Yixian smiled gently at them, "You have all misunderstood. I am not going to become a Celestial anytime soon. In fact, I am asking you to witness my demise."

They were shocked.

Han Shaodong stammered, "Xian'Er, what do you mean?"

Yixian said gently, "Only the virtuous can ascend as a Celestial. The Divine Calamity is just a divine tribulation that acts for the will of the Heaven. I have killed numerous exponents in my life. My Divine Calamity is the worst type and I probably won't be able to survive the ordeal. Even if you have the Golden Rejuvenation Pills, the Heavenly Relic, the blood of the Holy

Maiden and the auspicious signs of the seven stars to aid you, the result will still be the same; death awaits you."

Xiao Shuai was startled, "Is that the truth?"

Yixian said gently, "There no need for me to lie to you. After you have witnessed the Divine Calamity with your own eyes, you will understand."

The Martial Sage was stunned, "Xian'Er, you will die? How come?!"

Yixian smiled gently, "You do not need to feel regrets for me. I am really happy to meet and know all of you and…"

She paused and looked lovingly towards Yi Ping who was still being surrounded by the other maidens who were showering him with all kinds of love and concern. "…and knowing my husband Yi Ping is the best thing that has happened to me."

She looked at them and said, "The number of people that you have killed or ruined is enough to invite the wrathful retribution of the Divine Calamity. That is not something that mere mortals like us can overcome. That is why none of you will be able to survive the Divine Calamity. Look at the number of people that have already been killed today."

Shen Xingyue who had extremely keen hearing had overheard their conversation. She walked quietly besides Yixian, "There is a blessing in disguise too. Earlier, I have sensed the creation of the Universal Force when everyone was struck by it. Those who had survived this battle have the residue of the Universal Force in their bodies. Given time, it is still possible to become a Celestial without the aid of any external help. However it is still dependable upon the state of divinity of the practitioners and the providence of the Heavens. That Universal Force is actually the benevolent type. It just that its shockwaves are so great that many could not withstand it and hence, so many is killed by it."

Xiao Shuai was startled, "We can still become a Celestial?"

Shen Xingyue said, "In order to ascend, first know how to become a Human Sage and do no evil. That will clear the hurdles for you and makes the Divine Calamity less malevolent."

Xiao Shuai, Han Shaodong and the Martial Sage were all looking at each other as they stammered, "It is that simple?"

Shen Xingyue said, "It is that simple and it is all in the ancient classics. It is just that it is too obvious and everyone is looking the other way."

Xiao Shuai, Han Shaodong and the Martial Sage were extremely ashamed. They had read the ancient classics numerous times when they were young but as they grew up, they had forgotten about it.

All of a sudden, there was an evil laughter that resonated throughout the surroundings, startling everyone!

It was Zuo Tianyi and he was dragging Gu Tianle, who was motionless!

There was a frightening sword energy aura around Zuo Tianle and the air in the surroundings was chilly and filled with the spectral of death!

Yi Ping, Xiao Shuai, Han Shaodong and Lingfeng were to first to raise the alarm, "Is this the Infinity-Zero level?!"

Chapter 67: The Infinity-Zero

Zuo Tianyi was wrapped in an extraordinary powerful cold piercing sword energy as he looked murderously at everyone.

His aura was so malicious and cold that many exponents began to take frightful steps backward!

Zuo Tianyi was slightly startled to see the Joyful Goddess and the Celestial Fairy. He had recognized them and had borne a hatred for the Joyful Goddess.

It was because while he was at the Great Tranquil Mountains, she had interrupted his duel with Yi Ping by moving into the death zone of their sword energies. If he had been slower by a second, he would be killed by her. As a result of her attack, he had suffered a minor slash across his chest.

He had many puzzling questions that were on his mind.

How did she manage to get close to the killing sword energies that were rippling all around them that day without putting on any defenses? And why did she not get rip apart by their sword energies?

He was also perplexed to see the Celestial Fairy talking to Shen Xingyue, Xiao Shuai, Han Shaodong and the Martial Sage.

He could tell that even the insolent Xiao Shuai was talking respectfully to her.

Did Xiao Shuai not know that it was actually the Celestial Fairy that had fatally injured Yuan Shao?

But when he saw the state of condition that Xiao Shuai, Han Shaodong and the Three Sages were in, he almost wanted to laugh aloud at their uselessness.

He was dragging Gu Tianle. When he had stopped, he let loose of him.

Immediately, the exponents from the various martial clans were muttering. "Isn't that Gu Tianle, the Master of the Honor Manor? Is he dead?"

When the Universal Force had imploded and its shockwaves had rippled throughout the surrounding areas, Zuo Tianyi and Gu Tianle were recuperating from their injuries in the safety of the tent.

Zuo Tianyi who had developed a strong innate energy sense due to his superior sword energy level, had sensed a powerful shockwave towards them with a supersonic speed.

He had quickly grabbed Gu Tianle who was startled by surprise as he asked, "What are you doing…"

But before he could finish what he had wanted to say, the Universal Force had struck him directly!

Even though Zuo Tianyi had used Gu Tianle as a shield, he was still struck by the powerful Universal Force as it went past through to him!

He immediately coughed out a bout of black blood.

He had thought he was dead but he was feeling more energetic than ever. The Universal Force had completely forced out the sword energies that were caused by Yi Ping out of his body and had cleared his life and death channels!

As he looked in bewildered at himself, he noticed that his wounds were healing at a rapid rate and his agony pain was now endurable.

When he tried to muster his strength, he found that his internal energy was now very smoothing and he was even more energetic than ever before.

Zuo Tianyi picked out his sword and stared at it.

All of a sudden, he waved his sword as he tried to imbue his sword energy into his sword. But because he was not expecting his martial progression to improve, he was startled to see that the sword energy that he had imbued had flown out of the tent with a rippling slashing force!

Even though he was panting from the effort, he was excited; it was because his sword energies were limited to the length of his sword but now he could actually sent it flying out!

He laughed, "Providence is kind to me. To think that I have finally mastered the Infinity-Zero and can kill invisibly from afar. Now I am truly Invincible. Xiao Shuai, Han Shaodong, Yi Ping and Shen Xingyue, I have tolerated all of you long enough. This is the day that the entire fraternity will only know who is Zuo Tianyi and the Infinity Sword Clan will take the leadership away from the Honor Manor!"

That was how he had attained the Infinity-Zero and he was now looking disdainfully at everyone!

Two elders of the Infinity Sword Clan stepped forward as they called out respectfully to him, "Congratulations to our Protégé Leader for mastering the Infinity-Zero Technique! But how are your injuries? Are you well? Master Gu is…"

Zuo Tianyi looked at them coldly, saying. "If I am not well, will I be standing here?"

He pointed his sword towards Yi Ping, "That man has killed Master Gu. If I don't take vengeance for him, can I still consider myself as a righteous hero?"

The elder on the right, who had a short black beard said weakly, "The Honor Manor and the Virtuous Palace have conceded. The battle is over and the Young Hero Yi Ping has won. Therefore we should also retreat peacefully back to the Central Fraternity. The Holy Hex Sect has given their word that they won't be pursuing this matter anymore. Too many lives have already been lost…"

Zuo Tianyi said coldly, "Evil can only reign for a time but good will eventually triumph. Look at the number of dead around us. Are we going to let their sacrifices be in vain? Don't forget that this expedition is to avenge the Old Sword Saint. Even if the other martial orthodox clans are too cowardly to oppose the Holy Hex Sect and the Celestial Palace, the Infinity Sword Clan is not going to put it to rest so easily!"

Han Shaodong said coldly, "This battle is meaningless. Put down your sword…"

Zuo Tianyi interrupted as he looked at the hundreds of orthodox exponents who were still standing, pointing at Han Shaodong and Xiao Shuai. "If the Honor Manor and the Virtuous Palace are unable to uphold the honor of the orthodox clans, maybe it is time for the Infinity Sword Clan to take the mantle of leadership."

Xiao Shuai appraised him coldly before he said weakly, "So you have the lofty ambition to head the orthodox clans. But I wonder if you are capable."

Zuo Tianyi was clearly provoked and his murderous intent was evident.

The two elders quickly tried to persuade him, "Protégé Leader, this is unnecessary. Let's us go now…"

But Zuo Tianyi ignored them and shouted to Yi Ping, "Yi Ping, do you dare to accept my challenge?!"

Yi Ping was startled.

He coughed weakly and was being supported by Lingfeng, Youxue and the rest of the maidens but he replied defiantly, "Tianyi, give it up. This fight is meaningless. What do you hope to achieve even if you have defeated me?"

Zuo Tianyi laughed aloud, "Everything that I have lost, every honor that I have lost will be regained if you are killed by me."

Yunzi said, "There are certain things that once you have lost it, you will never be able to regain again."

Zuo Tianyi looked bitterly at them and he had also noticed that for the very first time, all the martial exponents were on the same side and were all staring at him hostility!

But Zuo Tianyi disregarded their hostility for these injured exponents were not a threat to him.

Zuo Tianyi said coldly, "Those who are on my side and willingly to follow me to greater glory, come over to my side. From now on, I will take on the legacy of the Old Sword Saint and will also lead the righteous martial orthodox clans to exterminate all the unorthodox clans."

Except for the remnants of the thirty odd protégés of the Infinity Sword Clan, no one else made a single move!

Zuo Tianyi said coldly, "It seems that the orthodox exponents are all cowed by the presence of the heretics. In this case, don't blame me for being ruthless."

All of a sudden, the 'dead' Gu Tianle raised a loud shout with the last bout of his strength. "Zuo Tianyi, you despicable man. You try to kill me!"

He had taken a fatal blow from the Universal Force when Zuo Tianyi had used him as a shield. It was only then did he realize that this Zuo Tianyi was an unscrupulous man that would do anything to satisfy his own desires.

Using the last reserve of his internal strength, he had used the basic heart intricacy formula of the Divine Rejuvenation Force which Han Shaodong had imparted to him to halt his heart beat and breathing, faking his own death.

Zuo Tianyi was startled that Gu Tianle was still alive. When he was startled by Gu Tianle, he reacted immediately by slashing him into two!

Immediately the entire congregation of martial exponents were all stunned and they had all broken into incessant mutterings!

Zuo Tianyi was looking at them and he was imagining that they were all scorning him!

Han Shaodong shouted angrily, "Zuo Tianyi, you dare to kill Gu Tianle!"

Zuo Tianyi shouted, "Shut your crap! I am going to use your blood as a sacrificial offering for my newly acquainted Infinity-Zero!"

He drawn out his beaming precious sword and waved in three different directions, stirring out the sand from the ground. Immediately, three rippling windforce energized by sword energies had flown with startling bursting speed towards the martial exponents!

As the rippling windforce swept across the field, it ripped apart everything that the invisible windforce had come into contact with as it shattered weapons, bodies and powdered rocks into dust!

Shen Xingyue, Xiao Shuai and Han Shaodong quickly shouted aloud to everyone, "Run! These sword energies cannot be blocked!"

To the astonishment of everyone, Yixian, Lele and Lie Qing had leapt forward in three different directions with a startling speed towards the three wavering sword energies!

Yixian had raised her fingers forward and had shattered the incoming wavering sword energy apart with a loud implosion using her Divine Emerald Skill!

Lele had drawn out her long black scythe and sliced the ground in front of her with her martial force, creating a wall of inertia force. As the wavering sword energies struck her wall of inertia force, it exploded and she was sent moving back a few steps but she was otherwise unharmed.

Lele exclaimed with a soft relief, "Lucky!"

At the same time, Lie Qing had surrounded herself with her Invincible Divine Force and had drawn out her Perpetual Darkness as she executed her sword technique with a soft shout, "The Seventh Heavens Stroke!"

The Seventh Heavens Stroke was an epitome sword technique that was similar to the Infinity-Zero. It was a sword energy technique that Lie Qing only reserved for her strongest opponents. She had used it in the past against the Celestial Fairy.

As she executed it, seven beaming blue visible blue beams of sword energies flew and clashed against Zuo Tianyi's incoming sword energy waves.

There was a thunderous implosion as the sword energies imploded against one another!

Zuo Tianyi's sword energies were dissipated by Lie Qing's sword energies as seven beaming bluish sword energies continued to fly towards Zuo Tianyi with astonishing speed!

Zuo Tianyi, unlike the majority of the exponents who were astonished that Lie Qing had the same level of energy technique as him was not surprised. It was because he had previously witnessed the duel between the Celestial Fairy and Lie Qing. That had the remarkable effect of helping him to progress his Infinity-Two to the Infinity-One at that time!

Unlike his invisible sword energy, her sword energies were visible and radiated a light hue. But the fact that she could unleash seven beaming continuous sword energies was a feat onto itself.

He immediately raised his sword and circulated his entire vital energies to block her sword energies, via the principle of using sword energy technique to guard against sword energy technique. Only a person of his level could be able to block sword energy with sword energy!

He smiled to himself. This would be a good time that he could prove to everyone that his Infinity-Zero was the most superior sword technique. He had decided that after he had defeated all of them, he would make this Lie Qing surrendered her sword techniques and sword manuals to him. He was particular interested in her sword energy as it may help to advance his future sword energy attainment.

Thereafter, he would demolish all his opponents, destroy the heretic sects and demolished the mysticism of the Celestial Palace! From this day onward, his renown and that of the Infinity Sword Clan would resonate throughout the martial fraternity!

All of a sudden when the seven beaming sword energies were about to approach him, he was startled and began to move backward!

It was because he had suddenly sensed seven extraordinary powerful energy bursts approaching at a terrifying speed. He was suddenly trembling and there was fear in his eyes!

As Zuo Tianyi had raised his precious sword, imbuing it with his sword energy and timed it against the seven flying bluish sword energies, he was ripped to pieces even before the bluish sword energies had even come within twenty paces of his body!

This development stunned the onlookers who were all gasping with startled disbelief!

While the super exponents could roughly guessed the reasons for that, only Shen Xingyue and Lele who had reached the Transverse state of divinity could see Lie Qing's invisible sword energies!

Zuo Tianyi had ill-timed his defense too late and as soon as he had raised his long precious sword, seven beaming invisible sword energies had went through his body, ripping him apart instantly!

The bluish sword energies that everyone had seen were just the aftermath and trail of Lie Qing's invisible sword energies; because it was speeding so fast and the intense heat was so great, it condensed the air behind the sword energies resulting in seven bluish trails!

Xiao Shuai muttered as he observed the nine hovering faint glow around Lie Qing, "She has not only mastered the Invincible Divine Force that the Virtuous Palace have been coveting but she has also reached the sword energy level of the Invincible Divine Force. Alas, it is a terrible mistake to fight her in the first place. If we have fought her one at a time, our fates would be the same as this Zuo Tianyi…"

Yixian sighed quietly, "This Zuo Tianyi has progressed too fast in his swordplay and has fought against too few powerful opponents that he has underestimated Qing'Er sword energy bursts and has allowed his eyes to deceive him."

She took a quick glance at the breathless Lie Qing who had thrust her sword into the ground as she used it as a support.

The execution of sword energies was an extremely exhausting affair for any practitioner. But because Lie Qing still had her Invincible Divine Force around her and that did not dissipated with her Seventh Heavens Stroke, Yixian knew that her martial foundation had shown a marked progression since they had last fought.

She began to wonder if her epitome Divine Emerald Skill would be able to withstand her Seventh Heavens Stroke?

Shen Xingyue looked at the three Celestial Star Sisters of Fate with a startled expression. These three sisters had just stopped the Infinity-Zero and their martial skills were startling.

She sighed softly, "It is going to be interesting in the future…"

Yi Ping had taken a few steps forward as he sighed weakly, "Zuo Tianyi, this shouldn't be your fate if you have repented of your past wrongdoings…"

The two elders of the Infinity Sword Clan and the three dozen protégés of the Infinity Sword Clan threw their long swords on the ground before walking towards Yi Ping, Xiao Shuai and Han Shaodong respectfully.

The black beard elder of the Infinity Sword Clan sighed as he said, "I am Zuo Ziya, elder of the Infinity Sword Clan. I hope the heroes of the fraternity will forgive our clan transgression and let this matter rest."

Yi Ping took a quick glance at Lie Qing who was stroking her long hair before he replied weakly, "If the Infinity Sword Clan does not pursue Maiden Lie Qing for your protégé leader's death and our transgressions over the deaths of your martial clan, I am naturally happy to let matters rest."

Zuo Ziya sighed, "This entire expedition is but a mistake in the first place…"

Han Shaodong said regretfully, "The mistake is mine too. Go in peace. My protégé disciple's death has nothing to do with the Infinity Sword Clan."

Xiao Shuai nodded weakly, "The mistake is mine as well. I only hope that we can make amends for the wrongs that we did…"

Zuo Ziya bowed respectfully before he shouted to the protégés of the Infinity Sword Clan, "Let's us go now!"

But before they could depart, there were columns of dust in the horizon!

Everyone was startled as they looked nervously at the horizons.

Had the heretic sects returned?

Or had a new enemy arrived to take advantage of the situation?

Ji Wuzheng shouted to his protégés, "Get ready for battle!"

He turned to address the orthodox exponents, "This is the territory of the Holy Hex Sect. Let us deal with the intruders. Evacuate all the wounded people behind our battle lines!"

Immediately, the injured martial exponents began to move to the back.

Xiao Shuai coughed weakly as he gripped his long sword, "Xiao Fei, Xiao Ao can you still fight?"

Xiao Fei said coolly, "I can still kill a few enemies."

Xiao Ao said, "The same goes for me!"

Xiao Shuai laughed aloud, "Good, good! You have not disgraced the Virtuous Palace. Even if we all perish today, the honor of the Virtuous Palace shall still remain for all posterity!"

There were also scores of orthodox exponents that despite their injuries had also stepped forward and shouted, "We are willing to be deployed by the Master of the Holy Hex Sect and to fight alongside you!"

Yi Ping too had gripped his swords and had stood beside Ji Wuzheng, "Elder Brother, let me fight with you."

Ji Wuzheng said, "Brother Yi Ping, you should take a rest first. You are in no condition to fight. No matter who the enemy is, the Holy Hex Sect has more than enough men to handle it…"

Lingfeng said coldly, "He wants to court his own death so fast, brother. So let him be."

Yi Ping smiled bitterly at her.

Lele closed her eyes for a second before she said solemnly, "The approaching enemies are numerous, probably in the thousands!"

Ji Wuzheng, Yi Ping, Xiao Shuai, Han Shaodong, Yan Nanfei, Shangguan Qingyun and the Three Sages were startled.

The Sword Sage coughed weakly, "Thousands? Who else could muster so many fighters?"

Yi Ping looked at everyone.

Yixian smiled gently at him as she held his hand tenderly, "Life and death is predetermined. I am content enough to know you and to listen to your voice. Ping'Er, are you afraid?"

Yi Ping looked tenderly at her, "Xian'Er, with you by my side I am not afraid. I just wish that I have my strength now…"

Shen Xingyue sighed softly, "Even if I have to destroy my attainments today, I would be willing."

She looked at Lele and Lie Qing who were also looking intently at the horizon and knew that they were also thinking the same because she could feel their disguised killing intent, however slight it had been.

Yu'Er said melancholy to Yi Ping, "You know I don't care about being a Celestial."

Mei'Er blinked at Yi Ping, "Master, you should take a step back to rest. You have been fighting nonstop all this while. How about this? Let's us form the Celestial Star Formation and you can watch in the middle while we fight off the intruders?"

Dugu Yunzi said demurely, "Mei'Er, this is an excellent idea!"

Youxue said coldly, "It doesn't matter how many they are. They are not getting past me."

Xiao Shuai laughed faintly, "That is my good daughter!"

Lingfeng said coolly, "Don't be alarmed. Things may not be as bad it looked."

Yi Ping nodded as he stared at the horizons.

They could see thousands of men with martial banners approaching in the horizon now.

All of a sudden, Ji Wuzheng and Yi Ping stared blankly at each other!

It was because they had quickly caught sight of Huo Fu who was leading his protégés, Nangong Le, Qiu Wufeng, Gongsun Jing, Sufeng, Suxin, Suyue, Priest Ling Kongquan, Priest Liu Qingcheng, Priest Bai Chongzhen and many other martial clans that were from the Western Fraternity!

Huo Fu, Nangong Le, Qiu Wufeng, Gongsun Jing, Sufeng, Suxin and Suyue were worried for Ji Wuzheng and Yi Ping. Despite their injuries, the four sworn brothers were determined to offer whatever aid they could to Yi Ping and Ji Wuzheng. The daughters of Ji Wuzheng were worried for their parents and they were also worried for Qiu Wufeng, Gongsun Jing and Nangong Le. Therefore, they had forced them to bring them along.

When they were at the foot of the mountains, they had met Priest Liu Qingcheng and Priest Bai Chongzhen who had led more than thirty other martial clans of the Western Fraternity to aid Yi Ping and to fight against the dominating ambitions of the Honor Manor!

Priest Bai Chongzhen was startled to see Yi Ping and Xiao Shuai standing on the same side, "Young Hero, whose side are you on now?"

Yi Ping smiled as he bowed respectfully with both his hands, "The battle is already over. We have made peace. There are no more feuds."

Immediately, the fighters that had just newly arrived shouted thunderously; their shouts shook the ground with excitement and joy!

Everyone who could move was hugging one another in joyous exclamations at the announcement, regardless of their clan and fraction affiliations!

Priest Bai Chongzhen was relieved, "That's good to hear…all men from four corners of the fraternity are brothers…"

Lele laughed heartily, "Yi Ping, you should thank me for this."

Yi Ping was startled, "Why should I?"

Lele was not happy that Yi Ping was questioning her so she replied, "Why do you think there are so many reinforcements coming to aid you?"

Yi Ping was surprised, "You have a help in mustering them?"

Priest Bai Chongzhen bowed respectfully to the Joyful Goddess, "The Joyful Goddess is the envoy from the Celestial Palace. With her token, we manage to persuade a large number of martial clans that were still neutral in the Western Fraternity to join our cause."

He turned to Yi Ping to say, "Young Hero, you must know that in the Western Fraternity, the Celestial Palace has a powerful presence."

Lele blinked at Yi Ping, "Now you know who you should thank?"

Yi Ping smiled bitterly at her.

Priest Bai Chongzhen saw that Yi Ping did not know what to say so he laughed aloud, "The credit naturally belongs to the Joyful Goddess. We are just doing our part to help."

Lele clapped her hands delightfully as she said to Priest Chongzhen, "The Celestial Palace will definitely reward you handsomely for accomplishing this task so well!"

Priest Chongzhen said humbly, "We are honored that the Joyful Goddess has appointed me as the Celestial Messenger and the Traverse Clan as the guardian clan of the Celestial Palace…"

Priest Liu Qingcheng quickly interrupted, "The Tranquil City also plays a major role in this. Why is that all the credits now belongs to the Traverse Clan?"

Priest Bai Chongzhen smiled, "Why didn't you ask the Joyful Goddess for a reward then?"

Lele said delightfully as she clapped her hands, "Both of you will be rewarded handsomely!"

Lie Qing almost fainted from the scene as she thought miserly, "She seems to be enjoying herself as she makes a fool out of them. She is a fake Celestial Envoy…"

Yixian, Youxue and Lingfeng were sighing…

Yi Ping could only smile bitterly…

When Ji Wuzheng saw the awkward smile that was on Yi Ping, he thought that Yi Ping did not believe in the far reaching influence of the Celestial Palace, so he said. "Brother Yi Ping, do you still remember the Celestial Liege? He…"

He was suddenly interrupted by Lele who exclaimed with surprise, "What?! You have seen my bro…the Celestial Liege?"

Ji Wuzheng said respectfully, "Indeed. The Celestial Palace has paid us a visit not too long ago."

Lele had turned ashen as she whispered softly, "He didn't take anything from you or ask for anything? What did he say to you?"

While Ji Wuzheng was explaining to the Joyful Goddess, Priest Liu Qingcheng said to Yi Ping, "Brother Yi Ping! I have also come to warn you to be wary of the seven maidens! Do you still remember the silver scroll that I have shown you?"

Yi Ping smiled bitterly, "Which seven of the maidens are you talking about?"

Priest Liu Qingcheng was also smiling bitterly as he looked at the hostile stares of the maidens that were standing behind Yi Ping.

Youxue said coldly, "Be wary of who? Do you want to say that again?"

Priest Liu Qingcheng broke into a cold sweat as he stammered, "Nothing…"

Nangong Le suddenly clapped him on his back, "I think you are in trouble, brother…"

Priest Liu Qingcheng stared at him, "Brother? I thought that I am your protégé teacher and master now."

Nangong Le laughed, "I haven't mastered your Dual Inertness Intricacy Skill yet…"

Priest Ling Kongquan hit him on his head, "Stop being so slippery and accept your fate!"

Suyue looked at them shyly, "Why are you bullying Brother Nangong Le?"

Priest Ling Kongquan and Priest Liu Qingcheng looked at each other before they roared with laughter!

Suyue was startled, "Why so funny about that?"

Yi Ping quickly tried to change the conversation as he turned to Yixian and Lele with an earnest sigh, "Xian'Er, Lele. I am so sorry…"

Lele asked curiously, "Why are you sorry?"

Yixian smiled at him gently, "Ping'Er, what's wrong?"

Yi Ping sighed, "I have promised Lele to find a miracle pill to help her grandpa. I have got a Divine Dragon Pill…"

He looked at Yixian with a sad expression, "But my heart wants to give this Divine Dragon Pill to you first. This may be the only thing that can help you..."

Lele was startled, "You have the Divine Dragon Pill…where did you find it?"

Yixian smiled gently, "Ping'Er, you can give it to Lele. Life and death is predetermined. Even if you have given me the Divine Dragon Pill, I may not be able to overcome the Divine Calamity. Rather than let it be wasted, it is better that you give it to Lele."

When Xiao Shuai, Han Shaodong and the Three Sages heard that Yi Ping had the Divine Dragon Pill with him, they were startled and they were already drooling to see it. In fact, they wished they could take it from him and swallowed it immediately!

The Martial Sage was the most impatient, "Young Hero Yi Ping, can you show it to us? I am really curious to see what it is like."

Xiao Shuai was trembling, "This pill is a legendary martial treasure…those who can consume it are able to become a Celestial Being…"

Shangguan Qingyun said, "Young Hero Yi Ping, do you still remember that I am the one that gives you this Divine Dragon Pill? I don't regret giving it to you but I hope that you can give it to Xian'Er instead. I don't want her to die…"

Xiao Shuai, Han Shaodong and the Three Martial Sages were shocked.

Han Shaodong interrupted him, "You have the Divine Dragon Pill all the time and you have actually given it away?!"

But Shangguan Qingyun ignored them.

Yi Ping said to Shangguan Qingyun, "The one that you have given me, I have actually given to Maiden Lie Qing to save her life. I have since found another one."

Shangguan Qingyun was startled as he muttered, "You really found another one?"

Ji Wuzheng said, "My wife and I can be the witness!"

Gongsun Jing and Qiu Wufeng said at the same time, "We can vouch for Brother Yi Ping as well!"

Yi Ping sighed as he reached into his garment to take out the Divine Dragon Pill that he had carefully concealed, "This is the only one Divine Dragon Pill now. I wish that there are two in the world…"

Yixian smiled gently at him, "Ping'Er, do the right thing and give it to Lele. Don't worry about me."

Lele looked tearfully at Yixian as she fell into her embrace, "Sister! I don't want you to die either! I…don't know what to do…"

Lie Qing moved quietly next to Lele and held her hands…

All of a sudden, Yi Ping had turned ashen as he searched panicky. He muttered aloud in alarm. "Where is it? I can't find it!"

Lingfeng had turned around and looked away…

Yunzi and Youxue were quiet too. They had witnessed how Lingfeng had stolen the Divine Dragon Pill and giving it to Yi Ping to save his life…

Chapter 68: Melancholy Farewell

A few days later and somewhere in one of the desolate peaks of the Holy Amalgamate Mountains range.

Yixian and Yi Ping was in a cave looking the majestic Holy Amalgamate Mountains range while waiting for the rest of their acquaintances to arrive.

The only signs that disturbed the scenic view were the endless rumbling and tremors of the unceasing earthquakes.

While waiting, Yixian gently examined Yi Ping's pulses for signs of injuries.

She pondered for a while before saying quietly, "It seemed that you have already broken through the Life and Death Channels. These two are the most difficult of the eight wondrous meridians and until now, not many practitioners know their effects. That you are alive and able to recover can be considered miraculous. I have never seen anything such as this."

Yi Ping was curious as he asked, "What are the Life and Death channels?"

Yixian asked, "You really do not know?"

Yi Ping was awkward. It was true that he did not know. That was because he was actually a greenhorn in the martial fraternity. Like many of the pugilists, Yi Ping knew only the fighting principles. He did not meet anyone that could teach him other principles like knowledge in internal strength, the vital channels, martial thoughts, martial schools and many others.

Yixian could see it from his expressions. She smiled and explained gently, "The Life and Death Channels controlled and restricted the flow of martial power in the body. That is only so much that the body would be able to take before internal injuries are sustained. Therefore the Life Channel restricted it and in a way is helping to protect the body. Severing the Death Channel stops air from being absorbs and kills the practitioner."

She smiles and added, "Try holding your breathe for as long as possible."

Yi Ping did as he was told. He continued to hold his breath for twenty minutes and he could feel his heart slowing down and it was as though he had been solidified into a stone.

Yi Ping was astonished, "It is as though I don't need air?"

Shui Yixian smiled, "Not true but your body have other means to obtain air through your vital energies. I once heard from my protégé mistress that most people have only one means of obtaining vital breath through breathing. But for some others, they have other means to do so. Exactly how, I do not know. Maybe they practiced some unknown martial skills that we did not know of. But nevertheless, without the life and death channel hindering us, our martial power growth will be unrestricted and replenished much faster."

All of a sudden Yi Ping asked, "If we are born with such inherent ability, then why are these abilities sealed in the first place?"

Shui Yixian said woefully, "I do not know. Maybe a higher power seals it and there is a heavy price in obtaining it. Anyone that tries to do it forcefully is likely to lose their life. Even if they have succeeded, they are unlikely to remain in the mortal realm for too long."

Yi Ping could not understand and he asked, "We will die?"

Shui Yixian smiled gently, "We will all die eventually. That is natural. You may not die but I am going to very soon."

Yi Ping had a jolt in his head and he said to her, "We have just been reunited. Do you know how happy I am to see you alive and well! We are not going to part anymore and will be together!"

Shui Yixian looked at him melancholy, "I really appreciate what you have said to me. That is what my heart is hoping for as well. I really wish I can have more time with you but it is already too late for me."

She sighed, "These tremors are a sign of the forthcoming Divine Calamity that is about to come…"

Yi Ping interrupted woefully, "Xian'Er, let hide in the deepest reach of a cave and avoid the Divine Calamity. How about that?"

Shui Yixian shook her head and said, "My protégé mistress was killed by the Divine Calamity. Before she died, I have told her exactly the same thing. And she told me that, no past protégé leaders had ever survived the 'Divine Calamity'. There was a past protégé leader that hid in the deepest reach of the Eternal Ice Palace but in the end, she was still killed by the Divine Calamity and the Eternal Ice Palace was almost completely destroyed back then."

Shui Yixian said, "That is why past protégé leaders instructed us to face the 'Divine Calamity' outside the Eternal Ice Palace to prevent unnecessary loss of life."

Yi Ping said, "I don't understand. What is this 'Divine Calamity' and why did it have to occur?"

When he had said this, another earthquake occurred and the cave began to vibrate for a while.

Shui Yixian said, "I do not know the reasons too. I only know that it happens only to those that practice the Divine Emerald Skill and the practitioner progression must reach a point when the Divine Calamity would forcefully occur. The Divine Calamity is a type of supernatural force. I once witness my protégé mistress died in that occurrence."

Yi Ping sighed heavily, "Surely, there must be a way to avert it?"

Shui Yixian shook her head and said nothing.

Yi Ping said, "I still find it so hard to believe. We have been through so much and yet Heavens have to separate us…"

Shui Yixian smiled gently, "You shouldn't blame Heavens for it. Heavens is already kind enough for let us acquaint with each other. At least I know that I have a husband that is a real hero. It is actually my fault for not being appreciative of you while you are at the Eternal Ice Palace. "

Yi Ping said, "Xian'Er, don't say that. That's not true. It is not your fault. What exactly is the Divine Calamity? Is it really so powerful?"

Shui Yixian said, "I have witnessed it twice before. The first time was when I was still very young. My grand protégé mistress perished in the fiery fireball from the skies while my protégé mistress died when a lightning bolt struck her."

Yi Ping was stunned, "These are natural forces? Fire would fall from the skies?"

Shui Yixian said, "I would never believe it in the past. But after I have seen it, I am convinced it is all too real."

Yi Ping asked, "Why were the two divine calamities so different?"

Shui Yixian said, "Your mother, my protégé sister told me that it might be because our protégé mistress was trying to dodge the divine calamity with her extraordinary swiftness skill therefore the divine calamity was a lightning bolt. What we fear most, the more it is unavoidable."

Yi Ping was startled, "This Divine Calamity actually is a sentient?"

Shui Yixian said, "I do not know. That is just our conclusion. Past protégé leaders told us that the Divine Calamity is unavoidable and we must overcome it with all our might."

Yi Ping asked, "The Divine Calamity always occur when past protégé leaders of the Eternal Ice Palace was almost a hundred and twenty?"

Shui Yixian nodded gently, "That is true."

Yi Ping said, "But this time it seems to occur three decades earlier for you?"

Shui Yixian shook her head, "I really do not know the reason. It may be the tenth stage of the Divine Emerald Skill that is causing this."

Yi Ping was at a loss. He really did not know if it was fiction or the truth. But no matter what happened, he was determined not to lose Yixian again.

Meanwhile…

Ji Wuzheng said, "I did not know that such a scenic place exist these mountains."

Dugu Zhen smiled at him, "Indeed!"

Lingfeng smiled to her brother, "There are three hundred mountains and peaks in the Holy Amalgamate Mountains range alone. There are many more inaccessible and even more beautiful scenic places here that you think."

Ji Wuzheng sighed, "I have been too buzy in the sect affairs and martial pursuits to appreciate the beauty around me. That is why I am missing the obvious…"

Even though he was saying that to himself, Xiao Shuai and Han Shaodong were also sighing to themselves.

Yixian, Yi Ping, Lele and Shen Xingyue had advanced ahead of them to find a suitable place for Yixian to overcome the Divine Calamity.

Following them were Lie Qing, Lingfeng, Yu'Er, Mei'Er, Yunzi, Youxue, Ji Wuzheng, Dugu Zhen, Huo Fu, Priest Liu Qingcheng, Priest Bai Chongzhen, Priest Ling Kongquan, Suxin, Sufeng, Suyue, Nangong Le, Gongsun Jing and Qiu Wufeng.

Besides Yi Ping's friends, there were Xiao Shuai, Han Shaodong, Shangguan Qingyun, Yan Nanfei, the Three Martial Sages, Xiao Fei, Xiao Ao, Xiao Fan and Chi Zhengqi!

Those were the ones that had been invited for the Celestial Fairy had no wish for anyone else to witness her tragic demise.

Most of the martial exponents in the fraternity would never have the opportunity to encounter the Divine Calamity. So this was an eye-opening for them.

Along the way, Xiao Shuai, Han Shaodong and the Three Martial Sages' heart were still very heavy. Not only would Xian'Er, the person that they had long to find was going to meet her end soon but they were also thinking of the Divine Dragon Pill that Yi Ping had taken!

When Yi Ping had uttered out that he had lost the mythical Divine Dragon Pill, everyone was frantically searching on the ground for it. After all, finder was the keeper in the pugilistic fraternity!

However, Lingfeng said to them. "There is no need to search for it. Yi Ping didn't drop it. When Xiao Shuai's flying sword had struck him, I took his Divine Dragon Pill to save his life. He didn't know about it. Other than the Divine Dragon Pill, is there another miracle in the entire fraternity that could heal his wounds and expended strength so quickly?"

Xiao Shuai was stunned and was muttering, "I have caused Xian'Er to lose the only chance that could have saved her life…"

Even Yi Ping was stunned and was muttered to himself, "I have taken two Divine Dragon Pills. Now I cannot save Xian'Er or Lele's Grandpa. I would rather die in Xian'Er place…"

Yixian knew what Yi Ping was thinking so she smiled gently, "This is my destiny. Remember what you have told me before? Our fate is in our own hands and not in the destinies of others. Moreover, this Divine Dragon Pill may be too potent for me and not suitable for cold and negative martial practitioners."

Lele too smiled at him, "Don't worry about your promise too. Now that I am a true Celestial, I may be able to help my grandpa to overcome his forthcoming Divine Calamity. Moreover…"

She blinked at Lie Qing, Yu'Er, Mei'Er and Shen Xingyue, "We have four other true Celestials here who are able to help me. Right, sisters?"

Lie Qing laughed softly, "Surely!"

Yu'Er said, "I am curious to test my skills against the Divine Calamity."

Mei'Er laughed jovially, "For sure I help!"

Shen Xingyue just smiled gently with a nod.

She was a little amused because even though she did not know who was the Jade Emperor was but for him to encounter into difficulties with his Divine Calamity only meant that his crisis was not an easy matter for the twin sisters who had just attained into Celestials to handle.

All of a sudden, Shen Xingyue called out. "Xiao Shuai, Han Shaodong."

She had tossed a pouch to Han Shaodong who caught it.

Han Shaodong asked curiously, "What is that?"

Shen Xingyue smiled, "This is the Heavenly Dreams Divine Pills that I have concocted in the event that I would get injure. If you treasure your lives, quickly take the pills. Don't say I am heartless."

Han Shaodong was startled and he bowed on the ground immediately!

Xiao Shuai stammered, "This is also a miracle pill? I can live?"

Shen Xingyue said, "Indeed. It is good for internal injuries and I have concocted it for the aftermath of my Divine Calamities."

Martial practitioners like Shen Xingyue and Lie Qing who had attained a high state of divinity and who were aware of the Divine Calamity were careful to have with them several life-saving pills to be used for emergencies.

Lie Qing had previously taken several miracle pills after her failure to battle the Divine Calamity hoping that somehow she would be able to survive her injuries. However her injuries were simply too serious and she did not regain her conscious.

Back to the present and just when the martial exponents were wondering which of the mountain paths to take; they had caught sight of Shen Xingyue and Lele who were on top of a cliff.

Lele said aloud, "Here!"

The martial exponents could see that this cliff was extremely steep and was dangerous to scale. However, it was not a daunting task for these veteran exponents except for a few.

Nangong Le was sighing, "Let's hope I don't fall to my death later…"

Suyue laughed softly, "Don't worry, I won't let you slip."

Qiu Wufeng was rubbing his chin and looking at Chi Zhengqi, who was also looking at Gongsun Jing.

Sufeng blinked at Qiu Wufeng, "So Windless Swordsman, do you need any help?"

Qiu Wufeng smiled bitterly.

Suxin said to Gongsun Jing, "Do you need help too?"

Gongsun Jing smiled, "My martial skills are not that weak. I have learnt how to scale this type of cliff before."

Suxin asked, "Oh really? Let's compete to see who can reach the top first then!"

Gongsun Jing smiled bitterly, "The Fairy Breeze swiftness skill of the Holy Hex Sect is renowned for its weightless feat and swiftness speed…"

Suxin asked again, "You dare not? Then don't you talk to me ever again."

Gongsun Jing quickly said, "But what if I have won?"

Suxin smiled, "Wait till you have won first!"

Just as they were talking and looking for the best way up the cliff, Lele had taken five hops down the extremely steep cliff and landed in front of them effortlessly!

She had landed lightly with her long black scythe and there was barely even any expression on her. It was as though it was just a casual five walking steps!

She smiled, "Hurry! What are you all waiting for? Yi Ping and Sister Xian'Er are still waiting for us!"

Even though many of the martial exponents here like Huo Fu, Ji Wuzheng, Xiao Shuai, Lingfeng and Youxue were exceptional skillful in their swiftness skill, they were still stunned to see her martial display!

Lie Qing walked quietly to Lele and whispered softly, "Sister, you are pregnant now. You ought to be more careful…"

Lele whispered softly, "I am alright. This is still the early stage. I don't want to let anyone knows, especially Ping'Er!"

Lie Qing sighed softly.

Lele smiled and in a blink of an eye, she had taken fifteen hops up the sheer cliff and was besides Shen Xingyue in an instant!

Lele laughed softly as soon as she was on the top of the cliff again, "Hurry!"

Going up was ten times much harder than going down and she had scaled the sheer cliff so effortless.

The Martial Sage patted his potted belly and asked, "Is there any way up?"

Huo Fu who was famed for his swiftness movement skill also said, "Even though I am a good runner but I am not really good in climbing…"

Qiu Wufeng was sighing, "She didn't even uses her hands…"

Chi Zhengqi asked, "Anyone have a rope here? I am weighted down by my five swords…"

Lingfeng said, "This sheer cliff is not impossible to scale. It just requires some time."

Youxue smiled, "That's right!"

Lie Qing was actually groaning. It was because she knew that her swiftness and weightless skill was not as superior as Lingfeng and Youxue.

Xiao Shuai took charge, "Let us climb up the cliff then and let's don't waste any more time. Xian'Er is still waiting for us!"

There seemed to be a charisma pull in his voice as he issued the command but yet Shangguan Qingyun and Yan Nanfei failed to make a move.

Xiao Shuai looked sternly at them, "Why are you not making a move yet? Are you not eager to see Xian'Er?"

Shangguan Qingyun smiled bitterly, "I wish I am able to climb but have you forgotten that I have cut off my thumb and I have difficulty grabbing…"

Yan Nanfei was also smiling bitterly, "I as well…"

Xiao Shuai and Han Shaodong looked at each other awkwardly.

Han Shaodong said, "Perhaps it is best that we can find another way up."

Lie Qing quickly said with her mesmerizing eyes, "That's right. I don't want to dirty my beautiful dress. Moreover, I am shy to climb in the full view of so many others. My pose will be ugly."

Yunzi smiled quietly as she said, "I am sure that there are other ways to go up."

Lele was looking at them with disapproval from above as she said aloud, "You guys are not climbing up?!"

Chapter 69: The Divine Calamity

When the others had arrived in the cave, Yixian was standing regally besides Yi Ping and they were sharing some nuts together.

When Yixian saw their approach, she smiled gently at them, "You are all here. Do you want to have some nuts too?"

Lele sighed softly as she looked at Yi Ping, "I have no appetite."

None of them had any appetite.

Xiao Shuai and Han Shaodong had a solemn look on their faces.

Yi Ping was looking at the gathering dark clouds and the flurrying winds that were sweeping into the dimly lit cave.

But they waited patiently for Yixian to finish her last meal.

Han Shaodong asked, "Xian'Er, you eat so simple…"

Yixian smiled comfortingly, "Brother Han, have you forgotten that I am a vegetarian? These are delicacies to me."

Han Shaodong sighed, "That's right. Time flies and I have forgotten…"

Yixian smiled gently as she looked calmly at everyone, "If only there are some good wines to be shared among us. That will be nice too."

Xiao Shuai sighed, "It is a pity that there are none right now…"

The Martial Sage sighed, "That's right."

Yi Ping immediately said, "Xian'Er, wait for me. I go get the wines…"

Xian'Er caught hold of him immediately with a quiet smile, "Silly! By the time you have returned, more than a day will have passed. That is just a casual remark. Don't go, alright?"

Yi Ping hesitated for a while before he was interrupted by Yixian. Her melancholically eyes were gazing at the gathering dark clouds, "It has come. Remember to stay back and don't come out of the cave."

Yi Ping said bitterly, "Xian'Er! You cannot go out. It is too dangerous…surely we can think of another way?"

Xiao Shuai said gravely, "Xian'Er, is there another way?"

Yixian smiled gently, "Brother Shuai, it is already too late. Everywhere that I go, the Divine Calamity will follow me. This is also the reason why this cave is picked for you to witness the furies of the Divine Calamity. Remember to do more good, stay away from evil and avoid needless killings."

She paused for a while before adding woefully, "It is precisely because I have killed so many people that my Divine Calamity will be difficult to overcome. Let my fate be a lesson to all."

Xiao Shuai stammered, "You call me Brother Shuai…I am still your Brother Shuai? After all that I did?"

Yixian nodded gently, "That's right."

Xiao Shuai murmured, "Xian'Er…"

Han Shaodong said quietly, "Xian'Er, be strong. I know that you can overcome the Divine Calamity."

Yixian said gently to him, "Thank you Brother Han. Let the past be the past. You should put the past aside and look forward. Given your intelligence, you can easily ascend to be a Celestial eventually."

Han Shaodong smiled bitterly, "I have the blood of many in my hands as well. Can I still hope for that?"

The Martial Sage quickly said, "Xian'Er, I know that you can surely overcome the Divine Calamity. You don't have to worry about my safety. Later when you are in trouble, I will surely…"

All of a sudden, Yixian had raised her fingers and had struck the Martial Sage three times on his chest!

The windforce of her fingers were so resonate and the blows received by the Martial Sage were so loud that the entire cave could feel the windforce that was generated by her fingers!

Xiao Shuai and Han Shaodong was startled that Yixian's finger skills would be so astonishing that she could even penetrated through the Martial Sage's Iron shroud skill and to numb him!

The Element Sage praised Yixian, "Xian'Er, your skills have improved! Even with my skills, I am not confident of striking through his Iron Shroud Skill and hit his pressure points."

The Martial Sage was suddenly gasping for breathe and he had fallen on his knees, "My foot! Quickly help me to clear my channels!"

The Element Sage smiled bitterly, "I just say I am not confident of bypassing your Iron Shroud Skill. If I fail to hit your channels properly, I may even worsen your numbness. I think you have better wait for your channels to clear on its own. Unless of course, you want to tell me the weakness of your Iron Shroud Skill…"

The Martial Sage interrupted him, "Do you think that I am foolish and senile?"

But he quickly turned to Yixian to say, "Xian'Er, why did you do that for…"

Yixian said gently, "Brother Ironfist, I know that you will surely come to aid me. That is what I am most afraid of. I have temporary disable your internal strength. With your internal strength, it won't be long before you clear your channels and regain your strength. But that will be enough to stop you for acting recklessly."

The Martial Sage hit his fists on the ground as he wailed aloud, "Xian'Er, I…if you are gone, I really don't know what my existence is for!"

The Sword Sage sighed and helped him up, "Maybe Xian'Er will live. Don't you think too much."

Yu'Er was downhearted as she tried very hard to withhold her tears, "Protégé Mistress will surely survive the Divine Calamity."

What she had said did not match her emotions.

As everyone looked at Yu'Er and her fluffy eyes, they could sense her heartfelt emotions.

Yi Ping sighed sadly. But at this moment, he refused to say anything because he did not want to distract Yixian!

He could only lend her his silent support!

After Yu'Er had ascended as a Celestial, her Dual Inertness Intricacy had advanced to the level of the 'Reflective Emotions'. Her emotions were like a mirror that affected everyone and her feeling could be felt mutually by all the others!

Immediately, those who were already saddened by her voice found themselves shedding silent tears!

Yi Ping and Lingfeng managed to suppress their emotions with their present attainment of the Emptiness Translucence but only barely…

Lingfeng was unaffected but she was sighing melancholy…

Yixian sighed softly. This was really something that she did not want to see.

Even with her cultivation in the Emotionless Rhyme, she was already brimming with tears as she embraced Yu'Er.

Yixian said gently, "Yu'Er, you are always more mature than Mei'Er. Take good care of Mei'Er for me. She needs your care and support…"

Even as Yu'Er nodded, Mei'Er had already flown into her embrace as she began to sob uncontrollable, "I don't want protégé mistress to leave us! You are more than our protégé mistress to me…I…mistress, I don't want you to leave us…"

Yunzi and Youxue had already looked away with silently tears as they could not bear to look anymore.

Yixian caressed Meijian's face gently, smiling fondly at her. "Mei'Er, don't be willful anymore. Be a good wife to Ping'Er and take good care of him on my behalf."

Mei'Er cried, "I will…I will…"

Yixian held Yujian and Meijian with loving hold as she said, "I'm so happy that both of you are Celestial Being now. This is the lifelong wish of our clan patriarchs to overcome the Divine Calamity and see the world beyond. Finally, we have the two of you. I am so proud of you…"

Yu'Er pursed her lips as she cried aloud, "This is not Yu'Er wish at all! Without protégé mistress to guide us, we really don't have confident to survive even the next celestial crisis! I only want mistress to be with us forever!"

Mei'Er cried, "Yes. Without protégé mistress to guide us, what hope do we have? We are so young and there are so many things we don't know yet. We can never be as good as protégé mistress. Why is Heavens so unfair to us? The one that should be a Celestial Being is Protégé Mistress and not us!"

Yixian smiled gently and looked at Lele and Lie Qing with a soft sigh, "Sisters, help me to take care of them as your dear sisters too. And Ping'Er…"

Lele glanced at Yi Ping unhappily, "Ping'Er, you do not have any last words to say?!"

Yi Ping sighed softly, "I have already said all I want to say when we are alone."

It was true. There was nothing he could do now at this point.

He had of course, his own decisions but he was determined to keep it to himself. In order not to make the others worry for him, he refused to say anything!

Yunzi sighed softly as she looked keenly at Yi Ping as she thought, "I don't believe you will not do a thing."

She had witnessed his fearless gut and how he had stand in front of adversity many times. The first time was when she had met him at the Honor Manor. The second time was when he dared to battle Yuan Shao alone so that she could escape and the third time was when he battled the Three Evils of the West, refusing to put down Lie Qing.

If her analysis was correct, he would surely rush into the Divine Calamity to take the blunt of it!

Therefore she had decided to keep a watchful look on him…

In the meantime, Lie Qing pulled Lele's sleeves, "Sister, surely you know that this is the inevitable and is irrational to ask Yi Ping to do anything at this moment. Let Heavens decide the forthcoming outcome and lets us just pray for Sister Xian'Er."

Even Suxin, Sufeng and Suyue who did not know Yixian were also embracing her and they were also inconsolable!

Shangguan Qingyun recited aloud, "Sorrowful partings, sorrowful farewells. Destinies meeting, destinies parting. When will Provident be kind to the empty soul?"

As he recited, he began to draw his long sword with his left hand and engraved the words that he had just recited into the wall!

Yan Nanfei immediately said, "You, you…!"

Shangguan Qingyun laughed bitterly, "What's the matter, Brother Yan? You didn't expect that my calligraphy skills and my swordsmanship to be this good?"

Yan Nanfei said bitterly, "Indeed! I am really surprise!"

Shangguan Qingyun sighed, "If only all these praises would turn my solemn mood into joyous mood…"

Yan Nanfei interrupted angrily, "You really think I am praising you? I feel like beating you up instead!"

Everyone was startled.

It was because Yan Nanfei had suddenly turned hostile and he was looking dead serious.

The Sword Sage was startled, "What's the matter with you brothers?"

Shangguan Qingyun quickly asked, "Yes, what's the matter? You seem upset with me all of a sudden?"

Yan Nanfei smiled bitterly, "I only realize that you are a left-handed swordsman today. You have cut off your thumb on your right hand and I did the same. You have not lost your sword skills but I have. Now tell me, why shouldn't I be angry with you?"

Shangguan Qingyun was stammering as he tried to pacify him, "Don't be angry, Brother Yan…I can explain…"

In his melancholy mood, he had actually forgotten to conceal the fact that he was also an ambidextrous swordsman and had accidentally let his secret slipped out…

The Element Sage said, "Both of you cut your thumbs willingly. Now it is not the time to quarrel. You will only be distracting Xian'Er."

Shangguan Qingyun said quickly, "That's right. We will only be distracting Xian'Er…"

Yan Nanfei kept quiet immediately but he was sighing heavily…

He was not really upset and was just venting. He took a quick glance at Yixian who was smiling to him and immediately he was not gloomy anymore.

He said aloud, "Forget it. This is just a small trivial. I don't really like to fight…"

Shangguan Qingyun interrupted, "Of course it is trivial to you. Everyone knows you are more renowned for your Vacuum Fist than your swordplay. As for me, not able to use a sword in the Divine Sword Clan is a big handicap and is a subject of scorn."

Yan Nanfei stammered, "You! You are the Old Master of the Divine Sword Clan. Who will dare to ridicule you and get away from it? And your swordplay isn't even impaired…"

Yi Ping was amused that these two Old Seniors were poking fun at one another. But he knew that the two of them were old friends and had also aided him in the past. Moreover Shangguan Qingyun had given him the precious Divine Dragon Pill...

He murmured to himself, "They are good men..."

Even Yixian was amused as she giggled softly, "Stop it. I really got to go now."

Shangguan Qingyun and Yan Nanfei sighed as they called out at the same time, "Xian'Er..."

Yixian was now standing at the entrance and the heavy, powerful winds were sweeping into the cave. The entire skies had turned dark even though it was still noon.

The winds were lashing so furiously now that everyone could barely stand straight!

Yi Ping had mustered his martial power immediately to steady himself while his attention was still on Yixian.

Yixian was about to exit the cave when Shen Xingyue called out to her, "Sister Xian'Er. Can I call you sister?"

Yixian nodded gently and held her hands.

Shen Xingyue smiled and took out a pouch, "Inside the pouch are three Heavenly Dreams Divine Pills. Take it when you are in desperate needs. These pills can grant a temporary boast to your internal strength and can even treats internal injuries. But be warned, these pills are also lethal and are poisonous."

Yixian nodded as she smiled faintly, "Thank you, my good sister..."

Xiao Shuai immediately interrupted, "If these are poisonous then where are the antidotes? You didn't give it to us..."

Shen Xingyue blinked at him, "There are no antidotes. I haven't managed to concoct one successfully yet. The only way to prevent the poison from reacting is to suppress it with another Heavenly Dreams Divine Pills periodically."

Han Shaodong stammered, "What happens when the poison reacts?"

Shen Xingyue sighed softly, "Then you will feel like a thousand scorpions stinging on you all at the same time."

The Element Sage was well versed in herbalism and he quickly asked, "What are the main ingredients of this Heavenly Dreams Divine Pill that cause it to be so poisonous and lethal?"

Shen Xingyue said coolly, "I am afraid I cannot tell you or else you will not be able to sleep or eat for days."

Han Shaodong, Xiao Shuai, the Element Sage, the Sword Sage and the Martial Sage were all smiling bitterly at her...

While they were talking, Yixian had quietly walked out of the cave as she struggled to walk in the fury winds to the platform outside the cave.

Yi Ping clenched his fists as he watched her walking towards the rugged platform.

The entire skies above the platform had turned eerily dark and the winds were howling so loud that it seemed almost supernatural. And in the middle of the skies, a dark whirling vortex had appeared!

It was a lucky thing that they were in a cave shelter or else they would be swept off their feet by the wailing winds!

Yi Ping had never seen such a powerful gale before.

He immediately increased his martial power again and executed the Thousand Weighed Skill to steady himself, as did the rest too!

Even though they were in the cave shelter, they could already feel the powerful might of the howling windforce. They could only imagine how strong the windforce was and the difficulties that Yixian had to brave outside!

As the intensity of the windforce grew in fury, Yujian and Meijian were forced to use the Divine Emerald Skill continuously to stay on their feet.

Yujian said to her sister as she stood in front of her, "Mei'Er, at this rate we will surely exhaust our martial power. Let's take turn to use the Divine Emerald Skill."

Meijian nodded silently as she withdrew her Emerald Intricate Energy and just steadied herself with her internal strength!

Lie Qing was besides the Martial Sage at a startling speed as she quickly struck him several times on his body, freeing him from his immobilization.

The Martial Sage sighed, "Thank you…"

Lie Qing combed her long hair as she laughed softly, "Quickly clear your channels. Things are getting more dangerous soon."

The Martial Sage nodded as he gasped for breathe.

Chi Zhengqi, Qiu Wufeng, Gongsun Jing and Nangong Le had already broken into cold sweat. They had already mustered all their strength and yet this windforce seemed to be trying to suck them out of the cave!

Lele quickly thrust her long sickle into the hard rocky ground with a large implosion as she said anxiously, "Everyone, stand behind Yu'Er quick! This is not an ordinary Divine Calamity. In all my years, I have never seen anything like this before! Grab my pole everyone!"

Xiao Shuai and Han Shaodong were startled at her internal strength.

The Sword Sage murmured, "She can pierce through this rocky ground with her pole. That is some amazing feat…"

Chi Zhengqi was puzzled. He quickly drawn his long sword and tried to thrust his long sword into the rocky rock; his long sword could only pierce just a little of the rocky rock before it got deflected! There was no way his long sword could go into the hard rocky ground…

When he had diverted part of his martial power away, he had lost his balance and in that instant he was swept off his feet; the powerful vortex had threatened to suck him out of the cave when the Element Sage caught hold of his foot, "Careful nephew!"

Priest Liu Qingcheng, Priest Bai Chongzhen and Priest Ling Kongquan were all sweating as they exercised their entire martial power to keep themselves on the ground!

Even Xiao Shuai who had profound internal strength was panicky as he asked, "Does anyone knows how long this wind vortex will last? We can't maintain our martial power like this!"

Xiao Shuai was right. Martial power was a sudden burst of a practitioner's internal strength and using martial power itself was physical demanding.

Ji Wuzheng had just mustered a martial shout as he raised his palms continuously to fight off the sucking wind vortex with his Holy Amalgamate Force by absorbing and neutralizing the windforce. He too, was sweating heavily and was worried for his wife and daughters, "At this rate, we will all be forced out of this cave and sweep into the skies!"

Shen Xingyue had turned pale completely, "Be careful. This windforce is not just trying to knock us to the ground. It is trying to pull us towards the dark vortex up the skies above."

She too, had never seen anything like this before!

Yujian was already standing at the entrance of the cave where it was the strongest as she lifted her fingers to deflect the furious vortex!

If she was not there, many of them would have already been swept out of the cave by now!

A tree that was outside the cave had just been uprooted by the strong winds and was swept in a circular motion up to the skies above. As it touched the vortex, it was ripped apart!

Only Yi Ping, Shen Xingyue, Lele, Youxue and the Element Sage could still maintain their balance through the Thousand Weight internal skill but from their expressions, it was also taking considerable effort to do so!

Xiao Shuai cursed aloud as he grabbed the Element Sage to steady himself, "If I know this would happen and that the Divine Calamity would be like this, I would have focused on internal strength training rather than martial power training!"

The Element Sage managed a weak smile, "Don't envy me. Maybe it is because Xian'Er is an internal strength practitioner so that is why this Divine Calamity was a test on internal strength foundation."

Yujian almost cried. Like Yi Ping, she had wanted to aid her protégé mistress but she could barely move at all!

Earlier, Shen Xingyue had emphasized to Lie Qing, Lele, Mei'Er and her that on no circumstances must she lend any lending hand to the Celestial Fairy. It was because once they had decided to aid her, the Divine Calamity would transfigure and that would cause Yixian to ascend as a Dark Celestial.

But when Yu'Er saw how terrifying this Divine Calamity was and the worst had yet to come, she did not care for that warning anymore and just wanted her protégé mistress to live!

Yi Ping had steadied himself with his martial power as beads of sweat dripped down his forehead. He saw that Yixian was now standing in the midst of the furious winds.

Without giving any prior warning to the others, he began to take slow steps as he walked out of the cave towards her!

Yi Ping could only move very slowly, lifting his feet slowly. As he stepped onto the ground, he left behind a deep imprint onto the rocky ground. Each step of his was likened to a ton of force as he concentrated all his martial force into his center of gravity.

He could see that Yixian was now sitting in mediation in the middle of the platform. He was in awe of her internal strength. As he moved closer to the platform, he could feel the lashing of the furious winds that continuously seek to cause him to lose his balance and blown him into the skies.

He could only move very slowly for each step was extremely tedious and difficult now.

Shen Xingyue and Ji Lingfeng called out panicky to him but their voices were quickly drowned as Yi Ping had already stepped out of the cave!

Shen Xingyue was stunned and she was not sure if Yi Ping could hear her even though she had traversed her words through the Thousand Mile Skill.

Lingfeng sighed softly, "It is no use. Even if you have used the Thousand Mile Skill and even if Yi Ping has heard you, he probably won't turn back. He is this stubborn…"

Dugu Yunzi was breathless as she raised the martial power of her Invincible Divine Force once again to maintain her balance, "That's right. Right now, we can only pray."

Youxue was battling the furious vortex with her Divine Emerald Skill beside Yu'Er and Mei'Er, pursing her lips silently as she watched helplessness when Yi Ping had walked past her…

Yu'Er and Mei'Er called after Yi Ping but their concerned voices were drowned out by the howling winds. They had tried to move forward but could not resist the slaughtering of the winds so they were forced to remain in the cave shelter.

Dugu Zhen said aloud, "Everyone, save your strength. We can only pray for now. I got a very bad feeling about this and this is best that we conserve as much strength as possible."

Shen Xingyue sighed softly and said, "That's right. We are in equally precaution position as well. I have thought that we are out of reach from the Divine Calamity but it seemed that this is a most unusual Divine Calamity. I have never seen anything like this before…"

Her voice was soft but everyone could hear her clearly despite the howling winds. That spoke volumes of her internal strength.

Lingfeng said quietly, "This is the Divine Wrath."

Lele, Lie Qing and Shen Xingyue had an astonished look in their expressions.

Lele asked, "You have never even seen a Divine Calamity before. How do you know what it is?"

Lingfeng who was the Heaveness and had recovered her memories kept quiet and did not reply to Lele. Instead she was looking intently at what happened outside.

Shen Xingyue's suspicious was immediately aroused. It was only now that she had noticed that Lingfeng was able to maintain her balance in perfect harmony and seemingly effortlessly!

She immediately thought, "What martial skill is she using? And she is not even using the stance of the Thousand Weight Skill for her posture was too casual. That isn't a skill from the Holy Hex Sect as even Ji Wuzheng, Dugu Zhen and Dugu Yunzi are all struggling against this forceful vortex."

Lie Qing and Lele were also exchanging curious looks to one another…

Lie Qing was already thinking, "If this is the legendary Divine Wrath, how can mortals like us overcome this?"

All of a sudden, she had felt mortal and was even afraid. Even though she was a Celestial but she felt no different from the others…

Not only was she trembling with fear, Shen Xingyue was also trembling and a sense of petrifying fear had also began to creep into everyone!

Suxin was already gasping as she struggled against her fatigue, "I cannot hold much longer. I am too tired…"

Lingfeng said softly, "Everyone, sit on the ground and hold each other hands. This divine storm isn't something that we can handle alone."

Nangong Le said panicky, "That's right. Let us hold hands. I have already exhausted all my strength." He tried to move towards Lingfeng and Shen Xingyue when he caught an angry glance coming from Suyue. He smiled bitterly and walked towards her instead.

As soon as everyone had sat down and holding each other hands, there was a loud rumbling earthquake as the ground began to shake violently and at the same time, multiple flashes of purple lightning began to flash thunderous across the entire skies!

Lele gasped, "This is an electric thunderstorm!"

There was a light drizzle and all of a sudden, a fireball freaked from the sky and headed right towards the middle of the platform where Yixian was mediating!

Everyone was shocked at the sudden appearance of the huge fireball that had burst out of the blue from the darkened skies!

Lingfeng said quietly, "This is just the beginning of the Divine Wrath and more are yet to come."

Chapter 70: The Lightning Calamity

Yixian the Celestial Fairy raised both her hands and stood up, displaying a defense stance. This defense stance was a lot more difficult to her than other times as she had to divert most of her internal strength to maintain her balance and to battle the furious vortex that was threatening to blow her to the whirling dark heavens above.

Yi Ping was panicky when he saw the huge fireball trekking down from the skies as he gave a martial shout and tried to hasten his steps amidst the hurricane winds!

Yixian was startled as she turned and saw his shadowy figure in the hazy windstorm, "Ping'Er, why are you here?!"

But her attention soon returned to the fiery fireball that was above her.

As the fireball drew close, Yixian and Yi Ping could feel the fiery heat and the suffocating pressure of the huge. The ground below them was shaking violently and fissure cracks appeared on the ground as the fireball fell!

Yixian was terrified when she saw the fireball but her will was resolute. She was determined to do her very best and she quickly regained her composure.

She did not dare to be careless as she quickly displayed the Divine Emerald Skill to the ninth level, the Absolute Defense Stance. With some difficulty, she managed to raise her internal strength to its zenith and raised the level of the Divine Emerald Skill to the tenth level in a nick of time as the fireball had impacted directly over her, sending multiple smaller fireballs in many different directions!

As the fireball exploded and imploded over her, the ground beneath her gave way as the sheer pressure of her fireball and her Divine Emerald Skill collided violently!

Just when she thought that she could not withstand the sheer collision anymore, the shattered fireball began to break apart and flew in all directions and most of the fireballs were eventually sucked into the dark vortex above.

Yixian was startled as she thought curiously, "It seems that the dark vortex above me is also indirectly helping me? If there isn't the powerful wind vortex above me, I doubt very much I can hold the fireball in place with just my martial skill alone. Is the Divine Calamity a test of one's courage and resolute?"

In the end, she had only suffered a few minor burns but was otherwise unscathed.

Yi Ping was almost swept forcefully aside when the huge fireball impacted upon Yixian. He displayed the Asper Continuum Horizon Hands with his martial power, imploding and deflecting the smaller fireballs with multiple forceful blows when it flew towards him!

The huge fireball had exploded with a thunderous impact, stirring the dust like a huge mushroom and sending flurry of burning windforce in all directions!

When the dust had cleared, Yi Ping was relieved to see that Yixian was still standing but she was gasping breathlessly. She was otherwise unharmed but the shock that she had received was evidenced in her...

Yixian was aware all of a sudden that Yi Ping was besides her.

Yixian said, "Ping'Er, why are you here? You shouldn't have come. It is very dangerous. I can sense that this is just the start. Move away quickly!"

Yi Ping said with a soft sigh, "Xian'Er, I know I won't be much help but if you were gone, I don't have the courage to live too. I really want to brave through this with you."

Yixian saw the determination in his eyes and knew that he would not listen. She did not have much strength to protest either. She simply closed her eyes to recuperate as much as possible while waiting for the next calamity to happen.

She simply said, "Be very careful!"

Yi Ping said, "I will. Don't worry about me. Don't let me be your distractions. I will look out for myself. I am not the target of the divine calamity."

They began to hold hands as they resisted the furious winds with their internal strength together.

The ground below them was rumbling loudly and tremors could be felt nonstop.

At this moment, the skies grew even darker and ominous.

Purple lightning began to streak across the dark clouds and the sounds of thunder grew even louder. Purple lightning bolts were flashing and striking the ground all around them, zapping and stirring up dust storms all around them!

At the same time, the relentless powerful winds that were generated from the dark vortex were also increasing in fury and attempting to pull them toward it!

Yixian had turned paled, "Ping'Er, this is the lightning calamity. You must leave immediately. The shockwave of the lightning is able to hit the surroundings. You will be in grave danger!"

She had heard from Lele and Lie Qing that among all the Divine Calamities, the lightning Calamity was the most feared. It was sometimes called the Divine Triple Lightning as it would strike three times before it could cease. Each time a lightning had struck, the next one would be even more deadly than the last!

Yi Ping looked gently into her eyes and he placed his hands on her shoulder, "Xian'Er, you focus on the incoming lightning calamity. I will use my martial power to steady you. Don't bother about me…"

Yixian knew she could not persuade Yi Ping in time and if she did not have sufficient preparation, she would cause both of them to be killed instantly. Therefore, she lifted her martial power once again and formed the 'Absolute Defense Stance' as she braced herself for the incoming lightning calamity.

All of a sudden, a white streak of lightning thundered and landed right in front of the Celestial Fairy! This lightning bolt had appeared out of the blue and descended so fast in a blink of an eye that if she did not prepare herself, she would surely be electrified instantly.

As the lightning bolt struck her 'Absolute Defense Stance', the impact was so thunderous that Yi Ping thought that they would perish immediately!

Yixian's fingers were trembling as she barely deflected the force of the lightning bolt. She turned around and asked, "Yi Ping, are you alright?"

Yi Ping had felt a surge of electricity energy bursting through him. It was as though his heart would burst at that time. He immediately inhaled and exercised the Divine Revelation to control his heartbeat.

He said, "Xian'Er, I am alright. My joints feel a little stiff. Is it over?"

Shui Yixian lifted her martial power again and shook her head, "If the divine calamity ceased, then the winds will die down as well. But it is not ceasing and in fact blows even stronger."

Yi Ping turned pale immediately. In the past he would never have believed that fire and lightning would descend from the skies and would descend upon a person so vengefully as though it had a will on its own!

Both Shui Yixian and Yi Ping tried to raise their martial powers as much as they could to brace themselves for the next calamity attack. It was an effort to muster their martial power as they were also using the bulk of their martial power to resist the threatening forceful winds that could at any time uproot them from the ground and sucked them into the dark vortex above them.

A bigger and blue lightning bolt thundered and zapped towards Yixian.

It struck the invisible barrier created by her 'Absolute Defense Stance' and this time she screamed and fell onto the ground. It was as though there was no resistance between her 'Absolute Defense Stance' and the wicked blue lightning bolt.

Yi Ping too, was thrown onto the ground as he felt the terrifying power of the blue lightning bolt!

There was small sparks of fire and burning smell around them.

But Yi Ping quickly struggled to stand as he called out panicky, "Xian'Er, are you alright?"

Yixian was also gasping, "Yi Ping, how are you?" In her most critical moment, her one and only concern was Yi Ping and not herself. She grabbed his hands and held him onto the ground as she could feel his vanishing martial power. It was to prevent him from being spiraled away to the dark vortex above as the strong violent windforce did not cease its furies; instead it was growing stronger every moment!

Yi Ping had suffered severe burning as the lightning bolt had passed through Yixian and through his body!

As Yixian called out to him, he quickly recovered his senses. "Xian'Er, I am alright." He exercised his martial power again and steadied himself as he said weakly to Yixian. "You must concentrate, I am really alright."

Yixian looked woefully at him, "Yi Ping, I…"

It was because she had discovered that the Divine Emerald Skill could only halt the power of the lightning bolt so much and could not prevent it from piercing her. Just when the blue lightning bolt passed through her, she had felt a severe shock but that shock was quickly alleviated by another force; Yi Ping had drawn away much of the power of the lightning bolt with his martial power.

And now, Yi Ping was reaching his limit; his heart would not be able to take anymore shock and to handle the burning temperatures of another lightning bolt.

Yi Ping reminded her, "Xian'Er, you must concentrate. I think the third lightning is coming!"

Yixian reluctantly turned her back from him and after a great deal of difficulty raised the 'Absolute Defense Stance' again. Her fingers were trembling, her footing was not steady and even her body was swaying!

But she knew that Yi Ping had suffered even greater injuries than her.

That gave her the resolute to muster her struggling internal strength as she was determined not to let Yi Ping come to further harm!

The winds grew even stronger and lightning streaked across the skies continuously! It was as though heavens were testing the limits of their endurance!

Yi Ping mused as sweat covered his entire face, "If the divine lightning did not strike now, we will die of exhaustion first!"

Indeed, he was right.

Yixian had broken into cold sweat as she struggled to maintain the 'Absolute Defense Stance'. She dare not cease the flow of her internal power for the Divine Lightning would strike at any time!

Yixian said gently, without losing her enchanting demeanor, "If we can survive this last tribulation then we can survive! Ping'Er, please hold on!"

Yi Ping said weakly, "Xian'Er, you must hold on too…"

All of a sudden, a purple lightning bolt, more powerful than the two previous lightning bolts flashed with a brilliant purplish light upon them!

As soon as Yixian saw the lightning bolt, she immediately lifted all her martial power to its zenith and Yi Ping did the same too!

Yi Ping saw that Yixian was losing her strength rapidly so he supported Yixian with his left hand to root her onto the ground and used the remaining of his martial power to display the Asper Divinity Horizon Hand as he clashed with the incoming purple lightning bolt!

All of a sudden and at the same time, there was another brilliant bolt of light from the other part of the sky that struck the purple lightning bolt!

There was a brilliant clash of explosion and binding flash of light as the ground beneath them exploded thunderously!

Yi Ping and Yixian were both flung across the platform!

The roaring winds suddenly died down and the dark clouds suddenly dispersed. It was as though it had never happened!

The cloudy skies had three opening as three rays of brilliant white light seemed to descend gently upon the fallen Yixian.

Yi Ping was convulsing as he could feel a gentle calming force entering his body!

His first thought was, "Am I about to become a Celestial? We have overcome the Divine Calamity?"

But when he had thought of Yunzi, Youxue and Lingfeng who had not overcome the Divine Calamity, he felt a terrible sadness as he recalled the lingering memories of the White Sage.

If he was a Celestial, then he would not be able to aid them in the future. It was an outcome that he did not want to see.

Not wanting to be separated from them, he did not hesitate at all as he rejected the Divine Force that was entering his body.

As he got up weakly, he saw that Yixian was already standing quietly besides him.

She was smiling gently at him.

Her eyes had turned crimson and now she had a divine air around her that was similar to Lele, Lie Qing, Yu'Er, Mei'Er and Shen Xingyue.

Yixian was looking at the white gold sword that was thrust into the ground. It was enveloped by a golden halo and it had landed exactly at where they were standing just a moment ago.

She muttered, "This sword has just saved our lives by absorbing the lightning. I wonder what it is. It just appeared out of the blue from the heavens above…"

Just as she was pondering this question, she was greeted by joyous cries as everyone had run out of the cave excitedly!

Lele was already hugging her as she said excitedly, "You have now awakened as a Celestial! Congratulation Sister! I know that you will surely overcome the Divine Calamity! What's more, you have just overcome the Divine Three Lightning! That's one of the most dreadful Divine Calamities that can happen. I almost faint from fright when I saw it!"

Lie Qing, Yu'Er and Mei'Er were swiping the tears away from their eyes.

Lie Qing and Lele were particular excited. It was because Yixian had finally overcome the Divine Calamity on her first attempt, a tribulation that they had failed in their first attempt. That failure had caused their confident to plummet and they were afraid that the same fate would be met by Yixian too.

Shen Xingyue was gasping as she pointed at the golden sword that was thrust into the ground, "That is the Heavenly Earth Sword! This sword is the pinnacle sword of the Celestial Star Formation and it is the only celestial sword that can unleash the Universal Force and withstand the Divine Calamity!"

Yixian smiled weakly, "Is that so? I wonder why it is here…"

Shen Xingyue was also pondering the same too, "I do not know but this sword is originally yours and it seems that the Heavenly Earth Sword is here to help you…"

She was interrupted by Mei'Er and Yu'Er who were embracing Yixian with soft cries of joy, followed by the rest!

Youxue was holding hands with Yunzi as they looked delightfully at the Celestial Fairy.

Xiao Shuai, Han Shaodong, the Three Sages, Shangguan Qingyun, Yan Nanfei, Huo Fu, Ji Wuzheng, Dugu Zhen and the rest of the maidens were crowding around Yi Ping and Yixian excitedly, expressing concerns and joyous applauds!

Lingfeng was secretly startled, "This is the Heavenly Earth Sword?"

She had silently raised her trembling fingers in its direction and was startled to find that the sword was indeed exuding vestiges of the Universal Force!

She was already thinking, "This is the secret key that the Celestials in Beyond have been searching for all these while?"

Her thoughts were interrupted by the startled gasp of Lie Qing who was looking tenderly at Yi Ping, "Ping'Er, why aren't you a Celestial yet?"

Immediately, Shen Xingyue and Lele turned pale!

Shen Xingyue murmured with a surprise expression, "I have never heard of anyone that can reject the Divine Force of the Divine Calamity. You supposed to be a Celestial after overcoming the Lightning Calamity. This is not possible…"

Yi Ping was silent as he stole a look at Yunzi, Youxue and Lingfeng, "I just don't want to be a Celestial yet…"

Yunzi sighed softly but she was secretly glad…

Youxue was touched. She knew that he was doing it for her. If Yi Ping becomes a Celestial and if she did not in the future, they would be separated.

Lingfeng was looking at Yi Ping tenderly and her eyes were affectionate…

But Lele was obviously unhappy!

She said melancholy, "You may have given up the one and only chance that you could have to possibly awaken as a Celestial Sage. Goodness knows what are the consequences and implications that will be in the future?"

Yi Ping said weakly, "That's alright…"

Lele interrupted, "That's not alright. That is because from now on, Yixian and I will have to leave you to continue on our celestial progression or the consequences in the future will be dire for us!"

Yi Ping was startled, "Lele, Xian'Er, you are going? Where are you going?"

Lie Qing said quietly, "That's right. We are all leaving. That includes Yu'Er, Mei'Er and Shen Xingyue too. Even though Sister Xian'Er has now awakened but this is just the beginning. Most of us have not even cleared the first celestial stage yet. That is also the most critical stage that will determine our future progression and fate. That's why we must leave so that we will not be distracted by worldly attachments. If you have become a Celestial, you can come with us to continue training. But you have not and we cannot wait for you."

Shen Xingyue added softly as she eyed Yi Ping with soft tears, "I will wait for you. You must also persist, till we meet again."

Yi Ping was stunned as he muttered, "Must we part?"

Xiao Shuai and Han Shaodong were also startled and they had said aloud at the same time, "Xian'Er, you will be leaving us?!"

Yixian nodded uncomfortably as she stole a glance towards Yi Ping.

The Martial Sage stammered, "Xian'Er, I want to become a Celestial too. Wait for me. Don't go yet…"

Shangguan Qingyun was also stammering, "Xian'Er, you are leaving us so soon?"

Yixian sighed softly as she picked up the Heavenly Earth Sword, "If destiny allows, we will surely meet again."

Shen Xingyue said, "Be careful of the Dark Celestials while we are not around."

Lele emphasized, "Not all the Dark Celestials are from the Celestial Palace. Be careful of the heretic sects."

Yi Ping was startled, "Other than the Dark Celestials from the Celestial Palace, there are other Dark Celestials elsewhere?"

Shen Xingyue nodded, "There are many more Dark Celestials and Celestials than you think. The battles between the Dark Celestials and the Celestials have never ceased."

Lele had discreetly turned away and her eyes were melancholy. It was because she had been hiding a secret. She had long suspected that her grandpa had already turned into a Dark Celestial...

CPSIA information can be obtained at www.ICGtesting.com
Printed in the USA
BVOW08s1049310316

442463BV00001B/63/P